THE VIKING CRITICAL LIBRARY

A PORTRAIT OF
THE ARTIST AS
A YOUNG MAN

THE VIKING CRITICAL LIBRARY

Malcolm Cowley, *General Editor*

Winesburg, Ohio
by Sherwood Anderson
Edited by John H. Ferres

Death of a Salesman
by Arthur Miller
Edited by Gerald Weales

*A Portrait of the Artist
as a Young Man*
by James Joyce
Edited by Chester G. Anderson

Sons and Lovers
by D.H. Lawrence
Edited by Julian Moynahan

Dubliners
by James Joyce
Edited by Robert Scholes
and A. Walton Litz

The Power and the Glory
by Graham Greene
Edited by R.W.B. Lewis
and Peter J. Conn

The Crucible
by Arthur Miller
Edited by Gerald Weales

The Grapes of Wrath
by John Steinbeck
Edited by Peter Lisca

*One Flew Over the
Cuckoo's Nest*
by Ken Kesey
Edited by John C. Pratt

THE VIKING CRITICAL LIBRARY

JAMES JOYCE

A Portrait of the Artist as a Young Man

TEXT, CRITICISM, AND NOTES

EDITED BY CHESTER G. ANDERSON

COLUMBIA UNIVERSITY

NEW YORK: THE VIKING PRESS

CONTENTS

Editor's Preface   1

I   *A Portrait of the Artist as a Young Man:* The
    Text   5
    A NOTE ON THE TEXT   254

II   *Related Texts by Joyce*   255
    EDITORIAL NOTE   256
    A Portrait of the Artist   257
    Epiphanies   267
    From *Stephen Hero*   273
      Emma Cleary   274
      I Will Not Submit   277
      The Convent Girls   283
      You Are Mad, Stephen   284
      Epiphanies   286
    The Trieste Notebook   290
    From *Ulysses*   299
      Let Me Be and Let Me Live   300
      The Only True Thing in Life?   303
      Nothung!   305
    From *Finnegans Wake*   310
      Shem the Penman   310
      The Haunted Inkbottle   312

III   *A Portrait of the Artist as a Young Man:*
    Criticism   315

    *Early Comment   317
    Ezra Pound, Letter to Joyce   317
    Edward Garnett, Reader's Report   319

Ezra Pound, James Joyce: At Last the Novel
   Appears   321
Diego Angeli, Extracts from *Il Marzocco*   325
H. G. Wells, James Joyce   329
The Egoist, Extracts from Press Notices   334
The Egoist, James Joyce and His Critics: Some
   Classified Comments   337

The Tradition and The New Novel   340
  Maurice Beebe, The Artist as Hero   340
  Irene Hendry Chayes, Joyce's Epiphanies   358
  Frank O'Connor, Joyce and Dissociated Metaphor   371
  William York Tindall, The Literary Symbol   378

General Readings   388
  Richard Ellmann, The Growth of Imagination   388
  Harry Levin, The Artist   399
  Hugh Kenner, The *Portrait* in Perspective   416
  Kenneth Burke, Definitions   440

Controversy: The Question of Esthetic Distance   446
  Editor's Introduction   446
  Wayne Booth, The Problem of Distance in
    A Portrait of the Artist   455
  Robert Scholes, Stephen Dedalus, Poet or
    Esthete?   468

IV   Explanatory Notes   481

Chronology   551
Topics for Discussion and Papers   556
Selected Bibliography   563

Editor's Preface

The pages of James Joyce's A *Portrait of the Artist as a Young Man* are, as Stephen Dedalus says of those in his second-hand copy of Horace, "human pages." They tell the story of the growth of a human soul from early childhood to young manhood—his revolt against his "nice mother" and the mother Church; his attempts to distance through comic formulation his improvident father; his real and phantasmal movements of love toward immaculate virgins and prostitutes; his encounter with sin, injustice and cruelty and hypocrisy and a million other faces of the "reality of experience," as he goes forth from the Eden of his childhood.

But it is also the story of the growth of the artist trying to "see" his life as "that thing which it is and no other thing"; trying to find the words, the individuating rhythms, the shapes of sentences, the mythy paradigms to give that flowing growth the "wholeness, harmony, and radiance" which writer and then reader rejoice to see and to understand.

The growth of both man and artist is told in a new way. Joyce called the new way a presentation of the past as a "fluid succession of presents," a succession in which nothing is lost. There is no past in the book: only a continuous present with a style that shifts to follow every curve in the fluid continuum, expressing or "discovering" it. Joyce did not have a style in the sense in which we understand that the "style is the man," as with a Henry James or a William Faulkner. He has no "voice"— the style is mimetic, tracing the shape of the object rather than revealing the author.

To surround these human pages with analysis, commentary, erudition—with what publishers in an epiphanic word often call "apparatus"—may seem to dehumanize them. Many readers, therefore, may "prefer the Joyce novel without an introduction by anyone," as did Ezra Pound, one of its first readers. But gradually in the years since 1916, when the novel was first published in book form and when Pound wrote of his preference to Harriet Shaw Weaver, the *Portrait* has become human in another sense: it has taken its place among the select works of the imagination which, studied in schools and colleges, form the core of humane learning in our time. Willy-nilly, since we have eyes to see, we must now read Joyce's novel in the perspectives of such study.

Accommodating the inevitable, this volume aims, first of all, to provide an accurate text of Joyce's book. The chronology of Joyce's life, made particularly detailed for the twenty years or so covered by the novel, and the map of Dublin help to show how the "daily bread of experience" was transmuted by the artist, whom Joyce pictured as a "priest of eternal imagination," into "the radiant body of everliving life." Some notion of the complexity of this alchemical act can be gained by studying the related texts by Joyce included here. The "Epiphanies," the essay "Portrait" of 1904, and the selections from *Stephen Hero* can help us see the stages through which the experiences passed before reaching final form in the *Portrait*; and the selections from *Ulysses* and *Finnegans Wake* show later stages in the "book of himself" which Joyce kept reading and writing.

The "Early Comment," some of it collected and some even sponsored by Joyce, is a selection from the earliest public discussion of the *Portrait* in all its diversity. Diversity is the keynote, too, of the several scholarly and critical essays reprinted here.

They range from attempts to place the *Portrait* in the traditions of the *Künstlerroman* and the symbolic novel to particular explications of the book. The "Explanatory Notes" present the work of many scholars (including Joyce himself, who was pleased to help the Spanish translator of the book understand the meaning of "slim jim" and other words) to make the *Portrait* literally clear. Finally, the "Topics for Discussion and Papers" and the Bibliography invite the student to go beyond the apparatus to understandings of his own.

Joyce might have approved of a volume like this—he is, after all, the main contributor. Besides, though he knew his work demanded attention in every way and even saw himself in *Finnegans Wake* keeping "the professors busy for centuries arguing over what I meant," he insisted that his work is clear. He helped explicators like Stuart Gilbert and Frank Budgen explain *Ulysses*. He told Samuel Beckett that unlike obscure modern writers, he could "justify every line" of his work. Time and attention have made this boast good.

Joyce did not, in fact, approve of obscure art. He said that he wished modern painters and musicians "could or would be as explicit as I try to be when people ask me: And what's this here, Guvnor?" Above all, this volume aims to answer that question.

For their help in approaching the answer I would like to thank the authors of the essays reprinted and their publishers. The curators of Joyce collections in several libraries have made possible the textual editing, the printing of manuscript material, and the preparation of the explanatory notes—R. J. Hayes of the National Library of Ireland, Marjorie Wynne of the Yale University Library, David Posner of the Lockwood Memorial Library at the State University of New York in Buffalo, and George H. Healey of the Cornell University Library. The notes also owe obvious debts to almost everyone who has written on Joyce, not least to Richard Ellmann of Northwestern University, and to a few who have not written, particularly John Ryan of the Bailey pub in Dublin. The notes were completed with the aid of a grant from the Council on Research in the Humanities of Columbia University. At Columbia, too, Kevin Sullivan prepared the Bibliography and helped with advice. Marshall Best, Malcolm Cowley, and Charles Noyes of The Viking Press have proved patient and intelligent. Catharine Carver, now of Chatto and Windus, Ltd., was very helpful in the early planning of the book. And to the wise students and teachers with whom I have read Joyce—especially Howard Hong of St. Olaf College, the late E. K. Brown, and Miles Dillon, then of the University of Chicago, and William York Tindall of Columbia—I owe debts I cannot pay, nor do they dun me.

C.G.A.

I

*A Portrait of
the Artist as
a Young Man*

The Text

Et ignotas animum dimittit in artes.
—Ovid, *Metamorphoses*, VIII, 188

Dublin and Environs

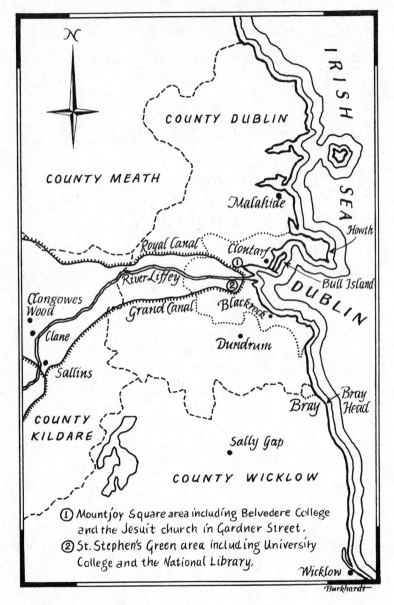

N

COUNTY DUBLIN

COUNTY MEATH

IRISH SEA

Malahide

Royal Canal

Clontarf

①

River Liffey

②

Howth

Bull Island

DUBLIN

Clongowes Wood

Grand Canal

Blackrock

Clane

Dundrum

Sallins

COUNTY KILDARE

Bray

Bray Head

Sally Gap

COUNTY WICKLOW

① Mountjoy Square area including Belvedere College and the Jesuit church in Gardner Street.

② St. Stephen's Green area including University College and the National Library.

Wicklow

Burkhardt

I

O<small>NCE</small> upon a time and a very good time it was there was a moocow coming down along the road and this moocow that was coming down along the road met a nicens little boy named baby tuckoo. . . .

His father told him that story: his father looked at him through a glass: he had a hairy face.

He was baby tuckoo. The moocow came down the road where Betty Byrne lived: she sold lemon platt.

> *O, the wild rose blossoms*
> *On the little green place.*

He sang that song. That was his song.

> *O, the green wothe botheth.*

When you wet the bed first it is warm then it gets cold. His mother put on the oilsheet. That had the queer smell.

His mother had a nicer smell than his father. She played on the piano the sailor's hornpipe for him to dance. He danced:

> *Tralala lala*
> *Tralala tralaladdy*
> *Tralala lala*
> *Tralala lala.*

Uncle Charles and Dante clapped. They were older than his father and mother but uncle Charles was older than Dante.

Dante had two brushes in her press. The brush with the maroon velvet back was for Michael Davitt and the brush with the green velvet back was for Parnell. Dante gave him a cachou every time he brought her a piece of tissue paper.

7

The Vances lived in number seven. They had a different father and mother. They were Eileen's father and mother. When they were grown up he was going to marry Eileen. He hid under the table. His mother said:

—O, Stephen will apologise.

Dante said:

—O, if not, the eagles will come and pull out his eyes.

> *Pull out his eyes,*
> *Apologise,*
> *Apologise,*
> *Pull out his eyes.*
>
> *Apologise,*
> *Pull out his eyes,*
> *Pull out his eyes,*
> *Apologise.*

*　　　*　　　*

The wide playgrounds were swarming with boys. All were shouting and the prefects urged them on with strong cries. The evening air was pale and chilly and after every charge and thud of the footballers the greasy leather orb flew like a heavy bird through the grey light. He kept on the fringe of his line, out of sight of his prefect, out of the reach of the rude feet, feigning to run now and then. He felt his body small and weak amid the throng of players and his eyes were weak and watery. Rody Kickham was not like that: he would be captain of the third line all the fellows said.

Rody Kickham was a decent fellow but Nasty Roche was a stink. Rody Kickham had greaves in his number and a hamper in the refectory. Nasty Roche had big hands. He called the Friday pudding dog-in-the-blanket. And one day he had asked:

—What is your name?

Stephen had answered:

—Stephen Dedalus.

Then Nasty Roche had said:

—What kind of a name is that?

And when Stephen had not been able to answer Nasty Roche had asked:

—What is your father?

Stephen had answered:

—A gentleman.

Then Nasty Roche had asked:

—Is he a magistrate?

He crept about from point to point on the fringe of his line, making little runs now and then. But his hands were bluish with cold. He kept his hands in the sidepockets of his belted grey suit. That was a belt round his pocket. And belt was also to give a fellow a belt. One day a fellow had said to Cantwell:

—I'd give you such a belt in a second.

Cantwell had answered:

—Go and fight your match. Give Cecil Thunder a belt. I'd like to see you. He'd give you a toe in the rump for yourself.

That was not a nice expression. His mother had told him not to speak with the rough boys in the college. Nice mother! The first day in the hall of the castle when she had said goodbye she had put up her veil double to her nose to kiss him: and her nose and eyes were red. But he had pretended not to see that she was going to cry. She was a nice mother but she was not so nice when she cried. And his father had given him two fiveshilling pieces for pocket money. And his father had told him if he wanted anything to write home to him and, whatever he did, never to peach on a fellow. Then at the door of the castle the rector had shaken hands with his father and mother, his soutane fluttering in the breeze, and the car had driven off with his father and mother on it. They had cried to him from the car, waving their hands:

—Goodbye, Stephen, goodbye!

—Goodbye, Stephen, goodbye!

He was caught in the whirl of a scrimmage and, fearful of the flashing eyes and muddy boots, bent down to look through the legs. The fellows were struggling and groaning and their legs were rubbing and kicking and stamping. Then Jack Lawton's yellow boots dodged out the ball and all the other boots and legs ran after. He ran after them a little way and then stopped. It was useless to run on. Soon they would be going home for the holidays. After supper in the studyhall he would change the number pasted up inside his desk from seventy-seven to seventysix.

It would be better to be in the studyhall than out there in the cold. The sky was pale and cold but there were lights in the castle. He wondered from which window Hamilton Rowan had thrown his hat on the haha and had there been flowerbeds at that time under the windows. One day when he had been called to the castle the butler had shown him the marks of the soldiers' slugs in the wood of the door and had given him a piece of shortbread that the community ate. It was nice and warm to see the lights in the castle. It was like something in a book. Perhaps Leicester Abbey was like that. And there were nice sentences in Doctor Cornwell's Spelling Book. They were like poetry but they were only sentences to learn the spelling from.

> *Wolsey died in Leicester Abbey*
> *Where the abbots buried him.*
> *Canker is a disease of plants,*
> *Cancer one of animals.*

It would be nice to lie on the hearthrug before the fire, leaning his head upon his hands, and think on those sentences. He shivered as if he had cold slimy water next his skin. That was mean of Wells to shoulder him into the square ditch because he would not swop his little snuffbox for Wells's seasoned hacking chestnut, the conqueror of forty. How cold and slimy the water had been! A fellow had once seen a big rat jump into the scum. Mother was sitting at the fire with Dante waiting for Brigid to bring in the tea. She had her feet on the fender and her jewelly slippers were so hot and they had such a lovely warm smell! Dante knew a lot of things. She had taught him where the Mozambique Channel was and what was the longest river in America and what was the name of the highest mountain in the moon. Father Arnall knew more than Dante because he was a priest but both his father and uncle Charles said that Dante was a clever woman and a wellread woman. And when Dante made that noise after dinner and then put up her hand to her mouth: that was heartburn.

A voice cried far out on the playground:

—All in!

Then other voices cried from the lower and third lines:

—All in! All in!

The players closed around, flushed and muddy, and he went among them, glad to go in. Rody Kickham held the ball by its greasy lace. A fellow asked him to give it one last: but he walked on without even answering the fellow. Simon Moonan told him not to because the prefect was looking. The fellow turned to Simon Moonan and said:

—We all know why you speak. You are McGlade's suck.

Suck was a queer word. The fellow called Simon Moonan that name because Simon Moonan used to tie the prefect's false sleeves behind his back and the prefect used to let on to be angry. But the sound was ugly. Once he had washed his hands in the lavatory of the Wicklow Hotel and his father pulled the stopper up by the chain after and the dirty water went down through the hole in the basin. And when it had all gone down slowly the hole in the basin had made a sound like that: suck. Only louder.

To remember that and the white look of the lavatory made him feel cold and then hot. There were two cocks that you turned and water came out: cold and hot. He felt cold and then a little hot: and he could see the names printed on the cocks. That was a very queer thing.

And the air in the corridor chilled him too. It was queer and wettish. But soon the gas would be lit and in burning it made a light noise like a little song. Always the same: and when the fellows stopped talking in the playroom you could hear it.

It was the hour for sums. Father Arnall wrote a hard sum on the board and then said:

—Now then, who will win? Go ahead, York! Go ahead, Lancaster!

Stephen tried his best but the sum was too hard and he felt confused. The little silk badge with the white rose on it that was pinned on the breast of his jacket began to flutter. He was no good at sums but he tried his best so that York might not lose. Father Arnall's face looked very black but he was not in a wax: he was laughing. Then Jack Lawton cracked his fingers and Father Arnall looked at his copybook and said:

—Right. Bravo Lancaster! The red rose wins. Come on now, York! Forge ahead!

Jack Lawton looked over from his side. The little silk badge with the red rose on it looked very rich because he had a blue sailor top on. Stephen felt his own face red too, thinking of all the bets about who would get first place in elements, Jack Lawton or he. Some weeks Jack Lawton got the card for first and some weeks he got the card for first. His white silk badge fluttered and fluttered as he worked at the next sum and heard Father Arnall's voice. Then all his eagerness passed away and he felt his face quite cool. He thought his face must be white because it felt so cool. He could not get out the answer for the sum but it did not matter. White roses and red roses: those were beautiful colours to think of. And the cards for first place and second place and third place were beautiful colours too: pink and cream and lavender. Lavender and cream and pink roses were beautiful to think of. Perhaps a wild rose might be like those colours and he remembered the song about the wild rose blossoms on the little green place. But you could not have a green rose. But perhaps somewhere in the world you could.

The bell rang and then the classes began to file out of the rooms and along the corridors towards the refectory. He sat looking at the two prints of butter on his plate but could not eat the damp bread. The tablecloth was damp and limp. But he drank off the hot weak tea which the clumsy scullion, girt with a white apron, poured into his cup. He wondered whether the scullion's apron was damp too or whether all white things were cold and damp. Nasty Roche and Saurin drank cocoa that their people sent them in tins. They said they could not drink the tea; that it was hogwash. Their fathers were magistrates, the fellows said.

All the boys seemed to him very strange. They had all fathers and mothers and different clothes and voices. He longed to be at home and lay his head on his mother's lap. But he could not: and so he longed for the play and study and prayers to be over and to be in bed.

He drank another cup of hot tea and Fleming said:

—What's up? Have you a pain or what's up with you?

—I don't know, Stephen said.

—Sick in your breadbasket, Fleming said, because your face looks white. It will go away.

—O yes, Stephen said.

But he was not sick there. He thought that he was sick in his heart if you could be sick in that place. Fleming was very decent to ask him. He wanted to cry. He leaned his elbows on the table and shut and opened the flaps of his ears. Then he heard the noise of the refectory every time he opened the flaps of his ears. It made a roar like a train at night. And when he closed the flaps the roar was shut off like a train going into a tunnel. That night at Dalkey the train had roared like that and then, when it went into the tunnel, the roar stopped. He closed his eyes and the train went on, roaring and then stopping; roaring again, stopping. It was nice to hear it roar and stop and then roar out of the tunnel again and then stop.

Then the higher line fellows began to come down along the matting in the middle of the refectory, Paddy Rath and Jimmy Magee and the Spaniard who was allowed to smoke cigars and the little Portuguese who wore the woolly cap. And then the lower line tables and the tables of the third line. And every single fellow had a different way of walking.

He sat in a corner of the playroom pretending to watch a

game of dominos and once or twice he was able to hear for an instant the little song of the gas. The prefect was at the door with some boys and Simon Moonan was knotting his false sleeves. He was telling them something about Tullabeg.

Then he went away from the door and Wells came over to Stephen and said:

—Tell us, Dedalus, do you kiss your mother before you go to bed?

Stephen answered:

—I do.

Wells turned to the other fellows and said:

—O, I say, here's a fellow says he kisses his mother every night before he goes to bed.

The other fellows stopped their game and turned round, laughing. Stephen blushed under their eyes and said:

—I do not.

Wells said:

—O, I say, here's a fellow says he doesn't kiss his mother before he goes to bed.

They all laughed again. Stephen tried to laugh with them. He felt his whole body hot and confused in a moment. What was the right answer to the question? He had given two and still Wells laughed. But Wells must know the right answer for he was in third of grammar. He tried to think of Wells's mother but he did not dare to raise his eyes to Wells's face. He did not like Wells's face. It was Wells who had shouldered him into the square ditch the day before because he would not swop his little snuffbox for Wells's seasoned hacking chestnut, the conqueror of forty. It was a mean thing to do; all the fellows said it was. And how cold and slimy the water had been! And a fellow had once seen a big rat jump plop into the scum.

The cold slime of the ditch covered his whole body; and, when the bell rang for study and the lines filed out of the playrooms, he felt the cold air of the corridor and staircase inside his clothes. He still tried to think what was the right answer. Was it right to kiss his mother or wrong to kiss his mother? What did that mean, to kiss? You put your face up like that to say goodnight and then his mother put her face down. That was to kiss. His mother put her lips on his cheek; her lips were soft and they wetted his cheek; and they made a tiny little noise: kiss. Why did people do that with their two faces?

Sitting in the studyhall he opened the lid of his desk and changed the number pasted up inside from seventyseven to seventysix. But the Christmas vacation was very far away: but one time it would come because the earth moved round always.

There was a picture of the earth on the first page of his geography: a big ball in the middle of clouds. Fleming had a box of crayons and one night during free study he had coloured the earth green and the clouds maroon. That was like the two brushes in Dante's press, the brush with the green velvet back for Parnell and the brush with the maroon velvet back for Michael Davitt. But he had not told Fleming to colour them those colours. Fleming had done it himself.

He opened the geography to study the lesson; but he could not learn the names of places in America. Still they were all different places that had those different names. They were all in different countries and the countries were in continents and the continents were in the world and the world was in the universe.

He turned to the flyleaf of the geography and read what he had written there: himself, his name and where he was.

Stephen Dedalus
Class of Elements
Clongowes Wood College
Sallins
County Kildare
Ireland
Europe
The World
The Universe

That was in his writing: and Fleming one night for a cod had written on the opposite page:

> *Stephen Dedalus is my name,*
> *Ireland is my nation.*
> *Clongowes is my dwellingplace*
> *And heaven my expectation.*

He read the verses backwards but then they were not poetry. Then he read the flyleaf from the bottom to the top till he came to his own name. That was he: and he read down the page again. What was after the universe? Nothing. But was there anything round the universe to show where it stopped before the nothing place began? It could not be a wall but there could be a thin thin line there all round everything. It was very big to think about everything and everywhere. Only God could do that. He tried to think what a big thought that must be but he could think only of God. God was God's name just as his name was Stephen. *Dieu* was the French for God and that was God's name too; and when anyone prayed to God and said *Dieu* then God knew at once that it was a French person that was praying. But though there were different names for God in all the different languages in the world and God understood what all the people who prayed said in their different languages still God remained always the same God and God's real name was God.

It made him very tired to think that way. It made him feel his head very big. He turned over the flyleaf and looked wearily at the green round earth in the middle of the maroon clouds. He wondered which was right, to be for the green or for the maroon, because Dante had ripped the green velvet back off the brush that was for Parnell one day with her scissors and had told him that Parnell was a bad man. He wondered if they were arguing at home about that. That was called politics. There were two sides in it: Dante was on one side and his father and Mr Casey were on the other side but his mother and uncle Charles were on no side. Every day there was something in the paper about it.

It pained him that he did not know well what politics meant and that he did not know where the universe ended. He felt small and weak. When would he be like the fellows in poetry and rhetoric? They had big voices and big boots and they studied trigonometry. That was very far away. First came the vacation and then the next term and then vacation again and then again another term and then again the vacation. It was like a train going in and out of tunnels and that was like the noise of the boys eating in the refectory when you opened and closed the flaps of the ears. Term, vacation; tunnel, out; noise, stop. How far away it was! It was better to go to bed to sleep. Only prayers in the chapel and then bed. He shivered and yawned. It would be lovely in bed after the sheets got a bit hot. First they were so cold to get into. He shivered to think how cold they were first. But then they got hot and then he could sleep. It was lovely to be tired. He yawned again. Night prayers and then bed: he shivered and wanted to yawn. It would be lovely in a few minutes. He felt a warm glow creeping up from the cold shivering sheets, warmer and warmer till he felt warm all over, ever so warm; ever so warm and yet he shivered a little and still wanted to yawn.

The bell rang for night prayers and he filed out of the study-hall after the others and down the staircase and along the corridors to the chapel. The corridors were darkly lit and the chapel was darkly lit. Soon all would be dark and sleeping. There was cold night air in the chapel and the marbles were the colour the sea was at night. The sea was cold day and night: but it was colder at night. It was cold and dark under the seawall beside his father's house. But the kettle would be on the hob to make punch.

The prefect of the chapel prayed above his head and his memory knew the responses:

> *O Lord, open our lips*
> *And our mouth shall announce Thy praise.*
> *Incline unto our aid, O God!*
> *O Lord, make haste to help us!*

There was a cold night smell in the chapel. But it was a holy smell. It was not like the smell of the old peasants who knelt at the back of the chapel at Sunday mass. That was a smell of air and rain and turf and corduroy. But they were very holy peasants. They breathed behind him on his neck and sighed as they prayed. They lived in Clane, a fellow said: there were little cottages there and he had seen a woman standing at the halfdoor of a cottage with a child in her arms, as the cars had come past from Sallins. It would be lovely to sleep for one night in that cottage before the fire of smoking turf, in the dark lit by the fire, in the warm dark, breathing the smell of the peasants, air and rain and turf and corduroy. But, O, the road there between the trees was dark! You would be lost in the dark. It made him afraid to think of how it was.

He heard the voice of the prefect of the chapel saying the last prayer. He prayed it too against the dark outside under the trees.

> *Visit, we beseech Thee, O Lord, this habitation and drive away from it all the snares of the enemy. May Thy holy angels dwell herein to preserve us in peace and may Thy blessing be always upon us through Christ, Our Lord. Amen.*

His fingers trembled as he undressed himself in the dormitory. He told his fingers to hurry up. He had to undress and then kneel and say his own prayers and be in bed before the gas was lowered so that he might not go to hell when he died. He rolled his stockings off and put on his nightshirt quickly and knelt trembling at his bedside and repeated his prayers quickly quickly, fearing that the gas would go down. He felt his shoulders shaking as he murmured:

> *God bless my father and my mother and spare them to me!*
> *God bless my little brothers and sisters and spare them to me!*
> *God bless Dante and uncle Charles and spare them to me!*

He blessed himself and climbed quickly into bed and, tucking the end of the nightshirt under his feet, curled himself together under the cold white sheets, shaking and trembling. But he would not go to hell when he died; and the shaking would stop. A voice bade the boys in the dormitory goodnight. He peered out for an instant over the coverlet and saw the yellow curtains round and before his bed that shut him off on all sides. The light was lowered quietly.

The prefect's shoes went away. Where? Down the staircase and along the corridors or to his room at the end? He saw the dark. Was it true about the black dog that walked there at night with eyes as big as carriagelamps? They said it was the ghost of a murderer. A long shiver of fear flowed over his body. He saw the dark entrance hall of the castle. Old servants in old dress were in the ironingroom above the staircase. It was long ago. The old servants were quiet. There was a fire there but the hall was still dark. A figure came up the staircase from the hall. He wore the white cloak of a marshal; his face was pale and strange; he held his hand pressed to his side. He looked out of strange eyes at the old servants. They looked at him and saw their master's face and cloak and knew that he had received his deathwound. But only the dark was where they looked: only dark silent air. Their master had received his deathwound on the battlefield of Prague far away over the sea. He was standing on the field; his hand was pressed to his side; his face was pale and strange and he wore the white cloak of a marshal.

O how cold and strange it was to think of that! All the dark was cold and strange. There were pale strange faces there, great eyes like carriagelamps. They were the ghosts of murderers, the figures of marshals who had received their deathwound on battlefields far away over the sea. What did they wish to say that their faces were so strange?

Visit, we beseech Thee, O Lord, this habitation and drive away from it all . . .

Going home for the holidays! That would be lovely: the fellows had told him. Getting up on the cars in the early wintry morning outside the door of the castle. The cars were rolling on the gravel. Cheers for the rector!

Hurray! Hurray! Hurray!

The cars drove past the chapel and all caps were raised. They drove merrily along the country roads. The drivers pointed with their whips to Bodenstown. The fellows cheered. They passed the farmhouse of the Jolly Farmer. Cheer after cheer after cheer. Through Clane they drove, cheering and cheered. The peasant women stood at the halfdoors, the men stood here and there. The lovely smell there was in the wintry air: the smell of Clane: rain and wintry air and turf smouldering and corduroy.

The train was full of fellows: a long long chocolate train with cream facings. The guards went to and fro opening, closing, locking, unlocking the doors. They were men in dark blue and silver; they had silvery whistles and their keys made a quick music: click, click: click, click.

And the train raced on over the flat lands and past the Hill of Allen. The telegraphpoles were passing, passing. The train went on and on. It knew. There were coloured lanterns in the hall of his father's house and ropes of green branches. There were holly and ivy round the pierglass and holly and ivy, green and red, twined round the chandeliers. There were red holly and green ivy round the old portraits on the walls. Holly and ivy for him and for Christmas.

Lovely . . .

All the people. Welcome home, Stephen! Noises of welcome. His mother kissed him. Was that right? His father was a marshal now: higher than a magistrate. Welcome home, Stephen!

Noises . . .

There was a noise of curtainrings running back along the rods, of water being splashed in the basins. There was a noise of rising and dressing and washing in the dormitory: a noise of clapping of hands as the prefect went up and down telling the fellows to look sharp. A pale sunlight showed the yellow curtains drawn back, the tossed beds. His bed was very hot and his face and body were very hot.

He got up and sat on the side of his bed. He was weak. He tried to pull on his stocking. It had a horrid rough feel. The sunlight was queer and cold.

Fleming said:

—Are you not well?

He did not know; and Fleming said:

—Get back into bed. I'll tell McGlade you're not well.

—He's sick.

—Who is?

—Tell McGlade.

—Get back into bed.

—Is he sick?

A fellow held his arms while he loosened the stocking clinging to his foot and climbed back into the hot bed.

He crouched down between the sheets, glad of their tepid glow. He heard the fellows talk among themselves about him as they dressed for mass. It was a mean thing to do, to shoulder him into the square ditch, they were saying.

Then their voices ceased; they had gone. A voice at his bed said:

—Dedalus, don't spy on us, sure you won't?

Wells's face was there. He looked at it and saw that Wells was afraid.

—I didn't mean to. Sure you won't?

His father had told him, whatever he did, never to peach on a fellow. He shook his head and answered no and felt glad. Wells said:

—I didn't mean to, honour bright. It was only for cod. I'm sorry.

The face and the voice went away. Sorry because he was afraid. Afraid that it was some disease. Canker was a disease of plants and cancer one of animals: or another different. That was a long time ago then out on the playgrounds in the evening light, creeping from point to point on the fringe of his line, a heavy bird flying low through the grey light. Leicester Abbey lit up. Wolsey died there. The abbots buried him themselves.

It was not Wells's face, it was the prefect's. He was not foxing. No, no: he was sick really. He was not foxing. And he felt the prefect's hand on his forehead; and he felt his forehead warm and damp against the prefect's cold damp hand. That was the way a rat felt, slimy and damp and cold. Every rat had two eyes to look out of. Sleek slimy coats, little little feet tucked up to jump, black shiny eyes to look out of. They could understand how to jump. But the minds of rats could not understand trigonometry. When they were dead they lay on their sides. Their coats dried then. They were only dead things.

The prefect was there again and it was his voice that was saying that he was to get up, that Father Minister had said he was to get up and dress and go to the infirmary. And while he was dressing himself as quickly as he could the prefect said:

—We must pack off to Brother Michael because we have the collywobbles! Terrible thing to have the collywobbles! How we wobble when we have the collywobbles!

He was very decent to say that. That was all to make him laugh. But he could not laugh because his cheeks and lips were all shivery: and then the prefect had to laugh by himself.

The prefect cried:

—Quick march! Hayfoot! Strawfoot!

They went together down the staircase and along the corridor and past the bath. As he passed the door he remembered with a vague fear the warm turfcoloured bogwater, the warm moist air, the noise of plunges, the smell of the towels, like medicine.

Brother Michael was standing at the door of the infirmary and from the door of the dark cabinet on his right came a smell like medicine. That came from the bottles on the shelves. The prefect spoke to Brother Michael and Brother

Michael answered and called the prefect sir. He had reddish hair mixed with grey and a queer look. It was queer that he would always be a brother. It was queer too that you could not call him sir because he was a brother and had a different kind of look. Was he not holy enough or why could he not catch up on the others?

There were two beds in the room and in one bed there was a fellow: and when they went in he called out:

—Hello! It's young Dedalus! What's up?

—The sky is up, Brother Michael said.

He was a fellow out of the third of grammar and, while Stephen was undressing, he asked Brother Michael to bring him a round of buttered toast.

—Ah, do! he said.

—Butter you up! said Brother Michael. You'll get your walking papers in the morning when the doctor comes.

—Will I? the fellow said. I'm not well yet.

Brother Michael repeated:

—You'll get your walking papers, I tell you.

He bent down to rake the fire. He had a long back like the long back of a tramhorse. He shook the poker gravely and nodded his head at the fellow out of third of grammar.

Then Brother Michael went away and after a while the fellow out of third of grammar turned in towards the wall and fell asleep.

That was the infirmary. He was sick then. Had they written home to tell his mother and father? But it would be quicker for one of the priests to go himself to tell them. Or he would write a letter for the priest to bring.

Dear Mother

I am sick. I want to go home. Please come and take me home. I am in the infirmary.

Your fond son,
Stephen

How far away they were! There was cold sunlight outside the window. He wondered if he would die. You could die just the same on a sunny day. He might die before his mother came. Then he would have a dead mass in the chapel like the way the fellows had told him it was when Little had died. All the fellows would be at the mass, dressed in black, all with sad faces. Wells too would be there but no fellow would look at him. The rector would be there in a cope of black and gold and there would be tall yellow candles on the altar and round the catafalque. And they would carry the coffin out of the chapel slowly and he would be buried in the little graveyard of the community off the main avenue of limes. And Wells would be sorry then for what he had done. And the bell would toll slowly.

He could hear the tolling. He said over to himself the song that Brigid had taught him.

> *Dingdong! The castle bell!*
> *Farewell, my mother!*
> *Bury me in the old churchyard*
> *Beside my eldest brother.*
> *My coffin shall be black,*
> *Six angels at my back,*
> *Two to sing and two to pray*
> *And two to carry my soul away.*

How beautiful and sad that was! How beautiful the words were where they said *Bury me in the old churchyard!* A tremor passed over his body. How sad and how beautiful! He wanted to cry quietly but not for himself: for the words, so beautiful and sad, like music. The bell! The bell! Farewell! O farewell!

The cold sunlight was weaker and Brother Michael was standing at his bedside with a bowl of beeftea. He was glad for his mouth was hot and dry. He could hear them playing on the playgrounds. And the day was going on in the college just as if he were there.

Then Brother Michael was going away and the fellow out of third of grammar told him to be sure and come back and tell him all the news in the paper. He told Stephen that his name was Athy and that his father kept a lot of racehorses that were spiffing jumpers and that his father would give a good tip to Brother Michael any time he wanted it because Brother Michael was very decent and always told him the news out of the paper they got every day up in the castle. There was every kind of news in the paper: accidents, shipwrecks, sports and politics.

—Now it is all about politics in the paper, he said. Do your people talk about that too?

—Yes, Stephen said.

—Mine too, he said.

Then he thought for a moment and said:

—You have a queer name, Dedalus, and I have a queer name too, Athy. My name is the name of a town. Your name is like Latin.

Then he asked:

—Are you good at riddles?

Stephen answered:

—Not very good.

Then he said:

—Can you answer me this one? Why is the county Kildare like the leg of a fellow's breeches?

Stephen thought what could be the answer and then said:

—I give it up.

—Because there is a thigh in it, he said. Do you see the joke? Athy is the town in the county Kildare and a thigh is the other thigh.

—O, I see, Stephen said.

—That's an old riddle, he said.

After a moment he said:

—I say!

—What? asked Stephen.

—You know, he said, you can ask that riddle another way?

—Can you? said Stephen.

—The same riddle, he said. Do you know the other way to ask it?

—No, said Stephen.

—Can you not think of the other way? he said.

He looked at Stephen over the bedclothes as he spoke. Then he lay back on the pillow and said:

—There is another way but I won't tell you what it is.

Why did he not tell it? His father, who kept the racehorses, must be a magistrate too like Saurin's father and Nasty Roche's father. He thought of his own father, of how he sang songs while his mother played and of how he always gave him a shilling when he asked for sixpence and he felt sorry for him that he was not a magistrate like the other boys' fathers. Then why was he sent to that place with them? But his father had told him that he would be no stranger there because his granduncle had presented an address to the liberator there fifty years before. You could know the people of that time by their old dress. It seemed to him a solemn time: and he wondered if that was the time when the fellows in Clongowes wore blue coats with brass buttons and yellow waistcoats and caps of rabbitskin and drank beer like grownup people and kept greyhounds of their own to course the hares with.

He looked at the window and saw that the daylight had grown weaker. There would be cloudy grey light over the playgrounds. There was no noise on the playgrounds. The class must be doing the themes or perhaps Father Arnall was reading a legend out of the book.

It was queer that they had not given him any medicine. Perhaps Brother Michael would bring it back when he came. They said you got stinking stuff to drink when you were in the infirmary. But he felt better now than before. It would be nice getting better slowly. You could get a book then. There was a book in the library about Holland. There were lovely foreign names in it and pictures of strangelooking cities and ships. It made you feel so happy.

How pale the light was at the window! But that was nice. The fire rose and fell on the wall. It was like waves. Someone had put coal on and he heard voices. They were talking. It was the noise of the waves. Or the waves were talking among themselves as they rose and fell.

He saw the sea of waves, long dark waves rising and falling, dark under the moonless night. A tiny light twinkled at the pierhead where the ship was entering: and he saw a multitude of people gathered by the waters' edge to see the ship that was entering their harbour. A tall man stood on the deck, looking out towards the flat dark land: and by the light at the pierhead he saw his face, the sorrowful face of Brother Michael.

He saw him lift his hand towards the people and heard him say in a loud voice of sorrow over the waters:

—He is dead. We saw him lying upon the catafalque.

A wail of sorrow went up from the people.

—Parnell! Parnell! He is dead!

They fell upon their knees, moaning in sorrow.

And he saw Dante in a maroon velvet dress and with a green velvet mantle hanging from her shoulders walking proudly and silently past the people who knelt by the waters' edge.

*   *   *

A great fire, banked high and red, flamed in the grate and under the ivytwined branches of the chandelier the Christmas table was spread. They had come home a little late and still dinner was not ready: but it would be ready in a jiffy, his mother had said. They were waiting for the door to open and for the servants to come in, holding the big dishes covered with their heavy metal covers.

All were waiting: uncle Charles, who sat far away in the shadow of the window, Dante and Mr Casey, who sat in the easychairs at either side of the hearth, Stephen, seated on a chair between them, his feet resting on the toasted boss. Mr Dedalus looked at himself in the pierglass above the mantelpiece, waxed out his moustache-ends and then, parting his coattails, stood with his back to the glowing fire: and still, from time to time, he withdrew a hand from his coattail to wax out one of his moustache-ends. Mr Casey leaned his head to one side and, smiling, tapped the gland of his neck with his fingers. And Stephen smiled too for he knew now that it was not true that Mr Casey had a purse of silver in his throat. He smiled to think how the silvery noise which Mr Casey used to make had deceived him. And when he had tried to open Mr Casey's hand to see if the purse of silver was hidden there he had seen that the fingers could not be straightened out: and Mr Casey had told him that he had got those three cramped fingers making a birthday present for Queen Victoria.

Mr Casey tapped the gland of his neck and smiled at Stephen with sleepy eyes: and Mr Dedalus said to him:

—Yes. Well now, that's all right. O, we had a good walk, hadn't we, John? Yes . . . I wonder if there's any likelihood of dinner this evening. Yes. . . . O, well now, we got a good breath of ozone round the Head today. Ay, bedad.

He turned to Dante and said:

—You didn't stir out at all, Mrs Riordan?

Dante frowned and said shortly:

—No.

Mr Dedalus dropped his coattails and went over to the sideboard. He brought forth a great stone jar of whisky from the locker and filled the decanter slowly, bending now and then to see how much he had poured in. Then replacing the jar in the locker he poured a little of the whisky into two glasses, added a little water and came back with them to the fireplace.

—A thimbleful, John, he said, just to whet your appetite.

Mr Casey took the glass, drank, and placed it near him on the mantelpiece. Then he said:

—Well, I can't help thinking of our friend Christopher manufacturing . . .

He broke into a fit of laughter and coughing and added:

—. . . manufacturing that champagne for those fellows.

Mr Dedalus laughed loudly.

—Is it Christy? he said. There's more cunning in one of those warts on his bald head than in a pack of jack foxes.

He inclined his head, closed his eyes, and, licking his lips profusely, began to speak with the voice of the hotelkeeper.

—And he has such a soft mouth when he's speaking to you, don't you know. He's very moist and watery about the dewlaps, God bless him.

Mr Casey was still struggling through his fit of coughing and laughter. Stephen, seeing and hearing the hotelkeeper through his father's face and voice, laughed.

Mr Dedalus put up his eyeglass and, staring down at him, said quietly and kindly:

—What are you laughing at, you little puppy, you?

The servants entered and placed the dishes on the table. Mrs Dedalus followed and the places were arranged.

—Sit over, she said.

Mr Dedalus went to the end of the table and said:

—Now, Mrs Riordan, sit over. John, sit you down, my hearty.

He looked round to where uncle Charles sat and said:

—Now then, sir, there's a bird here waiting for you.

When all had taken their seats he laid his hand on the cover and then said quickly, withdrawing it:

—Now, Stephen.

Stephen stood up in his place to say the grace before meals:

Bless us, O Lord, and these Thy gifts which through Thy bounty we are about to receive through Christ Our Lord. Amen.

All blessed themselves and Mr Dedalus with a sigh of pleasure lifted from the dish the heavy cover pearled around the edge with glistening drops.

Stephen looked at the plump turkey which had lain, trussed and skewered, on the kitchen table. He knew that his father had paid a guinea for it in Dunn's of D'Olier Street and that the man had prodded it often at the breastbone to show how good it was: and he remembered the man's voice when he had said:

—Take that one, sir. That's the real Ally Daly.

Why did Mr Barrett in Clongowes call his pandybat a turkey? But Clongowes was far away: and the warm heavy smell of turkey and ham and celery rose from the plates and dishes and the great fire was banked high and red in the grate and the green ivy and red holly made you feel so happy and when dinner was ended the big plumpudding would be carried in, studded with peeled almonds and sprigs of holly, with bluish fire running around it and a little green flag flying from the top.

It was his first Christmas dinner and he thought of his little brothers and sisters who were waiting in the nursery, as he had often waited, till the pudding came. The deep low collar and the Eton jacket made him feel queer and oldish: and that morning when his mother had brought him down to the parlour, dressed for mass, his father had cried. That was because he was thinking of his own father. And uncle Charles had said so too.

Mr Dedalus covered the dish and began to eat hungrily. Then he said:

—Poor old Christy, he's nearly lopsided now with roguery.

—Simon, said Mrs Dedalus, you haven't given Mrs Riordan any sauce.

Mr Dedalus seized the sauceboat.

—Haven't I? he cried. Mrs Riordan, pity the poor blind.

Dante covered her plate with her hands and said:

—No, thanks.

Mr Dedalus turned to uncle Charles.

—How are you off, sir?

—Right as the mail, Simon.

—You, John?

—I'm all right. Go on yourself.

—Mary? Here, Stephen, here's something to make your hair curl.

He poured sauce freely over Stephen's plate and set the boat again on the table. Then he asked uncle Charles was it tender. Uncle Charles could not speak because his mouth was full but he nodded that it was.

—That was a good answer our friend made to the canon. What? said Mr Dedalus.

—I didn't think he had that much in him, said Mr Casey.

—*I'll pay you your dues, father, when you cease turning the house of God into a pollingbooth.*

—A nice answer, said Dante, for any man calling himself a catholic to give to his priest.

—They have only themselves to blame, said Mr Dedalus suavely. If they took a fool's advice they would confine their attention to religion.

—It is religion, Dante said. They are doing their duty in warning the people.

—We go to the house of God, Mr Casey said, in all humility to pray to our Maker and not to hear election addresses.

—It is religion, Dante said again. They are right. They must direct their flocks.

—And preach politics from the altar, is it? asked Mr Dedalus.

—Certainly, said Dante. It is a question of public morality. A priest would not be a priest if he did not tell his flock what is right and what is wrong.

Mrs Dedalus laid down her knife and fork, saying:

—For pity's sake and for pity sake let us have no political discussion on this day of all days in the year.

—Quite right, ma'am, said uncle Charles. Now, Simon, that's quite enough now. Not another word now.

—Yes, yes, said Mr Dedalus quickly.

He uncovered the dish boldly and said:

—Now then, who's for more turkey?

Nobody answered. Dante said:

—Nice language for any catholic to use!

—Mrs Riordan, I appeal to you, said Mrs Dedalus, to let the matter drop now.

Dante turned on her and said:

—And am I to sit here and listen to the pastors of my church being flouted?

—Nobody is saying a word against them, said Mr Dedalus, so long as they don't meddle in politics.

—The bishops and priests of Ireland have spoken, said Dante, and they must be obeyed.

—Let them leave politics alone, said Mr Casey, or the people may leave their church alone.

—You hear? said Dante turning to Mrs Dedalus.

—Mr Casey! Simon! said Mrs Dedalus. Let it end now.

—Too bad! Too bad! said uncle Charles.

—What? cried Mr Dedalus. Were we to desert him at the bidding of the English people?

—He was no longer worthy to lead, said Dante. He was a public sinner.

—We are all sinners and black sinners, said Mr Casey coldly.

—*Woe be to the man by whom the scandal cometh!* said Mrs Riordan. *It would be better for him that a millstone were tied about his neck and that he were cast into the depth of the sea rather than that he should scandalise one of these, my least little ones.* That is the language of the Holy Ghost.

—And very bad language if you ask me, said Mr Dedalus coolly.

—Simon! Simon! said uncle Charles. The boy.

—Yes, yes, said Mr Dedalus. I meant about the . . . I was thinking about the bad language of that railway porter. Well now, that's all right. Here, Stephen, show me your plate, old chap. Eat away now. Here.

He heaped up the food on Stephen's plate and served uncle Charles and Mr Casey to large pieces of turkey and splashes of sauce. Mrs Dedalus was eating little and Dante sat with her hands in her lap. She was red in the face. Mr Dedalus rooted with the carvers at the end of the dish and said:

—There's a tasty bit here we call the pope's nose. If any lady or gentleman . . .

He held a piece of fowl up on the prong of the carvingfork. Nobody spoke. He put it on his own plate, saying:

—Well, you can't say but you were asked. I think I had better eat it myself because I'm not well in my health lately.

He winked at Stephen and, replacing the dishcover, began to eat again.

There was a silence while he ate. Then he said:

—Well now, the day kept up fine after all. There were plenty of strangers down too.

Nobody spoke. He said again:

—I think there were more strangers down than last Christmas.

He looked round at the others whose faces were bent towards their plates and, receiving no reply, waited for a moment and said bitterly:

—Well, my Christmas dinner has been spoiled anyhow.

—There could be neither luck nor grace, Dante said, in a house where there is no respect for the pastors of the church.

Mr Dedalus threw his knife and fork noisily on his plate.

—Respect! he said. Is it for Billy with the lip or for the tub of guts up in Armagh? Respect!

—Princes of the church, said Mr Casey with slow scorn.

—Lord Leitrim's coachman, yes, said Mr Dedalus.

—They are the Lord's anointed, Dante said. They are an honour to their country.

—Tub of guts, said Mr Dedalus coarsely. He has a handsome face, mind you, in repose. You should see that fellow lapping up his bacon and cabbage of a cold winter's day. O Johnny!

He twisted his features into a grimace of heavy bestiality and made a lapping noise with his lips.

—Really, Simon, said Mrs Dedalus, you should not speak that way before Stephen. It's not right.

—O, he'll remember all this when he grows up, said Dante hotly—the language he heard against God and religion and priests in his own home.

—Let him remember too, cried Mr Casey to her from across the table, the language with which the priests and the priests' pawns broke Parnell's heart and hounded him into his grave. Let him remember that too when he grows up.

—Sons of bitches! cried Mr Dedalus. When he was down they turned on him to betray him and rend him like rats in a sewer. Lowlived dogs! And they look it! By Christ, they look it!

—They behaved rightly, cried Dante. They obeyed their bishops and their priests. Honour to them!

—Well, it is perfectly dreadful to say that not even for one day in the year, said Mrs Dedalus, can we be free from these dreadful disputes!

Uncle Charles raised his hands mildly and said:

—Come now, come now, come now! Can we not have our opinions whatever they are without this bad temper and this bad language? It is too bad surely.

Mrs Dedalus spoke to Dante in a low voice but Dante said loudly:

—I will not say nothing. I will defend my church and my religion when it is insulted and spit on by renegade catholics.

Mr Casey pushed his plate rudely into the middle of the table and, resting his elbows before him, said in a hoarse voice to his host:

—Tell me, did I tell you that story about a very famous spit?

—You did not, John, said Mr Dedalus.

—Why then, said Mr Casey, it is a most instructive story. It happened not long ago in the county Wicklow where we are now.

He broke off and, turning towards Dante, said with quiet indignation:

—And I may tell you, ma'am, that I, if you mean me, am no renegade catholic. I am a catholic as my father was and his father before him and his father before him again when we gave up our lives rather than sell our faith.

—The more shame to you now, Dante said, to speak as you do.

—The story, John, said Mr Dedalus smiling. Let us have the story anyhow.

—Catholic indeed! repeated Dante ironically. The blackest protestant in the land would not speak the language I have heard this evening.

Mr Dedalus began to sway his head to and fro, crooning like a country singer.

—I am no protestant, I tell you again, said Mr Casey flushing.

Mr Dedalus, still crooning and swaying his head, began to sing in a grunting nasal tone:

> *O, come all you Roman catholics*
> *That never went to mass.*

He took up his knife and fork again in good humour and set to eating, saying to Mr Casey:

—Let us have the story, John. It will help us to digest.

Stephen looked with affection at Mr Casey's face which stared across the table over his joined hands. He liked to sit near him at the fire, looking up at his dark fierce face. But his dark eyes were never fierce and his slow voice was good to listen to. But why was he then against the priests? Because Dante must be right then. But he had heard his father say that she was a spoiled nun and that she had come out of the convent in the Alleghanies when her brother had got the money from the savages for the trinkets and the chainies. Perhaps that made her severe against Parnell. And she did not like him to play with Eileen because Eileen was a protestant and when she was young she knew children that used to play with protestants and the protestants used to make fun of the litany of the Blessed Virgin. *Tower of Ivory,* they used to say, *House of Gold!* How could a woman be a tower of ivory or a house of gold? Who was right then? And he remembered the evening in the infirmary in Clongowes, the dark waters, the light at the pierhead and the moan of sorrow from the people when they had heard.

Eileen had long white hands. One evening when playing tig she had put her hands over his eyes: long and white and thin and cold and soft. That was ivory: a cold white thing. That was the meaning of *Tower of Ivory*.

—The story is very short and sweet, Mr Casey said. It was one day down in Arklow, a cold bitter day, not long before the chief died. May God have mercy on him!

He closed his eyes wearily and paused. Mr Dedalus took a bone from his plate and tore some meat from it with his teeth, saying:

—Before he was killed, you mean.

Mr Casey opened his eyes, sighed and went on:

—It was down in Arklow one day. We were down there at a meeting and after the meeting was over we had to make our way to the railway station through the crowd. Such booing and baaing, man, you never heard. They called us all the names in the world. Well there was one old lady, and a drunken old harridan she was surely, that paid all her attention to me. She kept dancing along beside me in the mud bawling and screaming into my face: *Priesthunter! The Paris Funds! Mr Fox! Kitty O'Shea!*

—And what did you do, John? asked Mr Dedalus.

—I let her bawl away, said Mr Casey. It was a cold day and to keep up my heart I had (saving your presence, ma'am) a quid of Tullamore in my mouth and sure I couldn't say a word in any case because my mouth was full of tobacco juice.

—Well, John?

—Well. I let her bawl away, to her heart's content, *Kitty O'-Shea* and the rest of it till at last she called that lady a name that I won't sully this Christmas board nor your ears, ma'am, nor my own lips by repeating.

He paused. Mr Dedalus, lifting his head from the bone, asked:

—And what did you do, John?

—Do! said Mr Casey. She stuck her ugly old face up at me when she said it and I had my mouth full of tobacco juice. I bent down to her and *Phth!* says I to her like that.

He turned aside and made the act of spitting.

—*Phth!* says I to her like that, right into her eye.

He clapped a hand to his eye and gave a hoarse scream of pain.

—*O Jesus, Mary and Joseph!* says she. *I'm blinded! I'm blinded and drownded!*

He stopped in a fit of coughing and laughter, repeating:

—*I'm blinded entirely.*

Mr Dedalus laughed loudly and lay back in his chair while uncle Charles swayed his head to and fro.

Dante looked terribly angry and repeated while they laughed:

—Very nice! Ha! Very nice!

It was not nice about the spit in the woman's eye. But what was the name the woman had called Kitty O'Shea that Mr Casey would not repeat? He thought of Mr Casey walking through the crowds of people and making speeches from a wagonette. That was what he had been in prison for and he remembered that one night Sergeant O'Neill had come to the house and had stood in the hall, talking in a low voice with his father and chewing nervously at the chinstrap of his cap. And that night Mr Casey had not gone to Dublin by train but a car had come to the door and he had heard his father say something about the Cabinteely road.

He was for Ireland and Parnell and so was his father: and so was Dante too for one night at the band on the esplanade she had hit a gentleman on the head with her umbrella because he had taken off his hat when the band played *God save the Queen* at the end.

Mr Dedalus gave a snort of contempt.

—Ah, John, he said. It is true for them. We are an unfortunate priestridden race and always were and always will be till the end of the chapter.

Uncle Charles shook his head, saying:

—A bad business! A bad business!

Mr Dedalus repeated:

—A priestridden Godforsaken race!

He pointed to the portrait of his grandfather on the wall to his right.

—Do you see that old chap up there, John? he said. He was a good Irishman when there was no money in the job. He was condemned to death as a whiteboy. But he had a saying about our clerical friends, that he would never let one of them put his two feet under his mahogany.

Dante broke in angrily:

—If we are a priestridden race we ought to be proud of it! They are the apple of God's eye. *Touch them not,* says Christ, *for they are the apple of My eye.*

—And can we not love our country then? asked Mr Casey. Are we not to follow the man that was born to lead us?

—A traitor to his country! replied Dante. A traitor, an adulterer! The priests were right to abandon him. The priests were always the true friends of Ireland.

—Were they, faith? said Mr Casey.

He threw his fist on the table and, frowning angrily, protruded one finger after another.

—Didn't the bishops of Ireland betray us in the time of the union when bishop Lanigan presented an address of loyalty to the Marquess Cornwallis? Didn't the bishops and priests sell the aspirations of their country in 1829 in return for catholic emancipation? Didn't they denounce the fenian movement from the pulpit and in the confessionbox? And didn't they dishonour the ashes of Terence Bellew MacManus?

His face was glowing with anger and Stephen felt the glow rise to his own cheek as the spoken words thrilled him. Mr Dedalus uttered a guffaw of coarse scorn.

—O, by God, he cried, I forgot little old Paul Cullen! Another apple of God's eye!

Dante bent across the table and cried to Mr Casey:

—Right! Right! They were always right! God and morality and religion come first.

Mrs Dedalus, seeing her excitement, said to her:

—Mrs Riordan, don't excite yourself answering them.

—God and religion before everything! Dante cried. God and religion before the world!

Mr Casey raised his clenched fist and brought it down on the table with a crash.

—Very well, then, he shouted hoarsely, if it comes to that, no God for Ireland!

—John! John! cried Mr Dedalus, seizing his guest by the coatsleeve.

Dante stared across the table, her cheeks shaking. Mr Casey struggled up from his chair and bent across the table towards her, scraping the air from before his eyes with one hand as though he were tearing aside a cobweb.

—No God for Ireland! he cried. We have had too much God in Ireland. Away with God!

—Blasphemer! Devil! screamed Dante, starting to her feet and almost spitting in his face.

Uncle Charles and Mr Dedalus pulled Mr Casey back into his chair again, talking to him from both sides reasonably. He stared before him out of his dark flaming eyes, repeating:

—Away with God, I say!

Dante shoved her chair violently aside and left the table, upsetting her napkinring which rolled slowly along the carpet and came to rest against the foot of an easychair. Mrs Dedalus rose quickly and followed her towards the door. At the door Dante turned round violently and shouted down the room, her cheeks flushed and quivering with rage:

—Devil out of hell! We won! We crushed him to death! Fiend!

The door slammed behind her.

Mr Casey, freeing his arms from his holders, suddenly bowed his head on his hands with a sob of pain.

—Poor Parnell! he cried loudly. My dead king!

He sobbed loudly and bitterly.

Stephen, raising his terrorstricken face, saw that his father's eyes were full of tears.

*　　　*　　　*

The fellows talked together in little groups.

One fellow said:

—They were caught near the Hill of Lyons.

—Who caught them?

—Mr Gleeson and the minister. They were on a car.

The same fellow added:

—A fellow in the higher line told me.

Fleming asked:

—But why did they run away, tell us?

—I know why, Cecil Thunder said. Because they had fecked cash out of the rector's room.

—Who fecked it?

—Kickham's brother. And they all went shares in it.

But that was stealing. How could they have done that?

—A fat lot you know about it, Thunder! Wells said. I know why they scut.

—Tell us why.

—I was told not to, Wells said.

—O, go on, Wells, all said. You might tell us. We won't let it out.

Stephen bent forward his head to hear. Wells looked round to see if anyone was coming. Then he said secretly:

—You know the altar wine they keep in the press in the sacristy?

—Yes.

—Well, they drank that and it was found out who did it by the smell. And that's why they ran away, if you want to know.

And the fellow who had spoken first said:

—Yes, that's what I heard too from the fellow in the higher line.

The fellows were all silent. Stephen stood among them, afraid to speak, listening. A faint sickness of awe made him feel weak. How could they have done that? He thought of the dark silent sacristy. There were dark wooden presses there where the crimped surplices lay quietly folded. It was not the chapel but still you had to speak under your breath. It was a holy place. He remembered the summer evening he had been there to be dressed as boatbearer, the evening of the procession to the little altar in the wood. A strange and holy place. The boy that held the censer had swung it gently to and fro near the door with the silvery cap lifted by the middle chain to keep the coals lighting. That was called charcoal: and it had burned quietly as the fellow had swung it gently and had given off a weak sour smell. And then when all were vested he had stood holding out the boat to the rector and the rector had put a spoonful of incense in it and it had hissed on the red coals.

The fellows were talking together in little groups here and there on the playground. The fellows seemed to him to have grown smaller: that was because a sprinter had knocked him down the day before, a fellow out of second of grammar. He had been thrown by the fellow's machine lightly on the cinderpath and his spectacles had been broken in three pieces and some of the grit of the cinders had gone into his mouth.

That was why the fellows seemed to him smaller and farther away and the goalposts so thin and far and the soft grey sky so high up. But there was no play on the football grounds for cricket was coming: and some said that Barnes would be the prof and some said it would be Flowers. And all over the playgrounds they were playing rounders and bowling twisters and lobs. And from here and from there came the sounds of the cricketbats through the soft grey air. They said: pick, pack, pock, puck: like drops of water in a fountain slowly falling in the brimming bowl.

Athy, who had been silent, said quietly:

—You are all wrong.

All turned towards him eagerly.

—Why?

—Do you know?

—Who told you?

—Tell us, Athy.

Athy pointed across the playground to where Simon Moonan was walking by himself kicking a stone before him.

—Ask him, he said.

The fellows looked there and then said:

—Why him?

—Is he in it?

—Tell us, Athy. Go on. You might if you know.

Athy lowered his voice and said:

—Do you know why those fellows scut? I will tell you but you must not let on you know.

He paused for a moment and then said mysteriously:

—They were caught with Simon Moonan and Tusker Boyle in the square one night.

The fellows looked at him and asked:

—Caught?

—What doing?

Athy said:

—Smugging.

All the fellows were silent: and Athy said:

—And that's why.

Stephen looked at the faces of the fellows but they were all looking across the playground. He wanted to ask somebody about it. What did that mean about the smugging in the square? Why did the five fellows out of the higher line run away for that? It was a joke, he thought. Simon Moonan had nice clothes and one night he had shown him a ball of creamy sweets that the fellows of the football fifteen had rolled down to him along the carpet in the middle of the refectory when he was at the door. It was the night of the match against the Bective Rangers and the ball was made just like a red and green apple only it opened and it was full of the creamy sweets. And one day Boyle had said that an elephant had two tuskers instead of two tusks and that was why he was called Tusker Boyle but some fellows called him Lady Boyle because he was always at his nails, paring them.

Eileen had long thin cool white hands too because she was a girl. They were like ivory; only soft. That was the meaning of *Tower of Ivory* but protestants could not understand it and made fun of it. One day he had stood beside her looking into the hotel grounds. A waiter was running up a trail of bunting on the flagstaff and a fox terrier was scampering to and fro on the sunny lawn. She had put her hand into his pocket where his hand was and he had felt how cool and thin and soft her hand was. She had said that pockets were funny things to have: and then all of a sudden she had broken away and had run laughing down the sloping curve of the path. Her fair hair had streamed out behind her like gold in the sun. *Tower of Ivory. House of Gold.* By thinking of things you could understand them.

But why in the square? You went there when you wanted to do something. It was all thick slabs of slate and water trickled all day out of tiny pinholes and there was a queer smell of stale water there. And behind the door of one of the closets there was a drawing in red pencil of a bearded man in a Roman dress with a brick in each hand and underneath was the name of the drawing:

Balbus was building a wall.

Some fellows had drawn it there for a cod. It had a funny face but it was very like a man with a beard. And on the wall of another closet there was written in backhand in beautiful writing:

Julius Cæsar wrote The Calico Belly.

Perhaps that was why they were there because it was a place where some fellows wrote things for cod. But all the same it was queer what Athy said and the way he said it. It was not a cod because they had run away. He looked with the others in silence across the playground and began to feel afraid.

At last Fleming said:

—And we are all to be punished for what other fellows did?

—I won't come back, see if I do, Cecil Thunder said. Three days' silence in the refectory and sending us up for six and eight every minute.

—Yes, said Wells. And old Barrett has a new way of twisting the note so that you can't open it and fold it again to see how many ferulæ you are to get. I won't come back too.

—Yes, said Cecil Thunder, and the prefect of studies was in second of grammar this morning.

—Let us get up a rebellion, Fleming said. Will we?

All the fellows were silent. The air was very silent and you could hear the cricketbats but more slowly than before: pick, pock.

Wells asked:

—What is going to be done to them?

—Simon Moonan and Tusker are going to be flogged, Athy said, and the fellows in the higher line got their choice of flogging or being expelled.

—And which are they taking? asked the fellow who had spoken first.

—All are taking expulsion except Corrigan, Athy answered. He's going to be flogged by Mr Gleeson.

—Is it Corrigan that big fellow? said Fleming. Why, he'd be able for two of Gleeson!

—I know why, Cecil Thunder said. He is right and the other fellows are wrong because a flogging wears off after a bit but a fellow that has been expelled from college is known all his life on account of it. Besides Gleeson won't flog him hard.

—It's best of his play not to, Fleming said.

—I wouldn't like to be Simon Moonan and Tusker, Cecil Thunder said. But I don't believe they will be flogged. Perhaps they will be sent up for twice nine.

—No, no, said Athy. They'll both get it on the vital spot.

Wells rubbed himself and said in a crying voice:

—Please, sir, let me off!

Athy grinned and turned up the sleeves of his jacket, saying:

> *It can't be helped;*
> *It must be done.*
> *So down with your breeches*
> *And out with your bum.*

The fellows laughed; but he felt that they were a little afraid. In the silence of the soft grey air he heard the cricket-bats from here and from there: pock. That was a sound to hear but if you were hit then you would feel a pain. The pandybat made a sound too but not like that. The fellows said it was made of whalebone and leather with lead inside: and he wondered what was the pain like. There were different kinds of pains for all the different kinds of sounds. A long thin cane would have a high whistling sound and he wondered what was that pain like. It made him shivery to think of it and cold: and what Athy said too. But what was there to laugh at in it? It made him shivery: but that was because you always felt like a shiver when you let down your trousers. It was the same in the bath when you undressed yourself. He wondered who had to let them down, the master or the boy himself. O how could they laugh about it that way?

He looked at Athy's rolledup sleeves and knuckly inky hands. He had rolled up his sleeves to show how Mr Gleeson would roll up his sleeves. But Mr Gleeson had round shiny cuffs and clean white wrists and fattish white hands and the nails of them were long and pointed. Perhaps he pared them too like Lady Boyle. But they were terribly long and pointed nails. So long and cruel they were though the white fattish hands were not cruel but gentle. And though he trembled with cold and fright to think of the cruel long nails and of the high whistling sound of the cane and of the chill you felt at the end of your shirt when you undressed yourself yet he felt a feeling of queer quiet pleasure inside him to think of the white fattish hands, clean and strong and gentle. And he thought of what Cecil Thunder had said; that Mr Gleeson would not flog Corrigan hard. And Fleming had said he would not because it was best of his play not to. But that was not why.

A voice from far out on the playground cried:

—All in!

And other voices cried:

—All in! All in!

During the writing lesson he sat with his arms folded, listening to the slow scraping of the pens. Mr Harford went to and fro making little signs in red pencil and sometimes sitting beside the boy to show him how to hold the pen. He had tried to spell out the headline for himself though he knew already what it was for it was the last of the book. *Zeal without prudence is like a ship adrift.* But the lines of the letters were like fine invisible threads and it was only by closing his right eye tight tight and staring out of the left eye that he could make out the full curves of the capital.

But Mr Harford was very decent and never got into a wax. All the other masters got into dreadful waxes. But why were they to suffer for what fellows in the higher line did? Wells had said that they had drunk some of the altar wine out of the press in the sacristy and that it had been found out who had done it by the smell. Perhaps they had stolen a monstrance to run away with it and sell it somewhere. That must have been a terrible sin, to go in there quietly at night, to open the dark press and steal the flashing gold thing into which God was put on the altar in the middle of flowers and candles at benediction while the incense went up in clouds at both sides as the fellow swung the censer and Dominic Kelly sang the first part by himself in the choir. But God was not in it of course when they stole it. But still it was a strange and a great sin even to touch it. He thought of it with deep awe; a terrible and strange sin: it thrilled him to think of it in the silence when the pens scraped lightly. But to drink the altar wine out of the press and be found out by the smell was a sin too: but it was not terrible and strange. It only made you feel a little sickish on account of the smell of the wine. Because on the day when he had made his first holy communion in the chapel he had shut his eyes and opened his mouth and put out his tongue a little: and when the rector had stooped down to give him the holy communion he had smelt a faint winy smell off the rector's breath after the wine of the mass. The word was beautiful: wine. It made you think of dark purple because the grapes were dark purple that grew in Greece outside houses like white temples. But the faint smell off the rector's breath had made him feel a sick feeling on the morning of his first communion. The day of your first communion was the happiest day of your life. And once a lot of generals had asked Napoleon what was the happiest day of his life. They thought he would say the day he won some great battle or the day he was made an emperor. But he said:

—Gentlemen, the happiest day of my life was the day on which I made my first holy communion.

Father Arnall came in and the Latin lesson began and he remained still, leaning on the desk with his arms folded. Father Arnall gave out the themebooks and he said that they were scandalous and that they were all to be written out again with the corrections at once. But the worst of all was Fleming's theme because the pages were stuck together by a blot: and Father Arnall held it up by a corner and said it was an insult to any master to send him up such a theme. Then he asked Jack Lawton to decline the noun *mare* and Jack Lawton stopped at the ablative singular and could not go on with the plural.

—You should be ashamed of yourself, said Father Arnall sternly. You, the leader of the class!

Then he asked the next boy and the next and the next. Nobody knew. Father Arnall became very quiet, more and more quiet as each boy tried to answer and could not. But his face was blacklooking and his eyes were staring though his voice was so quiet. Then he asked Fleming and Fleming said that that word had no plural. Father Arnall suddenly shut the book and shouted at him:

—Kneel out there in the middle of the class. You are one of the idlest boys I ever met. Copy out your themes again the rest of you.

Fleming moved heavily out of his place and knelt between the two last benches. The others boys bent over their themebooks and began to write. A silence filled the classroom and

Stephen, glancing timidly at Father Arnall's dark face, saw that it was a little red from the wax he was in.

Was that a sin for Father Arnall to be in a wax or was he allowed to get into a wax when the boys were idle because that made them study better or was he only letting on to be in a wax? It was because he was allowed because a priest would know what a sin was and would not do it. But if he did it one time by mistake what would he do to go to confession? Perhaps he would go to confession to the minister. And if the minister did it he would go to the rector: and the rector to the provincial: and the provincial to the general of the jesuits. That was called the order: and he had heard his father say that they were all clever men. They could all have become highup people in the world if they had not become jesuits. And he wondered what Father Arnall and Paddy Barrett would have become and what Mr McGlade and Mr Gleeson would have become if they had not become jesuits. It was hard to think what because you would have to think of them in a different way with different coloured coats and trousers and with beards and moustaches and different kinds of hats.

The door opened quietly and closed. A quick whisper ran through the class: the prefect of studies. There was an instant of dead silence and then the loud crack of a pandybat on the last desk. Stephen's heart leapt up in fear.

—Any boys want flogging here, Father Arnall? cried the prefect of studies. Any lazy idle loafers that want flogging in this class?

He came to the middle of the class and saw Fleming on his knees.

—Hoho! he cried. Who is this boy? Why is he on his knees? What is your name, boy?

—Fleming, sir.

—Hoho, Fleming! An idler of course. I can see it in your eye. Why is he on his knees, Father Arnall?

—He wrote a bad Latin theme, Father Arnall said, and he missed all the questions in grammar.

—Of course he did! cried the prefect of studies. Of course he did! A born idler! I can see it in the corner of his eye.

He banged his pandybat down on the desk and cried:

—Up, Fleming! Up, my boy!

Fleming stood up slowly.

—Hold out! cried the prefect of studies.

Fleming held out his hand. The pandybat came down on it with a loud smacking sound: one, two, three, four, five, six.

—Other hand!

The pandybat came down again in six loud quick smacks.

—Kneel down! cried the prefect of studies.

Fleming knelt down squeezing his hands under his armpits, his face contorted with pain, but Stephen knew how hard his hands were because Fleming was always rubbing rosin into them. But perhaps he was in great pain for the noise of the pandies was terrible. Stephen's heart was beating and fluttering.

—At your work, all of you! shouted the prefect of studies. We want no lazy idle loafers here, lazy idle little schemers. At your work, I tell you. Father Dolan will be in to see you every day. Father Dolan will be in tomorrow.

He poked one of the boys in the side with the pandybat, saying:

—You, boy! When will Father Dolan be in again?

—Tomorrow, sir, said Tom Furlong's voice.

—Tomorrow and tomorrow and tomorrow, said the prefect of studies. Make up your minds for that. Every day Father Dolan. Write away. You, boy, who are you?

Stephen's heart jumped suddenly.

—Dedalus, sir.

—Why are you not writing like the others?

—I . . . my . . .

He could not speak with fright.

—Why is he not writing, Father Arnall?

—He broke his glasses, said Father Arnall, and I exempted him from work.

—Broke? What is this I hear? What is this your name is? said the prefect of studies.

—Dedalus, sir.

—Out here, Dedalus. Lazy little schemer. I see schemer in your face. Where did you break your glasses?

Stephen stumbled into the middle of the class, blinded by fear and haste.

—Where did you break your glasses? repeated the prefect of studies.

—The cinderpath, sir.

—Hoho! The cinderpath! cried the prefect of studies. I know that trick.

Stephen lifted his eyes in wonder and saw for a moment Father Dolan's whitegrey not young face, his baldy whitegrey head with fluff at the sides of it, the steel rims of his spectacles and his nocoloured eyes looking through the glasses. Why did he say he knew that trick?

—Lazy idle little loafer! cried the prefect of studies. Broke my glasses! An old schoolboy trick! Out with your hand this moment!

Stephen closed his eyes and held out in the air his trembling hand with the palm upwards. He felt the prefect of studies touch it for a moment at the fingers to straighten it and then the swish of the sleeve of the soutane as the pandybat was lifted to strike. A hot burning stinging tingling blow like the loud crack of a broken stick made his trembling hand crumple together like a leaf in the fire: and at the sound and the pain scalding tears were driven into his eyes. His whole body was shaking with fright, his arm was shaking and his crumpled burning livid hand shook like a loose leaf in the air. A cry sprang to his lips, a prayer to be let off. But though the tears scalded his eyes and his limbs quivered with pain and fright he held back the hot tears and the cry that scalded his throat.

—Other hand! shouted the prefect of studies.

Stephen drew back his maimed and quivering right arm and held out his left hand. The soutane sleeve swished again as the pandybat was lifted and a loud crashing sound and a fierce maddening tingling burning pain made his hand shrink together with the palms and fingers in a livid quivering mass. The scalding water burst forth from his eyes and, burning with shame and agony and fear, he drew back his shaking arm in terror and burst out into a whine of pain. His body shook with a palsy of fright and in shame and rage he felt the scalding cry come from his throat and the scalding tears falling out of his eyes and down his flaming cheeks.

—Kneel down! cried the prefect of studies.

Stephen knelt down quickly pressing his beaten hands to his sides. To think of them beaten and swollen with pain all in a moment made him feel so sorry for them as if they were not his own but someone else's that he felt sorry for. And as he knelt, calming the last sobs in his throat and feeling the burning tingling pain pressed in to his sides, he thought of the hands which he had held out in the air with the palms up and of the firm touch of the prefect of studies when he had steadied the shaking fingers and of the beaten swollen reddened mass of palm and fingers that shook helplessly in the air.

—Get at your work, all of you, cried the prefect of studies from the door. Father Dolan will be in every day to see if any boy, any lazy idle little loafer wants flogging. Every day. Every day.

The door closed behind him.

The hushed class continued to copy out the themes. Father Arnall rose from his seat and went among them, helping the boys with gentle words and telling them the mistakes they had made. His voice was very gentle and soft. Then he returned to his seat and said to Fleming and Stephen:

—You may return to your places, you two.

Fleming and Stephen rose and, walking to their seats, sat down. Stephen, scarlet with shame, opened a book quickly with one weak hand and bent down upon it, his face close to the page.

It was unfair and cruel because the doctor had told him not

to read without glasses and he had written home to his father that morning to send him a new pair. And Father Arnall had said that he need not study till the new glasses came. Then to be called a schemer before the class and to be pandied when he always got the card for first or second and was the leader of the Yorkists! How could the prefect of studies know that it was a trick? He felt the touch of the prefect's fingers as they had steadied his hand and at first he had thought he was going to shake hands with him because the fingers were soft and firm: but then in an instant he had heard the swish of the soutane sleeve and the crash. It was cruel and unfair to make him kneel in the middle of the class then: and Father Arnall had told them both that they might return to their places without making any difference between them. He listened to Father Arnall's low and gentle voice as he corrected the themes. Perhaps he was sorry now and wanted to be decent. But it was unfair and cruel. The prefect of studies was a priest but that was cruel and unfair. And his whitegrey face and the nocoloured eyes behind the steelrimmed spectacles were cruel looking because he had steadied the hand first with his firm soft fingers and that was to hit it better and louder.

—It's a stinking mean thing, that's what it is, said Fleming in the corridor as the classes were passing out in file to the refectory, to pandy a fellow for what is not his fault.

—You really broke your glasses by accident, didn't you? Nasty Roche asked.

Stephen felt his heart filled by Fleming's words and did not answer.

—Of course he did! said Fleming. I wouldn't stand it. I'd go up and tell the rector on him.

—Yes, said Cecil Thunder eagerly, and I saw him lift the pandybat over his shoulder and he's not allowed to do that.

—Did they hurt much? Nasty Roche asked.

—Very much, Stephen said.

—I wouldn't stand it, Fleming repeated, from Baldyhead or any other Baldyhead. It's a stinking mean low trick, that's what it is. I'd go straight up to the rector and tell him about it after dinner.

—Yes, do. Yes, do, said Cecil Thunder.

—Yes, do. Yes, go up and tell the rector on him, Dedalus, said Nasty Roche, because he said that he'd come in tomorrow again to pandy you.

—Yes, yes. Tell the rector, all said.

And there were some fellows out of second of grammar listening and one of them said:

—The senate and the Roman people declared that Dedalus had been wrongly punished.

It was wrong; it was unfair and cruel: and, as he sat in the refectory, he suffered time after time in memory the same humiliation until he began to wonder whether it might not really be that there was something in his face which made him look like a schemer and he wished he had a little mirror to see. But there could not be; and it was unjust and cruel and unfair.

He could not eat the blackish fish fritters they got on Wednesdays in Lent and one of his potatoes had the mark of the spade in it. Yes, he would do what the fellows had told him. He would go up and tell the rector that he had been wrongly punished. A thing like that had been done before by somebody in history, by some great person whose head was in the books of history. And the rector would declare that he had been wrongly punished because the senate and the Roman people always declared that the men who did that had been wrongly punished. Those were the great men whose names were in Richmal Magnall's Questions. History was all about those men and what they did and that was what Peter Parley's Tales about Greece and Rome were all about. Peter Parley himself was on the first page in a picture. There was a road over a heath with grass at the side and little bushes: and Peter Parley had a broad hat like a protestant minister and a big stick and he was walking fast along the road to Greece and Rome.

It was easy what he had to do. All he had to do was when the dinner was over and he came out in his turn to go on walking but not out to the corridor but up the staircase on the right that led to the castle. He had nothing to do but that: to turn to the right and walk fast up the staircase and in half a minute he would be in the low dark narrow corridor that led through the castle to the rector's room. And every fellow had said that it was unfair, even the fellow out of second of grammar who had said that about the senate and the Roman people.

What would happen? He heard the fellows of the higher line stand up at the top of the refectory and heard their steps as they came down the matting: Paddy Rath and Jimmy Magee and the Spaniard and the Portuguese and the fifth was big Corrigan who was going to be flogged by Mr Gleeson. That was why the prefect of studies had called him a schemer and pandied him for nothing: and, straining his weak eyes, tired with the tears, he watched big Corrigan's broad shoulders and big hanging black head passing in the file. But he had done something and besides Mr Gleeson would not flog him hard: and he remembered how big Corrigan looked in the bath. He had skin the same colour as the turfcoloured bogwater in the shallow end of the bath and when he walked along the side his feet slapped loudly on the wet tiles and at every step his thighs shook a little because he was fat.

The refectory was half empty and the fellows were still passing out in file. He could go up the staircase because there was never a priest or a prefect outside the refectory door. But he could not go. The rector would side with the prefect of studies and think it was a schoolboy trick and then the prefect of studies would come in every day the same only it would be worse because he would be dreadfully waxy at any fellow going up to the rector about him. The fellows had told him to go but they would not go themselves. They had forgotten all about it. No, it was best to forget all about it and perhaps the prefect of studies had only said he would come in. No, it was best to hide out of the way because when you were small and young you could often escape that way.

The fellows at his table stood up. He stood up and passed out among them in the file. He had to decide. He was coming near the door. If he went on with the fellows he could never go up to the rector because he could not leave the playground for that. And if he went and was pandied all the same all the fellows would make fun and talk about young Dedalus going up to the rector to tell on the prefect of studies.

He was walking down along the matting and he saw the door before him. It was impossible: he could not. He thought of the baldy head of the prefect of studies with the cruel nocoloured eyes looking at him and he heard the voice of the prefect of studies asking him twice what his name was. Why could he not remember the name when he was told the first time? Was he not listening the first time or was it to make fun out of the name? The great men in the history had names like that and nobody made fun of them. It was his own name that he should have made fun of if he wanted to make fun. Dolan: it was like the name of a woman that washed clothes.

He had reached the door and, turning quickly up to the right, walked up the stairs and, before he could make up his mind to come back, he had entered the low dark narrow corridor that led to the castle. And as he crossed the threshold of the door of the corridor he saw, without turning his head to look, that all the fellows were looking after him as they went filing by.

He passed along the narrow dark corridor, passing little doors that were the doors of the rooms of the community. He peered in front of him and right and left through the gloom and thought that those must be portraits. It was dark and silent and his eyes were weak and tired with tears so that he could not see. But he thought they were the portraits of the saints and great men of the order who were looking down on him silently as he passed: saint Ignatius Loyola holding an open book and pointing to the words *Ad Majorem Dei*

Gloriam in it, saint Francis Xavier pointing to his chest, Lorenzo Ricci with his berretta on his head like one of the prefects of the lines, the three patrons of holy youth, saint Stanislaus Kostka, saint Aloysius Gonzaga and blessed John Berchmans, all with young faces because they died when they were young, and Father Peter Kenny sitting in a chair wrapped in a big cloak.

He came out on the landing above the entrance hall and looked about him. That was where Hamilton Rowan had passed and the marks of the soldiers' slugs were there. And it was there that the old servants had seen the ghost in the white cloak of a marshal.

An old servant was sweeping at the end of the landing. He asked him where was the rector's room and the old servant pointed to the door at the far end and looked after him as he went on to it and knocked.

There was no answer. He knocked again more loudly and his heart jumped when he heard a muffled voice say:

—Come in!

He turned the handle and opened the door and fumbled for the handle of the green baize door inside. He found it and pushed it open and went in.

He saw the rector sitting at a desk writing. There was a skull on the desk and a strange solemn smell in the room like the old leather of chairs.

His heart was beating fast on account of the solemn place he was in and the silence of the room: and he looked at the skull and at the rector's kindlooking face.

—Well, my little man, said the rector, what is it?

Stephen swallowed down the thing in his throat and said:

—I broke my glasses, sir.

The rector opened his mouth and said:

—O!

Then he smiled and said:

—Well, if we broke our glasses we must write home for a new pair.

—I wrote home, sir, said Stephen, and Father Arnall said I am not to study till they come.

—Quite right! said the rector.

Stephen swallowed down the thing again and tried to keep his legs and his voice from shaking.

—But, sir . . .

—Yes?

—Father Dolan came in today and pandied me because I was not writing my theme.

The rector looked at him in silence and he could feel the blood rising to his face and the tears about to rise to his eyes.

The rector said:

—Your name is Dedalus, isn't it?

—Yes, sir.

—And where did you break your glasses?

—On the cinderpath, sir. A fellow was coming out of the bicycle house and I fell and they got broken. I don't know the fellow's name.

The rector looked at him again in silence. Then he smiled and said:

—O, well, it was a mistake; I am sure Father Dolan did not know.

—But I told him I broke them, sir, and he pandied me.

—Did you tell him that you had written home for a new pair? the rector asked.

—No, sir.

—O well then, said the rector, Father Dolan did not understand. You can say that I excuse you from your lessons for a few days.

Stephen said quickly for fear his trembling would prevent him:

—Yes, sir, but Father Dolan said he will come in tomorrow to pandy me again for it.

—Very well, the rector said, it is a mistake and I shall speak to Father Dolan myself. Will that do now?

Stephen felt the tears wetting his eyes and murmured:

—O yes sir, thanks.

The rector held his hand across the side of the desk where the skull was and Stephen, placing his hand in it for a moment, felt a cool moist palm.

—Good day now, said the rector, withdrawing his hand and bowing.

—Good day, sir, said Stephen.

He bowed and walked quietly out of the room, closing the doors carefully and slowly.

But when he had passed the old servant on the landing and was again in the low narrow dark corridor he began to walk faster and faster. Faster and faster he hurried on through the gloom excitedly. He bumped his elbow against the door at the end and, hurrying down the staircase, walked quickly through the two corridors and out into the air.

He could hear the cries of the fellows on the playgrounds. He broke into a run and, running quicker and quicker, ran across the cinderpath and reached the third line playground, panting.

The fellows had seen him running. They closed round him in a ring, pushing one against another to hear.

—Tell us! Tell us!

—What did he say?

—Did you go in?

—What did he say?

—Tell us! Tell us!

He told them what he had said and what the rector had said and, when he had told them, all the fellows flung their caps spinning up into the air and cried:

—Hurroo!

They caught their caps and sent them up again spinning skyhigh and cried again:

—Hurroo! Hurroo!

They made a cradle of their locked hands and hoisted him up among them and carried him along till he struggled to get free. And when he had escaped from them they broke away in all directions, flinging their caps again into the air and whistling as they went spinning up and crying:

—Hurroo!

And they gave three groans for Baldyhead Dolan and three cheers for Conmee and they said he was the decentest rector that was ever in Clongowes.

The cheers died away in the soft grey air. He was alone. He was happy and free: but he would not be anyway proud with Father Dolan. He would be very quiet and obedient: and he wished that he could do something kind for him to show him that he was not proud.

The air was soft and grey and mild and evening was coming. There was the smell of evening in the air, the smell of the fields in the country where they digged up turnips to peel them and eat them when they went out for a walk to Major Barton's, the smell there was in the little wood beyond the pavilion where the gallnuts were.

The fellows were practising long shies and bowing lobs and slow twisters. In the soft grey silence he could hear the bump of the balls: and from here and from there through the quiet air the sound of the cricket bats: pick, pack, pock, puck: like drops of water in a fountain falling softly in the brimming bowl.

U NCLE Charles smoked such black twist that at last his
nephew suggested to him to enjoy his morning smoke in
a little outhouse at the end of the garden.

—Very good, Simon. All serene, Simon, said the old man
tranquilly. Anywhere you like. The outhouse will do me
nicely: it will be more salubrious.

—Damn me, said Mr Dedalus frankly, if I know how you
can smoke such villainous awful tobacco. It's like gunpowder,
by God.

—It's very nice, Simon, replied the old man. Very cool and
mollifying.

Every morning, therefore, uncle Charles repaired to his
outhouse but not before he had creased and brushed scrupulously his back hair and brushed and put on his tall hat. While
he smoked the brim of his tall hat and the bowl of his pipe
were just visible beyond the jambs of the outhouse door. His
arbour, as he called the reeking outhouse which he shared
with the cat and the garden tools, served him also as a sound-
ingbox: and every morning he hummed contentedly one of his
favourite songs: *O, twine me a bower* or *Blue eyes and golden
hair* or *The Groves of Blarney* while the grey and blue coils of
smoke rose slowly from his pipe and vanished in the pure air.

During the first part of the summer in Blackrock uncle
Charles was Stephen's constant companion. Uncle Charles
was a hale old man with a welltanned skin, rugged features
and white side whiskers. On week days he did messages between the house in Carysfort Avenue and those shops in the
main street of the town with which the family dealt. Stephen
was glad to go with him on these errands for uncle Charles

6 o

helped him very liberally to handfuls of whatever was exposed in open boxes and barrels outside the counter. He would seize a handful of grapes and sawdust or three or four American apples and thrust them generously into his grand-nephew's hand while the shopman smiled uneasily; and, on Stephen's feigning reluctance to take them, he would frown and say:

—Take them, sir. Do you hear me, sir? They're good for your bowels.

When the order list had been booked the two would go on to the park where an old friend of Stephen's father, Mike Flynn, would be found seated on a bench, waiting for them. Then would begin Stephen's run round the park. Mike Flynn would stand at the gate near the railway station, watch in hand, while Stephen ran round the track in the style Mike Flynn favoured, his head high lifted, his knees well lifted and his hands held straight down by his sides. When the morning practice was over the trainer would make his comments and sometimes illustrate them by shuffling along for a yard or so comically in an old pair of blue canvas shoes. A small ring of wonderstruck children and nursemaids would gather to watch him and linger even when he and uncle Charles had sat down again and were talking athletics and politics. Though he had heard his father say that Mike Flynn had put some of the best runners of modern times through his hands Stephen often glanced with mistrust at his trainer's flabby stubblecovered face, as it bent over the long stained fingers through which he rolled his cigarette, and with pity at the mild lustreless blue eyes which would look up suddenly from the task and gaze vaguely into the blue distance while the long swollen fingers ceased their rolling and grains and fibres of tobacco fell back into the pouch.

On the way home uncle Charles would often pay a visit to the chapel and, as the font was above Stephen's reach, the old man would dip his hand and then sprinkle the water briskly about Stephen's clothes and on the floor of the porch. While he prayed he knelt on his red handkerchief and read above his breath from a thumbblackened prayerbook wherein catchwords were printed at the foot of every page. Stephen knelt at his side respecting, though he did not share, his piety. He often wondered what his granduncle prayed for so seriously. Perhaps he prayed for the souls in purgatory or for the grace of a happy death or perhaps he prayed that God might send him back a part of the big fortune he had squandered in Cork.

On Sundays Stephen with his father and his granduncle took their constitutional. The old man was a nimble walker in spite of his corns and often ten or twelve miles of the road were covered. The little village of Stillorgan was the parting of the ways. Either they went to the left towards the Dublin mountains or along the Goatstown road and thence into Dundrum, coming home by Sandyford. Trudging along the road or standing in some grimy wayside publichouse his elders spoke constantly of the subjects nearer their hearts, of Irish politics, of Munster and of the legends of their own family, to all of which Stephen lent an avid ear. Words which he did not understand he said over and over to himself till he had learned them by heart: and through them he had glimpses of the real world about him. The hour when he too would take part in the life of that world seemed drawing near and in secret he began to make ready for the great part which he felt awaited him the nature of which he only dimly apprehended.

His evenings were his own; and he pored over a ragged translation of *The Count of Monte Cristo*. The figure of that dark avenger stood forth in his mind for whatever he had heard or divined in childhood of the strange and terrible. At night he built up on the parlour table an image of the wonderful island cave out of transfers and paper flowers and coloured tissue paper and strips of the silver and golden paper in which chocolate is wrapped. When he had broken up this scenery, weary of its tinsel, there would come to his mind the bright picture of Marseilles, of sunny trellisses and of Mercedes. Outside Blackrock, on the road that led to the mountains, stood a small whitewashed house in the garden of which grew many rosebushes: and in this house, he told himself, another Mercedes lived. Both on the outward and on the homeward journey he measured distance by this landmark: and in his imagination he lived through a long train of adventures, marvellous as those in the book itself, towards the close of which there appeared an image of himself, grown older and sadder, standing in a moonlit garden with Mercedes who had so many years before slighted his love, and with a sadly proud gesture of refusal, saying:

—Madam, I never eat muscatel grapes.

He became the ally of a boy named Aubrey Mills and founded with him a gang of adventurers in the avenue. Aubrey carried a whistle dangling from his buttonhole and a bicycle lamp attached to his belt while the others had short sticks thrust daggerwise through theirs. Stephen, who had read of Napoleon's plain style of dress, chose to remain unadorned and thereby heightened for himself the pleasure of taking counsel with his lieutenant before giving orders. The gang made forays into the gardens of old maids or went down to the castle and fought a battle on the shaggy weedgrown rocks, coming home after it weary stragglers with the stale odours of the foreshore in their nostrils and the rank oils of the seawrack upon their hands and in their hair.

Aubrey and Stephen had a common milkman and often they drove out in the milkcar to Carrickmines where the cows were at grass. While the men were milking the boys would take turns in riding the tractable mare round the field. But when autumn came the cows were driven home from the grass: and the first sight of the filthy cowyard at Stradbrook with its foul green puddles and clots of liquid dung and steaming brantroughs sickened Stephen's heart. The cattle which had seemed so beautiful in the country on sunny days revolted him and he could not even look at the milk they yielded.

The coming of September did not trouble him this year for he was not to be sent back to Clongowes. The practice in the park came to an end when Mike Flynn went into hospital. Aubrey was at school and had only an hour or two free in the evening. The gang fell asunder and there were no more nightly forays or battles on the rocks. Stephen sometimes went round with the car which delivered the evening milk: and these chilly drives blew away his memory of the filth of the cowyard and he felt no repugnance at seeing the cowhairs and hayseeds on the milkman's coat. Whenever the car drew up before a house he waited to catch a glimpse of a wellscrubbed kitchen or of a softlylighted hall and to see how the servant would hold the jug and how she would close the door. He thought it should be a pleasant life enough, driving along the roads every evening to deliver milk, if he had warm gloves and a fat bag of ginger-nuts in his pocket to eat from. But the same foreknowledge which had sickened his heart and made his legs sag suddenly as he raced round the park, the same intuition which had made him glance with mistrust at his trainer's flabby stub-blecovered face as it bent heavily over his long stained fingers, dissipated any vision of the future. In a vague way he under-stood that his father was in trouble and that this was the reason why he himself had not been sent back to Clongowes. For some time he had felt the slight changes in his house; and these changes in what he had deemed unchangeable were so many slight shocks to his boyish conception of the world. The ambition which he felt astir at times in the darkness of his soul sought no outlet. A dusk like that of the outer world obscured his mind as he heard the mare's hoofs clattering along the tramtrack on the Rock Road and the great can swaying and rattling behind him.

He returned to Mercedes and, as he brooded upon her image, a strange unrest crept into his blood. Sometimes a fever gathered within him and led him to rove alone in the evening along the quiet avenue. The peace of the gardens and the kindly lights in the windows poured a tender influence into his restless heart. The noise of children at play annoyed him and their silly voices made him feel, even more keenly than he had felt at Clongowes, that he was different from others. He did not want to play. He wanted to meet in the real world the unsubstantial image which his soul so constantly beheld. He did not know where to seek it or how: but a premonition which led him on told him that this image would, without any overt act of his, encounter him. They would meet quietly as if they had known each other and had made their tryst, perhaps at one of the gates or in some more secret place. They would be alone, surrounded by darkness and silence: and in that moment of supreme tenderness he would be transfigured. He would fade into something impalpable under her eyes and then in a moment, he would be transfigured. Weakness and timidity and inexperience would fall from him in that magic moment.

* * *

Two great yellow caravans had halted one morning before the door and men had come tramping into the house to dismantle it. The furniture had been hustled out through the front garden which was strewn with wisps of straw and rope ends and into the huge vans at the gate. When all had been safely stowed the vans had set off noisily down the avenue: and from the window of the railway carriage, in which he had sat with his redeyed mother, Stephen had seen them lumbering heavily along the Merrion Road.

The parlour fire would not draw that evening and Mr Dedalus rested the poker against the bars of the grate to attract the flame. Uncle Charles dozed in a corner of the half furnished uncarpeted room and near him the family portraits leaned against the wall. The lamp on the table shed a weak light over the boarded floor, muddied by the feet of the vanmen. Stephen sat on a footstool beside his father listening to a long and incoherent monologue. He understood little or nothing of it at first but he became slowly aware that his father had enemies and that some fight was going to take place. He felt too that he was being enlisted for the fight, that some duty was being laid upon his shoulders. The sudden flight from the comfort and revery of Blackrock, the passage through the gloomy foggy city, the thought of the bare cheerless house in which they were now to live made his heart heavy: and again an intuition or foreknowledge of the future came to him. He understood also why the servants had often whispered together in the hall and why his father had often stood on the hearthrug, with his back to the fire, talking loudly to uncle Charles who urged him to sit down and eat his dinner.

—There's a crack of the whip left in me yet, Stephen, old chap, said Mr Dedalus, poking at the dull fire with fierce energy. We're not dead yet, sonny. No, by the Lord Jesus (God forgive me) nor half dead.

Dublin was a new and complex sensation. Uncle Charles had grown so witless that he could no longer be sent out on errands and the disorder in settling in the new house left Stephen freer than he had been in Blackrock. In the beginning he contented himself with circling timidly round the neighbouring square or, at most, going half way down one of the side streets: but when he had made a skeleton map of the city in his mind he followed boldly one of its central lines until he reached the customhouse. He passed unchallenged among the docks and along the quays wondering at the multitude of corks that lay bobbing on the surface of the water in a thick yellow scum, at the crowds of quay porters and the rumbling carts and the illdressed bearded policeman. The vastness and strangeness of the life suggested to him by the bales of merchandise stocked along the walls or swung aloft out of the holds of steamers wakened again in him the unrest which had sent him wandering in the evening from garden to garden in search of Mercedes. And amid this new bustling life he might have fancied himself in another Marseilles but that he missed the bright sky and the sunwarmed trellisses of the wineshops. A vague dissatisfaction grew up within him as he looked on the quays and on the river and on the lowering skies and yet he continued to wander up and down day after day as if he really sought someone that eluded him.

He went once or twice with his mother to visit their relatives: and, though they passed a jovial array of shops lit up and adorned for Christmas, his mood of embittered silence did not leave him. The causes of his embitterment were many, remote and near. He was angry with himself for being young and the prey of restless foolish impulses, angry also with the change of fortune which was reshaping the world about him into a vision of squalor and insincerity. Yet his anger lent nothing to the vision. He chronicled with patience what he saw, detaching himself from it and testing its mortifying flavour in secret.

He was sitting on the backless chair in his aunt's kitchen. A lamp with a reflector hung on the japanned wall of the fireplace and by its light his aunt was reading the evening paper that lay on her knees. She looked a long time at a smiling picture that was set in it and said musingly:

—The beautiful Mabel Hunter!

A ringletted girl stood on tiptoe to peer at the picture and said softly:

—What is she in, mud?

—In the pantomime, love.

The child leaned her ringletted head against her mother's sleeve, gazing on the picture, and murmured as if fascinated:

—The beautiful Mabel Hunter!

As if fascinated, her eyes rested long upon those demurely taunting eyes and she murmured again devotedly:

—Isn't she an exquisite creature?

And the boy who came in from the street, stamping crookedly under his stone of coal, heard her words. He dropped his load promptly on the floor and hurried to her side to see. But she did not raise her easeful head to let him see. He mauled the edges of the paper with his reddened and blackened hands, shouldering her aside and complaining that he could not see.

He was sitting in the narrow breakfast room high up in the old darkwindowed house. The firelight flickered on the wall and beyond the window a spectral dusk was gathering upon the river. Before the fire an old woman was busy making tea and, as she bustled at her task, she told in a low voice of what the priest and the doctor had said. She told too of certain changes she had seen in her of late and of her odd ways and sayings. He sat listening to the words and following the ways of adventure that lay open in the coals, arches and vaults and winding galleries and jagged caverns.

Suddenly he became aware of something in the doorway. A skull appeared suspended in the gloom of the doorway. A feeble creature like a monkey was there, drawn thither by the sound of voices at the fire. A whining voice came from the door, asking:

—Is that Josephine?

The old bustling woman answered cheerily from the fireplace:

—No, Ellen. It's Stephen.

—O . . . O, good evening, Stephen.

He answered the greeting and saw a silly smile break over the face in the doorway.

—Do you want anything, Ellen? asked the old woman at the fire.

But she did not answer the question and said:

—I thought it was Josephine. I thought you were Josephine, Stephen.

And, repeating this several times, she fell to laughing feebly.

He was sitting in the midst of a children's party at Harold's Cross. His silent watchful manner had grown upon him and he took little part in the games. The children, wearing the spoils of their crackers, danced and romped noisily and, though he tried to share their merriment, he felt himself a gloomy figure amid the gay cocked hats and sunbonnets.

But when he had sung his song and withdrawn into a snug corner of the room he began to taste the joy of his loneliness. The mirth, which in the beginning of the evening had seemed to him false and trivial, was like a soothing air to him, passing gaily by his senses, hiding from other eyes the feverish agitation of his blood while through the circling of the dancers and amid the music and laughter her glance travelled to his corner, flattering, taunting, searching, exciting his heart.

In the hall the children who had stayed latest were putting on their things: the party was over. She had thrown a shawl about her and, as they went together towards the tram, sprays of her fresh warm breath flew gaily above her cowled head and her shoes tapped blithely on the glassy road.

It was the last tram. The lank brown horses knew it and shook their bells to the clear night in admonition. The conductor talked with the driver, both nodding often in the green light of the lamp. On the empty seats of the tram were scattered a few coloured tickets. No sound of footsteps came up or down the road. No sound broke the peace of the night save when the lank brown horses rubbed their noses together and shook their bells.

They seemed to listen, he on the upper step and she on the lower. She came up to his step many times and went down to hers again between their phrases and once or twice stood close beside him for some moments on the upper step, forgetting to go down, and then went down. His heart danced upon her movements like a cork upon a tide. He heard what her eyes said to him from beneath their cowl and knew that in some dim past, whether in life or in revery, he had heard their tale before. He saw her urge her vanities, her fine dress and sash and long black stockings, and knew that he had yielded to them a thousand times. Yet a voice within him spoke above the noise of his dancing heart, asking him would he take her gift to which he had only to stretch out his hand. And he remembered the day when he and Eileen had stood looking into the hotel grounds, watching the waiters running up a trail of bunting on the flagstaff and the fox terrier scampering to and fro on the sunny lawn, and how, all of a sudden, she had broken out into a peal of laughter and had run down the sloping curve of the path. Now, as then, he stood listlessly in his place, seemingly a tranquil watcher of the scene before him.

—She too wants me to catch hold of her, he thought. That's why she came with me to the tram. I could easily catch hold of her when she comes up to my step: nobody is looking. I could hold her and kiss her.

But he did neither: and, when he was sitting alone in the deserted tram, he tore his ticket into shreds and stared gloomily at the corrugated footboard.

The next day he sat at his table in the bare upper room for many hours. Before him lay a new pen, a new bottle of ink and a new emerald exercise. From force of habit he had written at the top of the first page the initial letters of the jesuit motto: A.M.D.G. On the first line of the page appeared the title of the verses he was trying to write: To E—— C——. He knew it was right to begin so for he had seen similar titles in the collected poems of Lord Byron. When he had written this title and drawn an ornamental line underneath he fell into a daydream and began to draw diagrams on the cover of the book. He saw himself sitting at his table in Bray the morning after the discussion at the Christmas dinnertable, trying to write a poem about Parnell on the back of one of his father's second moiety notices. But his brain had then refused to grapple with the theme and, desisting, he had covered the page with the names and addresses of certain of his classmates:

> Roderick Kickham
> John Lawton
> Anthony MacSwiney
> Simon Moonan

Now it seemed as if he would fail again but, by dint of brooding on the incident, he thought himself into confidence. During this process all these elements which he deemed common and insignificant fell out of the scene. There remained no trace of the tram itself nor of the trammen nor of the horses: nor did he and she appear vividly. The verses told only of the night and the balmy breeze and the maiden lustre of the moon. Some undefined sorrow was hidden in the hearts of the protagonists as they stood in silence beneath the leafless trees and when the moment of farewell had come the kiss, which had been withheld by one, was given by both. After this the letters L.D.S. were written at the foot of the page and, having hidden the book, he went into his mother's bedroom and gazed at his face for a long time in the mirror of her dressingtable.

But his long spell of leisure and liberty was drawing to its end. One evening his father came home full of news which kept his tongue busy all through dinner. Stephen had been awaiting his father's return for there had been mutton hash that day and he knew that his father would make him dip his bread in the gravy. But he did not relish the hash for the mention of Clongowes had coated his palate with a scum of disgust.

—I walked bang into him, said Mr Dedalus for the fourth time, just at the corner of the square.

—Then I suppose, said Mrs Dedalus, he will be able to arrange it. I mean about Belvedere.

—Of course he will, said Mr Dedalus. Don't I tell you he's provincial of the order now?

—I never liked the idea of sending him to the christian brothers myself, said Mrs Dedalus.

—Christian brothers be damned! said Mr Dedalus. Is it with Paddy Stink and Mickey Mud? No, let him stick to the jesuits in God's name since he began with them. They'll be of service to him in after years. Those are the fellows that can get you a position.

—And they're a very rich order, aren't they, Simon?

—Rather. They live well, I tell you. You saw their table at Clongowes. Fed up, by God, like gamecocks.

Mr Dedalus pushed his plate over to Stephen and bade him finish what was on it.

—Now then, Stephen, he said, you must put your shoulder to the wheel, old chap. You've had a fine long holiday.

—O, I'm sure he'll work very hard now, said Mrs Dedalus, especially when he has Maurice with him.

—O, Holy Paul, I forgot about Maurice, said Mr Dedalus.

Here, Maurice! Come here, you thickheaded ruffian! Do you know I'm going to send you to a college where they'll teach you to spell c.a.t. cat. And I'll buy you a nice little penny handkerchief to keep your nose dry. Won't that be grand fun?

Maurice grinned at his father and then at his brother. Mr Dedalus screwed his glass into his eye and stared hard at both his sons. Stephen mumbled his bread without answering his father's gaze.

—By the bye, said Mr Dedalus at length, the rector, or provincial, rather, was telling me that story about you and Father Dolan. You're an impudent thief, he said.

—O, he didn't, Simon!

—Not he! said Mr Dedalus. But he gave me a great account of the whole affair. We were chatting, you know, and one word borrowed another. And, by the way, who do you think he told me will get that job in the corporation? But I'll tell you that after. Well, as I was saying, we were chatting away quite friendly and he asked me did our friend here wear glasses still and then he told me the whole story.

—And was he annoyed, Simon?

—Annoyed! Not he! *Manly little chap!* he said.

Mr Dedalus imitated the mincing nasal tone of the provincial.

—Father Dolan and I, when I told them all at dinner about it, Father Dolan and I had a great laugh over it. *You better mind yourself, Father Dolan,* said I, *or young Dedalus will send you up for twice nine.* We had a famous laugh together over it. Ha! Ha! Ha!

Mr Dedalus turned to his wife and interjected in his natural voice:

—Shows you the spirit in which they take the boys there. O, a jesuit for your life, for diplomacy!

He reassumed the provincial's voice and repeated:

—*I told them all at dinner about it and Father Dolan and I and all of us we had a hearty laugh together over it. Ha! Ha! Ha!*

*   *   *

The night of the Whitsuntide play had come and Stephen from the window of the dressingroom looked out on the small grassplot across which lines of Chinese lanterns were stretched. He watched the visitors come down the steps from the house and pass into the theatre. Stewards in evening dress, old Belvedereans, loitered in groups about the entrance to the theatre and ushered in the visitors with ceremony. Under the sudden glow of a lantern he could recognise the smiling face of a priest.

The Blessed Sacrament had been removed from the tabernacle and the first benches had been driven so as to leave the dais of the altar and the space before it free. Against the walls stood companies of barbells and Indian clubs; the dumbbells were piled in one corner: and in the midst of countless hillocks of gymnasium shoes and sweaters and singlets in untidy brown parcels there stood the stout leatherjacketed vaulting horse waiting its turn to be carried up on the stage. A large bronze shield, tipped with silver, leaned against the panel of the altar also waiting its turn to be carried up on the stage and set in the middle of the winning team at the end of the gymnastic display.

Stephen, though in deference to his reputation for essaywriting he had been elected secretary to the gymnasium, had had no part in the first section of the programme but in the play which formed the second section he had the chief part, that of a farcical pedagogue. He had been cast for it on account of his stature and grave manners for he was now at the end of his second year at Belvedere and in number two.

A score of the younger boys in white knickers and singlets came pattering down from the stage, through the vestry and into the chapel. The vestry and chapel were peopled with eager masters and boys. The plump bald sergeantmajor was testing with his foot the springboard of the vaulting horse. The lean young man in a long overcoat, who was to give a special display of intricate club swinging, stood near watching with interest, his silvercoated clubs peeping out of his deep sidepockets. The hollow rattle of the wooden dumbbells was heard as another team made ready to go up on the stage: and in another moment the excited prefect was hustling the boys through the vestry like a flock of geese, flapping the wings of his soutane nervously and crying to the laggards to make haste. A little troop of Neapolitan peasants were practising their steps at the end of the chapel, some circling their arms above their heads, some swaying their baskets of paper violets and curtseying. In a dark corner of the chapel at the gospel side of the altar a stout old lady knelt amid her copious black skirts. When she stood up a pinkdressed figure, wearing a curly golden wig and an oldfashioned straw sunbonnet, with black pencilled eyebrows and cheeks delicately rouged and powdered, was discovered. A low murmur of curiosity ran round the chapel at the discovery of this girlish figure. One of the prefects, smiling and nodding his head, approached the dark corner and, having bowed to the stout old lady, said pleasantly:

—Is this a beautiful young lady or a doll that you have here, Mrs Tallon?

Then, bending down to peer at the smiling painted face under the leaf of the bonnet, he exclaimed:

—No! Upon my word I believe it's little Bertie Tallon after all!

Stephen at his post by the window heard the old lady and the priest laugh together and heard the boys' murmur of admiration behind him as they passed forward to see the little boy who had to dance the sunbonnet dance by himself. A movement of impatience escaped him. He let the edge of the blind fall and, stepping down from the bench on which he had been standing, walked out of the chapel.

He passed out of the schoolhouse and halted under the shed that flanked the garden. From the theatre opposite came the muffled noise of the audience and sudden brazen clashes of the soldiers' band. The light spread upwards from the glass roof making the theatre seem a festive ark, anchored among the hulks of houses, her frail cables of lanterns looping her to her moorings. A sidedoor of the theatre opened suddenly and a shaft of light flew across the grassplots. A sudden burst of music issued from the ark, the prelude of a waltz: and when the sidedoor closed again the listener could hear the faint rhythm of the music. The sentiment of the opening bars, their languor and supple movement, evoked the incommunicable emotion which had been the cause of all his day's unrest and of his impatient movement of a moment before. His unrest issued from him like a wave of sound: and on the tide of flowing music the ark was journeying, trailing her cables of lanterns in her wake. Then a noise like dwarf artillery broke the movement. It was the clapping that greeted the entry of the dumbbell team on the stage.

At the far end of the shed near the street a speck of pink light showed in the darkness and as he walked towards it he became aware of a faint aromatic odour. Two boys were standing in the shelter of a doorway, smoking, and before he reached them he had recognised Heron by his voice.

—Here comes the noble Dedalus! cried a high throaty voice. Welcome to our trusty friend!

This welcome ended in a soft peal of mirthless laughter as Heron salaamed and then began to poke the ground with his cane.

—Here I am, said Stephen, halting and glancing from Heron to his friend.

The latter was a stranger to him but in the darkness, by the aid of the glowing cigarettetips, he could make out a pale dandyish face, over which a smile was travelling slowly, a tall overcoated figure and a hard hat. Heron did not trouble himself about an introduction but said instead:

—I was just telling my friend Wallis what a lark it would be tonight if you took off the rector in the part of the schoolmaster. It would be a ripping good joke.

Heron made a poor attempt to imitate for his friend Wallis the rector's pedantic bass and then, laughing at his failure, asked Stephen to do it.

—Go on, Dedalus, he urged, you can take him off rippingly. *He that will not hear the churcha let him be to theea as the heathena and the publicana.*

The imitation was prevented by a mild expression of anger from Wallis in whose mouthpiece the cigarette had become too tightly wedged.

—Damn this blankety blank holder, he said, taking it from his mouth and smiling and frowning upon it tolerantly. It's always getting stuck like that. Do you use a holder?

—I don't smoke, answered Stephen.

—No, said Heron, Dedalus is a model youth. He doesn't smoke and he doesn't go to bazaars and he doesn't flirt and he doesn't damn anything or damn all.

Stephen shook his head and smiled in his rival's flushed and mobile face, beaked like a bird's. He had often thought it strange that Vincent Heron had a bird's face as well as a bird's name. A shock of pale hair lay on the forehead like a ruffled crest: the forehead was narrow and bony and a thin hooked nose stood out between the closeset prominent eyes which were light and inexpressive. The rivals were school friends. They sat together in class, knelt together in the chapel, talked together after beads over their lunches. As the fellows in number one were undistinguished dullards Stephen and Heron had been during the year the virtual heads of the school. It was they who went up to the rector together to ask for a free day or to get a fellow off.

—O by the way, said Heron suddenly, I saw your governor going in.

The smile waned on Stephen's face. Any allusion made to his father by a fellow or by a master put his calm to rout in a moment. He waited in timorous silence to hear what Heron might say next. Heron, however, nudged him expressively with his elbow and said:

—You're a sly dog, Dedalus!

—Why so? said Stephen.

—You'd think butter wouldn't melt in your mouth, said Heron. But I'm afraid you're a sly dog.

—Might I ask you what you are talking about? said Stephen urbanely.

—Indeed you might, answered Heron. We saw her, Wallis, didn't we? And deucedly pretty she is too. And so inquisitive! *And what part does Stephen take, Mr Dedalus? And will Stephen not sing, Mr Dedalus?* Your governor was staring at her through that eyeglass of his for all he was worth so that I think the old man has found you out too. I wouldn't care a bit, by Jove. She's ripping, isn't she, Wallis?

—Not half bad, answered Wallis quietly as he placed his holder once more in the corner of his mouth.

A shaft of momentary anger flew through Stephen's mind at these indelicate allusions in the hearing of a stranger. For him there was nothing amusing in a girl's interest and regard. All day he had thought of nothing but their leavetaking on the steps of the tram at Harold's Cross, the stream of moody emotions it had made to course through him, and the poem he had written about it. All day he had imagined a new meeting with her for he knew that she was to come to the play. The old restless moodiness had again filled his breast as it had done on the night of the party but had not found an outlet in verse. The growth and knowledge of two years of boyhood stood between then and now, forbidding such an outlet: and all day the stream of gloomy tenderness within him had started forth and returned upon itself in dark courses and eddies, wearying him in the end until the pleasantry of the prefect and the painted little boy had drawn from him a movement of impatience.

—So you may as well admit, Heron went on, that we've fairly found you out this time. You can't play the saint on me any more, that's one sure five.

A soft peal of mirthless laughter escaped from his lips and, bending down as before, he struck Stephen lightly across the calf of the leg with his cane, as if in jesting reproof.

Stephen's movement of anger had already passed. He was neither flattered nor confused but simply wished the banter to end. He scarcely resented what had seemed to him at first a silly indelicateness for he knew that the adventure in his mind stood in no danger from their words: and his face mirrored his rival's false smile.

—Admit! repeated Heron, striking him again with his cane across the calf of the leg.

The stroke was playful but not so lightly given as the first one had been. Stephen felt the skin tingle and glow slightly and almost painlessly; and bowing submissively, as if to meet his companion's jesting mood, began to recite the *Confiteor*. The episode ended well for both Heron and Wallis laughed indulgently at the irreverence.

The confession came only from Stephen's lips and, while they spoke the words, a sudden memory had carried him to another scene called up, as if by magic, at the moment when he had noted the faint cruel dimples at the corners of Heron's smiling lips and had felt the familiar stroke of the cane against his calf and had heard the familiar word of admonition:

—Admit.

It was towards the close of his first term in the college when he was in number six. His sensitive nature was still smarting under the lashes of an undivined and squalid way of life. His soul was still disquieted and cast down by the dull phenomenon of Dublin. He had emerged from a two years' spell of revery to find himself in the midst of a new scene, every event and figure of which affected him intimately, disheartened him or allured and, whether alluring or disheartening, filled him always with unrest and bitter thoughts. All the leisure which his school life left him was passed in the company of subversive writers whose gibes and violence of speech set up a ferment in his brain before they passed out of it into his crude writings.

The essay was for him the chief labour of his week and every Tuesday, as he marched from home to the school, he read his fate in the incidents of the way, pitting himself against some figure ahead of him and quickening his pace to outstrip it before a certain goal was reached or planting his steps scrupulously in the spaces of the patchwork of the footpath and telling himself that he would be first and not first in the weekly essay.

On a certain Tuesday the course of his triumphs was rudely broken. Mr Tate, the English master, pointed his finger at him and said bluntly:

—This fellow has heresy in his essay.

A hush fell on the class. Mr Tate did not break it but dug with his hand between his crossed thighs while his heavily starched linen creaked about his neck and wrists. Stephen did not look up. It was a raw spring morning and his eyes were still smarting and weak. He was conscious of failure and of detection, of the squalor of his own mind and home, and felt against his neck the raw edge of his turned and jagged collar.

A short loud laugh from Mr Tate set the class more at ease.

—Perhaps you didn't know that, he said.

—Where? asked Stephen.

Mr Tate withdrew his delving hand and spread out the essay.

—Here. It's about the Creator and the soul. Rrm . . . rrm . . . rrm. . . . Ah! *without a possibility of ever approaching nearer*. That's heresy.

Stephen murmured:

—I meant *without a possibility of ever reaching*.

It was a submission and Mr Tate, appeased, folded up the essay and passed it across to him, saying:

—O . . . Ah! *ever reaching*. That's another story.

But the class was not so soon appeased. Though nobody spoke to him of the affair after class he could feel about him a vague general malignant joy.

A few nights after this public chiding he was walking with a letter along the Drumcondra Road when he heard a voice cry:

—Halt!

He turned and saw three boys of his own class coming towards him in the dusk. It was Heron who had called out and, as he marched forward between his two attendants, he cleft the air before him with a thin cane, in time to their steps. Boland, his friend, marched beside him, a large grin on his face, while Nash came on a few steps behind, blowing from the pace and wagging his great red head.

As soon as the boys had turned into Clonliffe Road together they began to speak about books and writers, saying what books they were reading and how many books there were in their fathers' bookcases at home. Stephen listened to them in some wonderment for Boland was the dunce and Nash the idler of the class. In fact after some talk about their favourite writers Nash declared for Captain Marryat who, he said, was the greatest writer.

—Fudge! said Heron. Ask Dedalus. Who is the greatest writer, Dedalus?

Stephen noted the mockery in the question and said:

—Of prose do you mean?

—Yes.

—Newman, I think.

—Is it Cardinal Newman? asked Boland.

—Yes, answered Stephen.

The grin broadened on Nash's freckled face as he turned to Stephen and said:

—And do you like Cardinal Newman, Dedalus?

—O, many say that Newman has the best prose style, Heron said to the other two in explanation. Of course he's not a poet.

—And who is the best poet, Heron? asked Boland.

—Lord Tennyson, of course, answered Heron.

—O, yes, Lord Tennyson, said Nash. We have all his poetry at home in a book.

At this Stephen forgot the silent vows he had been making and burst out:

—Tennyson a poet! Why, he's only a rhymester!

—O, get out! said Heron. Everyone knows that Tennyson is the greatest poet.

—And who do you think is the greatest poet? asked Boland, nudging his neighbour.

—Byron, of course, answered Stephen.

Heron gave the lead and all three joined in a scornful laugh.

—What are you laughing at? asked Stephen.

—You, said Heron. Byron the greatest poet! He's only a poet for uneducated people.

—He must be a fine poet! said Boland.

—You may keep your mouth shut, said Stephen, turning on him boldly. All you know about poetry is what you wrote up on the slates in the yard and were going to be sent to the loft for.

Boland, in fact, was said to have written on the slates in the yard a couplet about a classmate of his who often rode home from the college on a pony:

> *As Tyson was riding into Jerusalem*
> *He fell and hurt his Alec Kafoozelum.*

This thrust put the two lieutenants to silence but Heron went on:

—In any case Byron was a heretic and immoral too.

—I don't care what he was, cried Stephen hotly.

—You don't care whether he was a heretic or not? said Nash.

—What do you know about it? shouted Stephen. You never read a line of anything in your life except a trans or Boland either.

—I know that Byron was a bad man, said Boland.

—Here, catch hold of this heretic, Heron called out.

In a moment Stephen was a prisoner.

—Tate made you buck up the other day, Heron went on, about the heresy in your essay.

—I'll tell him tomorrow, said Boland.

—Will you? said Stephen. You'd be afraid to open your lips.

—Afraid?

—Ay. Afraid of your life.

—Behave yourself! cried Heron, cutting at Stephen's legs with his cane.

It was the signal for their onset. Nash pinioned his arms behind while Boland seized a long cabbage stump which was lying in the gutter. Struggling and kicking under the cuts of the cane and the blows of the knotty stump Stephen was borne back against a barbed wire fence.

—Admit that Byron was no good.

—No.

—Admit.

—No.

—Admit.

—No. No.

At last after a fury of plunges he wrenched himself free. His tormentors set off towards Jones's Road, laughing and jeering at him, while he, torn and flushed and panting, stumbled after them half blinded with tears, clenching his fists madly and sobbing.

While he was still repeating the *Confiteor* amid the indulgent laughter of his hearers and while the scenes of that malignant episode were still passing sharply and swiftly before his mind he wondered why he bore no malice now to those who had tormented him. He had not forgotten a whit of their cowardice and cruelty but the memory of it called forth no anger from him. All the descriptions of fierce love and hatred which he had met in books had seemed to him therefore unreal. Even that night as he stumbled homewards along Jones's Road he had felt that some power was divesting him of that suddenwoven anger as easily as a fruit is divested of its soft ripe peel.

He remained standing with his two companions at the end of the shed, listening idly to their talk or to the bursts of applause in the theatre. She was sitting there among the others perhaps waiting for him to appear. He tried to recall her appearance but could not. He could remember only that she had worn a shawl about her head like a cowl and that her dark eyes had invited and unnerved him. He wondered had he been in her thoughts as she had been in his. Then in the dark and unseen by the other two he rested the tips of the fingers of one hand upon the palm of the other hand, scarcely touching it and yet pressing upon it lightly. But the pressure of her fingers had been lighter and steadier: and suddenly the memory of their touch traversed his brain and body like an invisible warm wave.

A boy came towards them, running along under the shed. He was excited and breathless.

—O, Dedalus, he cried, Doyle is in a great bake about you. You're to go in at once and get dressed for the play. Hurry up, you better.

—He's coming now, said Heron to the messenger with a haughty drawl, when he wants to.

The boy turned to Heron and repeated:

—But Doyle is in an awful bake.

—Will you tell Doyle with my best compliments that I damned his eyes? answered Heron.

—Well, I must go now, said Stephen, who cared little for such points of honour.

—I wouldn't, said Heron, damn me if I would. That's no way to send for one of the senior boys. In a bake, indeed! I think it's quite enough that you're taking a part in his bally old play.

This spirit of quarrelsome comradeship which he had observed lately in his rival had not seduced Stephen from his habits of quiet obedience. He mistrusted the turbulence and doubted the sincerity of such comradeship which seemed to him a sorry anticipation of manhood. The question of honour here raised was, like all such questions, trivial to him. While his mind had been pursuing its intangible phantoms and turning in irresolution from such pursuit he had heard about him the constant voices of his father and of his masters, urging him to be a gentleman above all things and urging him to be a good catholic above all things. These voices had now come to be hollowsounding in his ears. When the gymnasium had been opened he had heard another voice urging him to be

strong and manly and healthy and when the movement towards national revival had begun to be felt in the college yet
another voice had bidden him be true to his country and help
to raise up her fallen language and tradition. In the profane
world, as he foresaw, a worldly voice would bid him raise up
his father's fallen state by his labours and, meanwhile, the
voice of his school comrades urged him to be a decent fellow,
to shield others from blame or to beg them off and to do his
best to get free days for the school. And it was the din of all
these hollowsounding voices that made him halt irresolutely in
the pursuit of phantoms. He gave them ear only for a time but
he was happy only when he was far from them, beyond their
call, alone or in the company of phantasmal comrades.

In the vestry a plump freshfaced jesuit and an elderly man,
in shabby blue clothes, were dabbling in a case of paints and
chalks. The boys who had been painted walked about or stood
still awkwardly, touching their faces in a gingerly fashion with
their furtive fingertips. In the middle of the vestry a young
jesuit, who was then on a visit to the college, stood rocking
himself rhythmically from the tips of his toes to his heels and
back again, his hands thrust well forward into his sidepockets.
His small head set off with glossy red curls and his newly
shaven face agreed well with the spotless decency of his soutane and with his spotless shoes.

As he watched this swaying form and tried to read for
himself the legend of the priest's mocking smile there came
into Stephen's memory a saying which he had heard from his
father before he had been sent to Clongowes, that you could
always tell a jesuit by the style of his clothes. At the same
moment he thought he saw a likeness between his father's
mind and that of this smiling welldressed priest: and he was
aware of some desecration of the priest's office or of the vestry
itself, whose silence was now routed by loud talk and joking
and its air pungent with the smells of the gasjets and the
grease.

While his forehead was being wrinkled and his jaws painted

black and blue by the elderly man he listened distractedly to the voice of the plump young jesuit which bade him speak up and make his points clearly. He could hear the band playing *The Lily of Killarney* and knew that in a few moments the curtain would go up. He felt no stage fright but the thought of the part he had to play humiliated him. A remembrance of some of his lines made a sudden flush rise to his painted cheeks. He saw her serious alluring eyes watching him from among the audience and their image at once swept away his scruples, leaving his will compact. Another nature seemed to have been lent him: the infection of the excitement and youth about him entered into and transformed his moody mistrustfulness. For one rare moment he seemed to be clothed in the real apparel of boyhood: and, as he stood in the wings among the other players, he shared the common mirth amid which the drop scene was hauled upwards by two ablebodied priests with violent jerks and all awry.

A few moments after he found himself on the stage amid the garish gas and the dim scenery, acting before the innumerable faces of the void. It surprised him to see that the play which he had known at rehearsals for a disjointed lifeless thing had suddenly assumed a life of its own. It seemed now to play itself, he and his fellow actors aiding it with their parts. When the curtain fell on the last scene he heard the void filled with applause and, through a rift in the side scene, saw the simple body before which he had acted magically deformed, the void of faces breaking at all points and falling asunder into busy groups.

He left the stage quickly and rid himself of his mummery and passed out through the chapel into the college garden. Now that the play was over his nerves cried for some further adventure. He hurried onwards as if to overtake it. The doors of the theatre were all open and the audience had emptied out. On the lines which he had fancied the moorings of an ark a few lanterns swung in the night breeze, flickering cheerlessly. He mounted the steps from the garden in haste, eager that some prey should not elude him, and forced his way through the crowd in the hall and past the two jesuits who stood watching the exodus and bowing and shaking hands with the visitors. He pushed onward nervously, feigning a still greater haste and faintly conscious of the smiles and stares and nudges which his powdered head left in its wake.

When he came out on the steps he saw his family waiting for him at the first lamp. In a glance he noted that every figure of the group was familiar and ran down the steps angrily.

—I have to leave a message down in George's Street, he said to his father quickly. I'll be home after you.

Without waiting for his father's questions he ran across the road and began to walk at breakneck speed down the hill. He hardly knew where he was walking. Pride and hope and desire like crushed herbs in his heart sent up vapours of maddening incense before the eyes of his mind. He strode down the hill amid the tumult of suddenrisen vapours of wounded pride and fallen hope and baffled desire. They streamed upwards before his anguished eyes in dense and maddening fumes and passed away above him till at last the air was clear and cold again.

A film still veiled his eyes but they burned no longer. A power, akin to that which had often made anger or resentment fall from him, brought his steps to rest. He stood still and gazed up at the sombre porch of the morgue and from that to the dark cobbled laneway at its side. He saw the word *Lotts* on the wall of the lane and breathed slowly the rank heavy air.

—That is horse piss and rotted straw, he thought. It is a good odour to breathe. It will calm my heart. My heart is quite calm now. I will go back.

*   *   *

Stephen was once again seated beside his father in the corner of a railway carriage at Kingsbridge. He was travelling with his father by the night mail to Cork. As the train steamed out of the station he recalled his childish wonder of years before and every event of his first day at Clongowes. But he felt no wonder now. He saw the darkening lands slipping past him, the silent telegraphpoles passing his window swiftly every four seconds, the little glimmering stations, manned by a few silent sentries, flung by the mail behind her and twinkling for a moment in the darkness like fiery grains flung backwards by a runner.

He listened without sympathy to his father's evocation of Cork and of scenes of his youth, a tale broken by sighs or draughts from his pocketflask whenever the image of some dead friend appeared in it or whenever the evoker remembered suddenly the purpose of his actual visit. Stephen heard but could feel no pity. The images of the dead were all strange to him save that of uncle Charles, an image which had lately been fading out of memory. He knew, however, that his father's property was going to be sold by auction and in the manner of his own dispossession he felt the world give the lie rudely to his phantasy.

At Maryborough he fell asleep. When he awoke the train had passed out of Mallow and his father was stretched asleep on the other seat. The cold light of the dawn lay over the country, over the unpeopled fields and the closed cottages. The terror of sleep fascinated his mind as he watched the silent country or heard from time to time his father's deep breath or sudden sleepy movement. The neighbourhood of unseen sleepers filled him with strange dread as though they could harm him; and he prayed that the day might come quickly. His prayer, addressed neither to God nor saint, began with a shiver, as the chilly morning breeze crept through the chink of the carriage door to his feet, and ended in a trail of foolish words which he made to fit the insistent rhythm of the train; and silently, at intervals of four seconds, the telegraphpoles held the galloping notes of the music between punctual bars. This furious music allayed his dread and, leaning against the windowledge, he let his eyelids close again.

They drove in a jingle across Cork while it was still early morning and Stephen finished his sleep in a bedroom of the

Victoria Hotel. The bright warm sunlight was streaming through the window and he could hear the din of traffic. His father was standing before the dressingtable, examining his hair and face and moustache with great care, craning his neck across the waterjug and drawing it back sideways to see the better. While he did so he sang softly to himself with quaint accent and phrasing:

> *'Tis youth and folly*
> *Makes young men marry,*
> *So here, my love, I'll*
>   *No longer stay.*
> *What can't be cured, sure,*
> *Must be injured, sure,*
>   *So I'll go to*
>   *Amerikay.*

> *My love she's handsome,*
> *My love she's bonny:*
> *She's like good whisky*
>   *When it is new;*
> *But when 'tis old*
> *And growing cold*
> *It fades and dies like*
>   *The mountain dew.*

The consciousness of the warm sunny city outside his window and the tender tremors with which his father's voice festooned the strange sad happy air, drove off all the mists of the night's ill humour from Stephen's brain. He got up quickly to dress and, when the song had ended, said:

—That's much prettier than any of your other *come-all-yous*.

—Do you think so? asked Mr Dedalus.

—I like it, said Stephen.

—It's a pretty old air, said Mr Dedalus, twirling the points of his moustache. Ah, but you should have heard Mick Lacy sing it! Poor Mick Lacy! He had little turns for it, grace notes he used to put in that I haven't got. That was the boy who could sing a *come-all-you,* if you like.

Mr Dedalus had ordered drisheens for breakfast and during the meal he crossexamined the waiter for local news. For the most part they spoke at crosspurposes when a name was mentioned, the waiter having in mind the present holder and Mr Dedalus his father or perhaps his grandfather.

—Well, I hope they haven't moved the Queen's College anyhow, said Mr Dedalus, for I want to show it to this young-ster of mine.

Along the Mardyke the trees were in bloom. They entered the grounds of the college and were led by the garrulous porter across the quadrangle. But their progress across the gravel was brought to a halt after every dozen or so paces by some reply of the porter's.

—Ah, do you tell me so? And is poor Pottlebelly dead?

—Yes, sir. Dead, sir.

During these halts Stephen stood awkwardly behind the two men, weary of the subject and waiting restlessly for the slow march to begin again. By the time they had crossed the quad-rangle his restlessness had risen to fever. He wondered how his father, whom he knew for a shrewd suspicious man, could be duped by the servile manners of the porter; and the lively southern speech which had entertained him all the morning now irritated his ears.

They passed into the anatomy theatre where Mr Dedalus, the porter aiding him, searched the desks for his initials. Stephen remained in the background, depressed more than ever by the darkness and silence of the theatre and by the air it wore of jaded and formal study. On the desk before him he read the word *Fœtus* cut several times in the dark stained wood. The sudden legend startled his blood: he seemed to feel the absent students of the college about him and to shrink from their company. A vision of their life, which his father's words had been powerless to evoke, sprang up before him out of the word cut in the desk. A broadshouldered student with a moustache was cutting in the letters with a jackknife, seriously. Other students stood or sat near him laughing at his handiwork. One jogged his elbow. The big student turned on him, frowning. He was dressed in loose grey clothes and had tan boots.

Stephen's name was called. He hurried down the steps of the theatre so as to be as far away from the vision as he could be and, peering closely at his father's initials, hid his flushed face.

But the word and the vision capered before his eyes as he walked back across the quadrangle and towards the college gate. It shocked him to find in the outer world a trace of what he had deemed till then a brutish and individual malady of his own mind. His recent monstrous reveries came thronging into his memory. They too had sprung up before him, suddenly and furiously, out of mere words. He had soon given in to them and allowed them to sweep across and abase his intellect, wondering always where they came from, from what den of monstrous images, and always weak and humble towards others, restless and sickened of himself when they had swept over him.

—Ay, bedad! And there's the Groceries sure enough! cried Mr Dedalus. You often heard me speak of the Groceries, didn't you, Stephen. Many's the time we went down there when our names had been marked, a crowd of us, Harry Peard and little Jack Mountain and Bob Dyas and Maurice Moriarty, the Frenchman, and Tom O'Grady and Mick Lacy that I told you of this morning and Joey Corbet and poor little good hearted Johnny Keevers of the Tantiles.

The leaves of the trees along the Mardyke were astir and whispering in the sunlight. A team of cricketers passed, agile young men in flannels and blazers, one of them carrying the long green wicketbag. In a quiet bystreet a German band of five players in faded uniforms and with battered brass instruments was playing to an audience of street arabs and leisurely messenger boys. A maid in a white cap and apron was watering a box of plants on a sill which shone like a slab of limestone in the warm glare. From another window open to the air came the sound of a piano, scale after scale rising into the treble.

Stephen walked on at his father's side, listening to stories he had heard before, hearing again the names of the scattered and dead revellers who had been the companions of his father's youth. And a faint sickness sighed in his heart. He recalled his own equivocal position in Belvedere, a free boy, a leader afraid of his own authority, proud and sensitive and suspicious, battling against the squalor of his life and against the riot of his mind. The letters cut in the stained wood of the desk stared upon him, mocking his bodily weakness and futile enthusiasms and making him loathe himself for his own mad and filthy orgies. The spittle in his throat grew bitter and foul to swallow and the faint sickness climbed to his brain so that for a moment he closed his eyes and walked on in darkness.

He could still hear his father's voice.

—When you kick out for yourself, Stephen—as I daresay you will one of those days—remember, whatever you do, to mix with gentlemen. When I was a young fellow I tell you I enjoyed myself. I mixed with fine decent fellows. Everyone of us could do something. One fellow had a good voice, another fellow was a good actor, another could sing a good comic song, another was a good oarsman or a good racketplayer, another could tell a good story and so on. We kept the ball rolling anyhow and enjoyed ourselves and saw a bit of life and we were none the worse of it either. But we were all gentlemen, Stephen—at least I hope we were—and bloody good honest Irishmen too. That's the kind of fellows I want you to associate with, fellows of the right kidney. I'm talking to you as a friend, Stephen. I don't believe in playing the stern father. I don't believe a son should be afraid of his father. No, I treat you as your grandfather treated me when I was a young chap. We were more like brothers than father and son. I'll never forget the first day he caught me smoking. I was standing at the end of the South Terrace one day with some maneens like myself and sure we thought we were grand fellows because we had pipes stuck in the corners of our mouths. Suddenly the governor passed. He didn't say a word, or stop even. But the next day, Sunday, we were out for a walk together and when we were coming home he took out his cigar case and said: *By the bye, Simon, I didn't know you smoked:* or something like that. Of course I tried to carry it off as best I could. *If you want a good smoke,* he said, *try one of these cigars. An American captain made me a present of them last night in Queenstown.*

Stephen heard his father's voice break into a laugh which was almost a sob.

—He was the handsomest man in Cork at that time, by God he was! The women used to stand to look after him in the street.

He heard the sob passing loudly down his father's throat and opened his eyes with a nervous impulse. The sunlight breaking suddenly on his sight turned the sky and clouds into a fantastic world of sombre masses with lakelike spaces of dark rosy light. His very brain was sick and powerless. He could scarcely interpret the letters of the signboards of the shops. By his monstrous way of life he seemed to have put himself beyond the limits of reality. Nothing moved him or spoke to him from the real world unless he heard in it an echo of the infuriated cries within him. He could respond to no earthly or human appeal, dumb and insensible to the call of summer and gladness and companionship, wearied and dejected by his father's voice. He could scarcely recognise as his his own thoughts, and repeated slowly to himself:

—I am Stephen Dedalus. I am walking beside my father whose name is Simon Dedalus. We are in Cork, in Ireland. Cork is a city. Our room is in the Victoria Hotel. Victoria and Stephen and Simon. Simon and Stephen and Victoria. Names.

The memory of his childhood suddenly grew dim. He tried

to call forth some of its vivid moments but could not. He recalled only names: Dante, Parnell, Clane, Clongowes. A little boy had been taught geography by an old woman who kept two brushes in her wardrobe. Then he had been sent away from home to a college. In the college he had made his first communion and eaten slim jim out of his cricketcap and watched the firelight leaping and dancing on the wall of a little bedroom in the infirmary and dreamed of being dead, of mass being said for him by the rector in a black and gold cope, of being buried then in the little graveyard of the community off the main avenue of limes. But he had not died then. Parnell had died. There had been no mass for the dead in the chapel and no procession. He had not died but he had faded out like a film in the sun. He had been lost or had wandered out of existence for he no longer existed. How strange to think of him passing out of existence in such a way, not by death but by fading out in the sun or by being lost and forgotten somewhere in the universe! It was strange to see his small body appear again for a moment: a little boy in a grey belted suit. His hands were in his sidepockets and his trousers were tucked in at the knees by elastic bands.

On the evening of the day on which the property was sold Stephen followed his father meekly about the city from bar to bar. To the sellers in the market, to the barmen and barmaids, to the beggars who importuned him for a lob Mr Dedalus told the same tale, that he was an old Corkonian, that he had been trying for thirty years to get rid of his Cork accent up in Dublin and that Peter Pickackafax beside him was his eldest son but that he was only a Dublin jackeen.

They had set out early in the morning from Newcombe's coffeehouse where Mr Dedalus' cup had rattled noisily against its saucer, and Stephen had tried to cover that shameful sign of his father's drinkingbout of the night before by moving his chair and coughing. One humiliation had succeeded another: the false smiles of the market sellers, the curvettings and oglings of the barmaids with whom his father flirted, the compliments and encouraging words of his father's friends. They had told him that he had a great look of his grandfather and Mr Dedalus had agreed that he was an ugly likeness. They had unearthed traces of a Cork accent in his speech and made him admit that the Lee was a much finer river than the Liffey. One of them in order to put his Latin to the proof had made him translate short passages from Dilectus and asked him whether it was correct to say: *Tempora mutantur nos et mutamur in illis* or *Tempora mutantur et nos mutamur in illis.* Another, a brisk old man, whom Mr Dedalus called Johnny Cashman, had covered him with confusion by asking him to say which were prettier, the Dublin girls or the Cork girls.

——He's not that way built, said Mr Dedalus. Leave him alone. He's a levelheaded thinking boy who doesn't bother his head about that kind of nonsense.

—Then he's not his father's son, said the little old man.

—I don't know, I'm sure, said Mr Dedalus, smiling complacently.

—Your father, said the little old man to Stephen, was the boldest flirt in the city of Cork in his day. Do you know that?

Stephen looked down and studied the tiled floor of the bar into which they had drifted.

——Now don't be putting ideas into his head, said Mr Dedalus. Leave him to his Maker.

—Yerra, sure I wouldn't put any ideas into his head. I'm old enough to be his grandfather. And I am a grandfather, said the little old man to Stephen. Do you know that?

—Are you? asked Stephen.

—Bedad I am, said the little old man. I have two bouncing grandchildren out at Sunday's Well. Now then! What age do you think I am? And I remember seeing your grandfather in his red coat riding out to hounds. That was before you were born.

—Ay, or thought of, said Mr Dedalus.

—Bedad I did, repeated the little old man. And, more than that, I can remember even your greatgrandfather, old John

Stephen Dedalus, and a fierce old fireeater he was. Now then! There's a memory for you!

—That's three generations—four generations, said another of the company. Why, Johnny Cashman, you must be nearing the century.

—Well, I'll tell you the truth, said the little old man. I'm just twentyseven years of age.

—We're as old as we feel, Johnny, said Mr Dedalus. And just finish what you have there, and we'll have another. Here, Tim or Tom or whatever your name is, give us the same again here. By God, I don't feel more than eighteen myself. There's that son of mine there not half my age and I'm a better man than he is any day of the week.

—Draw it mild now, Dedalus. I think it's time for you to take a back seat, said the gentleman who had spoken before.

—No, by God! asserted Mr Dedalus. I'll sing a tenor song against him or I'll vault a fivebarred gate against him or I'll run with him after the hounds across the country as I did thirty years ago along with the Kerry Boy and the best man for it.

—But he'll beat you here, said the little old man, tapping his forehead and raising his glass to drain it.

—Well, I hope he'll be as good a man as his father. That's all I can say, said Mr Dedalus.

—If he is, he'll do, said the little old man.

—And thanks be to God, Johnny, said Mr Dedalus, that we lived so long and did so little harm.

—But did so much good, Simon, said the little old man gravely. Thanks be to God we lived so long and did so much good.

Stephen watched the three glasses being raised from the counter as his father and his two cronies drank to the memory of their past. An abyss of fortune or of temperament sundered him from them. His mind seemed older than theirs: it shone coldly on their strifes and happiness and regrets like a moon upon a younger earth. No life or youth stirred in him as it had stirred in them. He had known neither the pleasure of companionship with others nor the vigour of rude male health nor filial piety. Nothing stirred within his soul but a cold and cruel and loveless lust. His childhood was dead or lost and with it his soul capable of simple joys, and he was drifting amid life like the barren shell of the moon.

> *Art thou pale for weariness*
> *Of climbing heaven and gazing on the earth,*
> *Wandering companionless . . . ?*

He repeated to himself the lines of Shelley's fragment. Its alternation of sad human ineffectualness with vast inhuman cycles of activity chilled him, and he forgot his own human and ineffectual grieving.

* * *

Stephen's mother and his brother and one of his cousins waited at the corner of quiet Foster Place while he and his father went up the steps and along the colonnade where the highland sentry was parading. When they had passed into the great hall and stood at the counter Stephen drew forth his orders on the governor of the bank of Ireland for thirty and three pounds; and these sums, the moneys of his exhibition and essay prize, were paid over to him rapidly by the teller in notes and in coin respectively. He bestowed them in his pockets with feigned composure and suffered the friendly teller, to whom his father chatted, to take his hand across the broad counter and wish him a brilliant career in after life. He was impatient of their voices and could not keep his feet at rest. But the teller still deferred the serving of others to say he was living in changed times and that there was nothing like giving a boy the best education that money could buy. Mr Dedalus lingered in the hall gazing about him and up at the roof and telling Stephen, who urged him to come out, that they were standing in the house of commons of the old Irish parliament.

—God help us! he said piously, to think of the men of those times, Stephen, Hely Hutchinson and Flood and Henry Grattan and Charles Kendal Bushe, and the noblemen we have now, leaders of the Irish people at home and abroad. Why, by God, they wouldn't be seen dead in a tenacre field with them. No, Stephen, old chap, I'm sorry to say that they are only as I roved out one fine May morning in the merry month of sweet July.

A keen October wind was blowing round the bank. The three figures standing at the edge of the muddy path had pinched cheeks and watery eyes. Stephen looked at his thinly clad mother and remembered that a few days before he had seen a mantle priced at twenty guineas in the windows of Barnardo's.

—Well that's done, said Mr Dedalus.

—We had better go to dinner, said Stephen. Where?

—Dinner? said Mr Dedalus. Well, I suppose we had better, what?

—Some place that's not too dear, said Mrs Dedalus.

—Underdone's?

—Yes. Some quiet place.

—Come along, said Stephen quickly. It doesn't matter about the dearness.

He walked on before them with short nervous steps, smiling. They tried to keep up with him, smiling also at his eagerness.

—Take it easy like a good young fellow, said his father. We're not out for the half mile, are we?

For a swift season of merrymaking the money of his prizes ran through Stephen's fingers. Great parcels of groceries and delicacies and dried fruits arrived from the city. Every day he drew up a bill of fare for the family and every night led a party of three or four to the theatre to see *Ingomar* or *The Lady of Lyons*. In his coat pockets he carried squares of Vienna chocolate for his guests while his trousers' pockets bulged with masses of silver and copper coins. He bought presents for everyone, overhauled his room, wrote out resolutions, marshalled his books up and down their shelves, pored upon all kinds of price lists, drew up a form of commonwealth for the household by which every member of it held some office, opened a loan bank for his family and pressed loans on willing borrowers so that he might have the pleasure of making out receipts and reckoning the interests on the sums lent. When he could do no more he drove up and down the city in trams. Then the season of pleasure came to an end. The pot of pink enamel paint gave out and the wainscot of his bedroom remained with its unfinished and illplastered coat.

His household returned to its usual way of life. His mother had no further occasion to upbraid him for squandering his money. He too returned to his old life at school and all his novel enterprises fell to pieces. The commonwealth fell, the loan bank closed its coffers and its books on a sensible loss, the rules of life which he had drawn about himself fell into desuetude.

How foolish his aim had been! He had tried to build a breakwater of order and elegance against the sordid tide of life without him and to dam up, by rules of conduct and active interests and new filial relations, the powerful recurrence of the tides within him. Useless. From without as from within the water had flowed over his barriers: their tides began once more to jostle fiercely above the crumbled mole.

He saw clearly too his own futile isolation. He had not gone one step nearer the lives he had sought to approach nor bridged the restless shame and rancour that divided him from mother and brother and sister. He felt that he was hardly of the one blood with them but stood to them rather in the mystical kinship of fosterage, fosterchild and fosterbrother.

He burned to appease the fierce longings of his heart before which everything else was idle and alien. He cared little that he was in mortal sin, that his life had grown to be a tissue of subterfuge and falsehood. Beside the savage desire within him to realise the enormities which he brooded on nothing was sacred. He bore cynically with the shameful details of his secret riots in which he exulted to defile with patience whatever image had attracted his eyes. By day and by night he moved among distorted images of the outer world. A figure that had seemed to him by day demure and innocent came towards him by night through the winding darkness of sleep, her face transfigured by a lecherous cunning, her eyes bright with brutish joy. Only the morning pained him with its dim memory of dark orgiastic riot, its keen and humiliating sense of transgression.

He returned to his wanderings. The veiled autumnal evenings led him from street to street as they had led him years before along the quiet avenues of Blackrock. But no vision of trim front gardens or of kindly lights in the windows poured a tender influence upon him now. Only at times, in the pauses of his desire, when the luxury that was wasting him gave room to a softer languor, the image of Mercedes traversed the background of his memory. He saw again the small white house and the garden of rosebushes on the road that led to the mountains and he remembered the sadly proud gesture of refusal which he was to make there, standing with her in the moonlit garden after years of estrangement and adventure. At those moments the soft speeches of Claude Melnotte rose to his lips and eased his unrest. A tender premonition touched him of the tryst he had then looked forward to and, in spite of the horrible reality which lay between his hope of then and now, of the holy encounter he had then imagined at which weakness and timidity and inexperience were to fall from him.

Such moments passed and the wasting fires of lust sprang up again. The verses passed from his lips and the inarticulate cries and the unspoken brutal words rushed forth from his brain to force a passage. His blood was in revolt. He wandered up and down the dark slimy streets peering into the gloom of lanes and doorways, listening eagerly for any sound. He moaned to himself like some baffled prowling beast. He wanted to sin with another of his kind, to force another being to sin with him and to exult with her in sin. He felt some dark presence moving irresistibly upon him from the darkness, a presence subtle and murmurous as a flood filling him wholly with itself. Its murmur besieged his ears like the murmur of some multitude in sleep; its subtle streams penetrated his being. His hands clenched convulsively and his teeth set together as he suffered the agony of its penetration. He stretched out his arms in the street to hold fast the frail swooning form that eluded him and incited him: and the cry that he had strangled for so long in his throat issued from his lips. It broke from him like a wail of despair from a hell of sufferers and died in a wail of furious entreaty, a cry for an iniquitous abandonment, a cry which was but the echo of an obscene scrawl which he had read on the oozing wall of a urinal.

He had wandered into a maze of narrow and dirty streets. From the foul laneways he heard bursts of hoarse riot and wrangling and the drawling of drunken singers. He walked onward, undismayed, wondering whether he had strayed into the quarter of the jews. Women and girls dressed in long vivid gowns traversed the street from house to house. They were leisurely and perfumed. A trembling seized him and his eyes grew dim. The yellow gasflames arose before his troubled vision against the vapoury sky, burning as if before an altar. Before the doors and in the lighted halls groups were gathered arrayed as for some rite. He was in another world: he had awakened from a slumber of centuries.

He stood still in the middle of the roadway, his heart clamouring against his bosom in a tumult. A young woman dressed in a long pink gown laid her hand on his arm to detain him and gazed into his face. She said gaily:

—Good night, Willie dear!

Her room was warm and lightsome. A huge doll sat with her legs apart in the copious easychair beside the bed. He tried to bid his tongue speak that he might seem at ease, watching her as she undid her gown, noting the proud conscious movements of her perfumed head.

As he stood silent in the middle of the room she came over to him and embraced him gaily and gravely. Her round arms held him firmly to her and he, seeing her face lifted to him in serious calm and feeling the warm calm rise and fall of her breast, all but burst into hysterical weeping. Tears of joy and relief shone in his delighted eyes and his lips parted though they would not speak.

She passed her tinkling hand through his hair, calling him a little rascal.

—Give me a kiss, she said.

His lips would not bend to kiss her. He wanted to be held firmly in her arms, to be caressed slowly, slowly, slowly. In her arms he felt that he had suddenly become strong and fearless and sure of himself. But his lips would not bend to kiss her.

With a sudden movement she bowed his head and joined her lips to his and he read the meaning of her movements in her frank uplifted eyes. It was too much for him. He closed his eyes, surrendering himself to her, body and mind, conscious of nothing in the world but the dark pressure of her softly parting lips. They pressed upon his brain as upon his lips as though they were the vehicle of a vague speech; and between them he felt an unknown and timid pressure, darker than the swoon of sin, softer than sound or odour.

THE swift December dusk had come tumbling clown-
ishly after its dull day and, as he stared through the dull
square of the window of the schoolroom, he felt his belly crave
for its food. He hoped there would be stew for dinner, turnips
and carrots and bruised potatoes and fat mutton pieces to be
ladled out in thick peppered flourfattened sauce. Stuff it into
you, his belly counselled him.

It would be a gloomy secret night. After early nightfall the
yellow lamps would light up, here and there, the squalid
quarter of the brothels. He would follow a devious course up
and down the streets, circling always nearer and nearer in a
tremor of fear and joy, until his feet led him suddenly round a
dark corner. The whores would be just coming out of their
houses making ready for the night, yawning lazily after their
sleep and settling the hairpins in their clusters of hair. He
would pass by them calmly waiting for a sudden movement of
his own will or a sudden call to his sinloving soul from their
soft perfumed flesh. Yet as he prowled in quest of that call, his
senses, stultified only by his desire, would note keenly all that
wounded or shamed them; his eyes, a ring of porter froth on a
clothless table or a photograph of two soldiers standing to
attention or a gaudy playbill; his ears, the drawling jargon of
greeting:

—Hello, Bertie, any good in your mind?

—Is that you, pigeon?

—Number ten. Fresh Nelly is waiting on you.

—Goodnight, husband! Coming in to have a short time?

The equation on the page of his scribbler began to spread

out a widening tail, eyed and starred like a peacock's; and, when the eyes and stars of its indices had been eliminated, began slowly to fold itself together again. The indices appearing and disappearing were eyes opening and closing; the eyes opening and closing were stars being born and being quenched. The vast cycle of starry life bore his weary mind outward to its verge and inward to its centre, a distant music accompanying him outward and inward. What music? The music came nearer and he recalled the words, the words of Shelley's fragment upon the moon wandering companionless, pale for weariness. The stars began to crumble and a cloud of fine stardust fell through space.

The dull light fell more faintly upon the page whereon another equation began to unfold itself slowly and to spread abroad its widening tail. It was his own soul going forth to experience, unfolding itself sin by sin, spreading abroad the balefire of its burning stars and folding back upon itself, fading slowly, quenching its own lights and fires. They were quenched: and the cold darkness filled chaos.

A cold lucid indifference reigned in his soul. At his first violent sin he had felt a wave of vitality pass out of him and had feared to find his body or his soul maimed by the excess. Instead the vital wave had carried him on its bosom out of himself and back again when it receded: and no part of body or soul had been maimed but a dark peace had been established between them. The chaos in which his ardour extinguished itself was a cold indifferent knowledge of himself. He had sinned mortally not once but many times and he knew that, while he stood in danger of eternal damnation for the first sin alone, by every succeeding sin he multiplied his guilt and his punishment. His days and works and thoughts could make no atonement for him, the fountains of sanctifying grace having ceased to refresh his soul. At most, by an alms given to a beggar whose blessing he fled from, he might hope wearily to win for himself some measure of actual grace. Devotion had gone by the board. What did it avail to pray when he knew that his soul lusted after its own destruction? A certain pride, a certain awe, withheld him from offering to God even one prayer at night though he knew it was in God's power to take away his life while he slept and hurl his soul hellward ere he could beg for mercy. His pride in his own sin, his loveless awe of God, told him that his offence was too grievous to be atoned for in whole or in part by a false homage to the Allseeing and Allknowing.

—Well now, Ennis, I declare you have a head and so has my stick! Do you mean to say that you are not able to tell me what a surd is?

The blundering answer stirred the embers of his contempt of his fellows. Towards others he felt neither shame nor fear. On Sunday mornings as he passed the churchdoor he glanced coldly at the worshippers who stood bareheaded, four deep, outside the church, morally present at the mass which they could neither see nor hear. Their dull piety and the sickly smell of the cheap hairoil with which they had anointed their heads repelled him from the altar they prayed at. He stooped to the evil of hypocrisy with others, sceptical of their innocence which he could cajole so easily.

On the wall of his bedroom hung an illuminated scroll, the certificate of his prefecture in the college of the sodality of the Blessed Virgin Mary. On Saturday mornings when the sodality met in the chapel to recite the little office his place was a cushioned kneelingdesk at the right of the altar from which he led his wing of boys through the responses. The falsehood of his position did not pain him. If at moments he felt an impulse to rise from his post of honour and, confessing before them all his unworthiness, to leave the chapel, a glance at their faces restrained him. The imagery of the psalms of prophecy soothed his barren pride. The glories of Mary held his soul captive: spikenard and myrrh and frankincense, symbolising the preciousness of God's gifts to her soul, rich garments, symbolising her royal lineage, her emblems, the lateflowering plant and lateblossoming tree, symbolising the agelong gradual growth of her cultus among men. When it fell to him to read the lesson towards the close of the office he read it in a veiled voice, lulling his conscience to its music.

Quasi cedrus exaltata sum in Libanon et quasi cupressus in monte Sion. Quasi palma exaltata sum in Gades et quasi plantatio rosae in Jericho. Quasi uliva speciosa in campis et quasi platanus exaltata sum juxta aquam in plateis. Sicut cinnamomum et balsamum aromatizans odorem dedi et quasi myrrha electa dedi suavitatem odoris.

His sin, which had covered him from the sight of God, had led him nearer to the refuge of sinners. Her eyes seemed to regard him with mild pity; her holiness, a strange light glowing faintly upon her frail flesh, did not humiliate the sinner who approached her. If ever he was impelled to cast sin from him and to repent the impulse that moved him was the wish to be her knight. If ever his soul, reentering her dwelling shyly after the frenzy of his body's lust had spent itself, was turned towards her whose emblem is the morning star, *bright and musical, telling of heaven and infusing peace,* it was when her names were murmured softly by lips whereon there still lingered foul and shameful words, the savour itself of a lewd kiss.

That was strange. He tried to think how it could be but the dusk, deepening in the schoolroom, covered over his thoughts. The bell rang. The master marked the sums and cuts to be done for the next lesson and went out. Heron, beside Stephen, began to hum tunelessly.

My excellent friend Bombados.

Ennis, who had gone to the yard, came back, saying:

—The boy from the house is coming up for the rector.

A tall boy behind Stephen rubbed his hands and said:

—That's game ball. We can scut the whole hour. He won't be in till after half two. Then you can ask him questions on the catechism, Dedalus.

Stephen, leaning back and drawing idly on his scribbler, listened to the talk about him which Heron checked from time to time by saying:

—Shut up, will you. Don't make such a bally racket!

It was strange too that he found an arid pleasure in following up to the end the rigid lines of the doctrines of the church and penetrating into obscure silences only to hear and feel the more deeply his own condemnation. The sentence of saint James which says that he who offends against one commandment becomes guilty of all had seemed to him first a swollen phrase until he had begun to grope in the darkness of his own state. From the evil seed of lust all other deadly sins had sprung forth: pride in himself and contempt of others, covetousness in using money for the purchase of unlawful pleasure, envy of those whose vices he could not reach to and calumnious murmuring against the pious, gluttonous enjoyment of food, the dull glowering anger amid which he brooded upon his longing, the swamp of spiritual and bodily sloth in which his whole being had sunk.

As he sat in his bench gazing calmly at the rector's shrewd harsh face his mind wound itself in and out of the curious questions proposed to it. If a man had stolen a pound in his youth and had used that pound to amass a huge fortune how much was he obliged to give back, the pound he had stolen only or the pound together with the compound interest accruing upon it or all his huge fortune? If a layman in giving baptism pour the water before saying the words is the child baptised? Is baptism with a mineral water valid? How comes it that while the first beatitude promises the kingdom of heaven to the poor of heart the second beatitude promises also to the meek that they shall possess the land? Why was the sacrament of the eucharist instituted under the two species of bread and wine if Jesus Christ be present body and blood, soul and divinity, in the bread alone and in the wine alone? Does a tiny particle of the consecrated bread contain all the body and blood of Jesus Christ or a part only of the body and blood? If the wine change into vinegar and the host crumble into corruption after they have been consecrated is Jesus Christ still present under their species as God and as man?

—Here he is! Here he is!

A boy from his post at the window had seen the rector come from the house. All the catechisms were opened and all heads bent upon them silently. The rector entered and took his seat on the dais. A gentle kick from the tall boy in the bench behind urged Stephen to ask a difficult question.

The rector did not ask for a catechism to hear the lesson from. He clasped his hands on the desk and said:

—The retreat will begin on Wednesday afternoon in honour of saint Francis Xavier whose feast day is Saturday. The retreat will go on from Wednesday to Friday. On Friday confession will be heard all the afternoon after beads. If any boys have special confessors perhaps it will be better for them not to change. Mass will be on Saturday morning at nine o'clock and general communion for the whole college. Saturday will be a free day. Sunday of course. But Saturday and Sunday being free days some boys might be inclined to think that Monday is a free day also. Beware of making that mistake. I think you, Lawless, are likely to make that mistake.

—I, sir? Why, sir?

A little wave of quiet mirth broke forth over the class of boys from the rector's grim smile. Stephen's heart began slowly to fold and fade with fear like a withering flower.

The rector went on gravely:

—You are all familiar with the story of the life of saint Francis Xavier, I suppose, the patron of your college. He came of an old and illustrious Spanish family and you remember that he was one of the first followers of saint Ignatius. They met in Paris where Francis Xavier was professor of philosophy at the university. This young and brilliant nobleman and man of letters entered heart and soul into the ideas of our glorious founder, and you know that he, at his own desire, was sent by saint Ignatius to preach to the Indians. He is called, as you know, the apostle of the Indies. He went from country to country in the east, from Africa to India, from India to Japan, baptising the people. He is said to have baptised as many as ten thousand idolaters in one month. It is said that his right arm had grown powerless from having been raised so often over the heads of those whom he baptised. He wished then to go to China to win still more souls for God but he died of fever on the island of Sancian. A great saint, saint Francis Xavier! A great soldier of God!

The rector paused and then, shaking his clasped hands before him, went on:

—He had the faith in him that moves mountains. Ten thousand souls won for God in a single month! That is a true conqueror, true to the motto of our order: *ad majorem Dei gloriam!* A saint who has great power in heaven, remember: power to intercede for us in our grief, power to obtain whatever we pray for if it be for the good of our souls, power above all to obtain for us the grace to repent if we be in sin. A great saint, saint Francis Xavier! A great fisher of souls!

He ceased to shake his clasped hands and, resting them against his forehead, looked right and left of them keenly at his listeners out of his dark stern eyes.

In the silence their dark fire kindled the dusk into a tawny glow. Stephen's heart had withered up like a flower of the desert that feels the simoom coming from afar.

*   *   *

—*Remember only thy last things and thou shalt not sin for ever*—words taken, my dear little brothers in Christ, from the book of Ecclesiastes, seventh chapter, fortieth verse. In the name of the Father and of the Son and of the Holy Ghost. Amen.

Stephen sat in the front bench of the chapel. Father Arnall sat at a table to the left of the altar. He wore about his shoulders a heavy cloak; his pale face was drawn and his voice broken with rheum. The figure of his old master, so strangely rearisen, brought back to Stephen's mind his life at Clongowes: the wide playgrounds, swarming with boys, the square ditch, the little cemetery off the main avenue of limes where he had dreamed of being buried, the firelight on the wall of the infirmary where he lay sick, the sorrowful face of Brother Michael. His soul, as these memories came back to him, became again a child's soul.

—We are assembled here today, my dear little brothers in Christ, for one brief moment far away from the busy bustle of the outer world to celebrate and to honour one of the greatest of saints, the apostle of the Indies, the patron saint also of your college, saint Francis Xavier. Year after year for much longer than any of you, my dear little boys, can remember or than I can remember the boys of this college have met in this very chapel to make their annual retreat before the feast day of their patron saint. Time has gone on and brought with it its changes. Even in the last few years what changes can most of you not remember? Many of the boys who sat in those front benches a few years ago are perhaps now in distant lands, in the burning tropics or immersed in professional duties or in seminaries or voyaging over the vast expanse of the deep or, it may be, already called by the great God to another life and to the rendering up of their stewardship. And still as the years roll by, bringing with them changes for good and bad, the memory of the great saint is honoured by the boys of his college who make every year their annual retreat on the days preceding the feast day set apart by our holy mother the church to transmit to all the ages the name and fame of one of the greatest sons of catholic Spain.

—Now what is the meaning of this word *retreat* and why is it allowed on all hands to be a most salutary practice for all who desire to lead before God and in the eyes of men a truly christian life? A retreat, my dear boys, signifies a withdrawal for a while from the cares of our life, the cares of this worka-day world, in order to examine the state of our conscience, to reflect on the mysteries of holy religion and to understand better why we are here in this world. During these few days I intend to put before you some thoughts concerning the four last things. They are, as you know from your catechism, death, judgment, hell and heaven. We shall try to understand them fully during these few days so that we may derive from the understanding of them a lasting benefit to our souls. And remember, my dear boys, that we have been sent into this world for one thing and for one thing alone: to do God's holy will and to save our immortal souls. All else is worthless. One thing alone is needful, the salvation of one's soul. What doth it profit a man to gain the whole world if he suffer the loss of his immortal soul? Ah, my dear boys, believe me there is nothing in this wretched world that can make up for such a loss.

—I will ask you therefore, my dear boys, to put away from your minds during these few days all worldly thoughts, whether of study or pleasure or ambition, and to give all your attention to the state of your souls. I need hardly remind you that during the days of the retreat all boys are expected to preserve a quiet and pious demeanour and to shun all loud unseemly pleasure. The elder boys, of course, will see that this custom is not infringed and I look especially to the prefects and officers of the sodality of Our Blessed Lady and of the sodality of the holy angels to set a good example to their fellowstudents.

—Let us try therefore to make this retreat in honour of saint Francis with our whole heart and our whole mind. God's blessing will then be upon all your year's studies. But, above and beyond all, let this retreat be one to which you can look back in after years when maybe you are far from this college and among very different surroundings, to which you can look back with joy and thankfulness and give thanks to God for having granted you this occasion of laying the first foundation of a pious honourable zealous christian life. And if, as may so happen, there be at this moment in these benches any poor soul who has had the unutterable misfortune to lose God's holy grace and to fall into grievous sin I fervently trust and pray that this retreat may be the turningpoint in the life of that soul. I pray to God through the merits of its zealous servant Francis Xavier that such a soul may be led to sincere repentance and that the holy communion on saint Francis' day of this year may be a lasting covenant between God and that soul. For just and unjust, for saint and sinner alike, may this retreat be a memorable one.

—Help me, my dear little brothers in Christ. Help me by your pious attention, by your own devotion, by your outward demeanour. Banish from your minds all worldly thoughts and think only of the last things, death, judgment, hell and heaven. He who remembers these things, says Ecclesiastes, shall not sin for ever. He who remembers the last things will act and think with them always before his eyes. He will live a good life and die a good death, believing and knowing that, if he has sacrificed much in this earthly life, it will be given to him a hundredfold and a thousandfold more in the life to come, in the kingdom without end—a blessing, my dear boys, which I wish you from my heart, one and all, in the name of the Father and of the Son and of the Holy Ghost. Amen.

As he walked home with silent companions a thick fog seemed to compass his mind. He waited in stupor of mind till it should lift and reveal what it had hidden. He ate his dinner with surly appetite and, when the meal was over and the greasestrewn plates lay abandoned on the table, he rose and went to the window, clearing the thick scum from his mouth with his tongue and licking it from his lips. So he had sunk to the state of a beast that licks his chaps after meat. This was the end; and a faint glimmer of fear began to pierce the fog of his mind. He pressed his face against the pane of the window and gazed out into the darkening street. Forms passed this way and that through the dull light. And that was life. The letters of the name of Dublin lay heavily upon his mind, pushing one another surlily hither and thither with slow boorish insistence. His soul was fattening and congealing into a gross grease, plunging ever deeper in its dull fear into a sombre threatening dusk, while the body that was his stood, listless and dishonoured, gazing out of darkened eyes, helpless, perturbed and human for a bovine god to stare upon.

The next day brought death and judgment, stirring his soul slowly from its listless despair. The faint glimmer of fear became a terror of spirit as the hoarse voice of the preacher blew death into his soul. He suffered its agony. He felt the deathchill touch the extremities and creep onward towards the heart, the film of death veiling the eyes, the bright centres of the brain extinguished one by one like lamps, the last sweat oozing upon the skin, the powerlessness of the dying limbs, the speech thickening and wandering and failing, the heart throbbing faintly and more faintly, all but vanquished, the breath, the poor breath, the poor helpless human spirit, sobbing and sighing, gurgling and rattling in the throat. No help! No help! He, he himself, his body to which he had yielded was dying. Into the grave with it! Nail it down into a wooden box, the corpse. Carry it out of the house on the shoulders of hirelings. Thrust it out of men's sight into a long hole in the ground, into the grave, to rot, to feed the mass of its creeping worms and to be devoured by scuttling plumpbellied rats.

And while the friends were still standing in tears by the bedside the soul of the sinner was judged. At the last moment of consciousness the whole earthly life passed before the vision of the soul and, ere it had time to reflect, the body had died and the soul stood terrified before the judgmentseat. God, who had long been merciful, would then be just. He had long been patient, pleading with the sinful soul, giving it time to repent, sparing it yet awhile. But that time had gone. Time was to sin and to enjoy, time was to scoff at God and at the warnings of His holy church, time was to defy His majesty, to disobey His commands, to hoodwink one's fellow men, to commit sin after sin and sin after sin and to hide one's corruption from the sight of men. But that time was over. Now it was God's turn: and He was not to be hoodwinked or deceived. Every sin would then come forth from its lurkingplace, the most rebellious against the divine will and the most degrading to our poor corrupt nature, the tiniest imperfection and the most heinous atrocity. What did it avail then to have been a great emperor, a great general, a marvellous inventor, the most learned of the learned? All were as one before the judgmentseat of God. He would reward the good and punish the wicked. One single instant was enough for the trial of a man's soul. One single instant after the body's death, the soul had been weighed in the balance. The particular judgment was over and the soul had passed to the abode of bliss or to the prison of purgatory or had been hurled howling into hell.

Nor was that all. God's justice had still to be vindicated before men: after the particular there still remained the general judgment. The last day had come. Doomsday was at hand. The stars of heaven were falling upon the earth like the figs cast by the figtree which the wind has shaken. The sun, the great luminary of the universe, had become as sackcloth of hair. The moon was bloodred. The firmament was as a scroll rolled away. The archangel Michael, the prince of the heavenly host, appeared glorious and terrible against the sky. With one foot on the sea and one foot on the land he blew from the archangelical trumpet the brazen death of time. The three blasts of the angel filled all the universe. Time is, time was but time shall be no more. At the last blast the souls of universal humanity throng towards the valley of Jehoshaphat, rich and poor, gentle and simple, wise and foolish, good and wicked. The soul of every human being that has ever existed, the souls of all those who shall yet be born, all the sons and daughters of Adam, all are assembled on that supreme day. And lo the supreme judge is coming! No longer the lowly Lamb of God, no longer the meek Jesus of Nazareth, no longer the Man of Sorrows, no longer the Good Shepherd, He is seen now coming upon the clouds, in great power and majesty, attended by nine choirs of angels, angels and archangels, principalities, powers and virtues, thrones and dominations, cherubim and seraphim, God Omnipotent, God Everlasting. He speaks: and His voice is heard even at the farthest limits of space, even in the bottomless abyss. Supreme Judge, from His sentence there will be and can be no appeal. He calls the just to His side, bidding them enter into the kingdom, the eternity of bliss, prepared for them. The unjust He casts from Him, crying in His offended majesty: *Depart from me, ye cursed, into everlasting fire which was prepared for the devil and his angels.* O what agony then for the miserable sinners! Friend is torn apart from friend, children are torn from their parents, husbands from their wives. The poor sinner holds out his arms to those who were dear to him in this earthly world, to those whose simple piety perhaps he made a mock of, to those who counselled him and tried to lead him on the right path, to a kind brother, to a loving sister, to the mother and father who loved him so dearly. But it is too late: the just turn away from the wretched damned souls which now appear before the eyes of all in their hideous and evil character. O you hypocrites, O you whited sepulchres, O you who present a smooth smiling face to the world while your soul within is a foul swamp of sin, how will it fare with you in that terrible day?

And this day will come, shall come, must come; the day of death and the day of judgment. It is appointed unto man to die and after death the judgment. Death is certain. The time and manner are uncertain, whether from long disease or from some unexpected accident; the Son of God cometh at an hour when you little expect Him. Be therefore ready every moment, seeing that you may die at any moment. Death is the end of us all. Death and judgment, brought into the world by the sin of our first parents, are the dark portals that close our earthly existence, the portals that open into the unknown and the unseen, portals through which every soul must pass, alone, unaided save by its good works, without friend or brother or parent or master to help it, alone and trembling. Let that thought be ever before our minds and then we cannot sin. Death, a cause of terror to the sinner, is a blessed moment for him who has walked in the right path, fulfilling the duties of his station in life, attending to his morning and evening prayers, approaching the holy sacrament frequently and performing good and merciful works. For the pious and believing catholic, for the just man, death is no cause of terror. Was it not Addison, the great English writer, who, when on his deathbed, sent for the wicked young earl of Warwick to let him see how a christian can meet his end. He it is and he alone, the pious and believing christian, who can say in his heart:

> *O grave, where is thy victory?*
> *O death, where is thy sting?*

Every word of it was for him. Against his sin, foul and secret, the whole wrath of God was aimed. The preacher's knife had probed deeply into his diseased conscience and he felt now that his soul was festering in sin. Yes, the preacher was right. God's turn had come. Like a beast in its lair his soul had lain down in its own filth but the blasts of the angel's trumpet had driven him forth from the darkness of sin into the light. The words of doom cried by the angel shattered in an instant his presumptuous peace. The wind of the last day blew through his mind; his sins, the jeweleyed harlots of his imagination, fled before the hurricane, squeaking like mice in their terror and huddled under a mane of hair.

As he crossed the square, walking homeward, the light laughter of a girl reached his burning ear. The frail gay sound smote his heart more strongly than a trumpetblast, and, not daring to lift his eyes, he turned aside and gazed, as he walked, into the shadow of the tangled shrubs. Shame rose from his smitten heart and flooded his whole being. The image of Emma appeared before him and, under her eyes, the flood of shame rushed forth anew from his heart. If she knew to what his mind had subjected her or how his brutelike lust had torn and trampled upon her innocence! Was that boyish love? Was that chivalry? Was that poetry? The sordid details of his orgies stank under his very nostrils: the sootcoated packet of pictures which he had hidden in the flue of the fireplace and in the presence of whose shameless or bashful wantonness he lay for hours sinning in thought and deed; his monstrous dreams, peopled by apelike creatures and by harlots with gleaming jewel eyes; the foul long letters he had written in the joy of guilty confession and carried secretly for days and days only to throw them under cover of night among the grass in the corner of a field or beneath some hingeless door or in some niche in the hedges where a girl might come upon them as she walked by and read them secretly. Mad! Mad! Was it possible he had done these things? A cold sweat broke out upon his forehead as the foul memories condensed within his brain.

When the agony of shame had passed from him he tried to raise his soul from its abject powerlessness. God and the Blessed Virgin were too far from him: God was too great and stern and the Blessed Virgin too pure and holy. But he imagined that he stood near Emma in a wide land and, humbly and in tears, bent and kissed the elbow of her sleeve.

In the wide land under a tender lucid evening sky, a cloud drifting westward amid a pale green sea of heaven, they stood together, children that had erred. Their error had offended deeply God's majesty though it was the error of two children, but it had not offended her whose beauty *is not like earthly beauty, dangerous to look upon, but like the morning star which is its emblem, bright and musical.* The eyes were not offended which she turned upon them nor reproachful. She placed their hands together, hand in hand, and said, speaking to their hearts:

—Take hands, Stephen and Emma. It is a beautiful evening now in heaven. You have erred but you are always my children. It is one heart that loves another heart. Take hands together, my dear children, and you will be happy together and your hearts will love each other.

The chapel was flooded by the dull scarlet light that filtered through the lowered blinds; and through the fissure between the last blind and the sash a shaft of wan light entered like a spear and touched the embossed brasses of the candlesticks upon the altar that gleamed like the battleworn mail armour of angels.

Rain was falling on the chapel, on the garden, on the college. It would rain for ever, noiselessly. The water would rise inch by inch, covering the grass and shrubs, covering the trees and houses, covering the monuments and the mountain tops. All life would be choked off, noiselessly: birds, men, elephants, pigs, children: noiselessly floating corpses amid the litter of the wreckage of the world. Forty days and forty nights the rain would fall till the waters covered the face of the earth.

It might be. Why not?

—*Hell has enlarged its soul and opened its mouth without any limits*—words taken, my dear little brothers in Christ Jesus, from the book of Isaias, fifth chapter, fourteenth verse. In the name of the Father and of the Son and of the Holy Ghost. Amen.

The preacher took a chainless watch from a pocket within his soutane and, having considered its dial for a moment in silence, placed it silently before him on the table.

He began to speak in a quiet tone.

—Adam and Eve, my dear boys, were, as you know, our first parents and you will remember that they were created by God in order that the seats in heaven left vacant by the fall of Lucifer and his rebellious angels might be filled again. Lucifer, we are told, was a son of the morning, a radiant and mighty angel; yet he fell: he fell and there fell with him a third part of the host of heaven: he fell and was hurled with his rebellious angels into hell. What his sin was we cannot say. Theologians consider that it was the sin of pride, the sinful thought conceived in an instant: *non serviam: I will not serve.* That instant was his ruin. He offended the majesty of God by the sinful thought of one instant and God cast him out of heaven into hell for ever.

—Adam and Eve were then created by God and placed in Eden, in the plain of Damascus, that lovely garden resplendent with sunlight and colour, teeming with luxuriant vegetation. The fruitful earth gave them her bounty: beasts and birds were their willing servants: they knew not the ills our flesh is heir to, disease and poverty and death: all that a great and generous God could do for them was done. But there was one condition imposed on them by God: obedience to His word. They were not to eat of the fruit of the forbidden tree.

—Alas, my dear little boys, they too fell. The devil, once a shining angel, a son of the morning, now a foul fiend, came in the shape of a serpent, the subtlest of all the beasts of the field. He envied them. He, the fallen great one, could not bear to think that man, a being of clay, should possess the inheritance which he by his sin had forfeited for ever. He came to the woman, the weaker vessel, and poured the poison of his eloquence into her ear, promising her—O, the blasphemy of that promise!—that if she and Adam ate of the forbidden fruit they would become as gods, nay as God Himself. Eve yielded to the wiles of the archtempter. She ate the apple and gave it also to Adam who had not the moral courage to resist her. The poison tongue of Satan had done its work. They fell.

—And then the voice of God was heard in that garden, calling His creature man to account: and Michael, prince of the heavenly host, with a sword of flame in his hand appeared before the guilty pair and drove them forth from Eden into the world, the world of sickness and striving, of cruelty and disappointment, of labour and hardship, to earn their bread in the sweat of their brow. But even then how merciful was God! He took pity on our poor degraded parents and promised that in the fulness of time He would send down from heaven One who would redeem them, make them once more children of God and heirs to the kingdom of heaven: and that One, that Redeemer of fallen man, was to be God's onlybegotten Son, the Second Person of the Most Blessed Trinity, the Eternal Word.

—He came. He was born of a virgin pure, Mary the virgin mother. He was born in a poor cowhouse in Judea and lived as a humble carpenter for thirty years until the hour of His mission had come. And then, filled with love for men, He went forth and called to men to hear the new gospel.

—Did they listen? Yes, they listened but would not hear. He was seized and bound like a common criminal, mocked at as a fool, set aside to give place to a public robber, scourged with five thousand lashes, crowned with a crown of thorns, hustled through the streets by the jewish rabble and the Roman soldiery, stripped of His garments and hanged upon a gibbet and His side was pierced with a lance and from the wounded body of Our Lord water and blood issued continually.

—Yet even then, in that hour of supreme agony, Our Merciful Redeemer had pity for mankind. Yet even there, on the hill of Calvary, He founded the holy catholic church against which, it is promised, the gates of hell shall not prevail. He founded it upon the rock of ages and endowed it with His grace, with sacraments and sacrifice, and promised that if men would obey the word of His church they would still enter into eternal life but if, after all that had been done for them, they still persisted in their wickedness there remained for them an eternity of torment: hell.

The preacher's voice sank. He paused, joined his palms for an instant, parted them. Then he resumed:

—Now let us try for a moment to realise, as far as we can, the nature of that abode of the damned which the justice of an offended God has called into existence for the eternal punishment of sinners. Hell is a strait and dark and foulsmelling prison, an abode of demons and lost souls, filled with fire and smoke. The straitness of this prisonhouse is expressly designed by God to punish those who refused to be bound by His laws. In earthly prisons the poor captive has at least some liberty of movement, were it only within the four walls of his cell or in the gloomy yard of his prison. Not so in hell. There, by reason of the great number of the damned, the prisoners are heaped together in their awful prison, the walls of which are said to be four thousand miles thick: and the damned are so utterly bound and helpless that, as a blessed saint, saint Anselm, writes in his book on similitudes, they are not even able to remove from the eye a worm that gnaws it.

—They lie in exterior darkness. For, remember, the fire of hell gives forth no light. As, at the command of God, the fire of the Babylonian furnace lost its heat but not its light so, at the command of God, the fire of hell, while retaining the intensity of its heat, burns eternally in darkness. It is a never-ending storm of darkness, dark flames and dark smoke of burning brimstone, amid which the bodies are heaped one upon another without even a glimpse of air. Of all the plagues with which the land of the Pharaohs was smitten one plague alone, that of darkness, was called horrible. What name, then, shall we give to the darkness of hell which is to last not for three days alone but for all eternity?

—The horror of this strait and dark prison is increased by its awful stench. All the filth of the world, all the offal and scum of the world, we are told, shall run there as to a vast reeking sewer when the terrible conflagration of the last day has purged the world. The brimstone too which burns there in such prodigious quantity fills all hell with its intolerable stench; and the bodies of the damned themselves exhale such a pestilential odour that as saint Bonaventure says, one of them alone would suffice to infect the whole world. The very air of this world, that pure element, becomes foul and unbreathable when it has been long enclosed. Consider then what must be the foulness of the air of hell. Imagine some foul and putrid corpse that has lain rotting and decomposing in the grave, a jellylike mass of liquid corruption. Imagine such a corpse a prey to flames, devoured by the fire of burning brimstone and giving off dense choking fumes of nauseous loathsome decomposition. And then imagine this sickening stench, multiplied a millionfold and a millionfold again from the millions upon millions of fetid carcasses massed together in the reeking darkness, a huge and rotting human fungus. Imagine all this and you will have some idea of the horror of the stench of hell.

—But this stench is not, horrible though it is, the greatest physical torment to which the damned are subjected. The torment of fire is the greatest torment to which the tyrant has ever subjected his fellowcreatures. Place your finger for a moment in the flame of a candle and you will feel the pain of fire. But our earthly fire was created by God for the benefit of man, to maintain in him the spark of life and to help him in the useful arts whereas the fire of hell is of another quality and was created by God to torture and punish the unrepentant sinner. Our earthly fire also consumes more or less rapidly according as the object which it attacks is more or less combustible so that human ingenuity has even succeeded in inventing chemical preparations to check or frustrate its action. But the sulphurous brimstone which burns in hell is a substance which is specially designed to burn for ever and for ever with unspeakable fury. Moreover our earthly fire destroys at the same time as it burns so that the more intense it is the shorter is its duration: but the fire of hell has this property that it preserves that which it burns and though it rages with incredible intensity it rages for ever.

—Our earthly fire again, no matter how fierce or widespread it may be, is always of a limited extent: but the lake of fire in hell is boundless, shoreless and bottomless. It is on record that the devil himself, when asked the question by a certain soldier, was obliged to confess that if a whole mountain were thrown into the burning ocean of hell it would be burned up in an instant like a piece of wax. And this terrible fire will not afflict the bodies of the damned only from without but each lost soul will be a hell unto itself, the boundless fire raging in its very vitals. O, how terrible is the lot of those wretched beings! The blood seethes and boils in the veins, the brains are boiling in the skull, the heart in the breast glowing and bursting, the bowels a redhot mass of burning pulp, the tender eyes flaming like molten balls.

—And yet what I have said as to the strength and quality and boundlessness of this fire is as nothing when compared to its intensity, an intensity which it has as being the instrument chosen by divine design for the punishment of soul and body alike. It is a fire which proceeds directly from the ire of God, working not of its own activity but as an instrument of divine vengeance. As the waters of baptism cleanse the soul with the body so do the fires of punishment torture the spirit with the flesh. Every sense of the flesh is tortured and every faculty of the soul therewith: the eyes with impenetrable utter darkness, the nose with noisome odours, the ears with yells and howls and execrations, the taste with foul matter, leprous corruption, nameless suffocating filth, the touch with redhot goads and spikes, with cruel tongues of flame. And through the several torments of the senses the immortal soul is tortured eternally in its very essence amid the leagues upon leagues of glowing fires kindled in the abyss by the offended majesty of the Omnipotent God and fanned into everlasting and ever increasing fury by the breath of the anger of the Godhead.

—Consider finally that the torment of this infernal prison is increased by the company of the damned themselves. Evil company on earth is so noxious that even the plants, as if by instinct, withdraw from the company of whatsoever is deadly or hurtful to them. In hell all laws are overturned: there is no thought of family or country, of ties, of relationships. The damned howl and scream at one another, their torture and rage intensified by the presence of beings tortured and raging like themselves. All sense of humanity is forgotten. The yells of the suffering sinners fill the remotest corners of the vast abyss. The mouths of the damned are full of blasphemies against God and of hatred for their fellowsufferers and of curses against those souls which were their accomplices in sin. In olden times it was the custom to punish the parricide, the man who had raised his murderous hand against his father, by casting him into the depths of the sea in a sack in which were placed a cock, a monkey and a serpent. The intention of those lawgivers who framed such a law, which seems cruel in our times, was to punish the criminal by the company of hateful and hurtful beasts. But what is the fury of those dumb beasts compared with the fury of execration which bursts from the parched lips and aching throats of the damned in hell when they behold in their companions in misery those who aided and abetted them in sin, those whose words sowed the first seeds of evil thinking and evil living in their minds, those whose immodest suggestions led them on to sin, those whose eyes tempted and allured them from the path of virtue. They turn upon those accomplices and upbraid them and curse them. But they are helpless and hopeless: it is too late now for repentance.

—Last of all consider the frightful torment to those damned souls, tempters and tempted alike, of the company of the devils. These devils will afflict the damned in two ways, by their presence and by their reproaches. We can have no idea of how horrible these devils are. Saint Catherine of Siena once saw a devil and she has written that, rather than look again for one single instant on such a frightful monster, she would prefer to walk until the end of her life along a track of red coals. These devils, who were once beautiful angels, have become as hideous and ugly as they once were beautiful. They mock and jeer at the lost souls whom they dragged down to ruin. It is they, the foul demons, who are made in hell the voices of conscience. Why did you sin? Why did you lend an ear to the temptings of fiends? Why did you turn aside from your pious practices and good works? Why did you not shun the occasions of sin? Why did you not leave that evil companion? Why did you not give up that lewd habit, that impure habit? Why did you not listen to the counsels of your confessor? Why did you not, even after you had fallen the first or the second or the third or the fourth or the hundredth time, repent of your evil ways and turn to God who only waited for your repentance to absolve you of your sins? Now the time for repentance has gone by. Time is, time was, but time shall be no more! Time was to sin in secrecy, to indulge in that sloth and pride, to covet the unlawful, to yield to the promptings of your lower nature, to live like the beasts of the field, nay worse than the beasts of the field for they, at least, are but brutes and have not reason to guide them: time was but time shall be no more. God spoke to you by so many voices but you would not hear. You would not crush out that pride and anger in your heart, you would not restore those illgotten goods, you would not obey the precepts of your holy church nor attend to your religious duties, you would not abandon those wicked companions, you would not avoid those dangerous temptations. Such is the language of those fiendish tormentors, words of taunting and of reproach, of hatred and of disgust. Of disgust, yes! For even they, the very devils, when they sinned sinned by such a sin as alone was compatible with such angelical natures, a rebellion of the intellect: and they, even they, the foul devils must turn away, revolted and disgusted, from the contemplation of those unspeakable sins by which degraded man outrages and defiles the temple of the Holy Ghost, defiles and pollutes himself.

—O, my dear little brothers in Christ, may it never be our lot to hear that language! May it never be our lot, I say! In the last day of terrible reckoning I pray fervently to God that not a single soul of those who are in this chapel today may be found among those miserable beings whom the Great Judge shall command to depart for ever from His sight, that not one of us may ever hear ringing in his ears the awful sentence of rejection: *Depart from me, ye cursed, into everlasting fire which was prepared for the devil and his angels!*

He came down the aisle of the chapel, his legs shaking and the scalp of his head trembling as though it had been touched by ghostly fingers. He passed up the staircase and into the corridor along the walls of which the overcoats and waterproofs hung like gibbeted malefactors, headless and dripping and shapeless. And at every step he feared that he had already died, that his soul had been wrenched forth of the sheath of his body, that he was plunging headlong through space.

He could not grip the floor with his feet and sat heavily at his desk, opening one of his books at random and poring over it. Every word for him! It was true. God was almighty. God could call him now, call him as he sat at his desk, before he had time to be conscious of the summons. God had called him. Yes? What? Yes? His flesh shrank together as it felt the approach of the ravenous tongues of flames, dried up as it felt about it the swirl of stifling air. He had died. Yes. He was judged. A wave of fire swept through his body: the first. Again a wave. His brain began to glow. Another. His brain was simmering and bubbling within the cracking tenement of the skull. Flames burst forth from his skull like a corolla, shrieking like voices:

—Hell! Hell! Hell! Hell! Hell!

Voices spoke near him:

—On hell.

—I suppose he rubbed it into you well.

—You bet he did. He put us all into a blue funk.

—That's what you fellows want: and plenty of it to make you work.

He leaned back weakly in his desk. He had not died. God had spared him still. He was still in the familiar world of the school. Mr Tate and Vincent Heron stood at the window, talking, jesting, gazing out at the bleak rain, moving their heads.

—I wish it would clear up. I had arranged to go for a spin on the bike with some fellows out by Malahide. But the roads must be kneedeep.

—It might clear up, sir.

The voices that he knew so well, the common words, the quiet of the classroom when the voices paused and the silence was filled by the sound of softly browsing cattle as the other boys munched their lunches tranquilly, lulled his aching soul.

There was still time. O Mary, refuge of sinners, intercede for him! O Virgin Undefiled, save him from the gulf of death!

The English lesson began with the hearing of the history. Royal persons, favourites, intriguers, bishops, passed like mute phantoms behind their veil of names. All had died: all had been judged. What did it profit a man to gain the whole world if he lost his soul? At last he had understood: and human life lay around him, a plain of peace whereon antlike men laboured in brotherhood, their dead sleeping under quiet mounds. The elbow of his companion touched him and his heart was touched: and when he spoke to answer a question of his master he heard his own voice full of the quietude of humility and contrition.

His soul sank back deeper into depths of contrite peace, no longer able to suffer the pain of dread, and sending forth, as she sank, a faint prayer. Ah yes, he would still be spared; he would repent in his heart and be forgiven; and then those above, those in heaven, would see what he would do to make up for the past: a whole life, every hour of life. Only wait.

—All, God! All, all!

A messenger came to the door to say that confessions were being heard in the chapel. Four boys left the room; and he heard others passing down the corridor. A tremulous chill blew round his heart, no stronger than a little wind, and yet, listening and suffering silently, he seemed to have laid an ear against the muscle of his own heart, feeling it close and quail, listening to the flutter of its ventricles.

No escape. He had to confess, to speak out in words what he had done and thought, sin after sin. How? How?

—Father, I . . .

The thought slid like a cold shining rapier into his tender flesh: confession. But not there in the chapel of the college. He would confess all, every sin of deed and thought, sincerely: but not there among his school companions. Far away from there in some dark place he would murmur out his own shame: and he besought God humbly not to be offended with him if he did not dare to confess in the college chapel: and in utter abjection of spirit he craved forgiveness mutely of the boyish hearts about him.

Time passed.

He sat again in the front bench of the chapel. The daylight

without was already failing and, as it fell slowly through the dull red blinds, it seemed that the sun of the last day was going down and that all souls were being gathered for the judgment.

—*I am cast away from the sight of Thine eyes:* words taken, my dear little brothers in Christ, from the Book of Psalms, thirtieth chapter, twentythird verse. In the name of the Father and of the Son and of the Holy Ghost. Amen.

The preacher began to speak in a quiet friendly tone. His face was kind and he joined gently the fingers of each hand, forming a frail cage by the union of their tips.

—This morning we endeavoured, in our reflection upon hell, to make what our holy founder calls in his book of spiritual exercises, the composition of place. We endeavoured, that is, to imagine with the senses of the mind, in our imagination, the material character of that awful place and of the physical torments which all who are in hell endure. This evening we shall consider for a few moments the nature of the spiritual torments of hell.

—Sin, remember, is a twofold enormity. It is a base consent to the promptings of our corrupt nature to the lower instincts, to that which is gross and beastlike; and it is also a turning away from the counsel of our higher nature, from all that is pure and holy, from the Holy God Himself. For this reason mortal sin is punished in hell by two different forms of punishment, physical and spiritual.

—Now of all these spiritual pains by far the greatest is the pain of loss, so great, in fact, that in itself it is a torment greater than all the others. Saint Thomas, the greatest doctor of the church, the angelic doctor, as he is called, says that the worst damnation consists in this that the understanding of man is totally deprived of divine light and his affection obstinately turned away from the goodness of God. God, remember, is a being infinitely good and therefore the loss of such a being must be a loss infinitely painful. In this life we have not a very clear idea of what such a loss must be but the damned in hell, for their greater torment, have a full understanding of that which they have lost and understand that they have lost it through their own sins and have lost it for ever. At the very instant of death the bonds of the flesh are broken asunder and the soul at once flies towards God. The soul tends towards God as towards the centre of her existence. Remember, my dear little boys, our souls long to be with God. We come from God, we live by God, we belong to God: we are His, inalienably His. God loves with a divine love every human soul and every human soul lives in that love. How could it be otherwise? Every breath that we draw, every thought of our brain, every instant of life proceed from God's inexhaustible goodness. And if it be pain for a mother to be parted from her child, for a man to be exiled from hearth and home, for friend to be sundered from friend, O think what pain, what anguish, it must be for the poor soul to be spurned from the presence of the supremely good and loving Creator Who has called that soul into existence from nothingness and sustained it in life and loved it with an immeasurable love. This, then, to be separated for ever from its greatest good, from God, and to feel the anguish of that separation, knowing full well that it is unchangeable, this is the greatest torment which the created soul is capable of bearing, *pœna damni,* the pain of loss.

—The second pain which will afflict the souls of the damned in hell is the pain of conscience. Just as in dead bodies worms are engendered by putrefaction so in the souls of the lost there arises a perpetual remorse from the putrefaction of sin, the sting of conscience, the worm, as Pope Innocent the Third calls it, of the triple sting. The first sting inflicted by this cruel worm will be the memory of past pleasures. O what a dreadful memory will that be! In the lake of alldevouring flame the proud king will remember the pomps of his court, the wise but wicked man his libraries and instruments of research, the lover of artistic pleasures his marbles and pictures and other art treasures, he who delighted in the pleasures of the table his gorgeous feasts, his dishes prepared with such delicacy, his choice wines; the miser will remember his hoard of gold, the robber his illgotten wealth, the angry and revengeful and merciless murderers their deeds of blood and violence in which they revelled, the impure and adulterous the unspeakable and filthy pleasures in which they delighted. They will remember all this and loathe themselves and their sins. For how miserable will all those pleasures seem to the soul condemned to suffer in hellfire for ages and ages. How they will rage and fume to think that they have lost the bliss of heaven for the dross of earth, for a few pieces of metal, for vain honours, for bodily comforts, for a tingling of the nerves. They will repent indeed: and this is the second sting of the worm of conscience, a late and fruitless sorrow for sins committed. Divine justice insists that the understanding of those miserable wretches be fixed continually on the sins of which they were guilty and moreover, as saint Augustine points out, God will impart to them His own knowledge of sin so that sin will appear to them in all its hideous malice as it appears to the eyes of God Himself. They will behold their sins in all their foulness and repent but it will be too late and then they will bewail the good occasions which they neglected. This is the last and deepest and most cruel sting of the worm of conscience. The conscience will say: You had time and opportunity to repent and would not. You were brought up religiously by your parents. You had the sacraments and graces and indulgences of the church to aid you. You had the minister of God to preach to you, to call you back when you had strayed, to forgive you your sins, no matter how many, how abominable, if only you had confessed and repented. No. You would not. You flouted the ministers of holy religion, you turned your back on the confessional, you wallowed deeper and deeper in the mire of sin. God appealed to you, threatened you, entreated you to return to Him. O what shame, what misery! The Ruler of the universe entreated you, a creature of clay, to love Him Who made you and to keep His law. No. You would not. And now, though you were to flood all hell with your tears if you could still weep, all that sea of repentance would not gain for you what a single tear of true repentance shed during your mortal life would have gained for you. You implore now a moment of earthly life wherein to repent: in vain. That time is gone: gone for ever.

—Such is the threefold sting of conscience, the viper which gnaws the very heart's core of the wretches in hell so that filled with hellish fury they curse themselves for their folly and curse the evil companions who have brought them to such ruin and curse the devils who tempted them in life and now mock them and torture them in eternity and even revile and curse the Supreme Being Whose goodness and patience they scorned and slighted but Whose justice and power they cannot evade.

—The next spiritual pain to which the damned are subjected is the pain of extension. Man, in this earthly life, though he be capable of many evils, is not capable of them all at once inasmuch as one evil corrects and counteracts another just as one poison frequently corrects another. In hell on the contrary one torment, instead of counteracting another, lends it still greater force: and moreover as the internal faculties are more perfect than the external senses, so are they more capable of suffering. Just as every sense is afflicted with a fitting torment so is every spiritual faculty; the fancy with horrible images, the sensitive faculty with alternate longing and rage, the mind and understanding with an interior darkness more terrible even than the exterior darkness which reigns in that dreadful prison. The malice, impotent though it be, which possesses these demon souls is an evil of boundless extension, of limitless duration, a frightful state of wickedness which we can scarcely realise unless we bear in mind the enormity of sin and the hatred God bears to it.

—Opposed to this pain of extension and yet coexistent with it we have the pain of intensity. Hell is the centre of evils and, as you know, things are more intense at their centres than at their remotest points. There are no contraries or admixtures of any kind to temper or soften in the least the pains of hell. Nay, things which are good in themselves become evil in hell.

Company, elsewhere a source of comfort to the afflicted, will be there a continual torment: knowledge, so much longed for as the chief good of the intellect, will there be hated worse than ignorance: light, so much coveted by all creatures from the lord of creation down to the humblest plant in the forest, will be loathed intensely. In this life our sorrows are either not very long or not very great because nature either overcomes them by habits or puts an end to them by sinking under their weight. But in hell the torments cannot be overcome by habit. For while they are of terrible intensity they are at the same time of continual variety, each pain, so to speak, taking fire from another and reendowing that which has enkindled it with a still fiercer flame. Nor can nature escape from these intense and various tortures by succumbing to them for the soul is sustained and maintained in evil so that its suffering may be the greater. Boundless extension of torment, incredible intensity of suffering, unceasing variety of torture—this is what the divine majesty, so outraged by sinners, demands, this is what the holiness of heaven, slighted and set aside for the lustful and low pleasures of the corrupt flesh, requires, this is what the blood of the innocent Lamb of God, shed for the redemption of sinners, trampled upon by the vilest of the vile, insists upon.

—Last and crowning torture of all the tortures of that awful place is the eternity of hell. Eternity! O, dread and dire word. Eternity! What mind of man can understand it? And, remember, it is an eternity of pain. Even though the pains of hell were not so terrible as they are yet they would become infinite as they are destined to last for ever. But while they are everlasting they are at the same time, as you know, intolerably intense, unbearably extensive. To bear even the sting of an insect for all eternity would be a dreadful torment. What must it be, then, to bear the manifold tortures of hell for ever? For ever! For all eternity! Not for a year or for an age but for ever. Try to imagine the awful meaning of this. You have often seen the sand on the seashore. How fine are its tiny grains! And how many of those tiny little grains go to make up the small handful which a child grasps in its play. Now imagine a mountain of that sand, a million miles high, reaching from the earth to the farthest heavens, and a million miles broad, extending to remotest space, and a million miles in thickness: and imagine such an enormous mass of countless particles of sand multiplied as often as there are leaves in the forest, drops of water in the mighty ocean, feathers on birds, scales on fish, hairs on animals, atoms in the vast expanse of the air: and imagine that at the end of every million years a little bird came to that mountain and carried away in its beak a tiny grain of that sand. How many millions upon millions of centuries would pass before that bird had carried away even a square foot of that mountain, how many eons upon eons of ages before it had carried away all. Yet at the end of that immense stretch of time not even one instant of eternity could be said to have ended. At the end of all those billions and trillions of years eternity would have scarcely begun. And if that mountain rose again after it had been all carried away and if the bird came again and carried it all away again grain by grain: and if it so rose and sank as many times as there are stars in the sky, atoms in the air, drops of water in the sea, leaves on the trees, feathers upon birds, scales upon fish, hairs upon animals, at the end of all those innumerable risings and sinkings of that immeasurably vast mountain not one single instant of eternity could be said to have ended; even then, at the end of such a period, after that eon of time the mere thought of which makes our very brain reel dizzily, eternity would have scarcely begun.

—A holy saint (one of our own fathers I believe it was) was once vouchsafed a vision of hell. It seemed to him that he stood in the midst of a great hall, dark and silent save for the ticking of a great clock. The ticking went on unceasingly; and it seemed to this saint that the sound of the ticking was the ceaseless repetition of the words: ever, never; ever, never. Ever to be in hell, never to be in heaven; ever to be shut off from the presence of God, never to enjoy the beatific vision; ever to be eaten with flames, gnawed by vermin, goaded with burning spikes, never to be free from those pains; ever to have the conscience upbraid one, the memory enrage, the mind filled with darkness and despair, never to escape; ever to curse and revile the foul demons who gloat fiendishly over the misery of their dupes, never to behold the shining raiment of the blessed spirits; ever to cry out of the abyss of fire to God for an instant, a single instant, of respite from such awful agony, never to receive, even for an instant, God's pardon; ever to suffer, never to enjoy; ever to be damned, never to be saved; ever, never; ever, never. O what a dreadful punishment! An eternity of endless agony, of endless bodily and spiritual torment, without one ray of hope, without one moment of cessation, of agony limitless in extent, limitless in intensity, of torment infinitely lasting, infinitely varied, of torture that sustains eternally that which it eternally devours, of anguish that everlastingly preys upon the spirit while it racks the flesh, an eternity, every instant of which is itself an eternity, and that eternity an eternity of woe. Such is the terrible punishment decreed for those who die in mortal sin by an almighty and a just God.

—Yes, a just God! Men, reasoning always as men, are astonished that God should mete out an everlasting and infinite punishment in the fires of hell for a single grievous sin. They reason thus because, blinded by the gross illusion of the flesh and the darkness of human understanding, they are unable to comprehend the hideous malice of mortal sin. They reason thus because they are unable to comprehend that even venial sin is of such a foul and hideous nature that even if the omnipotent Creator could end all the evil and misery in the world, the wars, the diseases, the robberies, the crimes, the deaths, the murders, on condition that He allowed a single venial sin to pass unpunished, a single venial sin, a lie, an angry look, a moment of wilful sloth, He, the great omnipotent God, could not do so because sin, be it in thought or deed, is a transgression of His law and God would not be God if He did not punish the transgressor.

—A sin, an instant of rebellious pride of the intellect, made

Lucifer and a third part of the cohorts of angels fall from their glory. A sin, an instant of folly and weakness, drove Adam and Eve out of Eden and brought death and suffering into the world. To retrieve the consequences of that sin the Only Begotten Son of God came down to earth, lived and suffered and died a most painful death, hanging for three hours on the cross.

—O, my dear little brethren in Christ Jesus, will we then offend that good Redeemer and provoke His anger? Will we trample again upon that torn and mangled corpse? Will we spit upon that face so full of sorrow and love? Will we too, like the cruel jews and the brutal soldiers, mock that gentle and compassionate Saviour Who trod alone for our sake the awful winepress of sorrow? Every word of sin is a wound in His tender side. Every sinful act is a thorn piercing His head. Every impure thought, deliberately yielded to, is a keen lance transfixing that sacred and loving heart. No, no. It is impossible for any human being to do that which offends so deeply the divine majesty, that which is punished by an eternity of agony, that which crucifies again the Son of God and makes a mockery of Him.

—I pray to God that my poor words may have availed today to confirm in holiness those who are in a state of grace, to strengthen the wavering, to lead back to the state of grace the poor soul that has strayed if any such be among you. I pray to God, and do you pray with me, that we may repent of our sins. I will ask you now, all of you, to repeat after me the act of contrition, kneeling here in this humble chapel in the presence of God. He is there in the tabernacle burning with love for mankind, ready to comfort the afflicted. Be not afraid. No matter how many or how foul the sins if only you repent of them they will be forgiven you. Let no worldly shame hold you back. God is still the merciful Lord Who wishes not the eternal death of the sinner but rather that he be converted and live.

—He calls you to Him. You are His. He made you out of

nothing. He loved you as only a God can love. His arms are open to receive you even though you have sinned against Him. Come to Him, poor sinner, poor vain and erring sinner. Now is the acceptable time. Now is the hour.

The priest rose and, turning towards the altar, knelt upon the step before the tabernacle in the fallen gloom. He waited till all in the chapel had knelt and every least noise was still. Then, raising his head, he repeated the act of contrition, phrase by phrase, with fervour. The boys answered him phrase by phrase. Stephen, his tongue cleaving to his palate, bowed his head, praying with his heart.

—*O my God!*—
—*O my God!*—
—*I am heartily sorry*—
—*I am heartily sorry*—
—*for having offended Thee*—
—*for having offended Thee*—
—*and I detest my sins*—
—*and I detest my sins*—
—*above every other evil*—
—*above every other evil*—
—*because they displease Thee, my God*—
—*because they displease Thee, my God*—
—*Who art so deserving*—
—*Who art so deserving*—
—*of all my love*—
—*of all my love*—
—*and I firmly purpose*—
—*and I firmly purpose*—
—*by Thy holy grace*—
—*by Thy holy grace*—
—*never more to offend Thee*—
—*never more to offend Thee*—
—*and to amend my life*—
—*and to amend my life*—

* * *

He went up to his room after dinner in order to be alone with his soul: and at every step his soul seemed to sigh: at every step his soul mounted with his feet, sighing in the ascent, through a region of viscid gloom.

He halted on the landing before the door and then, grasping the porcelain knob, opened the door quickly. He waited in fear, his soul pining within him, praying silently that death might not touch his brow as he passed over the threshold, that the fiends that inhabit darkness might not be given power over him. He waited still at the threshold as at the entrance to some dark cave. Faces were there; eyes: they waited and watched.

—We knew perfectly well of course that although it was bound to come to the light he would find considerable difficulty in endeavouring to try to induce himself to try to endeavour to ascertain the spiritual plenipotentiary and so we knew of course perfectly well—

Murmuring faces waited and watched; murmurous voices filled the dark shell of the cave. He feared intensely in spirit and in flesh but, raising his head bravely, he strode into the room firmly. A doorway, a room, the same room, same window. He told himself calmly that those words had absolutely no sense which had seemed to rise murmurously from the dark. He told himself that it was simply his room with the door open.

He closed the door and, walking swiftly to the bed, knelt beside it and covered his face with his hands. His hands were cold and damp and his limbs ached with chill. Bodily unrest and chill and weariness beset him, routing his thoughts. Why was he kneeling there like a child saying his evening prayers? To be alone with his soul, to examine his conscience, to meet his sins face to face, to recall their times and manners and circumstances, to weep over them. He could not weep. He could not summon them to his memory. He felt only an ache of soul and body, his whole being, memory, will, understanding, flesh, benumbed and weary.

That was the work of devils, to scatter his thoughts and

overcloud his conscience, assailing him at the gates of the cowardly and sincorrupted flesh: and, praying God timidly to forgive him his weakness, he crawled up on to the bed and, wrapping the blankets closely about him, covered his face again with his hands. He had sinned. He had sinned so deeply against heaven and before God that he was not worthy to be called God's child.

Could it be that he, Stephen Dedalus, had done those things? His conscience sighed in answer. Yes, he had done them, secretly, filthily, time after time, and, hardened in sinful impenitence, he had dared to wear the mask of holiness before the tabernacle itself while his soul within was a living mass of corruption. How came it that God had not struck him dead? The leprous company of his sins closed about him, breathing upon him, bending over him from all sides. He strove to forget them in an act of prayer, huddling his limbs closer together and binding down his eyelids: but the senses of his soul would not be bound and, though his eyes were shut fast, he saw the places where he had sinned and, though his ears were tightly covered, he heard. He desired with all his will not to hear or see. He desired till his frame shook under the strain of his desire and until the senses of his soul closed. They closed for an instant and then opened. He saw.

A field of stiff weeds and thistles and tufted nettlebunches. Thick among the tufts of rank stiff growth lay battered canisters and clots and coils of solid excrement. A faint marshlight struggled upwards from all the ordure through the bristling greygreen weeds. An evil smell, faint and foul as the light, curled upwards sluggishly out of the canisters and from the stale crusted dung.

Creatures were in the field; one, three, six: creatures were moving in the field, hither and thither. Goatish creatures with human faces, hornybrowed, lightly bearded and grey as indiarubber. The malice of evil glittered in their hard eyes, as they moved hither and thither, trailing their long tails behind them. A rictus of cruel malignity lit up greyly their old bony faces.

One was clasping about his ribs a torn flannel waistcoat, another complained monotonously as his beard stuck in the tufted weeds. Soft language issued from their spittleless lips as they swished in slow circles round and round the field, winding hither and thither through the weeds, dragging their long tails amid the rattling canisters. They moved in slow circles, circling closer and closer to enclose, to enclose, soft language issuing from their lips, their long swishing tails besmeared with stale shite, thrusting upwards their terrific faces . . .

Help!

He flung the blankets from him madly to free his face and neck. That was his hell. God had allowed him to see the hell reserved for his sins: stinking, bestial, malignant, a hell of lecherous goatish fiends. For him! For him!

He sprang from the bed, the reeking odour pouring down his throat, clogging and revolting his entrails. Air! The air of heaven! He stumbled towards the window, groaning and almost fainting with sickness. At the washstand a convulsion seized him within; and, clasping his cold forehead wildly, he vomited profusely in agony.

When the fit had spent itself he walked weakly to the window and, lifting the sash, sat in a corner of the embrasure and leaned his elbow upon the sill. The rain had drawn off; and amid the moving vapours from point to point of light the city was spinning about herself a soft cocoon of yellowish haze. Heaven was still and faintly luminous and the air sweet to breathe, as in a thicket drenched with showers: and amid peace and shimmering lights and quiet fragrance he made a covenant with his heart.

He prayed:

—He once had meant to come on earth in heavenly glory but we sinned: and then He could not safely visit us but with a shrouded majesty and a bedimmed radiance for He was God. So He came Himself in weakness not in power and He sent thee, a creature in His stead, with a creature's comeliness and

*lustre suited to our state. And now thy very face and form,
dear mother, speak to us of the Eternal; not like earthly
beauty, dangerous to look upon, but like the morning star
which is thy emblem, bright and musical, breathing purity,
telling of heaven and infusing peace. O harbinger of day! O
light of the pilgrim! Lead us still as thou hast led. In the dark
night, across the bleak wilderness guide us on to our Lord
Jesus, guide us home.*

His eyes were dimmed with tears and, looking humbly up to
heaven, he wept for the innocence he had lost.

When evening had fallen he left the house and the first
touch of the damp dark air and the noise of the door as it
closed behind him made ache again his conscience, lulled by
prayer and tears. Confess! Confess! It was not enough to lull
the conscience with a tear and a prayer. He had to kneel
before the minister of the Holy Ghost and tell over his hidden
sins truly and repentantly. Before he heard again the footboard of the housedoor trail over the threshold as it opened to
let him in, before he saw again the table in the kitchen set for
supper he would have knelt and confessed. It was quite simple.

The ache of conscience ceased and he walked onward
swiftly through the dark streets. There were so many flag-
stones on the footpath of that street and so many streets in that
city and so many cities in the world. Yet eternity had no end.
He was in mortal sin. Even once was a mortal sin. It could
happen in an instant. But how so quickly? By seeing or by
thinking of seeing. The eyes see the thing, without having
wished first to see. Then in an instant it happens. But does
that part of the body understand or what? The serpent, the
most subtle beast of the field. It must understand when it
desires in one instant and then prolongs its own desire instant
after instant, sinfully. It feels and understands and desires.
What a horrible thing! Who made it to be like that, a bestial
part of the body able to understand bestially and desire

bestially? Was that then he or an inhuman thing moved by a lower soul than his soul? His soul sickened at the thought of a torpid snaky life feeding itself out of the tender marrow of his life and fattening upon the slime of lust. O why was that so? O why?

He cowered in the shadow of the thought, abasing himself in the awe of God Who had made all things and all men. Madness. Who could think such a thought? And, cowering in darkness and abject, he prayed mutely to his angel guardian to drive away with his sword the demon that was whispering to his brain.

The whisper ceased and he knew then clearly that his own soul had sinned in thought and word and deed wilfully through his own body. Confess! He had to confess every sin. How could he utter in words to the priest what he had done? Must, must. Or how could he explain without dying of shame? Or how could he have done such things without shame? A madman, a loathsome madman! Confess! O he would indeed to be free and sinless again! Perhaps the priest would know. O dear God!

He walked on and on through illlit streets, fearing to stand still for a moment lest it might seem that he held back from what awaited him, fearing to arrive at that towards which he still turned with longing. How beautiful must be a soul in the state of grace when God looked upon it with love!

Frowsy girls sat along the curbstones before their baskets. Their dank hair hung trailed over their brows. They were not beautiful to see as they crouched in the mire. But their souls were seen by God; and if their souls were in a state of grace they were radiant to see: and God loved them, seeing them.

A wasting breath of humiliation blew bleakly over his soul to think of how he had fallen, to feel that those souls were dearer to God than his. The wind blew over him and passed on to the myriads and myriads of other souls on whom God's favour shone now more and now less, stars now brighter and now dimmer, sustained and failing. And the glimmering souls passed away, sustained and failing, merged in a moving breath. One soul was lost; a tiny soul: his. It flickered once and went out, forgotten, lost. The end: black cold void waste.

Consciousness of place came ebbing back to him slowly over a vast tract of time unlit, unfelt, unlived. The squalid scene composed itself around him; the common accents, the burning gasjets in the shops, odours of fish and spirits and wet sawdust, moving men and women. An old woman was about to cross the street, an oilcan in her hand. He bent down and asked her was there a chapel near.

—A chapel, sir? Yes, sir. Church Street chapel.

—Church?

She shifted the can to her other hand and directed him: and, as she held out her reeking withered right hand under its fringe of shawl, he bent lower towards her, saddened and soothed by her voice.

—Thank you.

—You are quite welcome, sir.

The candles on the high altar had been extinguished but the fragrance of incense still floated down the dim nave. Bearded workmen with pious faces were guiding a canopy out through a sidedoor, the sacristan aiding them with quiet gestures and words. A few of the faithful still lingered, praying before one of the sidealtars or kneeling in the benches near the confessionals. He approached timidly and knelt at the last bench in the body, thankful for the peace and silence and fragrant shadow of the church. The board on which he knelt was narrow and worn and those who knelt near him were humble followers of Jesus. Jesus too had been born in poverty and had worked in the shop of a carpenter, cutting boards and planing them, and had first spoken of the kingdom of God to poor fishermen, teaching all men to be meek and humble of heart.

He bowed his head upon his hands, bidding his heart be meek and humble that he might be like those who knelt beside him and his prayer as acceptable as theirs. He prayed beside them but it was hard. His soul was foul with sin and he dared not ask forgiveness with the simple trust of those whom Jesus, in the mysterious ways of God, had called first to His side, the carpenters, the fishermen, poor and simple people following a lowly trade, handling and shaping the wood of trees, mending their nets with patience.

A tall figure came down the aisle and the penitents stirred: and at the last moment, glancing up swiftly, he saw a long grey beard and the brown habit of a capuchin. The priest entered the box and was hidden. Two penitents rose and entered the confessional at either side. The wooden slide was drawn back and the faint murmur of a voice troubled the silence.

His blood began to murmur in his veins, murmuring like a sinful city summoned from its sleep to hear its doom. Little flakes of fire fell and powdery ashes fell softly, alighting on the houses of men. They stirred, waking from sleep, troubled by the heated air.

The slide was shot back. The penitent emerged from the side of the box. The farther slide was drawn. A woman entered quietly and deftly where the first penitent had knelt. The faint murmur began again.

He could still leave the chapel. He could stand up, put one foot before the other and walk out softly and then run, run, run swiftly through the dark streets. He could still escape from the shame. Had it been any terrible crime but that one sin! Had it been murder! Little fiery flakes fell and touched him at all points, shameful thoughts, shameful words, shameful acts. Shame covered him wholly like fine glowing ashes falling continually. To say it in words! His soul, stifling and helpless, would cease to be.

The slide was shot back. A penitent emerged from the farther side of the box. The near slide was drawn. A penitent entered where the other penitent had come out. A soft whispering noise floated in vaporous cloudlets out of the box. It was the woman: soft whispering cloudlets, soft whispering vapour, whispering and vanishing.

He beat his breast with his fist humbly, secretly under cover of the wooden armrest. He would be at one with others and with God. He would love his neighbour. He would love God Who had made and loved him. He would kneel and pray with others and be happy. God would look down on him and on them and would love them all.

It was easy to be good. God's yoke was sweet and light. It was better never to have sinned, to have remained always a child, for God loved little children and suffered them to come to Him. It was a terrible and a sad thing to sin. But God was merciful to poor sinners who were truly sorry. How true that was! That was indeed goodness.

The slide was shot to suddenly. The penitent came out. He was next. He stood up in terror and walked blindly into the box.

At last it had come. He knelt in the silent gloom and raised his eyes to the white crucifix suspended above him. God could see that he was sorry. He would tell all his sins. His confession would be long, long. Everybody in the chapel would know then what a sinner he had been. Let them know. It was true. But God had promised to forgive him if he was sorry. He was sorry. He clasped his hands and raised them towards the white form, praying with his darkened eyes, praying with all his trembling body, swaying his head to and fro like a lost creature, praying with whimpering lips.

—Sorry! Sorry! O sorry!

The slide clicked back and his heart bounded in his breast. The face of an old priest was at the grating, averted from him, leaning upon a hand. He made the sign of the cross and prayed of the priest to bless him for he had sinned. Then, bowing his head, he repeated the *Confiteor* in fright. At the words *my most grievous fault* he ceased, breathless.

—How long is it since your last confession, my child?

—A long time, father.

—A month, my child?

—Longer, father.

—Three months, my child?

—Longer, father.

—Six months?

—Eight months, father.

He had begun. The priest asked:

—And what do you remember since that time?

He began to confess his sins: masses missed, prayers not said, lies.

—Anything else, my child?

Sins of anger, envy of others, gluttony, vanity, disobedience.

—Anything else, my child?

—Sloth.

—Anything else, my child?

There was no help. He murmured:

—I . . . committed sins of impurity, father.

The priest did not turn his head.

—With yourself, my child?

—And . . . with others.

—With women, my child?

—Yes, father.

—Were they married women, my child?

He did not know. His sins trickled from his lips, one by one, trickled in shameful drops from his soul festering and oozing like a sore, a squalid stream of vice. The last sins oozed forth, sluggish, filthy. There was no more to tell. He bowed his head, overcome.

The priest was silent. Then he asked:

—How old are you, my child?

—Sixteen, father.

The priest passed his hand several times over his face. Then, resting his forehead against his hand, he leaned towards the grating and, with eyes still averted, spoke slowly. His voice was weary and old.

—You are very young, my child, he said, and let me implore of you to give up that sin. It is a terrible sin. It kills the body and it kills the soul. It is the cause of many crimes and misfortunes. Give it up, my child, for God's sake. It is dishonourable and unmanly. You cannot know where that wretched habit will lead you or where it will come against you. As long as you commit that sin, my poor child, you will never be worth one farthing to God. Pray to our mother Mary to help you. She will help you, my child. Pray to Our Blessed Lady when that sin comes into your mind. I am sure you will do that, will you not? You repent of all those sins. I am sure you do. And you will promise God now that by His holy grace you will never offend Him any more by that wicked sin. You will make that solemn promise to God, will you not?

—Yes, father.

The old and weary voice fell like sweet rain upon his quaking parching heart. How sweet and sad!

—Do so, my poor child. The devil has led you astray. Drive him back to hell when he tempts you to dishonour your body in that way—the foul spirit who hates Our Lord. Promise God now that you will give up that sin, that wretched wretched sin.

Blinded by his tears and by the light of God's mercifulness he bent his head and heard the grave words of absolution spoken and saw the priest's hand raised above him in token of forgiveness.

—God bless you, my child. Pray for me.

He knelt to say his penance, praying in a corner of the dark nave: and his prayers ascended to heaven from his purified heart like perfume streaming upwards from a heart of white rose.

The muddy streets were gay. He strode homeward, conscious of an invisible grace pervading and making light his limbs. In spite of all he had done it. He had confessed and God had pardoned him. His soul was made fair and holy once more, holy and happy.

It would be beautiful to die if God so willed. It was beautiful to live if God so willed, to live in grace a life of peace and virtue and forbearance with others.

He sat by the fire in the kitchen, not daring to speak for happiness. Till that moment he had not known how beautiful and peaceful life could be. The green square of paper pinned round the lamp cast down a tender shade. On the dresser was a plate of sausages and white pudding and on the shelf there were eggs. They would be for the breakfast in the morning after the communion in the college chapel. White pudding and eggs and sausages and cups of tea. How simple and beautiful was life after all! And life lay all before him.

In a dream he fell asleep. In a dream he rose and saw that it was morning. In a waking dream he went through the quiet morning towards the college.

The boys were all there, kneeling in their places. He knelt among them, happy and shy. The altar was heaped with fragrant masses of white flowers: and in the morning light the pale flames of the candles among the white flowers were clear and silent as his own soul.

He knelt before the altar with his classmates, holding the altar cloth with them over a living rail of hands. His hands were trembling, and his soul trembled as he heard the priest pass with the ciborium from communicant to communicant.

—*Corpus Domini nostri.*

Could it be? He knelt there sinless and timid: and he would hold upon his tongue the host and God would enter his purified body.

—*In vitam eternam. Amen.*

Another life! A life of grace and virtue and happiness! It was true. It was not a dream from which he would wake. The past was past.

—*Corpus Domini nostri.*

The ciborium had come to him.

I V

SUNDAY was dedicated to the mystery of the Holy Trinity, Monday to the Holy Ghost, Tuesday to the Guardian Angels, Wednesday to Saint Joseph, Thursday to the Most Blessed Sacrament of the Altar, Friday to the Suffering Jesus, Saturday to the Blessed Virgin Mary.

Every morning he hallowed himself anew in the presence of some holy image or mystery. His day began with an heroic offering of its every moment of thought or action for the intentions of the sovereign pontiff and with an early mass. The raw morning air whetted his resolute piety; and often as he knelt among the few worshippers at the sidealtar, following with his interleaved prayerbook the murmur of the priest, he glanced up for an instant towards the vested figure standing in the gloom between the two candles which were the old and the new testaments and imagined that he was kneeling at mass in the catacombs.

His daily life was laid out in devotional areas. By means of ejaculations and prayers he stored up ungrudgingly for the souls in purgatory centuries of days and quarantines and years; yet the spiritual triumph which he felt in achieving with ease so many fabulous ages of canonical penances did not wholly reward his zeal of prayer since he could never know how much temporal punishment he had remitted by way of suffrage for the agonising souls: and, fearful lest in the midst of the purgatorial fire, which differed from the infernal only in that it was not everlasting, his penance might avail no more than a drop of moisture, he drove his soul daily through an increasing circle of works of supererogation.

Every part of his day, divided by what he regarded now as the duties of his station in life, circled about its own centre of spiritual energy. His life seemed to have drawn near to eternity; every thought, word and deed, every instance of consciousness could be made to revibrate radiantly in heaven: and at times his sense of such immediate repercussion was so lively that he seemed to feel his soul in devotion pressing like fingers the keyboard of a great cash register and to see the amount of his purchase start forth immediately in heaven, not as a number but as a frail column of incense or as a slender flower.

The rosaries too which he said constantly—for he carried his beads loose in his trousers' pockets that he might tell them as he walked the streets—transformed themselves into coronals of flowers of such vague unearthly texture that they seemed to him as hueless and odourless as they were nameless. He offered up each of his three daily chaplets that his soul might grow strong in each of the three theological virtues, in faith in the Father, Who had created him, in hope in the Son Who had redeemed him, and in love of the Holy Ghost Who had sanctified him, and this thrice triple prayer he offered to the Three persons through Mary in the name of her joyful and sorrowful and glorious mysteries.

On each of the seven days of the week he further prayed that one of the seven gifts of the Holy Ghost might descend upon his soul and drive out of it day by day the seven deadly sins which had defiled it in the past; and he prayed for each gift on its appointed day, confident that it would descend upon him, though it seemed strange to him at times that wisdom and understanding and knowledge were so distinct in their nature that each should be prayed for apart from the others. Yet he believed that at some future stage of his spiritual progress this difficulty would be removed when his sinful soul had been raised up from its weakness and enlightened by the Third Person of the Most Blessed Trinity. He believed this all the more, and with trepidation, because of the divine gloom and silence wherein dwelt the unseen Paraclete, Whose symbols were a dove and a mighty wind, to sin against Whom was a sin beyond forgiveness, the eternal, mysterious secret Being to Whom, as God, the priests offered up mass once a year, robed in the scarlet of the tongues of fire.

The imagery through which the nature and kinship of the Three Persons of the Trinity were darkly shadowed forth in the books of devotion which he read—the Father contemplating from all eternity as in a mirror His Divine Perfections and thereby begetting eternally the Eternal Son and the Holy Spirit proceeding out of Father and Son from all eternity—were easier of acceptance by his mind by reason of their august incomprehensibility than was the simple fact that God had loved his soul from all eternity, for ages before he had been born into the world, for ages before the world itself had existed.

He had heard the names of the passions of love and hate pronounced solemnly on the stage and in the pulpit, had found them set forth solemnly in books, and had wondered why his soul was unable to harbour them for any time or to force his lips to utter their names with conviction. A brief anger had often invested him but he had never been able to make it an abiding passion and had always felt himself passing out of it as if his very body were being divested with ease of some outer skin or peel. He had felt a subtle, dark and murmurous presence penetrate his being and fire him with a brief iniquitous lust: it too had slipped beyond his grasp leaving his mind lucid and indifferent. This, it seemed, was the only love and that the only hate his soul would harbour.

But he could no longer disbelieve in the reality of love since God Himself had loved his individual soul with divine love from all eternity. Gradually, as his soul was enriched with spiritual knowledge, he saw the whole world forming one vast symmetrical expression of God's power and love. Life became a divine gift for every moment and sensation of which, were it even the sight of a single leaf hanging on the twig of a tree, his soul should praise and thank the Giver. The world for all its solid substance and complexity no longer existed for his soul save as a theorem of divine power and love and universality. So entire and unquestionable was this sense of the divine meaning in all nature granted to his soul that he could scarcely understand why it was in any way necessary that he should continue to live. Yet that was part of the divine purpose and he dared not question its use, he above all others who had sinned so deeply and so foully against the divine purpose. Meek and abased by this consciousness of the one eternal omnipresent perfect reality his soul took up again her burden of pieties, masses and prayers and sacraments and mortifications, and only then for the first time since he had brooded on the great mystery of love did he feel within him a warm movement like that of some newly born life or virtue of the soul itself. The attitude of rapture in sacred art, the raised and parted hands, the parted lips and eyes as of one about to swoon, became for him an image of the soul in prayer, humiliated and faint before her Creator.

But he had been forewarned of the dangers of spiritual exaltation and did not allow himself to desist from even the least or lowliest devotion, striving also by constant mortification to undo the sinful past rather than to achieve a saintliness fraught with peril. Each of his senses was brought under a rigorous discipline. In order to mortify the sense of sight he made it his rule to walk in the street with downcast eyes, glancing neither to right nor left and never behind him. His eyes shunned every encounter with the eyes of women. From time to time also he balked them by a sudden effort of the will, as by lifting them suddenly in the middle of an unfinished sentence and closing the book. To mortify his hearing he exerted no control over his voice which was then breaking, neither sang nor whistled and made no attempt to flee from noises which caused him painful nervous irritation such as the sharpening of knives on the knifeboard, the gathering of cinders on the fireshovel and the twigging of the carpet. To mortify his smell was more difficult as he found in himself no instinctive repugnance to bad odours, whether they were the odours of the outdoor world such as those of dung and tar or the odours of his own person among which he had made many curious comparisons and experiments. He found in the end that the only odour against which his sense of smell revolted was a certain stale fishy stink like that of longstanding urine: and whenever it was possible he subjected himself to this unpleasant odour. To mortify the taste he practised strict habits at table, observed to the letter all the fasts of the church and sought by distraction to divert his mind from the savours of different foods. But it was to the mortification of touch that he brought the most assiduous ingenuity of inventiveness. He never consciously changed his position in bed, sat in the most uncomfortable positions, suffered patiently every itch and pain, kept away from the fire, remained on his knees all through the mass except at the gospels, left parts of his neck and face undried so that air might sting them and, whenever he was not saying his beads, carried his arms stiffly at his sides like a runner and never in his pockets or clasped behind him.

He had no temptations to sin mortally. It surprised him however to find that at the end of his course of intricate piety and selfrestraint he was so easily at the mercy of childish and unworthy imperfections. His prayers and fasts availed him little for the suppression of anger at hearing his mother sneeze or at being disturbed in his devotions. It needed an immense effort of his will to master the impulse which urged him to give outlet to such irritation. Images of the outbursts of trivial anger which he had often noted among his masters, their twitching mouths, closeshut lips and flushed cheeks, recurred to his memory, discouraging him, for all his practice of humility, by the comparison. To merge his life in the common tide of other lives was harder for him than any fasting or prayer, and it was his constant failure to do this to his own satisfaction which caused in his soul at last a sensation of spiritual dryness together with a growth of doubts and scruples. His soul traversed a period of desolation in which the sacraments themselves seemed to have turned into dried up sources. His confession became a channel for the escape of scrupulous and unrepented imperfections. His actual reception of the eucharist did not bring him the same dissolving moments of virginal selfsurrender as did those spiritual communions made by him sometimes at the close of some visit to the Blessed Sacrament. The book which he used for these visits was an old neglected book written by saint Alphonsus Liguori, with fading characters and sere foxpapered leaves. A faded world of fervent love and virginal responses seemed to be evoked for his soul by the reading of its pages in which the imagery of the canticles was interwoven with the communicant's prayers. An inaudible voice seemed to caress the soul, telling her names and glories, bidding her arise as for espousal and come away, bidding her look forth, a spouse, from Amana and from the mountains of the leopards; and the soul seemed to answer with the same inaudible voice, surrendering herself: *Inter ubera mea commorabitur.*

This idea of surrender had a perilous attraction for his mind now that he felt his soul beset once again by the insistent voices of the flesh which began to murmur to him again during his prayers and meditations. It gave him an intense sense of power to know that he could by a single act of consent, in a moment of thought, undo all that he had done. He seemed to feel a flood slowly advancing towards his naked feet and to be waiting for the first faint timid noiseless wavelet to touch his fevered skin. Then, almost at the instant of that touch, almost at the verge of sinful consent, he found himself standing far away from the flood upon a dry shore, saved by a sudden act of the will or a sudden ejaculation: and, seeing the silver line of the flood far away and beginning again its slow advance towards his feet, a new thrill of power and satisfaction shook his soul to know that he had not yielded nor undone all.

When he had eluded the flood of temptation many times in

this way he grew troubled and wondered whether the grace which he had refused to lose was not being filched from him little by little. The clear certitude of his own immunity grew dim and to it succeeded a vague fear that his soul had really fallen unawares. It was with difficulty that he won back his old consciousness of his state of grace by telling himself that he had prayed to God at every temptation and that the grace which he had prayed for must have been given to him inasmuch as God was obliged to give it. The very frequency and violence of temptations showed him at last the truth of what he had heard about the trials of the saints. Frequent and violent temptations were a proof that the citadel of the soul had not fallen and that the devil raged to make it fall.

Often when he had confessed his doubts and scruples, some momentary inattention at prayer, a movement of trivial anger in his soul or a subtle wilfulness in speech or act, he was bidden by his confessor to name some sin of his past life before absolution was given him. He named it with humility and shame and repented of it once more. It humiliated and shamed him to think that he would never be freed from it wholly, however holily he might live or whatever virtues or perfections he might attain. A restless feeling of guilt would always be present with him: he would confess and repent and be absolved, confess and repent again and be absolved again, fruitlessly. Perhaps that first hasty confession wrung from him by the fear of hell had not been good? Perhaps, concerned only for his imminent doom, he had not had sincere sorrow for his sin? But the surest sign that his confession had been good and that he had had sincere sorrow for his sin was, he knew, the amendment of his life.

—I have amended my life, have I not? he asked himself.

*　　*　　*

The director stood in the embrasure of the window, his back to the light, leaning an elbow on the brown crossblind and, as he spoke and smiled, slowly dangling and looping the cord of the other blind. Stephen stood before him, following for a moment with his eyes the waning of the long summer daylight above the roofs or the slow deft movements of the priestly fingers. The priest's face was in total shadow but the waning daylight from behind him touched the deeply grooved temples and the curves of the skull. Stephen followed also with his ears the accents and intervals of the priest's voice as he spoke gravely and cordially of indifferent themes, the vacation which had just ended, the colleges of the order abroad, the transference of masters. The grave and cordial voice went on easily with its tale, and in the pauses Stephen felt bound to set it on again with respectful questions. He knew that the tale was a prelude and his mind waited for the sequel. Ever since the message of summons had come for him from the director his mind had struggled to find the meaning of the message; and during the long restless time he had sat in the college parlour waiting for the director to come in his eyes had wandered from one sober picture to another around the walls and his mind wandered from one guess to another until the meaning of the summons had almost become clear. Then, just as he was wishing that some unforeseen cause might prevent the director from coming, he had heard the handle of the door turning and the swish of a soutane.

The director had begun to speak of the dominican and franciscan orders and of the friendship between saint Thomas and saint Bonaventure. The capuchin dress, he thought, was rather too . . .

Stephen's face gave back the priest's indulgent smile and, not being anxious to give an opinion, he made a slight dubitative movement with his lips.

—I believe, continued the director, that there is some talk now among the capuchins themselves of doing away with it and following the example of the other franciscans.

—I suppose they would retain it in the cloister, said Stephen.

—O, certainly, said the director. For the cloister it is all right but for the street I really think it would be better to do away with, don't you?

—It must be troublesome, I imagine?

—Of course it is, of course. Just imagine when I was in Belgium I used to see them out cycling in all kinds of weather with this thing up about their knees! It was really ridiculous. *Les jupes,* they call them in Belgium.

The vowel was so modified as to be indistinct.

—What do they call them?

—*Les jupes.*

—O.

Stephen smiled again in answer to the smile which he could not see on the priest's shadowed face, its image or spectre only passing rapidly across his mind as the low discreet accent fell upon his ear. He gazed calmly before him at the waning sky, glad of the cool of the evening and the faint yellow glow which hid the tiny flame kindling upon his cheek.

The names of articles of dress worn by women or of certain soft and delicate stuffs used in their making brought always to his mind a delicate and sinful perfume. As a boy he had imagined the reins by which horses are driven as slender silken bands and it shocked him to feel at Stradbrook the greasy leather of harness. It had shocked him too when he had felt for the first time beneath his tremulous fingers the brittle texture of a woman's stocking for, retaining nothing of all he read save that which seemed to him an echo or a prophecy of his own state, it was only amid softworded phrases or within rosesoft stuffs that he dared to conceive of the soul or body of a woman moving with tender life.

But the phrase on the priest's lips was disingenuous for he knew that a priest should not speak lightly on that theme. The phrase had been spoken lightly with design and he felt that his face was being searched by the eyes in the shadow. Whatever he had heard or read of the craft of jesuits he had put aside frankly as not borne out by his own experience. His masters, even when they had not attracted him, had seemed to him always intelligent and serious priests, athletic and highspirited prefects. He thought of them as men who washed their bodies briskly with cold water and wore clean cold linen. During all the years he had lived among them in Clongowes and in Belvedere he had received only two pandies and, though these had been dealt him in the wrong, he knew that he had often escaped punishment. During all those years he had never heard from any of his masters a flippant word: it was they who had taught him christian doctrine and urged him to live a good life and, when he had fallen into grievous sin, it was they who had led him back to grace. Their presence had made him diffident of himself when he was a muff in Clongowes and it had made him diffident of himself also while he had held his equivocal position in Belvedere. A constant sense of this had remained with him up to the last year of his school life. He had never once disobeyed or allowed turbulent companions to seduce him from his habit of quiet obedience: and, even when he doubted some statement of a master, he had never presumed to doubt openly. Lately some of their judgments had sounded a little childish in his ears and had made him feel a regret and pity as though he were slowly passing out of an accustomed world and were hearing its language for the last time. One day when some boys had gathered round a priest under the shed near the chapel, he had heard the priest say:

—I believe that Lord Macaulay was a man who probably never committed a mortal sin in his life, that is to say, a deliberate mortal sin.

Some of the boys had then asked the priest if Victor Hugo were not the greatest French writer. The priest had answered that Victor Hugo had never written half so well when he had turned against the church as he had written when he was a catholic.

—But there are many eminent French critics, said the priest, who consider that even Victor Hugo, great as he certainly was, had not so pure a French style as Louis Veuillot.

The tiny flame which the priest's allusion had kindled upon

Stephen's cheek had sunk down again and his eyes were still fixed calmly on the colorless sky. But an unresting doubt flew hither and thither before his mind. Masked memories passed quickly before him: he recognised scenes and persons yet he was conscious that he had failed to perceive some vital circumstance in them. He saw himself walking about the grounds watching the sports in Clongowes and eating slim jim out of his cricketcap. Some jesuits were walking round the cycletrack in the company of ladies. The echoes of certain expressions used in Clongowes sounded in remote caves of his mind.

His ears were listening to these distant echoes amid the silence of the parlour when he became aware that the priest was addressing him in a different voice.

—I sent for you today, Stephen, because I wished to speak to you on a very important subject.

—Yes, sir.

—Have you ever felt that you had a vocation?

Stephen parted his lips to answer yes and then withheld the word suddenly. The priest waited for the answer and added:

—I mean have you ever felt within yourself, in your soul, a desire to join the order. Think.

—I have sometimes thought of it, said Stephen.

The priest let the blindcord fall to one side and, uniting his hands, leaned his chin gravely upon them, communing with himself.

—In a college like this, he said at length, there is one boy or perhaps two or three boys whom God calls to the religious life. Such a boy is marked off from his companions by his piety, by the good example he shows to others. He is looked up to by them; he is chosen perhaps as prefect by his fellow sodalists. And you, Stephen, have been such a boy in this college, prefect of Our Blessed Lady's sodality. Perhaps you are the boy in this college whom God designs to call to Himself.

A strong note of pride reinforcing the gravity of the priest's voice made Stephen's heart quicken in response.

—To receive that call, Stephen, said the priest, is the greatest honour that the Almighty God can bestow upon a man. No king or emperor on this earth has the power of the priest of God. No angel or archangel in heaven, no saint, not even the Blessed Virgin herself has the power of a priest of God: the power of the keys, the power to bind and to loose from sin, the power of exorcism, the power to cast out from the creatures of God the evil spirits that have power over them, the power, the authority, to make the great God of Heaven come down upon the altar and take the form of bread and wine. What an awful power, Stephen!

A flame began to flutter again on Stephen's cheek as he heard in this proud address an echo of his own proud musings. How often had he seen himself as a priest wielding calmly and humbly the awful power of which angels and saints stood in reverence! His soul had loved to muse in secret on this desire. He had seen himself, a young and silentmannered priest, entering a confessional swiftly, ascending the altarsteps, incensing, genuflecting, accomplishing the vague acts of the priesthood which pleased him by reason of their semblance of reality and of their distance from it. In that dim life which he had lived through in his musings he had assumed the voices and gestures which he had noted with various priests. He had bent his knee sideways like such a one, he had shaken the thurible only slightly like such a one, his chasuble had swung open like that of such another as he had turned to the altar again after having blessed the people. And above all it had pleased him to fill the second place in those dim scenes of his imagining. He shrank from the dignity of celebrant because it displeased him to imagine that all the vague pomp should end in his own person or that the ritual should assign to him so clear and final an office. He longed for the minor sacred offices, to be vested with the tunicle of subdeacon at high mass, to stand aloof from the altar, forgotten by the people, his shoulders covered with a humeral veil, holding the paten within its folds, or, when the sacrifice had been accomplished, to stand as deacon in a dalmatic of cloth of gold on the step below the celebrant, his hands joined and his face towards the people, and sing the chant *Ite, missa est.* If ever he had seen himself celebrant it was as in the pictures of the mass in his child's massbook, in a church without worshippers, save for the angel of the sacrifice, at a bare altar and served by an acolyte scarcely more boyish than himself. In vague sacrificial or sacramental acts alone his will seemed drawn to go forth to encounter reality: and it was partly the absence of an appointed rite which had always constrained him to inaction whether he had allowed silence to cover his anger or pride or had suffered only an embrace he longed to give.

He listened in reverent silence now to the priest's appeal and through the words he heard even more distinctly a voice bidding him approach, offering him secret knowledge and secret power. He would know then what was the sin of Simon Magus and what the sin against the Holy Ghost for which there was no forgiveness. He would know obscure things, hidden from others, from those who were conceived and born children of wrath. He would know the sins, the sinful longings and sinful thoughts and sinful acts, of others, hearing them murmured into his ears in the confessional under the shame of a darkened chapel by the lips of women and of girls: but rendered immune mysteriously at his ordination by the imposition of hands his soul would pass again uncontaminated to the white peace of the altar. No touch of sin would linger upon the hands with which he would elevate and break the host; no touch of sin would linger on his lips in prayer to make him eat and drink damnation to himself, not discerning the body of the Lord. He would hold his secret knowledge and secret power, being as sinless as the innocent: and he would be a priest for ever according to the order of Melchisedec.

—I will offer up my mass tomorrow morning, said the director, that Almighty God may reveal to you His holy will. And let you, Stephen, make a novena to your holy patron saint, the first martyr, who is very powerful with God, that

God may enlighten your mind. But you must be quite sure, Stephen, that you have a vocation because it would be terrible if you found afterwards that you had none. Once a priest always a priest, remember. Your catechism tells you that the sacrament of Holy Orders is one of those which can be received only once because it imprints on the soul an indelible spiritual mark which can never be effaced. It is before you must weigh well, not after. It is a solemn question, Stephen, because on it may depend the salvation of your eternal soul. But we will pray to God together.

He held open the heavy hall door and gave his hand as if already to a companion in the spiritual life. Stephen passed out on to the wide platform above the steps and was conscious of the caress of mild evening air. Towards Findlater's church a quartet of young men were striding along with linked arms, swaying their heads and stepping to the agile melody of their leader's concertina. The music passed in an instant, as the first bars of sudden music always did, over the fantastic fabrics of his mind, dissolving them painlessly and noiselessly as a sudden wave dissolves the sandbuilt turrets of children. Smiling at the trivial air he raised his eyes to the priest's face and, seeing in it a mirthless reflection of the sunken day, detached his hand slowly which had acquiesced faintly in that companionship.

As he descended the steps the impression which effaced his troubled selfcommunion was that of a mirthless mask reflecting a sunken day from the threshold of the college. The shadow, then, of the life of the college passed gravely over his consciousness. It was a grave and ordered and passionless life that awaited him, a life without material cares. He wondered how he would pass the first night in the novitiate and with what dismay he would wake the first morning in the dormitory. The troubling odour of the long corridors of Clongowes came back to him and he heard the discreet murmur of the burning gasflames. At once from every part of his being unrest began to irradiate. A feverish quickening of his pulses followed and a din of meaningless words drove his reasoned thoughts hither and thither confusedly. His lungs dilated and sank as if he were inhaling a warm moist unsustaining air and he smelt again the warm moist air which hung in the bath in Clongowes above the sluggish turfcoloured water.

Some instinct, waking at these memories, stronger than education or piety, quickened within him at every near approach to that life, an instinct subtle and hostile, and armed him against acquiescence. The chill and order of the life repelled him. He saw himself rising in the cold of the morning and filing down with the others to early mass and trying vainly to struggle with his prayers against the fainting sickness of his stomach. He saw himself sitting at dinner with the community of a college. What, then, had become of that deeprooted shyness of his which had made him loth to eat or drink under a strange roof? What had come of the pride of his spirit which had always made him conceive himself as a being apart in every order?

The Reverend Stephen Dedalus, S. J.

His name in that new life leaped into characters before his eyes and to it there followed a mental sensation of an undefined face or colour of a face. The colour faded and became strong like a changing glow of pallid brick red. Was it the raw reddish glow he had so often seen on wintry mornings on the shaven gills of the priests? The face was eyeless and sourfavoured and devout, shot with pink tinges of suffocated anger. Was it not a mental spectre of the face of one of the jesuits whom some of the boys called Lantern Jaws and others Foxy Campbell?

He was passing at that moment before the jesuit house in Gardiner Street, and wondered vaguely which window would be his if he ever joined the order. Then he wondered at the vagueness of his wonder, at the remoteness of his soul from what he had hitherto imagined her sanctuary, at the frail hold which so many years of order and obedience had of him when once a definite and irrevocable act of his threatened to end for ever, in time and in eternity, his freedom. The voice of the director urging upon him the proud claims of the church and the mystery and power of the priestly office repeated itself idly in his memory. His soul was not there to hear and greet it and he knew now that the exhortation he had listened to had already fallen into an idle formal tale. He would never swing the thurible before the tabernacle as priest. His destiny was to be elusive of social or religious orders. The wisdom of the priest's appeal did not touch him to the quick. He was destined to learn his own wisdom apart from others or to learn the wisdom of others himself wandering among the snares of the world.

The snares of the world were its ways of sin. He would fall. He had not yet fallen but he would fall silently, in an instant. Not to fall was too hard, too hard: and he felt the silent lapse of his soul, as it would be at some instant to come, falling, falling but not yet fallen, still unfallen but about to fall.

He crossed the bridge over the stream of the Tolka and turned his eyes coldly for an instant towards the faded blue shrine of the Blessed Virgin which stood fowlwise on a pole in the middle of a hamshaped encampment of poor cottages. Then, bending to the left, he followed the lane which led up to his house. The faint sour stink of rotted cabbages came towards him from the kitchengardens on the rising ground above the river. He smiled to think that it was this disorder, the misrule and confusion of his father's house and the stagnation of vegetable life, which was to win the day in his soul. Then a short laugh broke from his lips as he thought of that solitary farmhand in the kitchengardens behind their house whom they had nicknamed the man with the hat. A second laugh, taking rise from the first after a pause, broke from him involuntarily as he thought of how the man with the hat worked, considering in turn the four points of the sky and then regretfully plunging his spade in the earth.

He pushed open the latchless door of the porch and passed through the naked hallway into the kitchen. A group of his brothers and sisters was sitting round the table. Tea was nearly over and only the last of the second watered tea remained in the bottoms of the small glassjars and jampots which did service for teacups. Discarded crusts and lumps of sugared bread, turned brown by the tea which had been poured over them, lay scattered on the table. Little wells of tea lay here and there on the board and a knife with a broken ivory handle was stuck through the pith of a ravaged turnover.

The sad quiet greyblue glow of the dying day came through the window and the open door, covering over and allaying quietly a sudden instinct of remorse in Stephen's heart. All that had been denied them had been freely given to him, the eldest: but the quiet glow of evening showed him in their faces no sign of rancour.

He sat near them at the table and asked where his father and mother were. One answered:

—Goneboro toboro lookboro atboro aboro houseboro.

Still another removal! A boy named Fallon in Belvedere had often asked him with a silly laugh why they moved so often. A frown of scorn darkened quickly his forehead as he heard again the silly laugh of the questioner.

He asked:

—Why are we on the move again, if it's a fair question?

The same sister answered:

—Becauseboro theboro landboro lordboro willboro putboro usboro outboro.

The voice of his youngest brother from the farther side of the fireplace began to sing the air *Oft in the Stilly Night*. One by one the others took up the air until a full choir of voices was singing. They would sing so for hours, melody after melody, glee after glee, till the last pale light died down on the horizon, till the first dark nightclouds came forth and night fell.

He waited for some moments, listening, before he too took up the air with them. He was listening with pain of spirit to the overtone of weariness behind their frail fresh innocent voices.

Even before they set out on life's journey they seemed weary already of the way.

He heard the choir of voices in the kitchen echoed and multiplied through an endless reverberation of the choirs of endless generations of children: and heard in all the echoes an echo also of the recurring note of weariness and pain. All seemed weary of life even before entering upon it. And he remembered that Newman had heard this note also in the broken lines of Virgil *giving utterance, like the voice of Nature herself, to that pain and weariness yet hope of better things which has been the experience of her children in every time.*

*   *   *

He could wait no longer.

From the door of Byron's publichouse to the gate of Clontarf Chapel, from the gate of Clontarf Chapel to the door of Byron's publichouse and then back again to the chapel and then back again to the publichouse he had paced slowly at first, planting his steps scrupulously in the spaces of the patchwork of the footpath, then timing their fall to the fall of verses. A full hour had passed since his father had gone in with Dan Crosby, the tutor, to find out for him something about the university. For a full hour he had paced up and down, waiting: but he could wait no longer.

He set off abruptly for the Bull, walking rapidly lest his father's shrill whistle might call him back; and in a few moments he had rounded the curve at the police barrack and was safe.

Yes, his mother was hostile to the idea, as he had read from her listless silence. Yet her mistrust pricked him more keenly than his father's pride and he thought coldly how he had watched the faith which was fading down in his soul aging and strengthening in her eyes. A dim antagonism gathered force within him and darkened his mind as a cloud against her disloyalty: and when it passed, cloudlike, leaving his mind serene and dutiful towards her again, he was made aware dimly and without regret of a first noiseless sundering of their lives.

The university! So he had passed beyond the challenge of the sentries who had stood as guardians of his boyhood and had sought to keep him among them that he might be subject to them and serve their ends. Pride after satisfaction uplifted him like long slow waves. The end he had been born to serve yet did not see had led him to escape by an unseen path: and now it beckoned to him once more and a new adventure was about to be opened to him. It seemed to him that he heard notes of fitful music leaping upwards a tone and downwards a diminished fourth, upwards a tone and downwards a major third, like triplebranching flames leaping fitfully, flame after flame, out of a midnight wood. It was an elfin prelude, endless and formless; and, as it grew wilder and faster, the flames leaping out of time, he seemed to hear from under the boughs and grasses wild creatures racing, their feet pattering like rain upon the leaves. Their feet passed in pattering tumult over his mind, the feet of hares and rabbits, the feet of harts and hinds and antelopes, until he heard them no more and remembered only a proud cadence from Newman: *Whose feet are as the feet of harts and underneath the everlasting arms.*

The pride of that dim image brought back to his mind the dignity of the office he had refused. All through his boyhood he had mused upon that which he had so often thought to be his destiny and when the moment had come for him to obey the call he had turned aside, obeying a wayward instinct. Now time lay between: the oils of ordination would never anoint his body. He had refused. Why?

He turned seaward from the road at Dollymount and as he passed on to the thin wooden bridge he felt the planks shaking with the tramp of heavily shod feet. A squad of christian brothers was on its way back from the Bull and had begun to pass, two by two, across the bridge. Soon the whole bridge was trembling and resounding. The uncouth faces passed him two by two, stained yellow or red or livid by the sea, and as

he strove to look at them with ease and indifference, a faint
stain of personal shame and commiseration rose to his own
face. Angry with himself he tried to hide his face from their
eyes by gazing down sideways into the shallow swirling water
under the bridge but he still saw a reflection therein of their
topheavy silk hats, and humble tapelike collars and loosely
hanging clerical clothes.

—Brother Hickey.

Brother Quaid.

Brother MacArdle.

Brother Keogh.

Their piety would be like their names, like their faces, like
their clothes, and it was idle for him to tell himself that their
humble and contrite hearts, it might be, paid a far richer
tribute of devotion than his had ever been, a gift tenfold more
acceptable than his elaborate adoration. It was idle for him to
move himself to be generous towards them, to tell himself that
if he ever came to their gates, stripped of his pride, beaten and
in beggar's weeds, that they would be generous towards him,
loving him as themselves. Idle and embittering, finally, to
argue, against his own dispassionate certitude, that the commandment of love bade us not to love our neighbour as ourselves with the same amount and intensity of love but to love
him as ourselves with the same kind of love.

He drew forth a phrase from his treasure and spoke it softly
to himself:

—A day of dappled seaborne clouds.

The phrase and the day and the scene harmonised in a
chord. Words. Was it their colours? He allowed them to glow
and fade, hue after hue: sunrise gold, the russet and green of
apple orchards, azure of waves, the greyfringed fleece of
clouds. No, it was not their colours: it was the poise and
balance of the period itself. Did he then love the rhythmic rise
and fall of words better than their associations of legend and
colour? Or was it that, being as weak of sight as he was shy of
mind, he drew less pleasure from the reflection of the glowing

sensible world through the prism of a language manycoloured and richly storied than from the contemplation of an inner world of individual emotions mirrored perfectly in a lucid supple periodic prose?

He passed from the trembling bridge on to firm land again. At that instant, as it seemed to him, the air was chilled and looking askance towards the water he saw a flying squall darkening and crisping suddenly the tide. A faint click at his heart, a faint throb in his throat told him once more of how his flesh dreaded the cold infrahuman odour of the sea: yet he did not strike across the downs on his left but held straight on along the spine of rocks that pointed against the river's mouth.

A veiled sunlight lit up faintly the grey sheet of water where the river was embayed. In the distance along the course of the slowflowing Liffey slender masts flecked the sky and, more distant still, the dim fabric of the city lay prone in haze. Like a scene on some vague arras, old as man's weariness, the image of the seventh city of christendom was visible to him across the timeless air, no older nor more weary nor less patient of subjection than in the days of the thingmote.

Disheartened, he raised his eyes towards the slowdrifting clouds, dappled and seaborne. They were voyaging across the deserts of the sky, a host of nomads on the march, voyaging high over Ireland, westward bound. The Europe they had come from lay out there beyond the Irish Sea, Europe of strange tongues and valleyed and woodbegirt and citadelled and of entrenched and marshalled races. He heard a confused music within him as of memories and names which he was almost conscious of but could not capture even for an instant; then the music seemed to recede, to recede, to recede: and from each receding trail of nebulous music there fell always one longdrawn calling note, piercing like a star the dusk of silence. Again! Again! Again! A voice from beyond the world was calling.

—Hello, Stephanos!

—Here comes The Dedalus!

—Ao! . . . Eh, give it over, Dwyer, I'm telling you or I'll give you a stuff in the kisser for yourself. . . . Ao!

—Good man, Towser! Duck him!

—Come along, Dedalus! Bous Stephanoumenos! Bous Stephaneforos!

—Duck him! Guzzle him now, Towser!

—Help! Help! . . . Ao!

He recognised their speech collectively before he distinguished their faces. The mere sight of that medley of wet nakedness chilled him to the bone. Their bodies, corpsewhite or suffused with a pallid golden light or rawly tanned by the suns, gleamed with the wet of the sea. Their divingstone, poised on its rude supports and rocking under their plunges, and the roughhewn stones of the sloping breakwater over which they scrambled in their horseplay, gleamed with cold wet lustre. The towels with which they smacked their bodies were heavy with cold seawater: and drenched with cold brine was their matted hair.

He stood still in deference to their calls and parried their banter with easy words. How characterless they looked: Shuley without his deep unbuttoned collar, Ennis without his scarlet belt with the snaky clasp, and Connolly without his Norfolk coat with the flapless sidepockets! It was a pain to see them and a swordlike pain to see the signs of adolescence that made repellent their pitiable nakedness. Perhaps they had taken refuge in number and noise from the secret dread in their souls. But he, apart from them and in silence, remembered in what dread he stood of the mystery of his own body.

—Stephanos Dedalos! Bous Stephanoumenos! Bous Stephaneforos!

Their banter was not new to him and now it flattered his mild proud sovereignty. Now, as never before, his strange name seemed to him a prophecy. So timeless seemed the grey warm air, so fluid and impersonal his own mood, that all ages were as one to him. A moment before the ghost of the ancient kingdom of the Danes had looked forth through the vesture of the hazewrapped city. Now, at the name of the fabulous artificer, he seemed to hear the noise of dim waves and to see a winged form flying above the waves and slowly climbing the air. What did it mean? Was it a quaint device opening a page of some medieval book of prophecies and symbols, a hawklike man flying sunward above the sea, a prophecy of the end he had been born to serve and had been following through the mists of childhood and boyhood, a symbol of the artist forging anew in his workshop out of the sluggish matter of the earth a new soaring impalpable imperishable being?

His heart trembled; his breath came faster and a wild spirit passed over his limbs as though he were soaring sunward. His heart trembled in an ecstasy of fear and his soul was in flight. His soul was soaring in an air beyond the world and the body he knew was purified in a breath and delivered of incertitude and made radiant and commingled with the element of the spirit. An ecstasy of flight made radiant his eyes and wild his breath and tremulous and wild and radiant his windswept limbs.

—One! Two! . . . Look out!

—O, cripes, I'm drownded!

—One! Two! Three and away!

—Me next! Me next!

—One! . . . Uk!

—Stephaneforos!

His throat ached with a desire to cry aloud, the cry of a hawk or eagle on high, to cry piercingly of his deliverance to the winds. This was the call of life to his soul not the dull gross voice of the world of duties and despair, not the inhuman voice that had called him to the pale service of the altar. An instant of wild flight had delivered him and the cry of triumph which his lips withheld cleft his brain.

—Stephaneforos!

What were they now but cerements shaken from the body of death—the fear he had walked in night and day, the incertitude that had ringed him round, the shame that had abased him within and without—cerements, the linens of the grave?

His soul had arisen from the grave of boyhood, spurning her graveclothes. Yes! Yes! Yes! He would create proudly out of the freedom and power of his soul, as the great artificer whose name he bore, a living thing, new and soaring and beautiful, impalpable, imperishable.

He started up nervously from the stoneblock for he could no longer quench the flame in his blood. He felt his cheeks aflame and his throat throbbing with song. There was a lust of wandering in his feet that burned to set out for the ends of the earth. On! On! his heart seemed to cry. Evening would deepen above the sea, night fall upon the plains, dawn glimmer before the wanderer and show him strange fields and hills and faces. Where?

He looked northward towards Howth. The sea had fallen below the line of seawrack on the shallow side of the breakwater and already the tide was running out fast along the foreshore. Already one long oval bank of sand lay warm and dry amid the wavelets. Here and there warm isles of sand gleamed above the shallow tide, and about the isles and around the long bank and amid the shallow currents of the beach were lightclad gayclad figures, wading and delving.

In a few moments he was barefoot, his stockings folded in his pockets and his canvas shoes dangling by their knotted laces over his shoulders: and, picking a pointed salteaten stick out of the jetsam among the rocks, he clambered down the slope of the breakwater.

There was a long rivulet in the strand: and, as he waded slowly up its course, he wondered at the endless drift of seaweed. Emerald and black and russet and olive, it moved beneath the current, swaying and turning. The water of the rivulet was dark with endless drift and mirrored the high-drifting clouds. The clouds were drifting above him silently and silently the seatangle was drifting below him; and the grey warm air was still: and a new wild life was singing in his veins.

Where was his boyhood now? Where was the soul that had hung back from her destiny, to brood alone upon the shame of her wounds and in her house of squalor and subterfuge to queen it in faded cerements and in wreaths that withered at the touch? Or where was he?

He was alone. He was unheeded, happy and near to the wild heart of life. He was alone and young and wilful and wildhearted, alone amid a waste of wild air and brackish waters and the seaharvest of shells and tangle and veiled grey sunlight and gayclad lightclad figures, of children and girls and voices childish and girlish in the air.

A girl stood before him in midstream, alone and still, gazing out to sea. She seemed like one whom magic had changed into the likeness of a strange and beautiful seabird. Her long slender bare legs were delicate as a crane's and pure save where an emerald trail of seaweed had fashioned itself as a sign upon the flesh. Her thighs, fuller and softhued as ivory, were bared almost to the hips where the white fringes of her drawers were like featherings of soft white down. Her slateblue skirts were kilted boldly about her waist and dovetailed behind her. Her bosom was as a bird's soft and slight, slight and soft as the breast of some darkplumaged dove. But her long fair hair was girlish: and girlish, and touched with the wonder of mortal beauty, her face.

She was alone and still, gazing out to sea; and when she felt his presence and the worship of his eyes her eyes turned to him in quiet sufferance of his gaze, without shame or wantonness. Long, long she suffered his gaze and then quietly withdrew her eyes from his and bent them towards the stream, gently stirring the water with her foot hither and thither. The first faint noise of gently moving water broke the silence, low and faint and whispering, faint as the bells of sleep; hither and thither, hither and thither: and a faint flame trembled on her cheek.

—Heavenly God! cried Stephen's soul, in an outburst of profane joy.

He turned away from her suddenly and set off across the strand. His cheeks were aflame; his body was aglow; his limbs were trembling. On and on and on and on he strode, far out over the sands, singing wildly to the sea, crying to greet the advent of the life that had cried to him.

Her image had passed into his soul for ever and no word had broken the holy silence of his ecstasy. Her eyes had called him and his soul had leaped at the call. To live, to err, to fall, to triumph, to recreate life out of life! A wild angel had appeared to him, the angel of mortal youth and beauty, an envoy from the fair courts of life, to throw open before him in an instant of ecstasy the gates of all the ways of error and glory. On and on and on and on!

He halted suddenly and heard his heart in the silence. How far had he walked? What hour was it?

There was no human figure near him nor any sound borne to him over the air. But the tide was near the turn and already the day was on the wane. He turned landward and ran towards the shore and, running up the sloping beach, reckless of the sharp shingle, found a sandy nook amid a ring of tufted sand-knolls and lay down there that the peace and silence of the evening might still the riot of his blood.

He felt above him the vast indifferent dome and the calm processes of the heavenly bodies; and the earth beneath him, the earth that had borne him, had taken him to her breast.

He closed his eyes in the languor of sleep. His eyelids trembled as if they felt the vast cyclic movement of the earth and her watchers, trembled as if they felt the strange light of some new world. His soul was swooning into some new world, fantastic, dim, uncertain as under sea, traversed by cloudy shapes and beings. A world, a glimmer, or a flower? Glimmering and trembling, trembling and unfolding, a breaking light, an opening flower, it spread in endless succession to itself, breaking in full crimson and unfolding and fading to palest rose, leaf by leaf and wave of light by wave of light, flooding all the heavens with its soft flushes, every flush deeper than other.

Evening had fallen when he woke and the sand and arid grasses of his bed glowed no longer. He rose slowly and, recalling the rapture of his sleep, sighed at its joy.

He climbed to the crest of the sandhill and gazed about him. Evening had fallen. A rim of the young moon cleft the pale waste of sky like the rim of a silver hoop embedded in grey sand; and the tide was flowing in fast to the land with a low whisper of her waves, islanding a few last figures in distant pools.

V

H E DRAINED his third cup of watery tea to the dregs and
set to chewing the crusts of fried bread that were scattered near him, staring into the dark pool of the jar. The
yellow dripping had been scooped out like a boghole and the
pool under it brought back to his memory the dark turfcoloured water of the bath in Clongowes. The box of pawntickets at his elbow had just been rifled and he took up idly
one after another in his greasy fingers the blue and white
dockets, scrawled and sanded and creased and bearing the
name of the pledger as Daly or MacEvoy.

1 Pair Buskins.
1 D. Coat.
3 Articles and White.
1 Man's Pants.

Then he put them aside and gazed thoughtfully at the lid of
the box, speckled with lousemarks, and asked vaguely:

—How much is the clock fast now?

His mother straightened the battered alarmclock that was
lying on its side in the middle of the kitchen mantelpiece until
its dial showed a quarter to twelve and then laid it once more
on its side.

—An hour and twentyfive minutes, she said. The right time
now is twenty past ten. The dear knows you might try to be in
time for your lectures.

—Fill out the place for me to wash, said Stephen.

—Katey, fill out the place for Stephen to wash.

—Boody, fill out the place for Stephen to wash.

—I can't, I'm going for blue. Fill it out, you, Maggie.

When the enamelled basin had been fitted into the well of

the sink and the old washingglove flung on the side of it he allowed his mother to scrub his neck and root into the folds of his ears and into the interstices at the wings of his nose.

—Well, it's a poor case, she said, when a university student is so dirty that his mother has to wash him.

—But it gives you pleasure, said Stephen calmly.

An earsplitting whistle was heard from upstairs and his mother thrust a damp overall into his hands, saying:

—Dry yourself and hurry out for the love of goodness.

A second shrill whistle, prolonged angrily, brought one of the girls to the foot of the staircase.

—Yes, father?

—Is your lazy bitch of a brother gone out yet?

—Yes, father.

—Sure?

—Yes, father.

—Hm!

The girl came back making signs to him to be quick and go out quietly by the back. Stephen laughed and said:

—He has a curious idea of genders if he thinks a bitch is masculine.

—Ah, it's a scandalous shame for you, Stephen, said his mother, and you'll live to rue the day you set your foot in that place. I know how it has changed you.

—Good morning, everybody, said Stephen, smiling and kissing the tips of his fingers in adieu.

The lane behind the terrace was waterlogged and as he went down it slowly, choosing his steps amid heaps of wet rubbish, he heard a mad nun screeching in the nuns' madhouse beyond the wall.

—Jesus! O Jesus! Jesus!

He shook the sound out of his ears by an angry toss of his head and hurried on, stumbling through the mouldering offal, his heart already bitten by an ache of loathing and bitterness. His father's whistle, his mother's mutterings, the screech of an unseen maniac were to him now so many voices offending and threatening to humble the pride of his youth. He drove their echoes even out of his heart with an execration: but, as he walked down the avenue and felt the grey morning light falling about him through the dripping trees and smelt the strange wild smell of the wet leaves and bark, his soul was loosed of her miseries.

The rainladen trees of the avenue evoked in him, as always, memories of the girls and women in the plays of Gerhart Hauptmann; and the memory of their pale sorrows and the fragrance falling from the wet branches mingled in a mood of quiet joy. His morning walk across the city had begun, and he foreknew that as he passed the sloblands of Fairview he would think of the cloistral silverveined prose of Newman, that as he walked along the North Strand Road, glancing idly at the windows of the provision shops, he would recall the dark humour of Guido Cavalcanti and smile, that as he went by Baird's stonecutting works in Talbot Place the spirit of Ibsen would blow through him like a keen wind, a spirit of wayward boyish beauty, and that passing a grimy marinedealer's shop beyond the Liffey he would repeat the song by Ben Jonson which begins:

I was not wearier where I lay.

His mind, when wearied of its search for the essence of beauty amid the spectral words of Aristotle or Aquinas, turned often for its pleasure to the dainty songs of the Elizabethans. His mind, in the vesture of a doubting monk, stood often in shadow under the windows of that age, to hear the grave and mocking music of the lutenists or the frank laughter of waistcoaters until a laugh too low, a phrase, tarnished by time, of chambering and false honour, stung his monkish pride and drove him on from his lurkingplace.

The lore which he was believed to pass his days brooding upon so that it had rapt him from the companionships of youth was only a garner of slender sentences from Aristotle's poetics and psychology and a *Synopsis Philosophiæ Scho-*

lasticæ ad mentem divi Thomæ. His thinking was a dusk of doubt and selfmistrust lit up at moments by the lightnings of intuition, but lightnings of so clear a splendour that in those moments the world perished about his feet as if it had been fireconsumed: and thereafter his tongue grew heavy and he met the eyes of others with unanswering eyes for he felt that the spirit of beauty had folded him round like a mantle and that in revery at least he had been acquainted with nobility. But, when this brief pride of silence upheld him no longer, he was glad to find himself still in the midst of common lives, passing on his way amid the squalor and noise and sloth of the city fearlessly and with a light heart.

Near the hoardings on the canal he met the consumptive man with the doll's face and the brimless hat coming towards him down the slope of the bridge with little steps, tightly buttoned into his chocolate overcoat, and holding his furled umbrella a span or two from him like a diviningrod. It must be eleven, he thought, and peered into a dairy to see the time. The clock in the dairy told him that it was five minutes to five but, as he turned away, he heard a clock somewhere near him, but unseen, beating eleven strokes in swift precision. He laughed as he heard it for it made him think of MacCann and he saw him a squat figure in a shooting jacket and breeches and with a fair goatee, standing in the wind at Hopkins' corner, and heard him say:

—Dedalus, you're an antisocial being, wrapped up in yourself. I'm not. I'm a democrat: and I'll work and act for social liberty and equality among all classes and sexes in the United States of the Europe of the future.

Eleven! Then he was late for that lecture too. What day of the week was it? He stopped at a newsagent's to read the headline of a placard. Thursday. Ten to eleven, English; eleven to twelve, French; twelve to one, physics. He fancied to himself the English lecture and felt, even at that distance, restless and helpless. He saw the heads of his classmates meekly bent as they wrote in their notebooks the points they were bidden to note, nominal definitions, essential definitions and examples or dates of birth or death, chief works, a favourable and an unfavourable criticism side by side. His own head was unbent for his thoughts wandered abroad and whether he looked around the little class of students or out of the window across the desolate gardens of the green an odour assailed him of cheerless cellardamp and decay. Another head than his, right before him in the first benches, was poised squarely above its bending fellows like the head of a priest appealing without humility to the tabernacle for the humble worshippers about him. Why was it that when he thought of Cranly he could never raise before his mind the entire image of his body but only the image of the head and face? Even now against the grey curtain of the morning he saw it before him like the phantom of a dream, the face of a severed head or deathmask, crowned on the brows by its stiff black upright hair as by an iron crown. It was a priestlike face, priestlike in its pallor, in the widewinged nose, in the shadowings below the eyes and along the jaws, priestlike in the lips that were long and bloodless and faintly smiling: and Stephen, remembering swiftly how he had told Cranly of all the tumults and unrest and longings in his soul, day after day and night by night, only to be answered by his friend's listening silence, would have told himself that it was the face of a guilty priest who heard confessions of those whom he had not power to absolve but that he felt again in memory the gaze of its dark womanish eyes.

Through this image he had a glimpse of a strange dark cavern of speculation but at once turned away from it, feeling that it was not yet the hour to enter it. But the nightshade of his friend's listlessness seemed to be diffusing in the air around him a tenuous and deadly exhalation and he found himself glancing from one casual word to another on his right or left in stolid wonder that they had been so silently emptied of instantaneous sense until every mean shop legend bound his mind like the words of a spell and his soul shrivelled up, sighing with age as he walked on in a lane among heaps of dead language. His own consciousness of language was ebbing from his brain and trickling into the very words themselves which set to band and disband themselves in wayward rhythms:

> *The ivy whines upon the wall*
> *And whines and twines upon the wall*
> *The ivy whines upon the wall*
> *The yellow ivy on the wall*
> *Ivy, ivy up the wall.*

Did any one ever hear such drivel? Lord Almighty! Who ever heard of ivy whining on a wall? Yellow ivy: that was all right. Yellow ivory also. And what about ivory ivy?

The word now shone in his brain, clearer and brighter than any ivory sawn from the mottled tusks of elephants. *Ivory, ivoire, avorio, ebur.* One of the first examples that he had learnt in Latin had run: *India mittit ebur;* and he recalled the shrewd northern face of the rector who had taught him to construe the Metamorphoses of Ovid in a courtly English, made whimsical by the mention of porkers and potsherds and chines of bacon. He had learnt what little he knew of the laws of Latin verse from a ragged book written by a Portuguese priest.

> *Contrahit orator, variant in carmine vates.*

The crises and victories and secessions in Roman history were handed on to him in the trite words *in tanto discrimine* and he had tried to peer into the social life of the city of cities through the words *implere ollam denariorum* which the rector had rendered sonorously as the filling of a pot with denaries. The pages of his timeworn Horace never felt cold to the touch even when his own fingers were cold: they were human pages: and fifty years before they had been turned by the human fingers of John Duncan Inverarity and by his brother, William Malcolm Inverarity. Yes, those were noble names on the dusky flyleaf and, even for so poor a Latinist as he, the dusky verses were as fragrant as though they had lain all those years in myrtle and lavender and vervain; but yet it wounded him to think that he would never be but a shy guest at the feast of the world's culture and that the monkish learning, in terms of which he was striving to forge out an esthetic philosophy, was held no higher by the age he lived in than the subtle and curious jargons of heraldry and falconry.

The grey block of Trinity on his left, set heavily in the city's ignorance like a great dull stone set in a cumbrous ring, pulled his mind downward; and while he was striving this way and that to free his feet from the fetters of the reformed conscience he came upon the droll statue of the national poet of Ireland.

He looked at it without anger: for, though sloth of the body and of the soul crept over it like unseen vermin, over the shuffling feet and up the folds of the cloak and around the servile head, it seemed humbly conscious of its indignity. It was a Firbolg in the borrowed cloak of a Milesian; and he thought of his friend Davin, the peasant student. It was a jesting name between them but the young peasant bore with it lightly saying:

—Go on, Stevie, I have a hard head, you tell me. Call me what you will.

The homely version of his christian name on the lips of his friend had touched Stephen pleasantly when first heard for he was as formal in speech with others as they were with him. Often, as he sat in Davin's rooms in Grantham Street, wondering at his friend's wellmade boots that flanked the wall pair by pair and repeating for his friend's simple ear the verses and cadences of others which were the veils of his own longing and dejection, the rude Firbolg mind of his listener had drawn his mind towards it and flung it back again, drawing it by a quiet inbred courtesy of attention or by a quaint turn of old English speech or by the force of its delight in rude bodily skill—for Davin had sat at the feet of Michael Cusack, the Gael—repelling swiftly and suddenly by a grossness of intelligence or by a bluntness of feeling or by a dull stare of terror in the eyes, the terror of soul of a starving Irish village in which the curfew was still a nightly fear.

Side by side with his memory of the deeds of prowess of his uncle Mat Davin, the athlete, the young peasant worshipped the sorrowful legend of Ireland. The gossip of his fellowstudents which strove to render the flat life of the college significant at any cost loved to think of him as a young fenian. His nurse had taught him Irish and shaped his rude imagination by the broken lights of Irish myth. He stood towards this myth upon which no individual mind had ever drawn out a line of beauty and to its unwieldy tales that divided themselves as they moved down the cycles in the same attitude as towards the Roman catholic religion, the attitude of a dullwitted loyal serf. Whatsoever of thought or of feeling came to him from England or by way of English culture his mind stood armed against in obedience to a password: and of the world that lay beyond England he knew only the foreign legion of France in which he spoke of serving.

Coupling this ambition with the young man's humour Stephen had often called him one of the tame geese: and there was even a point of irritation in the name pointed against that very reluctance of speech and deed in his friend which seemed so often to stand between Stephen's mind, eager of speculation, and the hidden ways of Irish life.

One night the young peasant, his spirit stung by the violent or luxurious language in which Stephen escaped from the cold silence of intellectual revolt, had called up before Stephen's mind a strange vision. The two were walking slowly towards Davin's room through the dark narrow streets of the poorer jews.

—A thing happened to myself, Stevie, last autumn, coming on winter, and I never told it to a living soul and you are the first person now I ever told it to. I disremember if it was October or November. It was October because it was before I came up here to join the matriculation class.

Stephen had turned his smiling eyes towards his friend's

face, flattered by his confidence and won over to sympathy by the speaker's simple accent.

—I was away all that day from my own place over in Butt-evant—I don't know if you know where that is—at a hurling match between the Croke's Own Boys and the Fearless Thurles and by God, Stevie, that was the hard fight. My first cousin, Fonsy Davin, was stripped to his buff that day minding cool for the Limericks but he was up with the forwards half the time and shouting like mad. I never will forget that day. One of the Crokes made a woeful wipe at him one time with his camaun and I declare to God he was within an aim's ace of getting it at the side of the temple. O, honest to God, if the crook of it caught him that time he was done for.

—I am glad he escaped, Stephen had said with a laugh, but surely that's not the strange thing that happened you?

—Well, I suppose that doesn't interest you but leastways there was such noise after the match that I missed the train home and I couldn't get any kind of a yoke to give me a lift for, as luck would have it, there was a mass meeting that same day over in Castletownroche and all the cars in the country were there. So there was nothing for it only to stay the night or to foot it out. Well, I started to walk and on I went and it was coming on night when I got into the Ballyhoura hills; that's better than ten miles from Kilmallock and there's a long lonely road after that. You wouldn't see the sign of a christian house along the road or hear a sound. It was pitch dark almost. Once or twice I stopped by the way under a bush to redden my pipe and only for the dew was thick I'd have stretched out there and slept. At last, after a bend of the road, I spied a little cottage with a light in the window. I went up and knocked at the door. A voice asked who was there and I answered I was over at the match in Buttevant and was walking back and that I'd be thankful for a glass of water. After a while a young woman opened the door and brought me out a big mug of milk. She was half undressed as if she was going to bed when I knocked and she had her hair hanging; and I thought by her figure and by something in the look of her eyes that she must be carrying a child. She kept me in talk a long while at the door and I thought it strange because her breast and her shoulders were bare. She asked me was I tired and would I like to stop the night there. She said she was all alone in the house and that her husband had gone that morning to Queenstown with his sister to see her off. And all the time she was talking, Stevie, she had her eyes fixed on my face and she stood so close to me I could hear her breathing. When I handed her back the mug at last she took my hand to draw me in over the threshold and said: *Come in and stay the night here. You've no call to be frightened. There's no-one in it but ourselves. . . .* I didn't go in, Stevie. I thanked her and went on my way again, all in a fever. At the first bend of the road I looked back and she was standing at the door.

The last words of Davin's story sang in his memory and the figure of the woman in the story stood forth, reflected in other figures of the peasant women whom he had seen standing in the doorways at Clane as the college cars drove by, as a type of her race and his own, a batlike soul waking to the consciousness of itself in darkness and secrecy and loneliness and, through the eyes and voice and gesture of a woman without guile, calling the stranger to her bed.

A hand was laid on his arm and a young voice cried:

—Ah, gentleman, your own girl, sir! The first handsel today, gentleman. Buy that lovely bunch. Will you, gentleman?

The blue flowers which she lifted towards him and her young blue eyes seemed to him at that instant images of guilelessness; and he halted till the image had vanished and he saw only her ragged dress and damp coarse hair and hoydenish face.

—Do, gentleman! Don't forget your own girl, sir!

—I have no money, said Stephen.

—Buy them lovely ones, will you, sir? Only a penny.

—Did you hear what I said? asked Stephen, bending towards her. I told you I had no money. I tell you again now.

—Well, sure, you will some day, sir, please God, the girl answered after an instant.

—Possibly, said Stephen, but I don't think it likely.

He left her quickly, fearing that her intimacy might turn to gibing and wishing to be out of the way before she offered her ware to another, a tourist from England or a student of Trinity. Grafton Street, along which he walked, prolonged that moment of discouraged poverty. In the roadway at the head of the street a slab was set to the memory of Wolfe Tone and he remembered having been present with his father at its laying. He remembered with bitterness that scene of tawdry tribute. There were four French delegates in a brake and one, a plump smiling young man, held, wedged on a stick, a card on which were printed the words: *Vive l'Irlande!*

But the trees in Stephen's Green were fragrant of rain and the rainsodden earth gave forth its mortal odour, a faint incense rising upward through the mould from many hearts. The soul of the gallant venal city which his elders had told him of had shrunk with time to a faint mortal odour rising from the earth and he knew that in a moment when he entered the sombre college he would be conscious of a corruption other than that of Buck Egan and Burnchapel Whaley.

It was too late to go upstairs to the French class. He crossed the hall and took the corridor to the left which led to the physics theatre. The corridor was dark and silent but not unwatchful. Why did he feel that it was not unwatchful? Was it because he had heard that in Buck Whaley's time there was a secret staircase there? Or was the jesuit house extraterritorial and was he walking among aliens? The Ireland of Tone and of Parnell seemed to have receded in space.

He opened the door of the theatre and halted in the chilly grey light that struggled through the dusty windows. A figure was crouching before the large grate and by its leanness and greyness he knew that it was the dean of studies lighting the fire. Stephen closed the door quietly and approached the fireplace.

—Good morning, sir! Can I help you?

The priest looked up quickly and said:

—One moment now, Mr Dedalus, and you will see. There is an art in lighting a fire. We have the liberal arts and we have the useful arts. This is one of the useful arts.

—I will try to learn it, said Stephen.

—Not too much coal, said the dean, working briskly at his task, that is one of the secrets.

He produced four candlebutts from the sidepockets of his soutane and placed them deftly among the coals and twisted papers. Stephen watched him in silence. Kneeling thus on the flagstone to kindle the fire and busied with the disposition of his wisps of paper and candlebutts he seemed more than ever a humble server making ready the place of sacrifice in an empty temple, a levite of the Lord. Like a levite's robe of plain linen the faded worn soutane draped the kneeling figure of one whom the canonicals or the bellbordered ephod would irk and trouble. His very body had waxed old in lowly service of the Lord—in tending the fire upon the altar, in bearing tidings secretly, in waiting upon worldlings, in striking swiftly when bidden—and yet had remained ungraced by aught of saintly or of prelatic beauty. Nay, his very soul had waxed old in that service without growing towards light and beauty or spreading abroad a sweet odour of her sanctity—a mortified will no more responsive to the thrill of its obedience than was to the thrill of love or combat his aging body, spare and sinewy, greyed with a silverpointed down.

The dean rested back on his hunkers and watched the sticks catch. Stephen, to fill the silence, said:

—I am sure I could not light a fire.

—You are an artist, are you not, Mr Dedalus? said the dean, glancing up and blinking his pale eyes. The object of the artist is the creation of the beautiful. What the beautiful is is another question.

He rubbed his hands slowly and drily over the difficulty.

—Can you solve that question now? he asked.

—Aquinas, answered Stephen, says *Pulcra sunt quæ visa placent*.

—This fire before us, said the dean, will be pleasing to the eye. Will it therefore be beautiful?

—In so far as it is apprehended by the sight, which I suppose means here esthetic intellection, it will be beautiful. But Aquinas also says *Bonum est in quod tendit appetitus*. In so far as it satisfies the animal craving for warmth fire is a good. In hell however it is an evil.

—Quite so, said the dean, you have certainly hit the nail on the head.

He rose nimbly and went towards the door, set it ajar and said:

—A draught is said to be a help in these matters.

As he came back to the hearth, limping slightly but with a brisk step, Stephen saw the silent soul of a jesuit look out at him from the pale loveless eyes. Like Ignatius he was lame but in his eyes burned no spark of Ignatius' enthusiasm. Even the legendary craft of the company, a craft subtler and more secret than its fabled books of secret subtle wisdom, had not fired his soul with the energy of apostleship. It seemed as if he used the shifts and lore and cunning of the world, as bidden to do, for the greater glory of God, without joy in their handling or hatred of that in them which was evil but turning them, with a firm gesture of obedience, back upon themselves: and for all this silent service it seemed as if he loved not at all the master and little, if at all, the ends he served. *Similiter atque senis baculus,* he was, as the founder would have had him, like a staff in an old man's hand, to be left in a corner, to be leaned on in the road at nightfall or in stress of weather, to lie with a lady's nosegay on a garden seat, to be raised in menace.

The dean returned to the hearth and began to stroke his chin.

—When may we expect to have something from you on the esthetic question? he asked.

—From me! said Stephen in astonishment. I stumble on an idea once a fortnight if I am lucky.

—These questions are very profound, Mr Dedalus, said the dean. It is like looking down from the cliffs of Moher into the depths. Many go down into the depths and never come up. Only the trained diver can go down into those depths and explore them and come to the surface again.

—If you mean speculation, sir, said Stephen, I also am sure that there is no such thing as free thinking inasmuch as all thinking must be bound by its own laws.

—Ha!

—For my purpose I can work on at present by the light of one or two ideas of Aristotle and Aquinas.

—I see. I quite see your point.

—I need them only for my own use and guidance until I have done something for myself by their light. If the lamp smokes or smells I shall try to trim it. If it does not give light enough I shall sell it and buy another.

—Epictetus also had a lamp, said the dean, which was sold for a fancy price after his death. It was the lamp he wrote his philosophical dissertations by. You know Epictetus?

—An old gentleman, said Stephen coarsely, who said that the soul is very like a bucketful of water.

—He tells us in his homely way, the dean went on, that he put an iron lamp before a statue of one of the gods and that a thief stole the lamp. What did the philosopher do? He reflected that it was in the character of a thief to steal and determined to buy an earthen lamp next day instead of the iron lamp.

A smell of molten tallow came up from the dean's candlebutts and fused itself in Stephen's consciousness with the jingle of the words, bucket and lamp and lamp and bucket. The priest's voice too had a hard jingling tone. Stephen's mind halted by instinct, checked by the strange tone and the imagery and by the priest's face which seemed like an unlit lamp or a reflector hung in a false focus. What lay behind it or within it? A dull torpor of the soul or the dullness of the thundercloud, charged with intellection and capable of the gloom of God?

—I meant a different kind of lamp, sir, said Stephen.

—Undoubtedly, said the dean.

—One difficulty, said Stephen, in esthetic discussion is to know whether words are being used according to the literary tradition or according to the tradition of the marketplace. I remember a sentence of Newman's in which he says of the Blessed Virgin that she was detained in the full company of the saints. The use of the word in the marketplace is quite different. *I hope I am not detaining you.*

—Not in the least, said the dean politely.

—No, no, said Stephen, smiling, I mean . . .

—Yes, yes: I see, said the dean quickly, I quite catch the point: *detain.*

He thrust forward his under jaw and uttered a dry short cough.

—To return to the lamp, he said, the feeding of it is also a nice problem. You must choose the pure oil and you must be careful when you pour it in not to overflow it, not to pour in more than the funnel can hold.

—What funnel? asked Stephen.

—The funnel through which you pour the oil into your lamp.

—That? said Stephen. Is that called a funnel? Is it not a tundish?

—What is a tundish?

—That. The . . . the funnel.

—Is that called a tundish in Ireland? asked the dean. I never heard the word in my life.

—It is called a tundish in Lower Drumcondra, said Stephen laughing, where they speak the best English.

—A tundish, said the dean reflectively. That is a most interesting word. I must look that word up. Upon my word I must.

His courtesy of manner rang a little false, and Stephen

looked at the English convert with the same eyes as the elder brother in the parable may have turned on the prodigal. A humble follower in the wake of clamorous conversions, a poor Englishman in Ireland, he seemed to have entered on the stage of jesuit history when that strange play of intrigue and suffering and envy and struggle and indignity had been all but given through—a late comer, a tardy spirit. From what had he set out? Perhaps he had been born and bred among serious dissenters, seeing salvation in Jesus only and abhorring the vain pomps of the establishment. Had he felt the need of an implicit faith amid the welter of sectarianism and the jargon of its turbulent schisms, six principle men, peculiar people, seed and snake baptists, supralapsarian dogmatists? Had he found the true church all of a sudden in winding up to the end like a reel of cotton some finespun line of reasoning upon insufflation or the imposition of hands or the procession of the Holy Ghost? Or had Lord Christ touched him and bidden him follow, like that disciple who had sat at the receipt of custom, as he sat by the door of some zincroofed chapel, yawning and telling over his church pence?

The dean repeated the word yet again.

—Tundish! Well now, that is interesting!

—The question you asked me a moment ago seems to me more interesting. What is that beauty which the artist struggles to express from lumps of earth, said Stephen coldly.

The little word seemed to have turned a rapier point of his sensitiveness against this courteous and vigilant foe. He felt with a smart of dejection that the man to whom he was speaking was a countryman of Ben Jonson. He thought:

—The language in which we are speaking is his before it is mine. How different are the words *home, Christ, ale, master,* on his lips and on mine! I cannot speak or write these words without unrest of spirit. His language, so familiar and so foreign, will always be for me an acquired speech. I have not made or accepted its words. My voice holds them at bay. My soul frets in the shadow of his language.

—And to distinguish between the beautiful and the sublime, the dean added. To distinguish between moral beauty and material beauty. And to inquire what kind of beauty is proper to each of the various arts. These are some interesting points we might take up.

Stephen, disheartened suddenly by the dean's firm dry tone, was silent. The dean also was silent: and through the silence a distant noise of many boots and confused voices came up the staircase.

—In pursuing these speculations, said the dean conclusively, there is however the danger of perishing of inanition. First you must take your degree. Set that before you as your first aim. Then little by little, you will see your way. I mean in every sense, your way in life and in thinking. It may be uphill pedalling at first. Take Mr Moonan. He was a long time before he got to the top. But he got there.

—I may not have his talent, said Stephen quietly.

—You never know, said the dean brightly. We never can say what is in us. I most certainly should not be despondent. *Per aspera ad astra.*

He left the hearth quickly and went towards the landing to oversee the arrival of the first arts' class.

Leaning against the fireplace Stephen heard him greet briskly and impartially every student of the class and could almost see the frank smiles of the coarser students. A desolating pity began to fall like a dew upon his easily embittered heart for this faithful servingman of the knightly Loyola, for this halfbrother of the clergy, more venal than they in speech, more steadfast of soul than they, one whom he would never call his ghostly father: and he thought how this man and his companions had earned the name of worldlings at the hands not of the unworldly only but of the worldly also for having pleaded, during all their history, at the bar of God's justice for the souls of the lax and the lukewarm and the prudent.

The entry of the professor was signalled by a few rounds of Kentish fire from the heavy boots of those students who sat on the highest tier of the gloomy theatre under the grey cobwebbed windows. The calling of the roll began and the responses to the names were given out in all tones until the name of Peter Byrne was reached.

—Here!

A deep base note in response came from the upper tier, followed by coughs of protest along the other benches.

The professor paused in his reading and called the next name:

—Cranly!

No answer.

—Mr Cranly!

A smile flew across Stephen's face as he thought of his friend's studies.

—Try Leopardstown! said a voice from the bench behind.

Stephen glanced up quickly but Moynihan's snoutish face, outlined on the grey light, was impassive. A formula was given out. Amid the rustling of the notebooks Stephen turned back again and said:

—Give me some paper for God's sake.

—Are you as bad as that? asked Moynihan with a broad grin.

He tore a sheet from his scribbler and passed it down, whispering:

—In case of necessity any layman or woman can do it.

The formula which he wrote obediently on the sheet of paper, the coiling and uncoiling calculations of the professor, the spectrelike symbols of force and velocity fascinated and jaded Stephen's mind. He had heard some say that the old professor was an atheist freemason. O the grey dull day! It seemed a limbo of painless patient consciousness through which souls of mathematicians might wander, projecting long slender fabrics from plane to plane of ever rarer and paler twilight, radiating swift eddies to the last verges of a universe ever vaster, farther and more impalpable.

—So we must distinguish between elliptical and ellipsoidal. Perhaps some of you gentlemen may be familiar with the works of Mr W. S. Gilbert. In one of his songs he speaks of the billiard sharp who is condemned to play:

> *On a cloth untrue*
> *With a twisted cue*
> *And elliptical billiard balls.*

—He means a ball having the form of the ellipsoid of the principal axes of which I spoke a moment ago.

Moynihan leaned down towards Stephen's ear and murmured:

—What price ellipsoidal balls! Chase me, ladies, I'm in the cavalry!

His fellowstudent's rude humour ran like a gust through the cloister of Stephen's mind, shaking into gay life limp priestly vestments that hung upon the walls, setting them to sway and caper in a sabbath of misrule. The forms of the community emerged from the gustblown vestments, the dean of studies, the portly florid bursar with his cap of grey hair, the president, the little priest with feathery hair who wrote devout verses, the squat peasant form of the professor of economics, the tall form of the young professor of mental science discussing on the landing a case of conscience with his class like a giraffe cropping high leafage among a herd of antelopes, the grave troubled prefect of the sodality, the plump roundheaded professor of Italian with his rogue's eyes. They came ambling and stumbling, tumbling and capering, kilting their gowns for leap frog, holding one another back, shaken with deep fast laughter, smacking one another behind and laughing at their rude malice, calling to one another by familiar nicknames, protesting with sudden dignity at some rough usage, whispering two and two behind their hands.

The professor had gone to the glass cases on the sidewall from a shelf of which he took down a set of coils, blew away the dust from many points and, bearing it carefully to the table, held a finger on it while he proceeded with his lecture. He explained that the wires in modern coils were of a compound called platinoid lately discovered by F. W. Martino.

He spoke clearly the initials and surname of the discoverer. Moynihan whispered from behind:

—Good old Fresh Water Martin!

—Ask him, Stephen whispered back with weary humour, if he wants a subject for electrocution. He can have me.

Moynihan, seeing the professor bend over the coils, rose in his bench and, clacking noiselessly the fingers of his right hand, began to call with the voice of a slobbering urchin:

—Please, teacher! Please, teacher! This boy is after saying a bad word, teacher.

—Platinoid, the professor said solemnly, is preferred to German silver because it has a lower coefficient of resistance variation by changes of temperature. The platinoid wire is insulated and the covering of silk that insulates it is wound on the ebonite bobbins just where my finger is. If it were wound single an extra current would be induced in the coils. The bobbins are saturated in hot paraffin wax . . .

A sharp Ulster voice said from the bench below Stephen:

—Are we likely to be asked questions on applied science?

The professor began to juggle gravely with the terms pure science and applied science. A heavybuilt student wearing gold spectacles stared with some wonder at the questioner. Moynihan murmured from behind in his natural voice:

—Isn't MacAlister a devil for his pound of flesh?

Stephen looked down coldly on the oblong skull beneath him overgrown with tangled twinecoloured hair. The voice, the accent, the mind of the questioner offended him and he allowed the offence to carry him towards wilful unkindness, bidding his mind think that the student's father would have done better had he sent his son to Belfast to study and have saved something on the train fare by so doing.

The oblong skull beneath did not turn to meet this shaft of thought and yet the shaft came back to its bowstring: for he saw in a moment the student's wheypale face.

—That thought is not mine, he said to himself quickly. It came from the comic Irishman in the bench behind. Patience. Can you say with certitude by whom the soul of your race was bartered and its elect betrayed—by the questioner or by the mocker? Patience. Remember Epictetus. It is probably in his character to ask such a question at such a moment in such a tone and to pronounce the word *science* as a monosyllable.

The droning voice of the professor continued to wind itself slowly round and round the coils it spoke of, doubling, trebling, quadrupling its somnolent energy as the coil multiplied its ohms of resistance.

Moynihan's voice called from behind in echo to a distant bell:

—Closing time, gents!

The entrance hall was crowded and loud with talk. On a table near the door were two photographs in frames and between them a long roll of paper bearing an irregular tail of signatures. MacCann went briskly to and fro among the students, talking rapidly, answering rebuffs and leading one after another to the table. In the inner hall the dean of studies stood talking to a young professor, stroking his chin gravely and nodding his head.

Stephen, checked by the crowd at the door, halted irresolutely. From under the wide falling leaf of a soft hat Cranly's dark eyes were watching him.

—Have you signed? Stephen asked.

Cranly closed his long thinlipped mouth, communed with himself an instant and answered:

—*Ego habeo.*

—What is it for?

—*Quod?*

—What is it for?

Cranly turned his pale face to Stephen and said blandly and bitterly:

—*Per pax universalis.*

Stephen pointed to the Csar's photograph and said:

—He has the face of a besotted Christ.

The scorn and anger in his voice brought Cranly's eyes back from a calm survey of the walls of the hall.

—Are you annoyed? he asked.

—No, answered Stephen.

—Are you in bad humour?

—No.

—*Credo ut vos sanguinarius mendax estis,* said Cranly, *quia facies vostra monstrat ut vos in damno malo humore estis.*

Moynihan, on his way to the table, said in Stephen's ear:

—MacCann is in tiptop form. Ready to shed the last drop. Brandnew world. No stimulants and votes for the bitches.

Stephen smiled at the manner of this confidence and, when Moynihan had passed, turned again to meet Cranly's eyes.

—Perhaps you can tell me, he said, why he pours his soul so freely into my ear. Can you?

A dull scowl appeared on Cranly's forehead. He stared at the table where Moynihan had bent to write his name on the roll, and then said flatly:

—A sugar!

—*Quis est in malo humore,* said Stephen, *ego aut vos?*

Cranly did not take up the taunt. He brooded sourly on his judgment and repeated with the same flat force:

—A flaming bloody sugar, that's what he is!

It was his epitaph for all dead friendships and Stephen wondered whether it would ever be spoken in the same tone over his memory. The heavy lumpish phrase sank slowly out of hearing like a stone through a quagmire. Stephen saw it sink as he had seen many another, feeling its heaviness depress his heart. Cranly's speech, unlike that of Davin, had neither rare phrases of Elizabethan English nor quaintly turned versions of Irish idioms. Its drawl was an echo of the quays of Dublin given back by a bleak decaying seaport, its energy an echo of the sacred eloquence of Dublin given back flatly by a Wicklow pulpit.

The heavy scowl faded from Cranly's face as MacCann marched briskly towards them from the other side of the hall.

—Here you are! said MacCann cheerily.

—Here I am! said Stephen.

—Late as usual. Can you not combine the progressive tendency with a respect for punctuality?

—That question is out of order, said Stephen. Next business.

His smiling eyes were fixed on a silverwrapped tablet of milk chocolate which peeped out of the propagandist's breastpocket. A little ring of listeners closed round to hear the war of wits. A lean student with olive skin and lank black hair thrust his face between the two, glancing from one to the other at each phrase and seeming to try to catch each flying phrase in his open moist mouth. Cranly took a small grey handball from his pocket and began to examine it closely, turning it over and over.

—Next business? said MacCann. Hom!

He gave a loud cough of laughter, smiled broadly and tugged twice at the strawcoloured goatee which hung from his blunt chin.

—The next business is to sign the testimonial.

—Will you pay me anything if I sign? asked Stephen.

—I thought you were an idealist, said MacCann.

The gipsylike student looked about him and addressed the onlookers in an indistinct bleating voice.

—By hell, that's a queer notion. I consider that notion to be a mercenary notion.

His voice faded into silence. No heed was paid to his words. He turned his olive face, equine in expression, towards Stephen, inviting him to speak again.

MacCann began to speak with fluent energy of the Csar's rescript, of Stead, of general disarmament, arbitration in cases of international disputes, of the signs of the times, of the new humanity and the new gospel of life which would make it the business of the community to secure as cheaply as possible the greatest possible happiness of the greatest possible number.

The gipsy student responded to the close of the period by crying:

—Three cheers for universal brotherhood!

—Go on, Temple, said a stout ruddy student near him. I'll stand you a pint after.

—I'm a believer in universal brotherhood, said Temple, glancing about him out of his dark, oval eyes. Marx is only a bloody cod.

Cranly gripped his arm tightly to check his tongue, smiling uneasily, and repeated:

—Easy, easy, easy!

Temple struggled to free his arm but continued, his mouth flecked by a thin foam:

—Socialism was founded by an Irishman and the first man in Europe who preached the freedom of thought was Collins. Two hundred years ago. He denounced priestcraft, the philosopher of Middlesex. Three cheers for John Anthony Collins!

A thin voice from the verge of the ring replied:

—Pip! pip!

Moynihan murmured beside Stephen's ear:

—And what about John Anthony's poor little sister:

> *Lottie Collins lost her drawers;*
> *Won't you kindly lend her yours?*

Stephen laughed and Moynihan, pleased with the result, murmured again:

—We'll have five bob each way on John Anthony Collins.

—I am waiting for your answer, said MacCann briefly.

—The affair doesn't interest me in the least, said Stephen wearily. You know that well. Why do you make a scene about it?

—Good! said MacCann, smacking his lips. You are a reactionary then?

—Do you think you impress me, Stephen asked, when you flourish your wooden sword?

—Metaphors! said MacCann bluntly. Come to facts.

Stephen blushed and turned aside. MacCann stood his ground and said with hostile humour:

—Minor poets, I suppose, are above such trivial questions as the question of universal peace.

Cranly raised his head and held the handball between the two students by way of a peaceoffering, saying:

—*Pax super totum sanguinarium globum.*

Stephen, moving away the bystanders, jerked his shoulder angrily in the direction of the Csar's image, saying:

—Keep your icon. If we must have a Jesus, let us have a legitimate Jesus.

—By hell, that's a good one! said the gipsy student to those about him. That's a fine expression. I like that expression immensely.

He gulped down the spittle in his throat as if he were gulping down the phrase and, fumbling at the peak of his tweed cap, turned to Stephen, saying:

—Excuse me, sir, what do you mean by that expression you uttered just now?

Feeling himself jostled by the students near him, he said to them:

—I am curious to know now what he meant by that expression.

He turned again to Stephen and said in a whisper:

—Do you believe in Jesus? I believe in man. Of course, I don't know if you believe in man. I admire you, sir. I admire the mind of man independent of all religions. Is that your opinion about the mind of Jesus?

—Go on, Temple, said the stout ruddy student, returning, as was his wont, to his first idea, that pint is waiting for you.

—He thinks I'm an imbecile, Temple explained to Stephen, because I'm a believer in the power of mind.

Cranly linked his arms into those of Stephen and his admirer and said:

—*Nos ad manum ballum jocabimus.*

Stephen, in the act of being led away, caught sight of MacCann's flushed bluntfeatured face.

—My signature is of no account, he said politely. You are right to go your way. Leave me to go mine.

—Dedalus, said MacCann crisply, I believe you're a good

fellow but you have yet to learn the dignity of altruism and the responsibility of the human individual.

A voice said:

—Intellectual crankery is better out of this movement than in it.

Stephen, recognising the harsh tone of MacAlister's voice, did not turn in the direction of the voice. Cranly pushed solemnly through the throng of students, linking Stephen and Temple like a celebrant attended by his ministers on his way to the altar.

Temple bent eagerly across Cranly's breast and said:

—Did you hear MacAlister what he said? That youth is jealous of you. Did you see that? I bet Cranly didn't see that. By hell, I saw that at once.

As they crossed the inner hall the dean of studies was in the act of escaping from the student with whom he had been conversing. He stood at the foot of the staircase, a foot on the lowest step, his threadbare soutane gathered about him for the ascent with womanish care, nodding his head often and repeating:

—Not a doubt of it, Mr Hackett! Very fine! Not a doubt of it!

In the middle of the hall the prefect of the college sodality was speaking earnestly, in a soft querulous voice, with a boarder. As he spoke he wrinkled a little his freckled brow and bit, between his phrases, at a tiny bone pencil.

—I hope the matric men will all come. The first arts men are pretty sure. Second arts too. We must make sure of the newcomers.

Temple bent again across Cranly, as they were passing through the doorway, and said in a swift whisper:

—Do you know that he is a married man? He was a married man before they converted him. He has a wife and children somewhere. By hell, I think that's the queerest notion I ever heard! Eh?

His whisper trailed off into sly cackling laughter. The moment they were through the doorway Cranly seized him rudely by the neck and shook him, saying:

—You flaming floundering fool! I'll take my dying bible there isn't a bigger bloody ape, do you know, than you in the whole flaming bloody world!

Temple wriggled in his grip, laughing still with sly content, while Cranly repeated flatly at every rude shake:

—A flaming flaring bloody idiot!

They crossed the weedy garden together. The president, wrapped in a heavy loose cloak, was coming towards them along one of the walks, reading his office. At the end of the walk he halted before turning and raised his eyes. The students saluted, Temple fumbling as before at the peak of his cap. They walked forward in silence. As they neared the alley Stephen could hear the thuds of the players' hands and the wet smacks of the ball and Davin's voice crying out excitedly at each stroke.

The three students halted round the box on which Davin sat to follow the game. Temple, after a few moments, sidled across to Stephen and said:

—Excuse me, I wanted to ask you do you believe that Jean Jacques Rousseau was a sincere man?

Stephen laughed outright. Cranly, picking up the broken stave of a cask from the grass at his foot, turned swiftly and said sternly:

—Temple, I declare to the living God if you say another word, do you know, to anybody on any subject I'll kill you *super spottum*.

—He was like you, I fancy, said Stephen, an emotional man.

—Blast him, curse him! said Cranly broadly. Don't talk to him at all. Sure, you might as well be talking, do you know, to a flaming chamberpot as talking to Temple. Go home, Temple. For God's sake, go home.

—I don't care a damn about you, Cranly, answered Temple, moving out of reach of the uplifted stave and pointing at

Stephen. He's the only man I see in this institution that has an individual mind.

—Institution! Individual! cried Cranly. Go home, blast you, for you're a hopeless bloody man.

—I'm an emotional man, said Temple. That's quite rightly expressed. And I'm proud that I'm an emotionalist.

He sidled out of the alley, smiling slily. Cranly watched him with a blank expressionless face.

—Look at him! he said. Did you ever see such a go-by-the-wall?

His phrase was greeted by a strange laugh from a student who lounged against the wall, his peaked cap down on his eyes. The laugh, pitched in a high key and coming from a so muscular frame, seemed like the whinny of an elephant. The student's body shook all over and, to ease his mirth, he rubbed both his hands delightedly, over his groins.

—Lynch is awake, said Cranly.

Lynch, for answer, straightened himself and thrust forward his chest.

—Lynch puts out his chest, said Stephen, as a criticism of life.

Lynch smote himself sonorously on the chest and said:

—Who has anything to say about my girth?

Cranly took him at the word and the two began to tussle. When their faces had flushed with the struggle they drew apart, panting. Stephen bent down towards Davin who, intent on the game, had paid no heed to the talk of the others.

—And how is my little tame goose? he asked. Did he sign too?

Davin nodded and said:

—And you, Stevie?

Stephen shook his head.

—You're a terrible man, Stevie, said Davin, taking the short pipe from his mouth. Always alone.

—Now that you have signed the petition for universal peace, said Stephen, I suppose you will burn that little copybook I saw in your room.

As Davin did not answer Stephen began to quote:

—Long pace, fianna! Right incline, fianna! Fianna, by numbers, salute, one, two!

—That's a different question, said Davin. I'm an Irish nationalist, first and foremost. But that's you all out. You're a born sneerer, Stevie.

—When you make the next rebellion with hurleysticks, said Stephen, and want the indispensable informer, tell me. I can find you a few in this college.

—I can't understand you, said Davin. One time I hear you talk against English literature. Now you talk against the Irish informers. What with your name and your ideas . . . Are you Irish at all?

—Come with me now to the office of arms and I will show you the tree of my family, said Stephen.

—Then be one of us, said Davin. Why don't you learn Irish? Why did you drop out of the league class after the first lesson?

—You know one reason why, answered Stephen.

Davin tossed his head and laughed.

—O, come now, he said. Is it on account of that certain young lady and Father Moran? But that's all in your own mind, Stevie. They were only talking and laughing.

Stephen paused and laid a friendly hand upon Davin's shoulder.

—Do you remember, he said, when we knew each other first? The first morning we met you asked me to show you the way to the matriculation class, putting a very strong stress on the first syllable. You remember? Then you used to address the jesuits as father, you remember? I ask myself about you: *Is he as innocent as his speech?*

—I'm a simple person, said Davin. You know that. When you told me that night in Harcourt Street those things about your private life, honest to God, Stevie, I was not able to eat my dinner. I was quite bad. I was awake a long time that night. Why did you tell me those things?

—Thanks, said Stephen. You mean I am a monster.

—No, said Davin, but I wish you had not told me.

A tide began to surge beneath the calm surface of Stephen's friendliness.

—This race and this country and this life produced me, he said. I shall express myself as I am.

—Try to be one of us, repeated Davin. In your heart you are an Irishman but your pride is too powerful.

—My ancestors threw off their language and took another, Stephen said. They allowed a handful of foreigners to subject them. Do you fancy I am going to pay in my own life and person debts they made? What for?

—For our freedom, said Davin.

—No honourable and sincere man, said Stephen, has given up to you his life and his youth and his affections from the days of Tone to those of Parnell but you sold him to the enemy or failed him in need or reviled him and left him for another. And you invite me to be one of you. I'd see you damned first.

—They died for their ideals, Stevie, said Davin. Our day will come yet, believe me.

Stephen, following his own thought, was silent for an instant.

—The soul is born, he said vaguely, first in those moments I told you of. It has a slow and dark birth, more mysterious than the birth of the body. When the soul of a man is born in this country there are nets flung at it to hold it back from flight. You talk to me of nationality, language, religion. I shall try to fly by those nets.

Davin knocked the ashes from his pipe.

—Too deep for me, Stevie, he said. But a man's country comes first. Ireland first, Stevie. You can be a poet or mystic after.

—Do you know what Ireland is? asked Stephen with cold violence. Ireland is the old sow that eats her farrow.

Davin rose from his box and went towards the players,

shaking his head sadly. But in a moment his sadness left him and he was hotly disputing with Cranly and the two players who had finished their game. A match of four was arranged, Cranly insisting, however, that his ball should be used. He let it rebound twice or thrice to his hand and struck it strongly and swiftly towards the base of the alley, exclaiming in answer to its thud:

—Your soul!

Stephen stood with Lynch till the score began to rise. Then he plucked him by the sleeve to come away. Lynch obeyed, saying:

—Let us eke go, as Cranly has it.

Stephen smiled at this sidethrust. They passed back through the garden and out through the hall where the doddering porter was pinning up a notice in the frame. At the foot of the steps they halted and Stephen took a packet of cigarettes from his pocket and offered it to his companion.

—I know you are poor, he said.

—Damn your yellow insolence, answered Lynch.

This second proof of Lynch's culture made Stephen smile again.

—It was a great day for European culture, he said, when you made up your mind to swear in yellow.

They lit their cigarettes and turned to the right. After a pause Stephen began:

—Aristotle has not defined pity and terror. I have. I say . . .

Lynch halted and said bluntly:

—Stop! I won't listen! I am sick. I was out last night on a yellow drunk with Horan and Goggins.

Stephen went on:

—Pity is the feeling which arrests the mind in the presence of whatsoever is grave and constant in human sufferings and unites it with the human sufferer. Terror is the feeling which arrests the mind in the presence of whatsoever is grave and constant in human sufferings and unites it with the secret cause.

—Repeat, said Lynch.

Stephen repeated the definitions slowly.

—A girl got into a hansom a few days ago, he went on, in London. She was on her way to meet her mother whom she had not seen for many years. At the corner of a street the shaft of a lorry shivered the window of the hansom in the shape of a star. A long fine needle of the shivered glass pierced her heart. She died on the instant. The reporter called it a tragic death. It is not. It is remote from terror and pity according to the terms of my definitions.

—The tragic emotion, in fact, is a face looking two ways, towards terror and towards pity, both of which are phases of it. You see I use the word *arrest*. I mean that the tragic emotion is static. Or rather the dramatic emotion is. The feelings excited by improper art are kinetic, desire or loathing. Desire urges us to possess, to go to something; loathing urges us to abandon, to go from something. These are kinetic emotions. The arts which excite them, pornographical or didactic, are therefore improper arts. The esthetic emotion (I use the general term) is therefore static. The mind is arrested and raised above desire and loathing.

—You say that art must not excite desire, said Lynch. I told you that one day I wrote my name in pencil on the backside of the Venus of Praxiteles in the Museum. Was that not desire?

—I speak of normal natures, said Stephen. You also told me that when you were a boy in that charming carmelite school you ate pieces of dried cowdung.

Lynch broke again into a whinny of laughter and again rubbed both his hands over his groins but without taking them from his pockets.

—O I did! I did! he cried.

Stephen turned towards his companion and looked at him for a moment boldly in the eyes. Lynch, recovering from his laughter, answered his look from his humbled eyes. The long slender flattened skull beneath the long pointed cap brought before Stephen's mind the image of a hooded reptile. The eyes, too, were reptilelike in glint and gaze. Yet at that instant, humbled and alert in their look, they were lit by one tiny human point, the window of a shrivelled soul, poignant and selfembittered.

—As for that, Stephen said in polite parenthesis, we are all animals. I also am an animal.

—You are, said Lynch.

—But we are just now in a mental world, Stephen continued. The desire and loathing excited by improper esthetic means are really unesthetic emotions not only because they are kinetic in character but also because they are not more than physical. Our flesh shrinks from what it dreads and responds to the stimulus of what it desires by a purely reflex action of the nervous system. Our eyelid closes before we are aware that the fly is about to enter our eye.

—Not always, said Lynch critically.

—In the same way, said Stephen, your flesh responded to the stimulus of a naked statue but it was, I say, simply a reflex action of the nerves. Beauty expressed by the artist cannot awaken in us an emotion which is kinetic or a sensation which is purely physical. It awakens, or ought to awaken, or induces, or ought to induce, an esthetic stasis, an ideal pity or an ideal terror, a stasis called forth, prolonged and at last dissolved by what I call the rhythm of beauty.

—What is that exactly? asked Lynch.

—Rhythm, said Stephen, is the first formal esthetic relation of part to part in any esthetic whole or of an esthetic whole to its part or parts or of any part to the esthetic whole of which it is a part.

—If that is rhythm, said Lynch, let me hear what you call beauty: and, please remember, though I did eat a cake of cowdung once, that I admire only beauty.

Stephen raised his cap as if in greeting. Then, blushing slightly, he laid his hand on Lynch's thick tweed sleeve.

—We are right, he said, and the others are wrong. To speak of these things and to try to understand their nature and, having understood it, to try slowly and humbly and constantly to express, to press out again, from the gross earth or what it brings forth, from sound and shape and colour which are the prison gates of our soul, an image of the beauty we have come to understand—that is art.

They had reached the canal bridge and, turning from their course, went on by the trees. A crude grey light, mirrored in the sluggish water, and a smell of wet branches over their heads seemed to war against the course of Stephen's thought.

—But you have not answered my question, said Lynch. What is art? What is the beauty it expresses?

—That was the first definition I gave you, you sleepy-headed wretch, said Stephen, when I began to try to think out the matter for myself. Do you remember the night? Cranly lost his temper and began to talk about Wicklow bacon.

—I remember, said Lynch. He told us about them flaming fat devils of pigs.

—Art, said Stephen, is the human disposition of sensible or intelligible matter for an esthetic end. You remember the pigs and forget that. You are a distressing pair, you and Cranly.

Lynch made a grimace at the raw grey sky and said:

—If I am to listen to your esthetic philosophy give me at least another cigarette. I don't care about it. I don't even care about women. Damn you and damn everything. I want a job of five hundred a year. You can't get me one.

Stephen handed him the packet of cigarettes. Lynch took the last one that remained, saying simply:

—Proceed!

—Aquinas, said Stephen, says that is beautiful the apprehension of which pleases.

Lynch nodded.

—I remember that, he said. *Pulcra sunt quæ visa placent.*

—He uses the word *visa,* said Stephen, to cover esthetic apprehensions of all kinds, whether through sight or hearing or through any other avenue of apprehension. This word, though it is vague, is clear enough to keep away good and evil which excite desire and loathing. It means certainly a stasis and not a kinesis. How about the true? It produces also a stasis of the mind. You would not write your name in pencil across the hypothenuse of a rightangled triangle.

—No, said Lynch, give me the hypothenuse of the Venus of Praxiteles.

—Static therefore, said Stephen. Plato, I believe, said that beauty is the splendour of truth. I don't think that it has a meaning but the true and the beautiful are akin. Truth is beheld by the intellect which is appeased by the most satisfying relations of the intelligible: beauty is beheld by the imagination which is appeased by the most satisfying relations of the sensible. The first step in the direction of truth is to understand the frame and scope of the intellect itself, to comprehend the act itself of intellection. Aristotle's entire system of philosophy rests upon his book of psychology and that, I think, rests on his statement that the same attribute cannot at the same time and in the same connection belong to and not belong to the same subject. The first step in the direction of beauty is to understand the frame and scope of the imagination, to comprehend the act itself of esthetic apprehension. Is that clear?

—But what is beauty? asked Lynch impatiently. Out with another definition. Something we see and like! Is that the best you and Aquinas can do?

—Let us take woman, said Stephen.

—Let us take her! said Lynch fervently.

—The Greek, the Turk, the Chinese, the Copt, the Hottentot, said Stephen, all admire a different type of female beauty. That seems to be a maze out of which we cannot escape. I see however two ways out. One is this hypothesis: that every physical quality admired by men in women is in direct connection with the manifold functions of women for the propagation of the species. It may be so. The world, it seems, is drearier than even you, Lynch, imagined. For my part I dislike that way out. It leads to eugenics rather than to esthetic. It leads you out of the maze into a new gaudy lectureroom where Mac-

Cann, with one hand on *The Origin of Species* and the other hand on the new testament, tells you that you admired the great flanks of Venus because you felt that she would bear you burly offspring and admired her great breasts because you felt that she would give good milk to her children and yours.

—Then MacCann is a sulphuryellow liar, said Lynch energetically.

—There remains another way out, said Stephen, laughing.

—To wit? said Lynch.

—This hypothesis, Stephen began.

A long dray laden with old iron came round the corner of sir Patrick Dun's hospital covering the end of Stephen's speech with the harsh roar of jangled and rattling metal. Lynch closed his ears and gave out oath after oath till the dray had passed. Then he turned on his heel rudely. Stephen turned also and waited for a few moments till his companion's illhumour had had its vent.

—This hypothesis, Stephen repeated, is the other way out: that, though the same object may not seem beautiful to all people, all people who admire a beautiful object find in it certain relations which satisfy and coincide with the stages themselves of all esthetic apprehension. These relations of the sensible, visible to you through one form and to me through another, must be therefore the necessary qualities of beauty. Now, we can return to our old friend saint Thomas for another pennyworth of wisdom.

Lynch laughed.

—It amuses me vastly, he said, to hear you quoting him time after time like a jolly round friar. Are you laughing in your sleeve?

—MacAlister, answered Stephen, would call my esthetic theory applied Aquinas. So far as this side of esthetic philosophy extends Aquinas will carry me all along the line. When we come to the phenomena of artistic conception, artistic gestation and artistic reproduction I require a new terminology and a new personal experience.

—Of course, said Lynch. After all Aquinas, in spite of his

intellect, was exactly a good round friar. But you will tell me about the new personal experience and new terminology some other day. Hurry up and finish the first part.

—Who knows? said Stephen, smiling. Perhaps Aquinas would understand me better than you. He was a poet himself. He wrote a hymn for Maundy Thursday. It begins with the words *Pange lingua gloriosi*. They say it is the highest glory of the hymnal. It is an intricate and soothing hymn. I like it: but there is no hymn that can be put beside that mournful and majestic processional song, the *Vexilla Regis* of Venantius Fortunatus.

Lynch began to sing softly and solemnly in a deep bass voice:

> *Impleta sunt quæ concinit*
> *David fideli carmine*
> *Dicendo nationibus*
> *Regnavit a ligno Deus.*

—That's great! he said, well pleased. Great music!

They turned into Lower Mount Street. A few steps from the corner a fat young man, wearing a silk neckcloth, saluted them and stopped.

—Did you hear the results of the exams? he asked. Griffin was plucked. Halpin and O'Flynn are through the home civil. Moonan got fifth place in the Indian. O'Shaughnessy got fourteenth. The Irish fellows in Clarke's gave them a feed last night. They all ate curry.

His pallid bloated face expressed benevolent malice and, as he had advanced through his tidings of success, his small fatencircled eyes vanished out of sight and his weak wheezing voice out of hearing.

In reply to a question of Stephen's his eyes and his voice came forth again from their lurkingplaces.

—Yes, MacCullagh and I, he said. He's taking pure mathematics and I'm taking constitutional history. There are twenty subjects. I'm taking botany too. You know I'm a member of the field club.

He drew back from the other two in a stately fashion and placed a plump woollengloved hand on his breast, from which muttered wheezing laughter at once broke forth.

—Bring us a few turnips and onions the next time you go out, said Stephen drily, to make a stew.

The fat student laughed indulgently and said:

—We are all highly respectable people in the field club. Last Saturday we went out to Glenmalure, seven of us.

—With women, Donovan? said Lynch.

Donovan again laid his hand on his chest and said:

—Our end is the acquisition of knowledge.

Then he said quickly:

—I hear you are writing some essay about esthetics.

Stephen made a vague gesture of denial.

—Goethe and Lessing, said Donovan, have written a lot on that subject, the classical school and the romantic school and all that. The *Laocoon* interested me very much when I read it. Of course it is idealistic, German, ultraprofound.

Neither of the others spoke. Donovan took leave of them urbanely.

—I must go, he said softly and benevolently. I have a strong suspicion, amounting almost to a conviction, that my sister intended to make pancakes today for the dinner of the Donovan family.

—Goodbye, Stephen said in his wake. Don't forget the turnips for me and my mate.

Lynch gazed after him, his lip curling in slow scorn till his face resembled a devil's mask:

—To think that that yellow pancakeeating excrement can get a good job, he said at length, and I have to smoke cheap cigarettes!

They turned their faces towards Merrion Square and went on for a little in silence.

—To finish what I was saying about beauty, said Stephen, the most satisfying relations of the sensible must therefore correspond to the necessary phases of artistic apprehension. Find these and you find the qualities of universal beauty.

Aquinas says: *ad pulcritudinem tria requiruntur, integritas, consonantia, claritas*. I translate it so: *Three things are needed for beauty, wholeness, harmony and radiance*. Do these correspond to the phases of apprehension? Are you following?

—Of course, I am, said Lynch. If you think I have an excrementitious intelligence run after Donovan and ask him to listen to you.

Stephen pointed to a basket which a butcher's boy had slung inverted on his head.

—Look at that basket, he said.

—I see it, said Lynch.

—In order to see that basket, said Stephen, your mind first of all separates the basket from the rest of the visible universe which is not the basket. The first phase of apprehension is a bounding line drawn about the object to be apprehended. An esthetic image is presented to us either in space or in time. What is audible is presented in time, what is visible is presented in space. But, temporal or spatial, the esthetic image is first luminously apprehended as selfbounded and selfcontained upon the immeasurable background of space or time which is not it. You apprehend it as *one* thing. You see it as one whole. You apprehend its wholeness. That is *integritas*.

—Bull's eye! said Lynch, laughing. Go on.

—Then, said Stephen, you pass from point to point, led by its formal lines; you apprehend it as balanced part against part within its limits; you feel the rhythm of its structure. In other words the synthesis of immediate perception is followed by the analysis of apprehension. Having first felt that it is *one* thing you feel now that it is a *thing*. You apprehend it as complex, multiple, divisible, separable, made up of its parts, the result of its parts and their sum, harmonious. That is *consonantia*.

—Bull's eye again! said Lynch wittily. Tell me now what is *claritas* and you win the cigar.

—The connotation of the word, Stephen said, is rather vague. Aquinas uses a term which seems to be inexact. It baffled me for a long time. It would lead you to believe that he had in mind symbolism or idealism, the supreme quality of beauty being a light from some other world, the idea of which the matter is but the shadow, the reality of which it is but the symbol. I thought he might mean that *claritas* is the artistic discovery and representation of the divine purpose in anything or a force of generalisation which would make the esthetic image a universal one, make it outshine its proper conditions. But that is literary talk. I understand it so. When you have apprehended that basket as one thing and have then analysed it according to its form and apprehended it as a thing you make the only synthesis which is logically and esthetically permissible. You see that it is that thing which it is and no other thing. The radiance of which he speaks is the scholastic *quidditas,* the *whatness* of a thing. This supreme quality is felt by the artist when the esthetic image is first conceived in his imagination. The mind in that mysterious instant Shelley likened beautifully to a fading coal. The instant wherein that supreme quality of beauty, the clear radiance of the esthetic image, is apprehended luminously by the mind which has been arrested by its wholeness and fascinated by its harmony is the luminous silent stasis of esthetic pleasure, a spiritual state very like to that cardiac condition which the Italian physiologist Luigi Galvani, using a phrase almost as beautiful as Shelley's, called the enchantment of the heart.

Stephen paused and, though his companion did not speak, felt that his words had called up around them a thoughten-chanted silence.

—What I have said, he began again, refers to beauty in the wider sense of the word, in the sense which the word has in the literary tradition. In the marketplace it has another sense. When we speak of beauty in the second sense of the term our judgment is influenced in the first place by the art itself and by the form of that art. The image, it is clear, must be set be-tween the mind or senses of the artist himself and the mind or senses of others. If you bear this in memory you will see that art necessarily divides itself into three forms progressing from one to the next. These forms are: the lyrical form, the form wherein the artist presents his image in immediate relation to himself; the epical form, the form wherein he presents his image in mediate relation to himself and to others; the dramatic form, the form wherein he presents his image in immediate relation to others.

—That you told me a few nights ago, said Lynch, and we began the famous discussion.

—I have a book at home, said Stephen, in which I have written down questions which are more amusing than yours were. In finding the answers to them I found the theory of esthetic which I am trying to explain. Here are some questions I set myself: *Is a chair finely made tragic or comic? Is the portrait of Mona Lisa good if I desire to see it? Is the bust of Sir Philip Crampton lyrical, epical or dramatic? Can excrement or a child or a louse be a work of art? If not, why not?*

—Why not, indeed? said Lynch, laughing.

—*If a man hacking in fury at a block of wood,* Stephen continued, *make there an image of a cow, is that image a work of art? If not, why not?*

—That's a lovely one, said Lynch, laughing again. That has the true scholastic stink.

—Lessing, said Stephen, should not have taken a group of statues to write of. The art, being inferior, does not present the forms I spoke of distinguished clearly one from another. Even in literature, the highest and most spiritual art, the forms are often confused. The lyrical form is in fact the simplest verbal vesture of an instant of emotion, a rhythmical cry such as ages ago cheered on the man who pulled at the oar or dragged stones up a slope. He who utters it is more conscious of the instant of emotion than of himself as feeling emotion. The simplest epical form is seen emerging out of lyrical literature when the artist prolongs and broods upon himself as the centre of an epical event and this form progresses till the centre of emotional gravity is equidistant from the artist himself and from others. The narrative is no longer purely personal. The personality of the artist passes into the narration itself, flowing round and round the persons and the action like a vital sea. This progress you will see easily in that old English ballad *Turpin Hero* which begins in the first person and ends in the third person. The dramatic form is reached when the vitality which has flowed and eddied round each person fills every person with such vital force that he or she assumes a proper and intangible esthetic life. The personality of the artist, at first a cry or a cadence or a mood and then a fluid and lambent narrative, finally refines itself out of existence, impersonalises itself, so to speak. The esthetic image in the dramatic form is life purified in and reprojected from the human imagination. The mystery of esthetic like that of material creation is accomplished. The artist, like the God of the creation, remains within or behind or beyond or above his handiwork, invisible, refined out of existence, indifferent, paring his fingernails.

—Trying to refine them also out of existence, said Lynch.

A fine rain began to fall from the high veiled sky and they turned into the duke's lawn, to reach the national library before the shower came.

—What do you mean, Lynch asked surlily, by prating about beauty and the imagination in this miserable God-forsaken island? No wonder the artist retired within or behind his handiwork after having perpetrated this country.

The rain fell faster. When they passed through the passage beside the royal Irish academy they found many students sheltering under the arcade of the library. Cranly, leaning against a pillar, was picking his teeth with a sharpened match, listening to some companions. Some girls stood near the entrance door. Lynch whispered to Stephen:

—Your beloved is here.

Stephen took his place silently on the step below the group of students, heedless of the rain which fell fast, turning his eyes towards her from time to time. She too stood silently among her companions. She has no priest to flirt with, he thought with conscious bitterness, remembering how he had seen her last. Lynch was right. His mind, emptied of theory and courage, lapsed back into a listless peace.

He heard the students talking among themselves. They spoke of two friends who had passed the final medical examination, of the chances of getting places on ocean liners, of poor and rich practices.

—That's all a bubble. An Irish country practice is better.

—Hynes was two years in Liverpool and he says the same. A frightful hole he said it was. Nothing but midwifery cases. Half a crown cases.

—Do you mean to say it is better to have a job here in the country than in a rich city like that? I know a fellow . . .

—Hynes has no brains. He got through by stewing, pure stewing.

—Don't mind him. There's plenty of money to be made in a big commercial city.

—Depends on the practice.

—*Ego credo ut vita pauperum est simpliciter atrox, simpliciter sanguinarius atrox, in Liverpoolio.*

Their voices reached his ears as if from a distance in interrupted pulsation. She was preparing to go away with her companions.

The quick light shower had drawn off, tarrying in clusters of diamonds among the shrubs of the quadrangle where an exhalation was breathed forth by the blackened earth. Their trim boots prattled as they stood on the steps of the colonnade, talking quietly and gaily, glancing at the clouds, holding their umbrellas at cunning angles against the few last raindrops, closing them again, holding their skirts demurely.

And if he had judged her harshly? If her life were a simple rosary of hours, her life simple and strange as a bird's life, gay in the morning, restless all day, tired at sundown? Her heart simple and wilful as a bird's heart?

*   *   *

Towards dawn he awoke. O what sweet music! His soul was all dewy wet. Over his limbs in sleep pale cool waves of light had passed. He lay still, as if his soul lay amid cool waters, conscious of faint sweet music. His mind was waking slowly to a tremulous morning knowledge, a morning inspiration. A spirit filled him, pure as the purest water, sweet as dew, moving as music. But how faintly it was inbreathed, how passionlessly, as if the seraphim themselves were breathing upon him! His soul was waking slowly, fearing to awake wholly. It was that windless hour of dawn when madness wakes and strange plants open to the light and the moth flies forth silently.

An enchantment of the heart! The night had been enchanted. In a dream or vision he had known the ecstasy of seraphic life. Was it an instant of enchantment only or long hours and days and years and ages?

The instant of inspiration seemed now to be reflected from all sides at once from a multitude of cloudy circumstance of what had happened or of what might have happened. The instant flashed forth like a point of light and now from cloud on cloud of vague circumstance confused form was veiling softly its afterglow. O! In the virgin womb of the imagination the word was made flesh. Gabriel the seraph had come to the virgin's chamber. An afterglow deepened within his spirit, whence the white flame had passed, deepening to a rose and ardent light. That rose and ardent light was her strange wilful heart, strange that no man had known or would know, wilful from before the beginning of the world: and lured by that ardent roselike glow the choirs of the seraphim were falling from heaven.

> *Are you not weary of ardent ways,*
> *Lure of the fallen seraphim?*
> *Tell no more of enchanted days.*

The verses passed from his mind to his lips and, murmuring them over, he felt the rhythmic movement of a villanelle pass through them. The roselike glow sent forth its rays of rhyme; ways, days, blaze, praise, raise. Its rays burned up the world, consumed the hearts of men and angels: the rays from the rose that was her wilful heart.

> *Your eyes have set man's heart ablaze*
> *And you have had your will of him.*
> *Are you not weary of ardent ways?*

And then? The rhythm died away, ceased, began again to move and beat. And then? Smoke, incense ascending from the altar of the world.

> *Above the flame the smoke of praise*
> *Goes up from ocean rim to rim.*
> *Tell no more of enchanted days.*

Smoke went up from the whole earth, from the vapoury oceans, smoke of her praise. The earth was like a swinging smoking swaying censer, a ball of incense, an ellipsoidal ball. The rhythm died out at once; the cry of his heart was broken. His lips began to murmur the first verses over and over; then went on stumbling through half verses, stammering and baffled; then stopped. The heart's cry was broken.

The veiled windless hour had passed and behind the panes of the naked window the morning light was gathering. A bell beat faintly very far away. A bird twittered; two birds, three. The bell and the bird ceased: and the dull white light spread itself east and west, covering the world, covering the roselight in his heart.

Fearing to lose all, he raised himself suddenly on his elbow to look for paper and pencil. There was neither on the table; only the soupplate he had eaten the rice from for supper and the candlestick with its tendrils of tallow and its paper socket, singed by the last flame. He stretched his arm wearily towards the foot of the bed, groping with his hand in the pockets of the coat that hung there. His fingers found a pencil and then a cigarette packet. He lay back and, tearing open the packet, placed the last cigarette on the windowledge and began to write out the stanzas of the villanelle in small neat letters on the rough cardboard surface.

Having written them out he lay back on the lumpy pillow, murmuring them again. The lumps of knotted flock under his head reminded him of the lumps of knotted horsehair in the sofa of her parlour on which he used to sit, smiling or serious, asking himself why he had come, displeased with her and with himself, confounded by the print of the Sacred Heart above the untenanted sideboard. He saw her approach him in a lull of the talk and beg him to sing one of his curious songs. Then he saw himself sitting at the old piano, striking chords softly from its speckled keys and singing, amid the talk which had risen again in the room, to her who leaned beside the mantel-piece a dainty song of the Elizabethans, a sad and sweet loth to depart, the victory chant of Agincourt, the happy air of Greensleeves. While he sang and she listened, or feigned to listen, his heart was at rest but when the quaint old songs had ended and he heard again the voices in the room he remembered his own sarcasm: the house where young men are called by their christian names a little too soon.

At certain instants her eyes seemed about to trust him but he had waited in vain. She passed now dancing lightly across his memory as she had been that night at the carnival ball, her white dress a little lifted, a white spray nodding in her hair. She danced lightly in the round. She was dancing towards him and, as she came, her eyes were a little averted and a faint glow was on her cheek. At the pause in the chain of hands her hand had lain in his an instant, a soft merchandise.

—You are a great stranger now.

—Yes. I was born to be a monk.

—I am afraid you are a heretic.

—Are you much afraid?

For answer she had danced away from him along the chain of hands, dancing lightly and discreetly, giving herself to none. The white spray nodded to her dancing and when she was in shadow the glow was deeper on her cheek.

A monk! His own image started forth a profaner of the

cloister, a heretic franciscan, willing and willing not to serve, spinning like Gherardino da Borgo San Donnino, a lithe web of sophistry and whispering in her ear.

No, it was not his image. It was like the image of the young priest in whose company he had seen her last, looking at him out of dove's eyes, toying with the pages of her Irish phrasebook.

—Yes, yes, the ladies are coming round to us. I can see it every day. The ladies are with us. The best helpers the language has.

—And the church, Father Moran?

—The church too. Coming round too. The work is going ahead there too. Don't fret about the church.

Bah! he had done well to leave the room in disdain. He had done well not to salute her on the steps of the library. He had done well to leave her to flirt with her priest, to toy with a church which was the scullerymaid of christendom.

Rude brutal anger routed the last lingering instant of ecstasy from his soul. It broke up violently her fair image and flung the fragments on all sides. On all sides distorted reflections of her image started from his memory: the flowergirl in the ragged dress with damp coarse hair and a hoyden's face who had called herself his own girl and begged his handsel, the kitchengirl in the next house who sang over the clatter of her plates with the drawl of a country singer the first bars of *By Killarney's Lakes and Fells,* a girl who had laughed gaily to see him stumble when the iron grating in the footpath near Cork Hill had caught the broken sole of his shoe, a girl he had glanced at, attracted by her small ripe mouth as she passed out of Jacob's biscuit factory, who had cried to him over her shoulder:

—Do you like what you seen of me, straight hair and curly eyebrows?

And yet he felt that, however he might revile and mock her image, his anger was also a form of homage. He had left the classroom in disdain that was not wholly sincere, feeling that perhaps the secret of her race lay behind those dark eyes upon which her long lashes flung a quick shadow. He had told himself bitterly as he walked through the streets that she was a figure of the womanhood of her country, a batlike soul waking to the consciousness of itself in darkness and secrecy and loneliness, tarrying awhile, loveless and sinless, with her mild lover and leaving him to whisper of innocent transgressions in the latticed ear of a priest. His anger against her found vent in coarse railing at her paramour, whose name and voice and features offended his baffled pride: a priested peasant, with a brother a policeman in Dublin and a brother a potboy in Moycullen. To him she would unveil her soul's shy nakedness, to one who was but schooled in the discharging of a formal rite rather than to him, a priest of eternal imagination, transmuting the daily bread of experience into the radiant body of everliving life.

The radiant image of the eucharist united again in an instant his bitter and despairing thoughts, their cries arising unbroken in a hymn of thanksgiving.

> *Our broken cries and mournful lays*
> *Rise in one eucharistic hymn.*
> *Are you not weary of ardent ways?*
>
> *While sacrificing hands upraise*
> *The chalice flowing to the brim,*
> *Tell no more of enchanted days.*

He spoke the verses aloud from the first lines till the music and rhythm suffused his mind, turning it to quiet indulgence; then copied them painfully to feel them the better by seeing them; then lay back on his bolster.

The full morning light had come. No sound was to be heard: but he knew that all around him life was about to awaken in common noises, hoarse voices, sleepy prayers. Shrinking from that life he turned towards the wall, making a cowl of the blanket and staring at the great overblown scarlet flowers of the tattered wallpaper. He tried to warm his perishing joy in their scarlet glow, imagining a roseway from where he lay upwards to heaven all strewn with scarlet flowers. Weary! Weary! He too was weary of ardent ways.

A gradual warmth, a languorous weariness passed over him, descending along his spine from his closely cowled head. He felt it descend and, seeing himself as he lay, smiled. Soon he would sleep.

He had written verses for her again after ten years. Ten years before she had worn her shawl cowlwise about her head, sending sprays of her warm breath into the night air, tapping her foot upon the glassy road. It was the last tram; the lank brown horses knew it and shook their bells to the clear night in admonition. The conductor talked with the driver, both nodding often in the green light of the lamp. They stood on the steps of the tram, he on the upper, she on the lower. She came up to his step many times between their phrases and went down again and once or twice remained beside him forgetting to go down and then went down. Let be! Let be!

Ten years from that wisdom of children to his folly. If he sent her the verses? They would be read out at breakfast amid the tapping of eggshells. Folly indeed! The brothers would laugh and try to wrest the page from each other with their strong hard fingers. The suave priest, her uncle, seated in his armchair, would hold the page at arm's length, read it smiling and approve of the literary form.

No, no: that was folly. Even if he sent her the verses she would not show them to others. No, no: she could not.

He began to feel that he had wronged her. A sense of her innocence moved him almost to pity her, an innocence he had never understood till he had come to the knowledge of it through sin, an innocence which she too had not understood while she was innocent or before the strange humiliation of her nature had first come upon her. Then first her soul had begun to live as his soul had when he had first sinned: and a tender compassion filled his heart as he remembered her frail pallor and her eyes, humbled and saddened by the dark shame of womanhood.

While his soul had passed from ecstasy to languor where had she been? Might it be, in the mysterious ways of spiritual life, that her soul at those same moments had been conscious of his homage? It might be.

A glow of desire kindled again his soul and fired and fulfilled all his body. Conscious of his desire she was waking from odorous sleep, the temptress of his villanelle. Her eyes, dark and with a look of languor, were opening to his eyes. Her nakedness yielded to him, radiant, warm, odorous and lavish-limbed, enfolded him like a shining cloud, enfolded him like water with a liquid life: and like a cloud of vapour or like waters circumfluent in space the liquid letters of speech, symbols of the element of mystery, flowed forth over his brain.

> *Are you not weary of ardent ways,*
> *Lure of the fallen seraphim?*
> *Tell no more of enchanted days.*
>
> *Your eyes have set man's heart ablaze*
> *And you have had your will of him.*
> *Are you not weary of ardent ways?*
>
> *Above the flame the smoke of praise*
> *Goes up from ocean rim to rim.*
> *Tell no more of enchanted days.*
>
> *Our broken cries and mournful lays*
> *Rise in one eucharistic hymn.*
> *Are you not weary of ardent ways?*
>
> *While sacrificing hands upraise*
> *The chalice flowing to the brim,*
> *Tell no more of enchanted days.*
>
> *And still you hold our longing gaze*
> *With languorous look and lavish limb!*

Are you not weary of ardent ways?
Tell no more of enchanted days.

*   *   *

What birds were they? He stood on the steps of the library to look at them, leaning wearily on his ashplant. They flew round and round the jutting shoulder of a house in Molesworth Street. The air of the late March evening made clear their flight, their dark darting quivering bodies flying clearly against the sky as against a limphung cloth of smoky tenuous blue.

He watched their flight; bird after bird: a dark flash, a swerve, a flash again, a dart aside, a curve, a flutter of wings. He tried to count them before all their darting quivering bodies passed: six, ten, eleven: and wondered were they odd or even in number. Twelve, thirteen: for two came wheeling down from the upper sky. They were flying high and low but ever round and round in straight and curving lines and ever flying from left to right, circling about a temple of air.

He listened to the cries: like the squeak of mice behind the wainscot: a shrill twofold note. But the notes were long and shrill and whirring, unlike the cry of vermin, falling a third or a fourth and trilled as the flying beaks clove the air. Their cry was shrill and clear and fine and falling like threads of silken light unwound from whirring spools.

The inhuman clamour soothed his ears in which his mother's sobs and reproaches murmured insistently and the dark frail quivering bodies wheeling and fluttering and swerving round an airy temple of the tenuous sky soothed his eyes which still saw the image of his mother's face.

Why was he gazing upwards from the steps of the porch, hearing their shrill twofold cry, watching their flight? For an augury of good or evil? A phrase of Cornelius Agrippa flew through his mind and then there flew hither and thither shapeless thoughts from Swedenborg on the correspondence of birds to things of the intellect and of how the creatures of the air have their knowledge and know their times and seasons because they, unlike man, are in the order of their life and have not perverted that order by reason.

And for ages men had gazed upward as he was gazing at birds in flight. The colonnade above him made him think vaguely of an ancient temple and the ashplant on which he leaned wearily of the curved stick of an augur. A sense of fear of the unknown moved in the heart of his weariness, a fear of symbols and portents, of the hawklike man whose name he bore soaring out of his captivity on osierwoven wings, of Thoth, the god of writers, writing with a reed upon a tablet and bearing on his narrow ibis head the cusped moon.

He smiled as he thought of the god's image for it made him think of a bottlenosed judge in a wig, putting commas into a document which he held at arm's length and he knew that he would not have remembered the god's name but that it was like an Irish oath. It was folly. But was it for this folly that he was about to leave for ever the house of prayer and prudence into which he had been born and the order of life out of which he had come?

They came back with shrill cries over the jutting shoulder of the house, flying darkly against the fading air. What birds were they? He thought that they must be swallows who had come back from the south. Then he was to go away for they were birds ever going and coming, building ever an unlasting home under the eaves of men's houses and ever leaving the homes they had built to wander.

> *Bend down your faces, Oona and Aleel,*
> *I gaze upon them as the swallow gazes*
> *Upon the nest under the eave before*
> *He wander the loud waters.*

A soft liquid joy like the noise of many waters flowed over his memory and he felt in his heart the soft peace of silent spaces of fading tenuous sky above the waters, of oceanic silence, of swallows flying through the seadusk over the flowing waters.

A soft liquid joy flowed through the words where the soft long vowels hurtled noiselessly and fell away, lapping and flowing back and ever shaking the white bells of their waves in mute chime and mute peal and soft low swooning cry; and he felt that the augury he had sought in the wheeling darting birds and in the pale space of sky above him had come forth from his heart like a bird from a turret quietly and swiftly.

Symbol of departure or of loneliness? The verses crooned in the ear of his memory composed slowly before his remembering eyes the scene of the hall on the night of the opening of the national theatre. He was alone at the side of the balcony, looking out of jaded eyes at the culture of Dublin in the stalls and at the tawdry scenecloths and human dolls framed by the garish lamps of the stage. A burly policeman sweated behind him and seemed at every moment about to act. The catcalls and hisses and mocking cries ran in rude gusts round the hall from his scattered fellowstudents.

—A libel on Ireland!

—Made in Germany!

—Blasphemy!

—We never sold our faith!

—No Irish woman ever did it!

—We want no amateur atheists.

—We want no budding buddhists.

A sudden swift hiss fell from the windows above him and he knew that the electric lamps had been switched on in the reader's room. He turned into the pillared hall, now calmly lit, went up the staircase and passed in through the clicking turnstile.

Cranly was sitting over near the dictionaries. A thick book, opened at the frontispiece, lay before him on the wooden rest. He leaned back in his chair, inclining his ear like that of a confessor to the face of the medical student who was reading to him a problem from the chess page of a journal. Stephen sat down at his right and the priest at the other side of the table closed his copy of *The Tablet* with an angry snap and stood up.

Cranly gazed after him blandly and vaguely. The medical student went on in a softer voice:

—Pawn to king's fourth.

—We had better go, Dixon, said Stephen in warning. He has gone to complain.

Dixon folded the journal and rose with dignity, saying:

—Our men retired in good order.

—With guns and cattle, added Stephen, pointing to the titlepage of Cranly's book on which was printed *Diseases of the Ox*.

As they passed through a lane of the tables Stephen said:

—Cranly, I want to speak to you.

Cranly did not answer or turn. He laid his book on the counter and passed out, his wellshod feet sounding flatly on the floor. On the staircase he paused and gazing absently at Dixon repeated:

—Pawn to king's bloody fourth.

—Put it that way if you like, Dixon said.

He had a quiet toneless voice and urbane manners and on a finger of his plump clean hand he displayed at moments a signet ring.

As they crossed the hall a man of dwarfish stature came towards them. Under the dome of his tiny hat his unshaven face began to smile with pleasure and he was heard to murmur. The eyes were melancholy as those of a monkey.

—Good evening, captain, said Cranly, halting.

—Good evening, gentlemen, said the stubblegrown monkeyish face.

—Warm weather for March, said Cranly. They have the windows open upstairs.

Dixon smiled and turned his ring. The blackish monkeypuckered face pursed its human mouth with gentle pleasure: and its voice purred:

—Delightful weather for March. Simply delightful.

—There are two nice young ladies upstairs, captain, tired of waiting, Dixon said.

Cranly smiled and said kindly:

—The captain has only one love: sir Walter Scott. Isn't that so, captain?

—What are you reading now, captain? Dixon asked. *The Bride of Lammermoor?*

—I love old Scott, the flexible lips said. I think he writes something lovely. There is no writer can touch sir Walter Scott.

He moved a thin shrunken brown hand gently in the air in time to his praise and his thin quick eyelids beat often over his sad eyes.

Sadder to Stephen's ear was his speech: a genteel accent, low and moist, marred by errors: and listening to it he wondered was the story true and was the thin blood that flowed in his shrunken frame noble and come of an incestuous love?

The park trees were heavy with rain and rain fell still and ever in the lake, lying grey like a shield. A game of swans flew there and the water and the shore beneath were fouled with their greenwhite slime. They embraced softly, impelled by the grey rainy light, the wet silent trees, the shieldlike witnessing lake, the swans. They embraced without joy or passion, his arm about his sister's neck. A grey woollen cloak was wrapped athwart her from her shoulder to her waist: and her fair head was bent in willing shame. He had loose redbrown hair and tender shapely strong freckled hands. Face. There was no face seen. The brother's face was bent upon her fair rainfragrant hair. The hand freckled and strong and shapely and caressing was Davin's hand.

He frowned angrily upon his thought and on the shrivelled mannikin who had called it forth. His father's gibes at the Bantry gang leaped out of his memory. He held them at a distance and brooded uneasily on his own thought again. Why were they not Cranly's hands? Had Davin's simplicity and innocence stung him more secretly?

He walked on across the hall with Dixon, leaving Cranly to take leave elaborately of the dwarf.

Under the colonnade Temple was standing in the midst of a little group of students. One of them cried:

—Dixon, come over till you hear. Temple is in grand form.

Temple turned on him his dark gipsy eyes.

—You're a hypocrite, O'Keeffe, he said, and Dixon's a smiler. By hell, I think that's a good literary expression.

He laughed slily, looking in Stephen's face, repeating:

—By hell, I'm delighted with that name. A smiler.

A stout student who stood below them on the steps said:

—Come back to the mistress, Temple. We want to hear about that.

—He had, faith, Temple said. And he was a married man too. And all the priests used to be dining there. By hell, I think they all had a touch.

—We shall call it riding a hack to spare the hunter, said Dixon.

—Tell us, Temple, O'Keeffe said, how many quarts of porter have you in you?

—All your intellectual soul is in that phrase, O'Keeffe, said Temple with open scorn.

He moved with a shambling gait round the group and spoke to Stephen.

—Did you know that the Forsters are the kings of Belgium? he asked.

Cranly came out through the door of the entrance hall, his hat thrust back on the nape of his neck and picking his teeth with care.

—And here's the wiseacre, said Temple. Do you know that about the Forsters?

He paused for an answer. Cranly dislodged a figseed from his teeth on the point of his rude toothpick and gazed at it intently.

—The Forster family, Temple said, is descended from Baldwin the First, king of Flanders. He was called the Forester. Forester and Forster are the same name. A descendant of

Baldwin the First, captain Francis Forster, settled in Ireland and married the daughter of the last chieftain of Clanbrassil. Then there are the Blake Forsters. That's a different branch.

—From Baldhead, king of Flanders, Cranly repeated, rooting again deliberately at his gleaming uncovered teeth.

—Where did you pick up all that history? O'Keeffe asked.

—I know all the history of your family too, Temple said, turning to Stephen. Do you know what Giraldus Cambrensis says about your family?

—Is he descended from Baldwin too? asked a tall consumptive student with dark eyes.

—Baldhead, Cranly repeated, sucking at a crevice in his teeth.

—*Pernobilis et pervetusta familia,* Temple said to Stephen.

The stout student who stood below them on the steps farted briefly. Dixon turned towards him saying in a soft voice:

—Did an angel speak?

Cranly turned also and said vehemently but without anger:

—Goggins, you're the flamingest dirty devil I ever met, do you know.

—I had it on my mind to say that, Goggins answered firmly. It did no-one any harm, did it?

—We hope, Dixon said suavely, that it was not of the kind known to science as a *paulo post futurum.*

—Didn't I tell you he was a smiler? said Temple, turning right and left. Didn't I give him that name?

—You did. We're not deaf, said the tall consumptive.

Cranly still frowned at the stout student below him. Then, with a snort of disgust, he shoved him violently down the steps.

—Go away from here, he said rudely. Go away, you stinkpot. And you are a stinkpot.

Goggins skipped down on to the gravel and at once returned to his place with good humour. Temple turned back to Stephen and asked:

—Do you believe in the law of heredity?

—Are you drunk or what are you or what are you trying to say? asked Cranly, facing round on him with an expression of wonder.

—The most profound sentence ever written, Temple said with enthusiasm, is the sentence at the end of the zoology. Reproduction is the beginning of death.

He touched Stephen timidly at the elbow and said eagerly:

—Do you feel how profound that is because you are a poet?

Cranly pointed his long forefinger.

—Look at him! he said with scorn to the others. Look at Ireland's hope!

They laughed at his words and gesture. Temple turned on him bravely, saying:

—Cranly, you're always sneering at me. I can see that. But I am as good as you any day. Do you know what I think about you now as compared with myself?

—My dear man, said Cranly urbanely, you are incapable, do you know, absolutely incapable of thinking.

—But do you know, Temple went on, what I think of you and of myself compared together?

—Out with it, Temple! the stout student cried from the steps. Get it out in bits!

Temple turned right and left, making sudden feeble gestures as he spoke.

—I'm a ballocks, he said, shaking his head in despair. I am. And I know I am. And I admit it that I am.

Dixon patted him lightly on the shoulder and said mildly:

—And it does you every credit, Temple.

—But he, Temple said, pointing to Cranly. He is a ballocks too like me. Only he doesn't know it. And that's the only difference I see.

A burst of laughter covered his words. But he turned again to Stephen and said with a sudden eagerness:

—That word is a most interesting word. That's the only English dual number. Did you know?

—Is it? Stephen said vaguely.

He was watching Cranly's firmfeatured suffering face, lit up now by a smile of false patience. The gross name had passed over it like foul water poured over an old stone image, patient of injuries: and, as he watched him, he saw him raise his hat in salute and uncover the black hair that stood up stiffly from his forehead like an iron crown.

She passed out from the porch of the library and bowed across Stephen in reply to Cranly's greeting. He also? Was there not a slight flush on Cranly's cheek? Or had it come forth at Temple's words? The light had waned. He could not see.

Did that explain his friend's listless silence, his harsh comments, the sudden intrusions of rude speech with which he had shattered so often Stephen's ardent wayward confessions? Stephen had forgiven freely for he had found this rudeness also in himself towards himself. And he remembered an evening when he had dismounted from a borrowed creaking bicycle to pray to God in a wood near Malahide. He had lifted up his arms and spoken in ecstasy to the sombre nave of the trees, knowing that he stood on holy ground and in a holy hour. And when two constabularymen had come into sight round a bend in the gloomy road he had broken off his prayer to whistle loudly an air from the last pantomime.

He began to beat the frayed end of his ashplant against the base of a pillar. Had Cranly not heard him? Yet he could wait. The talk about him ceased for a moment: and a soft hiss fell again from a window above. But no other sound was in the air and the swallows whose flight he had followed with idle eyes were sleeping.

She had passed through the dusk. And therefore the air was silent save for one soft hiss that fell. And therefore the tongues about him had ceased their babble. Darkness was falling.

Darkness falls from the air.

A trembling joy, lambent as a faint light, played like a fairy host around him. But why? Her passage through the darkening air or the verse with its black vowels and its opening sound, rich and lutelike?

He walked away slowly towards the deeper shadows at the end of the colonnade, beating the stone softly with his stick to hide his revery from the students whom he had left: and allowed his mind to summon back to itself the age of Dowland and Byrd and Nash.

Eyes, opening from the darkness of desire, eyes that dimmed the breaking east. What was their languid grace but the softness of chambering? And what was their shimmer but the shimmer of the scum that mantled the cesspool of the court of a slobbering Stuart. And he tasted in the language of memory ambered wines, dying fallings of sweet airs, the proud pavan: and saw with the eyes of memory kind gentlewomen in Covent Garden wooing from their balconies with sucking mouths and the poxfouled wenches of the taverns and young wives that, gaily yielding to their ravishers, clipped and clipped again.

The images he had summoned gave him no pleasure. They were secret and enflaming but her image was not entangled by them. That was not the way to think of her. It was not even the way in which he thought of her. Could his mind then not trust itself? Old phrases, sweet only with a disinterred sweetness like the figseeds Cranly rooted out of his gleaming teeth.

It was not thought nor vision though he knew vaguely that her figure was passing homeward through the city. Vaguely first and then more sharply he smelt her body. A conscious unrest seethed in his blood. Yes, it was her body he smelt: a wild and languid smell: the tepid limbs over which his music had flowed desirously and the secret soft linen upon which her flesh distilled odour and a dew.

A louse crawled over the nape of his neck and, putting his thumb and forefinger deftly beneath his loose collar, he caught it. He rolled its body, tender yet brittle as a grain of rice, between thumb and finger for an instant before he let it fall from him and wondered would it live or die. There came to his mind a curious phrase from Cornelius a Lapide which said that the lice born of human sweat were not created by God with the other animals on the sixth day. But the tickling of the skin of his neck made his mind raw and red. The life of his body, illclad, illfed, louseeaten, made him close his eyelids in a sudden spasm of despair: and in the darkness he saw the brittle bright bodies of lice falling from the air and turning often as they fell. Yes; and it was not darkness that fell from the air. It was brightness.

Brightness falls from the air.

He had not even remembered rightly Nash's line. All the images it had awakened were false. His mind bred vermin. His thoughts were lice born of the sweat of sloth.

He came back quickly along the colonnade towards the group of students. Well then, let her go and be damned to her. She could love some clean athlete who washed himself every morning to the waist and had black hair on his chest. Let her.

Cranly had taken another dried fig from the supply in his pocket and was eating it slowly and noisily. Temple sat on the pediment of a pillar, leaning back, his cap pulled down on his sleepy eyes. A squat young man came out of the porch, a leather portfolio tucked under his armpit. He marched towards the group, striking the flags with the heels of his boots and with the ferule of his heavy umbrella. Then, raising the umbrella in salute, he said to all:

—Good evening, sirs.

He struck the flags again and tittered while his head trembled with a slight nervous movement. The tall consumptive student and Dixon and O'Keeffe were speaking in Irish and did not answer him. Then, turning to Cranly, he said:

—Good evening, particularly to you.

He moved the umbrella in indication and tittered again. Cranly, who was still chewing the fig, answered with loud movements of his jaws.

—Good? Yes. It is a good evening.

The squat student looked at him seriously and shook his umbrella gently and reprovingly.

—I can see, he said, that you are about to make obvious remarks.

—Um, Cranly answered, holding out what remained of the halfchewed fig and jerking it towards the squat student's mouth in sign that he should eat.

The squat student did not eat it but, indulging his special humour, said gravely, still tittering and prodding his phrase with his umbrella:

—Do you intend that . . .

He broke off, pointed bluntly to the munched pulp of the fig and said loudly:

—I allude to that.

—Um, Cranly said as before.

—Do you intend that now, the squat student said, as *ipso facto* or, let us say, as so to speak?

Dixon turned aside from his group, saying:

—Goggins was waiting for you, Glynn. He has gone round to the Adelphi to look for you and Moynihan. What have you there? he asked, tapping the portfolio under Glynn's arm.

—Examination papers, Glynn answered. I give them monthly examinations to see that they are profiting by my tuition.

He also tapped the portfolio and coughed gently and smiled.

—Tuition! said Cranly rudely. I suppose you mean the barefooted children that are taught by a bloody ape like you. God help them!

He bit off the rest of the fig and flung away the butt.

—I suffer little children to come unto me, Glynn said amiably.

—A bloody ape, Cranly repeated with emphasis, and a blasphemous bloody ape!

Temple stood up and, pushing past Cranly, addressed Glynn:

—That phrase you said now, he said, is from the new testament about suffer the children to come to me.

—Go to sleep again, Temple, said O'Keeffe.

—Very well, then, Temple continued, still addressing

Glynn, and if Jesus suffered the children to come why does the church send them all to hell if they die unbaptised? Why is that?

—Were you baptised yourself, Temple? the consumptive student asked.

—But why are they sent to hell if Jesus said they were all to come? Temple said, his eyes searching in Glynn's eyes.

Glynn coughed and said gently, holding back with difficulty the nervous titter in his voice and moving his umbrella at every word:

—And, as you remark, if it is thus I ask emphatically whence comes this thusness.

—Because the church is cruel like all old sinners, Temple said.

—Are you quite orthodox on that point, Temple? Dixon said suavely.

—Saint Augustine says that about unbaptised children going to hell, Temple answered, because he was a cruel old sinner too.

—I bow to you, Dixon said, but I had the impression that limbo existed for such cases.

—Don't argue with him, Dixon, Cranly said brutally. Don't talk to him or look at him. Lead him home with a sugan the way you'd lead a bleating goat.

—Limbo! Temple cried. That's a fine invention too. Like hell.

—But with the unpleasantness left out, Dixon said.

He turned smiling to the others and said:

—I think I am voicing the opinions of all present in saying so much.

—You are, Glynn said in a firm tone. On that point Ireland is united.

He struck the ferule of his umbrella on the stone floor of the colonnade.

—Hell, Temple said. I can respect that invention of the grey spouse of Satan. Hell is Roman, like the walls of the Romans, strong and ugly. But what is limbo?

—Put him back into the perambulator, Cranly, O'Keeffe called out.

Cranly made a swift step towards Temple, halted, stamping his foot, crying as if to a fowl:

—Hoosh!

Temple moved away nimbly.

—Do you know what limbo is? he cried. Do you know what we call a notion like that in Roscommon?

—Hoosh! Blast you! Cranly cried, clapping his hands.

—Neither my arse nor my elbow! Temple cried out scornfully. And that's what I call limbo.

—Give us that stick here, Cranly said.

He snatched the ashplant roughly from Stephen's hand and sprang down the steps: but Temple, hearing him move in pursuit, fled through the dusk like a wild creature, nimble and fleetfooted. Cranly's heavy boots were heard loudly charging across the quadrangle and then returning heavily, foiled and spurning the gravel at each step.

His step was angry and with an angry abrupt gesture he thrust the stick back into Stephen's hand. Stephen felt that his anger had another cause but, feigning patience, touched his arm slightly and said quietly:

—Cranly, I told you I wanted to speak to you. Come away.

Cranly looked at him for a few moments and asked:

—Now?

—Yes, now, Stephen said. We can't speak here. Come away.

They crossed the quadrangle together without speaking. The birdcall from *Siegfried* whistled softly followed them from the steps of the porch. Cranly turned: and Dixon, who had whistled, called out:

—Where are you fellows off to? What about that game, Cranly?

They parleyed in shouts across the still air about a game of billiards to be played in the Adelphi hotel. Stephen walked on alone and out into the quiet of Kildare Street. Opposite Maple's hotel he stood to wait, patient again. The name of the hotel, a colourless polished wood, and its colourless quiet front stung him like a glance of polite disdain. He stared angrily back at the softly lit drawingroom of the hotel in which he imagined the sleek lives of the patricians of Ireland housed in calm. They thought of army commissions and land agents: peasants greeted them along the roads in the country: they knew the names of certain French dishes and gave orders to jarvies in highpitched provincial voices which pierced through their skintight accents.

How could he hit their conscience or how cast his shadow over the imaginations of their daughters, before their squires begat upon them, that they might breed a race less ignoble than their own? And under the deepened dusk he felt the thoughts and desires of the race to which he belonged flitting like bats, across the dark country lanes, under trees by the edges of streams and near the poolmottled bogs. A woman had waited in the doorway as Davin had passed by at night and, offering him a cup of milk, had all but wooed him to her bed; for Davin had the mild eyes of one who could be secret. But him no woman's eyes had wooed.

His arm was taken in a strong grip and Cranly's voice said:

—Let us eke go.

They walked southward in silence. Then Cranly said:

—That blithering idiot Temple! I swear to Moses, do you know, that I'll be the death of that fellow one time.

But his voice was no longer angry and Stephen wondered was he thinking of her greeting to him under the porch.

They turned to the left and walked on as before. When they had gone on so for some time Stephen said:

—Cranly, I had an unpleasant quarrel this evening.

—With your people? Cranly asked.

—With my mother.

—About religion?

—Yes, Stephen answered.

After a pause Cranly asked:

—What age is your mother?

—Not old, Stephen said. She wishes me to make my easter duty.

—And will you?

—I will not, Stephen said.

—Why not? Cranly said.

—I will not serve, answered Stephen.

—That remark was made before, Cranly said calmly.

—It is made behind now, said Stephen hotly.

Cranly pressed Stephen's arm, saying:

—Go easy, my dear man. You're an excitable bloody man, do you know.

He laughed nervously as he spoke and, looking up into Stephen's face with moved and friendly eyes, said:

—Do you know that you are an excitable man?

—I daresay I am, said Stephen, laughing also.

Their minds, lately estranged, seemed suddenly to have been drawn closer, one to the other.

—Do you believe in the eucharist? Cranly asked.

—I do not, Stephen said.

—Do you disbelieve then?

—I neither believe in it nor disbelieve in it, Stephen answered.

—Many persons have doubts, even religious persons, yet they overcome them or put them aside, Cranly said. Are your doubts on that point too strong?

—I do not wish to overcome them, Stephen answered.

Cranly, embarrassed for a moment, took another fig from his pocket and was about to eat it when Stephen said:

—Don't, please. You cannot discuss this question with your mouth full of chewed fig.

Cranly examined the fig by the light of a lamp under which he halted. Then he smelt it with both nostrils, bit a tiny piece, spat it out and threw the fig rudely into the gutter. Addressing it as it lay, he said:

—Depart from me, ye cursed, into everlasting fire!

Taking Stephen's arm, he went on again and said:

—Do you not fear that those words may be spoken to you on the day of judgment?

—What is offered me on the other hand? Stephen asked. An eternity of bliss in the company of the dean of studies?

—Remember, Cranly said, that he would be glorified.

—Ay, Stephen said somewhat bitterly, bright, agile, impassible and, above all, subtle.

—It is a curious thing, do you know, Cranly said dispassionately, how your mind is supersaturated with the religion in which you say you disbelieve. Did you believe in it when you were at school? I bet you did.

—I did, Stephen answered.

—And were you happier then? Cranly asked softly. Happier than you are now, for instance?

—Often happy, Stephen said, and often unhappy. I was someone else then.

—How someone else? What do you mean by that statement?

—I mean, said Stephen, that I was not myself as I am now, as I had to become.

—Not as you are now, not as you had to become, Cranly repeated. Let me ask you a question. Do you love your mother?

Stephen shook his head slowly.

—I don't know what your words mean, he said simply.

—Have you never loved anyone? Cranly asked.

—Do you mean women?

—I am not speaking of that, Cranly said in a colder tone. I ask you if you ever felt love towards anyone or anything.

Stephen walked on beside his friend, staring gloomily at the footpath.

—I tried to love God, he said at length. It seems now I failed. It is very difficult. I tried to unite my will with the will of God instant by instant. In that I did not always fail. I could perhaps do that still . . .

Cranly cut him short by asking:

—Has your mother had a happy life?

—How do I know? Stephen said.

—How many children had she?

—Nine or ten, Stephen answered. Some died.

—Was your father. . . . Cranly interrupted himself for an instant: and then said: I don't want to pry into your family affairs. But was your father what is called well-to-do? I mean when you were growing up?

—Yes, Stephen said.

—What was he? Cranly asked after a pause.

Stephen began to enumerate glibly his father's attributes.

—A medical student, an oarsman, a tenor, an amateur actor, a shouting politician, a small landlord, a small investor, a drinker, a good fellow, a storyteller, somebody's secretary, something in a distillery, a taxgatherer, a bankrupt and at present a praiser of his own past.

Cranly laughed, tightening his grip on Stephen's arm, and said:

—The distillery is damn good.

—Is there anything else you want to know? Stephen asked.

—Are you in good circumstances at present?

—Do I look it? Stephen asked bluntly.

—So then, Cranly went on musingly, you were born in the lap of luxury.

He used the phrase broadly and loudly as he often used technical expressions as if he wished his hearer to understand that they were used by him without conviction.

—Your mother must have gone through a good deal of suffering, he said then. Would you not try to save her from suffering more even if . . . or would you?

—If I could, Stephen said. That would cost me very little.

—Then do so, Cranly said. Do as she wishes you to do. What is it for you? You disbelieve in it. It is a form: nothing else. And you will set her mind at rest.

He ceased and, as Stephen did not reply, remained silent. Then, as if giving utterance to the process of his own thought, he said:

—Whatever else is unsure in this stinking dunghill of a

world a mother's love is not. Your mother brings you into the world, carries you first in her body. What do we know about what she feels? But whatever she feels, it, at least, must be real. It must be. What are our ideas or ambitions? Play. Ideas! Why, that bloody bleating goat Temple has ideas. MacCann has ideas too. Every jackass going the roads thinks he has ideas.

Stephen, who had been listening to the unspoken speech behind the words, said with assumed carelessness:

—Pascal, if I remember rightly, would not suffer his mother to kiss him as he feared the contact of her sex.

—Pascal was a pig, said Cranly.

—Aloysius Gonzaga, I think, was of the same mind, Stephen said.

—And he was another pig then, said Cranly.

—The church calls him a saint, Stephen objected.

—I don't care a flaming damn what anyone calls him, Cranly said rudely and flatly. I call him a pig.

Stephen, preparing the words neatly in his mind, continued:

—Jesus, too, seems to have treated his mother with scant courtesy in public but Suarez, a jesuit theologian and Spanish gentleman, has apologised for him.

—Did the idea ever occur to you, Cranly asked, that Jesus was not what he pretended to be?

—The first person to whom that idea occurred, Stephen answered, was Jesus himself.

—I mean, Cranly said, hardening in his speech, did the idea ever occur to you that he was himself a conscious hypocrite, what he called the jews of his time, a whited sepulchre? Or, to put it more plainly, that he was a blackguard?

—That idea never occurred to me, Stephen answered. But I am curious to know are you trying to make a convert of me or a pervert of yourself?

He turned towards his friend's face and saw there a raw smile which some force of will strove to make finely significant.

Cranly asked suddenly in a plain sensible tone:

—Tell me the truth. Were you at all shocked by what I said?

—Somewhat, Stephen said.

—And why were you shocked, Cranly pressed on in the same tone, if you feel sure that our religion is false and that Jesus was not the son of God?

—I am not at all sure of it, Stephen said. He is more like a son of God than a son of Mary.

—And is that why you will not communicate, Cranly asked, because you are not sure of that too, because you feel that the host too may be the body and blood of the son of God and not a wafer of bread? And because you fear that it may be?

—Yes, Stephen said quietly. I feel that and I also fear it.

—I see, Cranly said.

Stephen, struck by his tone of closure, reopened the discussion at once by saying:

—I fear many things: dogs, horses, firearms, the sea, thunderstorms, machinery, the country roads at night.

—But why do you fear a bit of bread?

—I imagine, Stephen said, that there is a malevolent reality behind those things I say I fear.

—Do you fear then, Cranly asked, that the God of the Roman catholics would strike you dead and damn you if you made a sacrilegious communion?

—The God of the Roman catholics could do that now, Stephen said. I fear more than that the chemical action which would be set up in my soul by a false homage to a symbol behind which are massed twenty centuries of authority and veneration.

—Would you, Cranly asked, in extreme danger commit that particular sacrilege? For instance, if you lived in the penal days?

—I cannot answer for the past, Stephen replied. Possibly not.

—Then, said Cranly, you do not intend to become a protestant?

—I said that I had lost the faith, Stephen answered, but not that I had lost selfrespect. What kind of liberation would that be to forsake an absurdity which is logical and coherent and to embrace one which is illogical and incoherent?

They had walked on towards the township of Pembroke and now, as they went on slowly along the avenues, the trees and the scattered lights in the villas soothed their minds. The air of wealth and repose diffused about them seemed to comfort their neediness. Behind a hedge of laurel a light glimmered in the window of a kitchen and the voice of a servant was heard singing as she sharpened knives. She sang, in short broken bars, *Rosie O'Grady*.

Cranly stopped to listen, saying:

—*Mulier cantat.*

The soft beauty of the Latin word touched with an enchanting touch the dark of the evening, with a touch fainter and more persuading than the touch of music or of a woman's hand. The strife of their minds was quelled. The figure of woman as she appears in the liturgy of the church passed silently through the darkness: a whiterobed figure, small and slender as a boy and with a falling girdle. Her voice, frail and high as a boy's, was heard intoning from a distant choir the first words of a woman which pierce the gloom and clamour of the first chanting of the passion:

—*Et tu cum Jesu Galilæo eras.*

And all hearts were touched and turned to her voice, shining like a young star, shining clearer as the voice intoned the proparoxyton and more faintly as the cadence died.

The singing ceased. They went on together, Cranly repeating in strongly stressed rhythm the end of the refrain:

> *And when we are married,*
> *O, how happy we'll be*
> *For I love sweet Rosie O'Grady*
> *And Rosie O'Grady loves me.*

—There's real poetry for you, he said. There's real love.

He glanced sideways at Stephen with a strange smile and said:

—Do you consider that poetry? Or do you know what the words mean?

—I want to see Rosie first, said Stephen.

—She's easy to find, Cranly said.

His hat had come down on his forehead. He shoved it back: and in the shadow of the trees Stephen saw his pale face, framed by the dark, and his large dark eyes. Yes. His face was handsome: and his body was strong and hard. He had spoken of a mother's love. He felt then the sufferings of women, the weaknesses of their bodies and souls: and would shield them with a strong and resolute arm and bow his mind to them.

Away then: it is time to go. A voice spoke softly to Stephen's lonely heart, bidding him go and telling him that his friendship was coming to an end. Yes; he would go. He could not strive against another. He knew his part.

—Probably I shall go away, he said.

—Where? Cranly asked.

—Where I can, Stephen said.

—Yes, Cranly said. It might be difficult for you to live here now. But is it that that makes you go?

—I have to go, Stephen answered.

—Because, Cranly continued, you need not look upon yourself as driven away if you do not wish to go or as a heretic or an outlaw. There are many good believers who think as you do. Would that surprise you? The church is not the stone building nor even the clergy and their dogmas. It is the whole mass of those born into it. I don't know what you wish to do in life. Is it what you told me the night we were standing outside Harcourt Street station?

—Yes, Stephen said, smiling in spite of himself at Cranly's way of remembering thoughts in connection with places. The night you spent half an hour wrangling with Doherty about the shortest way from Sallygap to Larras.

—Pothead! Cranly said with calm contempt. What does he know about the way from Sallygap to Larras? Or what does he know about anything for that matter? And the big slobbering washingpot head of him!

He broke out into a loud long laugh.

—Well? Stephen said. Do you remember the rest?

—What you said, is it? Cranly asked. Yes, I remember it. To discover the mode of life or of art whereby your spirit could express itself in unfettered freedom.

Stephen raised his hat in acknowledgment.

—Freedom! Cranly repeated. But you are not free enough yet to commit a sacrilege. Tell me, would you rob?

—I would beg first, Stephen said.

—And if you got nothing, would you rob?

—You wish me to say, Stephen answered, that the rights of property are provisional and that in certain circumstances it is not unlawful to rob. Everyone would act in that belief. So I will not make you that answer. Apply to the jesuit theologian Juan Mariana de Talavera who will also explain to you in what circumstances you may lawfully kill your king and whether you had better hand him his poison in a goblet or smear it for him upon his robe or his saddlebow. Ask me rather would I suffer others to rob me or, if they did, would I call down upon them what I believe is called the chastisement of the secular arm?

—And would you?

—I think, Stephen said, it would pain me as much to do so as to be robbed.

—I see, Cranly said.

He produced his match and began to clean the crevice between two teeth. Then he said carelessly:

—Tell me, for example, would you deflower a virgin?

—Excuse me, Stephen said politely, is that not the ambition of most young gentlemen?

—What then is your point of view? Cranly asked.

His last phrase, soursmelling as the smoke of charcoal and disheartening, excited Stephen's brain, over which its fumes seemed to brood.

—Look here, Cranly, he said. You have asked me what I would do and what I would not do. I will tell you what I will do and what I will not do. I will not serve that in which I no longer believe whether it call itself my home, my fatherland or my church: and I will try to express myself in some mode of life or art as freely as I can and as wholly as I can, using for my defence the only arms I allow myself to use—silence, exile, and cunning.

Cranly seized his arm and steered him round so as to head back towards Leeson Park. He laughed almost slily and pressed Stephen's arm with an elder's affection.

—Cunning indeed! he said. Is it you? You poor poet, you!

—And you made me confess to you, Stephen said, thrilled by his touch, as I have confessed to you so many other things, have I not?

—Yes, my child, Cranly said, still gaily.

—You made me confess the fears that I have. But I will tell you also what I do not fear. I do not fear to be alone or to be spurned for another or to leave whatever I have to leave. And I am not afraid to make a mistake, even a great mistake, a lifelong mistake and perhaps as long as eternity too.

Cranly, now grave again, slowed his pace and said:

—Alone, quite alone. You have no fear of that. And you know what that word means? Not only to be separate from all others but to have not even one friend.

—I will take the risk, said Stephen.

—And not to have any one person, Cranly said, who would be more than a friend, more even than the noblest and truest friend a man ever had.

His words seemed to have struck some deep chord in his own nature. Had he spoken of himself, of himself as he was or wished to be? Stephen watched his face for some moments in silence. A cold sadness was there. He had spoken of himself, of his own loneliness which he feared.

—Of whom are you speaking? Stephen asked at length.

Cranly did not answer.

*   *   *

20 *March:* Long talk with Cranly on the subject of my revolt. He had his grand manner on. I supple and suave. Attacked me on the score of love for one's mother. Tried to

imagine his mother: cannot. Told me once, in a moment of thoughtlessness, his father was sixtyone when he was born. Can see him. Strong farmer type. Pepper and salt suit. Square feet. Unkempt grizzled beard. Probably attends coursing matches. Pays his dues regularly but not plentifully to Father Dwyer of Larras. Sometimes talks to girls after nightfall. But his mother? Very young or very old? Hardly the first. If so, Cranly would not have spoken as he did. Old then. Probably, and neglected. Hence Cranly's despair of soul: the child of exhausted loins.

21 *March, morning:* Thought this in bed last night but was too lazy and free to add it. Free, yes. The exhausted loins are those of Elisabeth and Zachary. Then he is the precursor. Item: he eats chiefly belly bacon and dried figs. Read locusts and wild honey. Also, when thinking of him, saw always a stern severed head or deathmask as if outlined on a grey curtain or veronica. Decollation they call it in the fold. Puzzled for the moment by saint John at the Latin gate. What do I see? A decollated precursor trying to pick the lock.

21 *March, night:* Free. Soulfree and fancyfree. Let the dead bury the dead. Ay. And let the dead marry the dead.

22 *March:* In company with Lynch followed a sizable hospital nurse. Lynch's idea. Dislike it. Two lean hungry greyhounds walking after a heifer.

23 *March:* Have not seen her since that night. Unwell? Sits at the fire perhaps with mamma's shawl on her shoulders. But not peevish. A nice bowl of gruel? Won't you now?

24 *March:* Began with a discussion with my mother. Subject: B.V.M. Handicapped by my sex and youth. To escape held up relations between Jesus and Papa against those between Mary and her son. Said religion was not a lying-in hospital. Mother indulgent. Said I have a queer mind and have read too much. Not true. Have read little and understood less. Then she said I would come back to faith because I had a restless mind. This means to leave church by backdoor of sin and reenter through the skylight of repentance. Cannot repent. Told her so and asked for sixpence. Got threepence.

Then went to college. Other wrangle with little roundhead rogue'seye Ghezzi. This time about Bruno the Nolan. Began in Italian and ended in pidgin English. He said Bruno was a terrible heretic. I said he was terribly burned. He agreed to this with some sorrow. Then gave me recipe for what he calls *risotto alla bergamasca*. When he pronounces a soft *o* he protrudes his full carnal lips as if he kissed the vowel. Has he? And could he repent? Yes, he could: and cry two round rogue's tears, one from each eye.

Crossing Stephen's, that is, my green, remembered that his countrymen and not mine had invented what Cranly the other night called our religion. A quartet of them, soldiers of the ninetyseventh infantry regiment, sat at the foot of the cross and tossed up dice for the overcoat of the crucified.

Went to library. Tried to read three reviews. Useless. She is not out yet. Am I alarmed? About what? That she will never be out again.

Blake wrote:

> *I wonder if William Bond will die*
> *For assuredly he is very ill.*

Alas, poor William!

I was once at a diorama in Rotunda. At the end were pictures of big nobs. Among them William Ewart Gladstone, just then dead. Orchestra played *O, Willie, we have missed you*.

A race of clodhoppers!

25 *March, morning:* A troubled night of dreams. Want to get them off my chest.

A long curving gallery. From the floor ascend pillars of dark vapours. It is peopled by the images of fabulous kings, set in stone. Their hands are folded upon their knees in token of weariness and their eyes are darkened for the errors of men go up before them for ever as dark vapours.

Strange figures advance from a cave. They are not as tall as men. One does not seem to stand quite apart from another. Their faces are phosphorescent, with darker streaks. They peer at me and their eyes seem to ask me something. They do not speak.

30 *March:* This evening Cranly was in the porch of the library, proposing a problem to Dixon and her brother. A mother let her child fall into the Nile. Still harping on the mother. A crocodile seized the child. Mother asked it back. Crocodile said all right if she told him what he was going to do with the child, eat it or not eat it.

This mentality, Lepidus would say, is indeed bred out of your mud by the operation of your sun.

And mine? Is it not too? Then into Nilemud with it!

1 *April:* Disapprove of this last phrase.

2 *April:* Saw her drinking tea and eating cakes in Johnston, Mooney and O'Brien's. Rather, lynxeyed Lynch saw her as we passed. He tells me Cranly was invited there by brother. Did he bring his crocodile? Is he the shining light now? Well, I discovered him. I protest I did. Shining quietly behind a bushel of Wicklow bran.

3 *April:* Met Davin at the cigar shop opposite Findlater's church. He was in a black sweater and had a hurleystick. Asked me was it true I was going away and why. Told him the shortest way to Tara was *via* Holyhead. Just then my father came up. Introduction. Father, polite and observant. Asked Davin if he might offer him some refreshment. Davin could not, was going to a meeting. When we came away father told me he had a good honest eye. Asked me why I did not join a rowingclub. I pretended to think it over. Told me then how he broke Pennyfeather's heart. Wants me to read law. Says I was cut out for that. More mud, more crocodiles.

5 *April:* Wild spring. Scudding clouds. O life! Dark stream of swirling bogwater on which appletrees have cast down their delicate flowers. Eyes of girls among the leaves. Girls demure and romping. All fair or auburn: no dark ones. They blush better. Houp-la!

6 *April:* Certainly she remembers the past. Lynch says all women do. Then she remembers the time of her childhood—

and mine if I was ever a child. The past is consumed in the present and the present is living only because it brings forth the future. Statues of women, if Lynch be right, should always be fully draped, one hand of the woman feeling regretfully her own hinder parts.

6 *April, later:* Michael Robartes remembers forgotten beauty and, when his arms wrap her round, he presses in his arms the loveliness which has long faded from the world. Not this. Not at all. I desire to press in my arms the loveliness which has not yet come into the world.

10 *April:* Faintly, under the heavy night, through the silence of the city which has turned from dreams to dreamless sleep as a weary lover whom no caresses move, the sound of hoofs upon the road. Not so faintly now as they come near the bridge: and in a moment as they pass the darkened windows the silence is cloven by alarm as by an arrow. They are heard now far away, hoofs that shine amid the heavy night as gems, hurrying beyond the sleeping fields to what journey's end—what heart?—bearing what tidings?

11 *April:* Read what I wrote last night. Vague words for a vague emotion. Would she like it? I think so. Then I should have to like it also.

13 *April:* That tundish has been on my mind for a long time. I looked it up and find it English and good old blunt English too. Damn the dean of studies and his funnel! What did he come here for to teach us his own language or to learn it from us? Damn him one way or the other!

14 *April:* John Alphonsus Mulrennan has just returned from the west of Ireland. (European and Asiatic papers please copy.) He told us he met an old man there in a mountain cabin. Old man had red eyes and short pipe. Old man spoke Irish. Mulrennan spoke Irish. Then old man and Mulrennan spoke English. Mulrennan spoke to him about universe and stars. Old man sat, listened, smoked, spat. Then said:

—Ah, there must be terrible queer creatures at the latter end of the world.

I fear him. I fear his redrimmed horny eyes. It is with him I must struggle all through this night till day come, till he or I lie dead, gripping him by the sinewy throat till . . . Till what? Till he yield to me? No. I mean him no harm.

15 *April:* Met her today pointblank in Grafton Street. The crowd brought us together. We both stopped. She asked me why I never came, said she had heard all sorts of stories about me. This was only to gain time. Asked me, was I writing poems? About whom? I asked her. This confused her more and I felt sorry and mean. Turned off that valve at once and opened the spiritual-heroic refrigerating apparatus, invented and patented in all countries by Dante Alighieri. Talked rapidly of myself and my plans. In the midst of it unluckily I made a sudden gesture of a revolutionary nature. I must have looked like a fellow throwing a handful of peas into the air. People began to look at us. She shook hands a moment after and, in going away, said she hoped I would do what I said.

Now I call that friendly, don't you?

Yes, I liked her today. A little or much? Don't know. I liked her and it seems a new feeling to me. Then, in that case, all the rest, all that I thought I thought and all that I felt I felt, all the rest before now, in fact . . . O, give it up, old chap! Sleep it off!

16 *April:* Away! Away!

The spell of arms and voices: the white arms of roads, their promise of close embraces and the black arms of tall ships that stand against the moon, their tale of distant nations. They are held out to say: We are alone. Come. And the voices say with them: We are your kinsmen. And the air is thick with their company as they call to me, their kinsman, making ready to go, shaking the wings of their exultant and terrible youth.

26 *April:* Mother is putting my new secondhand clothes in order. She prays now, she says, that I may learn in my own life and away from home and friends what the heart is and what it feels. Amen. So be it. Welcome, O life! I go to encoun-

ter for the millionth time the reality of experience and to forge in the smithy of my soul the uncreated conscience of my race.

27 *April:* Old father, old artificer, stand me now and ever in good stead.

Dublin 1904
Trieste 1914

A NOTE ON THE TEXT

The preceding is the 1964 Viking Compass edition text, with pagination unchanged. It was prepared by comparing Joyce's final fair-copy manuscript, in his own handwriting, now in the National Library of Ireland, with all the texts published in England and America during Joyce's lifetime, and with lists of corrections and changes noted by Joyce, some of which were never made in any of the published versions. An extensive list of possible corrections in the current Viking Compass edition was then prepared. Richard Ellmann, Joyce's biographer and editor of his letters, was asked to act as arbiter, and reviewed the final selection. The text is discussed in detail in Chester G. Anderson's "The Text of James Joyce's *Portrait of the Artist as a Young Man*" (see Bibliography).

This 1964 edition was set as nearly as possible page-for-page with the old text, so that references based on the old would not differ by more than one page.

C.G.A.

II

❖◇

Related Texts by Joyce

All footnotes in Parts II and III of this volume are mine unless they carry the author's initials. Omissions, of course, are indicated by ellipses. Abbreviations used in the references to Joyce texts are explained in the Explanatory Notes, p. 481. All material reprinted in this edition is cited in full in the Bibliography.

C.G.A.

❖◈❖

A PORTRAIT OF THE ARTIST

Joyce first attempted to draw his self-portrait on January 7, 1904, four months after the death of his mother. On that day, commissioned by the editors of a new Dublin magazine called *Dana*, he wrote the following narrative essay in a notebook belonging to his sister Mabel and called it "A Portrait of the Artist." In it he incorporated a few of his epiphanies (see p. 267), broadly sketched the story he wished to tell, and gave one of his clearest statements of the intention which remained constant for later versions of the *Portrait*—the presentation of the past as "a fluid succession of presents" in a prose supple enough to follow "the curve of an emotion."

Much of the essay "Portrait" was quarried by Joyce when he rewrote it as *Stephen Hero*. As he re-used lines, he sometimes crossed them out in the manuscript. These are printed here between the signs « ».

The features of infancy are not commonly reproduced in the adolescent portrait for, so capricious are we, that we cannot or will not conceive the past in any other than its iron, memorial aspect. Yet the past assuredly implies a fluid succession of presents, the development of an entity of which our actual

The essay has been edited from the manuscript which is in the Lockwood Memorial Library of the State University of New York at Buffalo. Because the manuscript has a few lacunae caused by the flaking of its pages, it has been supplemented by the typed copy which Stanislaus Joyce had made in Trieste in 1928, which is now in the Mennen Collection at the Cornell University Library. The manuscript was first printed by Richard M. Kain and Robert Scholes in the *Yale Review*, XLIX (Spring 1960), 355-369, and reprinted by them in *The Workshop of Daedalus*, pp. 60-68. Used by permission of The Society of Authors.

present is a phase only. Our world, again, recognises its acquaintance chiefly by the characters of beard and inches and is, for the most part, estranged from those of its members who seek through some art, by some process of the mind as yet untabulated, to liberate from the personalised lumps of matter that which is their individuating rhythm, the first or formal relation of their parts.[1] But for such as these a portrait is not an identificative paper but rather the curve of an emotion.

Use of reason is by popular judgment antedated by some seven years and so it is not easy [to?—Ms torn] set down the exact age at which the natural sensibility of the subject of this portrait awoke to the ideas of eternal damnation, the necessity of penitence and the efficacy of prayer. «His training had early developed a very lively sense of spiritual obligations at the expense of what is called 'common sense.' He ran through his measure like a spendthrift saint, astonishing many by ejaculatory fervours, offending many by airs of the cloister. One day in a wood near Malahide a labourer had marvelled to see a boy of fifteen praying in an ecstasy of Oriental posture. It was indeed a long time before this boy understood the nature of the most marketable goodness which makes it possible to give comfortable assent to propositions without ordering one's life in accordance with them. The digestive value of religion he never appreciated and he chose, as more fitting his case those poorer humbler orders in which a confessor did not seem anxious to reveal himself, in theory at least, a man of the world. In spite, however, of continued shocks, which drove him from breathless flights of zeal shamefully inwards, he was still soothed by devotional exercises when he entered the University.

About this period the enigma of a manner was put up at all corners to protect the crisis. He was quick enough now to see that he must disentangle his affairs in secrecy and reserve had ever been a light penance. His reluctance to

---

[1] Cf. *P*, 206.26.

debate scandal, to seem curious of others, aided him in his real indictment and was not without a satisfactory flavour of the heroic. It was part of that ineradicable egoism which he was afterwards to call redeemer that he imagined converging to him the deeds and thoughts of the microcosm. Is the mind of boyhood medieval that it is so divining of intrigue? Field sports (or their correspondent in the world of mentality) are perhaps the most effective cure, but for the fantastic idealist, eluding the grunting booted apparition with a bound, the mimic hunt was no less ludicrous than unequal in a ground chosen to his disadvantage. But behind the rapidly indurating shield the sensitive answered. Let the pack of enmities come tumbling and sniffing to the highlands after their game—there was his ground: and he flung them disdain from flashing antlers.» There was evident self-flattery in the image but a danger of complacence too. Wherefore, neglecting the wheezier bayings in that chorus which leagues of distance could make musical, he began loftily diagnosis of the younglings. His judgment was exquisite, deliberate, sharp; his sentence sculptural. «These young men saw in the sudden death of a dull French novelist[2] the hand of Emmanuel God with us; they admired Gladstone,[3] physical science and the tragedies of Shakespeare; and they believed in the adjustment of Catholic teaching to everyday needs, in the church diplomatic. In their relations among themselves and towards their superiors they displayed a nervous and (wherever there was question of authority) a very English liberalism.» He remarked the half-admiring, half-reproving demeanour of a class, implicitly pledged to abstinences towards «others among whom (the fame went) wild living was not unknown. Though the union of faith and fatherland was ever sacred in that world of easily inflammable enthusiasms a couplet from Davis,[4] accusing the least docile of tempers, never failed of its ap-

---

[2] Emile Zola (1840-1902).
[3] For a similar sarcasm about Gladstone, see *P*, 249.23.
[4] Thomas Davis (1814-1845). Irish patriot and patriotic poet.

plause and the memory of McManus[5] was hardly less revered than that of Cardinal Cullen.» [6] They had many reasons to respect authority; and even if «a student were forbidden to go to *Othello* ("There are some coarse expressions in it" he was told) what a little cross was that? Was it not rather an evidence of watchful care and interest, and were they not assured that in their future lives this care would continue, this interest be maintained? The exercise of authority might be sometimes (rarely) questionable, its intention never. Who, therefore, readier than these young men to acknowledge gratefully the sallies of some genial professor or the surliness of some door porter, who more solicitous to cherish in every way and to advance in person the honour of Alma Mater? For his part he was at the difficult age, dispossessed and necessitous, sensible of all that was ignoble in such manners who, in revery at least, had been acquainted with nobility. An earnest Jesuit had prescribed a clerkship in Guinness's and doubtless the clerk designate of a brewery would not have had scorn and pity only for an admirable community had it not been that he desired (in the language of the schoolmen) an arduous good. It was impossible that he should find solace in societies for the encouragement of thought among laymen or any other than bodily comfort in the warm sodality amid so many foolish or grotesque virginities.[7] Moreover, it was impossible that a temperament ever trembling towards its ecstasy should submit to acquiesce, that a soul should decree servitude for its portion over which the image of beauty had fallen as a mantle. One night in early spring, standing at the foot of the staircase in the library, he said to his friend "I have left the Church." » And as they walked home through

---

[5] Terence Bellew MacManus (1823-1861). See *P*, 38.27 and Explanatory Notes.

[6] Cardinal Paul Cullen (1803-1878). See *P*, 38.31 and Explanatory Notes.

[7] For Stephen as hypocritical prefect of the Sodality of the Blessed Virgin, see *P*, 104. Jesus' parable of the wise and foolish virgins is told in Matthew 25.

the streets arm-in-arm he told, in words that seemed an echo of their closing, how he had left it through the gates of Assisi.[8]

Extravagance followed. The simple history of the Poverello[9] was soon out of mind and he established himself in the maddest of companies. Joachim Abbas,[10] Bruno the Nolan,[11] Michael Sendivogius,[12] all the hierarchs of initiation cast their spells upon him. He descended among the hells of Swedenborg[13] and abased himself in the gloom of Saint John of the Cross.[14] His heaven was suddenly illuminated by a horde of stars, the signature of all nature, the soul remembering ancient days. Like an alchemist he bent upon his handiwork, bringing together the mysterious elements, separating the subtle from the gross.[15] For the artist the rhythms of phrase and period, the symbols of word and allusion, were paramount things.[16] And was it any wonder that out of this marvellous life, wherein he had annihilated and rebuilt experience, laboured and despaired, he came forth at last with a simple purpose—to reunite the children of the spirit, jealous and long-divided, to reunite them against fraud and principality. A thousand eternities were to be reaffirmed, divine knowledge was to be re-established. Alas for Fatuity! as easily might he have summoned a regiment of the winds. They pleaded their natural pieties—social limitations, inherited apathy of race,

---

[8] See *P*, 237ff.

[9] St. Francis of Assisi (1181-1226). See *P*, 219.37-220.03.

[10] Joachim Abbas (1145-1202). Joachim, abbot of Floris, a Franciscan mystic named a heresiarch by the Council of Arles in 1260.

[11] Giordano Bruno of Nola (1548?-1600), a Dominican humanist, scientist, and theologian, declared a heretic by the Inquisition and burned at the stake. Joyce mentions him frequently in his work, beginning with "The Day of Rabblement" (1902) and continuing through *FW* (1939). See *P*, 249.02.

[12] A Polish alchemist also known as Michael Sedziwoj (1556-1636).

[13] See *P*, 224-234 and 224.32 in Explanatory Notes.

[14] St. John of the Cross (1549-1591), a Spanish mystic and poet of the Carmelite order of friars.

[15] Cf. *P*, 221.14, "transmuting the daily bread of experience . . ."

[16] Cf. *P*, 166.32, 35.

an adoring mother, the Christian fable.[17] Their treasons were
venial only. Wherever the social monster permitted they
would hazard the extremes of heterodoxy, reasons of an
imaginative determinant in ethics, of anarchy (the folk), of
blue triangles, of the fish-gods, proclaiming in a fervent moment the necessity for action. His revenge was a phrase and
isolation. He lumped the emancipates together—Venomous
Butter—and set away from the sloppy neighborhood.

Isolation, he had once written, is the first principle of
artistic economy but traditional and individual revelations
were at that time pressing their claims and self-communion
had been but shyly welcomed. But in the intervals of friendships (for he had outridden three) he had known the sister-
hood of meditative hours and now the hope began to grow
up within him of finding among them that serene emotion,
that certitude, which among men he had not found. An
impulse had led him forth in the dark season to silent and
lonely places where the mists hung streamerwise among the
trees; and as he had passed there amid the subduing night, in
the secret fall of leaves, the fragrant rain, the mesh of vapours
moon-transpierced, he had imagined an admonition of the
frailty of all things.[18] In summer it had led him seaward.
Wandering over the arid grassy hills or along the strand,
avowedly in quest of shellfish, he had grown almost impatient
of the day. Waders, into whose childish or girlish hair, girlish
or childish dresses, the very wilfulness of the sea had entered
—even they had not fascinated. But as day had waned it had
been pleasant to watch the few last figures islanded in distant
pools; and as evening deepened, the grey glow above the sea
he had gone out, out among the shallow waters, the holy
joys of solitude uplifting him, singing passionately to the
tide.[19] Sceptically, cynically, mystically, he had sought for an

---

[17] Cf. Stephen's discussion of mother and Church with Cranly, *SH*, pp.
137-143, reprinted, p. 277 and *P*, 240-247, and 203.28.
[18] Cf. "the rainladen trees" and "fragrance falling from the wet
branches," *P*, 176.07, 10.
[19] Cf. *P*, 171-173.

absolute satisfaction and now little by little he began to be
conscious of the beauty of mortal conditions. He remembered
a sentence in Augustine—"It was manifested unto me that
those things be good which yet are corrupted; which neither
if they were supremely good, nor unless they were good could
be corrupted: for had they been supremely good they would
have been incorruptible but if they were not good there would
be nothing in them which could be corrupted." A philosophy
of reconcilement .... possible ..... as eve The ....
of the ..... at lef .... bor lit up with dolphin lights but
the lights in the chambers of the heart were unextinguished,
nay, burning as for espousal [Ms torn].

Dearest of mortals! In spite of tributary verses and of the
comedy of meetings here and in the foolish society of sleep
the fountain of being (it seemed) had been interfused. Years
before, in boyhood, «the energy of sin opening a world before him» he had been made aware of thee.[20] «The yellow
gaslamps arising in his troubled vision against an autumnal
sky, gleaming mysteriously there before that violet altar—
the groups gathered at the doorways arranged as for some
rite—the glimpses of revel and fantasmal mirth—the vague
face of some welcomer seeming to awaken from a slumber of
centuries under his gaze—the blind confusion (iniquity! iniquity!) suddenly overtaking him—in all the ardent adventure
of lust didst thou not even then communicate?»[21] Beneficent
one! (the shrewdness of love was in the title) thou camest
timely, as a witch to the agony of self devourer, an envoy
from the fair courts of life.[22] How could he thank thee for
that enrichment of soul by thee consummated? Mastery of art
had been achieved in irony; asceticism of intellect had been
a mood of indignant pride: but who had revealed him to himself but thou alone? In ways of tenderness, simple, intuitive
tenderness, thy love had made to arise in him the central

---

[20] Cf. *P*, 222-223.
[21] Cf. *P*, 100.15-26.
[22] Cf. *P*, 172.09-12.

torrents of life. Thou hadst put thine arms about him and, intimately prisoned as thou hadst been, in the soft stir of thy bosom, the raptures of silence, the murmured words, thy heart had spoken to his heart. Thy disposition could refine and direct his passion holding more beauty at the cunningest angle. Thou wert sacramental imprinting thine indelible mark, of very visible grace. A litany must honour thee: Lady of Apple Trees, Kind Wisdom, Sweet Flower of Dusk. In another phase it had been not uncommon to devise dinners in white and purple upon the actuality of stirabout but here, surely, is sturdy or delicate food to hand; no need for devising. His way (abrupt creature!) lies out now to the measurable world and the broad expanses of activity. The blood hurries to a galop [*sic*] in his veins; his nerves accumulate an electric force; he is footed with flame. A kiss: and they leap together, indivisible, upwards, radiant lips and eyes, their bodies sounding with the triumph of harps! Again, beloved! Again, thou bride! Again, ere life is ours!

In calmer mood the critic in him could not but remark a strange prelude to the new crowning era in a season of melancholy and unrest. He made up his tale of losses—a dispiriting tale enough even were there no comments. The air of false Christ was manifestly the mask of a physical decrepitude, itself the brand and sign of vulgar ardours; whence ingenuousness, forbearance, sweet amiability and the whole tribe of domestic virtues. Sadly mindful of the worst[,] the vision of his dead, the vision (far more pitiful) of congenital lives shuffling onwards between yawn and howl, starvelings in mind and body, visions of which came a temporary failure of his olden, sustained manner, darkly beset him.[23] The cloud of difficulties about him allowed only peeps of light; even his rhetoric proclaimed transition. He could convict himself at least of a natural inability to prove everything at once and certain random attempts suggested the need for regular campaigning. His faith increased. It emboldened him to say to a patron of the fine

[23] Cf. Stephen's views of his brothers and sisters, *P*, 162-164.

arts[24] 'What advance upon spiritual goods?' and to a capitalist[25] 'I need two thousand pounds for a project.' He had interpreted for orthodox Greek scholarship the living doctrine of the *Poetics*[26] and, out of the burning bushes of excess, had declaimed to a night-policeman on the true status of public women: but there was no budge of those mountains, no perilous cerebration. In a moment of frenzy he called for the elves. Many in our day, it would appear, cannot avoid a choice between sensitiveness and dulness; they recommend themselves by proofs of culture[27] to a like-minded minority or dominate the huger world as lean of meat. But he saw between camps his ground of vantage, opportunities for the mocking devil in an isle twice removed from the mainland, under joint government of their Intensities and their Bullockships. His Nego,[28] therefore, written amid a chorus of peddling Jews' gibberish and Gentile clamour, was drawn up valiantly while true believers prophesied fried atheism and was hurled against the obscene hells of our Holy Mother: but, that outburst over, it was urbanity in warfare. Perhaps his state would pension off old tyranny—a mercy no longer hopelessly remote—in virtue of that mature civilisation to which (let all allow) it had in some way contributed. Already the messages of citizens were flashed along the wires of the world, already the generous idea had emerged from a thirty years' war in Germany and was directing the councils of the Latins. To those multitudes not as yet in the wombs of humanity but surely engenderable there, he would give the word.[29] Man and woman, out of you comes the nation that is

---

[24] Perhaps Lady Augusta Gregory, Yeats's patron, whom Joyce asked for help before leaving Dublin for Paris in 1902 and again in 1904.

[25] Probably Thomas F. Kelly, an American millionaire living near Dublin, to whom Joyce applied unsuccessfully in December 1903 for an advance of £2000, with which he and Francis Skeffington ("MacCann") planned to start a literary newspaper.

[26] Cf. *P*, 204ff.

[27] Cf. *P*, 204.20.

[28] In Latin, literally "I deny"—the opposite of a creed or *credo* ("I believe").

[29] Cf. *P*, 238.10-13.

to come, the lightning of your masses in travail; the competitive order is employed against itself, the aristocracies are supplanted; and amid the general paralysis of an insane society, the confederate will issues in action.

Jas. A. Joyce
7/1/1904

EPIPHANIES

Joyce defines the epiphany in *Stephen Hero* as "a sudden spiritual manifestation, whether in the vulgarity of speech or of gesture or in a memorable phase of the mind itself. He believed that it was for the man of letters to record these epiphanies with extreme care, seeing that they themselves are the most delicate and evanescent of moments." (The entire passage is printed on p. 288, and the epiphany as a part of Joyce's technique in longer works is discussed by Irene Hendry Chayes, p. 358.)

The forty epiphanies which survive as independent works are printed and discussed in Robert Scholes and Richard M. Kain, *The Workshop of Daedalus* (Evanston, Ill.: Northwestern University Press, 1965), pp. 3-54. They include the earlier collection of the twenty-two epiphanies at the University of Buffalo which was made by O. A. Silverman in *Epiphanies* (Buffalo, N.Y.: University of Buffalo, 1956). The eleven printed below comprise all the epiphanies separately extant which are used in the *Portrait*, though the reader may detect others embedded there.

[Bray: in the parlour of the house
in Martello Terrace]

MR VANCE—(*comes in with a stick*) . . . O, you know, he'll have to apologise, Mrs Joyce.

MRS JOYCE—O yes . . . Do you hear that, Jim?

The manuscript of the first of these is in the Lockwood Memorial Library of the State University of New York at Buffalo. The manuscripts for the others are from the Mennen Collection at the Cornell University Library. Used by permission of The Society of Authors.

Mr Vance—Or else—if he doesn't the eagles'll come and pull
  out his eyes.
Mrs Joyce—O, but I'm sure he will apologise.
Joyce—(*under the table, to himself*)

> —Pull out his eyes,
> Apologise,
> Apologise,
> Pull out his eyes.
>
> Apologise,
> Pull out his eyes,
> Pull out his eyes,
> Apologise.[1]

The children who have stayed latest are getting on their things
to go home for the party is over. This is the last tram. The lank
brown horses know it and shake their bells to the clear night, in
admonition. The conductor talks to the driver; both nod often
in the green light of the lamp. There is nobody near[.] We
seem to listen, I on the upper step and she on the lower. She
comes up to my step many times and goes down again, between
our phrases, and once or twice remains beside me, forgetting to
go down, and then goes down. . . . . Let be; let be. . . . .
And now she does not urge her vanities,—her fine dress and
sash and long black stockings,—for now (wisdom of children)
we seem to know that this end will please us better than any
end we have laboured for.[2]

High up in the old, dark-windowed house: firelight in the narrow room: dusk outside. An old woman bustles about, making

---

[1] See *P*, 8. The bracketed material is Joyce's. The incident took place
between 1887 and 1891, but no doubt the epiphany was written in 1901
or 1902. See the discussion of it by Kenner, p. 420.
[2] See *SH*, pp. 67-68, reprinted, p. 274, and *P*, 69-70, 77, 82, and 222.

tea; she tells of the changes, her odd ways, and what the priest and the doctor said. . . . . I hear her words in the distance. I wander among the coals, among the ways of adventure. . . . . . Christ! What is in the doorway? . . . . . A skull—a monkey; a creature drawn hither to the fire, to the voices: a silly creature.

—Is that Mary Ellen?—

—No, Eliza, it's Jim—

—O. . . . . . O, goodnight, Jim—

—D'ye want anything, Eliza?—

—I thought it was Mary Ellen. . . . . I thought you were Mary Ellen, Jim—[3]

A small field of stiff weeds and thistles alive with confused forms, half-men, half-goats. Dragging their great tails they move hither and thither, aggressively. Their faces are lightly bearded, pointed and grey as indiarubber. A secret personal sin directs them, holding them now, as in reaction, to constant malevolence. One is clasping about his body a torn flannel jacket; another complains monotonously as his beard catches in the stiff weeds. They move about me, enclosing me, that old sin sharpening their eyes to cruelty, swishing through the fields in slow circles, thrusting upwards their terrific faces. Help! [4]

Her arm is laid for a moment on my knees and then withdrawn and her eyes have revealed her—secret, vigilant, an enclosed garden—in a moment. I remember a harmony of red and white that was made for one like her, telling her names and glories, bidding her arise, as for espousal, and come away, bidding her look forth, a spouse, from Amana and from the mountains of the leopards. And I remember that response whereto the per-

---

[3] See *P*, 67-68.
[4] See *P*, 137-138.

fect tenderness of the body and the soul with all its mystery have gone: Inter ubera mea commorabitur.[5]

The quick light shower is over but tarries, a cluster of diamonds, among the shrubs of the quadrangle where an exhalation arises from the black earth. In the colonnade are the girls, an April company. They are leaving shelter, with many a doubting glance, with the prattle of trim boots and the pretty rescue of petticoats, under umbrellas, a light armoury, upheld at cunning angles. They are returning to the convent-demure corridors and simple dormitories, a white rosary of hours—having heard the fair promises of Spring, that well-graced ambassador. . . . .

Amid a flat rain-swept country stands a high plain building, with windows that filter the obscure daylight. Three hundred boys, noisy and hungry, sit at long tables eating beef fringed with green fat and vegetables that are still rank of the earth.[6]

She is engaged. She dances with them in the round—a white dress lightly lifted as she dances, a white spray in her hair; eyes a little averted, a faint glow on her cheek. Her hand is in mine for a moment, softest of merchandise.

—You very seldom come here now.—

—Yes I am becoming something of a recluse.

—I saw your brother the other day. . . . . . He is very like you.—

—Really?—

She dances with them in the round—evenly, discreetly, giving herself to none. The white spray is ruffled as she dances, and when she is in shadow the glow is deeper on her cheek.[7]

---

[5] See *P*, 152.
[6] See *SH*, 183, 184, reprinted on p. 283, and *P*, 216.
[7] See *P*, 219.

Faintly, under the heavy summer night, through the silence of the town which has turned from dreams to dreamless sleep as a weary lover whom no carresses [*sic*] move, the sound of hoofs upon the Dublin road. Not so faintly now as they come near the bridge: and in a moment as they pass the dark windows the silence is cloven by alarm as by an arrow. They are heard now far away—hoofs that shine amid the heavy night as diamonds, hurrying beyond the grey, still marshes to what journey's end— what heart—bearing what tidings? [8]

A long curving gallery: from the floor arise pillars of dark vapours. It is peopled by the images of fabulous kings, set in stone. Their hands are folded upon their knees, in token of weariness, and their eyes are darkened for the errors of men go up before them for ever as dark vapours.[9]

The spell of arms and voices—the white arms of roads, their promise of close embraces, and the black arms of tall ships that stand against the moon, their tale of distant nations. They are held out to say: We are alone,—come. And the voices say with them, We are your people. And the air is thick with their company as they call to me their kinsman, making ready to go, shaking the wings of their exultant and terrible youth.[10]

Here are we come together, wayfarers; here are we housed, amid intricate streets, by night and silence closely covered. In amity we rest together, well content, no more remembering the devious- ness of the ways that we have come. What moves upon me from

---

[8] See *P*, 251.
[9] See *P*, 249.
[10] See *SH*, 237, and *P*, 252.

the darkness subtle and murmurous as a flood, passionate and fierce with an indecent movement of the loins? What leaps, crying in answer, out of me, as eagle to eagle in mid air, crying to overcome, crying for an iniquitous abandonment? [11]

[11] See P, 100.

FROM *STEPHEN HERO*

As soon as the editors of *Dana* had rejected the essay "Portrait" (see p. 257) Joyce began to rework the material as a long naturalistic novel called *Stephen Hero*. According to the diary of his brother Stanislaus, Joyce began the novel on February 2, 1904 (his twenty-second birthday), to show the *Dana* editors that "in writing about himself he has a subject of more interest than their aimless discussion." Stanislaus said that Joyce told him that day that the novel was to be "autobiographical, and naturally as it comes from Jim, satirical. He is putting a large number of his acquaintances into it, and those Jesuits whom he has known. I don't think they will like themselves in it. . . . The title, like the book, is satirical."

By April 1904, Joyce had finished eleven chapters, but a little more than a year later he got stuck on Chapter XXV (about halfway through the book as he had planned it) and returned to writing *Dubliners* stories and to preparing *Chamber Music* for publication. The manuscript as it came down to the Harvard Library begins in the middle of Chapter XVI and breaks off in the middle of Chapter XXVI. Twenty-five additional pages from an earlier part of the manuscript were discovered and published in 1955.

The fragment of *Stephen Hero* contains many of the same characters and incidents refashioned in the *Portrait*. Some of them are included in the brief parts reprinted here. A comparison of the different treatments they are given should help the reader understand the artistic work which formed Joyce's *Portrait*.

Professor Theodore Spencer, the editor of the *Stephen Hero* manuscript, placed square brackets around words which Joyce crossed out and changed. He placed French quotation marks (« ») around words which Joyce marked with red or blue crayon, because "presumably he did not like them and intended to change them." (*SH*, Introduction, p. 18.)

From *Stephen Hero* by James Joyce. Used by permission of The Executors of The James Joyce Estate, Jonathan Cape Ltd., and The Society of Authors.

[EMMA CLERY][1]

. . . Every Friday evening he met Miss Clery, or, as he had
now returned to the Christian name, Emma. She lived near
Portobello and any evening that the meeting was over early she
walked home. She often delayed a long time chatting with a
low-sized young priest, a Father Moran, who had a neat head of
curly black hair and expressive black eyes. This young priest
was a pianist and sang sentimental songs and was for many
reasons a great favourite with the ladies. Stephen often watched
Emma and Father Moran. Father Moran, who sang tenor, had
once complimented Stephen saying he had heard many people
speak highly of his voice and hoping he would have the pleasure of hearing him some time. Stephen had said the same thing
to the priest adding that Miss Clery had told him great things
of *his* voice. At this the priest had smiled and looked archly at
Stephen. "One must not believe all the complimentary things
the ladies say of us" he had said. "The ladies are a little given to
—what shall I say—fibbing, I am afraid." And here the priest had
bit his lower rosy lip with two little white even teeth and smiled
with his expressive eyes and altogether looked such a pleasant
tender-hearted vulgarian that Stephen felt inclined to slap him
on the back admiringly. Stephen had continued talking for a
few minutes and once when the conversation had touch on
Irish matters the priest had become very serious and had said
very piously "Ah, yes. « God bless the work!" » Father Moran
was no lover of the old droning chants, he told Stephen. Of
course, he said, it is very grand music severe style of music
[sic]. But he held the opinion that the Church must not be
made too gloomy and he said with a charming smile that the

---

[1] *SH*, pp. 65-68. Cf. *P*, 69-70, 77, 82, 219-221, and 222, and the
epiphany, p. 270.

spirit of the Church was not gloomy. He said that one could not expect the people to take kindly to severe music and that the people needed more human religious music than the Gregorian and ended by advising Stephen to learn "The Holy City" by Adams.

—There is a song now, beautiful, full of lovely melody and yet—religious. It has the religious sentiment, a touching « melody, power—soul, in fact. »

Stephen watching this young priest and Emma together usually worked himself into a state of unsettled rage. It was not so much that he suffered personally as that the spectacle seemed to him typical of Irish ineffectualness. Often he felt his fingers itch. Father Moran's eyes were so clear and tender-looking, Emma stood to his gaze in such a poise of bold careless « pride of the flesh » that Stephen longed to precipitate the two into each other's arms and shock the room even though he knew the pain this impersonal generosity would cause himself. Emma allowed him to see her home several times but she did not seem to have reserved herself for him. The youth was piqued at this for above all things he hated to be compared with others and, had it not been that her body seemed so compact of pleasure, he would have preferred to have been ignominiously left behind. Her loud forced manners shocked him at first until his mind had thoroughly mastered the stupidity of hers. She criticised the Miss Daniels very sharply, assuming, much to Stephen's discomfort, an identical temper in him. She coquetted with knowledge, asking Stephen could he not persuade the President of his College to admit women to the college. Stephen told her to apply to McCann who was the champion of women. She laughed at this and said with « genuine dismay » "Well, honestly, isn't he a dreadful-looking artist?" She treated femininely everything that young men are supposed to regard as serious but she made polite exception for Stephen himself and for the Gaelic Revival. She asked him wasn't he reading a paper and what was it on. She would give anything to go and hear him: she was awfully fond of the theatre herself and a gypsy woman had once read her hand and told her she would be an actress. She had been three times to the pantomime and asked Stephen what he liked best in pantomime. Stephen said he liked a good clown but she said that she preferred ballets. Then she wanted to know did he go out much to dances and pressed him to join an Irish dancing-class of which she was a member. Her eyes had begun to « imitate the expression » of Father Moran's—an expression of tender « significance » when the conversation was at the lowest level of banality. Often as he walked beside her Stephen wondered how she had employed her time since he had last seen her and he congratulated himself that he had caught an impression of her when she was at her finest moment. In his heart he deplored the change in her for he would have liked nothing so well as an adventure with her now but he felt that even that warm ample body could hardly compensate him for her distressing pertness and middle-class affectations. « In the centre of her attitude towards him he thought he discerned a point of defiant illwill and he thought he understood the cause of it. » He had swept the moment into his memory, the figure and the landscape into his treasure-room, and conjuring with all three had brought forth some pages of « sorry verse. » One rainy night when the streets were too bad for walking she took the Rathmines tram at the Pillar and as she held down her hand to him from the step, thanking him for his kindness and wishing him good-night, that « episode of their childhood seemed to magnetise » the minds of both at the same instant. The change of circumstances had reversed their positions, giving her the upper hand. He took her hand caressingly, caressing one after another the three lines on the « back of her kid glove and numbering her knuckles, » caressing also his own past towards which this inconsistent hater of [antiquity] inheritances was always lenient. They smiled at each other; and again in the centre of her amiableness he discerned a [centre] point of illwill and he suspected that by her code of honour she was obliged to insist on the forbearance of the male and to despise him for forbearing.

[I WILL NOT SUBMIT]²

. . . They walked together up along Kildare St without speaking. When they came to the Green Cranly said:

—I'm going home on Saturday. Will you come as far as Harcourt St Station? I want to see the hour the train goes at.

—All right.

In the station Cranly spent a great deal of time reading the time-tables and making abstruse calculations. Then he went up to the platform and watched for a long time the shunting of the engine of a goods train on to a passenger train. The engine was steaming and blowing a deafening whistle and rolling billows of thick smoke towards the roof of the station. Cranly said that the engine-driver came from his part of the country and that he was the son of a cobbler in Tinahely. The engine executed a series of indecisive movements and finally settled itself on to the train. The engine-driver stuck his head out through the side and gazed languidly along the train:

—I suppose you would call him sooty Jaysus, said Cranly.

—Cranly, said Stephen, I have left the Church.

Cranly took his arm at the word and they turned away from the platform and went down the staircase. As soon as they had emerged into the street he said encouragingly:

—You have left the Church?

Stephen went over the interview phrase by phrase.

—Then you do not believe any longer?

—I cannot believe.

—But you could at one time.

—I cannot now.

—You could now if you wanted to.

—Well, I don't want to.

² *SH, pp.* 137-143. Cf. *P,* 237-247.

—Are you sure you do not believe?

—Quite sure.

—Why do you not go to the altar?

—Because I do not believe.

—Would you make a sacrilegious communion?

—Why should I?

—For your mother's sake.

—I don't see why I should.

—Your mother will suffer very much. You say you do not believe. The Host for you is a piece of ordinary bread. Would you not eat a piece of ordinary bread to avoid causing your mother pain?

—I would in many cases.

—And why not in this case? Have you any reluctance to commit a sacrilege? If you do not believe you should not have any.

—Wait a minute, said Stephen. At present I have a reluctance to commit a sacrilege. I am a product of Catholicism; I was sold to Rome before my birth. Now I have broken my slavery but I cannot in a moment destroy every feeling in my nature. That takes time. However if it were a case of needs must —for my life, for instance—I would commit any enormity with the host.

—Many Catholics would do the same, said Cranly, if their lives were at stake.

—Believers?

—Ay, believers. So by your own showing you are a believer.

—It is not from fear that I refrain from committing a sacrilege.

— Why then?

—I see no reason for committing sacrilege.

—But you have always made your Easter Duty. Why do you change? The thing for you is mockery, mummery.

—If I mum it is an act of submission, a public act of submission to the Church. I will not submit to the Church.

—Even so far as to mum?

—It is mumming with an intention. The outward show is nothing but it means a good deal.

—Again you are speaking like a Catholic. The host is nothing in outward show—a piece of bread.

—I admit: but all the same I insist on disobeying the Church. I will not submit any longer.

—But could you not be more diplomatic? Could you not rebel in your heart and yet conform out of contempt? You could be a rebel in spirit.

—That cannot be done for long by anyone who is sensitive. The Church knows the value of her services: her priest must hypnotise himself every morning before the tabernacle. If I get up every morning, go to the looking-glass and say to myself "You are the Son of God" at the end of twelve months I will want disciples.

—If you could make your religion pay like Christianity I would advise you to get up every morning and go to the looking-glass.

—That would be good for my vicars on earth but I would find crucifixion a personal inconvenience.

—But here in Ireland by following your new religion of unbelief you may be crucifying yourself like Jesus—only socially not physically.

—There is this difference. Jesus was good-humoured over it. I will die hard.

—How can you propose such a future to yourself and yet be afraid to trust yourself to perform even the simplest mumming in a church? said Cranly.

—That is my business, said Stephen, tapping at his forehead.

When they had come to the Green they crossed the streets and began to walk round the enclosure inside the chains. A few mechanics and their sweethearts were sitting on the swinging-chains turning the shadows to account. The footpath was deserted except for the metallic image of a distant policeman who had been posted well in the gaslight as an admonition. When the two young men passed the college they both looked up at the same moment towards the dark windows.

—May I ask you why you left the Church? asked Cranly.

—I could not observe the precepts.

—Not even with grace?

—No.

—Jesus gives very simple precepts. The Church is severe.

—Jesus or the Church—it's all the time to me. I can't follow him. I must have liberty to do as I please.

—No man can do as he pleases.

—Morally.

—No, not morally either.

—You want me, said Stephen, to toe the line with those sycophants and hypocrites in the college. I will never do so.

—No. I mentioned Jesus.

—Don't mention him. I have made it a common noun. They don't believe in him; they don't observe his precepts. In any case let us leave Jesus aside. My sight will only carry me as far as his lieutenant in Rome. It is quite useless: I will not be frightened into paying tribute in money or in thought.

—You told me—do you remember the evening we were standing at the top of the staircase talking about . . .

—Yes, yes, I remember, said Stephen who hated Cranly's « method of remembering » the past, what did I tell you?

—You told me the idea you had of Jesus on Good Friday, an ugly misshapen Jesus. Did it ever strike you that Jesus may have been a conscious impostor?

—I have never believed in his chastity—that is since I began to think about him. I am sure he [is] was no eunuch priest. His interest in loose women is too persistently humane. All the women associated with him are of dubious character.

—You don't think he was God?

—What a question! Explain it: explain the hypostatic union: tell me if the figure which « that policeman worships » as the Holy Ghost is intended for a spermatozoon with wings added. What a question! He makes general remarks on life, that's all I know: and I disagree with them.

—For example?

—For example . . . Look here, I cannot talk on this subject. I am not a scholar and I receive no pay as a minister of God. I want to live, do you understand. McCann wants air and food: I want them and a hell of a lot of other things too. I don't care whether I am right or wrong. There is always that risk in human affairs, I suppose. But even if I am wrong at least I shall not have to endure Father Butt's company for eternity.

Cranly laughed.

—Remember he would be glorified.

—Heaven for climate, isn't that it, and hell for society . . . the whole affair is too damn idiotic. Give it up. I am very young. When I have a beard to my middle I will study Hebrew and then write to you about it.

—Why are you so impatient with the Jesuits? asked Cranly.

Stephen did not answer and, when they arrived in the next region of light Cranly exclaimed:

—Your face is red!

—I feel it, said Stephen.

—Most people think you are self-restrained, said Cranly after a pause.

—So I am, said Stephen.

—Not on this subject. Why do you get so excited: I can't understand that. It is a thing for you to think out.

—I can think out things when I like. I have thought this affair out very carefully though you may not believe me when I tell you. But my escape excites me: I must talk as I do. I feel a flame in my face. I feel a wind rush through me.

—'Like a mighty wind rushing,' said Cranly.

—You urge me to postpone life—till when? Life is now—this is life: if I postpone it I may never live. To walk nobly on the surface of the earth, to express oneself without pretence, to acknowledge one's own humanity! You mustn't think I rhapsodise: I am quite serious. I speak from my soul.

—Soul?

—Yes: from my soul, my spiritual nature. Life is not a yawn. Philosophy, love, art will not disappear from my world because I no longer believe that by entertaining an emotion of desire for the tenth part of a second I prepare for myself an eternity of torture. I am happy.

—Can you say that?

—Jesus is sad. Why is he so sad? He is solitary . . . I say, you must feel the truth of what I say, You are holding up the Church against me . . .

—Allow me . . .

—But what is the Church? It is not Jesus, the magnificent solitary with his inimitable abstinences. The Church is made by me and my like[3]—her services, legends, practices, paintings, music, traditions. These her artists gave her. They made her what she is. They accepted Aquinas' commentary on Aristotle as the Word of God and made her what she is.

—And why will you not help her to be so still—you as an artist?

—I see you recognise the truth of what I say though you won't admit it.

—The Church allows the individual conscience to have great . . . in fact, if you believe . . . believe, that is, said Cranly stamping each heavy foot on the words, honestly and truly . . .

—Enough! said Stephen gripping his companion's arm. You need not defend me. I will take the odds as they are.

They paced along three sides of the Green in silence while the couples began to leave the chains and return meekly to their modest resting-places and after a while Cranly began to explain to Stephen how he too had felt a desire for life—a life of freedom and happiness—when he had been younger and how at that time he too had been about to leave the Church in search of happiness but that many considerations had restrained him.

---

[3] In the Ms the words "made by me and my like" are added in red crayon [T.S.].

[THE CONVENT GIRLS][4]

. . . Stephen leaned against one of the stone pillars and regarded the farther group. She stood in a ring of her companions, laughing and talking with them. The anger with which the new review had filled him gradually ebbed away and he chose to contemplate the spectacle which she and her companions offered him. As on his entrance into the grounds of Clonliffe College a « sudden sympathy arose out of a sudden reminiscence, a reminiscent sympathy toward a [sheltered] protected seminarist life the very virtues of which seemed to be set provokingly before the wild gaze of the world, so provokingly that only the strength of walls and watchdogs held them in a little circle of modish and timid ways. Though their affectations often lacked grace and their vulgarity wanted only lungs to be strident the rain brought him charity. The babble of the young students reached him » as if from a distance, in broken pulsations, and lifting his eyes he saw the high rain-clouds retreating across the rain-swept country. The quick light shower was over, tarrying, a cluster of diamonds, among the shrubs of the quadrangle where an exhalation ascended from the blackened earth. The company in the colonnade was leaving shelter, with many a doubting glance, with a prattle of trim boots, a pretty rescue of petticoats, under umbrellas, a light armoury, upheld at cunning angles. He saw them returning to the convent—demure corridors and simple dormitories, a quiet rosary of hours—while the rain-clouds retreated towards the west and the babble of the young men reached him in regular pulsations. He saw far away amid a flat rain-swept country a high plain building with windows that filtered the obscure daylight. Three hundred boys, noisy and hungry, sat at long tables eating beef fringed with green fat like

[4] *SH*, p. 183. Cf. the epiphany on p. 270; and *P*, 216 and 252.

blubber and junks of white damp bread, and one young boy, leaning upon his elbows, opened and closed the flaps of his ears while the noise of the diners reached him rhythmically as the wild gabble of animals.

[YOU ARE MAD, STEPHEN][5]

. . . —I was gazing out of the window, he answered, looking at the sky and the Green. Lord God! I felt so full of despair. Sometimes I am taken that way: I live such a strange life— without help or sympathy from anyone. Sometimes I am afraid of myself. I call those people in the college not men but vegetables . . . Then while I was cursing my own character I saw you.

—Yes? she said looking at the disorderly figure beside her out of her large oval eyes.

—You know I was delighted to see you. I had to jump up and rush out. I couldn't have sat there another minute . . . I said, Here is a human creature at last . . . I can't tell you how delighted I was.

—You strange boy! she said. You mustn't go running about like that. You must have more sense.

—Emma! cried Stephen, don't start talking to me like that today. I know you want to be very sensible. But you and I— we are both young, aren't we?

—Yes, Stephen.

—Very good, then. If we're young we feel happy. We feel full of desire.

—Desire?

—Do you know when I saw you . . .

---

[5] *SH*, pp. 197-199. Cf. *P*, 252.

—Yes, how did you know me?

—I knew the stride.

—Stride!

—Do you know, Emma, even from my window I could see your hips moving inside your waterproof? I saw a young woman walking proudly through the decayed city. Yes, that's the way you walk: you're proud of being young and proud of being a woman. Do you know when I caught sight of you from my window—do you know what I felt? [6]

There was no use in her essaying indifference now. Her cheeks were covered with a persistent flush and her eyes shone like gems. She gazed straight before her and her breath began to be agitated. They stood together in the deserted street and he continued speaking, a certain ingenuous disattachment guiding his excited passion.

—I felt that I longed to hold you in my arms—your body. I longed for you to take me in your arms. That's all . . . Then I thought I would run after you and say that to you . . . Just to live one night together, Emma, and then to say goodbye in the morning and never to see each other again! There is no such thing as love in the world: only people are young . . .

She tried to take her arm away from his and murmured as if she were repeating from memory:

—You are mad, Stephen.

Stephen let go her arm and took her hand in his, saying:

—Goodbye, Emma . . . I felt that I wanted to say that to you for my own sake but if I stand here in this stupid street beside you for much longer I shall begin to say more . . . You say I am mad because I do not bargain with you or say I love you or swear to you. But I believe you hear my words and understand me, don't you?

—I don't understand you indeed, she answered with a touch of anger.

—I will give you a chance, said Stephen, pressing her hand close in his two hands. Tonight when you are going to bed

---

[6] Written across this paragraph in red crayon are the words "pride of the flesh" [T.S.].

remember me and go to your window: I will be in the garden.
Open the window and call my name and ask me to come in.
Then come down and let me in. We will live one night together—one night, Emma, alone together and in the morning
we will say goodbye.

—Let go my hand, please, she said pulling her hand away
from him. If I had known [if] it was for this mad talk . . .
You must not speak to me any more, she said moving on a pace
or two and plucking her waterproof out of his reach. Who do
you think I am that you can speak to me like that?

—It is no insult, said Stephen colouring suddenly as the reverse of the image struck him, for a man to ask a woman what
I have asked you. You are annoyed at something else not at
that.

—You are mad, I think, she said, brushing past him swiftly
without taking any notice of his salute. She did not go quickly
enough, however, to hide the tears that were in her eyes and he,
surprised to see them and wondering at their cause, forgot to
say the goodbye that was on his lips. As he watched her walk
onward swiftly with her head slightly bowed he seemed to
feel her soul and his falling asunder swiftly and for ever after an
instant of all but union.

[EPIPHANIES] [7]

. . . The general attitude of women towards religion puzzled
and often maddened Stephen. His nature was incapable of
achieving such an attitude of insincerity or stupidity. By brooding constantly upon this he ended by anathemising [*sic*] Emma
as the most deceptive and cowardly of marsupials. He discovered that it was a menial fear and no spirit of chastity which

---

[7] *SH*, pp. 210-213. Cf. *P*, 208-213, 220, 221-224.

had prevented her from granting his request. Her eyes, he thought, must look strange when upraised to some holy image and her lips when poised for the reception of the host. He cursed her burgher cowardice and her beauty and he said to himself that though her eyes might cajole the half-witted God of the Roman Catholics they would not cajole him. In every stray image of the streets he saw her soul manifest itself and every such manifestation renewed the intensity of his disapproval. It did not strike him that the attitude of women towards holy things really implied a more genuine emancipation than his own and he condemned them out of a purely suppositious [*sic*] conscience. He exaggerated their iniquities and evil influence and returned them their antipathy in full measure. He toyed also with a theory of dualism which would symbolise the twin eternities of spirit and nature in the twin eternities of male and female and even thought of explaining the audacities of his verse as symbolical allusions. It was hard for him to compel his head to preserve the strict temperature of classicism. More than he had ever done before he longed for the season to lift and for spring—the misty Irish spring—to be over and gone. He was passing through Eccles' St one evening, one misty evening, with all these thoughts dancing the dance of unrest in his brain when a trivial incident set him composing some ardent verses which he entitled a "Vilanelle of the Temptress." A young lady was standing on the steps of one of those brown brick houses which seem the very incarnation of Irish paralysis. A young gentleman was leaning on the rusty railings of the area. Stephen as he passed on his quest heard the following fragment of colloquy out of which he received an impression keen enough to afflict his sensitiveness very severely.

The Young Lady—(drawling discreetly) . . . O, yes . . . I was . . . at the . . . cha . . . pel . . .

The Young Gentleman—(inaudibly) . . . I . . . (again inaudibly) . . . I . . .

The Young Lady—(softly) . . . O . . . but you're . . . ve . . . ry . . . wick . . . ed . . .

This triviality made him think of collecting many such moments together in a book of epiphanies. By an epiphany he meant a sudden spiritual manifestation, whether in the vulgarity of speech or of gesture or in a memorable phase of the mind itself. He believed that it was for the man of letters to record these epiphanies with extreme care, seeing that they themselves are the most delicate and evanescent of moments. He told Cranly that the clock of the Ballast Office was capable of an epiphany. Cranly questioned the inscrutable dial of the Ballast Office with his no less inscrutable countenance:

—Yes, said Stephen. I will pass it time after time, allude to it, refer to it, catch a glimpse of it. It is only an item in the catalogue of Dublin's street furniture. Then all at once I see it and I know at once what it is: epiphany.

—What?

—Imagine my glimpses at that clock as the gropings of a spiritual eye which seeks to adjust its vision to an exact focus. The moment the focus is reached the object is epiphanised. It is just in this epiphany that I find the third, the supreme quality of beauty.

—Yes? said Cranly absently.

—No esthetic theory, pursued Stephen relentlessly, is of any value which investigates with the aid of the lantern of tradition. What we symbolise in black the Chinaman may symbolise in yellow: each has his own tradition. Greek beauty laughs at Coptic beauty and the American Indian derides them both. It is almost impossible to reconcile all tradition whereas it is by no means impossible to find the justification of every form of beauty which has ever been adored on the earth by an examination into the mechanism of esthetic apprehension whether it be dressed in red, white, yellow or black. We have no reason for thinking that the Chinaman has a different system of digestion from that which we have though our diets are quite dissimilar. The apprehensive faculty must be scrutinised in action.

—Yes . . .

—You know what Aquinas says: The three things requisite for beauty are, integrity, a wholeness, symmetry and radiance. Some day I will expand that sentence into a treatise. Consider the performance of your own mind when confronted with any object, hypothetically beautiful. Your mind to apprehend that object divides the entire universe into two parts, the object, and the void which is not the object. To apprehend it you must lift it away from everything else: and then you perceive that it is one integral thing, that is *a* thing. You recognise its integrity. Isn't that so?

—And then?

—That is the first quality of beauty: it is declared in a simple sudden synthesis of the faculty which apprehends. What then? Analysis then. The mind considers the object in whole and in part, in relation to itself and to other objects, examines the balance of its parts, contemplates the form of the object, traverses every cranny of the structure. So the mind receives the impression of the symmetry of the object. The mind recognises that the object is in the strict sense of the word, a *thing*, a definitely constituted entity. You see?

—Let us turn back, said Cranly.

They had reached the corner of Grafton St and as the footpath was overcrowded they turned back northwards. Cranly had an inclination to watch the antics of a drunkard who had been ejected from a bar in Suffolk St but Stephen took his arm summarily and led him away.

—Now for the third quality. For a long time I couldn't make out what Aquinas meant. He uses a figurative word (a very unusual thing for him) but I have solved it. *Claritas* is *quidditas*. After the analysis which discovers the second quality the mind makes the only logically possible synthesis and discovers the third quality. This is the moment which I call epiphany. First we recognise that the object is *one* integral thing, then we recognise that it is an organised composite structure, a *thing* in fact: finally, when the relation of the parts is exquisite, when the parts are adjusted to the special point, we recognise that it is *that* thing which it is. Its soul, its whatness, leaps to us from the vestment of its appearance. The soul of the commonest object, the structure of which is so adjusted, seems to us radiant. The object achieves its epiphany. . . .

THE TRIESTE NOTEBOOK

After Joyce decided in 1907 that *Stephen Hero* gave a false picture of the artist and that he would start over again, for a few years he kept an alphabetical notebook in which he wrote key sentences about some of the characters who were to be used in the *Portrait* and *Ulysses*. Most of the notebook, including all the entries relating to the *Portrait*, is printed here from the manuscript in the Mennen Collection at the Cornell University Library. The entire notebook can be found in Kain and Scholes, *The Workshop of Daedalus*.

Byrne (John Francis) [Cranly in *P*]

He hears confessions without giving absolution: a guilty priest. [*P*, 178, 247, 248.]

His silence means that he has an answer to what puzzles me.

His speech has neither the rare phrases of Elizabethan English nor the quaintly turned versions of Irish idioms which I have heard with Clancy.[1] I hear in its drawl an echo of the Dublin quays, given back by the decaying seaport from which he comes, and in its energy an echo of the flat emphasis of Wicklow pulpits. [*P*, 195.]

He asked me if I would deflower a virgin. [*P*, 246.]

He has one epitaph for all dead friendships: A Sugar. [*P*, 195.]

Used by permission of The Society of Authors.

[1] That is, Davin in *P*. See, for example, *P*, 181-183 and the Explanatory Notes to those pages.

He spoke to me as: my dear man. [*P*, 239.]

On the steps of the National Library he dislodged an old figseed from a rotten tooth. [*P*, 229-239, 248.]

He said that I was reared in the lap of luxury [*P*, 241.]

He did not think that *Nicholas Nickleby* was true to life. He is exhausted. [Cf. *P*, 248.]

He calls a clock a wag-by-the-wall and Yeats a go-by-the-wall. [Cf. *P*, 201.]

Cosgrave (Vincent) [Lynch in *P*]

His laugh is like the whinny of an elephant. His trunk shakes all over and he rubs his hands delightedly over his groins. [*P*, 201, 205.] [2]

His hands are usually in his trousers' pockets. [*P*, 205.] They were in his trousers' pockets when I was knocked down on S. Stephen's Green.

Under his headgear he brought up the image of a hooded reptile. The long slender flattened skull under his cap brought up the image of a hooded reptile: the eyes, too, were reptilian in glint and gaze but with one human point, a tiny window of a shrivelled soul, poignant and embittered. [*P*, 205-206.]

He is a self-consumer.

He ate dried cowdung. [*P*, 205.]

Clancy (George Stephen) [Davin in *P*]

There is a stare of terror in his eyes [*P*, 180.]

He sat at the feet of Michael Cusack the Gael who hailed him as citizen. [*P*, 180.]

Chance did not bring us face to face on either of my visits

---

[2] Joyce apparently did not intend the pun on "trunk" here. At 201.14 he wrote, "The student's trunk shook all over . . ." in the fair-copy manuscript, but after it had been printed in the serialization in *The Egoist*, he changed "trunk" to "body" for the first edition.

to Ireland.[3] I wonder where he is at the present time. I don't know is he alive still.[4]

His use of "whatever."

It is equal to him

He wore a swanskin gansy. [Cf. *P*, 228.]

Dedalus (Stephen)

"Et ignotas animum dimittit in artes": Ovid: Metamorphoses VIII.188. [Epigraph.]

Girls laughing when he stumbled in the street were unchaste. [*P*, 220.]

He made duck in cricket.

Flowergirls and beggarboys came after him in the street for handsel, saying: Will you, gentleman? [*P*, 183, 220.]

The gratings in the path often caught the broken soles of his boots. [*P*, 220.]

He had an inborn distaste for fermented foods.

He was a dispossessed son. [Cf. *P*, 98.]

He disliked to be seen in the company of any woman.

At times as he walked through the streets of Dublin he felt that he was really invisible.

He dreaded the sea that would drown his body and the crowd that would drown his soul. [*P*, 167.]

He came to the knowledge of innocence through sin. [Cf. *P*, 100-101, 222.]

His heart was moved to a deep compassionate love by the frail pallor and humble eyes of girls, humbled and saddened by the dark shame of womanhood. [*P*, 222-223.]

He liked green. [Cf. *P*, 7.]

---

[3] Joyce probably refers to the visits he made to Ireland in 1909 and 1912.

[4] The omission of the conjunctions "whether" or "if" in the noun clause is one of the "versions of Irish idioms" to which Joyce refers under *Byrne*. The construction imitates Gaelic. Cf. the statement attributed above to Byrne, "He asked me *if* I would deflower a virgin." [My italics.]

He looked in vain for some poet of the people among his generation to be his whetstone.

He hoped that by sinning whole-heartedly his race might come in him to the knowledge of herself. [P, 238, 253.]

He disliked bottles.

He strove to shut his eyes against the disloyalty of others to himself

He gave what he got.

He devoured snowcake.

He pawned a Pali book.

He felt the growing pains of his soul in the painful process of life.

He shrank from limning the features of his soul for he feared that no everlasting image of beauty could shine through an immature being.

Girls called after him: *Hey, young fellow* . . . or . . . . *Straight hair and curly eyebrows* [P, 220.]

It annoyed him to hear a girl begin suddenly the first bars of a song and stop. [Cf. P, 244.]

The applause following the fall of the curtain fired his blood more than the scene on the stage. [Cf. P, 85.]

He felt the quaking of the earth.

He felt himself alone in the theatre.

Having left the city of the church by the gate of sin he might enter it again by the wicket of repentance if repentance were possible. [Cf. P, 246.]

He desired to be not a man of letters but a spirit expressing itself through language because shut off from the visible arts by an inheritance of servitude and from music by vigour of mind. [Cf. P, 246.]

Esthetic

An enchantment of the heart [P, 212, 217.]

Pornographic and cinematographic images act like those

stimuli which produce a reflex action of the nerves through channels which are independent of esthetic perception. [*P*, 205, 206.]

It relieves us to hear or see our own distress expressed by another person.

The instant of inspiration is a spark so brief as to be invisible. The reflection of it on many sides at once from a multitude of cloudy circumstances with no one of which it is united save by the bond of merest possibility veils its afterglow in an instant in a first confusion of form. This is the instant in which the word is made flesh. [Cf. *P*, 217.]

There is a morning inspiration as there is a morning knowledge about the windless hour when the moth escapes from the chrysalis, and certain plants bloom and the feverfit of madness comes on the insane. [*P*, 217.]

The rite is the poet's rest.

Art has the gift of tongues.

Pornography fails because whores are bad conductors of emotion.

The skeleton conditions the esthetic image.

Henry (Father William) [Rector of Belvedere College in *P*]

In translating Ovid he spoke of porkers and potsherds and of chines of bacon. [*P*, 179.]

When I listen I can still hear him reading sonorously: *In tanto discrimine. . . . . Implere ollam denariorum. . . . India mittit ebur.* [*P*, 179.]

Healy (Michael) [Nora Barnacle Joyce's uncle, whom Joyce visited in Galway in 1909]

Many pairs of boots stand in a row along the wall of his bedroom. [Used for Davin, *P*, 180.]

Ireland

Its learning is in the hands of the monks and their clerks and its art in the hands of blacklegs who still serve those ideas which their fellow artists in Europe have rebelled against.

One effect of the resurgence of the Irish nation would be the entry into the field of Europe of the Irish artist and thinker, a being without sexual education.

The sow that eats her young. [*P*, 203.]

Her state is like that of France after the Napoleonic wars or of Egypt after the slaughter of the first-born.

The first maxim in Irish morals is: *omertà* (the Sicilian law of silence) [Cf. *P*, 247.]

Irish wits follow in the footsteps of King James the Second who struck off base money for Ireland which the hoofs of cattle have trampled into her soil.

The curfew is still a nightly fear in her starving villages.

Irish art is the cracked looking-glass of a servant.

The Irish provinces not England and her tradition stand between me and Edward VII.

The cable of Catholicism that links Ireland to Latin Europe is eaten by two seas.

The shortest way from Cape of Good Hope to Cape Horn is to sail away from it. The shortest route to Tara is via Holyhead. [*P*, 250.]

Her rebellions are servile wars. [Cf. *P*, 202.]

The Irish are washed by the Gulf Stream

There is hope for her: in 500 years the coal supply of England will run out

Duns Scotus has won a poorer fame than S. Fiacre, whose legend sown in French soil, has grown up in a harvest of hackney-cabs.

If he and Columbanus the fiery, whose fingertips God illumined, and Fridolinus Viator can see as far as earth from their creepy-stools in heaven they know that Aquinas, the lucid sensual Latin, has won the day.

Jesus

His shadow is everywhere.

From the first instant of his existence his human soul was filled with divine knowledge.

He was discourteous to his mother in public but Suarez, a Jesuit theologian and Spanish gentleman, has apologised for him. [*P*, 242.]

The dove above his head is the *lex eterna* which overshadows the mind and will of God.

Jesuits

They breed atheists

I learnt Latin prosody from the rhymes of Father Alvarez. [*P*, 179.]

The nice terms of their philosophy are like the jargon of heraldry. [*P*, 180.]

They are levites. [*P*, 185.]

They do not love the end they serve. [*P*, 186.]

The houses of jesuits are extraterritorial. [*P*, 184]

They flatter the wealthy but they do not love them nor their ways. They flatter the clergy, their half brothers. [*P*, 190.]

They who live by the mob shall perish by the mob.

They judge by categories.

Are they venal of speech because venality is the only point of contact between pastor and flock? [*P*, 190.]

They are erotically preoccuppied [*sic*]

Mother

The drawer in her deadroom contained perfumed programmes and old feathers. When she was a girl a birdcage hung in the sunny window of her house. When she was a girl she went to the theatre to see the pantomime of Turko the Terrible and laughed when Old Royce the actor sang:

> *I am the boy*
> *That can enjoy*
> *Invisibility*

She came to me silently in a dream after her death: and her washed body within its loose brown habit gave out a faint odour of wax and rosewood and her breath a faint odour of wetted ashes.

Every first Friday she approached the altar and when she came home drank a glass of water before eating.

Her nails were reddened with the blood of lice.

She was taken sometimes to a performance of Christy minstrels in the Leinster Hall.

Sometimes she roasted an apple for herself on the hob.

She used to exclaim: *Merciful hour*.

She said I never went to church, mass or meeting.

Pappie [John Joyce]

He is an Irish suicide.

He read medicine

He cannot keep his pipe alight as the buccinator muscle is weak.

He gave me money to wire to Nora on Christmas Eve, saying: "Non ignorus [sic] malorum miseris soccorere [sic] disco." [5]

One morning he played the fiddle, sitting up in bed.

His college friends were: Tom O'Grady, Harry Peard, Mick Lacey, Maurice Moriarty, Jack Mountain, Joey Corbet, Bob Dyas and Keevers of the Tantiles. [P, 89, 90.]

He calls a prince of the church a tub of guts. [P, 33.]

The verses he quotes most are:

> *Conservio lies captured! He lies in the lowest dungeons*

---

[5] *Aeneid* I, 630.

With manacles and chains around his limbs
Weighing upwards of three tons.

When he is satirical he calls me sonny and bids me think of my Maker and give up the ghost.

He offers the pope's nose at table. [*P*, 32.]

He was proud of his hop step and jump.

He calls Canon Keon frosty face and Cardinal Logue a tub of guts. Had they been laymen he would condone their rancid fat. [*P*, 33.]

When something is mislaid he asks softly: *Have you tried the ashpit?*

He inquires: *Who said?*

He read *Modern Society* and the *Licensed Victuallers' Gazette*

He threatened to make me smell hell.

He called Eileen a confirmed bloody idiot.

He quarrelled with my friends.

When drunk he composes verses containing the word *perchance.*

Skeffington (Francis Joseph Christopher)
[MacCann in *P*.]

He wields a wooden sword. [*P*, 197.]

Shelley (Percy Bysshe)

He spoke his ecstatic verses with an English accent. [Cf. *P*, 96.]

Uncle William (*O'Connell*)
[Uncle Charles in *P*]

He agreed: *You may say that, ma'am.*

He sang *The Groves of the Pool.* [Cf. *The Groves of Blarney*, *P*, 60.]

❀◈❀

FROM *ULYSSES*

Stephen Dedalus at the end of the *Portrait* leaves Dublin for a self-imposed exile in Paris in the spring of 1902. In April 1903, as we know from *Ulysses*, he is called home by his father because his mother is dying. She dies in August, but Stephen remains in Dublin through the winter and into the next summer. The action of *Ulysses* takes place on June 16, 1904.

In the first selection reprinted here, Stephen is still troubled by his relationship to his mother and by the guilt which he feels because he refused to kneel down and pray at her deathbed. He discusses her death with Buck Mulligan, his "gay betrayer," with whom he lives in a round tower on the coast of Dublin Bay at Sandymount. He then meditates on her death and asks for his freedom to live.

In the second selection Stephen is teaching in Mr. Deasy's school in Dalkey. Helping his pupil Sargent understand how to add, Stephen thinks back over his own childhood and *amor matris* ("mother-love" and "love of mother").

The final, expressionistic selection is taken from the climactic scene in Bella Cohen's brothel, late in *Ulysses*. Stephen and the other characters have been "turned into swine" by Bella, a modern Circe. The ghost of Stephen's mother appears to him. He finally frees himself from her, from the Church, and from the guilt he feels, by smashing the chandelier with his ashplant. As he does so, he shouts "Nothung!" It is the name of the sword which Siegfried had forged from the fragments of his father's sword in order to slay the dragon and his foster father, Mime the smith, and to win Brünnhilde. This Wagnerian version of the story is referred to obliquely in the *Portrait*, p. 237, where Dixon whistles the birdcall from *Siegfried* as Stephen and Cranly set out on their walk to

discuss mother-love and Stephen's apostasy from the Roman Catholic
Church. (See Explanatory Notes, 237.29.)

[LET ME BE AND LET ME LIVE][1]

. . . Stephen, depressed by his own voice, said:

—Do you remember the first day I went to your house after
my mother's death?

Buck Mulligan frowned quickly and said:

—What? Where? I can't remember anything. I remember
only ideas and sensations. Why? What happened in the name
of God?

—You were making tea, Stephen said, and I went across the
landing to get more hot water. Your mother and some visitor
came out of the drawingroom. She asked you who was in your
room.

—Yes? Buck Mulligan said. What did I say? I forget.

—You said, Stephen answered, O, *it's only Dedalus whose
mother is beastly dead*.

A flush which made him seem younger and more engaging
rose to Buck Mulligan's cheek.

—Did I say that? he asked. Well? What harm is that?

He shook his constraint from him nervously.

—And what is death, he asked, your mother's or yours or
my own? You saw only your mother die. I see them pop off
every day in the Mater and Richmond and cut up into tripes
in the dissecting room. It's a beastly thing and nothing else.
It simply doesn't matter. You wouldn't kneel down to pray
for your mother on her deathbed when she asked you. Why?
Because you have the cursed jesuit strain in you, only it's in-
jected the wrong way. To me it's all a mockery and beastly.

---

[1] *U*, 8-10.

Her cerebral lobes are not functioning. She calls the doctor Sir Peter Teazle and picks buttercups off the quilt. Humour her till it's over. You crossed her last wish in death and yet you sulk with me because I don't whinge like some hired mute from Lalouette's. Absurd! I suppose I did say it. I didn't mean to offend the memory of your mother.

He had spoken himself into boldness. Stephen, shielding the gaping wounds which the words had left in his heart, said very coldly:

—I am not thinking of the offence to my mother.

—Of what, then? Buck Mulligan asked.

—Of the offence to me, Stephen answered.

Buck Mulligan swung round on his heel.

—O, an impossible person! he exclaimed.

He walked off quickly round the parapet. Stephen stood at his post, gazing over the calm sea towards the headland. Sea and headland now grew dim. Pulses were beating in his eyes, veiling their sight, and he felt the fever of his cheeks.

A voice within the tower called loudly:

—Are you up there, Mulligan?

—I'm coming, Buck Mulligan answered.

He turned towards Stephen and said:

—Look at the sea. What does it care about offences? Chuck Loyola, Kinch, and come on down. The Sassenach wants his morning rashers.

His head halted again for a moment at the top of the staircase, level with the roof.

—Don't mope over it all day, he said. I'm inconsequent. Give up the moody brooding.

His head vanished but the drone of his descending voice boomed out of the stairhead:

> *And no more turn aside and brood*
> *Upon love's bitter mystery*
> *For Fergus rules the brazen cars.*

Woodshadows floated silently by through the morning peace from the stairhead seaward where he gazed. Inshore and farther out the mirror of water whitened, spurned by lightshod hurrying feet. White breast of the dim sea. The twining stresses, two by two. A hand plucking the harpstrings merging their twining chords. Wavewhite wedded words shimmering on the dim tide.

A cloud began to cover the sun slowly, shadowing the bay in deeper green. It lay behind him, a bowl of bitter waters. Fergus' song: I sang it alone in the house, holding down the long dark chords. Her door was open: she wanted to hear my music. Silent with awe and pity I went to her bedside. She was crying in her wretched bed. For those words, Stephen: love's bitter mystery.

Where now?

Her secrets: old feather fans, tasselled dancecards, powdered with musk, a gaud of amber beads in her locked drawer. A birdcage hung in the sunny window of her house when she was a girl. She heard old Royce sing in the pantomime of Turko the terrible and laughed with others when he sang:

> *I am the boy*
> *That can enjoy*
> *Invisibility.*

Phantasmal mirth, folded away: muskperfumed.

And no more turn aside and brood

Folded away in the memory of nature with her toys. Memories beset his brooding brain. Her glass of water from the kitchen tap when she had approached the sacrament. A cored apple, filled with brown sugar, roasting for her at the hob on a dark autumn evening. Her shapely fingernails reddened by the blood of squashed lice from the children's shirts.

In a dream, silently, she had come to him, her wasted body within its loose graveclothes giving off an odour of wax and rosewood, her breath bent over him with mute secret words, a faint odour of wetted ashes.

Her glazing eyes, staring out of death, to shake and bend my soul. On me alone. The ghostcandle to light her agony. Ghostly light on the tortured face. Her hoarse loud breath rattling in horror, while all prayed on their knees. Her eyes on me to strike me down. *Liliata rutilantium te confessorum turma circumdet: iubilantium te virginum chorus excipiat.*[2]

Ghoul! Chewer of corpses!

No mother. Let me be and let me live. . . .

[THE ONLY TRUE THING IN LIFE?][3]

. . . A stick struck the door **and a voice** in the corridor called:
—Hockey!

They broke asunder, sidling out of their benches, leaping them. Quickly they were gone and from the lumberroom came the rattle of sticks and clamour of their boots and tongues.

Sargent who alone had lingered came forward slowly, show-ing an open copybook. His tangled hair and scraggy neck gave witness of unreadiness and through his misty glasses weak eyes looked up pleading. On his cheek, dull and bloodless, a soft stain of ink lay, dateshaped, recent and damp as a snail's bed.

He held out his copybook. The word *Sums* was written on the headline. Beneath were sloping figures and at the foot a crooked signature with blind loops and a blot. Cyril Sargent: his name and seal.

—Mr Deasy told me to write them out all again, he said, and show them to you, sir.

Stephen touched the edges of the book. Futility.

---

[2] "May a lily-bedecked crowd of blushing confessors surround you, a chorus of singing virgins receive you."

[3] *U,* 27-28.

—Do you understand how to do them now? he asked.

—Numbers eleven to fifteen, Sargent answered. Mr Deasy said I was to copy them off the board, sir.

—Can you do them yourself? Stephen asked.

—No, sir.

Ugly and futile: lean neck and tangled hair and a stain of ink, a snail's bed. Yet someone had loved him, borne him in her arms and in her heart. But for her the race of the world would have trampled him under foot, a squashed boneless snail. She had loved his weak watery blood drained from her own. Was that then real? The only true thing in life? His mother's prostrate body the fiery Columbanus in holy zeal bestrode. She was no more: the trembling skeleton of a twig burnt in the fire, an odour of rosewood and wetted ashes. She had saved him from being trampled under foot and had gone, scarcely having been. A poor soul gone to heaven: and on a heath beneath winking stars a fox, red reek of rapine in his fur, with merciless bright eyes scraped in the earth, listened, scraped up the earth, listened, scraped and scraped.

Sitting at his side Stephen solved out the problem. He proves by algebra that Shakespeare's ghost is Hamlet's grandfather. Sargent peered askance through his slanted glasses. Hockeysticks rattled in the lumberroom: the hollow knock of a ball and calls from the field.

Across the page the symbols moved in grave morrice, in the mummery of their letters, wearing quaint caps of squares and cubes. Give hands, traverse, bow to partner: so: imps of fancy of the Moors. Gone too from the world, Averroes and Moses Maimonides, dark men in mien and movement, flashing in their mocking mirrors the obscure soul of the world, a darkness shining in brightness which brightness could not comprehend.

—Do you understand now? Can you work the second for yourself?

—Yes, sir.

In long shady strokes Sargent copied the data. Waiting always for a word of help his hand moved faithfully the unsteady symbols, a faint hue of shame flickering behind his dull skin.

Amor matris: subjective and objective genitive. With her weak blood and wheysour milk she had fed him and hid from sight of others his swaddling bands.

Like him was I, these sloping shoulders, this gracelessness. My childhood bends beside me. Too far for me to lay a hand there once or lightly. Mine is far and his secret as our eyes. Secrets, silent, stony sit in the dark palaces of both our hearts: secrets weary of their tyranny: tyrants willing to be dethroned.

The sum was done.

—It is very simple, Stephen said as he stood up.

—Yes, sir. Thanks, Sargent answered.

He dried the page with a sheet of thin blottingpaper and carried his copybook back to his desk.

—You had better get your stick and go out to the others, Stephen said as he followed towards the door the boy's graceless form.

—Yes, sir. . . .

[NOTHUNG!][4]

. . . (*Stephen's mother, emaciated, rises stark through the floor in leper grey with a wreath of faded orange blossoms and a torn bridal veil, her face worn and noseless, green with grave mould. Her hair is scant and lank. She fixes her blue-circled hollow eyesockets on Stephen and opens her toothless mouth uttering a silent word. A choir of virgins and confessors sing voicelessly.*)

THE CHOIR

Lilliata rutilantium te confessorum . . .
Iubilantium te virginum . . .

[4] *U,* 579-583.

(*From the top of a tower Buck Mulligan, in particoloured jester's dress of puce and yellow and clown's cap with curling bell, stands gaping at her, a smoking buttered split scone in his hand.*)

BUCK MULLIGAN

She's beastly dead. The pity of it! Mulligan meets the afflicted mother. (*He upturns his eyes.*) Mercurial Malachi.

THE MOTHER

(*With the subtle smile of death's madness.*) I was once the beautiful May Goulding. I am dead.

STEPHEN

(*Horrorstruck.*) Lemur, who are you? What bogeyman's trick is this?

BUCK MULLIGAN

(*Shakes his curling capbell.*) The mockery of it! Kinch killed her dogsbody bitchbody. She kicked the bucket. (*Tears of molten butter fall from his eyes into the scone.*) Our great sweet mother! *Epi oinopa ponton.*[5]

THE MOTHER

(*Comes nearer, breathing upon him softly her breath of wetted ashes.*) All must go through it, Stephen. More women than men in the world. You too. Time will come.

STEPHEN

(*Choking with fright, remorse and horror.*) They said I killed you, mother. He offended your memory. Cancer did it, not I. Destiny.

---

[5] A famous Homeric epithet, usually translated as "the wine-dark sea."

THE MOTHER

(*A green rill of bile trickling from a side of her mouth.*) You sang that song to me. *Love's bitter mystery.*

STEPHEN

(*Eagerly.*) Tell me the word, mother, if you know now. The word known to all men.

THE MOTHER

Who saved you the night you jumped into the train at Dalkey with Paddy Lee? Who had pity for you when you were sad among the strangers? Prayer is all powerful. Prayer for the suffering souls in the Ursuline manual, and forty days' indulgence. Repent, Stephen.

STEPHEN

The ghoul! Hyena!

THE MOTHER

I pray for you in my other world. Get Dilly to make you that boiled rice every night after your brain work. Years and years I loved you, O my son, my firstborn, when you lay in my womb.

ZOE

(*Fanning herself with the grate fan.*) I'm melting!

FLORRY

(*Points to Stephen.*) Look! He's white.

BLOOM

(*Goes to the window to open it more.*) Giddy.

THE MOTHER

(*With smouldering eyes.*) Repent! O, the fire of hell!

STEPHEN

(*Panting.*) The corpsechewer! Raw head and bloody bones!

THE MOTHER

(*Her face drawing near and nearer, sending out an ashen breath.*) Beware! (*She raises her blackened, withered right arm slowly towards Stephen's breast with outstretched fingers.*) Beware! God's hand! (*A green crab with malignant red eyes sticks deep its grinning claws in Stephen's heart.*)

STEPHEN

(*Strangled with rage.*) Shite! (*His features grow drawn and grey and old.*)

BLOOM

(*At the window.*) What?

STEPHEN

Ah non, par exemple! The intellectual imagination! With me all or not at all. *Non serviam!*

FLORRY

Give him some cold water. Wait. (*She rushes out.*)

THE MOTHER

(*Wrings her hands slowly, moaning desperately.*) O Sacred Heart of Jesus, have mercy on him! Save him from hell, O divine Sacred Heart!

STEPHEN

No! No! No! Break my spirit all of you if you can! I'll bring you all to heel!

THE MOTHER

(*In the agony of her deathrattle.*) Have mercy on Stephen, Lord, for my sake! Inexpressible was my anguish when expiring with love, grief and agony on Mount Calvary.

STEPHEN

Nothung!

(*He lifts his ashplant high with both hands and smashes the chandelier. Time's livid final flame leaps and, in the following darkness, ruin of all space, shattered glass and toppling masonry.*)

FROM *FINNEGANS WAKE*

In writing *Finnegans Wake*, his last book, between 1923 and 1938, Joyce frequently returned to sketch himself as a young man in the character of Shem the Penman. The name alludes not only to Joyce's occupation as a writer, but also to Jim the Penman, a famous forger. Shem, therefore, is a "sham" (the answer to the "first riddle of the universe"—"When is a man not a man?"—in the first brief excerpt.) He sees his artistic career as having less of the motive of forging the conscience of his race within the smithy of his soul than of "uttering an epical forged check on the public."

The second selection also criticizes Shem for his "endlessly inartistic portraits of himself" and then paints another one by means of a catalogue of the contents of his "Inkbottle" house.

[SHEM THE PENMAN][1]

. . . Shem was a sham and a low sham and his lowness creeped out first via foodstuffs. So low was he that he preferred Gibsen's teatime salmon tinned, as inexpensive as pleasing, to the plumpest roeheavy lax or the friskiest parr or smolt troutlet that ever

---

From *Finnegans Wake* by James Joyce. Copyright 1939 by James Joyce, renewed 1967 by George Joyce and Lucia Joyce. Used by permission of The Viking Press, Inc., and The Society of Authors.

Some of the other passages in *Finnegans Wake* which portray the early life of the artist are on pp. 114-116, 152-155, 231-233, and 237-239.
[1] FW, 170-171.

was gaffed between Leixlip and Island Bridge and many was
the time he repeated in his botulism that no junglegrown pine-
apple ever smacked like the whoppers you shook out of Ana-
nias' cans, Findlater and Gladstone's, Corner House, Englend.
None of your inchthick blueblooded Balaclava fried-at-belief-
stakes or juicejelly legs of the Grex's molten mutton or greasily-
gristly grunters' goupons or slice upon slab of luscious goose-
bosom with lump after load of plumpudding stuffing all aswim
in a swamp of bogoakgravy for that greekenhearted yude! Rosbif
of Old Zealand! he could not attouch it. See what happens
when your somatophage merman takes his fancy to our virgi-
tarian swan? He even ran away with hunself and became a
farsoonerite, saying he would far sooner muddle through the
hash of lentils in Europe than meddle with Irrland's split
little pea. Once when among those rebels in a state of hopelessly
helpless intoxication the piscivore strove to lift a czitround peel
to either nostril, hiccupping, apparently impromptued by the
hibat he had with his glottal stop, that he kukkakould flowrish
for ever by the smell, as the czitr, as the kcedron, like a scedar,
of the founts, on mountains, with limon on, of Lebanon. O!
the lowness of him was beneath all up to that sunk to! No
likedbylike firewater or firstserved firstshot or gulletburn gin or
honest brewbarrett beer either. O dear no! Instead the tragic
jester sobbed himself wheywhingingly sick of life on some sort
of a rhubarbarous maundarin yellagreen funkleblue windigut
diodying applejack squeezed from sour grapefruice and, to hear
him twixt his sedimental cupslips when he had gulfed down
mmmmuch too mmmmany gourds of it retching off to almost
as low withswillera, who always knew notwithstanding when
they had had enough and were rightly indignant at the retch's
hospitality when they found to their horror they could not
carry another drop, it came straight from the noble white fat,
jo, openwide sat, jo, jo, her why hide that, jo jo jo, the winevat,
of the most serene magyansty az archdiochesse, if she is a duck,
she's a douches, and when she has a feherbour snot her fault,
now is it? artstouchups, funny you're grinning at, fancy you're
in her yet, Fanny Urinia. . . .

[THE HAUNTED INKBOTTLE][2]

. . . One cannot even begin to post figure out a statuesquo ante
as to how slow in reality the excommunicated Drumcondriac,
nate Hamis, really was. Who can say how many pseudostylic
shamiana, how few or how many of the most venerated public
impostures, how very many piously forged palimpsests slipped
in the first place by this morbid process from his pelagiarist pen?
 Be that as it may, but for that light phantastic of his gnose's
glow as it slid lucifericiously within an inch of its page (he
would touch at its from time to other, the red eye of his fear
in saddishness, to ensign the colours by the beerlitz in his
mathness and his educandees to outhue to themselves in the
cries of girlglee: gember! inkware! chonchambre! cinsero! zinn-
zabar! tincture and gin!) Nibs never would have quilled a seriph
to sheepskin. By that rosy lampoon's effluvious burning and
with help of the simulchronic flush in his pann (a ghinee a
ghirk he ghets there!) he scrabbled and scratched and scriob-
bled and skrevened nameless shamelessness about everybody
ever he met, even sharing a precipitation under the idlish tar-
riers' umbrella of a showerproof wall, while all over up and
down the four margins of this rancid Shem stuff the evilsmeller
(who was devoted to Uldfadar Sardanapalus) used to stipple
endlessly inartistic portraits of himself in the act of reciting old
Nichiabelli's monolook interyerear *Hanno, o Nonanno, acce'l
brubblemm'*as, ser Autore, q.e.d., a heartbreakingly handsome
young paolo with love lyrics for the goyls in his eyols, a plain-
tiff's tanner vuice, a jucal inkome of one hundred and thirtytwo
drachmas per yard from Broken Hill stranded estate, Came-
breech mannings, cutting a great dash in a brandnew two
guinea dress suit and a burled hogsford hired for a Fursday

[2] *FW*, 181-183.

evenin merry pawty, anna loavely long pair of inky Italian moostarshes glistering with boric vaseline and frangipani. Puh! How unwhisperably so!

The house O'Shea or O'Shame, *Quivapieno*, known as the Haunted Inkbottle, no number Brimstone Walk, Asia in Ireland, as it was infested with the raps, with his penname SHUT sepiascraped on the doorplate and a blind of black sailcloth over its wan phwinshogue, in which the soulcontracted son of the secret cell groped through life at the expense of the taxpayers, dejected into day and night with jesuit bark and bitter bite, calicohydrants of zolfor and scoppialamina by full and forty Queasisanos, every day in everyone's way more exceeding in violent abuse of self and others, was the worst, it is hoped, even in our western playboyish world for pure mousefarm filth. You brag of your brass castle or your tyled house in ballyfermont? Niggs, niggs, and niggs again. For this was a stinksome inkenstink, quite puzzonal to the wrottel. Smatterafact, Angles aftanon browsing there thought not Edam reeked more rare. My wud! The warped flooring of the lair and soundconducting walls thereof, to say nothing of the uprights and imposts, were persianly literatured with burst loveletters, telltale stories, stickyback snaps, doubtful eggshells, bouchers, flints, borers, puffers, amygdaloid almonds, rindless raisins, alphybettyformed verbage, vivlical viasses, ompiter dictas, visus umbique, ahems and ahahs, imeffible tries at speech unasyllabled, you owe mes, eyoldhyms, fluefoul smut, fallen lucifers, vestas which had served, showered ornaments, borrowed brogues, reversibles jackets, blackeye lenses, family jars, falsehair shirts, Godforsaken scapulars, neverworn breeches, cutthroat ties, counterfeit franks, best intentions, curried notes, upset latten tintacks, unused mill and stumpling stones, twisted quills, painful digests, magnifying wineglasses, solid objects cast at goblins, once current puns, quashed quotatoes, messes of mottage, unquestionable issue papers, seedy ejaculations, limerick damns, crocodile tears, spilt ink. . . .

III

✦◆

A Portrait of the Artist as a Young Man: *Criticism*

Early Comment

✿◊

EZRA POUND

Ezra Pound, poet, critic, and editor, besides inventing the "Imagiste"
school of poetry, founding imaginative translation, advising such
established writers as Yeats, and reviving such disestablished writers
as Henry James, "discovered" both James Joyce and T. S. Eliot.
The latter, in dedicating *The Waste Land* to Pound, called him
"il miglior fabbro" ("the best artificer"). In addition to giving
Joyce much encouragement, Pound used his influence to introduce
editors and publishers to Joyce's work, and to engineer financial help
for him during the First World War.

LETTER TO JOYCE

September 1915
5 Holland Place Chambers, Kensington

Dear Joyce I have just read the splendid end of 'The Portrait
of the Artist', and if I try to tell you how fine it is, I shall only
break out into inane hyperbole.

I think the Chapter V. went straight to the Egoist, or came
when I was away and had to be forwarded at once,,, anyhow I
have been reading it *in* the paper. I have been doing nothing
but write 15 page letters to New York about the new magazine
and my head is a squeezed rag, so don't expect le mot juste in
this letter.

However I read you[r] final instalment last night when I was
calm enough to know what I was doing, and I might have
written then with more lucidity.

Anyhow I think the book hard, perfect stuff. I doubt if you could have done it in 'the lap of luxury' or in the whirl of a metropolis with the attrition of endless small amusements and endless calls on one's time, and endless trivialities of enjoyment (or the reverse).

I think the book is permanent like Flaubert and Stendhal. Not so squarish as Stendhal, certainly not so varnished as Flaubert. In english I think you join on to Hardy and Henry James (I don't mean a resemblance, I mean that there's has [*sic*] been nothing of permanent value in prose in between. But I think you must soon, or at least sooner or later, get your recognition.

Hang it all, we dont get prose books that a man can *re*read. We don't get prose that gives us pleasure paragraph by paragraph. I know one man who occasionally burries a charming short chapter in a long inneffective novel . . . but that's another story.

It is the ten years spent on the book, the Dublin 1904, Trieste 1914, that counts. No man can dictate a novel, though there are a lot who try to. And for the other school. I am so damn sick of energetic stupidity. The 'strong' work . . . balls! And it is such a comfort to find an author who has read something and knows something. This deluge of work by subirban [*sic*] counter-jumpers on the one hand and gut-less Oxford graduates or flunktuates on the other . . . bah! And never any intensity, not in *any* of it.

The play has come, and I shall read it as soon as I can be sure of being uninterrupted. . . .

EDWARD GARNETT

Edward Garnett, critic and essayist, was literary adviser to the English publishing firm Duckworth and Company when the *Portrait* was first submitted to them. Among the writers whom he advised and whose careers he helped to launch were Joseph Conrad, John Galsworthy, D. H. Lawrence, W. H. Hudson, and Edward Thomas. Garnett's original report, written in early summer of 1915 in a Minute Book now owned by his son, is published here for the first time. The longer version which follows was sent by Duckworth to James B. Pinker, Joyce's agent, on June 26, 1916, on Pinker's requesting an explanation for the rejection of the *Portrait*. The long version is clearly based on the shorter, but there is some doubt whether Garnett actually wrote it. Later in 1915 he had joined the Italian Ambulance Unit organized by Sir Charles Trevelyan, so that he was fully occupied with the wounded on the Izonzo at the time Duckworth sent the long version to Pinker. That version was in fact transmitted to Pinker by Herbert J. Cape, who later as Jonathan Cape published an English edition of the *Portrait* in 1924.

A PORTRAIT OF THE ARTIST
AS A YOUNG MAN

By James Joyce
(From Edward Garnett: Minute Book, 1915)

Mr. Joyce published some very clever stories (with Maunsel) "Dubliners," in the summer, but the book was probably *not* successful, as the sketches were rather "realistic" studies of unprepossessing types. In the M.S. now submitted he gives us reminiscences of his schooldays, of his family life in Dublin and of his adolescence. It is all ably written and the picture is curious. But the style is too discursive and his point of view will be called "a little sordid." It isn't a book that would make a young man's reputation—it is too unconventional for our British public.

First version used by permission of Mr. David Garnett.

And in War Time it has less chance than at any other.
Decline with thanks.

READER'S REPORT

James Joyce's 'Portrait of the Artist as a Young Man' wants
going through carefully from start to finish. There are many
'longueurs.' Passages which, though the publisher's reader may
find them entertaining, will be tedious to the ordinary man
among the reading public. That public will call the book, as
it stands at present, realistic, unprepossessing, unattractive. We
call it ably written. The picture is 'curious,' it arouses interest
and attention. But the author must revise it and let us see it
again. It is too discursive, formless, unrestrained, and ugly
things, ugly words, are too prominent; indeed at times they
seem to be shoved in one's face, on purpose, unnecessarily.
The point of view will be voted 'a little sordid.' The picture of
life is good; the period well brought to the reader's eye, and
the types and characters are well drawn, but it is too 'unconventional.' This would stand against it in normal times. At the
present time, though the old conventions are in the background,
we can only see a chance for it if it is pulled into shape and
made more definite.

In the earlier portion of the MS. as submitted to us, a good
deal of pruning can be done. Unless the author will use re-
straint and proportion he will not gain readers. His pen and
his thoughts seem to have run away with him sometimes.

And at the end of the book there is a complete falling to
bits; the pieces of writing and the thoughts are all in pieces
and they fall like damp, ineffective rockets.

The author shows us he has art, strength and originality, but
this MS. wants time and trouble spent on it, to make it a more
finished piece of work, to shape it more carefully as the product of the craftsmanship, mind and imagination of an artist.

EZRA POUND

The *Portrait*, after serialization in *The Egoist* from February 1914 to September 1915, was turned down by every publisher in London to whom it was offered, and when Harriet Shaw Weaver tried to have it published in book form by *The Egoist* itself, the printers refused to print it. It was finally published in New York by B. W. Huebsch and Company (predecessor of The Viking Press) in December 1916. *The Egoist* imported printed sheets from America and brought out the first English edition of 750 copies in February 1917.

JAMES JOYCE:
At Last the Novel Appears

It is unlikely that I shall say anything new about Mr. Joyce's novel, *A Portrait of the Artist as a Young Man*. I have already stated that it is a book worth reading and that it is written in good prose. In using these terms I do not employ the looseness of the half-crown reviewer.

I am very glad that it is now possible for a few hundred people to read Mr. Joyce comfortably from a bound book, instead of from a much-handled file of Egoists or from a slippery bundle of type-script. After much difficulty THE EGOIST itself turns publisher and produces *A Portrait of the Artist* as a volume, for the hatred of ordinary English publishers for good prose is, like the hatred of the *Quarterly Review* for good poetry, deep-rooted, traditional.

Since Landor's *Imaginary Conversations* were bandied from pillar to post, I doubt if any manuscript has met with so much opposition, and no manuscript has been more worth supporting.

Landor is still an unpopular author. He is still a terror to fools. He is still concealed from the young (not for any alleged indecency, but simply because he did not acquiesce in certain popular follies). He, Landor, still plays an inconspicuous rôle in university courses. The amount of light which he would shed on the undergraduate mind would make students inconvenient to the average run of professors. But Landor is permanent.

Members of the "Fly-Fishers" and "Royal Automobile" clubs, and of the "Isthmian," may not read him. They will not read Mr. Joyce. *E pur si muove.* Despite the printers and publishers the British Government has recognized Mr. Joyce's literary merit. That is a definite gain for the party of intelligence. A number of qualified judges have acquiesced in my statement of two years ago, that Mr. Joyce was an excellent and important writer of prose.

The last few years have seen the gradual shaping of a party of intelligence, a party not bound by any central doctrine or theory. We cannot accurately define new writers by applying to them tag-names from old authors, but as there is no adequate means of conveying the general impression of their characteristics one may at times employ such terminology, carefully stating that the terms are nothing more than approximation.

With that qualification, I would say that James Joyce produces the nearest thing to Flaubertian prose that we have now in English, just as Wyndham Lewis has written a novel which is more like, and more fitly compared with, Dostoievsky than is the work of any of his contemporaries. In like manner Mr. T. S. Eliot comes nearer to filling the place of Jules Laforgue in our generation. (Doing the "nearest thing" need not imply an approach to a standard, from a position inferior.)

Two of these writers have met with all sorts of opposition. If Mr. Eliot probably has not yet encountered very much opposition, it is only because his work is not yet very widely known.

My own income was considerably docked because I dared

to say that Gaudier-Brzeska was a good sculptor and that Wyndham Lewis was a great master of design. It has, however, reached an almost irreducible minimum, and I am, perhaps, fairly safe in reasserting Joyce's ability as a writer. It will cost me no more than a few violent attacks from several sheltered, and therefore courageous, anonymities. When you tell the Irish that they are slow in recognizing their own men of genius they reply with street riots and politics.

Now, despite the jobbing of bigots and of their sectarian publishing houses, and despite the "Fly-Fishers" and the types which they represent, and despite the unwillingness of the print-packers (a word derived from pork-packers) and the initial objections of the Dublin publishers and the later unwillingness of the English publishers, Mr. Joyce's novel appears in book form, and intelligent readers gathering few by few will read it, and it will remain a permanent part of English literature—written by an Irishman in Trieste and first published in New York City. I doubt if a comparison of Mr. Joyce to other English writers or Irish writers would much help to define him. One can only say that he is rather unlike them. *The Portrait* is very different from *L'Education Sentimentale*, but it would be easier to compare it with that novel of Flaubert's than with anything else. Flaubert pointed out that if France had studied his work they might have been saved a good deal in 1870. If more people had read *The Portrait* and certain stories in Mr. Joyce's *Dubliners* there might have been less recent trouble in Ireland. A clear diagnosis is never without its value.

Apart from Mr. Joyce's realism—the school-life, the life in the University, the family dinner with the discussion of Parnell depicted in his novel—apart from, or of a piece with, all this is the style, the actual writing: hard, clear-cut, with no waste of words, no bundling up of useless phrases, no filling in with pages of slosh.

It is very important that there should be clear, unexaggerated, realistic literature. It is very important that there should be good prose. The hell of contemporary Europe is caused by the lack of representative government in Germany, *and* by the non-existence of decent prose in the German language. Clear thought and sanity depend on clear prose. They cannot live apart. The former produces the latter. The latter conserves and transmits the former.

The mush of the German sentence, the straddling of the verb out to the end, are just as much a part of the befoozlement of Kultur and the consequent hell, as was the rhetoric of later Rome the seed and the symptom of the Roman Empire's decadence and extinction. A nation that cannot write clearly cannot be trusted to govern, nor yet to think.

Germany has had two decent prose-writers, Frederick the Great and Heine—the one taught by Voltaire, and the other saturated with French and with Paris. Only a nation accustomed to muzzy writing could have been led by the nose and bamboozled as the Germans have been by their controllers.

The terror of clarity is not confined to any one people. The obstructionist and the provincial are everywhere, and in them alone is the permanent danger to civilization. Clear, hard prose is the safeguard and should be valued as such. The mind accustomed to it will not be cheated or stampeded by national phrases and public emotionalities.

These facts are true, even for the detesters of literature. For those who love good writing there is no need of argument. In the present instance it is enough to say to those who will believe one that Mr. Joyce's book is now procurable.

DIEGO ANGELI

Diego Angeli was a prominent Florentine book reviewer and commentator for Italian periodicals on the European cultural scene. The following review was translated by Joyce himself from "Un Romanzo di Gesuiti," from the Florentine newspaper *Il Marzocco*, August 12, 1917, and sent to Harriet Shaw Weaver for insertion in *The Egoist* for February 1917. Joyce's translation is accurate and straightforward.

Extract from IL MARZOCCO

Mr. James Joyce is a young Irish novelist whose last book, *A Portrait of the Artist as a Young Man*, has raised a great tumult of discussion among English-speaking critics. It is easy to see why. An Irishman, he has found in himself the strength to proclaim himself a citizen of a wider world; a catholic, he has had the courage to cast his religion from him and to proclaim himself an atheist; and a writer, inheriting the most traditionalist of all European literatures, he has found a way to break free from the tradition of the old English novel and to adopt a new style consonant with a new conception. In a word such an effort was bound to tilt against all the feelings and cherished beliefs of his fellowcountrymen but, carried out, as it is here, with a fine and youthful boldness, it has won the day. His book is not alone an admirable work of art and thought; it is also a cry of revolt: it is the desire of a new artist to look upon the world with other eyes, to bring to the front his individual theories and to compel a listless public to reflect that there are another literature and another esthetic apprehension beyond those foisted upon us, with a bountifulness at times nauseating, by the general purveying of pseudo-romantic prose and by fashionable publishers, with their seriocomic booklists, and by the weekly and monthly magazines. And let

---

us admit that such a cry of revolt has been uttered at the right moment and that it is in itself the promise of a fortunate renascence.

For, to tell the truth, English fiction seemed lately to have gone astray amid the sentimental niceties of Miss Beatrice Harraden, the police-aided plottiness of Sir Conan Doyle, the stupidities of Miss Corelli or, at best, the philosophical and sociological disquisitions of Mrs. Humphrey Ward. The intention seemed to be to satisfy the largest circle of readers and all that remain within the pale of tradition by trying to put again on the market old dusty ideas and by avoiding sedulously all conflict with the esthetic, moral and political susceptibilities of the majority. For this reason in the midst of the great revolution of the European novel English writers continued to remain in their "splendid isolation" and could not or would not open their eyes to what was going on around them. Literature, however, like all the other arts underwent a gradual transformation and Mr. Joyce's book marks its definite date in the chronology of English literature. I think it well to put so much on record here not only for that which it signifies actually but also for that which in time it may bring forth.

The phenomenon is all the more important in that Mr. Joyce's *Portrait* contains two separate elements, each of which is significant and worthy of analysis: its ethical content and the form wherewith this content is clothed. When one has read the book to the end one understands why most English and American critics have raised an outcry against both form and content, understanding, for the most part, neither one nor the other. Accustomed as they are to the usual novels, enclosed in a set framework, they found themselves in this case out of their depth and hence their talk of immorality, impiety, naturalism and exaggeration. They have not grasped the sublety of the psychological analysis nor the synthetic value of certain details and certain sudden arrests of movement. Possibly their own protestant upbringing renders the moral development of the central character incomprehensible to them. For Mr. Joyce is a catholic and, more than that, a catholic brought up in a jesuit college. One must have passed many years of one's own life in a seminary of the society of Jesus, one must have passed through the same experiences and undergone the same crises to understand the profound analysis, the keenness of observation shown in the character of Stephen Dedalus. No writer, so far as I know, has penetrated deeper in the examination of the influence, sensual rather than spiritual, of the society's exercises.

For this analysis so purely modern, so cruelly and boldly true, the writer needed a style which would break down the tradition of the six shilling novel: and this style Mr. Joyce has fashioned for himself. The brushwork of the novel reminds one of certain modern paintings in which the planes interpenetrate and the external vision seems to partake of the sensations of the onlooker. It is not so much the narrative of a life as its reminiscence but it is a reminiscence whole, complete and absolute, with all those incidents and details which tend to fix indelibly each feature of the whole. He does not lose time explaining the wherefore of these sensations of his nor even tell us their reason or origin: they leap up in his pages as do the memories of a life we ourselves have lived without apparent cause, without logical sequence. But it is exactly such a succession of past visions and memories which makes up the sum of every life. In this evocation of reality Mr. Joyce is truly a master. The majority of English critics remark, with easy superficiality, that he thinks himself a naturalist simply because he does not shrink from painting certain brutal episodes in words more brutal still. This is not so: his naturalism goes much deeper. Certainly there is a difference, formal no less than substantial, between his book and, let us say, *La Terre* of Emile Zola. Zola's naturalism is romantic whereas the naturalism of Mr. Joyce is impressionist, the profound synthetic naturalism of some pictures of Cézanne or Maquet, the naturalism of the late impressionists who single out the characteristic elements of a landscape or a scene or a human face. And all this he expresses in a rapid and concise style, free from every picturesque effect, every rhetorical redundancy, every needless image or epithet. Mr. Joyce tells us what he must tell in the least number of words; his palette is limited to a few colours. But he knows what to choose for his end and therefore half a page of his dry precise angular prose expresses much more (and with much more telling effect) than all that wearisome research of images and colour of which we have lately heard and read so much.

And that is why Mr. Joyce's book has raised such a great clamour of discussion. He is a new writer in the glorious company of English literature, a new writer with a new form of his own and new aims, and he comes at a moment when the world is making a new constitution and a new social ordinance. We must welcome him with joy. He is one of those rude craftsmen who open up paths whereon many will yet follow. It is the first streak of the dawn of a new art visible on the horizon. Let us hail it therefore as the herald of a new day.

H. G. WELLS

H. G. Wells was one of the best-known English novelists of the
late Victorian and Edwardian eras, though he is now more admired
for works of science fiction, such as *The Time Machine*, *The Island
of Dr. Moreau*, and *The War of the Worlds*. He was also a leading
spokesman for the critical establishment of his time, showing insight
into the writing of younger contemporaries such as Joyce and
Virginia Woolf, though he could not share their commitment to
experiment in the novel.

JAMES JOYCE

An eminent novelist was asked recently by some troublesome
newspaper what he thought of the literature of 1916. He answered publicly and loudly that he had heard of no literature in
1916; for his own part he had been reading "science." This was
kind neither to our literary nor our scientific activities. It was
not intelligent to make an opposition between literature and
science. It is no more legitimate than an opposition between
literature and "classics" or between literature and history. Good
writing about the actualities of the war too has been abundant,
that was only to be expected; it is an ungracious thing in the
home critic to sit at a confused feast and bewail its poverty
when he ought to be sorting out his discoveries. Criticism may
analyze, it may appraise and attack, but when it comes to the
mere grumbling of veterans no longer capable of novel perceptions, away with it! There is indeed small justification for grumbling at the writing of the present time. Quite apart from the
books and stories about the war, a brilliant literature in itself,
from that artless assured immortal Arthur Green (*The Story of
a Prisoner of War*) up to the already active historians, there is
a great amount of fresh and experimental writing that cannot
be ignored by anyone still alive to literary interests. There are,

for instance, Miss Richardson's *Pointed Roofs*, and *Backwater*, amusing experiments to write as the Futurists paint, and Mr. Caradoc Evan's invention in *My People*, and *Capel Sion*, of a new method of grimness, a pseudo-Welsh idiom that is as pleasing in its grotesque force to the intelligent story-reader as it must be maddening to every sensitive Welsh patriot. Nowhere have I seen anything like adequate praise for the romantic force and beauty of Mr. Thomas Burke's *Limehouse Nights*. In the earlier 'nineties when Henley was alive and discovering was in fashion that book would have made a very big reputation indeed. Even more considerable is *A Portrait of the Artist as a Young Man*, by James Joyce. It is a book to buy and read and lock up, but it is not a book to miss. Its claim to be literature is as good as the last book of *Gulliver's Travels*.

It is no good trying to minimize a characteristic that seems to be deliberately obtruded. Like Swift and another living Irish writer, Mr. Joyce has a cloacal obsession. He would bring back into the general picture of life aspects which modern drainage and modern decorum have taken out of ordinary intercourse and conversation. Coarse, unfamiliar words are scattered about the book unpleasantly, and it may seem to many, needlessly. If the reader is squeamish upon these matters, then there is nothing for it but to shun this book, but if he will pick his way, as one has to do at times on the outskirts of some picturesque Italian village with a view and a church and all sorts of things of that sort to tempt one, then it is quite worth while. And even upon this unsavory aspect of Swift and himself, Mr. Joyce is suddenly illuminating. He tells at several points how his hero Stephen is swayed and shocked and disgusted by harsh and loud *sounds*, and how he is stirred to intense emotion by music and the rhythms of beautiful words. But no sort of smell offends him like that. He finds olfactory sensations interesting or aesthetically displeasing, but they do not make him sick or excited as sounds do. This is a quite understandable turn over from the more normal state of affairs. Long ago I remember pointing out in a review the difference in the sensory basis of the stories of Robert Louis Stevenson and Sir J. M. Barrie; the former visualized and saw his story primarily as picture, the latter mainly heard it. We shall do Mr. Joyce an injustice if we attribute a normal sensory basis to him and then accuse him of deliberate offense.

But that is by the way. The value of Mr. Joyce's book has little to do with its incidental insanitary condition. Like some of the best novels in the world it is the story of an education; it is by far the most living and convincing picture that exists of an Irish Catholic upbringing. It is a mosaic of jagged fragments that does altogether render with extreme completeness the growth of a rather secretive, imaginative boy in Dublin. The technique is startling, but on the whole it succeeds. Like so many Irish writers from Sterne to Shaw Mr. Joyce is a bold experimentalist with paragraph and punctuation. He breaks away from scene to scene without a hint of the change of time and place; at the end he passes suddenly from the third person to the first; he uses no inverted commas to mark off his speeches. The first trick I found sometimes tiresome here and there, but then my own disposition, perhaps acquired at the blackboard, is to mark off and underline rather fussily, and I do not know whether I was so much put off the thing myself as anxious, which after all is not my business, about its effect on those others; the second trick, I will admit, seems entirely justified in this particular instance by its success; the third reduces Mr. Joyce to a free use of dashes. One conversation in this book is a superb success, the one in which Mr. Dedalus carves the Christmas turkey; I write with all due deliberation that Sterne himself could not have done it better; but most of the talk flickers blindingly with these dashes, one has the same wincing feeling of being flicked at that one used to have in the early cinema shows. I think Mr. Joyce has failed to discredit the inverted comma.

The interest of the book depends entirely upon its quintessential and unfailing reality. One believes in Stephen Dedalus as one believes in few characters in fiction. And the peculiar lie of the interest for the intelligent reader is the convincing revelation it makes of the limitations of a great mass of Irishmen.

Mr. Joyce tells us unsparingly of the adolescence of this young-ster under conditions that have passed almost altogether out of English life. There is an immense shyness, a profound se-crecy, about matters of sex, with its inevitable accompaniment of nightmare revelations and furtive scribblings in unpleasant places, and there is a living belief in a real hell. The descrip-tion of Stephen listening without a doubt to two fiery sermons on that tremendous theme, his agonies of fear, not disgust at dirtiness such as unorthodox children feel but just fear, his terror-inspired confession of his sins of impurity to a strange priest in a distant part of the city, is like nothing in any boy's experience who has been trained under modern conditions. Compare its stuffy horror with Conrad's account of how under analogous circumstances Lord Jim wept. And a second thing of immense significance is the fact that everyone in this Dublin story, every human being, accepts as a matter of course, as a thing in nature like the sky and the sea, that the English are to be hated. There is no discrimination in that hatred, there is no gleam of recognition that a considerable number of English-men have displayed a very earnest disposition to put matters right with Ireland, there is an absolute absence of any idea of a discussed settlement, any notion of helping the slow-witted Englishman in his three-cornered puzzle between North and South. It is just hate, a cant cultivated to the pitch of mono-mania, an ungenerous violent direction of the mind. That is the political atmosphere in which Stephen Dedalus grows up, and in which his essentially responsive mind orients itself. I am afraid it is only too true an account of the atmosphere in which a number of brilliant young Irishmen have grown up. What is the good of pretending that the extreme Irish "patriot" is an equivalent and parallel of the English or American liberal? He is narrower and intenser than any English Tory. He will be the natural ally of the Tory in delaying British social and economic reconstruction after the war. He will play into the hands of the Tories by threatening an outbreak and providing the excuse for a militarist reaction in England. It is time the American observer faced the truth of that. No reason in that why England should not do justice to Ireland, but excellent reason for bearing in mind that these bright-green young people across the Channel are something quite different from the liberal English in training and tradition, and absolutely set against helping them. No single book has ever shown how different they are, as completely as this most memorable novel.

THE EGOIST

Joyce and Harriet Shaw Weaver gathered the following excerpts from
reviews (the deletions are theirs) and printed them as an advertisement on the back cover of *The Egoist*. Joyce had more than a
thousand of these extras reprinted as handbills in 1917 to use in
advertising the *Portrait*.

[EXTRACTS FROM FIRST PRESS NOTICES]

The first edition of this masterpiece among works of modern
fiction (for which not only was no British publisher to be
found willing to publish, but *no British printer willing to print*)
is now nearly exhausted. Copies of the first edition, "Printed
in America," will be very valued possessions when *The Portrait*
becomes more widely recognized—as it certainly will—as an
outstanding feature in the permanent literature of the present
period. Readers of *The Egoist* who have not already secured a
copy should *order at once*.

EXTRACTS FROM FIRST PRESS NOTICES

. . . *The Times Literary Supplement:* We should like the book
to have as many readers as possible. . . . As one reads one remembers oneself in it. . . . Like all good fiction, it is as particular as it is universal. . . . Mr. Joyce can present the external
world excellently. . . . No living writer is better at conversations.
. . . The talk is more real than real talk. . . . His hero is one
of the many Irishmen who cannot reconcile themselves to things;
above all he cannot reconcile himself to himself. . . . His mind
is a mirror in which beauty and ugliness are intensified. . . . His
experience is so intense, such a conflict of beauty and disgust, that

---

From *The Egoist*, April 1917, p. 48.

for a time it drives him into an immoral life, in which there is also beauty and disgust. . . . But for all that he is not futile, because of the drifting passion and the flushing and fading beauty of his mind. . . . It is wild youth, as wild as Hamlet's, and full of music.

Manchester Guardian: When one recognizes genius in a book one had perhaps best leave criticism alone. Genius is so rare that humility must needs mingle with the gratitude it inspires. . . . There are many pages, and not a few whole scenes, in Mr. Joyce's book which are undoubtedly the work of a man of genius. . . . A subtle sense of art has worked amidst the chaos, making this hither-and-thither record of a young mind and soul . . . a complete and ordered thing. . . . Among the new-fangled heroes of the newest fiction devoted to the psychology of youth he is almost unique in having known at least once a genuine sense of sin and undergone a genuine struggle. There is drama in Stephen.

Scotsman: To readers who knew Mr. Joyce's former book, *Dubliners,* his new story may be at once described and recommended as a more elaborate work in the same vein. . . . It has the same accomplished literary craftsmanship in the realistic characterization of the young Irishmen of today. . . . Written with a rare skill in charging simple forcible language with an uncommon weight of original feeling.

Glasgow Herald: James Joyce is a remarkable writer. As a pure stylist he is equalled by few and surpassed by none. . . . His thought is crystalized out in clear sentences with many facets, transparent, full of meaning, free from unessentials. . . . His economy of words is wonderful . . . a ruthless excision of all that is irrelevant to the theme at hand. . . . The reader instead of moving across a laboriously bridged gulf . . . leaps confidently from one peak to another in the clear radiance emanating from the summits themselves. . . . We have acknowledged fully his greatness as an artist in form, and as fully acknowledge his sincerity of purpose, but we quarrel with him on aesthetic values.

Birmingham Post: Dubliners showed the author to be a relentless realist whose craftsmanship was undeniable. The qualities which won praise for that volume are emphasized in this novel, but its realism will displease many.

Liverpool Daily Post: A remarkable book, as original in style as it is abrupt. . . . A book which flashes its truth upon one like a searchlight and a moment later leaves the dazzled reader in darkness. The family quarrel over Parnell is the vividest piece of writing of modern times. The Roman Catholic school, the fear of Hell, the wild sinning and the melodramatic repentance pass in swift succession through a boy's imaginative brain . . . dizzy in a body thrilling with life.

Eastern Morning News: There is power in "A Portrait" and an originality that is almost overwhelming. . . . The book is immensely clever; whether it is pleasant or not we leave our readers to decide for themselves. Of its literary value there can be no doubt.

Mr. Ernest A. Boyd in *New Ireland:* With a frankness and veracity as appalling as they are impressive, Mr. Joyce sets forth the relentless chronicle of a soul stifled by material and intellectual squalor. . . . The pages of the book are redolent of the ooze of our shabby respectability, with its intolerable tolerance of most shameful barbarism. . . . A truly amazing piece of personal and social dissection.

Southport Guardian: A ruthless, relentless essay in realism; a conscious, candid effort at perfection in portraiture, with no reticences and no reserves—almost brutally frank.

Cambridge Review: His vivid chapters on life in a Catholic school place him at once amongst the few great masters of analytic reminiscence.

Literary World: Rather a study of a temperament than a story in the ordinary way. . . . It has the intimate veracity, or appearance of veracity, of the great writers of confessions. . . . At times the analysis reminds one of Andreyed [*sic*] . . . at others the writing is pure lyrical beauty.

Everyman: Garbage. . . . We feel that Mr. Joyce would be at his best in a treatise on drains.

THE EGOIST

This is a verbatim report of actual reviews, compiled by *The Egoist*.

JAMES JOYCE AND HIS CRITICS:
Some Classified Comments

CAUTION: It is very difficult to know quite what to say about this new book by Mr. Joyce.—*Literary World.*

DRAINS: Mr. Joyce is a clever novelist, but we feel he would be really at his best in a treatise on drains.—*Everyman.*

CLEANMINDEDNESS: This pseudo-autobiography of Stephen Dedalus, a weakling and a dreamer, makes fascinating reading. . . . No clean-minded person could possibly allow it to remain within reach of his wife, his sons or daughters.—*Irish Book Lover.*

OPPORTUNITIES OF DUBLIN: If one must accuse Mr. Joyce of anything, it is that he too wilfully ignores the opportunities which Dublin offers even to a Stephen Dedalus. . . . He has undoubtedly failed to bring out the undeniable superiority of many features of life in the capital. . . . He is as blind to the charm of its situation as to the stirrings of literary and civic consciousness which give an interest and zest to social and political intercourse.—*New Ireland.*

BEAUTY: There is much in the book to offend a good many varieties of readers, and little compensating beauty.—*New York Globe.*

The most obvious thing about the book is its beauty.—*New Witness.*

STYLE: It is possible that the author intends to write a sequel to the story. If so, he might acquire a firmer, more coherent and more lucid style by a study of Flaubert, Daudet, Thackeray and Thomas Hardy.—*Rochester* (New York) *Post-Express.*

The occasional lucid intervals in which one glimpses imminent setting forth of social elements and forces in Dublin, only to be disappointed, are similar to the eye or ear which appears in futurist portraits, but proves the more bewildering because no other recognizable feature is to be discerned among the chaos.—*Bellman* (U.S.A.). [*Editor's Note:* In the sentence quoted above, "lucid intervals" is to be parsed with "are similar" and "eye or ear" with "proves." The adjective "recognizable" is apparently pleonastic.]

REALISM: It is a ruthless, relentless essay in realism.—*Southport Guardian.*

To put the literary form of rude language in a book makes some authors feel realistic.—*Manchester Weekly Times.*

Mr. Joyce aims at being realistic, but his method is too chaotic to produce the effect of realism.—*Rochester* (New York) *Post-Express.*

Its realism will displease many.—*Birmingham Post.*

Mr. Joyce is unsparing in his realism, and his violent contrasts —the brothel, the confessional—jar on one's finer feelings.— *Irish Book Lover.*

The description of life in a Jesuit school, and later in a Dublin college, strikes one as being absolutely true to life—but what a life!—*Everyman.*

WISDOM: Is it even wise, from a worldly point of view— mercenary, if you will—to dissipate one's talents on a book which can only attain a limited circulation?—*Irish Book Lover.*

ADVANTAGES OF IRISH EDUCATION: One boy from Clongowes School is not a replica of all the other boys. I will reintroduce Mr. Wells to half a dozen Irish "old boys" of whom five—Sir Arthur Conan Doyle is one—were educated at Roman Catholic schools and have nevertheless become most conventional citizens of the Empire.—*Sphere.*

COMPARISON WITH OTHER IRISH AUTHORS: The book is not within a hundred miles of being as fine a work of art as "Limehouse Nights," the work of another young Irishman.—*Sphere.*

There are a good many talented young Irish writers to-day, and it will take a fellow of exceptional literary stature to tower above Lord Dunsany, for example, or James Stephens.—*New York Globe*.

IMAGINATION: He shows an astonishingly unCeltic absence of imagination and humour.—*Bellman* (U.S.A.).

RELIGION: The irreverent treatment of religion in the story must be condemned.—*Rochester* (New York) *Post-Express*.

TRUTH: It is an accident that Mr. Joyce's book should have Dublin as its background.—*Freeman's Journal* (Dublin).

He is justified, in so far as too many Dubliners are of the calibre described in this and the preceding volume.—*New Ireland*.

The Tradition and the New Novel

MAURICE BEEBE

Maurice Beebe has taught at Cornell University and the University of Kansas and is now Professor of English at Purdue University. He is the author of *Literary Symbolism* and *Ivory Towers and Sacred Founts*, to which the following essay is the introduction, and is co-author with L. A. Field of *All the King's Men: A Critical Handbook*.

[THE ARTIST AS HERO]

No sooner has Denis Stone, the young poet in Aldous Huxley's *Crome Yellow*, confessed that he is writing a novel than he is chagrined to hear a new acquaintance describe the plot of the story:

"Little Percy, the hero, was never good at games, but he was always clever. He passes through the usual public school and the usual university and comes to London, where he lives among the artists. He is bowed down with melancholy thought; he carries the whole weight of the universe upon his shoulders. He writes a novel of dazzling brilliance; he dabbles delicately in Amour and disappears, at the end of the book, into the Luminous Future."

Denis blushed scarlet. Mr. Scogan had described the plan of his novel with an accuracy that was appalling. He made an effort to laugh. "You're entirely wrong," he said. "My novel is not in the

---

least like that." It was a heroic lie. Luckily, he reflected, only two chapters were written. He would tear them up that evening when he unpacked.

Mr. Scogan paid no attention to his denial, but went on: "Why will you young men continue to write about things that are so entirely uninteresting as the mentality of adolescents and artists? . . . As for the artist, he is preoccupied with problems that are so utterly unlike those of the ordinary adult man—problems of pure aesthetics which don't so much as present themselves to people like myself—that a description of his mental processes is as boring to the ordinary reader as a piece of pure mathematics. A serious book about artists regarded as artists is unreadable; and a book about artists regarded as lovers, husbands, dipsomaniacs, heroes, and the like is really not worth writing again." [1]

Mr. Scogan is not clairvoyant; he is simply well read. The story of Percy could be that of several hundred sensitive young heroes of novels, for by 1921, when *Crome Yellow* was published, both the artist and the adolescent had become hackneyed subjects of fiction. The tradition of artist fiction, which had developed steadily for more than a century, reached a crest in the first two decades of the twentieth century. William York Tindall has gone so far as to say that "from 1903 onwards, almost every first novel by a serious novelist was a novel of adolescence." Mr. Scogan is justified in linking stories of adolescents with stories of artists, because the story of a sensitive young man is usually that of a potential artist; when the novel is autobiographical, as most are, it is the story of the artist who wrote the book.

Less justified is Mr. Scogan's blanket dismissal of a form of fiction which includes some of the most distinguished novels of the past century: *Pierre, Lost Illusions, Sentimental Education, The Way of All Flesh, Sons and Lovers, The Tragic Muse, Jean-Christophe, Remembrance of Things Past, The Counterfeiters, Doctor Faustus,* and *A Portrait of the Artist as a Young Man.* If it be objected that Mr. Scogan is speaking as the "ordinary adult

---

[1] (New York: Harper, 1922), pp. 30-32. [M.B.]

man" and that few of these novels have attained popular success, the list could easily be expanded to include such nineteenth-century classics as *Wilhelm Meister, David Copperfield, Pendennis,* and *The Ordeal of Richard Feverel;* or such twentieth-century best-sellers as *Of Human Bondage, Martin Eden, Maurice Guest, The Song of the Lark, The Constant Nymph, Lust for Life, Sparkenbroke, Sinister Street, The Fountainhead, The Horse's Mouth, The Alexandria Quartet,* and *Look Homeward, Angel.*

Fictional portraits of the artist are valuable in at least two ways. First, a portrait of the artist helps us to understand the novelist who wrote it. The novel can be seen in much the same manner as the writer's letters, diaries, notebooks, prefaces, or memoirs—though, of course, the careful critic will not make a one-to-one equation between a work of art and an autobiography. Nonetheless, the very fact that the artist-novel is a product of the imagination, in which the experience it uses is distorted and transcended, makes it often more revealing than primary documents, for writers frequently tell more about their true selves and convictions under the guise of fiction than they will confess publicly. The second main value of the portrait-of-the-artist novel is to be found in its cumulative impact. A comparative study of many portraits of the artist enables us better to understand the artist in general. Ideas that may seem eccentric or special in an individual portrait of the artist take on added significance when the same ideas are expressed again and again by other novelists. Thus a knowledge of the whole tradition helps to illuminate each work within that tradition.

Artists have always prided themselves on their individuality, but the most surprising fact about portrait-of-the-artist novels is their similarity. From the beginnings of the genre in the late eighteenth century to the present time, the artist-hero is an easily recognized type. The person blessed (or cursed?) with "artistic temperament" is always sensitive, usually introverted and self-centered, often passive, and sometimes so capable of abstracting himself mentally from the world around him that he appears absentminded or "possessed." Granted most or all of these traits, he has an excellent chance of becoming an artist if he also has talent and the ability to apply himself. In many artist-novels, however, the story concludes with the hero not yet an accomplished artist. Except in temperament, Stephen Dedalus, in Joyce's *A Portrait of the Artist as a Young Man,* is still more young man than artist at the novel's conclusion, and when we reach the end of Proust's *A la Recherche du Temps Perdu,* we find that Marcel is at last ready to write the book we have just read. In both instances, as in many others, the hero attains this state only after he has sloughed off the domestic, social, and religious demands imposed upon him by his environment. Narrative development in the typical artist-novel requires that the hero test and reject the claims of love and life, of God, home, and country, until nothing is left but his true self and his consecration as artist. Quest for self is the dominant theme of the artist-novel, and because the self is almost always in conflict with society, a closely related theme is the opposition of art to life. The artist-as-hero is usually therefore the artist-as-exile.

Although the artist-hero claims individuality in that he is different from the majority of men, his quest for his true self usually ends in the discovery that he is very much like other artists, that in fact he embodies the archetype of the artist. Joyce's novel is not a portrait of *an* artist, but a portrait of *the* artist, and the distinction is important. In artist-novels the same themes appear so frequently that they assume the dimension of myths that may express universal truths, and just as we can distinguish between *an* artist and *the* artist, we can best understand individual portraits of the artist if we establish first the nature of the genre by finding an overall pattern in the works as a group. That pattern can be found, I think, in three interlocking themes: the Divided Self, the Ivory Tower, and the Sacred Fount. Each must be considered individually before we can see how they function together to form an archetype of the artist-novel.

I

Much literary scholarship is based on the assumption that the more we know about the life and background of a man, the better we can understand him as an artist and the more capable we are of interpreting his works. But an underlying assumption in the artist-novel is that creative man is a divided being, man *and* artist, a historical personage who merely serves as the medium through which the creative spirit manifests itself. The man is a human being of normal appetites and desires, for whom life is essentially the process of dying. The artist is a free, detached spirit which looks down on the man from a distance and is concerned not so much with the consumption of life as with the transcendence of life through creative effort. The man must spend himself, but the artist-spirit saves itself by becoming one with its works and thus escaping the bonds of time.

The theme of the Divided Self has a psychological basis in the nature of the introverted person. Thoreau [in *Walden*], for example, writes:

With thinking we may be beside ourselves in a sane sense. By a conscious effort of the mind we can stand aloof from actions and their consequences; and all things, good and bad, go by us like a torrent. We are not wholly involved in Nature. I may be either the driftwood in the stream, or Indra in the sky looking down on it. I *may* be affected by a theatrical exhibition; on the other hand, I *may not* be affected by an actual event which appears to concern me much more. I only know myself as a human entity; the scene, so to speak, of thoughts and affections; and am sensible of a certain doubleness by which I can stand as remote from myself as from another. However intense my experience, I am conscious of the presence and criticism of a part of me, which, as it were, is not a part of me, but spectator, sharing no experience, but taking note of it; and that is no more I than it is you. When the play, it may be the tragedy, of life is over, the spectator goes his way. It was a kind of fiction, a work of the imagination only.

Alphonse Daudet recorded "that other self" which observed

himself weeping beside his father's deathbed, and Yeats, in *Per Amica Silentia Lunae,* built a theory of art around the second, inner self of the artist.

> I call to the mysterious one who yet
> Shall walk the wet sands by the water's edge
> And look most like me, being indeed my double,
> And prove of all imaginable things
> The most unlike, being my anti-self,
> And, standing by these characters, disclose
> All that I seek.

The artist's double, most theorists agree, comes from the artist's subconsciousness, yet seems to look down dispassionately on the artist himself. Coleridge must have had something like this in mind when he wrote, "The eye hath a two-fold power. It is, verily, a window through which you not only look out of the house, but can look into it too."

If the artist-hero is usually an introvert, it is perhaps because the artist-novel, especially when it is autobiographical, is by its very nature an act of introspection. At any rate, many of the artists of fiction share an ability to step outside the self and to recognize a difference between the artist and the man. Disraeli's Contarini Fleming reflects on "the separation of the mere individual from the universal poet." Arnold Bennett's frustrated artist, Edwin Clayhanger, discovers an "impartial observer" in himself. Dreiser's Eugene Witla "was troubled with a dual point of view—a condition based upon a peculiar power of analysis—self analysis in particular, which was constantly permitting him to tear himself up by the roots in order to see how he was getting along." The hero of St. John Ervine's *Changing Winds* "had a strange sense of fear that was inexplicable to him. He seemed to be outside himself, outside his own fear, looking on at it and wondering what had caused it." The ability to become detached from the self is shared by artist-heroes as different from each other in other respects as Michael Fane, the hero of Compton Mackenzie's *Sinister Street,* and Edouard of Gide's *The Counterfeiters.* The former confesses, "Sometimes

I feel as if there wasn't any me at all, and I'm surprised to see a letter come addressed to me." Edouard writes: "It seems to me sometimes that I do not really exist, but that I merely imagine I exist. The thing that I have the greatest difficulty in believing in is my own reality. I am constantly getting outside myself, and as I watch myself act I cannot understand how a person who acts is the same as the person who is watching him act, and who wonders in astonishment and doubt how he can be actor and watcher at the same moment!" So common are split selves in artists that Aldous Huxley was able to satirize the concept in his short story, "The Farcical History of Richard Greenow": from midnight to early morning the body of the sophisticated Greenow is occupied by the sentimental anti-self, "Pearl Bellairs," whose gushing best-sellers support, embarrass, and ultimately destroy the man through whom she acts. Huxley's story, like Henry James's "The Private Life," applies the *doppelgänger* theme common in fiction to the situation of the artist, but it may well be that there would be fewer stories about doubles if writers were not so peculiarly aware of a division in themselves.

Another psychological basis for the theme of the Divided Self may be found in the nature of the creative process. Any writer knows that there is a moment when calculation stops and the author seems to be carried along by a force beyond himself. Today we are likely to be scornful of "inspiration," and it may well be that the something that takes over in the creative process is not a divine afflatus descending upon the artist but a subconscious force arising from within. Whatever it is, thousands of artists have testified to the experience of inspiration, and there may be something after all in William Faulkner's insistence that "the writer's got to be demon-driven" or Joseph Conrad's reluctance to revise one of his works because "all my work is produced unconsciously (so to speak) and I cannot meddle to any purpose with what is within myself.—I am sure you understand what I mean—it isn't in me to improve what has got itself written." But the "I" here is not Conrad. It is Captain Korzeniowski, a humble seaman, who on another occasion said, "You know I take no credit to myself for what I do —and so I may judge my own performance. There is no mistake about this. . . . It [*Nostromo*] is a very genuine Conrad." Critics of fiction often confuse the "I" of the storyteller with the person who wrote the work, but as early as 1877, Edward Dowden, discussing George Eliot, another novelist who, like Conrad, wrote under a pseudonym, noted that the personality which dominates her novel is "one who, if not the real George Eliot, is that second self who writes her books, and lives and speaks through them." This "second self," he continued, is "more substantial than any mere human personality" and has "fewer reserves"; while "behind it, lurks well pleased the veritable historical self secure from impertinent observation and criticism."

Literary scholars may scoff at the separation of the person from the creator, but the psychologist Jung finds in this division the basis for his theory of the artist:

Every creative person is a duality or a synthesis of contradictory attitudes. On the one side he is a human being with a personal life, while on the other side he is an impersonal, creative process. Since as a human being he may be either sound or morbid, we must look at his psychic make-up to find the determinants of his personality. But we can only understand him in his capacity of artist by looking at his artistic achievement. We should make a sad mistake if we tried to explain the mode of life of an English gentleman, a Prussian officer, or a cardinal in terms of personal factors. The gentleman, the officer and the cleric function as such in an impersonal role, and their psychic make-up is qualified by a peculiar objectivity. We must grant that the artist does not function in an official capacity—the very opposite is nearer the truth. He nevertheless resembles the types I have named in one respect, for the specifically artistic disposition involves an overweight of collective psychic life as against the personal. Art is a kind of innate drive that seizes a human being and makes him its instrument. The artist is not a person endowed with a free will who seeks his own ends, but one who allows art to realize its purposes through him. As a human being he may have moods and a will and personal aims, but as an artist he is "man" in a higher sense—he is "collective man"—one who carries and shapes the unconscious, psychic life of mankind.[2]

Here, perhaps, is Stephen Dedalus' "uncreated conscience of my race." Willa Cather comes even closer to Jung's theory of the artist in her *The Song of the Lark.* Thea Kronborg becomes aware of a second, observing self when as a young girl she is seriously ill: "She did not realize that she was suffering pain. When she was conscious at all, she seemed to be separated from her body; to be perched on top of the piano, or on the hanging lamp, watching the doctor sew her up." When she reaches maturity and achieves prominence as a singer, she realizes that this other self is her artistic personality. Why do people care for her?

It was something that had to do with her that made them care, but it was not she. It was something they believed in, but it was not she. Perhaps each of them concealed another person in himself, just as she did. Why was it that they seemed to feel and to hunt for a second person in her and not in each other? . . . What if one's second self could somehow speak to all these second selves? . . . How deep they lay, these second persons, and how little one knew about them, except to guard them fiercely. It was to music, more than to anything else, that these hidden things in people responded.[3]

The time-and-eternity theme which appears frequently in artist-novels is, I think, closely related to the myth of the Divided Self. To escape death and become immortal, the artist-self would somehow remove himself from the bonds of the chronological time which drives him relentlessly from cradle to grave. Opposed to chronological time is subjective time, which cannot be clocked: minutes are sometimes hours, hours can be minutes. Subjective time is universal. But, for most of us, such time

---

[2] C. G. Jung, *Modern Man in Search of a Soul,* trans. W. S. Dell and Cary F. Barnes (London: Kegan Paul, Trench, Trubner and Company, 1945), pp. 194-195. [M.B.]

[3] *The Novels and Stories of Willa Cather,* Library Edition (Boston: Houghton Mifflin, 1937), II, 273. [M.B.]

is as fleeting, as transitory as the seconds the clock ticks off. What the artist tries to do is to capture lost time and imprison it in the form of his art-work. The man must die, but the artist in him can achieve immortality in his works. This is a common theme in literature from Keats's Grecian Urn to Yeats's Byzantium. For instance, Gerald Lovel, the poet-hero of J. Westland Marston's unwieldly novel in verse, *Gerald*, finds his motivation as a poet in his desire to transcend time through art:

> A Statue's silence—is the Sculptor's voice.
> The Painter's immortality resides
> In his own forms, and objects. . . .

Even the objective, imitative work of art is, in this sense, capable of being immortal. But when the work of art is subjective, when it reflects the consciousness of its creator, the artist feels that he can achieve a personal self-extension through eternity:

> And thus the Sons
> Of Genius have prerogative to stand
> Exempt from Time's decree; Immutable
> In change!

Joseph Frank, in his essay, "Spatial Form in Modern Literature," has shown that the attempt to capture time in the spatial form of the art-work is characteristic of many modern artists. To explain the simultaneous appearance of this trend in a number of writers working independently of one another, Frank relies, in part, upon the theories of Wilhelm Worringer. In *Abstraktion und Einfühlung*, Worringer demonstrated that historical fluctuations between naturalistic and nonnaturalistic art may be understood only if one substitutes what Alois Riegl called *Kunstwollen*, or will-to-form, for the will-to-imitate which had been considered responsible for the creative impulse. Naturalism is the prevailing style in cultures which have attained harmonious balance with their environment; abstract styles are produced when man is not in harmony with the universe, when the artist, distrustful of the outside world, directs the will-to-form to the subjective world. Because the modern era is of the second type and because one characteristic of non-naturalistic art is the attempt to remove all traces of time value, much modern art has utilized spatial form. By emphasizing "climates of feeling," the Worringer-Frank theory overlooks the fact that the psychology of the individual artist is also important in determining the art-form.

Acknowledging his debt to Riegl and Worringer, Otto Rank has extended the theory of *Kunstwollen* to include the "urge to eternalization" which he considers basic to the creative impulse: The artist would escape time through the medium of his immortal art. The kind of artistic personality, as well as the cultural environment, determines the art-form:

What the artist needs for true creative art . . . is life in one form or another; and the two artist-types differ essentially in the source from which they take this life that is so essential to production. The Classical type, who is possibly poorer within, but nearer to life, and himself more vital, takes it from without: that is, he creates immortal work from mortal life without necessarily having first transformed it into personal experience as is the case with the Romantic. For, to the Romantic, experience of his own appears to be an essential preliminary to productivity, although he does not use this experience for the enrichment of his own personality, but to economize the personal experience, the burden of which he would fain escape. Thus the one artist-type constantly makes use of other life than his own—in fact, nature—for the purpose of creating, while the other can create only by perpetually sacrificing his own life. From the spiritual point of view the work of the Classicist, more or less naturalistic, artist is essentially *partial*, and the work of the Romantic, produced from within, *total*. The totality-type spends itself perpetually in creative work without absorbing very much of life, while the partial type has continually to absorb life so that he may throw it off again in his work.[4]

Although Rank does not specifically relate his classification of artist types to the question of spatial form, it is the Romantic,

---

[4] *Art and Artist: Creative Urge and Personality* (New York: Knopf, 1932), pp. 48-49. [M.B.]

denying the chronology that common sense tells us exists in the world, who finds totality in the fusion of space and time within the individual consciousness. As Rank implies, it is the Romantic or totality-type of artist who is most likely to be alienated from the mundane world outside his ego. And it is this type of artist with whom I am dealing. Here again, though, we are faced with the paradox that what the artist is as artist is not necessarily what he is as man. In fictional portraits of the artist the artist-self is usually of the "totality-type," but this self may be in conflict with another self that yearns for experience and is of the partial type. The knowledge that "one must die to life in order to be utterly a creator" does not stop Thomas Mann's Tonio Kröger from envying and loving "the blond and blue-eyed, the fair and living, the happy, lovely, and commonplace." In fact, Mann implies that if Tonio is superior to his Bohemian friends, it is largely because he embodies the perfect balance of artist and bourgeois.

II

If we grant the divided nature of the artist, we can readily see why he is pulled in contrary directions. The man seeks personal fulfillment in experience, while the artist-self desires freedom from the demands of life. One result is that conflicting traditions of art have existed side by side for more than a century. What I call the Sacred Fount tradition tends to equate art with experience and assumes that the true artist is one who lives not less, but more fully and intensely than others. Within this tradition art is essentially the re-creation of experience. The Ivory Tower tradition, on the other hand, exalts art above life and insists that the artist can make use of life only if he stands aloof—"The artist, like the God of the creation, remains within or behind or beyond or above his handiwork, invisible, refined out of existence, indifferent, paring his fingernails." [5]

Crucial in this statement by Joyce is the comparison of the artist with God, for the Ivory Tower tradition equates art with

[5] *P*, 215.

religion rather than experience. The frequency with which the authors of artist-novels describe the creation of art as "divine," the sanctuary of the artist as "holy," or the nature of the artist as "godlike" or "priestly" is a heritage from the classic analogy of creator with Creator. Until the nineteenth century, the analogy between God and artist could be assimilated into orthodox religious faith: the artist is *like* God; he is a kind of secondary god whose power comes from God. The artist imitates God, and the world-in-itself which is the work of art is like God's world in that it is ordered and unified by a just and benevolent power. Poetic justice reflects divine justice. With the gradual collapse of religious values during the nineteenth century, however, an important change appears in the artist-as-God concept. When the artist loses his belief in God and can see in the universe no evidence of a divine plan, but only chaos and disorder, then he no longer considers himself a secondary god, but a successor to God. The old God, as in Joyce's description, is an "indifferent" one who pares his fingernails and leaves the world to its own direction. But because the modern artist retains control over his creation, he feels justified in claiming that a "well-made" work of art is superior to the real world.

God looks down on the world. It is for this reason perhaps that when the artist assumes the role of God, he visualizes his place as one from which he can look down on his fellowmen, secure in his superiority and closer to the heavens than the earth. Scholars have attempted to find the first recorded use of the Ivory Tower as a metaphor for the artist's ideal retreat, but who originated the phrase during the early nineteenth century matters little. That it was familiar by mid-century is shown by Gerard de Nerval's use of the term: "The only refuge left to us was the poet's ivory tower, which we climbed, ever higher, to isolate ourselves from the mob. Led by our masters to those high places we breathed at last the pure air of solitude, we drank oblivion in the legendary cup, and we got drunk on poetry and love." If ivory implies the purity of the absolute, the tower implies height and open vistas. Traditionally, artists have preferred garrets to cellars. In one of its many forms, the Ivory

Tower is that lofty perch from which Hawthorne, in "Sights from a Steeple," visualized himself a "spiritualized Paul Pry, hovering invisible round man and woman, witnessing their deeds, searching into their hearts, borrowing brightness from their felicity and shade from their sorrow, and retaining no emotion peculiar to himself." It is the Invisible Lodge of Jean Paul Richter, the Palace of Art of Tennyson, the Great Good Place of Henry James. It is the House of Usher, Axel's castle, Faust's alchemic chambers, and Joyce's Martello Tower. But whatever it may be called, the Ivory Tower is always the artist's private retreat.

In fact, the concept of the Ivory Tower is so familiar that it requires little elaboration. Just as Huxley satirized the theme of the Divided Self in his "Farcical History of Richard Greenow," Albert Camus could be sure that readers would recognize the target of his mock-serious story, "The Artist at Work." In this story Gilbert Jonas, a painter who believes only in his "star," is forced to work in a crowded apartment with his wife and children, where he is subjected to continual interruptions from his family, friends, and patrons. Fortunately the apartment has unusually high ceilings, and Jonas is able to build himself a loft high above the turmoil. As time passes, Jonas finds it increasingly disagreeable to leave his sanctuary. He begins to sleep there, and his meals and supplies are handed up to him by his wife, Louise, and his best friend, Rateau. His muse escapes him even there, and he sits in darkness patiently waiting for the return of the star that has abandoned him temporarily. The voices below become more and more distant, until finally

He put out the lamp and, in the darkness that suddenly returned, right there! wasn't that his star shining? It was the star, he recognized it with his heart full of gratitude, and he was still watching it when he fell, without a sound.

"It's nothing," the doctor they had called declared a little later. "He is working too much. In a week he will be on his feet again." "You are sure he will get well?" asked Louise with distorted face. "He will get well." In the other room Rateau was looking at the

canvas, completely blank, in the center of which Jonas had merely
written in very small letters a word that could be made out, but
without any certainty as to whether it should be read *solitary* or
solidary.[6]

Like other artist-thinkers of the past few decades, Camus
reacted against the concept of the Ivory Tower. "The Artist at
Work" suggests that when the artist denies his own humanity
and rejects the need for social engagement, he loses the ability
to produce. For Camus, the artist must leave his Ivory Tower to
tap the Sacred Fount of life.

III

The Sacred Fount tradition is rooted in the concept of art as
experience. Prior to Freud and the twentieth-century view that
the artist is one who compensates through his work for his inability to participate actively in society or to lead a satisfying
passional life, it was generally assumed that the artist differs
from other men by the intensity of his emotions and that he
therefore lives more rather than less fully than other men. For
Wordsworth a poet is a man "endowed with more lively sensibility, more enthusiasm and tenderness . . . a man pleased with
his own passions and volitions, and who rejoices more than
other men in the spirit of life which is in him." And George
Edward Woodberry summed up the conventional nineteenth-
century attitude when he wrote: "The sign of the poet . . . is
that by passion he enters into life more than other men. That
is his gift—the power to live. The lives of poets are but little
known; but from the fragments of their lives that come down
to us, the characteristic legend is that they have been singularly
creatures of passion."

To assume that the artist is by nature a man of feeling and
passion is to assume a close relation between art and experience.
In fact, one implication of the Sacred Fount myth is that life
and art are interchangeable. Life can be converted directly

---

[6] *Exile and the Kingdom*, trans. Justin O'Brien (New York: Knopf,
1958), pp. 157-158. [M.B.]

to art, but to do so is to destroy life. Similarly, art and the artist may be destroyed by life. In Henry James's *The Sacred Fount*, the artist-narrator theorizes that in any marriage or love affair one party becomes more vigorous, youthful, intelligent as the other is drained of these qualities. Ironically, the narrator himself indulges in a love affair with the life around him, turning human relationships into an elaborate, ingenious, artistic structure, but is himself left depleted when the life he has tried to control and manipulate proves stronger than he. In one of Balzac's parables of the artist, *La Peau de chagrin*, the fatal skin shrinks in direct ratio to the intensity with which the artist lives so that he can actually see the decreasing measure of his days. Much the same idea is behind the many variations of the "magic portrait" stories, such as Poe's "Oval Portrait," Hawthorne's "Prophetic Pictures," or Oscar Wilde's *Picture of Dorian Gray*. In such stories the assumption is made that life can literally be transferred from flesh to canvas: as the portrait takes on life, the model's life seems to wane away, or, in Wilde's reversal of the myth, the portrait ages while the model remains as he was painted. The inference of the Sacred Fount myth is that life and art are so closely related that one can exhaust or destroy the other. Because there is only so much life to be lived, that which is turned into art is made unavailable for living: the more kite-string in the air, the less in the hand, and one cannot have it in both places at once. Hence the continual struggle between life and art.

To assume that creativity must be expended *either* in life *or* in art often leads to a confusion between sex and art. The religious of all times have defended chastity as a means of preserving creative energy. Thoreau writes in *Walden:* "The generative energy, which, when we are loose, dissipates and makes us unclean, when we are continent invigorates and inspires us. Chastity is the flowering of man; and what are called Genius, Heroism, Holiness, and the like, are but various fruits which succeed it." And a century later the novelist-hero of Alberto Moravia's *Conjugal Love* feels that he cannot complete his book unless he abstains from sexual relations with his wife. To assume that there is only one kind of creative energy leads to the view that the artist must spend himself, sacrifice his physical being, in artistic creation. In an extreme form this idea is expressed allegorically in "The Artist's Secret," one of Olive Schreiner's *Dreams*.

There was an artist once, and he painted a picture. Other artists had colors richer and rarer, and painted more notable pictures. He painted his with one color, there was a wonderful red glow on it; and people went up and down, saying, "We like the picture, we like the glow."

The other artists came and said, "Where does he get his color from?" They asked him; and he smiled and said, "I cannot tell you"; and worked on with his head bent low. And one went to the far East and bought costly pigments, and made a rare color and painted, but after a time the picture faded. Another read in the old books, and made a color rich and rare, but when he had put it on the picture it was dead.

But the artist painted on. Always the work got redder and redder, and the artist grew whiter and whiter. At last one day they found him dead before his picture, and they took him up to bury him. The other men looked about in all the pots and crucibles, but found nothing they had not.

And when they undressed him to put his grave-clothes on him, they found above his left breast the mark of a wound—it was an old, old wound, that must have been there all his life, for the edges were old and hardened; but Death, who seals all things, had drawn the edges together, and closed it up.

And it came to pass that after a while the artist was forgotten—but the work lived.[7]

The necessity to preserve creative force is one justification for the Ivory Tower. However, most of the writers in that tradition think of the artist as a being distinct from ordinary men and thus not subject in the same degree to the carnal appetites; he finds the source of his art in observation or introspection. For such artists the problem of the single creative force is less cru-

---

[7] *So Here Then Are Dreams* (East Aurora, New York: Roycroft Press, 1901), p. 55. [M.B.]

cial than for those who find the source of art in experience. When the idea of the single force combines with the idea of art as experience, a conflict naturally arises. The artist *must* tap the Sacred Fount, but in doing so runs the risk of dissipating creative energy in the mere process of living and therefore proving incapable of transforming experience into art.

In the portrait-of-the-artist novel the Sacred Fount theme is most often expressed in terms of the artist's relationship to women. In many artist-novels—James's *Roderick Hudson*, Flaubert's *Sentimental Education* and Gissing's *New Grub Street*, to name but three—the artist is destroyed as artist because of his submission to love. In other novels, the artist feels that he cannot function without love. Hardy's *The Well-Beloved*, Wyndham Lewis's *Tarr*, Dreiser's *The "Genius"* and Norris's *Vandover and the Brute* are examples of novels in which the artist-hero must have romantic fulfillment to produce artistically. Although he may be destroyed by the search for such fulfillment, he must go to Woman in order to create—just as a man can father children only through women—and his artistic power is dependent on the Sacred Fount.

There are, of course, many variations of these three basic themes in the artist-novel, and there are many other themes as well. But the situation of the typical artist-hero is essentially what I have outlined here: the Divided Self of the artist-man wavering between the Ivory Tower and the Sacred Fount, between the "holy" or esthetic demands of his mission as artist and his natural desire as a human being to participate in the life around him.

IRENE HENDRY CHAYES

Irene Hendry Chayes has taught English at George Washington University, The Johns Hopkins University, the University of Maryland, Hollins College, the University of Illinois at Chicago Circle, and the State University of New York at Binghamton. She has published essays on the English romantic poets and is at work on a critical book on William Blake.

JOYCE'S EPIPHANIES

Stephen Dedalus' esthetic in A *Portrait of the Artist as a Young Man* has the same specious quality as his Hamlet thesis in *Ulysses* and is a product of the same talent for parody; as Stephen's friend Lynch remarks, it has "the true scholastic stink." Both theories are, of course, more than parody: the speculations on Hamlet serve to crystallize Stephen's broodings on his spiritual parentage, and the esthetic is actually Joyce's, which he followed faithfully in his own literary method. Just how closely method and principle were related in Joyce's work is shown by his little-noticed theory of epiphanies, which is mentioned fleetingly in *Ulysses* but is given explicit statement only in *Stephen Hero*, the fragmentary first draft of the *Portrait* recently published in book form for the first time.

The theory of epiphanies, presented as Stephen's, is bound up with the three cardinal esthetic principles, or conditions of beauty, that he expounds to Lynch in one of their dialogues in the *Portrait*. (In *Stephen Hero*, the passive listener is Cranly, a character apparently based on Joyce's own college friend Byrne.) These principles have a respectable philosophic origin in the *integritas, consonantia,* and *claritas* of Aquinas. *Integritas* Stephen explains in pseudoscholastic language as

---

From *The Sewanee Review* (Summer 1946). Copyright 1946 by the University of the South. Used by permission of *The Sewanee Review* and Irene Hendry Chayes.

"wholeness"—the perception of an esthetic image as *one* thing, "self-bounded and self-contained upon the immeasurable background of space or time which is not it." *Consonantia*, similarly, is symmetry and rhythm of structure, the esthetic image conceived as "complex, multiple, divisible, separable, made up of its parts and their sum, harmonious"; "the synthesis of immediate perception is followed by the analysis of apprehension." The third principle, *claritas*, is given the approximate meaning of "radiance" and equated with another Thomistic term, *quidditas*, or the "whatness" of a thing. *Quidditas* is the link with the theory of epiphanies; in this case, the definition in *Stephen Hero* is the more revealing:

Claritas is *quidditas*. After the analysis which discovers the second quality the mind makes the only logically possible synthesis and discovers the third quality. This is the moment which I call epiphany. First we recognise that the object is *one* integral thing, then we recognise that it is an organized composite structure, a *thing* in fact: finally, when the relation of the parts is exquisite, when the parts are adjusted to the special point, we recognise that it is *that* thing which it is. Its soul, its whatness, leaps to us from the vestment of its appearance. The soul of the commonest object, the structure of which is so adjusted, seems to us radiant. The object achieves its epiphany.[1]

Joyce's epiphanies are mentioned by Harry Levin, who had access to the manuscript of *Stephen Hero* in preparing his New Directions study, and by Theodore Spencer, who edited and wrote the preface to the published version of the fragment. Both Levin and Spencer, however, emphasize only the obvious aspect of the epiphany: its effect on the observer and his relation to the object "epiphanized." Spencer calls the theory one which "implies a lyrical rather than a dramatic view of life," thinking apparently of Stephen's definition of the "lyrical" form of art as "the form wherein the artist presents his image in immediate relation to himself." Levin takes the stories in *Dubliners* as pure examples of epiphany and the collection of

---

[1] See p. 289 for the entire passage.

which Stephen resolves (in *Ulysses*) to leave copies to all the
libraries of the world; Joyce's later works, he says, are "artificial
reconstructions of a transcendental view of experience," and
his "dizzying shifts" of technique attempt "to create a literary
substitute for the revelations of religion."

But these descriptions do justice to neither the concept nor
Joyce's use of it. In the first place, of course, the epiphany is
not peculiar to Joyce alone. Virtually every writer experiences
a sense of revelation when he beholds a fragment of his ordinary
world across what Bullough has called "psychic distance"—
dissociated from his subjective and practical concerns, fraught
with meaning beyond itself, with every detail of its physical
appearance relevant. It is a revelation quite as valid as the
religious; in fact, from our present secular viewpoint, it perhaps would be more accurate to say that the revelation of the
religious mystic is actually an esthetic revelation into which
the mystic projects himself—as a participant, not merely as an
observer and recorder—and to which he assigns a source, an
agent and an end, called God. What Joyce did was give
systematic formulation to a common esthetic experience, so
common that few others—writers, if not estheticians—have
thought it worth considering for its own sake.

Again, many writers use "revelation" as a technical device
in achieving their effects; Joyce, however, used it more consciously and with greater variation than anyone with whom
he can be compared. More than a "transcendental view of
experience" is involved in Joyce's application of his theory of
epiphanies, just as there is more than mysticism in religion,
particularly the Roman Catholicism that shaped his whole out-
look as a young man. The theory furnished Joyce with a technique of characterization which evolved generally in the
"lyrical-epical-dramatic" progression that Stephen describes:
from the first person to the third, from the personal to the
impersonal, from the kinetic to the static. It is a technique
in which *integritas* and *consonantia* are always necessary to *claritas*, and *claritas* itself comes more and more to reside in *quidditas*, the soul, the essential identifying quality of the thing,

than in a mystic, emotional exhilaration on the part of someone who looks on. *Claritas* is *quidditas* is the key the theory itself gives us.

In *Dubliners*, *claritas* is achieved most often, although not always, through an apparently trivial incident, action, or single detail which differs from the others making up the story only in that it illuminates them, integrates them, and gives them meaning. It is like the final piece which is added to the child's pile of lettered blocks and completes the spelling of a word or gives form to the "house" or "tower" he is building. Farrington's treatment of his son attaches to himself the petty tyranny we recognize first in his employer. Little Chandler's brief rebellion against domesticity frightens his child, and his dreams of being a poet are swept away by his remorse. . . . The *Dubliners* stories seem to conform to Stephen's definition of "dramatic" art as the form in which the artist "presents his image in immediate relation to others"; "life purified in and reprojected from the human imagination." Joyce was not satisfied with such an easy attainment of the esthetic stasis, however, and this may have been because the "block" technique did not fulfill equally all three of his basic principles of art. *Claritas* is achieved, but the *quidditas* that constitutes it is dilute; *consonantia*, the parts and their sum, is in evidence, but *integritas* is not, at least to the same degree.

II

The example of epiphany which Joyce employs in *Stephen Hero*—a fragment of conversation between a girl and a young man, overheard on Mr. Bloom's own Eccles Street—is actually the final "block" of the *Dubliners* method without the foundation; one may guess that the foundation in each story was laid down later, in an effort to insure the impersonality of the epiphany Joyce originally experienced in a very personal fashion. It may be, too, that the collection of epiphanies Stephen wishes to leave to posterity is not *Dubliners* at all but a collection of just such fragments as the one he acknowledges.

A number of these "most delicate and evanescent of moments" occur throughout both *Stephen Hero* and the *Portrait*, taking up residence in Stephen's consciousness with neither elucidation nor relation to anything beyond themselves: factory girls and boys coming out to lunch; the witless laughter of an old woman; the screeching of a mad nun; a servant singing; the salutation of a flower girl. In *Ulysses*, too, the peregrinations of Bloom and Stephen about Dublin are rich in epiphanies of this sort; the shout Stephen hears in the street and calls a "manifestation of God" is only the most obvious.

Occasionally we are given a suggestion of what is "revealed" in Joyce's epiphanies. The black straw hat and the greeting of the prostitute in *Stephen Hero* have an inordinate fascination for Dedalus; "mustn't the devil be annoyed to hear her described as an evil creature?" he asks. In order to fill in the background of an epiphany, he sometimes makes a reconstruction of an event in the past: a forgotten medical student cutting the word *Fœtus* in the wooden surface of his desk, or an imagined incestuous meeting in the rain, suggested by the dwarfish reader in the library and the rumors about his birth. And in at least three instances an epiphany helps Stephen to decide on the future course of his life: the snatch of song from the street, contrasting suddenly with the unsmiling face of the Jesuit who has been urging him to enter a novitiate; the vision of the girl wading at the shore; and the flight of birds about the college library, symbolizing the "fabulous artificer" after whom he is named.

The moment of revelation without its narrative base is the most conventional of Joyce's epiphanies; we find it elsewhere even in fiction which does not make use of revelation as a specific technique. . . .

Joyce's second epiphany technique does quite clearly conform to Stephen's definition of lyrical art. Although *claritas* is ultimately generated by *quidditas*, we are first aware of an effect on the beholder—Stephen, or ourselves through Stephen—not of an objectively apprehensible quality in the thing revealed; if we are to penetrate through to the *quidditas*, we must try to identify ourselves with Stephen or wrest a meaning of our own from the revelation. From the standpoint of eliminating the artist's personality from his work, this particular technique was a retrogression from the method of *Dubliners*, but it did have the advantage—in Joyce's esthetic theory, an extremely important one—of realizing the three principles, *integritas, consonantia*, and *claritas*, in a single image. The next step toward impersonal creation was to modify the image so that its *quidditas* would be unmistakable, with its radiance attached to itself rather than to a perceiving consciousness: Joyce's third epiphany technique, which explains the differences between *Stephen Hero* and *A Portrait of the Artist*.

In the *Portrait*, which covers in 93 pages events that require 234 pages in the *Hero* fragment, the original elements of Joyce's first novel, particularly the characters, are subjected to a process of compression and distillation that rejects all irrelevancies, all particularities and ambiguities, and leaves only their pure essence. In *Stephen Hero*, the common people at the Good Friday service are diverse in their submissive ignorance and their unquestioning respect for the clergy; the old women scrape their hands over the dry bottom of the holy-water font and speak in broad, realistic dialect. But in the *Portrait* the simple faithful are represented by pious sighs and a peasant smell "of air and rain and turf and corduroy," or by kneeling forms and whispering voices in the confessional box—"soft whispering cloudlets, soft whispering vapour, whispering and vanishing." In the first draft of the novel, Maurice and Isabel Dedalus appear specifically as characters; in the *Portrait*, Stephen's brothers and sisters are merely voices at the teatable, replying to his questions in pig Latin or singing with an "overtone of weariness behind their frail fresh innocent voices." "He heard the choir of voices in the kitchen echoed and multiplied through an endless reverberation of the choirs of endless generations of children: and heard in all the echoes an echo also of the recurring note of weariness and pain. All seemed weary of life even before entering upon it."

The character of Stephen itself undergoes a transformation

The *Hero* draft is often marred by adolescent particularities: Stephen baiting his cruder classmates, sneering at his mother's pious superstitions, or trying to convert his parents to Ibsen. In the *Portrait*, however, the Ibsen episode is omitted entirely, the intellectual distance between Stephen and his contemporaries is given less emphasis, and the quarrel with his mother over his failure to do his Easter duty is mentioned only indirectly. The details of Stephen's debauches similarly remain obscure; what we are shown, in the boy's dreams of temptation, the sermons he listens to during the retreat, and his hallucinations of damnation and punishment, is actually an apotheosis —or epiphany—of sin and repentance, far removed from the adventures of the Eugene Gants who for a generation have been storming the brothels of the world in imitation of Stephen.

But the most striking attenuation occurs in the character of Emma Clery. In the *Hero* fragment, she is a healthy, middle-class girl who studies Gaelic with enthusiasm, flirts with priests, and is only confused and offended by Stephen's unconventional offer of himself.[2] In the *Portrait*, however, we are told nothing of her appearance and are never allowed a clear conception of her as an individual. The Gaelic lessons shrink to an Irish phrasebook, the flirtation becomes a bitter recollection in Stephen's mind, associated with the scorn he feels for the Church, and there is only the barest hint of the circumstances of the rejection. The girl herself is never more than a shadowy presence—a provocative glance or speech, a shawled head, "fresh warm breath," laughter and tapping footsteps, a sash or a nodding hair ornament. Her etherealization extends even to her name, which in the *Portrait* becomes [merely "Emma" and] "E—— C——."

. . . . . .

The final epiphany in the *Portrait* is Stephen's famous journal entry marking the point at which the young man becomes

[2] See p. 284 for the entire passage.

an artist: "Welcome, O life! I go to encounter for the millionth time the reality of experience and to forge in the smithy of my soul the uncreated conscience of my race." Although we are supposed to think of it as written, this is pure oratory (Joyce refused to set off the written word from the spoken and exploited the possibilities of both to the utmost) and an exact formal counterpart of both Molly Bloom's remembered affirmation as she sinks into sleep and Anna Livia Plurabelle's valediction at dawn. Moreover, it is balanced by the fragmentary, unpersonalized impressions of the infant Stephen at the beginning of the book precisely as the soliloquies of Molly and Anna Livia are balanced by the impersonal narrative beginnings of *Ulysses* and *Finnegans Wake*. In a reversal of the progression in Stephen's theory (which actually describes the relation of the artist to his work rather than artistic form), Joyce moves from the third person to the first, and achieves in each case a simultaneous progression on another level. In the *Portrait*, the biological development from child to man becomes also a psychological and moral development, from passive receptivity to the self-conscious will. In *Ulysses*, with the progress of the day we are taken from the matter-of-fact blasphemies of Buck Mulligan to the nostalgia of middle age, a development away from the delusive optimism of the will. (For the eagerness of youth which Molly Bloom celebrates belongs as much to the past as the dead son Bloom himself has been seeking during the day, and Molly's memories—Anna Livia has them also—serve to bring into focus, or "reveal," what has gone before in much the same way as Gretta Conroy's story in "The Dead.") And in *Finnegans Wake* the concluding first-person passage is the final epiphany of the generalized human *quidditas*, the thinking and feeling soul (Joyce shows sensibility surviving will), before it enters a new cycle of existence and is dissolved in the inorganic beginnings we encountered on the first page of the book: "riverrun, past Eve and Adam's, from swerve of shore to bend of bay," the river flowing through the city. Here at last is a perfect unity of technique, theme, and

esthetic principle, and a distillation of essence so complete
that Being becomes quite literally the Word.

III

Joyce's work is a tissue of epiphanies, great and small, from
fleeting images to whole books, from the briefest revelation
in his lyrics to the epiphany that occupies one gigantic, en-
during "moment" in *Finnegans Wake*, running through 628
pages of text and then returning upon itself. His major technique and the best illustration of his theory is the one just
discussed, revelation through distillation of the pure, generalized *quidditas* from an impure whole, by which *consonantia*
(here analysis of the whole into its parts) and *integritas* (re-
synthesis of the parts into a larger whole through the agency
of language itself) interact to produce *claritas* directly. . . .

Although it is less conspicuous and plays a fixed and minor
role in the larger scheme of his work, Joyce makes use of one
more epiphany technique which is worth considering because
it is his closest approach to that austere impersonality of
creation Stephen describes to Lynch: when "the artist, like
the God of the creation, remains within or behind or above
his handiwork, invisible, refined out of existence, indifferent,
paring his fingernails." Under this, the intervention of a
consciousness, even indirectly through the medium of language, is ruled out. A character is broken down into its separate parts, as it is under the "distillation" technique, but only
one or two of the detached "parts"—"the vulgarity of speech
or of gesture," a detail of figure or expression, an item of
clothing—are recombined. Although it is free of irrelevancies,
the *quidditas* represented by the recombination is not the
quidditas of a generality but an individual; its function is to
identify rather than to abstract.

In *Stephen Hero* to some degree, and especially in *A Por-
trait of the Artist*, we can watch this technique take form.
A priest is invariably marked by the fluttering of his soutane.
Father Dolan steadies Stephen's hand before administering the

pandying, and the cruelty of his gesture extends to his "firm soft fingers," "his whitegrey face and the nocoloured eyes behind the steel-rimmed glasses"; when the priest reappears in *Ulysses*, he is signified only by the pandybat. In the same way, Mr. Casey's three cramped fingers symbolize his activities as an Irish patriot and hence his loyalty to Parnell, which for the boy Stephen is the peculiar essence of his father's friend. Again, the humility and joylessness of the church office are represented in the movements of the Jesuit dean of studies as he lights the fire, in his old, lean body—literally *similiter atque senis baculus* —and his face, compared by Stephen to "an unlit lamp or a reflection hung in a false focus."

Gesture and clothing, in particular, are as important in creating an individual *quidditas* as voice and breathing in creating a generalized *quidditas*. "There should be an art of gesture," Stephen tells Cranly in **Stephen Hero**. In the *Portrait*, he finds his "image of the soul in prayer" in "the raised and parted hands, the parted lips and eyes of one about to swoon" of religious art, and during his period of repentance visualizes himself "accomplishing the vague acts of the priesthood which pleased him by reason of their semblance of reality and of their distance from it." Clothes, in their turn, are true repositories of the soul, as they are for Lévy-Bruhl's primitives. When he comes upon his schoolmates, swimming, Stephen thinks pityingly of their nakedness: "How characterless they looked! Shuley without his deep unbuttoned collar, Ennis without his scarlet belt with the snaky clasp, and Connolly without his Norfolk coat with the flapless sidepockets!" In *Stephen Hero*, he is first impressed by the prostitute's black straw hat, the outward and visible sign of her essence, and the clothes of the characters in Joyce's play *Exiles* are so important that they are not only described in the stage directions but are mentioned by the characters themselves, with a green velvet jacket playing a significant part in the action. Finally, in the nighttown episode of *Ulysses*, changes of costume are as frequent as in the charades in which Stephen takes part at

Mr. Daniel's house (*Stephen Hero*), and the hallucinatory images of Bloom at successive stages of his past are all carefully dressed for their roles.

Gesture and clothing, details of physical appearance, peculiarities of speech, and intimate material appurtenances all serve to identify Stephen's friends in the *Portrait*, in dialogue passages which might be scenes from a play. Amid the profane, witty, or banal conversations of the students, the author intervenes only as a sort of property man, to mark each one with his objectified *quidditas*, which adheres to him from scene to scene virtually without change and in some instances even carries over into *Ulysses*: Cranly's "iron crown" of hair and priestly pallor, his profanity and Latin affectation of speech; Lynch's whinnying laugh, his habit of swearing "in yellow," and his gesture of putting out his chest; the shooting suit and fair goatee of MacCann, the reformer; Davin's brogue and Dixon's signet ring; Heron's cane and smile; the pedant Glynn's umbrella. In these scenes Stephen himself, the individual Stephen, is often a participant; he has his ashplant, his "familiar," which he carries also in *Ulysses*, and his soul moves rapidly and elusively through a series of metamorphoses which never quite leave the realm of the literal: the lamp mentioned in his conversation with the dean of studies; Epictetus' bucketful of water; Cranly's handball; the louse he picks from his neck; the fig Cranly tosses into the gutter.

This technique represents the ultimate in "objective" characterization, "revealing" an individual essence by means of a detail or an object to which it has only a fortuitous relation; the pandybat expresses Father Dolan's soul not because it resembles him in any way but because it is associated with him in an act that marks him forever in Stephen's eyes. Through Joyce's fourth epiphany technique (in which *claritas* is a tiny, perfunctory flash, all but absorbed by *quidditas*) we can trace out a virtual iconography of the characters, like the systematic recurrence of emblems and attitudes among the figures in sacred art. This was probably intentional on the part of Joyce, who was curiously "influenced" by medieval concepts and methods, probably more so than any other writer of our time, and whose preoccupation with symmetry and correspondence and the-microcosm-within-the-macrocosm would have been worthy of Dante. (There are indications in the *Portrait* of his attraction to religious iconography, which itself had a literary origin in the Middle Ages. During his period of sin, the adolescent Stephen still delights in the traditional symbols of Mary, and saints and their emblems—St. Ignatius Loyola with his book, St. Francis Xavier indicating his chest, Lorenzo Ricci and his berretta—are noted with particular interest by Stephen the boy in the paintings at Clongowes.) In *Ulysses*, where the individual Mr. Bloom is signified variously by his hat, his newspaper and cigar, the lemon soap, the yellow flower, and the pork kidney, much of the medieval flavor of the Witches' Sabbath passages is due to the highly formalized iconography of the apparitions: King Edward with his bucket ("for identification bucket in my hand," the king explains himself), the dead Rudy with his Eton suit and his lambkin (a genuine epiphany to Bloom as he appears over the prostrate body of Stephen), Gerty MacDowell with her bloody clout, Lord Tennyson and his Union Jack blazer, the corpse of Stephen's mother with her faded orange blossoms and torn bridal veil, her breath of "wetted ashes" and *Liliata rutilantium.*

. . . . . .

. . . Basically, perhaps, there is no difference between Joyce's final epiphany technique and the symbolism of other writers —such as the *leitmotiv* of Thomas Mann—but in its development and its use there are very real differences. Following Freud, we have come to think of a symbol chiefly in terms of its representational qualities (Pribislav Hippe's pencil in *The Magic Mountain*); through a combination of experimental science and philosophical idealism, we tend also to find a value of their own in "things," which we conceive more or less as absolutes. Joyce's conception of the symbol is much closer to the conception of the medieval Church: a symbol has a specific function to perform in a given situation, and, when that function has been performed, nothing prevents the use of the symbol again in a totally different context. This flexibility results eventually in the intimate interpenetration of the parts and the whole that is one of the chief manifestations of Joyce's principle of *consonantia*, reaching a high degree of complexity in his later work. In *Finnegans Wake*, where, as the writers of exegeses remind us, every part presupposes every other part and their sum as well, it is difficult to separate out the individual threads of the pattern. But we can see its outlines already in the "Christmas" symbolism of the *Portrait*, where the significance of the velvet-backed brushes (maroon for the *quidditas* of Michael Davitt, green for the *quidditas* of Parnell) is expanded in Stephen's "red and green" impressions as he anticipates the school holiday, and the Irish church and Irish politics are ironically united at the dinner party on Christmas day in the violent quarrel between Aunt Dante and Mr. Casey; we see it also in the "bowl" symbolism in the early pages of *Ulysses*, where the bowl of shaving-lather, introduced as the *quidditas* of Buck Mulligan, becomes successively the bay, the bowl of incense Stephen carried at Clongowes, and the bowl of green bile at his mother's deathbed. Although these are only minor examples of Joyce's method, few could illustrate it more effectively.

✿◇❀◇✿◇❀◇✿◇❀◇✿◇❀◇✿◇❀◇✿◇❀◇✿◇❀◇✿◇❀◇✿◇❀◇✿◇❀◇

FRANK O'CONNOR

Frank O'Connor (pseudonym of Michael O'Donovan), distinguished
Irish man of letters and short-story writer, lectured at Northwestern
and Harvard universities and the University of Chicago. He was
author or editor of more than twenty-five books, among them *An
Only Child*, an autobiography; *Stories of Frank O'Connor* and many
other story collections; several books of verse; and books of critical
studies, such as *The Mirror in the Roadway* and *The Lonely
Voice*.

JOYCE AND DISSOCIATED METAPHOR

. . . . .

Sir Desmond MacCarthy describes in one of his essays how
I first came to notice the peculiar cast of Joyce's mind. The
incident concerned a picture of Cork in his [Joyce's] hallway. I
could not detect what the frame was made of. "What is that?"
I asked. "Cork," he replied. "Yes," I said, "I know it's Cork,
but what's the frame?" "Cork," he replied with a smile. "I
had the greatest difficulty in finding a French frame-maker
who would make it."

Whether or not this indicated, as I thought, that he was
suffering from associative mania, it proved a valuable key in
my efforts to understand his work.

It also proved a necessary one, for though in his years of
fame Joyce had interpreters galore who propounded his work
to the public even before it was completed, we have no such
interpreters for the early stories and *A Portrait of the Artist as a
Young Man.*

This seems to me an exceedingly difficult book. The first
thing to notice is that the peculiar style used in the opening

of *Two Gallants* is now a regular device. It can best be described as "mechanical prose," for certain key words are repeated deliberately and mechanically to produce a feeling of hypnosis in the reader.

The soft beauty of the Latin word *touched* with an enchanting *touch* the *dark* of the evening, with a *touch* fainter and more persuading than the *touch* of music or of a *woman's* hand. The strife of their minds was quelled. The figure of a *woman* as she appears in the liturgy of the church *passed* silently through the *darkness*: a whiterobed figure, small and slender as a boy and with a falling girdle. Her *voice*, frail and high as a boy's, was heard intoning from a distant choir the first words of a *woman* which pierce the gloom and clamour of the first chanting of the passion:

—*Et tu cum Jesu Galilæo eras.*

And all hearts were *touched* and turned to her *voice*, shining like a young star, shining clearer as the *voice* intoned the proparoxyton and more faintly as the cadence died. [P, 244.]

I have italicized a few of the principal words to show how a chain of association is built up, but the reader can see for himself that other words are similarly repeated. The whole structure of the book is probably lost unless Joyce's notebooks give some indication of what it was, but I have an impression that Joyce wrote with a list of a couple of hundred words before him, each representing some association, and that at intervals the words were dropped in, like currants in a cake and a handful at a time, so that their presence would be felt rather than identified. I suspect that a number of those words, like the spotlighted word "touch" in the passage I have quoted, are of sensory significance, and are intended to maintain in our subconscious minds the metaphor of the Aristotelian scheme of psychology, while others, like the word "passed," seem to have a general significance in relation to the movement of the individual through time and space. Whenever the emotion overflows, it is represented by inversion and repetition. The whole subject should be studied in a few paragraphs like the following:

He was *alone*. He was unheeded, happy and near to the *wild heart* of life. He was *alone* and young and wilful and *wildhearted*, *alone* amid a waste of *wild air* and brackish waters and the *sea*-harvest of shells and tangle and veiled grey sunlight and gayclad lightclad figures, of *children* and *girls* and voices *childish* and *girlish* in the *air*.

A *girl* stood before him in *midstream*, *alone* and *still*, *gazing* out to *sea*. She seemed like one whom magic had changed into the likeness of a strange and beautiful *seabird*. Her *long* slender *bare* legs were delicate as a *crane's* and pure save where an emerald trail of *sea*weed had fashioned itself as a sign upon the flesh. Her thighs, fuller and *soft*hued as ivory, were *bared* almost to the hips where the *white* fringes of her drawers were like *featherings* of *soft white down*. Her slateblue skirts were kilted boldly about her waist and *dovetailed* behind her. Her bosom was as a *bird's soft and slight*, *slight and soft* as the breast of some dark*plumaged* dove. But her *long* fair hair was *girlish*: and *girlish*, and *touched* with the wonder of mortal beauty, her face.

She was *alone and still*, *gazing* out to *sea*, and when she felt his presence and the worship of his *eyes* her *eyes* turned to him in quiet *sufferance* of his *gaze*, without shame or wantonness. *Long*, *long* she *suffered* his *gaze* and then quietly withdrew her *eyes* from his and bent them towards the *stream*, gently stirring the water with her foot hither and thither. The first *faint* noise of gently moving water broke the silence, low and *faint* and whispering, *faint* as the bells of sleep; hither and thither, hither and thither: and a *faint* flame trembled on her cheek. [P, 171.]

I find it difficult to transcribe, let alone analyze, the passage because it seems to me insufferably self-conscious, as though Walter Pater had taken to business and commercialized his style for the use of schools and colleges, but those who admire such prose should, I feel, be compelled to consider how it is constructed. I suspect there are at least two movements in a passage of this sort, one a local movement that seems to rise and fall within the framework of the paragraph in relation to the dominant image, and which produces words like "crane," "feathering," "down," "dovetailed," and "plumaged"; and another, over-all movement in which key words, particularly words of sensory significance like "touch," "eyes," and "gazed," are repeated and varied. I fancy that these could be traced right through the book, and that the study of them would throw considerable light on Joyce's intentions.

It is important to note that this is something new in literature, and it represents the point, anticipated in Flaubert, at which style ceases to be a relationship between author and reader and becomes a relationship of a magical kind between author and object. Here *le mot juste* is no longer *juste* for the reader, but for the object. It is not an attempt at communicating the experience to the reader, who is supposed to be present only by courtesy, but at equating the prose with the experience. Indeed, one might say that it aims at replacing the experience by the prose, and the process may be considered complete when Joyce and his interpreters refer to one chapter in *Ulysses* as a canon fugue or, as they prefer to describe it in their idiomatic way, a *fuga per canonem*, which it is not and, by the nature of prose and of canon fugues, could not possibly be.

So far as I understand it, which is not very far, A *Portrait* is a study in differentiation based on Aristotle's *De Anima* and St. Thomas's *Commentary*. The first page, which looks like a long passage of baby talk, is an elaborate construct that relates the development of the senses to the development of the arts, a device later used in *Ulysses*, when we find the transmigration of souls discussed over an underlying metaphor of the transmutation of matter. "Once upon a time," the words with which the book opens, represent story-telling, the primary form of art. This whole passage is a fascinating piece of exposition. The first external person identified by the child is his father, whom he identifies first by sight, then by touch. Himself he identifies with a character in the story his father tells him, and from the abstract "road" of the bedtime story constructs a real road containing a real character whom he identifies by the sense of taste—"she sold lemon platt." He learns a song, the second of the arts, which contains the key words "rose" and "green," and he unconsciously identifies these with "hot" and "cold." When, instead of "O, the wild rose blossoms in the little green place," he remembers "O the green wothe botheth," we know that he has wet the bed because he has linked the symbols for hot and cold. From this episode the unconscious images become conscious, and the sense of touch, the primary sense, according to Aristotle, is clearly differentiated. "When you wet the bed first it is warm then it gets cold." The metaphor is carried through into the divided politics of the home, for "Dante had two brushes in her press. The brush with the maroon velvet back was for Michael Davitt and the brush with the green velvet back was for Parnell."

As the first chapter develops, we find the boy at school with a high temperature that causes him to feel hot and cold by turn. This is illustrated in the prose by alternations of metaphor. The boy remembers washing his hands in the Wicklow Hotel where there were two taps, hot and cold. At school his class is divided into two groups, York and Lancaster, red and white. When he goes to bed, we know he is shivering violently because he is thinking of ghost stories, of black dogs and white cloaks, of old people and of strange people. We know the bed is warming up when he begins to think of the holidays, of warm colors and familiar faces. Eventually, when delirium overtakes him, the civil war between Davitt and Parnell is also used as a metaphor. The little drama is played out against a background of other antitheses: big, small; nasty, nice; damp, dry. There are no mental or moral antitheses because the boy knows of "right" and "wrong" only in terms of answers to schoolbook questions. He cannot think. As he can only feel, the only quality that can be attributed to him is "heart," the organ to which Aristotle ascribes sensation, and so we get, casually tossed in, the phrase "He was sick in his heart if you could be sick in that place."

In the next section we get a repetition of the words "good" and "bad," "right" and "wrong," which still have no true meaning for the boy because mind has not yet been born in him. Mind emerges only when he has been unjustly punished, and once more Joyce tosses the casual reference in—"before he could make up his mind," to indicate that the miracle of differentiation has taken place. The soul, though born in all women with menstruation, is born in males only with mortal sin, so that it is scarcely mentioned until the boy has been with a prostitute. Then it overflows the pages.

The differentiation is marked also in the literary forms. Its aesthetic is propounded to Lynch in the final pages of the book.

. . . art necessarily divides itself into three forms progressing from one to the next. These forms are: the lyrical form, the form wherein the artist presents his image in immediate relation to himself; the epical form, the form wherein he presents his image in mediate relation to himself and to others; the dramatic form, the form wherein he presents his image in immediate relation to others. [*P*, 214.]

This progress is also used as part of the metaphorical structure of the book to illustrate the differentiation taking place in Stephen's character. It begins with lyrical forms; when he goes to college, it turns into epic; and, finally, when he makes up his mind to leave home (action), it becomes dramatic— the diary form. "The lyrical form," says Stephen, "is in fact the simplest verbal vesture of an instant of emotion, a rhythmical cry such as ages ago cheered on the man who pulled at the oar or dragged stone up a slope" [*P*, 214]. Accordingly, each of the early sections represents an "instant of emotion" and ends with a cry, though the cries seem to be differentiated according to the stage of self-consciousness which the individual has reached. Thus, the first cry "Parnell! Parnell! He is dead," though supposed to come from a crowd of imaginary figures on a shore, is the impersonal, unindividualized cry of the sick child in a state of delirium, attributing his own suffering to dream figures. In the next section, when Mr. Casey cries: "Poor Parnell! My dead king!" the cry, though impersonal, is individualized and is followed by tears, though the tears are not Stephen's own. It is not until he himself has been punished unjustly that he gives a scream of pain and his tears flow. Again he cries when he goes to the prostitute, but this time with lust, and his tears are tears of relief. He cries once more when terrified by the thought of his sins, and his tears are tears of repentance. Finally, in the scene with the bird-girl, he cries again, but there are no tears, for the artistic emotion is not kinetic.

In reading Joyce, one is reading Literature—Literature with a capital L. The tide rises about the little figures islanded here and there in a waste of waters, and gradually they disappear till nothing is left but the blank expanse of Literature, mirroring the blank face of the sky.

WILLIAM YORK TINDALL

William York Tindall has taught at New York and Northwestern universities and is Professor of English at Columbia University. He is the author of books on John Bunyan, D. H. Lawrence, and Dylan Thomas, among others, and has written five books on Joyce: *James Joyce: His Way of Interpreting the Modern World, Joyce's Chamber Music, James Joyce, Reader's Guide to James Joyce,* and *The Joyce Country.*

[THE LITERARY SYMBOL]

. . . The symbolists of the early twentieth century, Conrad, for example, and Joyce, owe a considerable debt to *Madame Bovary.* Referring to it several times in his letters, Conrad praises "the sheer sincerity of its method" and the marvelous "rendering of concrete things." What Flaubert did for him, he continues, was open his eyes and arouse his emulation. He did not read *Madame Bovary* until he had finished *Almayer's Folly,* but it was between that work and *Lord Jim* that Conrad developed his imagistic method. As for Joyce, who wrote the stories of *Dubliners* shortly after the appearance of Conrad's great symbolist work, he knew pages of Flaubert by heart. What he learned from him is expressed in *Stephen Hero* where Stephen, after rejecting naturalistic "portrayal of externals," says that the artist must free "the image from its mesh of defining circumstances . . . and re-embody it in artistic circumstances chosen as the most exact for it in its new office." In that office the details of observed reality, so precise that they have caused critics to confuse Joyce with the naturalists, are "transmuted," as he puts it in *A Portrait of the Artist,* into radiant images. Not only Flaubert, to be sure, but symbolist poets and the

Hermetic tradition led Joyce to his method; and it is fitting that *Chamber Music*, the sketch from which his poetic novel developed, is verse; but that Flaubert remained central in Joyce's mind is suggested not only by his concern with the observed image but with the *mot juste* and expressive rhythm. Many passages in Flaubert's letters, with which Joyce must have been familiar, anticipate and maybe helped to shape the aesthetics of Stephen Dedalus. Speaking as Stephen was to speak of the need for impersonality, Flaubert says in one of his letters that the artist must "be in his work like God in creation, present everywhere and visible nowhere. Since art is a second world, its creator must act by analogous methods."

A *Portrait of the Artist*, at once the residence and the creation of Stephen's nail-paring God, differs from most other novels of adolescence in detachment and method. At first glance, however, Joyce's improvement upon the *Bildungsroman* seems simple enough because the main burden is carried, as in ordinary novels of this sort, by character and action. We have plainly before us the story of a sensitive, gifted boy who is disappointed in his hope of communion with parents, country, and religion. Refusing the actual world at last, as in the role of the Count of Monte Cristo he refuses the muscatel grapes that Mercedes proffers, he constructs a better world to replace it. "If you have form'd a circle to go into," says cynical Blake, "go into it yourself, and see how you would do."

The theme of A *Portrait of the Artist* is normal enough. Joyce differs from most of his predecessors, as Flaubert from his, in greater dependence upon image, rhythm, juxtaposition, and tone to supplement the narrative and in giving attitudes and feelings body to support them. What Joyce in his notes for *Exiles* called "attendant images" could be omitted without destroying the outline of his book, but some of its quality and depth must be attributed to this accompaniment. At times, moreover, forgetting their capacity of attendants, images and other devices become essential and assume the principal burden as they were to do in *Ulysses*. Yielding place to other things at such times, the narrative grows "obscure," a word which means that narrative has given way to suggestion and discourse to nondiscursive elements having more effect on feeling than on mind. While still attendant, however, images may be too familiar or obvious to attract notice. Even Tolstoi used them.

When Vronsky in *Anna Karenina* rides his mare to death at the races, breaking her back by his awkwardness or zeal, his action, unnecessary to the plot and far from realistic, embodies his relationship with Anna. But Tolstoi's image of the mare is so narrowly assigned and painfully deliberate that it does little more than discourse could. Joyce's images, though partly assigned, however deliberate, are suggestive, indefinite, and not altogether explicable. Ambivalent, they reveal not only the quality of experience but its complexity. Without attendant or essential images, *A Portrait of the Artist* would be so much less immediate and less moving that few would pick it up again.

Images play other parts in the great design. Embodying Stephen's experience before he is entirely aware of it, and doing the same service for us, they prepare for moments of realization, which could not occur without them. Operating below conscious notice, the images, rhythms, and other forms project an unconscious process that comes to light at last. This function is no more important, however, than that of relating part to part and, composing a structure which, with the dominant narrative it supplements and complicates, creates what Stephen calls radiance or the meaning of the composite form.

The first two pages of *A Portrait of the Artist* present the images that, when elaborated, are to compose the supplementary structure and take their place in the form. We are confronted here with a moocow coming down the road, with a rose (maybe green), with wetting the bed, with a girl, and with an eagle that plucks out eyes—not to mention a number of other things such as dancing to another's tune. Without much context as yet, these images, acquiring fresh meanings from recurrence and relationship with others, carry aspects of Stephen and his trouble. Never was opening so dense as this or more important.

Take that road, long, narrow, and strictly bounded, along

which comes a moocow to meet the passive boy. Diction, rhythm, and the opening phrase (the traditional beginning of an Irish "story") suggest the condition of childhood and its helplessness. Confined to the road, the child cannot escape encounter with a creature traditionally associated with Irish legend and with everything maternal. Later, Stephen delights to accompany the milkman in his round of neighboring roads, although a little discouraged by the foul green puddles of the cowyard. Cows, which have seemed so beautiful in the country on sunny days, now revolt him and he can look no longer at their milk. Yet as he pursues "the Rock Road," he thinks a milkman's life pleasant enough, and looks forward with equanimity to adopting it as his own. Innumerable connotations of word and phrase make it almost plain at last that the road suggests tradition, that the cow suggests church, country, and all maternal things, and that the milkman suggests the priest. The little episode, far from being a sign of these meanings, is no more than the embodiment of possibilities. What it implies awaits corroboration from later episodes, Stephen's rejection of the priesthood, for example, or his aesthetic query about the man hacking a cow by accident from a block of wood. It is certain that none of these connected images is casual. As for the road itself, it develops into the circular track round which Mike Flynn, the old trainer, makes Stephen run; into the track at Clongowes where Stephen, breaking his glasses, is almost blinded; into the dark road alongside which Davin meets his peasant woman; and, after many reappearances, all of which confirm and enlarge the initial idea and feeling of tradition, into its opposite, the road that promises freedom on the final page.

The images of rose, water, girl, and bird are so intricately involved with one another that it seems all but impossible to separate them for analysis. Take the rose, however, a symbol which, carrying traditional significance, becomes, after much recurrence, Stephen's image of woman and creativity. Lacking sufficient context at its first appearance to have certain meaning, the rose, made green by Stephen, is not altogether without possibilities. Green is the color of Ireland, of immaturity, and of vegetable creation; yet a green rose is unnatural. Art is unnatural too. Could the green rose anticipate Stephen's immature desire for Irish art? We cannot tell for sure. At school Stephen is champion of the white rose that loses to the red in an academic war of roses; and during his period of "resolute piety" his prayers ascend to heaven "like perfume streaming upwards from a heart of white rose." It is the red rose, however, that attends his creative ecstasies near the Bull Wall, after he resolves to follow mortal beauty, and in bed, after composing a poem. His soul, "swooning into some new world," shares Dante's penultimate vision: "A world, a glimmer, or a flower? Glimmering and trembling, trembling and unfolding, a breaking light, an opening flower, it spread in endless succession to itself, breaking in full crimson and unfolding and fading to palest rose, leaf by leaf and wave of light by wave of light, flooding all the heavens with its soft flushes, every flush deeper than other." This heavenly vision, which follows the hell of the sermons and the purgatory of his repentance, anticipates his ultimate vision of Mrs. Bloom, the heavenly yet earthly rose of *Ulysses*.

Woman, associated with rose, embodies Stephen's aspiration and, increasingly, his creative power. Eileen, the girl who appears at the beginning of the book, unattainable because Protestant, is soon identified with sex and the Tower of Ivory, symbol of the Blessed Virgin. Mercedes, a dream who inhabits a garden of roses along the milkman's road, suggests the Virgin by her name while adding overtones of remoteness, exile, and revenge. At Cork, however, Stephen's "monstrous" adolescent thoughts injure her purity by desire. When Emma, a teaser, replaces Mercedes as object of desire and becomes in addition an image of his mother country and his church, Stephen transfers his devotion to the Virgin herself, over whose sodality he presides, and whose "office" becomes his formula. The wading girl near the Bull Wall, who embodies mortal beauty, unites all previous suggestions. Associating her with Emma, the Virgin, the rose, and the womb of the imagination, whose priest he becomes, he finds her an image of his own capacity: "Heavenly God!" his soul exclaims, its eye no doubt upon himself. His repeated "Yes" anticipates Mrs. Bloom's as the girl, stirring the waters "hither and thither," anticipates the hither and thithering waters of Anna Livia Plurabelle: "He would create."

Other women take their place in the great design. There is the common girl, persisting in memory, who stops Stephen on the street to offer flowers for which he cannot pay. Connected in his mind with a kitchen girl who sings Irish songs over the dishes, she develops near the end into the servant maid, who, singing "Rosie O'Grady" in her kitchen, proffers the suggestion at least of Irish flowers, green roses perhaps. Cranly's "*Mulier cantat*" unites her in Stephen's mind with "the figure of woman as she appears in the liturgy of the Church" and with all his symbolic women. Unprepared as yet to receive what she proffers in her song or unable to pay the price of acceptance, Stephen says, "I want to see Rosie first."

That Rosie, another anticipation of Mrs. Bloom, sings in a kitchen is not unimportant. After each of his ecstasies, Stephen comes back to the kitchen, which serves not only as an ironic device for deflating him but as an image of the reality to which, if he is to be an artist, he must return. It is notable that his acceptance of Mr. Bloom and the communion with mankind that precedes the vision of Mrs. Bloom takes place in a kitchen. Rosie in her kitchen, the last great image of woman in *A Portrait of the Artist,* unites the ideal with the actual. Neither the wading girl nor Mercedes, both ethereal, can present to Stephen the idea and feeling of a union which someday he will understand. Far from seeing Rosie first, he sees her last, but by her aid, of which he is not fully aware as yet, he comes nearer his vision of above and below, of heavenly roses to be sure but of roses in kitchens.

Woman is not only rose but bird and sometimes bat. The bird, which makes its first appearance as the eagle who is to punish Stephen's guilt by making him blind as a bat, makes its next appearance as Heron, who, looking and acting like a bird of prey, tries to make Stephen conform. Bad at first, birds become good as Stephen approaches mortal beauty at the beach. He thinks of Daedalus, "a hawklike man flying sunward," and wants to utter cries of hawk or eagle, images no longer of oppression but, retaining authority, of creation. The wading girl is "a strange and beautiful seabird." "Her bosom was as a bird's soft and slight, slight and soft as the breast of some darkplumaged dove." As Stephen observes their flight, birds also become what he calls a "symbol of departure or loneliness." When, becoming birdlike Daedalus, he takes flight across the sea to exile, he unites all these meanings and confirms their association with water. Bats are anticipated by images of blinding, not only those of the eye-plucking eagle, of glasses broken on the track, and of dull red blinds that keep light from boys of Belvedere during their retreat but that of the woman into whose eye Mr. Casey spits: " 'Phth! says I to her.' 'O Jesus, Mary and Joseph!' says she . . . 'I'm blinded and drownded . . . I'm blinded entirely.' " When they appear at last, bats gather up these anticipatory associations with woman, custom, and country. Davin's peasant woman at her door along the dark lonely road seems to Stephen "a type of her race and of his own, a batlike soul waking to the consciousness of itself in darkness and secrecy and loneliness." Seeming almost a bird for a moment, Emma, revisited, becomes another bat, but its darkness, secrecy, and loneliness connect it with himself as artist about to try silence, exile, and cunning. Blind to reality as yet, he may improve. Like the images of bird and flower, the bat is ambivalent, not only bad but good. If bat suggests things as they are, and bird things as they ought to be, it is the artist's job to reconcile them. If all these women are aspects of woman, and if woman is an aspect of himself, the creative part, he too is presented by images of bird, bat, and, besides these, water.

Ambivalent from the first, water is either warm or cold, agreeable or frightening. The making of water at the beginning of the *Portrait* seems an image of creation that includes the artist's two realities. At school Stephen is shouldered into the "square ditch," square not because of shape but because it receives the flow of the urinal or "square." Plainly maternal by context, this image warns Stephen of the perils of regression, to which like one of those rats who enjoy the ditch, he is tempted by the discomforts of external reality. The "warm turfcoloured bogwater" of the bath adds something peculiarly Irish to his complex. Dirty water down the drain at the Wicklow Hotel and the watery sound of cricket bats (connected in his mind with pandybats and bats) confirm his fears. The concluding image of the first chapter, assigned only by previous associations, embodies his infantile career: "Pick, pack, pock, puck," go the cricket bats, "like drops of water in a fountain falling softly in the brimming bowl." If Stephen himself is suggested by this bowl and his development by an ablaut series, water is not altogether bad. This possibility is established toward the middle of the book, where, changing character, water becomes good on the whole and unmistakably a symbol of creation. On his way to the beach, Stephen still finds the sea cold and "infra-human." The bathing boys repel him, but the sight of the wading girl gives water another aspect. Rolling up his trousers like J. Alfred Prufrock, he himself goes wading. From that moment of baptism and rebirth inaudible music and the sound of waters attend his creative ecstasies. It is true that, relapsing a little, Stephen fears water again in *Ulysses*, but Mr. Bloom, with whom he finally unites, is a water lover, and Anna Livia Plurabelle is the river Liffey.

These families of developing images that, supplementing the narrative, give it texture, immediacy, and more body are not the only symbolic devices Joyce commands. As we have noticed, large parallels, rhythms, shifts of tone, juxtaposition, and all else that Flaubert commended complicate the "significant form." But deferring these, I shall confine myself in this place to some of the relatively unassigned and unattached images that concentrate feeling at important points.

Consider, for example, the opening of the second chapter. Uncle Charles, who is addicted to black twist, is deported to the outhouse, whence rising smoke and the brim of his tall hat appear as he sings old songs in tranquillity. Position gives this image an importance that import cannot justify. Hints of exile, creation, and piety, all relevant to the theme, may divert our understanding without satisfying it entirely. Few of Joyce's images are so mysterious as this and, while occupying our feelings, so resistant to discourse. The scenery at Cork appeals more readily to the understanding. While in that town with his father, Stephen finds in the word "Foetus," carved in the wood of a desk, what Eliot would call an objective correlative of the "den of monstrous images" within him. After this corroboration of inner disorder, he emerges from schoolroom into the sunny street where he sees cricketers and a maid watering plants; hears a German band and scale after scale from a girl's piano. In another book this urban noise and scenery might serve as setting alone. Here, more functional that that, it presents a vision of the normal, the orderly, and the quotidian from which the discovery of his monstrous interior has separated him.

Characters are no less symbolic. The two dwarfish eccentrics that Stephen encounters, one on the street and the other in the library, seem caricatures of Stephen's possible future and of the soul of Ireland, but aside from that, they evade significance. By action, speech, and context, on the other hand, the figure of Cranly becomes more nearly definite. That last interview which drives Stephen to exile concentrates in Cranly the forces of admission, submission, confession, and retreat, and he becomes the embodiment of all that has plagued the imperfect hero. Cranly's preoccupation with a book called *Diseases of the Ox* adds to the picture. Since Stephen as "Bous Stephanoumenos" has been identified with the ox, Cranly's devotion to his book reveals him as Stephen's most reactionary critic, not, as we had supposed, his friend.

When Stephen turns seaward toward his great experience with the wading girl, an image which might escape casual notice not only suggests the finality of his action but adds to our understanding of his complexity: he crosses the bridge from Dollymount to the Bull. Readers of *Dubliners* may recall that crossing bridges in that work is as portentous as Caesar's crossing of the Rubicon; in *Ulysses* Stephen, a frustrated exile back from Paris, is "a disappointed bridge." In the *Portrait*, on the bridge which marks his passage from old custom to freedom and the waters of life, he meets a squad of uncouth, tall-hatted Christian Brothers, marching two by two, going the other way. Their direction, their appearance, and their regimentation are important, but what reveals Stephen's character is the contempt with which he regards those who are socially and intellectually inferior to Jesuits. The episode, therefore, includes both his escape from one tyranny and his submission to another, the greater tyranny of pride, which, until he understands the Blooms, will keep him from uniting the regions of reality by art. Stephen may think of charity or Joyce talk of pride, but this revealing episode contributes more than all that talk or thought to the portrait of an autist.

The writer of this kind of novel, says E. M. Forster, "is not necessarily going to 'say' anything about the universe; he proposes to sing." His song—and Forster has both Melville and Lawrence in mind—must "combine with the furniture of common sense." In *Aspects of the Novel*, where this reflection appears, Forster excludes Joyce from the great company to which he himself belongs. Rejecting symbolist as a term for it, he prefers prophetical. "A prophet does not reflect," he says. "That is why we exclude Joyce. Joyce has many qualities akin to prophecy and he has shown (especially in the *Portrait of the Artist*) an imaginative grasp of evil. But he undermines the universe in too workmanlike a manner, looking around for this tool or that: in spite of all his internal looseness he is too tight, he is never vague except after due deliberation; it is talk, talk, never song." As for *Ulysses*, it is "a dogged attempt to cover the universe with mud," an "epic of grubbiness and disillusion," and "a simplification of the human character in the interests of Hell." It seems a pity that one great symbolist cannot comprehend another, but the Irish Sea is wider than it looks and considerably deeper.

General Readings

✿◈✿

RICHARD ELLMANN

Richard Ellmann, Joyce's biographer and editor of his letters, holds the Franklin Bliss Snyder Chair of English at Northwestern University. His books include *The Identity of Yeats* and *Yeats: The Man and the Masks*, a biography. He is editor of *My Brother's Keeper*, by Stanislaus Joyce, and co-editor with Ellsworth Mason of *The Critical Writings of James Joyce*. His biography *James Joyce* won the 1959 National Book Award for nonfiction.

THE GROWTH OF IMAGINATION

. . . the childman weary, the manchild in the womb.—*Ulysses*

The agitation of Joyce's feelings during his visit to Dublin in 1909 laid bare for a moment topics of that conversation with himself which, like Yeats, he never ceased to conduct. One was his bond to Dublin, which his books indicate he thoroughly understood. Although Stephen Dedalus in both *Stephen Hero* and *A Portrait* assumes his isolation, he surrounds himself with friends and family to whom he can confide it. When he rebels he hastens to let them know of his rebellion so that he can measure their response to it. He searches for disciples who must share his motives vicariously. As he demands increasing allegiance from them, step by step, he brings them to the point where they will go no further, and their refusal, half-anticipated, enables him to feel forsaken and to forsake them. He buys his own ticket for Holyhead, but claims to have been deported. Yet his mother prepares his clothing for the journey;

---

she at any rate does not break with him. Of this young man it may be safely predicted that he will write letters home.

Joyce's life wears a similar aspect. Having stomped angrily out of the house, he circled back to peer in the window. He could not exist without close ties, no matter in what part of Europe he resided; and if he came to terms with absence, it was by bringing Ireland with him, in his memories, and in the persons of his wife, his brother, his sister. So in later life, when asked if he would go back to Ireland, he could reply, 'Have I ever left it?' In memory his closest ties to the past were with the scenes of his early childhood. This childhood was dominated rhetorically by his father, but emotionally by his mother with her practicality, her unquenchable indulgence, her tenacity, even her inveterate pregnancy. As a small boy he had gone to her to ask that she examine him in his school work; as a young man, the letters from Paris in 1902 and 1903 confirm, he asked her support for his ambitions and ideas. His confidences went to his mother, not to his father, a man (as his sister May remembered) impossible to confide in.

His attitude toward his mother is clarified by his attitude toward Nora Barnacle. In the letters he sent to Nora in that discomposed summer of 1909, there are many testimonies that Joyce longed to reconstitute, in his relation with her, the filial bond which his mother's death had broken. Explicitly he longs to make their relationship that of child and mother, as if the relationship of lovers was too remote. He covets an even more intimate dependence: 'O that I could nestle in your womb like a child born of your flesh and blood, be fed by your blood, sleep in the warm secret gloom of your body!' [*Letters*, I, pp. 296-297.]

Joyce seems to have thought with equal affection of the roles of mother and child. He said once to Stanislaus about the bond between the two, 'There are only two forms of love in the world, the love of a mother for her child and the love of a man for lies.' In later life, as Maria Jolas remarked, 'Joyce talked of fatherhood as if it were motherhood.' He seems to have longed to establish in himself all aspects of the bond of mother and child. He was attracted, particularly, by the image of himself as a weak child cherished by a strong woman, which seems closely connected with the images of himself as victim, whether as a deer pursued by hunters, as a passive man surrounded by burly extroverts, as a Parnell or a Jesus among traitors. His favorite characters are those who in one way or another retreat before masculinity, yet are loved regardless by motherly women.

The sense of his family life as warm and tranquil, which was established in Joyce's mind during his earliest years, was disturbed for him by his father's irresponsibility. To some extent John Joyce served his son as model, for he continually tried his wife's steadfastness, which however proved equal to every challenge, including the drunken attempt on her life. James, contesting for his mother's love, learned to use the same weapons with a difference. A merely good boy would have been submerged, unable to compete with his father in the inordinate demands upon a mother's affection, but a prodigal son had a better chance. His mother must be encouraged to love him more than his father because he was just as errant and much more gifted, so more pitiable and lovable. For his irresponsibility was the turbulence of genius, motivated—unlike his father's—by courage rather than by failure. At first it took the form of arousing his mother to question his conduct. His answers proved surprisingly sweeping and persuasive. Then he tried her further: John Joyce had been anticlerical, James exceeded him by becoming irreligious.

This change, which was not easy for him to undergo, presented an added complication. For one thing, in the figure of the Virgin he had found a mother image which he cherished. He had gone to prostitutes and then prayed to the Virgin as later he would drum up old sins with which to demand Nora's forgiveness; the Virgin's love, like his mother's and later his wife's, was of a sort especially suited to great sinners. But there was an aspect of Irish Catholicism which he was glad to abandon. It was not a mother church but a father church, harsh, repressive, masculine. To give it up was both consciously and unconsciously to offer his mother's love its supreme test, for his mother was deeply religious. She was disconcerted but did not abandon him. Yet her death not long after one of his open defiances of her belief seemed a punishment; he felt as if he had killed her by trying her too far. This thought he confided to Nora, who called him reproachfully, 'Woman-killer.'

When Joyce met Nora Barnacle in 1904, it was not enough for her to be his mistress; she must be his queen and even his goddess; he must be able to pray to her. But to gain all her love, and so increase her perfection, he must make sure she will accept even the worst in him. He must test her by making her his wife without calling her that, by denying legal sanction to the bond between them, just as in dealing with his mother he had wanted her to acknowledge him as her son even though in so many ways he was not filial. Nora Barnacle passed this test easily, no doubt aware that their attachment was indispensable to him. Then he tried her further, not by flouting her religion, which she did not care deeply about, but by doubting her fidelity. That the accusation might be false did not deter him; in a way, it encouraged him, for if he was accusing her falsely he could be, when reassured of her innocence, more humble and so more childlike than before. When this test too was surmounted, Joyce made a final trial of her: she must recognize all his impulses, even the strangest, and match his candor by confiding in him every thought she has found in herself, especially the most embarrassing. She must allow him to know her inmost life, to learn with odd exactitude what it is to be a woman. This test, the last, Nora passed successfully later in 1909. In so doing she accepted complicity, she indulged his reduction of her motherly purity just as she had indulged his insistence upon that purity. Joyce's letters during his two subsequent absences from her in Trieste were full of thoughts about 'adoration' and 'desecration' of her image, extravagant terms that he himself applied.

What was unusual about his attitude was not that he saw his wife as his mother or that he demanded inordinate fulfillment of either role. The novelty lay in his declining to confuse the two images and instead holding them remorsefully apart, opposing them to each other so that they became the poles of his mind. He was thereby enabled to feel that with Nora, as with his mother, he was a prodigal son, full of love and misbehavior; he was pleased that she 'saw through him,' as he said, and detected the boy in the man. This view of himself he encouraged. In *Ulysses* and *Finnegans Wake* he apportioned womanhood in its sexual aspect to Molly Bloom, and in its maternal aspect to Anna Livia Plurabelle. But he understood and marveled that Nora had no sense of the dichotomy that bothered him. He represented her attitude, which he took to be feminine in general, when Molly, though primarily the sensualist, thinks of Stephen Dedalus as child and as lover, without incompatibility, and Anna Livia, though primarily the mother, recollects her once passionate attachment to her husband.

Joyce studied his mental landscape and made use of it in his books. *Dubliners* is written on the assumption that Ireland is an inadequate mother, 'an old sow who eats her farrow,' and he associates himself with the masticated children. As he wrote to Georg Goyert, the book did not describe the way 'they' are in Dublin, but the way 'we' are. We are foolish, comic, motionless, corrupted; yet we are worthy of sympathy too, a sympathy which, if Ireland denies us, the international reader may give. But the reader must be tested like a loving mother by an errant child, must be forced to see the ugly, undecorated reality before he is allowed to extend his pity, a pity compounded of outraged affection, amusement, and understanding.

Joyce's own preoccupations emerge through the impersonal façade of *Dubliners*. Two stories, 'A Mother' and 'The Boarding House,' portray mothers who fail in their role by browbeating, a type Joyce could never endure. 'The Dead' represents in Gretta a woman with genuine maternal sympathy, which she extends both to the dead boy who loved her and to her inadequate husband. She overwhelms Gabriel's sexual passion by letting her thoughts dwell upon the boy, with whom Gabriel at the last associates himself. Other stories, especially

'Araby' and 'Ivy Day in the Committee Room,' play on the theme of the loss of warmth in the past: the bazaar closed, the radiant image of Parnell chilled by small feelings. Throughout the book the women usually hold together when the men do not, 'The Sisters' in that they survive so solidly their brother the priest, Chandler's wife in 'A Little Cloud' in her relegation of her husband in favor of her child. Yet there is pity for them too, especially for those who, like Corley's girl in 'Two Gallants,' like 'Eveline,' like Maria in 'Clay,' cannot achieve full maternal being, and for Gretta in 'The Dead' because of her inevitably lost girlhood. In the book women act (or fail to act) the mother, men drink, children suffer.

To write *A Portrait of the Artist as a Young Man* Joyce plunged back into his own past, mainly to justify, but also to expose it. The book's pattern, as he explained to Stanislaus, is that we are what we were; our maturity is an extension of our childhood, and the courageous boy is father of the arrogant young man. But in searching for a way to convert the episodic *Stephen Hero* into *A Portrait of the Artist*, Joyce hit upon a principle of structure which reflected his habits of mind as extremely as he could wish. The work of art, like a mother's love, must be achieved over the greatest obstacles, and Joyce, who had been dissatisfied with his earlier work as too easily done, now found the obstacles in the form of a most complicated pattern.

This is hinted at in his image of the creative process. As far back as his paper on Mangan, Joyce said that the poet takes into the vital center of his life 'the life that surrounds it, flinging it abroad again amid planetary music.' He repeated this image in *Stephen Hero*, then in *A Portrait of the Artist* developed it more fully. Stephen refers to the making of literature as 'the phenomenon of artistic conception, artistic gestation and artistic reproduction,' and then describes the progression from lyrical to epical and to dramatic art:

The simplest epical form is seen emerging out of lyrical literature when the artist prolongs and broods upon himself as the centre of an epical event and this form progresses till the centre of emotional gravity is equidistant from the artist himself and from others. The narrative is no longer purely personal. The personality of the artist passes into the narration itself, flowing round and round the persons and the action like a vital sea. . . . The dramatic form is reached when the vitality which has flowed and eddied round each person fills every person with such vital force that he or she assumes a proper and intangible esthetic life. . . . The mystery of esthetic like that of material creation is accomplished. [*P*, 214-215.]

This creator is not male but female; Joyce goes on to borrow an image of Flaubert by calling him a 'god,' [1] but he is really a goddess. Within this womb creatures come to life. No male intercession is necessary even; as Stephen says, 'In the virgin womb of the imagination the word was made flesh.'

Joyce did not take up such metaphors lightly. His brother records that in the first draft of A *Portrait*, Joyce thought of a man's character as developing 'from an embryo' with constant traits. Joyce acted upon this theory with his characteristic thoroughness, and his subsequent interest in the process of gestation, as conveyed to Stanislaus during Nora's first pregnancy, expressed a concern that was literary as well as anatomical. His decision to rewrite *Stephen Hero* as A *Portrait* in five chapters occurred appropriately just after Lucia's birth. For A *Portrait of the Artist as a Young Man* is in fact the gestation of a soul, and in the metaphor Joyce found his new principle of order. The book begins with Stephen's father and, just before the ending, it depicts the hero's severance from his mother. From the start the soul is surrounded by liquids, urine, slime, seawater, amniotic tides, 'drops of water' (as Joyce says at the end of the first chapter) 'falling softly in the brimming bowl.' The atmosphere of biological struggle is necessarily dark and melancholy until the light of life is glimpsed. In the first chapter the foetal soul is for a few pages only slightly

---

[1] Stephen says the artist is "like the God of the creation," remaining "within or behind or beyond or above his handiwork, invisible, refined out of existence, paring his fingernails." But Lynch sardonically qualifies this statement by saying, "Trying to refine them [the fingernails] also out of existence." Stephen makes no reply. [*P*, 215.] [R.E.]

individualized, the organism responds only to the most primitive sensory impressions, then the heart forms and musters its affections, the being struggles toward some unspecified, uncomprehended culmination, it is flooded in ways it cannot understand or control, it gropes wordlessly toward sexual differentiation. In the third chapter shame floods Stephen's whole body as conscience develops; the lower bestial nature is put by. Then at the end of the fourth chapter the soul discovers the goal towards which it has been mysteriously proceeding—the goal of life. It must swim no more but emerge into air, the new metaphor being flight. The final chapter shows the soul, already fully developed, fattening itself for its journey until at last it is ready to leave. In the last few pages of the book, Stephen's diary, the soul is released from its confinement, its individuality is complete, and the style shifts with savage abruptness.

The sense of the soul's development as like that of an embryo not only helped Joyce to the book's imagery, but also encouraged him to work and rework the original elements in the process of gestation. Stephen's growth proceeds in waves, in accretions of flesh, in particularization of needs and desires, around and around but always ultimately forward. The episodic framework of *Stephen Hero* was renounced in favor of a group of scenes radiating backwards and forwards.[2] In the new first chapter Joyce had three clusters of sensations: his earliest memories of infancy, his sickness at Clongowes (probably indebted like the ending of 'The Dead' to rheumatic fever in Trieste), and his pandying at Father Daly's hands. Under these he subsumed chains of related moments, with the effect of three fleshings in time rather than of a linear succession of

---

[2] It is a technique which William Faulkner was to carry even further in the opening section of *The Sound and the Fury*, where the extreme disconnection finds its justification, not, as in Joyce, in the haze of childhood memory, but in the blur of an idiot's mind. Faulkner, when he wrote his book, had read *Dubliners* and *A Portrait*; he did not read *Ulysses* until a year later, in 1930, but he knew about it from excerpts and from the conversation of friends. He has said that he considered himself the heir of Joyce in his methods in *The Sound and the Fury*. [R.E.]

events. The sequence became primarily one of layers rather than of years.

In this process other human beings are not allowed much existence except as influences upon the soul's development or features of it. The same figures appear and reappear, the schoolboy Heron for example, each time in an altered way to suggest growth in the soul's view of them. E—— C——, a partner in childhood games, becomes the object of Stephen's adolescent love poems; the master at Clongowes reappears as the preacher of the sermons at Belvedere.[3] The same words, 'Apologise,' 'admit,' 'maroon,' 'green,' 'cold,' 'warm,' 'wet,' and the like, keep recurring with new implications. The book moves from rudimentary meanings to more complex ones, as in the conceptions of the call and the fall. Stephen, in the first chapter fascinated by unformed images, is next summoned by the flesh and then by the church, the second chapter ending with a prostitute's lingual kiss, the third with his reception of the Host upon his tongue. The soul that has been enraptured by body in the second chapter and by spirit in the third (both depicted in sensory images) then hears the call of art and life, which encompass both without bowing before either, in the fourth chapter; the process is virtually complete. Similarly the fall into sin, at first a terror, gradually becomes an essential part of the discovery of self and life.

Now Stephen, his character still recomposing the same

---

[3] In both these instances Joyce changed the actual events. His freedom of recomposition is displayed also in the scene in the physics classroom in *A Portrait* [193], where he telescopes two lectures, one on electricity and one on mechanics, which as Professor Felix Hackett remembers, took place months apart. Moynihan's whispered remark, inspired by the lecturer's discussion of ellipsoidal balls, "Chase me, ladies, I'm in the cavalry!", was in fact made by a young man named Kinahan on one of these occasions. In the same way, as J. F. Byrne points out in *Silent Years* [see Notes, p. 525] the long scene with the dean of studies in *A Portrait* [185-190] happened not to Joyce but to him; he told it to Joyce and was later displeased to discover how his innocent description of Father Darlington lighting a fire had been converted into a reflection of Stephen's strained relations with the Church. [R.E.]

elements, leaves the Catholic priesthood behind him to become 'a priest of eternal imagination, transmuting the daily bread of experience into the radiant body of everliving life.' Having listened to sermons on ugliness in the third chapter, he makes his own sermons on beauty in the last. The Virgin is transformed into the girl wading on the strand, symbolizing a more tangible reality. In the last two chapters, to suit his new structure, Joyce minimizes Stephen's physical life to show the dominance of his mind, which has accepted but subordinated physical things. The soul is ready now, it throws off its sense of imprisonment, its melancholy, its no longer tolerable conditions of lower existence, to be born.

Joyce was obviously well-pleased with the paradox into which his method had put him, that he was, as the artist framing his own development in a constructed matrix, his own mother. The complications of this state are implied in Stephen's thought of himself as not his parents' true son, but a foster-son. In *Ulysses* Joyce was to carry the method much further; he makes that book the epic of the whole human body, the womb being the organ only of the *Oxen of the Sun* episode. In that episode, as Joyce said later, Stephen is again the embryo. But, in a parody of the method of *A Portrait*, Stephen emerges not to life but to Burke's pub. The theme of *Ulysses*, Joyce intimates, is reconciliation with the father. Of course, the father whom Joyce depicts in Bloom is in almost every way the opposite of his own father, and is much closer to himself. Insofar as the movement of the book is to bring Stephen, the young Joyce, into *rapport* with Bloom, the mature Joyce, the author becomes, it may be said, his own father. Stephen is aware enough of the potential ironies of this process to ponder all the paradoxes of the father as his own son in the Trinity, and of Shakespeare as both King Hamlet and Prince Hamlet. Yet the book is not without its strong woman; Bloom is appropriately under the influence of his wife, whom he dissatisfies (to some extent intentionally), and wishes to bring Stephen under her influence too.

In both these books Joyce seems to reconstitute his family relationships, to disengage himself from the contradictions of his view of himself as a child and so to exploit them, to overcome his mother's conventionality and his father's rancor, to mother and father himself, to become, by the superhuman effort of the creative process, no one but James Joyce.

HARRY LEVIN

Harry Levin is Irving Babbitt Professor of Comparative Literature at Harvard University and Chairman of the Department. He is author of, among other books, *Symbolism and Fiction*, *Contexts of Criticism*, and *The Question of Hamlet*, and is the editor of *The Portable James Joyce*.

THE ARTIST

The history of the realistic novel shows that fiction tends toward autobiography. The increasing demands for social and psychological detail that are made upon the novelist can only be satisfied out of his own experience. The forces which make him an outsider focus his observation upon himself. He becomes his own hero, and begins to crowd his other characters into the background. The background takes on a new importance for its influence on his own character. The theme of his novel is the formation of character; its habitual pattern is that of apprenticeship or education; and it falls into that category which has been distinguished, by German criticism at least, as the *Bildungsroman*. The novel of development, when it confines itself to the professional sphere of the novelist, becomes a novel of the artist, a *Künstlerroman*. Goethe's *Wilhelm Meister*, Stendhal's *Vie d'Henri Brulard*, and Butler's *Way of All Flesh* amply suggest the potentialities of the form.

The *Künstlerroman* offered a tentative solution to the dilemma of Joyce's generation, by enabling writers to apply the methods of realism to the subject of art. It enabled Marcel Proust to communicate experience more fully and subtly than had been done before, because it was his own experience that he was communicating, and because he was an artist to his

finger-tips. A *la recherche du temps perdu* has been described
as a novel that was written to explain why it was written. But,
having come to be written, it offers other novelists little stimulus
toward self-portraiture. It is singularly fitting that *Ulysses* should
have appeared in the year of Proust's death. The perverse logic
of André Gide can still present, in his *Journal des faux-mon-
nayeurs*, the diary of a novelist who is writing a novel about
a novelist who is keeping a diary about the novel he is writing.
Of course, the *Künstlerroman* has no logical limit; but, like
the label on the box of Quaker Oats, it has a vanishing-point.
Already it is beginning to look as old-fashioned as Murger's
Vie de Bohême.

The *Künstlerroman*, though it reverses the more normal
procedure of applying the methods of art to the subject of
reality, is the only conception of the novel that is specialized
enough to include *A Portrait of the Artist as a Young Man*.
In 1913, the year before Joyce finished his book, D. H. Lawrence
had published his own portrait of the artist, *Sons and Lovers*.
Both books convey the claustral sense of a young intelligence
swaddled in convention and constricted by poverty, and the
intensity of its first responses to esthetic experience and life at
large. The extent to which Lawrence warms to his theme
is the measure of Joyce's reserve. Characteristically, they may
be reacting from the very different institutions behind them—
evangelical English protestantism and Irish Catholic orthodoxy
—when Lawrence dwells on the attractions of life, and Joyce
on its repulsions. The respective mothers of the two artists
play a similar role, yet May Dedalus is a wraith beside the
full-bodied realization of Mrs. Morel. The characters in *Sons
and Lovers* seem to enjoy an independent existence; in the *Portrait of the Artist* they figure mainly in the hero's reveries and
resentments. Joyce's treatment of childhood is unrelieved in
its sadness: endless generations of choirs of children sounded,
for Stephen Dedalus, the same note of pain and weariness
that Newman had heard in Virgil. "All seemed weary of life
even before entering upon it."

The attitude of the novelist toward his subject is one of the critical questions considered by Joyce's subject. Stephen expounds his own esthetic theory, which he designates as "applied Aquinas," during a walk in the rain with his irreverent friend, Lynch. *Solvitur ambulando.* It should be noted that the principal action of the *Portrait of the Artist,* whether in conversation or revery, is walking. The lingering images of *Dubliners* are those of people—often children—in the streets. And it was reserved for Joyce to turn the wanderings of Ulysses into a peripatetic pilgrimage through Dublin. He was, in that respect, a good Aristotelian. But he added a personal touch to the critical theory of Aristotle and Aquinas, when he based the distinction between the various literary forms on the relation of the artist to his material. In the lyric, it is immediate; in the epic, the artist presents his material "in mediate relation to himself and others"; in drama, it is presented in immediate relation to others.

The lyrical form is in fact the simplest verbal vesture of an instant of emotion, a rhythmical cry such as ages ago cheered on the man who pulled at the oar or dragged stones up a slope. He who utters it is more conscious of the instant of emotion than of himself as feeling emotion. The simplest epical form is seen emerging out of lyrical literature when the artist prolongs and broods upon himself as the centre of an epical event and this form progresses till the centre of emotional gravity is equidistant from the artist himself and from others. The narrative is no longer purely personal. The personality of the artist passes into the narration itself, flowing round and round the persons and the action like a vital sea. This progress you will see easily in that old English ballad *Turpin Hero,* which begins in the first person and ends in the third person. The dramatic form is reached when the vitality which has flowed and eddied round each person fills every person with such vital force that he or she assumes a proper and intangible esthetic life. The personality of the artist, at first a cry or a cadence or a mood and then a fluid and lambent narrative, finally refines itself out of existence, impersonalises itself, so to speak, The esthetic image in the dramatic form is life purified in and reprojected from the human imagination. The mystery of esthetic like that of material creation is accomplished. The artist, like the God of the creation, remains within or behind or beyond or above his handiwork, invisible, refined out of existence, indifferent, paring his fingernails. [*P*, 214-215.]

This progress you will see easily in the succession of Joyce's works. The cry becomes a cadence in *Chamber Music*; the mood becomes a *nuance* in *Dubliners*. If *Exiles* is unsuccessful, it is because the epiphany is not manifest to others, the artist has failed to objectify the relations of his characters with each other or with the audience. The narrative of the *Portrait of the Artist* has scarcely emerged from the lyrical stage. Whereas *Dubliners* began in the first person and ended in the third, the *Portrait of the Artist* takes us back from an impersonal opening to the notes of the author at the end. The personality of the artist, prolonging and brooding upon itself, has not yet passed into the narration. The shift from the personal to the epic will come with *Ulysses*, and the center of emotional gravity will be equidistant from the artist himself and from others. And with *Finnegans Wake*, the artist will have retired within or behind, above or beyond his handiwork, refined out of existence.

Except for the thin incognito of its characters, the *Portrait of the Artist* is based on a literal transcript of the first twenty years of Joyce's life. If anything, it is more candid than other autobiographies. It is distinguished from them by its emphasis on the emotional and intellectual adventures of its protagonist. If we can trust the dates at the end of the book, Joyce started to write in Dublin during 1904, and continued to rewrite until 1914 in Trieste. There is reason to believe that he had accumulated almost a thousand pages—and brought Stephen to the point of departure for Paris—when the idea of *Ulysses* struck him, and he decided to reserve those further adventures for the sequel. His provisional title, *Stephen Hero*, with its echo of the ballad of Dick Turpin, marks the book as an early point in his stages of artistic impersonality. As the hero of a pedagogical novel, Stephen is significantly baptized. Saint Stephen Protomartyr was patron of the green on which University College was located, and therefore of the magazine with which Joyce had had his earliest literary misadventures.

Stephen is ever susceptible to the magic of names—particularly of his own last name. Names and words, copybook phrases and schoolboy slang, echoes and jingles, speeches and sermons float through his mind and enrich the restricted realism of the context. His own name is the wedge by which symbolism enters the book. One day he penetrates its secret. Brooding on the prefect of studies, who made him repeat the unfamiliar syllables of "Dedalus," he tells himself that it is a better name than Dolan. He hears it shouted across the surf by some friends in swimming, and the strangeness of the sound is for him a prophecy: "Now, at the name of the fabulous artificer, he seemed to hear the noise of dim waves and to see a winged form flying above the waves and slowly climbing the air. What did it mean? Was it a quaint device opening a page of some medieval book of prophecies and symbols, a hawklike man flying sunward above the sea, a prophecy of the end he had been born to serve and had been following through the mists of childhood and boyhood, a symbol of the artist forging anew in his workshop out of the sluggish matter of the earth a new soaring impalpable imperishable being?" [P, 169.]

The *Portrait of the Artist,* as we have it, is the result of an extended process of revision and refinement. The original version—if an *Ur-Portrait* can be remotely discerned—must have been securely founded upon the bedrock of naturalistic narrative. It must have been a human document, virtually a diary, to which Joyce confided his notions and reactions not very long after they occurred. In turning from a reproductive to a selective method, he has foreshortened his work. A fragmentary manuscript, now in the Harvard College Library, touches only the period covered by the last chapter of the printed book, and yet it is nearly as long as the book itself. What is obliquely implied in the final version is explicitly stated in this early draft. The economic situation, for example, as the Dedalus household declines from the genteel to the shabby, is attested by a series of moving vans. In the book there is just one such episode, when Stephen arrives home to hear from his brothers and sisters that the family is looking for another house. Even then the news is not put in plain English, but in evasive pig-Latin. And the book leaves us with only the vaguest impression of the brothers and sisters; Stephen himself is not sure how many there are.

With revision, the other characters seem to have retreated into the background. Stephen's mother, because of the tension between her love and his disbelief, should be the most poignant figure in the book, just as her memory is the most unforgettable thing in *Ulysses*. But the actual conflict is not dramatized; it is coldly analyzed by Stephen in the course of one of his interminable walks and talks—this time with the serious-minded Cranly. In the manuscript it gives rise to a powerful scene, on the death of Stephen's sister, when his mother's orthodox piety is humbled before the mysteries of the body. The heroine of the book has been refined out of existence; she survives only [as Emma] in veiled allusions and the initials E—— C——. Emma Clery, in the manuscript, is an enthusiastic young lady with whom Stephen attends a Gaelic class. Their prolonged and pallid romance comes to an unexpected climax when he sees her mackintosh flashing across the green, and abruptly leaves his lesson to confront her with the proposal that they spend the night together and say farewell in the morning. Her reaction explains the interview so cryptically reported in the book, when Stephen turns on the "spiritual-heroic refrigerating apparatus, invented and patented in all countries by Dante Alighieri."

The esthetic theory plays a more active part in the earlier version. Instead of being dogmatically expounded to Lynch, it is sounded in the debating society, where it occasions a bitter argument. As Joyce rewrote his book he seems to have transferred the scene of action from the social to the psychological sphere. As he recollected his "conflicts with orthodoxy" in the comparative tranquility of exile, he came to the conclusion that the actual struggles had taken place within the mind of Stephen. Discussions gave way to meditations, and scenes were replaced by *tableaux*. Evasion and indirection were ingrained in Joyce's narrative technique. The final effect is that which Shakespearean actors achieve by cutting out all the scenes in *Hamlet* where the hero does not appear. The continuity of dynastic feuds and international issues is obscured by the morbid atmosphere of introspection. Drama has retired before soliloquy.

The Stephen we finally meet is more sharply differentiated from his environment than the figure Joyce set out to describe. How can he be a poet—the other boys have asked him—and not wear long hair? The richness of his inner experience is continually played off against the grim reality of his external surroundings. He is trying "to build a breakwater of order and elegance against the sordid tide of life without him." He is marked by the aureole of the romantic hero, like Thomas Mann's outsiders, pressing their noses against the window panes of a bourgeois society from which they feel excluded. "To merge his life in the common tide of other lives was harder for him than any fasting or prayer, and it was his constant failure to do this to his own satisfaction which caused in his soul at last a sensation of spiritual dryness together with a growth of doubts and scruples." At school he takes an equivocal position, "a free boy, a leader afraid of his own authority, proud and sensitive and suspicious, battling against the squalor of his life and against the riot of his mind." At home he feels "his own futile isolation." He feels that he is scarcely of the same blood as his mother and brother and sister, but stands to them "rather in the mystical kinship of fosterage, fosterchild and fosterbrother."

Joyce's prose is the register of this intellectual and emotional cleavage. It preserves the contrast between his rather lush verse and his rather dry criticism, between the pathetic children and the ironic politicians of *Dubliners*. All his sensibility is reserved for himself; his attitude toward others is consistently caustic. The claims to objectivity of a subjective novel, however, must be based on its rendering of intimate experience. If Joyce's treatment of Stephen is true to himself, we have no right to interpose any other criteria. Mr. Eliot has made the plausible suggestion that Joyce's two masters in prose were Newman and Pater. Their alternating influence would account for the oscillations of style in the *Portrait of the Artist*. The sustaining tone, which it adopts toward the outside world, is that of precise and mordant description. Interpolated, at strategic points in Stephen's development, are a number of purple passages that have faded considerably.

Joyce's own contribution to English prose is to provide a more fluid medium for refracting sensations and impressions through the author's mind—to facilitate the transition from photographic realism to esthetic impressionism. In the introductory pages of the *Portrait of the Artist*, the reader is faced with nothing less than the primary impact of life itself, a presentational continuum of the tastes and smells and sights and sounds of earliest infancy. Emotion is integrated, from first to last, by words. Feelings, as they filter through Stephen's sensory apparatus, become associated with phrases. His conditioned reflexes are literary. In one of the later dialogues of the book, he is comparing his theory to a trimmed lamp. The dean of studies, taking up the metaphor, mentions the lamp of Epictetus, and Stephen's reply is a further allusion to the stoic doctrine that the soul is like a bucketful of water. In his mind this far-fetched chain of literary associations becomes attached to the sense impressions of the moment: "A smell of molten tallow came up from the dean's candle butts and fused itself in Stephen's consciousness with the jingle of the words, bucket and lamp and lamp and bucket."

This is the state of mind that confers upon language a magical potency. It exalts the habit of verbal association into a principle for the arrangement of experience. You gain power over a thing by naming it; you become master of a situation by putting it into words. It is psychological need, and not hyperfastidious taste, that goads the writer on to search for the *mot juste*, to loot the thesaurus. Stephen, in the more explicit manuscript, finds a treasure-house in Skeat's *Etymological Dictionary*. The crucial moment of the book, which leads to the revelation of his name and calling, is a moment he tries to make his own by drawing forth a phrase of his treasure:

—A day of dappled seaborne clouds.

The phrase and the day and the scene harmonised in a chord. Words. Was it their colours? He allowed them to glow and fade, hue after hue: sunrise gold, the russet and green of apple orchards, azure of waves, the greyfringed fleece of clouds. No, it was not their colours: it was the poise and balance of the period itself. Did he then love the rhythmic rise and fall of words better than their associations of legend and colour? Or was it that, being as weak of sight as he was shy of mind, he drew less pleasure from the reflection of the glowing sensible world through the prism of a language manycoloured and richly storied than from the contemplation of an inner world of individual emotions mirrored perfectly in a lucid supple periodic prose? [*P*, 166-167.]

The strength and weakness of his style, by Joyce's own diagnosis, are those of his mind and body. A few pages later he offers a cogent illustration, when Stephen dips self-consciously into his word-hoard for suitable epithets to describe a girl who is wading along the beach. We are given a paragraph of word-painting which is not easy to visualize. "Her bosom was as a bird's, soft and slight, slight and soft as the breast of some dark-plumaged dove," it concludes. "But her long fair hair was girlish: and girlish, and touched with the wonder of mortal beauty, her face." This is incantation, and not description. Joyce is thinking in rhythms rather than metaphors. Specification of the bird appeals to the sense of touch rather than to the sense of sight. What is said about the hair and face is intended to produce an effect without presenting a picture. The most striking effects in Joyce's imagery are those of coldness, whiteness, and dampness, like the bodies of the bathers who shout Stephen's name.

The most vital element in Joyce's writing, in the *Portrait of the Artist* as in *Dubliners*, is his use of conversation. As a reporter of Irish life, for all his reservations, Joyce is a faithful and appreciative listener. It is a tribute to Stephen's ear that, in spite of the antagonism between father and son, Simon

Dedalus is such a ripe and congenial character. Like Sean O'Casey's *Paycock*, with all his amiable failings, he is Ireland itself. Though he takes pride in showing Cork to Stephen, and in showing off his son to his own native city, he is really the embodiment of Dublin: "A medical student, an oarsman, a tenor, an amateur actor, a shouting politician, a small landlord, a small investor, a drinker, a good fellow, a storyteller, somebody's secretary, something in a distillery, a taxgatherer, a bankrupt and at present a praiser of his own past." The improvident worldliness of John Stanislaus Joyce had made him, in the unforgiving eyes of his son, a foster-parent. So young Charles Dickens, hastening from the blacking-factory to the Marshalsea, came to look upon his father as a horrible example of goodfellowship, a Mr. Micawber.

This disorder, "the misrule and confusion of his father's house," comes to stand in Stephen's mind for the plight of Ireland. Like Synge's *Playboy*, he must go through the motions of parricide to make good his revolt. Religion and politics, to his adult perception, are among the intimations of early childhood: harsh words and bitter arguments that spoil the taste of the Christmas turkey. Again, as in "Ivy Day in the Committee Room," or in Lennox Robinson's *Lost Leader* on the stage, it is the ghost of Parnell that turns conversation into drama. "Dante," the devout Mrs. Riordan, is true to the Catholic Church in denouncing the disgraced nationalist leader. Mr. Casey, the guest of honor, is of the anti-clerical faction. Mr. Dedalus is by no means a neutral, and some of his mellowest profanity is enlisted in the cause of his dead hero. Mrs. Dedalus softly rebukes him:

—Really, Simon, said Mrs Dedalus, you should not speak that way before Stephen. It's not right.

—O, he'll remember all this when he grows up, said Dante hotly— the language he heard against God and religion and priests in his own home.

—Let him remember too, cried Mr Casey to her from across the table, the language with which the priests and the priests' pawns broke Parnell's heart and hounded him into his grave. Let him remember that too when he grows up. [*P*, 33-34.]

The *Portrait of the Artist*, as Joyce's remembrance finally shaped it, is a volume of three hundred pages, symmetrically constructed around three undramatic climaxes, intimate crises of Stephen's youth. The first hundred pages, in two chapters, trace the awakening of religious doubts and sexual instincts, leading up to Stephen's carnal sin at the age of sixteen. The central portion, in two more chapters, continues the cycle of sin and repentance to the moment of Stephen's private apocalypse. The external setting for the education of the artist is, in the first chapter, Clongowes Wood College; in the second, third, and fourth, Belvedere College, Dublin. The fifth and final chapter, which is twice as long as the others, develops the theories and projects of Stephen's student days in University College, and brings him to the verge of exile. As the book advances, it becomes less sensitive to outside impressions, and more intent upon speculations of its own. Friends figure mainly as interlocutors to draw Stephen out upon various themes. Each epiphany—awakening of the body, literary vocation, farewell to Ireland—leaves him lonelier than the last.

A trivial episode at Clongowes Wood seems fraught for Joyce with a profoundly personal meaning. Young Stephen has been unable to get his lessons, because his glasses were broken on the playing-field. Father Dolan, the prefect of studies, is unwilling to accept this excuse, and disciplines Stephen with the boys who have shirked their books. Smarting with pain and a sense of palpable injustice, Stephen finally carries his case to the rector, who shows a humane understanding of the situation. Many years later Father Conmee, the rector, takes a walk through a chapter of *Ulysses*; and Father Dolan—who was actually a Father Daly—pops up with his "pandybat" in Stephen's nightmare. This schoolboy incident lays down a pattern for Joyce's later behavior. When he cabled Lloyd George, who had other things on his mind during the First World War, *re* a pair of trousers and *The Importance of Being Earnest*, he was behaving like an aggrieved schoolboy unjustly pandied.

The physical handicap, the public humiliation, the brooding sensibility, the sense of grievance, the contempt for convention, the desire for self-justification, and the appeal to higher authority—these are all elements of Joyce's attitude toward society and toward himself. He had begun his education by questioning the Jesuit discipline; he would finish by repudiating the Catholic faith. Having responded to the urgent prompting of his senses, he would be treated as a sinner; he would refer the ensuing conflict, over the head of religious authority, to the new light of his scientific and naturalistic studies; he would seek, in the end, to create his own authority by the light of his senses. In turning away from Ireland toward the world at large, he would appeal from the parochial Daly to the enlightened Conmee. That miserable day at Clongowes Wood, like that long evening at Combray when M. Swann's visit kept Marcel's mother downstairs, had unforeseen consequences.

Adolescence complicates the second chapter. Stephen is beginning to appreciate beauty, but as something illicit and mysterious, something apart from the common walks of life. Literature has begun to color his experience, and to stimulate his mind and his senses. His untimely enthusiasm for Lord Byron —"a heretic and immoral too"—provokes a beating at the hands of his classmates. Now in jest and again in earnest, he is forced to repeat the *confiteor*. One of his essays had been rewarded with the taunt of heresy from his English master, and he takes rueful consolation in the self-conscious part of the Byronic hero. He will not agree that Lord Tennyson is a poet, though he gives tacit consent to the assertion that Newman has the best prose style. But it is his other master, Pater, whose influence is felt at the climax of the chapter. Stephen's sexual initiation is presented in empurpled prose, as an esthetic ritual for which his literary heresies have been preparing him. In trying to find a cadence for his cry, he harks back to the lyricism of *Chamber Music* and the anguish of the small boy in *Dubliners:*

He stretched out his arms in the street to hold fast the frail swoon-ing form that eluded him and incited him: and the cry that he had strangled for so long in his throat issued from his lips. It broke from him like a wail of despair from a hell of sufferers and died in a wail of furious entreaty, a cry for an iniquitous abandonment, a cry which was but the echo of an obscene scrawl which he had read on the oozing wall of a urinal. [*P*, 100.]

The unromantic reader is prone to feel that a scrawl would have been more adequate to the occasion. The incidence of the word "swoon" is a humorless symptom of the Pateresque influence on Joyce's early writing. There is many "a swoon of shame" in *Chamber Music*, and "a slowly swooning soul" in the last paragraph of *Dubliners*. "His soul was swooning" at the end of the fourth chapter of the *Portrait of the Artist*, having been darkened by "the swoon of sin" at the end of the second chapter. Though the scene is clouded with decadent incense, it is clear that Stephen is still a child, and that the woman plays the part of a mother. Joyce's heroes are sons and lovers at the same time; his heroines are always maternal. It is like him to lavish his romantic sensibility on an encounter with a prostitute and to reserve his acrid satire for the domain of the church. In Stephen's mind a symbolic association between art and sex is established, and that precocious revelation helps him to decide his later conflict between art and religion.

Meanwhile, the third chapter is devoted to his remorse. It embodies at formidable length a sermon on hell, suffered by Stephen and his classmates during a retreat. The eloquent Jesuit preacher takes as his object-lesson the sin of Lucifer, pride of the intellect, his great refusal and his terrible fall. Stephen's repentant imagination is harrowed by the torments of the damned. This powerful discourse provides an ethical core for the book, as Father Mapple's sermon on Jonah does for *Moby-Dick*, or Ivan's legend of the Grand Inquisitor for *The Brothers Karamazov*. Joyce is orthodox enough to go on believing in hell, and—as Professor Curtius recognized—to set up his own *Inferno* in *Ulysses*. Like another tormented apostate, Christopher Marlowe, he lives in a world where there is still suffering, but no longer the prospect of salvation. Like Blake's Milton, he is a true poet, and of the devil's party. Stephen's ultimate text is the defiance of the fallen archangel: *"Non serviam!"*

Temporarily, there is confession and absolution. When Stephen sees the eggs and sausages laid out for the communion breakfast, life seems simple and beautiful after all. For a time his restlessness seems to be tranquilized by church and satisfied by school. Seeking to order his existence, he contemplates the possibilities of the Jesuit order itself: the Reverend Stephen Dedalus, S.J. After a conference with a member of that order, he is fascinated and terrified by the awful assumption of powers which ordination involves. In the fourth chapter the call comes unexpectedly—the call to another kind of priesthood. Stephen dedicates himself to art, and enters upon his peculiar novitiate. The church would have meant order,. but it would also have meant a denial of the life of the senses. A walk along the strand brings him his real vocation—an outburst of profane joy at the bird-like beauty of a girl, a realization of the fabulous artificer whose name he bears, a consciousness of the power of words to confer an order and life of their own. Like the birds that circle between the sea and the sky, his soul soars in "an ecstasy of flight," in a metaphor of sexual fulfilment and artistic creation. "To live, to err, to fall, to triumph, to recreate life out of life!"

The fifth chapter is the discursive chronicle of Stephen's rebellion. He moves among his fellow-students, an aloof and pharisaic figure, unwilling to share their indignation at the first performance of the *Countess Cathleen*, or their confidence in a petition to ensure world peace. His own struggle comes when his mother requests him to make his Easter duty and his diabolic pride of intellect asserts itself. Cranly, with the sharpest instruments of casuistry, tries to probe his stubborn refusal. It is less a question of faith than of observance. Stephen will not, to please his mother, do false homage to the symbols of authority, yet he is not quite unbeliever enough to take part in a sacrilegious communion. If he cannot accept the eucharist, he must be anathema; he respects the forms by refusing to observe them.

"I will not serve that in which I no longer believe, whether it call itself my home, my fatherland or my church: and I will try to express myself in some mode of life or art as freely as I can and as wholly as I can, using for my defence the only arms I allow myself to use, silence, exile and cunning."

With this peremptory gesture, emancipating himself from his petty-bourgeois family, and from Ireland and Catholicism at the same time, Stephen stands ready to take his solitary way wherever the creative life engages him. In a previous argument with other friends, he abandoned the possibility of fighting these issues out at home. "Ireland is the old sow that eats her farrow." Davin, the nationalist, is willing to admit that Stephen's position is thoroughly Irish, all too typical of their gifted countrymen. "In your heart you are an Irishman but your pride is too powerful." Stephen is unwilling to compromise: "When the soul of a man is born in this country there are nets flung at it to hold it back from flight. You talk to me of nationality, language, religion. I shall try to fly by those nets." In exile, silence, and cunning he trusts to find substitutes for those three forms of subjection.

On his way to and from Belvedere College, his soul was "disquieted and cast down by the dull phenomenon of Dublin." With his realization of the end he was soon to serve, a new vista of "the slowflowing Liffey" became visible "across the timeless air." Nomadic clouds, dappled and seaborne, voyaging westward from Europe, suggested strange tongues and marshalled races. "He heard a confused music within him as of memories and names . . ." At University College, the time-worn texts of Ovid and Horace have filled him with awe for the past and contempt of the present: ". . . it wounded him to think that he would never be but a shy guest at the feast of the world's culture and that the monkish learning, in terms of which he was striving to forge out an esthetic philosophy, was held no higher by the age he lived in than the subtle and curious jargons of heraldry and falconry."

English is as strange a tongue as Latin. "His language, so familiar and so foreign, will always be for me an acquired speech," Stephen reflects, while conversing with the dean of studies, an English convert to Catholicism. "I have not made or accepted its words. My voice holds them at bay. My soul frets in the shadow of his language." The last pages are fragments from Stephen's notebook, duly recording his final interviews with teachers and friends, with his family and "her." Spring finds him setting down "vague words for a vague emotion," his farewell to Dublin, and to sounds of the city which will never stop echoing in his ears:

10 *April:* Faintly, under the heavy night, through the silence of the city which has turned from dreams to dreamless sleep as a weary lover whom no caresses move, the sound of hoofs upon the road. [*P*, 251.]

Toward the end, his purpose stiffens into a flourish of blank verse:

26 *April:* Mother is putting my new secondhand clothes in order. She prays now, she says, that I may learn in my own life and away from home and friends what the heart is and what it feels. Amen. So be it. Welcome, O life! I go to encounter for the millionth time the reality of experience and to forge in the smithy of my soul the uncreated conscience of my race. [*P*, 252-253.]

On the eve of departure he makes his final entry:

27 *April:* Old father, old artificer, stand me now and ever in good stead. [*P*, 253.]

The mythical and priestly figure of Dædalus is known for more than one work of genius—for a pair of wings, as well as a labyrinth. Stephen invokes his namesake under both aspects, the hawklike man and the fabulous artificer. Sometimes it is the cunning of the craftsman, the smithy of the artist, that is symbolized. At other times, soaring, falling, flying by the nets of Ireland, it is life itself. Yet these images of aspiration can also be associated with Icarus, the son of Dædalus. That ill-fated and rebellious spirit, who borrowed his father's wings and flew too near the sun, is an equally prophetic symbol: in a classical drama, *Icaro*, the young anti-fascist poet, Lauro de

Bosis, adumbrated the heroism of his own death. The epigraph of Joyce's book is a quotation from Ovid—or rather a misquotation (the correct reference is to the *Metamorphoses*, VIII, 188). Here we are told that Dædalus abandoned his mind to obscure arts, "*et ignotas animum dimittit in artes*." But Joyce does not tell us Ovid's reason:

> . . . *longumque perosus*
> *exsilium, tractusque soli natalis amore* . . .

The artificer was weary of his long exile and lured by the love of his natal soil, the Roman poet and exile goes on to say, and the rest of his myth rehearses the filial tragedy. The father cries out for the son; Joyce's confused recollection, in *Ulysses*, makes the son cry out for the father: "*Pater, ait*." On the brink of expatriation, poised for his trial flight, Stephen, in the *Portrait of the Artist*, is more nearly akin to the son. His natural father, Simon Dedalus, is left standing in the mystical kinship of fosterage. The Jesuit fathers, who supervised his education, no longer call him son. He has appealed from Father Dolan to Father Conmee; now he appeals from the church to another paternity. His wings take him from the fatherland. The labyrinth leads toward a father.

HUGH KENNER

Hugh Kenner is Professor of English at the University of California, Santa Barbara, and is the author of *The Poetry of Ezra Pound*, *Wyndham Lewis*, and *Flaubert, Joyce, and Beckett: The Stoic Comedians*.

The PORTRAIT *in Perspective*

. . . . . .

LINKING THEMES

In the reconceived *Portrait* Joyce abandoned the original intention of writing the account of his own escape from Dublin. One cannot escape one's Dublin. He recast Stephen Dedalus as a figure who could not even detach himself from Dublin because he had formed himself on a denial of Dublin's values. He is the egocentric rebel become an ultimate. There is no question whatever of his regeneration. "Stephen no longer interests me to the same extent [as Bloom]," said Joyce to Frank Budgen one day. "He has a shape that can't be changed." His shape is that of aesthete. The Stephen of the first chapter of *Ulysses* who "walks wearily," constantly "leans" on everything in sight, invariably sits down before he has gone three paces, speaks "gloomily," "quietly," "with bitterness," and "coldly," and "suffers" his handkerchief to be pulled from his pocket by the exuberant Mulligan, is precisely the priggish, humourless Stephen of the last chapter of the *Portrait* who cannot remember what day of the week it is, sentimentalizes like Charles Lamb over the "human pages" of a second-hand Latin book, conducts the inhumanly pedantic dialogue with Cranly on mother-love, writes Frenchified verses in bed in an erotic swoon, and is epiphanized at full length, like Shem the Penman be-

From *Dublin's Joyce* by Hugh Kenner. Reprinted by permission of Indiana University Press and Chatto and Windus Ltd.

neath the bedclothes, shrinking from the "common noises" of daylight:

Shrinking from that life he turned towards the wall, making a cowl of the blanket and staring at the great overblown scarlet flowers of the tattered wallpaper. He tried to warm his perishing joy in their scarlet glow, imaging a roseway from where he lay upwards to heaven all strewn with scarlet flowers. Weary! Weary! He too was weary of ardent ways. [P, 221-222.]

This new primrose path is a private Jacob's ladder let down to his bed now that he is too weary to do anything but go to heaven.

To make epic and drama emerge naturally from the intrinsic stresses and distortions of the lyric material meant completely new lyric techniques for a constation exact beyond irony. The *Portrait* concentrates on stating themes, arranging apparently transparent words into configurations of the utmost symbolic density. Here is the director proposing that Stephen enter the priesthood:

The director stood in the embrasure of the window, his back to the light, leaning an elbow on the brown crossblind, and, as he spoke and smiled, slowly dangling and looping the cord of the other blind. Stephen stood before him, following for a moment with his eyes the waning of the long summer daylight above the roofs or the slow deft movements of the priestly fingers. The priest's face was in total shadow but the waning daylight from behind him touched the deeply grooved temples and the curves of the skull. [P, 153-154.]

The looped cord, the shadow, the skull, none of these is accidental. The "waning daylight," twice emphasized, conveys that denial of nature which the priest's office represented for Stephen; "his back to the light" co-operates toward a similar effect. So "crossblind": "blind to the cross"; "blinded by the cross." "The curves of the skull" introduces another death-image; the "deathbone" from Lévy-Bruhl's Australia, pointed by Shaun in *Finnegans Wake*, is the dramatic version of an identical symbol. But the central image, the epiphany of the interview, is contained in the movement of the priest's fingers: "slowly dangling and looping the cord of the other blind." That is to say, coolly proffering a noose. This is the lyric mode of *Ulysses'* epical hangman, "The lord of things as they are whom the most Roman of Catholics call *dio boia*, hangman god."

THE CONTRAPUNTAL OPENING

According to the practice inaugurated by Joyce when he rewrote "The Sisters" in 1906, the *Portrait*, like the two books to follow, opens amid elaborate counterpoint. The first two pages, terminating in a row of asterisks, enact the entire action in microcosm. An Aristotelian catalogue of senses, faculties, and mental activities is played against the unfolding of the infant conscience.

Once upon a time and a very good time it was there was a moo-cow coming down along the road and this moocow that was coming down along the road met a nicens little boy named baby tuckoo. . . .

His father told him that story: his father looked at him through a glass: he had a hairy face.

He was baby tuckoo. The moocow came down along the road where Betty Byrne lived: she sold lemon platt.

> O, *the wild rose blossoms*
> On *the little green place.*

He sang that song. That was his song.

> O, *the green wothe botheth.*

When you wet the bed first it is warm then it gets cold. His mother put on the oilsheet. That had the queer smell. [*P*, 7.]

This evocation of holes in oblivion is conducted in the mode of each of the five senses in turn; hearing (the story of the moocow), sight (his father's face), taste (lemon platt), touch (warm and cold), smell (the oil-sheet). The audible soothes: the visible disturbs. Throughout Joyce's work, the senses are symbolically disposed. Smell is the means of discriminating empirical realities ("His mother had a nicer smell than his father," is the next sentence), sight corresponds to the phantasms of oppression, hearing to the imaginative life. Touch and taste together are the modes of sex. Hearing, here, comes first, via a piece of imaginative literature. But as we can see from the vantage-point of *Finnegans Wake*, the whole book is about the encounter of baby tuckoo with the moocow: the Gripes with the mookse. The father with the hairy face is the first Mookse-avatar, the Freudian infantile analogue of God the Father.

In the *Wake*

. . . Derzherr, live wire, fired Benjermine Funkling outa th'Empyre, sin right hand son.

Der Erzherr (arch-lord), here a Teutonic Junker, is the God who visited his wrath on Lucifer; the hairy attribute comes through via the music-hall refrain, "There's hair, like wire, coming out of the Empire."

Dawning consciousness of his own identity ("He was baby tuckoo") leads to artistic performance ("He sang that song. That was his song."). This is hugely expanded in Chapter IV:

Now, as never before, his strange name seemed to him a prophecy . . . of the end he had been born to serve and had been following through the mists of childhood and boyhood, a symbol of the artist forging anew in his workshop out of the sluggish matter of the earth a new soaring impalpable imperishable being. [P, 168-169.]

By changing the red rose to a green and dislocating the spelling, he makes the song his own. ("But you could not have a green rose. But perhaps somewhere in the world you could.")

His mother had a nicer smell than his father. She played on the piano the sailor's hornpipe for him to dance. He danced:

> *Tralala lala,*
> *Tralala tralaladdy,*
> *Tralala lala*
> *Tralala lala.* [P, 7.]

Between this innocence and its Rimbaudian recapture through the purgation of the *Wake* there is to intervene the hallucination in Circe's sty:

THE MOTHER

(*With the subtle smile of death's madness.*) I was once the beautiful May Goulding. I am dead. . . .

STEPHEN

(*Eagerly.*) Tell me the word, mother, if you know it now. The word known to all men. . . .

THE MOTHER

(*With smouldering eyes.*) Repent! O, the fire of hell! [*U*, 580-581. Reprinted in this volume, p. 306.]

This is foreshadowed as the overture to the *Portrait* closes:

He hid under the table. His mother said:
—O, Stephen will apologise.
Dante said:
—O, if not, the eagles will come and pull out his eyes.

> Pull out his eyes,
> Apologise,
> Apologise,
> Pull out his eyes.
>
> Apologise,
> Pull out his eyes,
> Pull out his eyes,
> Apologise. [*P*, 8]

The eagles, eagles of Rome, are emissaries of the God with the hairy face: the punisher. They evoke Prometheus and gnawing guilt: again-bite. So the overture ends with Stephen hiding under the table awaiting the eagles. He is hiding under something most of the time: bedclothes, "the enigma of a manner," an indurated rhetoric, or some other carapace of his private world.

THEME WORDS

It is through their names that things have power over Stephen.

—The language in which we are speaking is his before it is mine. How different are the words *home, Christ, ale, master,* on his lips and on mine! I cannot speak or write these words without unrest of spirit. His language, so familiar and so foreign, will always be for me an acquired speech. I have not made or accepted its words. My voice holds them at bay. My soul frets in the shadow of his language. [*P,* 189.]

Not only is the Dean's English a conqueror's tongue; since the loss of Adam's words which perfectly mirrored things, all language has conquered the mind and imposed its own order, askew from the order of creation. Words, like the physical world, are imposed on Stephen from without, and it is in their canted mirrors that he glimpses a physical and moral world already dyed the colour of his own mind since absorbed, with language, into his personality.

Words which he did not understand he said over and over to himself till he had learnt them by heart; and through them he had glimpses of the real world about him. [*P,* 62.]

Language is a Trojan horse by which the universe gets into the mind. The first sentence in the book isn't something Stephen sees but a story he is told, and the overture climaxes in an insistent brainless rhyme, its jingle corrosively fascinating to the will. It has power to terrify a child who knows nothing of eagles, or of Prometheus, or of how his own grown-up failure to apologise will blend with gathering blindness.

It typifies the peculiar achievement of the *Portrait* that Joyce can cause patterns of words to make up the very moral texture of Stephen's mind:

Suck was a queer word. The fellow called Simon Moonan that name because Simon Moonan used to tie the prefect's false sleeves behind his back and the prefect used to let on to be angry. But the sound was ugly. Once he had washed his hands in the lavatory of the Wicklow hotel and his father pulled the stopper up by the chain after and the dirty water went down through the hole in the basin. And when it had all gone down slowly the hole in the basin had made a sound like that: suck. Only louder.

To remember that and the white look of the lavatory made him feel cold and then hot. There were two cocks that you turned and the water came out: cold and hot. He felt cold and then a little hot: and he could see the names printed on the cocks. That was a very queer thing. [_P_, 11.]

"Suck" joins two contexts in Stephen's mind: a playful sinner toying with his indulgent superior, and the disappearance of dirty water. The force of the conjunction is felt only after Stephen has lost his sense of the reality of the forgiveness of sins in the confessional. The habitually orthodox penitent tangles with a God who pretends to be angry; after a reconciliation the process is repeated. And the mark of that kind of play is disgraceful servility. Each time the sin disappears, the sinner is mocked by an impersonal voice out of nature: "Suck!"

This attitude to unreal good and evil furnishes a context for the next conjunction: whiteness and coldness. Stephen finds himself, like Simon Moonan,[1] engaged in the rhythm of obedience to irrational authority, bending his mind to a meaningless act, the arithmetic contest. He is being obediently "good." And the appropriate colour is adduced: "He thought his face must be white because it felt so cool."

The pallor of lunar obedient goodness is next associated with damp repulsiveness: the limpness of a wet blanket and of a servant's apron:

He sat looking at the two prints of butter on his plate but could not eat the damp bread. The tablecloth was damp and limp. But he drank off the hot weak tea which the clumsy scullion, girt with a

---

[1] Joyce's names should always be scrutinized. Simon Moonan: moon: the heatless (white) satellite reflecting virtue borrowed from Simon Peter. Simony, too, is an activity naturally derived from this casually businesslike attitude to priestly authority. [H.K.]

white apron, poured into his cup. He wondered whether the scullion's apron was damp too or whether all white things were cold and damp. [*P.* 12-13.]

Throughout the first chapter an intrinsic linkage, white-cold-damp-obedient, insinuates itself repeatedly. Stephen after saying his prayers, "his shoulders shaking," "so that he might not go to hell when he died," "curled himself together under the cold white sheets, shaking and trembling. But he would not go to hell when he died, and the shaking would stop." The sea, mysterious as the terrible power of God, "was cold day and night, but it was colder at night"; we are reminded of Anna Livia's gesture of submission: "My cold father, my cold mad father, my cold mad feary father" [in *FW*]. "There was a cold night smell in the chapel. But it was a holy smell." Stephen is puzzled by the phrase in the Litany of the Blessed Virgin: Tower of Ivory. "How could a woman be a tower of ivory or a house of gold?" He ponders until the revelation comes:

Eileen had long white hands. One evening when playing tig she had put her hands over his eyes: long and white and thin and cold and soft. That was ivory: a cold white thing. That was the meaning of *Tower of Ivory.* [*P,* 36.]

This instant of insight depends on a sudden reshuffling of associations, a sudden conviction that the Mother of God, and the symbols appropriate to her, belong with the cold, the white, and the unpleasant in a blindfold morality of obedience. Contemplation focussed on language is repaid:

Tower of Ivory. House of Gold. By thinking of things you could understand them. [*P,* 43.]

The white-damp-obedient association reappears when Stephen is about to make his confession after the celebrated retreat; its patterns provide the language in which he thinks. Sin has been associated with fire, while the prayers of the penitents are epiphanized as "soft whispering cloudlets, soft whispering vapour, whispering and vanishing." And having been absolved:

White pudding and eggs and sausages and cups of tea. How simple and beautiful was life after all! And life lay all before him. . . .

The boys were all there, kneeling in their places. He knelt among them, happy and shy. The altar was heaped with fragrant masses of white flowers: and in the morning light the pale flames of the candles among the white flowers were clear and silent as his own soul. [P, 146.]

We cannot read *Finnegans Wake* until we have realized the significance of the way the mind of Stephen Dedalus is bound in by language. He is not only an artist: he is a Dubliner.

THE PORTRAIT AS LYRIC

The "instant of emotion," of which this 300-page lyric is the "simplest verbal vesture" is the exalted instant, emerging at the end of the book, of freedom, of vocation, of Stephen's destiny, winging his way above the waters at the side of the hawklike man: the instant of promise on which the crushing ironies of *Ulysses* are to fall. The epic of the sea of matter is preceded by the lyric image of a growing dream: a dream that like Richard Rowan's in *Exiles* disregards the fall of man; a dream nourished by a sensitive youth of flying above the sea into an uncreated heaven:

The spell of arms and voices: the white arms of roads, their promise of close embraces and the black arms of tall ships that stand against the moon, their tale of distant nations. They are held out to say: We are alone. Come. And the voices say with them: We are your kinsmen. And the air is thick with their company as they call to me, their kinsman, making ready to go, shaking the wings of their exultant and terrible youth. [P, 252.]

The emotional quality of this is continuous with that of the *Count of Monte Cristo*, that fantasy of the exile returned for vengeance (the plot of the *Odyssey*) which kindled so many of Stephen's boyhood dreams:

The figure of that dark avenger stood forth in his mind for whatever he had heard or divined in childhood of the strange and terrible. At night he built up on the parlour table an image of the wonder-

ful island cave out of transfers and paper flowers and coloured tissue paper and strips of the silver and golden paper in which chocolate is wrapped. When he had broken up this scenery, weary of its
tinsel, there would come to his mind the bright picture of Marseilles, of sunny trellisses and of Mercedes. [P, 62.]

The prose surrounding Stephen's flight is empurpled with
transfers and paper flowers too. It is not immature prose, as
we might suppose by comparison with *Ulysses*. The prose of
"The Dead" is mature prose, and "The Dead" was written
in 1908. Rather, it is a meticulous pastiche of immaturity. Joyce
has his eye constantly on the epic sequel.

He wanted to meet in the real world the unsubstantial image which
his soul so constantly beheld. He did not know where to seek it or
how: but a premonition which led him on told him that this image
would, without any overt act of his, encounter him. They would
meet quietly as if they had known each other and had made their
tryst, perhaps at one of the gates or in some more secret place. They
would be alone, surrounded by darkness and silence: and in that
moment of supreme tenderness he would be transfigured. [P, 65.]

As the vaginal imagery of gates, secret places, and darkness implies, this is the dream that reaches temporary fulfilment in the
plunge into profane love, *P*, 100-101. But the ultimate "secret
place" is to be Mabbot Street, outside Bella Cohen's brothel;
the unsubstantial image of his quest, that of Leopold Bloom,
advertisement canvasser—Monte Cristo, returned avenger, Ulysses; and the transfiguration, into the phantasmal dead son of a
sentimental Jew:

*Against the dark wall a figure appears slowly, a fairy boy of
eleven, a changeling, kidnapped, dressed in an Eton suit with glass
shoes and a little bronze helmet, holding a book in his hand. He
reads from right to left inaudibly, smiling, kissing the page.* [U,
609.]

That Dedalus the artificer did violence to nature is the point
of the epigraph from Ovid, *Et ignotas animum dimittit in artes*;
the Icarian fall is inevitable.

> In tedious exile now too long detain'd
> Dedalus languish'd for his native land.
> The sea foreclos'd his flight; yet thus he said,
> Though earth and water in subjection laid,
> O cruel Minos, thy dominion be,
> We'll go through air; for sure the air is free.
> *Then to new arts his cunning thought applies,*
> *And to improve the work of nature tries.*

Stephen does not, as the careless reader may suppose, become an artist by rejecting church and country. Stephen does not become an artist at all. Country, church, and mission are an inextricable unity, and in rejecting the two that seem to hamper him, he rejects also the one on which he has set his heart. Improving the work of nature is his obvious ambition ("But you could not have a green rose. But perhaps somewhere in the world you could"), and it logically follows from the aesthetic he expounds to Lynch. It is a neo-platonic aesthetic; the crucial principle of epiphanization has been withdrawn. He imagines that "the loveliness that has not yet come into the world," is to be found in his own soul. The earth is gross, and what it brings forth is cowdung; sound and shape and colour are "the prison gates of our soul"; and beauty is something mysteriously gestated within. The genuine artist reads signatures, the fake artist forges them, a process adumbrated in the obsession of Shem the Penman (from *Jim the Penman*, a forgotten drama about a forger) with "Macfearsome's Ossean," the most famous of literary forgeries, studying "how cutely to copy all their various styles of signature so as one day to utter an epical forged cheque on the public for his own private profit."

One can sense all this in the first four chapters of the *Portrait*, and *Ulysses* is unequivocal:

Fabulous artificer, the hawklike man. You flew. Whereto? Newhaven-Dieppe, steerage passenger. Paris and back. [*U*, 210.]

The Stephen of the end of the fourth chapter, however, is still unstable; he had to be brought into a final balance, and shown at some length as a being whose development was virtually ended. Unfortunately, the last chapter makes the book a peculiarly difficult one for the reader to focus, because Joyce had to close it on a suspended chord. As a lyric, it is finished in its own terms; but the themes of the last forty pages, though they give the illusion of focussing, don't really focus until we have read well into *Ulysses*. The final chapter, which in respect to the juggernaut of *Ulysses* must be a vulnerable flank, in respect to what has gone before must be a conclusion. This problem Joyce didn't wholly solve; there remains a moral ambiguity (how seriously are we to take Stephen?) which makes the last forty pages painful reading.

Not that Stephen would stand indefinitely if *Ulysses* didn't topple him over; his equilibrium in Chapter V, though good enough to give him a sense of unusual integrity in University College, is precarious unless he can manage, in the manner of so many permanent undergraduates, to prolong the college context for the rest of his life. Each of the preceding chapters, in fact, works toward an equilibrium which is dashed when in the next chapter Stephen's world becomes larger and the frame of reference more complex. The terms of equilibrium are always stated with disquieting accuracy; at the end of Chapter I we find:

He was alone. He was happy and free: but he would not be anyway proud with Father Dolan. He would be very quiet and obedient: and he wished that he could do something kind for him to show him that he was not proud. [*P*, 59.]

And at the end of Chapter III:

He sat by the fire in the kitchen, not daring to speak for happiness. Till that moment he had not known how beautiful and peaceful life could be. The green square of paper pinned round the lamp cast down a tender shade. On the dresser was a plate of sausages and white pudding and on the shelf there were eggs. They would be for the breakfast in the morning after the communion in the college chapel. White pudding and eggs and sausages and cups of tea. How simple and beautiful was life after all! And life lay all before him. [*P*, 146.]

Not "irony" but simply the truth: the good life conceived in terms of white pudding and sausages is unstable enough to need no underlining.

The even-numbered chapters make a sequence of a different sort. The ending of IV, Stephen's panting submission to an artistic vocation:

Evening had fallen when he woke and the sand and arid grasses of his bed glowed no longer. He rose slowly and, recalling the rapture of his sleep, sighed at its joy. [*P*, 173],

—hasn't quite the finality often read into it when the explicit parallel with the ending of II is perceived:

He closed his eyes, surrendering himself to her, body and mind, conscious of nothing in the world but the dark pressure of her softly parting lips. They pressed upon his brain as upon his lips as though they were the vehicle of a vague speech; and between them he felt an unknown and timid pressure, darker than the swoon of sin, softer than sound or odour. [*P*, 101.]

When we link these passages with the fact that the one piece of literary composition Stephen actually achieves in the book comes out of a wet dream ("Towards dawn he awoke. O what sweet music! His soul was all dewy wet") we are in a position to see that the concluding "Welcome, O life!" has an air of finality and balance only because the diary-form of the last seven pages disarms us with an illusion of auctorial impartiality.

CONTROLLING IMAGES: CLONGOWES AND BELVEDERE

Ego *vs.* authority is the theme of the three odd-numbered chapters, Dublin *vs.* the dream that of the two even-numbered ones. The generic Joyce plot, the encounter with the alter ego, is consummated when Stephen at the end of the book identifies himself with the sanctified Stephen who was stoned by the Jews after reporting a vision (Acts VII, 56) and claims sonship with the classical Daedalus who evaded the ruler of land and sea by turning his soul to obscure arts. The episodes are built about adumbrations of this encounter: with Father Conmee, with Monte Cristo, with the whores, with the broad-shouldered moustached student who cut the word "Foetus" in a desk, with the weary mild confessor, with the bird-girl. Through this repeated plot intertwine controlling emotions and controlling images that mount in complexity as the book proceeds.

In Chapter I the controlling emotion is fear, and the dominant image Father Dolan and his pandybat; this, associated with the hangman-god and the priestly denial of the senses, was to become one of Joyce's standard images for Irish clericalism—hence the jack-in-the-box appearance of Father Dolan in Circe's nightmare imbroglio, his pandybat cracking twice like thunder [in *Ulysses*]. Stephen's comment, in the mode of Blake's repudiation of the God who slaughtered Jesus, emphasizes the inclusiveness of the image: "I never could read His handwriting except His criminal thumbprint on the haddock."

Chapter II opens with a triple image of Dublin's prepossessions: music, sport, religion. The first is exhibited via Uncle Charles singing sentimental ballads in the outhouse; the second via Stephen's ritual run around the park under the eye of a superannuated trainer, which his uncle enjoins on him as the whole duty of a Dubliner; the third via the clumsy piety of Uncle Charles, kneeling on a red handkerchief and reading above his breath "from a thumbblackened prayerbook wherein catchwords were printed at the foot of every page." This trinity of themes is unwound and entwined throughout the chapter, like a net woven round Stephen; it underlies the central incident, the Whitsuntide play in the Belvedere chapel (religion), which opens with a display by the dumb-bell team (sport) preluded by sentimental waltzes from the soldier's band (music).

While he is waiting to play his part, Stephen is taunted by fellow-students, who rally him on a fancied love-affair and smiting his calf with a cane bid him recite the *Confiteor*. His mind goes back to an analogous incident, when a similar punishment had been visited on his refusal to "admit that Byron was no good." The further analogy with Father Dolan is obvious; love, art, and personal independence are thus united in an ideogram of the prepossessions Stephen is determined to cultivate in the teeth of persecution.

The dream-world Stephen nourishes within himself is played against manifestations of music, sport, and religion throughout the chapter. The constant ironic clash of Dublin *vs.* the Dream animates Chapter II, as the clash of the ego *vs.* authority did Chapter I. All these themes come to focus during Stephen's visit with his father to Cork. The dream of rebellion he has silently cultivated is externalized by the discovery of the word *Foetus* carved in a desk by a forgotten medical student:

It shocked him to find in the outer world a trace of what he had deemed till then a brutish and individual malady of his own mind. His recent monstrous reveries came thronging into his memory. They too had sprung up before him, suddenly and furiously, out of mere words. [*P*, 90.]

The possibility of shame gaining the upper hand is dashed, however, by the sudden banal intrusion of his father's conversation ("When you kick out for yourself, Stephen—as I daresay you will one of those days—remember, whatever you do, to mix with gentlemen."). Against the standards of Dublin his monstrous reveries acquire a Satanic glamour, and the trauma is slowly diverted into a resolution to rebel. After his father has expressed a resolve to "leave him to his Maker" (religion), and offered to "sing a tenor song against him" (music) or "vault a fivebarred gate against him" (sport), Stephen muses, watching his father and two cronies drinking to the memory of their past:

An abyss of fortune or of temperament sundered him from them. His mind seemed older than theirs: it shone coldly on their strifes and happiness and regrets like a moon upon a younger earth. No life or youth stirred in him as it had stirred in them. He had known neither the pleasure of companionship with others nor the vigour of rude male health nor filial piety. Nothing stirred within his soul but a cold and cruel and loveless lust. [*P*, 95-96.]

After one final effort to compromise with Dublin on Dublin's terms has collapsed into futility ("The pot of pink enamel paint gave out and the wainscot of his bedroom remained with its unfinished and illplastered coat"), he fiercely cultivates his rebellious thoughts, and moving by day and night "among distorted images of the outer world," plunges at last into the arms of whores. "The holy encounter he had then imagined at which weakness and timidity and inexperience were to fall from him," finally arrives in inversion of Father Dolan's and Uncle Charles' religion: his descent into night-town is accompanied by lurid evocations of a Black Mass:

The yellow gasflames arose before his troubled vision against the vapoury sky, burning as if before an altar. Before the doors and in the lighted halls groups were gathered arrayed as for some rite. He was in another world: he had awakened from a slumber of centuries. [*P*, 100.]

CONTROLLING IMAGES:
SIN AND REPENTANCE

Each chapter in the *Portrait* gathers up the thematic material of the preceding ones and entwines them with a dominant theme of its own. In Chapter III the fear-pandybat motif is present in Father Arnall's crudely materialistic hell, of which even the thickness of the walls is specified; and the Dublin-*vs.*-dream motif has ironic inflections in Stephen's terror-stricken broodings, when the dream has been twisted into a dream of holiness, and even Dublin appears transfigured:

How beautiful must be a soul in the state of grace when God looked upon it with love!

Frowsy girls sat along the curbstones before their baskets. Their dank hair hung trailed over their brows. They were not beautiful to see as they crouched in the mire. But their souls were seen by God; and if their souls were in a state of grace they were radiant to see: and God loved them, seeing them. [*P*, 140.]

A *rapprochement* in these terms between the outer world and Stephen's desires is too inadequate to need commentary; and it makes vivid as nothing else could the hopeless inversion of his attempted self-sufficiency. It underlines, in yet another way, his persistent sin: and the dominant theme of Chapter III is Sin. A fugue-like opening plays upon the Seven Deadly Sins in turn; gluttony is in the first paragraph ("Stuff it into you, his belly counselled him"), followed by lust, then sloth ("A cold lucid indifference reigned in his soul"), pride ("His pride in his own sin, his loveless awe of God, told him that his offence was too grievous to be atoned for"), anger ("The blundering answer stirred the embers of his contempt for his fellows"); finally, a recapitulation fixes each term of the mortal catalogue in a phrase, enumerating how "from the evil seed of lust all the other deadly sins had sprung forth."

Priest and punisher inhabit Stephen himself as well as Dublin: when he is deepest in sin he is most thoroughly a theologian. A paragraph of gloomy introspection is juxtaposed with a list of theological questions that puzzle Stephen's mind as he awaits the preacher:

Is baptism with a mineral water valid? How comes it that while the first beatitude promises the kingdom of heaven to the poor of heart, the second beatitude promises also to the meek that they shall possess the land? . . . If the wine change into vinegar and the host crumble into corruption after they have been consecrated is Jesus Christ still present under their species as God and as man?
—Here he is! Here he is!
A boy from his post at the window had seen the rector come from the house. All the catechisms were opened and all heads bent upon them silently. [*P*, 106-107.]

Wine changed into vinegar and the host crumbled into corruption fits exactly the Irish clergy of "a church which was the scullery-maid of Christendom." The excited "Here he is! Here he is!" following hard on the mention of Jesus Christ and signalling nothing more portentous than the rector makes the point as dramatically as anything in the book, and the clinching sentence, with the students suddenly bending over their catechisms, places the rector as the vehicle of pandybat morality.

The last of the theological questions is the telling question.

Stephen never expresses doubt of the existence of God nor of the essential validity of the priestly office—his *Non serviam* is not a *non credo*, and he talks of a "malevolent reality" behind these appearances—but the wine and bread that were offered for his veneration were changed into vinegar and crumbled into corruption. And it was the knowledge of that underlying validity clashing with his refusal to do homage to vinegar and rot that evoked his ambivalent poise of egocentric despair. The hell of Father Arnall's sermon, so emotionally overwhelming, so picayune beside the horrors that Stephen's imagination can generate, had no more ontological content for Stephen than had "an eternity of bliss in the company of the dean of studies."

The conflict of this central chapter is again between the phantasmal and the real. What is real—psychologically real, because realized—is Stephen's anguish and remorse, and its context in the life of the flesh. What is phantasmal is the "heaven" of the Church and the "good life" of the priest. It is only fear that makes him clutch after the latter at all; his reaching out after orthodox salvation is, as we have come to expect, presented in terms that judge it:

The wind blew over him and passed on to the myriads and myriads of other souls on whom God's favour shone now more and now less, stars now brighter and now dimmer, sustained and failing. And the glimmering souls passed away, sustained and failing, merged in a moving breath. One soul was lost; a tiny soul: his. It flickered once and went out, forgotten, lost. The end: black cold void waste.

Consciousness of place came ebbing back to him slowly over a vast tract of time unlit, unfelt, unlived. The squalid scene composed itself around him; the common accents, the burning gasjets in the shops, odours of fish and spirits and wet sawdust, moving men and women. An old woman was about to cross the street, an oilcan in her hand. He bent down and asked her was there a chapel near. [*P*, 140-141.]

That wan waste world of flickering stars is the best Stephen has been able to do towards an imaginative grasp of the communion of Saints sustained by God; "unlit, unfelt, unlived" explains succinctly why it had so little hold on him, once fear had relaxed. Equally pertinent is the vision of human temporal occupations the sermon evokes:

What did it profit a man to gain the whole world if he lost his soul? At last he had understood: and human life lay around him, a plain of peace whereon antlike men laboured in brotherhood, their dead sleeping under quiet mounds. [*P*, 126.]

To maintain the life of grace in the midst of nature, sustained by so cramped a vision of the life of nature, would mean maintaining an intolerable tension. Stephen's unrelenting philosophic bias, his determination to understand what he is about, precludes his adopting the double standard of the Dubliners; to live both the life of nature and the life of grace he must enjoy an imaginative grasp of their relationship which stunts neither. "No one doth well against his will," writes Saint Augustine, "even though what he doth, be well"; and Stephen's will is firmly harnessed to his understanding. And there is no one in Dublin to help him achieve understanding. Father Arnall's sermon precludes rather than secures a desirable outcome, for it follows the modes of pandybat morality and Dublin materiality. Its only possible effect on Stephen is to lash his dormant conscience into a frenzy. The description of Hell as "a strait and dark and foulsmelling prison, an abode of demons and lost souls, filled with fire and smoke," with walls four thousand miles thick, its damned packed in so tightly that "they are not even able to remove from the eye the worm that gnaws it," is childishly grotesque beneath its sweeping eloquence; and the hair-splitting catalogues of pains—pain of loss, pain of conscience (divided into three heads), pain of extension, pain of intensity, pain of eternity—is cast in a brainlessly analytic mode that effectively prevents any corresponding Heaven from possessing any reality at all.

Stephen's unstable pact with the Church, and its dissolution, follows the pattern of composition and dissipation established by his other dreams: the dream for example of the tryst with "Mercedes," which found ironic reality among harlots. It parallels exactly his earlier attempt to "build a breakwater of order and elegance against the sordid tide of life without him," whose failure, with the exhaustion of his money, was epiphanized in the running-dry of a pot of pink enamel paint. His regimen at that time:

He bought presents for everyone, overhauled his rooms, wrote out resolutions, marshalled his books up and down their shelves, pored over all kinds of price lists . . . [*P*, 97-98.]

is mirrored by his searching after spiritual improvement:

His daily life was laid out in devotional areas. By means of ejaculations and prayers he stored up ungrudgingly for the souls in purgatory centuries of days and quarantines and years. . . . He offered up each of his three daily chaplets that his soul might grow strong in each of the three theological virtues. . . . On each of the seven days of the week he further prayed that one of the seven gifts of the Holy Ghost might descend upon his soul. . . . [*P*, 147-148.]

The "loan bank" he had opened for the family, out of which he had pressed loans on willing borrowers "that he might have the pleasure of making out receipts and reckoning the interests on sums lent" finds its counterpart in the benefits he stored up for souls in purgatory that he might enjoy the spiritual triumph of "achieving with ease so many fabulous ages of canonical penances." Both projects are parodies on the doctrine of economy of grace; both are attempts, corrupted by motivating self-interest, to make peace with Dublin on Dublin's own terms; and both are short-lived.

As this precise analogical structure suggests, the action of each of the five chapters is really the same action. Each chapter closes with a synthesis of triumph which the next destroys. The triumph of the appeal to Father Conmee from lower authority, of the appeal to the harlots from Dublin, of the appeal to the Church from sin, of the appeal to art from the priesthood (the bird-girl instead of the Virgin) is always the same triumph raised to a more comprehensive level. It is an attempt to find new parents; new fathers in the odd chapters, new objects of love in the even. The last version of Father Conmee is the "priest of the eternal imagination"; the last version of Mercedes is the "lure of the fallen seraphim." But the last version of the mother who said, "O, Stephen will apologise" is the mother who prays on the last page "that I may learn in my own life and away from home and friends what the heart is and what it feels." The mother remains.

THE DOUBLE FEMALE

As in *Dubliners* and *Exiles*, the female role in the *Portrait* is less to arouse than to elucidate masculine desires. Hence the complex function in the book of physical love: the physical is the analogue of the spiritual, as St. Augustine insisted in his *Confessions* (which, with Ibsen's *Brand*, is the chief archetype of Joyce's book). The poles between which this affection moves are those of St. Augustine and St. John: the Whore of Babylon and the Bride of Christ. The relation between the two is far from simple, and Stephen moves in a constant tension between them.

His desire, figured in the visions of Monte Cristo's Mercedes, "to meet in the real world the unsubstantial image which his soul so constantly beheld" draws him toward the prostitute ("In her arms he felt that he had suddenly become strong and fearless and sure of himself") and simultaneously toward the vaguely spiritual satisfaction represented with equal vagueness by the wraithlike E—— C——, to whom he twice writes verses. The Emma Clery of *Stephen Hero*, with her loud forced manners and her body compact of pleasure, was refined into a wraith with a pair of initials to parallel an intangible Church. She is continually assimilated to the image of the Blessed Virgin and of the heavenly Bride. The torture she costs him is the torture his apostasy costs him. His flirtation with her is his flirtation with Christ. His profane villanelle draws its imagery from religion—the incense, the eucharistic hymn, the chalice—and her heart, following Dante's image, is a rose, and in her praise "the earth was like a swinging swaying censer, a ball of incense."

The woman is the Church. His vision of greeting Mercedes with "a sadly proud gesture of refusal":

—Madam, I never eat muscatel grapes. [P, 63.]

is fulfilled when he refuses his Easter communion. Emma's eyes, in their one explicit encounter, speak to him from beneath a cowl. "The glories of Mary held his soul captive," and a temporary reconciliation of his lust and his spiritual thirst is achieved as he reads the Lesson out of the Song of Solomon. In the midst of his repentance she functions as imagined mediator: "The image of Emma appeared before him," and, repenting, "he imagined that he stood near Emma in a wide land, and, humbly and in tears, bent and kissed the elbow of her sleeve." Like Dante's Beatrice, she manifests in his earthly experience the Church Triumphant of his spiritual dream. And when he rejects her because she seems to be flirting with Father Moran, his anger is couched in the anti-clerical terms of his apostasy: "He had done well to leave her to flirt with her priest, to toy with a church which was the scullerymaid of christendom."

That Kathleen ni Houlihan can flirt with priests is the unforgivable sin underlying Stephen's rejection of Ireland. But he makes a clear distinction between the stupid clericalism which makes intellectual and communal life impossible, and his long-nourished vision of an artist's Church Triumphant upon earth. He rejects the actual for daring to fall short of his vision.

THE FINAL BALANCE

The climax of the book is of course Stephen's ecstatic discovery of his vocation at the end of Chapter IV. The prose rises in nervous excitement to beat again and again the tambours of a fin-de-siècle ecstasy:

His heart trembled; his breath came faster and a wild spirit passed over his limbs as though he were soaring sunward. His heart trembled in an ecstasy of fear and his soul was in flight. His soul was soaring in an air beyond the world and the body he knew was purified in a breath and delivered of incertitude and made radiant and commingled with the element of the spirit. An ecstasy of flight made radiant his eyes and wild his breath and tremulous and wild and radiant his windswept limbs.

—One! Two! . . . Look out!

—O, cripes, I'm drownded! [*P*, 169.]

The interjecting voices of course are those of bathers, but their ironic appropriateness to Stephen's Icarian "soaring sunward" is not meant to escape us: divers have their own "ecstasy of flight," and Icarus was "drownded." The imagery of Stephen's ecstasy is fetched from many sources; we recognize Shelley's skylark, Icarus, the glorified body of the Resurrection (cf. "His soul had arisen from the grave of boyhood, spurning her grave-clothes") and a tremulousness from which it is difficult to dissociate adolescent sexual dreams (which the Freudians tell us are frequently dreams of flying). The entire eight-page passage is cunningly organized with great variety of rhetoric and incident; but we cannot help noticing the limits set on vocabulary and figures of thought. The empurpled triteness of such a cadence as "radiant his eyes and wild his breath and tremulous and wild and radiant his windswept limbs" is enforced by recurrence: "But her long fair hair was girlish: and girlish, and touched with the wonder of mortal beauty, her face." "Ecstasy" is the keyword, indeed. This riot of feelings corresponds to no vocation definable in mature terms; the paragraphs come to rest on images of irresponsible motion:

He turned away from her suddenly and set off across the strand. His cheeks were aflame; his body was aglow; his limbs were trembling. On and on and on and on he strode, far out over the sands, singing wildly to the sea, crying to greet the advent of the life that had cried to him. [*P*, 172.]

What "life" connotes it skills not to ask; the word recurs and recurs. So does the motion onward and onward and onward:

A wild angel had appeared to him, the angel of mortal youth and beauty, an envoy from the fair courts of life, to throw open before him in an instant of ecstasy the gates of all the ways of error and glory. On and on and on and on! [*P*, 172.]

It may be well to recall Joyce's account of the romantic temper:

. . . an insecure, unsatisfied, impatient temper which sees no fit abode here for its ideals and chooses therefore to behold them under insensible figures. As a result of this choice it comes to disregard certain limitations. Its figures are blown to wild adventures, lacking the gravity of solid bodies. . . . [*SH.*]

Joyce also called *Prometheus Unbound* "the Schwärmerei of a young jew."

And it is quite plain from the final chapter of the *Portrait* that we are not to accept the mode of Stephen's "freedom" as the "message" of the book. The "priest of the eternal imagination" turns out to be indigestibly Byronic. Nothing is more obvious than his total lack of humour. The dark intensity of the first four chapters is moving enough, but our impulse on being confronted with the final edition of Stephen Dedalus is to laugh; and laugh at this moment we dare not; he is after all a victim being prepared for a sacrifice. His shape, as Joyce said, can no longer change. The art he has elected is not "the slow elaborative patience of the art of satisfaction." "On and on and on and on" will be its inescapable mode. He does not *see* the girl who symbolizes the full revelation; "she seemed like one whom magic had changed into the likeness of a strange and beautiful seabird," and he confusedly apprehends a sequence of downy and feathery incantations. What, in the last chapter, he does see he sees only to reject, in favour of an incantatory "loveliness which has not yet come into the world."

The only creative attitude to language exemplified in the book is that of Stephen's father:

—Is it Christy? he said. There's more cunning in one of those warts on his bald head than in a pack of jack foxes. [*P,* 28.]

His vitality is established before the book is thirty pages under way. Stephen, however, isn't enchanted at any time by the proximity of such talk. He isn't, as a matter of fact, even interested in it. Without a backward glance, he exchanges this father for a myth.

KENNETH BURKE

Kenneth Burke, critic, philosopher, poet, has lectured at the New School for Social Research, the Universities of Chicago and California, and Bennington College. His books include *Philosophy of Literary Form*, *The Grammar of Motives*, *The Rhetoric of Motives*, and *Language as Symbolic Action*.

[DEFINITIONS]

THE JOYCE PORTRAIT

Definition:

A serious prose narrative, imitating an agent's spiritual adventures, in the development of a new attitude, with its corresponding doctrine; it employs an intense, elevated, or otherwise exceptional diction (involving a principle of selectivity that makes it representative in the *culminative* sense rather than as tested by *statistical averages*); the unity of action centers in the unity of the main character, whose transformations coincide with the stages of the plot; like the lyric proper, it places great reliance upon sensory images, not merely for purposes of vividness (*enargeia*) but to serve structural ends (the images thus taking on "mythic" dimensions that transcend their specifically sensory significance); the seriousness of the agent and the magnitude of his trials serve to dignify the development towards which the work is directed.

Comments:

"A serious prose narrative." Some readers have shown an inclination to overrate the possibility that Joyce would have us "discount" Stephen. The work as a whole is complexly motivated; for instance, Lynch's "sulphuryellow" remarks to

From *The Kenyon Review*, XIII (Spring 1951). Copyright 1951 by *The Kenyon Review* and used by their permission and that of Kenneth Burke.

Stephen, while Stephen is explaining his *ars poetica*, should be taken as an integral part of the motivation, not merely as an irrelevant heckling. But we would not thereby conclude that the reader similarly is to "heckle" Stephen. Stephen is naïve and excessive, but his trials are to be viewed sympathetically. Even though we are not intended to take the hellfire sermon as seriously as he did, we are intended to feel that Stephen's agitation was quite "proper" to his condition. Even though we may partly smile, we take each stage of his development "seriously."

"Imitating an agent's spiritual adventures." Not the adventures of a Jason or an Odysseus—but in the order of meditation, scruples, "change of heart." (Nor is Joyce's *Ulysses* the adventures of an Odysseus.)

"In the development of a new attitude." Perhaps most would prefer "vision" to "attitude." (Should we also seek to include here the fact that the work as a whole gains unity in terms of the central agent's sensibility and development?)

"With its corresponding doctrine." It is surprising how many analysts, even when asked to discuss the over-all stages in the development of this work, will omit the "catechism," the *doctrinal* equivalent of Stephen's shift from religious to aesthetic vocation. (Here is the respect in which this "lyric novel" overlaps upon another species, an *Erziehungsroman* like Goethe's *Wilhelm Meister*. Ironically, though Joyce became a symbol of pure aestheticism, his novel is a *plea* for certain artistic policies.)

"Involving a principle of selectivity that makes it 'representative' in the *culminative* sense rather than as tested by statistical averages." Stephen is not "representative" in the "statistical" sense. He is a rarity. But many modern writers have in one way or another adapted religious coordinates to aesthetic ends. And Joyce imagines such a course "to perfection." This is what we mean by its "culminative" nature.

"The images may accordingly take on 'mythic' dimensions that transcend their specifically sensory significance." We have in mind here the development that Joyce called an "epiphany." Our remarks on the Platonic dialogue would indicate respects in which the Joycean form paralleled Plato's use of the "mythic image" for the figuring of a new motivational dimension. Insofar as the bathing girl stands for Stephen's new vocation, she is a "mythic" image, as distinct from a purely "sensory" image. She is "enigmatic," or "emblematic" of the motives that transcend her meaning as a "natural object."

"The seriousness of the agent and the magnitude of his trials serve to dignify the development towards which the work is directed." Elsewhere we have offered four ways of subdividing the idea of tragedy: (1) Tragedy as a species (as with Aristotle's definition of one particular kind of tragedy; a different kind of definition would be needed for, say, Cornelian tragedy); (2) the "tragic rhythm" (the progression from action, through passion, to learning); (3) the "tragic spirit" (the general cult of "mortification" or "resignation"; an ultimate or "cumulative" expression of social repressions voluntarily enacted by the self upon the self, in response to problems of private property in the social order); (4) "tragedy as a rhetorical device, as a means of dignification" (arguing for a cause by depicting a serious person who is willing to sacrifice himself in its behalf; the device has somewhat Satanistic aspects here, as with the heroics of Stephen's willingness to consider the possibility that eternal damnation might result from his aesthetic "pride").

"STAGES"

Consider Chapter XII in the *Poetics*, the listing of a tragedy's "quantitative" parts (Prologue, Episode, Exode, Parode, Stasimon, Commos). Here we touch upon the dialectic of "stages." But Aristotle was so eager to disassociate himself from the Platonist dialectic in general, and to establish a purely secular analysis of tragic "pleasure" (despite its vestiges of ritual "cure") his treatment here is quite perfunctory. The feeling for the "stages" of a development is slighted.

Our biggest loss here is unquestionably in Aristotle's unconcern with the trilogy as a form. His analysis of tragedy centers about individual works considered as separate units. Yet what of trilogies like Aeschylus' *Oresteia*, where each play carries the over-all development one step farther? (And, of course, if we had the material, we might further extend our theories of form until we also treated the contrasted fourth drama, the final burlesque or "satyr-play," as an integral part of the playwright's statement in its entirety.)

Modern anthropologists have supplied information and speculations that enable us to bring Chapter XII to life. (See George Thomson's *Aeschylus and Athens*, p. 192, for a chart suggesting how the "quantitative parts" of tragedy developed from patterns of religious ritual. Similarly, this Marxist-tempered variant of the Hegelian dialectic serves well for throwing light upon the trilogy as a form. Such considerations are directed two ways. First, the three stages of the only surviving trilogy are analyzed; next, a similar logic of the parts is assumed, in reasoned guesses as to the likely developments in the *Prometheus* trilogy, of which only the first play survives, though fragments of the others are extant.)

Often, however, anthropology has fed the present fad for "myth" in ways that mislead. For instance, many purely dialectical considerations are stated in an insufficiently generalized form; as a result, a term local to the study of ritual will be used to designate a process that is not necessarily ritualistic at all.

Thus, consider the most highly generalized resources of discursive reason: "composition and division." Because such resources are universal to human thinking, they will also be found exemplified in primitive rituals. The principle of "division," for instance, is present in *sparagmos*, the rending of the god's flesh in primitive religious practices. Or the principle of "composition" is present here, inasmuch as the members of the group are thought to be made consubstantial by thus ceremoniously eating of the same magical substance. Suppose, then, for "division" in general, we used the word *sparagmos*, or rending and tearing of the divine sacrifice, and for "composition" in general we used some term for the tribal love-feast. The most rational processes of science or everyday life would thus be expressed in terms that referred merely to the application of them in one specific subject matter. Scientific *analysis* might thus be treated as a vestigial survival of *sparagmos*. The current over-use of terms for the processes of ritual and myth has two bad effects: first, it can make even realistic common sense look like an attenuated survival of primitive magic; second, by thus misdirecting our attention, it can keep us from perceiving the mythic elements that really do infuse our culture (mythic elements rooted in the magic of property, with its avowed and unavowed, spontaneous and deliberate, forms of priestcraft).

While it is our job to brood over man's dismal bondage to the magic of social relations as rooted in property, and thus to mention this topic in a hit-and-run sort of way whenever the given subject offers such an inkling, for the moment we are trying to suggest that the dialectic of "stages" (sometimes called "levels") was not adequately considered in the case of the definition which we have taken as our model. So we suggested a possible corrective, plus a corrective to the possible misuse of that.

In the *Portrait*, considered from the standpoint of "stages," the first three chapters would be like courses "prerequisite" to the choice Stephen makes in Chapter IV, where he turns from priestly to artistic vocation. However, we should not overlook an intermediate stage here. After thought of *"ordination"* . . . of "a grave and *ordered* and passionless life that awaited him, a life without material cares" . . . of himself as "a being apart in every *order*" . . . of the window that might be his "if he ever joined the *order*" . . . of his destiny "to be elusive of social or religious *orders*," there is talk of himself as "about to fall," then "he crossed the bridge over the stream of the Tolka," whereat he contemplates the opposite of order: "Then, bending to the left, he followed the lane which led up to his house. The faint sour stink of rotted cabbages came towards him from the kitchengardens on the rising ground above the river. He smiled to think that it was this *disorder* [throughout, italics ours], the misrule and confusion of his father's house and the stagnation of vegetable life, which was to win the day in his soul." Not quite. For the next episode will detail the vision of the hawklike man and the bird-girl (flight away, flight up, a *transcending* of the rotted cabbages). Hence, all told: *from* the priestly calling, *through* the dismal alternative, *to* the new exaltation, the aesthetic jesuitry that will be his purging of the alternative disorder, that will fly above it. And since the disorder had been "to the left," and since Part I should "implicitly contain" what eventuates, we might appropriately recall young Stephen's first triumph, as regards the pandybat episode, when he had gone "not to the corridor but up the staircase on the right that led up to the castle." Here is accurate writing. . . .

$$\mathcal{C}ontroversy$$

❀◇❀◇❀◇❀◇❀◇❀◇❀◇❀◇❀◇❀◇❀◇❀◇❀◇❀◇❀◇❀◇❀◇❀◇❀◇

THE QUESTION OF ESTHETIC
DISTANCE

EDITOR'S INTRODUCTION

Among the controversial questions about Joyce's "Portrait," none has been asked more persistently than the one debated in this section by Wayne Booth and Robert Scholes—what is the attitude of James Joyce toward Stephen Dedalus?

Critics have given several different and sometimes contradictory answers to the question. It is implicit in almost every review and essay included in the present volume. Sometimes even the same critic has answered the question differently for himself as he has read and reread the book. John V. Kelleher, for instance, writes:

I remember that when I first encountered Stephen Dedalus I was twenty and I wondered how Joyce could have known so much about me. That is what I mean by the sort of reading the book will continue to get, whatever literary fashion may decree. Perhaps about the third reading it dawned on me that Stephen was, after all, a bit of a prig; and to that extent I no longer identified myself with him. (How could I?) Quite a while later I perceived that Joyce knew that Stephen was a prig; that, indeed, he looked on Stephen with quite an ironic eye. So then I understood. At least I did until I had to observe that the author's glance was not one of unmixed irony. There was compassion in it too, as well as a sort of tender, humorous pride.[1]

---

[1] John V. Kelleher, "The Perceptions of James Joyce," *Atlantic Monthly*, CCI (March 1958), p. 83.

Like Kelleher, other critics have assumed that Joyce has one of three attitudes toward Stephen, and on the basis of the assumptions they have reacted in several ways. The assumptions are these:

1. That Joyce sees Stephen as an autobiographical hero who triumphs over his tawdry environment of squalor, stupidity, and treachery, by rejecting it, flying past the "nets" of family, nation, and church to find his own identity. Joyce asks the reader to join him in approving of the hero and his triumph. The novel is "romantic" in the sense that writer and reader "identify with" the hero, and there is little "distance" between the painter and his portrait. (Most of the early reviewers of the book concur about this, whether they like the book or not.)

a. Some readers have agreed to join Joyce in this way. David Daiches is representative:

As indicated by the title, Stephen Dedalus, in all essentials, is James Joyce, and the *Portrait* is an autobiographical study as well as a piece of prose fiction. It is fiction in the sense that the selection and arrangement of the incidents produce an artistically patterned work, a totality in which there is nothing superfluous, in which every detail is artistically as well as biographically relevant. . . . As autobiography, the work has an almost terrifying honesty; as fiction, it has unity, consistency, probability, and all the other aesthetic qualities we look for in a work of art. Using the facts of his own life as material, memory as the principle of selection, and his own acute aesthetic sense as a guide to organization and arrangement, Joyce has found a way of fusing the Aristotelian categories of possible and probable. Thematic unity is provided by the single direction in which all the incidents move—the direction toward the hero's final rejection of his environment. Stephen is at once the product of his environment and its critic.[2]

b. Others, while accepting the same assumptions, have refused to join Joyce in approving Stephen. As early as 1927 Wyndham Lewis, in *Time and Western Man*, argued that "*The Portrait of the Artist* seemed . . . a rather cold and

---

[2] David Daiches, *The Novel and the Modern World* (Chicago: University of Chicago Press, 1939), pp. 101-102.

priggish book," and for forty years the adjective "priggish" has been trailed through Joyce criticism, along with the word "sentimentality," which Rebecca West added the next year. Miss West, characterizing Joyce in *The Strange Necessity* as "a great man who is entirely without taste," claimed that his lack of taste "is the source of . . . the gross sentimentality which is his most fundamental error." She continued:

There is working here a narcissism, a compulsion to make a self-image and to make it with an eye to the approval of others, which turns Stephen Dedalus into a figure oddly familiar for the protagonist of a book supposed to be revolutionary and unique. In his monologues on aesthetics . . . he enjoys the unnatural immunity from interruption that one might encounter not in life but in a typical Freudian wish-fulfilment dream.[3]

Even in more recent years perceptive critics like Hugh Kenner (see pp. 416-439) have joined the group which has come to be called "Stephen haters." Kenner speaks of the "insufferable Stephen of the final chapter" who is an "indigestibly Byronic hero," redeemed only by his reappearance in *Ulysses* and *Finnegans Wake*, and Denis Donoghue, though refusing to support Kenner in rejecting the final chapter, sees the book as seriously flawed because "the tender hero is endorsed in his own isolation":

The book would have freed itself from a pervading softness of focus if Joyce had caused his juxtapositions to evoke as much judgment as apprehension. Only a perverse reader will happily reject whole chapters of the *Portrait* as Pater-pastiche, but difficulties persist. . . . Drama or rhetoric should have warned Joyce that Stephen the aesthetic *alazon* needed nothing so urgently as a correspondingly deft *eiron*; lacking this, the book is blind in one eye.[4]

2. That Joyce sees Stephen as an autobiographical representation of the author, a "portrait of the artist" drawn "as a young

---

[3] Rebecca West, *The Strange Necessity: Essays* (Garden City, N.Y.: Doubleday Doran, 1928), p. 11.
[4] Denis Donoghue, "Joyce and the Finite Order," *Sewanee Review*, LXVIII, 3 (Spring 1960), 258.

man" by an older man. Joyce asks the reader to join him in seeing Stephen as a priggish, narcissistic young egoist. The *alazon* (romantic hero) does have his corresponding *eiron* (ironic commentator), not so much in Cranly or Lynch as in Joyce himself, who by means of his ironic tone constantly undercuts the hero, placing considerable distance between painter and portrait.

Beginning as early as 1950, William York Tindall became the main spokesman for this kind of reading:

Rebecca West's error is a confusion of Joyce with Stephen. As almost everybody knows, Joyce once said that the important words of his title are *as a Young Man*. From this remark and from a careful reading of the book it becomes evident that Joyce differs from Butler and Wolfe in having an artist's detachment from what he is using. Stephen is not Joyce but Joyce's past. Stephen is sentimental; Joyce is not. In *A Portrait of the Artist as a Young Man*, the mature man looks back at his adolescent self, not to praise it, but to give it shape as an artist must. Stephen is Joyce's material. Like any artist Joyce was fascinated with his material, but as he wrote, he formalized and "distanced it." By this process, which is that of all art, he composed the personal and gave it that symbolic form which, freed from the emotive and the personal, permits insight into reality.

Those who find a sentimental attachment in *A Portrait of the Artist* have failed to notice the tone. To his friend Frank Budgen, Joyce once said, "I haven't let this young man off very lightly, have I?" A careful reading makes it apparent that Joyce is aloof and generally ironic in his treatment of Stephen. But Joyce's attitude is never explicit. Stephen is allowed to expose himself. Joyce limits his assistance to arranging contrasts and juxtapositions and to using a style which, following the contours of the hero's passion, becomes that passion while parodying it. His attitude toward Stephen is more obvious in *Ulysses* where that priggish hero is subjected to Mulligan's deflation and permitted to display his humorless egocentricity.[5]

a. Tindall indicates one direction in which this answer to

---

[5] W. Y. Tindall, *James Joyce: His Way of Interpreting the Modern World* (New York: Scribner's, 1950), pp. 16-17.

the question of distance leads—the direction of style. He praises the "style which, following the contours of the hero's passion becomes that passion while parodying it." (Cf. Joyce's argument in the essay "Portrait" of 1904 [pp. 257-266] that he would shape the past as a "fluid succession of presents.")

Mark Schorer in 1948 had praised the style for similar reasons:

A *Portrait of the Artist as a Young Man*, like *Tono Bungay* and *Sons and Lovers*, is autobiographical, but unlike these it analyzes its material rigorously, and it defines the value and the quality of its experience not by appended comment or moral epithet, but by the texture of the style. The theme of A *Portrait*, a young artist's alienation from his environment, is explored and evaluated through three different styles and methods as Stephen Dedalus moves from childhood through boyhood into maturity. . . . In essence Stephen's alienation is a denial of the human environment; it is a loss; and the austere discourse of the final section, abstract and almost wholly without sensuous detail or strong rhythm, tells us of that loss. It is a loss so great that the texture of the notation-like prose here suggests that the end is really all an illusion, that when Stephen tells us and himself that he is going forth to forge in the smithy of his soul the uncreated conscience of his race, we are to infer from the very quality of the icy, abstract void he now inhabits, the implausibility of his aim. For *Ulysses* does not create the conscience of the race; it creates our consciousness.

Might one not say . . . that the final passage of A *Portrait* punctuates the illusory nature of the whole ambition? [6]

b. But Frank O'Connor, while agreeing with Schorer and Tindall that the style follows what Joyce calls in the essay "Portrait" the "curve of an emotion," objects that the style is "insufferably self-conscious, as though Walter Pater had taken to business and commercialized his style for the use of schools and colleges . . ." O'Connor argues that this is something new in literature.

---

[6] Mark Schorer, "Technique as Discovery," *Hudson Review*, I (Spring 1948), 78-80.

. . . it represents the point, anticipated in Flaubert, at which style ceases to be a relationship between author and reader and becomes a relationship of a magical kind between author and object. Here *le mot juste* is no longer *juste* for the reader, but for the object. It is not an attempt at communicating the experience to the reader, who is supposed to be present only by courtesy, but at equating the prose with the experience. Indeed, one might say that it aims at replacing the experience by the prose . . .[7]

D. S. Savage goes even further in condemning what he calls "the biggest question raised by Joyce . . . that of the entirely self-subsistent work of art."

Aestheticism I interpret as a malady of the spirit in which the poverty of a meaningless and static life is compensated by the transposition into living of properties borrowed from the artistic sphere. . . . Despite all efforts, art cannot be severed from its relation to experience, and the material of the artist-aesthete who rejects the echo and the dream cannot be other than his own intrinsically meaningless and impoverished existence. Joyce accepted this position, and, transferring the meaning and purpose which he repudiated in life to the realm of art, he brought art and life together in a relationship of unparalleled immediacy; it was, so to speak, a symbiotic relationship, in which art fed upon and incorporated life into itself . . . The psychic quality of Joyce's work is astonishingly primitive; it shows marked leanings towards plain animism.[8]

3. That Joyce's view of his own past in Stephen is mixed, both ironic and romantic or sympathetic. Kenneth Burke might have been answering Tindall's statement of 1950 when he said in 1951:

Some readers have shown an inclination to overrate the possibility that Joyce would have us "discount" Stephen. The work as a whole is complexly motivated; for instance, Lynch's "sulphur yellow" remarks to Stephen, while Stephen is explaining his *ars poetica,*

---

[7] See pp. 371-377 for O'Connor's essay.
[8] D. S. Savage, *The Withered Branch: Six Studies in the Modern Novel* (London: Eyre and Spottiswoode, 1950), pp. 157-159.

should be taken as an integral part of the motivation, not merely as an irrelevant heckling. But we would not thereby conclude that the reader similarly is to "heckle" Stephen. Stephen is naïve and excessive, but his trials are to be viewed sympathetically. Even though we are not intended to take the hell-fire sermons as seriously as he did, we are intended to feel that Stephen's agitation was quite "proper" to his condition. Even thought we may partly smile, we take each stage of his development "seriously." [9]

And Tindall himself in 1959, while still holding his general position, places more emphasis on the "compassion" Joyce feels for the young Stephen:

Taking a stand within a subject may forbid comedy, but a virtue of impressionism is that it allows the author to stand alongside his subject as well—at a little distance. Not enough for comedy, this distance is suitable for irony, as civilized and critical as comedy and far more disagreeable. Distance lends disenchantment to the view. A value of Joyce's method is that Stephen exposes himself while Joyce, at that little distance, exposes Stephen. The difference between their views of the same thing constitutes an irony so quiet that it escapes many readers, who, reducing two to one, take Stephen at his own estimate. To miss Joyce's estimate, however, is to miss half the meaning and all the fun.

That Stephen, less admirable than he thinks, is not Joyce seems proved again by Joyce's irony. "I have been rather hard on that young man," Joyce told his friend Frank Budgen, emphasizing the last words of his title. Young man no more, Joyce looks at a young man with compassion, to be sure, but with mocking eyes. The first word of his title, that indefinite article, also seems significant in this connection. Meaning not only one of several possible portraits, the article may imply a portrait of a particular kind, ironic perhaps. The kind of irony tenderly lavished upon one's self to enhance it may not be altogether absent; for though not Stephen, Joyce had been young. He was humane moreover and a creature of his romantic time. But his tone, generally more distant than sentiment prefers, seems the real thing, not its sentimental substitute. Rebecca West and Frank O'Connor think ironic Joyce sentimental; but she is English and O'Connor Irish. I am unable to share their

---

[9] See pp. 440-445 for part of Burke's essay.

detestable opinion. In judging Joyce national differences sometimes make all the difference; but there are texts to base my difference on.[10]

a. Some readers remain uneasy about this "double vision"
of irony and compassion. They see the book and Joyce's attitude as essentially "ambivalent." Stanley Poss, for example:

> But it is, after all, indispensable to locate as precisely as one can
> where an author stands in regard to his characters. Through explica-
> tion of the text of the *Portrait*, I hope to show that Joyce's evasive
> and ambivalent attitude toward Stephen lies closer to apotheosis
> than outright denigration, though it should not be identified with
> either extreme . . .
> In short, the rotten cabbages are parallel with the "sluggish
> matter of the earth" which he is to transmute, and both are the
> reciprocal of the "birdgirl," who is mortal beauty at its highest
> pitch, that is, cabbages and earth worked upon by art and changed
> utterly in the process. Thus, Stephen rhapsodically, as Joyce wryly,
> accepts life itself; but his rhapsodic words are not merely romantic
> vaporings. They are his only means of awakening The Old Woman,
> of recreating the girl, and they testify to a baffled patriotism, a
> frustrated love which, together with the self-asserting implications
> of the messianic impulse, complicates him considerably and alters
> fundamentally one's initial impression of him as an orthodox adoles-
> cent rebel.[11]

b. Richard Ellmann, while agreeing essentially with Tindall
and others that "Joyce plunged back into his own past, mainly
to justify, but also to expose it," sees the key to the book and
the answer to the question of aesthetic distance to lie in Joyce's
taking seriously the metaphor of "artistic reproduction." In
painting his portrait the artist becomes "his own mother" and
"seems to reconstitute his family relationships, to disengage
himself from the contradictions of his view of himself as a child
and so to exploit them, to overcome his mother's convention-

---

[10] W. Y. Tindall, *A Reader's Guide to James Joyce* (New York: Noonday Press, 1959), pp. 64-65.

[11] Stanley Poss, "A Portrait of the Artist as Hard-Boiled Messiah," *Modern Language Quarterly*, XXVII (March 1966), 69 and 79.

ality and his father's rancor, to mother and father himself, to become, by the superhuman effort of the creative process, no one but James Joyce." This opens up a new frame of reference for discussing the question. The book is not so much, in Ellmann's view, an acceptance of self and a rejection of environment, nor a rejection of youth by maturity, as it is a transformation of both environment and self into something new, the record of the growth of an identity (or "soul," as Joyce would have said) before our very eyes. (See pp. 388-398, this edition, for Ellmann's essay.)

The question of esthetic distance is not, perhaps, finally answered, and as Kelleher says, each reader may have to find a succession of answers for himself. Wayne Booth and Robert Scholes, in the essays which follow, at least help to make the question clearer.

WAYNE BOOTH

Wayne Booth has taught at Haverford College and Earlham College, and is George M. Pullman Professor of English at the University of Chicago and Dean of the College. He is the author of *The Rhetoric of Fiction*, and the editor of *Knowledge Most Worth Having*.

The Problem of Distance in
A PORTRAIT OF THE ARTIST

If a master puzzle maker had set out to give us the greatest possible difficulty, he could not have done more than has been done in some modern works in which this effect of deep involvement is combined with the implicit demand that we maintain our capacity for ironic judgment. The trouble with *Moll Flanders*, such a genius of confusion might be imagined as saying to himself, is that the obvious differences between the female heroine and the author provide too many clues. Let us then write a book that will look like the author's autobiography, using many details from his own life and opinions. But we cannot be satisfied with moral problems, which are after all much less subject to dispute than intellectual and aesthetic matters. Let us then call for the reader's precise judgment on a very elaborate set of opinions and actions in which the hero is sometimes right, sometimes slightly wrong, and sometimes absurdly astray. Just to make sure that things are not too obvious, let us finally bind the reader so tightly to the consciousness of the ambiguously misguided protagonist that nothing will interfere with his delight in inferring the precise though varying degrees of distance that operate from point to point throughout the book. We can be sure that some readers will

---

take the book as strictly autobiographical; others will go sadly astray in overlooking ironies that are intended and in discovering ironies that are not there. But for the rare reader who can make his way through this jungle, the delight will be great indeed.

The giant whom we all must wrestle with in this regard is clearly Joyce. Except for occasional outbursts of bravado nobody has ever really claimed that Joyce is clear. In all the skeleton keys and classroom guides there is an open assumption that his later works, *Ulysses* and *Finnegans Wake*, cannot be read; they can only be studied. Joyce himself was always explicating his works, and it is clear that he saw nothing wrong with the fact that they could not be thought of as standing entirely on their own feet. The reader's problems are handled, if they are to be handled at all, by rhetoric provided outside the work.

But the difficulties with distance that are pertinent here cannot be removed by simple study. Obscure allusions can be looked up, patterns of imagery and theme can be traced; gradually over the years a good deal of lore has accumulated, and about some of it by now there is even a certain amount of agreement. But about the more fundamental matters the skeleton keys and guides are of little help, because unfortunately they do not agree, they do not agree at all. It is fine to know that in *Ulysses* Stephen stands in some way for Telemachus and Bloom for his wandering father, Ulysses. But it would also be useful to know whether the work is comic or pathetic or tragic, or, if it is a combination, where the elements fall. Can two readers be said to have read the same book if one thinks it ends affirmatively and the other sees the ending as pessimistic? It is really no explanation to say that Joyce has succeeded in imitating life so well that like life itself his books seem totally ambiguous, totally open to whatever interpretation the reader wants to place on them. Even William Empson, that perceptive and somewhat overly ingenious prophet of ambiguity, finds himself unable to be completely permissive toward conflicting interpretations. In a long, curious essay arguing that the basic movement of *Ulysses* is toward a favorable ending, with the Blooms and Stephen united, he admits that there are difficulties, and that they spring from the kind of book it is: it "not only refuses to tell you the end of the story, it also refuses to tell you what the author thinks would have been a good end to the story." And yet almost in the same breath he can write as if he thought previous critics somehow at fault for not having come to *his* inferences about the book. "By the way, I have no patience with critics who say it is impossible ever to tell whether Joyce means a literary effect to be ironical or not; if they don't know this part isn't funny, they ought to." Well, but why should they be able to? Who is to mediate between Empson and those he attacks, or between Lawrance Thompson, in his interpretation of the book as comedy, and those critics with whom he is "decidedly at odds," Stuart Gilbert, Edmund Wilson, Harry Levin, David Daiches, and T. S. Eliot, each of whom assumes, he says, that "Joyce's artistic mode is essentially a non-comic mode, or that comedy in *Ulysses* is an effect rather than a cause"?

Can it possibly make no difference whether we laugh or do not laugh? Can we defend the book even as a realistic mixture, like life itself, unless we can state with some precision what the ingredients are that have been mixed together?

Rather than pursue such general questions about Joyce's admittedly difficult later works, it will be more useful to look closely at that earlier work for which no skeleton key has been thought necessary, *A Portrait of the Artist as a Young Man* (1916). Everyone seems by now agreed that it is a masterpiece in the modern mode. Perhaps we can accept it as that—indeed accept it as an unquestionably great work from any viewpoint —and still feel free to ask a few irreverent questions.

The structure of this "authorless" work is based on the growth of a sensitive boy to young manhood. The steps in his growth are obviously constructed with great care. Each of the first four sections ends a period of Stephen's life with what Joyce, in an earlier draft, calls an epiphany: a peculiar revelation of the inner reality of an experience, accompanied with great elation, as in a mystical religious experience. Each is followed by the opening of a new chapter on a very prosaic, even depressed level. Now here is clearly a careful structural preparation—for what? For a transformation, or for a merely cyclical return? Is the final exaltation a release from the depressing features of Irish life which have tainted the earlier experiences? Or is it the fifth turn in an endless cycle? And in either case, is Stephen always to be viewed with the same deadly seriousness with which he views himself? Is it to artistic maturity that he grows? As the young man goes into exile from Ireland, goes "to encounter for the millionth time the reality of experience and to forge in the smithy" of his soul "the uncreated conscience" of his race, are we to take this, with Harry Levin, as a fully serious portrait of the artist Dedalus, praying to his namesake Daedalus, to stand him "now and ever in good stead"? Or is the inflated style, as Mark Schorer tells us, Joyce's clue that the young Icarus is flying too close to the sun, with the "excessive lyric relaxation" of Stephen's final style punctuating "the illusory nature of the whole ambition"? The young man takes himself and his flight with deadly solemnity. Should we?

To see the difficulties clearly, let us consider three crucial episodes, all from the final section: his rejection of the priesthood, his exposition of what he takes to be Thomistic aesthetics, and his composition of a poem.

Is his rejection of the priesthood a triumph, a tragedy, or merely a comedy of errors? Most readers, even those who follow the new trend of reading Stephen ironically, seem to have read it as a triumph: the artist has rid himself of one of the chains that bound him. To Caroline Gordon, this is a serious misreading. "I suspect that Joyce's _Portrait_ has been misread by a whole generation." She sees the rejection as "the picture of a soul that is being damned for time and eternity caught in the act of foreseeing and foreknowing its damnation," and she cites in evidence the fall of Icarus and Stephen's own statement to Cranly that he is not afraid to make a mistake, "even a great mistake, a lifelong mistake and perhaps for eternity, too." Well, which *Portrait* do we choose, that of the artistic soul battling through successfully to his necessary freedom, or that of the child of God, choosing, like Lucifer, his own damnation? No two books could be further from each other than the two we envision here. There may be a sufficient core of what is simply interesting to salvage the book as a great work of the sensibility, but unless we are willing to retreat into babbling and incommunicable relativism, we cannot believe that it is *both* a portrait of the prisoner freed *and* a portrait of the soul placing itself in chains.

Critics have had even more difficulty with Stephen's aesthetic theory, ostensibly developed from Aquinas. Is the book itself, as Grant Redford tells us, an "objectification of an artistic proposition and a method announced by the central character," achieving for Joyce the "wholeness, harmony, and radiance" that Stephen celebrates in his theory? Or is it, as Father Noon says, an ironic portrait of Stephen's immature aesthetics? Joyce wanted to qualify Stephen's utterances, Father Noon tells us, "by inviting attention to his own more sophisticated literary concerns," and he stands apart from the Thomist aesthetics, watching Stephen miss the clue in his drive for an impersonal, dramatic narration. "The comparison of the artist with the God of the creation," taken "straight" by many critics, is for Father Noon "the climax of Joyce's ironic development of the Dedalus aesthetic."

Finally, what of the precious villanelle? Does Joyce intend it to be taken as a serious sign of Stephen's artistry, as a sign of his genuine but amusingly pretentious precocity, or as something else entirely?

> Are you not weary of ardent ways,
> Lure of the fallen seraphim?
> Tell no more of enchanted days.
>
> Your eyes have set man's heart ablaze
> And you have had your will of him.
> Are you not weary of ardent ways? . . .

Hardly anyone has committed himself in public about the

quality of this poem. Are we to smile at Stephen or pity him in his tortured longing? Are we to marvel at his artistry, or scoff at his conceit? Or are we merely to say, "How remarkable an insight into the kind of poem that would be written by an adolescent in love, if he were artistically inclined?" The poem, we are told, "enfolded him like a shining cloud, enfolded him like water with a liquid life: and like a cloud of vapour or like waters circumfluent in space the liquid letters of speech, symbols of the element of mystery, flowed forth over his brain." As we recall Jean Paul's formula for "romantic irony," "hot baths of sentiment followed by cold showers of irony," we can only ask here which tap has been turned on. Are we to swoon—or laugh?

Some critics will no doubt answer that all these questions are irrelevant. The villanelle is not to be judged but simply experienced; the aesthetic theory is, within the art work, neither true nor false but simply "true" to the art work—that is, true to Stephen's character at this point. To read modern literature properly we must refuse to ask irrelevant questions about it; we must accept the "portrait" and no more ask whether the character portrayed is good or bad, right or wrong than we ask whether a woman painted by Picasso is moral or immoral. "All facts of any kind," as Gilbert puts it, "mental or material, sublime or ludicrous, have an equivalence of value for the artist."

This answer, which can be liberating at one stage of our development in appreciating not only modern but all art, becomes less and less satisfactory the longer we look at it. It certainly does not seem to have been Joyce's basic attitude, though he was often misleading about it.[1] The creation and the enjoyment of art can never be a completely neutral activity. Though different works of art require different kinds of judgment for their enjoyment . . . no work, not even the shortest

---

[1] Richard Ellmann concludes that whether we know it or not, "Joyce's court is, like Dante's or Tolstoy's, always in session" (*James Joyce* [New York, 1959], p. 3). [W.B.]

lyric, can be written in complete moral, intellectual and aesthetic neutrality. We may judge falsely, we may judge unconsciously, but we cannot even bring the book to mind without judging its elements, seeing them as shaped into a given kind of thing. Even if we denied that the sequence of events has meaning in the sense of being truly sequential, that denial would itself be a judgment on the rightness of Stephen's actions and opinions at each stage: to decide that he is not growing is as much a judgment on his actions as to decide that he is becoming more and more mature. Actually everyone reads the book as some kind of progressive sequence, and to do so we judge succeeding actions and opinions to be more or less moral, sensitive, intellectually mature, than those they follow. If we felt that the question of Joyce's precise attitude toward Stephen's vocation, his aesthetics, and his villanelle were irrelevant, we would hardly dispute with each other about them. Yet I count in a recent check list at least fifteen articles and one full book disputing Joyce's attitude about the aesthetics alone.

Like most modern critics, I would prefer to settle such disputes by using internal rather than external evidence. But the experts themselves give me little hope of finding answers to my three problems by re-reading *Portrait* one more time. They all clutch happily at any wisp of comment or fragmentary document that might illuminate Joyce's intentions. And who can blame them?

The truth seems to be that Joyce was always a bit uncertain about his attitude toward Stephen. Anyone who reads Ellmann's masterful biography with this problem in mind cannot help being struck by the many shifts and turns Joyce took as he worked through the various versions. There is nothing especially strange in that, of course. Most "autobiographical" novelists probably encounter difficulty in trying to decide just how heroic their heroes are to be. But Joyce's explorations came just at a time when the traditional devices for control of distance were being repudiated, when doctrines of objectivity were in the air, and when people were taking seriously the idea that to evoke "reality" was a sufficient aim in art; the artist need not concern himself with judging or with specifying whether the reader should approve or disapprove, laugh or cry.

Now the traditional forms *had* specified in their very conceptions a certain degree of clarity about distance. If an author chose to write comedy, for example, he knew that his characters must at least to some degree be "placed" at a distance from the spectator's norms. This predetermination did not, of course, settle all of his problems. To balance sympathy and antipathy, admiration and contempt, was still a fundamental challenge, but it was a challenge for which there was considerable guidance in the practice of previous writers of comedy. If, on the other hand, he chose to write tragedy, or satire, or elegy, or celebration odes, or whatever, he could rely to some extent on conventions to guide him and his audience to a common attitude toward his characters.

The young Joyce had none of this to rely on, but he seems never to have sensed the full danger of his position. When, in his earliest years, he recorded his brief epiphanies—those bits of dialogue or description that were supposed to reveal the inner reality of things—there was always an implied identification of the recorder's norms and the reader's; both were spectators at the revealing moment, both shared in the vision of one moment of truth. Though some of the epiphanies are funny, some sad, and some mixed, the basic effect is always the same: an overwhelming sense—when they succeed—of what Joyce liked to call the "incarnation": Artistic Meaning has come to live in the world's body. The Poet has done his work.

Even in these early epiphanies there is difficulty with distance; the author inevitably expects the reader to share in his own preconceptions and interests sufficiently to catch, from each word or gesture, the precise mood or tone that they evoke for the author himself. But since complete identification with the author is a silent precondition for the success of such moments, the basic problem of distance is never a serious one. Even if the author and reader should differ in interpretation, they can share the sense of evoked reality.

It is only when Joyce places at the center of a long work a figure who experiences epiphanies, an epiphany-producing device, as it were, who is himself used by the real author as an object ambiguously distant from the norms of the work, that the complications of distance become incalculable. If he treats the author-figure satirically, as he does in much of *Stephen Hero*, that earlier, windier version of *Portrait*, then what happens to the quality of the epiphanies that *he* describes? Are they still genuine epiphanies or only what the misguided, callow youth *thinks* are epiphanies? If, as Joyce's brother Stanislaus has revealed, the word "hero" is satiric, can we take seriously that anti-hero's vision? Yet if the satirical mode is dropped, if the hero is made into a real hero, and if the reader is made to see things entirely as he sees them, what then happens to objectivity? The portrait is no longer an objective rendering of reality, looked at from a respectable aesthetic distance, but rather a mere subjective indulgence.

Joyce can be seen, in Ellmann's account, wrestling with this problem throughout the revisions. Unlike writers before Flaubert, he had no guidance from convention or tradition or fellow artists. Neither Flaubert nor James had established any sure ground to stand on. Both of them had, in fact, stumbled on the same hurdles, and though each had on occasion surmounted the difficulties, Joyce was in no frame of mind to look behind their claims as realists to the actual problems and lessons that lay beneath their evocative surfaces. A supreme egoist struggling to deal artistically with his own ego, a humorist who could not escape the comic consequences of his portrait of that inflated ego, he faced, in the completed *Stephen Hero*, what he had to recognize as a hodge-podge of irreconcilables. Is Stephen a pompous ass or not? Is his name deliberately ridiculous, as Stanislaus, who invented it, says? Or is it a serious act of symbolism? The way out seems inevitable, but it seems a retreat nonetheless: simply present the "reality" and let the reader judge. Cut all of the author's judgments, cut all of the adjectives, produce one long, ambiguous epiphany.[2]

Purged of the author's explicit judgment, the resulting work was so brilliant and compelling, its hero's vision so scintillating, that almost all readers overlooked the satiric and ironic content —except, of course, as the satire operated against *other* characters. So far as I know no one said anything about irony against Stephen until after *Ulysses* was published in 1922, with its opening in which Icarus-Stephen is shown with his wings clipped. Ironic readings did not become popular, in fact, until after the fragment of *Stephen Hero* was published in 1944. Readers of that work found, it is true, many authoritative confirmations of their exaltation of Stephen—for the most part in a form that might confirm anyone's prejudice against commentary. ". . . When he [Stephen] wrote it was always a mature and reasoned emotion which urged him." "This mood of indignation which was not guiltless of a certain superficiality was undoubtedly due to the excitement of release. . . . He acknowledged to himself in honest egoism that he could not take to heart the distress of a nation, the soul of which was antipathetic to his own, so bitterly as the indignity of a bad line of verse: but at the same time he was nothing in the world so little as an amateur artist." "Stephen did not attach himself to art in any spirit of youthful dilettantism but strove to pierce to the significant heart of everything." But readers were also faced with a good many denigrations of the hero. We can agree that *Portrait* is a better work because the immature author has been effaced; Joyce may indeed have found that effacing the com-

---

[2] See Denis Donoghue's "Joyce and the Finite Order," *Sewanee Review*, LXVIII (Spring, 1960), 256-73: "The objects [in *Portrait*] exist to provide a suitably piteous setting for Stephen as Sensitive Plant; they are meant to mark a sequence of experiences in the mode of *pathos*. . . . The lyric situation is insulated from probes, and there is far too much of this cosseting in the *Portrait*. . . . Drama or rhetoric should have warned Joyce that Stephen the aesthetic *alazon* needed nothing so urgently as a correspondingly deft *eiron;* lacking this, the book is blind in one eye" (p. 258). Joyce would no doubt reply—I think unfairly—that he intended Stephen as both *alazon* and *eiron*. [W.B.]

mentary was the only way he could obtain an air of maturity. But the fact remains that it is primarily to this immature commentary that we must go for evidence in deciphering the ironies of the later, purer work.

What we find in *Stephen Hero* is not a simple confirmation of any reading that we might have achieved on the basis of *Portrait* alone. Rather we find an extremely complicated view, combining irony and admiration in unpredictable mixtures. Thus the Thomist aesthetics "was in the main applied Aquinas and he set it forth plainly with a naif air of discovering novelties. This he did partly to satisfy his own taste for enigmatic roles and partly from a genuine predisposition in favour of all but the premisses of scholasticism." No one ever inferred, before this passage was available, anything like this precise and complex judgment on Stephen. The combination of blame and approval, we may be sure, is different in the finished *Portrait*; the implied author no doubt often repudiates the explicit judgments of the younger narrator who intrudes into *Stephen Hero*. But we can also be sure that his judgment has not become less complex. Where do we find, in any criticism of *Portrait* based entirely on internal evidence, the following kind of juxtaposition of Stephen's views with the author's superior insight? "Having by this *simple process* established the literary form of art as the most excellent he *proceeded to examine it in favour of his theory*, or, *as he rendered it*, to establish the relations which must subsist between the literary image, the work of art itself, and that energy which had imagined and fashioned it, that center of conscious, re-acting, particular life, the artist" (italics mine). Can we infer, from *Portrait*, that Joyce sees Stephen as simply rationalizing in favor of his theory? Did we guess that Joyce could refer to him mockingly as a "fiery-hearted revolutionary" and a "heaven-ascending essayist"? [3]

---

[3] One reviewer of *Stephen Hero* was puzzled to notice in it that the omniscient author, not yet purged in accordance with Joyce's theories of dramatic narration, frequently expresses biting criticism of the young Stephen. The earlier work thus seemed to him "much more cynical," and "much, much farther from the principles of detached classicism that had

In *Stephen Hero*, the author's final evaluation of the aesthetics is favorable but qualified: "Except for the eloquent and
arrogant peroration Stephen's essay was a careful exposition of
a carefully meditated theory of esthetic." Though it might be
argued that in the finished book he has cut out some of the
negative elements, such as the "eloquent and arrogant peroration," and has presented the pure theory in conversational form,
it is clear that Joyce himself judged his hero's theory in greater
detail than we could possibly infer from the final version alone.

Similar clarifications can be found in *Stephen Hero* of our
other two crucial problems, his rejection of the priesthood and
his poetic ability. For example, "He had swept the moment
into his memory . . . and . . . had brought forth some pages
of sorry verse." Can the hero of *Portrait* be thought of as writing
"sorry verse"? One would not think so, to read much of the
commentary by Joyce's critics.

But who is to blame them? Whatever intelligence Joyce
postulates in his reader—let us assume the unlikely case of its

---

been formulated before either book was written." How could the man
who wrote *Stephen Hero* go on and write, "in a mood of enraptured
fervour," a work like *Portrait? (Times Literary Supplement*, February 1,
1957, p. 64).

It is true that, once we have been alerted, signs of ironic intention
come rushing to our view. Those of us who now believe that Joyce is not
entirely serious in the passages on aesthetics must wonder, for example,
how we ever read them "straight." What did we make out of passages
like the following, in those old, benighted days before we saw what was
going on? "The lore which he was believed to pass his days brooding
upon so that it had rapt him from the companionship of youth was only
a garner of slender sentences from Aristotle's poetics and psychology and
a *Synopsis Philosophiæ Scholasticæ ad mentem divi Thomæ*. His thinking
was a dusk of doubt and selfmistrust, lit up at moments by the lightnings
of intuition. . . ." ". . . in those moments the world perished about his
feet as if it had been fireconsumed; and thereafter his tongue grew
heavy and he met the eyes of others with unanswering eyes for he felt that
the spirit of beauty had folded him round like a mantle and that in revery
at least he had been acquainted with nobility. But, when this brief pride
of silence upheld him no longer, he was glad to find himself still in the
midst of common lives, passing on his way amid the squalor and noise and
sloth of the city fearlessly and with a light heart" (opening pp. of Chap.
V). If this is not mockery, however tender, it is fustian. [W.B.]

being comparable to his own—will not be sufficient for precise inference of a pattern of judgments which is, after all, private to Joyce. And this will be true regardless of how much distance from his own hero we believe him to have achieved by the time he concluded his final version. We simply cannot avoid the conclusion that to some extent the book itself is at fault, regardless of its great virtues. Unless we make the absurd assumption that Joyce had in reality purged himself of all judgment by the time he completed his final draft, unless we see him as having really come to look upon all of Stephen's actions as equally wise or equally foolish, equally sensitive or equally meaningless, we must conclude that many of the refinements he intended in his finished *Portrait* are, for most of us, permanently lost. Even if we were now to do our homework like dutiful students, even if we were to study all of Joyce's work, even if we were to spend the lifetime that Joyce playfully said his novels demand, presumably we should never come to as rich, as refined, and as varied a conception of the quality of Stephen's last days in Ireland as Joyce had in mind. For some of us the air of detachment and objectivity may still be worth the price, but we must never pretend that a price was not paid.

ROBERT SCHOLES

Robert Scholes has taught at the University of Virginia and is Professor of English at the University of Iowa. He is the author of *Approaches to the Novel, The Cornell Joyce Collection: A Catalogue,* co-author with Richard Kain of *The Workshop of Daedalus,* and editor of *Learners and Discerners: A Newer Criticism.*

STEPHEN DEDALUS, POET OR ESTHETE?

The problem of Stephen Dedalus is one of the most curious and interesting in modern letters. One aspect of the problem has been brought to our attention recently in a very impressive book by Wayne C. Booth, *The Rhetoric of Fiction*. Mr. Booth notes that *A Portrait of the Artist as a Young Man* was not, by its first readers, thought to be an ironic work. It was after the publication of *Ulysses*, with its presentation of Stephen as the fallen Icarus, that the reassessment of Stephen's character began; and it was the publication of the *Stephen Hero* fragment in 1944 which really accelerated the movement toward a view of the novel as mainly ironic, with Stephen seen as a posturing esthete rather than an actual or even a potential artist. The most extreme version of this ironic view of Stephen has been proposed by Hugh Kenner, in his *Dublin's Joyce* (1955).

Joyce's Flaubertian refusal to provide authoritative commentary on his characters within his works seems to open the way to any possible interpretation, making a definitive or even a consensus interpretation extremely difficult. And, however much our new-critical yearnings make us want to consider *A Portrait* as a work-in-itself, we are led by Joyce's own writings in everwidening circles. If the Stephen in *Ulysses* is the same person

From *PMLA*, LXXXIX (September 1964), 484-489. Reprinted by permission of the Modern Language Association and Robert Scholes.

as the Stephen in *A Portrait*—and there seems to be no question about this—then we must consider *Ulysses* in interpreting *Portrait*. By a similar chain of reasoning we find ourselves led to *Stephen Hero*, with its theory of the epiphany, thence to Joyce's own Epiphanies—those little prose pieces which he wrote from his own observation and then often used as fictional incidents or descriptions in *Stephen Hero* and *A Portrait*—until finally we reluctantly discover that everything about Joyce is relevant in some way to our interpretation of *A Portrait*, and we either devote a large chunk of our lives to the problem of Joyce or give up the problem in despair. How much simpler the problem would be if we had only to consider Stephen as he appears in those works which Joyce meant for publication, in *A Portrait* and *Ulysses*; but the publication of *Stephen Hero* is equivalent for us to the opening of Pandora's box. It is too late now to go back. We can never recover our lost innocence.

I mean to suggest that since we cannot go back we must go on. Since we cannot rely on our innocence to preserve us from the dangers of misinterpretation, we must gain the maximum of experience. In a fallen critical world we must commit all the fallacies, including the intentional, in order to work out our own salvation. It is in this spirit that I wish to turn to one specific aspect of the problem of Stephen Dedalus, in the hope that it may illuminate the problem as a whole. The question is raised by Mr. Booth in his discussion of "The Problem of Distance in *A Portrait of the Artist*" (*Rhetoric of Fiction*, pp. 323-336). He focusses our attention on the poem which Stephen writes in the last chapter of the book: "Finally, what of the precious villanelle? Does Joyce intend it to be taken as a serious sign of Stephen's artistry, as a sign of his genuine but amusingly pretentious precocity, or as something else entirely. . . . Hardly anyone has committed himself in public about the quality of this poem. Are we to smile at Stephen or pity him in his tortured longing? Are we to marvel at his artistry, or scoff at his conceit?"

I think we can answer some of those questions, now, with considerable assurance—at least insofar as Joyce's intentions in the matter are concerned. And I hope to provide a generally satisfactory interpretation of the episode of the poem. We must begin by reviewing the composition of the poem in its narrative context. It follows directly the long episode of the esthetic discussion with Lynch, which closes with a rain-shower. Stephen and Lynch take refuge from the rain under the library arcade. There, after the shower, Stephen sees the girl who has most interested him in his youth. He has come to feel as alienated from her as from those aspects of Ireland he associates with her—the Gaelic League, the priests, and the comfortable hypocrisy of the Philistine citizens of Dublin, who are pre-occupied with piety but are neither spiritual nor religious. As he sees her going off demurely with some other girls after the shower, he wonders if he has judged her too harshly. At this point the episode closes. In the next sentence we are with Stephen as he wakes the following morning, after an enchanting dream in which he has "known the ecstasy of seraphic life."

As he wakes, Stephen finds that he has an idea for a poem, which he begins at once to compose. The composition of the poem is presented to us in detail during the next few pages of narration, along with Stephen's thoughts, which center on the girl, on other women who have called out to him in the street, and on the mysterious country woman who had invited the gentle Davin into her cottage; all of whom merge into a composite symbol of Irish womanhood—batlike souls waking to consciousness in darkness and secrecy. Between them and him lies the shadow of the Irish priesthood. To the priest, the girl (E.C.) "would unveil her soul's shy nakedness, to one who was but schooled in the discharging of a formal rite rather than to him, a priest of the eternal imagination, transmuting the daily bread of experience into the radiant body of everliving life." Despite his bitterness Stephen comes, through the composition of the poem, to an understanding of her innocence, an equilibrium, a stasis, in which his new understanding and pity balance his old desire and bitterness. He turns, finally, from thoughts of the girl to a vision of the temptress of his villanelle, a personification of a feminine ideal, something like the white goddess-muse of Robert Graves's mythology. Stephen's spiritual copulation with her is a symbolic equivalent for that moment of inspiration when "in the virgin womb of the imagination the word was made flesh."

A glow of desire kindled again his soul and fired and fulfilled all his body. Conscious of his desire she was waking from odorous sleep, the temptress of his villanelle. Her eyes, dark and with a look of languor, were opening to his eyes. Her nakedness yielded to him, radiant, warm, odorous and lavishlimbed, enfolded him like a shining cloud, enfolded him like water with a liquid life: and like a cloud of vapour or like waters circumfluent in space the liquid letters of speech, symbols of the element of mystery, flowed forth over his brain. [*P*, 223.]

The temptress of his dream suggests his service to art, just as at the end of the previous chapter the girl on the beach, the "envoy from the fair courts of life," symbolizes the freedom of life as opposed to the cloistered virtue offered Stephen in the priesthood: "To live, to err, to fall, to triumph, to recreate life out of life!" The creation of life out of life is the privilege of both the lover and the artist. The physical copulation of the human animal and the spiritual copulation of the artist in which the word is made flesh are valid and complementary manifestations of the same human impulse toward creation. There is no hint of mockery in Joyce's reverent attitude toward the creative process.

In order to fulfill the term of Stephen's esthetic gestation, it was necessary for Joyce to present us with a created thing, with a literary work which was the product of his inspiration. He chose for this purpose the Villanelle of the Temptress. Why? And what, as Mr. Booth asks, are we to make of it? Here we must turn to biographical information and manuscript material for help. The poem itself (or a version of it) was actually written by Joyce long before *A Portrait*. It dates from one of his early collections of verse, probably the lost "Shine and Dark" of 1900 or 1901 (see Stanislaus Joyce, *My Brother's Keeper*, pp. 85-86). It is a distinctly better poem than most of the surviving fragments of that collection, as the reader may verify by consulting Richard Ellmann's *James Joyce*, pp. 84-85, where these fragments have been published. That Joyce thought it superior is attested to by his keeping it for 15 years though he destroyed nearly every other sample of his pre-*Chamber Music* verse, leaving us only the tattered fragments which his brother saved. But Joyce's over-riding reason for using this particular poem must have been its subject. It was the perfect poem, and it had been written by himself when he was only slightly younger than Stephen. The poem thus satisfied both the naturalistic urge and the symbolic urge in Joyce. As fact and symbolic artifact it was indisputably the right thing. (His continuing interest in this subject and the poetic materials of the villanelle is evidenced by his re-use of them in the poem "Nightpiece" of *Pomes Penyeach*, which is very close to Stephen's poem in theme and imagery, though very different in prosody.)

How perfectly its subject matter suited Joyce's purposes can be seen only when the poem is understood. To this reader it seems obvious that the failure of critics to understand the function of the villanelle stems from their failure to understand what the poem is about. It is ironic that in this one instance, in which Joyce himself has provided a commentary on his own work, such problems in understanding should have arisen; for the poem comes to us, in *A Portrait*, imbedded not only in the circumstances of its creation but in an elaborate explication as well. But even with Joyce's explicatory narrative the poem is a difficult one. The difficulty stems from its complexity of thought. It is a far richer poem than the ninety-ish verses which it appears to resemble. So that my commentary may be specific, here is the full text of the poem:

> Are you not weary of ardent ways,
> Lure of the fallen seraphim?
> Tell no more of enchanted days.
>
> Your eyes have set man's heart ablaze
> And you have had your will of him.
> Are you not weary of ardent ways?

Above the flame the smoke of praise
Goes up from ocean rim to rim.
Tell no more of enchanted days.

Our broken cries and mournful lays
Rise in one eucharistic hymn.
Are you not weary of ardent ways?

While sacrificing hands upraise
The chalice flowing to the brim.
Tell no more of enchanted days.

And still you hold our longing gaze.
With languorous look and lavish limb!
Are you not weary of ardent ways?
Tell no more of enchanted days.

The first question which must be resolved is the nature of
the person addressed. She is, as I have suggested above, a
composite figure, but I want now to elaborate on her composition, taking my cues from the explication provided. In describing the moment of inspiration as that instant when "In the
virgin womb of the imagination the word was made flesh," the
narrator has established a parallel between artistic creation and
the divine begetting of the Son of God. The next sentences
gloss this parallel and provide an interpretation of the first
tercet:

Gabriel the seraph had come to the virgin's chamber. An afterglow
deepened within his spirit, whence the white flame had passed,
deepening into a rose and ardent light. That rose and ardent light
was her strange wilful heart, strange that no man had known
or would know, wilful from before the beginning of the world: and
lured by that ardent roselike glow the choirs of the seraphim were
falling from heaven. [*P*, 217.]

In this violently compressed fusion of myth and theology the
ardent heart of the virgin mother of the redeemer is seen
as the cause of the fall of the rebellious angels. This is a variation on the *felix culpa* notion that Adam's fall was fortunate

because its result was the birth of the redeemer. Joyce's version upsets chronology and causality as well as theology by making one of the results of Satan's fall function as the prime cause of that fall. Mary is the "Lure of the fallen seraphim." The poem is addressed, initially at any rate, to her.

The second tercet is explicated similarly: "The roselike glow sent forth its rays of rhyme: ways, days, blaze, praise, raise. Its rays burned up the world, consumed the hearts of men and angels: the rays from the rose that was her wilful heart." Here the ardent glow is seen to perform two functions. In Stephen's mind it inspires rays of rhyme for his artistic creation. In its more general manifestation it has consumed the hearts of men and angels.

In the third tercet the smoke from the burning heart of man rises as "incense ascending from the altar of the world." At this point Stephen's thoughts turn from the earth as a "ball of incense" to the phrase "an ellipsoidal ball," which is an echo of vulgar student scatology coming into Stephen's mind by association and breaking the spell of inspiration. His thoughts wander through all the various female associations mentioned above until his image of himself as "a priest of the eternal imagination transmuting the daily bread of experience into the radiant body of everliving life" returns his mind to the altar and incense of the villanelle and he composes the fourth and fifth tercets around the image of the eucharist. The "smoke of praise" and the rimmed ocean suggest the thurible and the chalice—images which Stephen handles in the poem, though he will "never swing the thurible before the tabernacle" in actuality. After his mind has wandered back again to E. C. and his youthful romantic feelings for her, his thoughts dissolve in the moment of spiritual copulation quoted above. Here he finds his image for the "languorous look and lavish limb" of the conclusion.

The paradox of the Virgin as Temptress has given the whole poem a peculiar tone, which, if we did not consider carefully, we might be tempted to write off as merely blasphemous. But the poem is not *merely* anything. It is a commonplace of Biblical exegesis that Eve, in the Old Testament, is a type of Mary in the New Testament, just as Adam is a type of Jesus. Joyce's awareness of this derives from his reading of St. Augustine and other Church Fathers, as shown in this passage from the "Oxen of the Sun" section of *Ulysses*:

Desire's wind blasts the thorntree but after it becomes from a bramblebush to be a rose upon the rood of time. Mark me now. In woman's womb word is made flesh but in the spirit of the maker all flesh that passes becomes the word that shall not pass away. This is the postcreation. *Omnis caro ad te veniet.* No question but her name is puissant who aventried the dear corse of our Agenbuyer, Healer and Herd, our mighty mother and mother most venerable and Bernardus saith aptly that she hath an *omnipotentiam deiparae supplicem,* that is to wit, an almightiness of petition because she is the second Eve and she won us, saith Augustine too, whereas that other, our grandam, which we are all linked upon with by successive anastomosis of navelcords sold us all, seed, breed and generation, for a penny pippin. [*U,* 39.]

Beyond the parallel between Eve and Mary, Joyce seems to have in mind a similar and even more paradoxical parallel between Satan and Gabriel. Satan literally fell from heaven, but Gabriel was lured "to the virgin's chamber" so that the word could be made flesh. And Stephen himself has known in the arms of his dream temptress "the ecstasy of *seraphic* life" [my italics]. Thus the term "fallen seraphim" of the first tercet applies not only to Satan but to Gabriel as well, and finally, by his own imaginative extension, to Stephen himself and the male principle in general—what may be said to be represented by that rising-fallen pheonix culprit HCE in *Finnegans Wake.* And, by a similar mental process the temptress can be Eve in relation to Satan, Mary to Gabriel, E. C. to Stephen, and the female principle in general—the Anna Livia Plurabelle of *Finnegans Wake.*

The medievalness of Joyce's mind can hardly be overemphasized. Not only is he capable of a medieval kind of religious parody without blasphemy (comparable to the *Second Shepherds' Play* and other Biblical romps) but he thinks in types and tropes constantly. The whole "metempsychosis" motif in *Ulysses* is allegorical in its operation, and the various multi-characters of *Finnegans Wake* are conceived in that medieval spirit which could not consider Hercules, even, without seeing Christ superimposed on him. The kind of mental process which culminates in *Finnegans Wake* seems to be operating in Joyce's handling of the villanelle in *A Portrait*. His original conception of the poem may even have been trivial. In *Stephen Hero* we are told that the insipid epiphany of the Young Lady and the Young Gentleman set Stephen composing "some ardent verses which he entitled 'Vilanelle [sic] of the Temptress'." But by the time he re-wrote the last part of *A Portrait* for publication he had seen larger possibilities in the poem, which he exploited by connecting its inspiration to Stephen's glimpse of E. C. at the library (instead of the Young Lady and Gentleman) and providing the poem with the narrative commentary which we now have. We can not be sure, of course, that we are dealing with the same poem. Joyce's drastic revision of "Tilly" for *Pomes Penyeach*, in which he completely reversed the mood and meaning of the poem from a sentimental idyll to a bitter cry of anguish, is warning enough to make us proceed with caution here. (See Chester Anderson's essay in *PMLA*, LXXIII [June 1958], 285.) But Joyce certainly reinterpreted the poem, possibly revising it in accordance with his new view, making it unmistakably clear from the context that the "you" addressed in the opening line is, initially at least, the Virgin Mary.

Eve is our first mother and Mary is our second, a "second Eve" as Augustine saith (according to Stephen in the "Oxen of the Sun"). But in the Bible Eve figures as first temptress as well as first mother. And this feminine principle—irrational, sensual, seductive—becomes in Joyce's inversion of traditional typology equally the property of Mary and Eve. The ardent heart of the Virgin lured Gabriel the seraph to her chamber and precipitated, in advance of her own birth, the fall of Satan and his seraphim; who, through Eve, caused the fall of man. Not only are Eve and Mary fused in the image of the Temptress (and that other temptress, Lilith, perhaps) but such other figures as E. C. herself, girls who have laughed at Stephen or called out to him in the street, and the mysterious woman who invited Davin into her cottage. The last woman is of especial significance. She brings the Celtic Twilight into Joyce's narrative. Davin rejected her offer partly through his innate goodness and innocence, and partly through a vague fear that she was not all she seemed to be. The Irish fairies, the Shee, hover over Davin's story. And one in particular hovers over Stephen's poem. "The Leanhaun Shee (fairy mistress)" [Yeats wrote in his collection of *Fairy and Folk Tales of the Irish Peasantry*, 1888],

seeks the love of mortals. If they refuse, she must be their slave; if they consent, they are hers, and can only escape by finding another to take their place. The fairy lives on their life, and they waste away. Death is no escape from her. She is the Gaelic muse, for she gives inspiration to those she persecutes. The Gaelic poets die young, for she is restless and will not let them remain long on earth —this malignant phantom. . . .

She is of the dreadful solitary fairies. To her have belonged the greatest of the Irish poets, from Oisin down to the last century. (Pp. 80, 146.)

Though Oliver Gogarty addressed him as the Wandering Ængus (letter in Ms at Cornell), Joyce had specifically repudiated the "Gaelic League" approach to literature. Stephen's poem is more Catholic than Celtic. Its literary models are the poems of the nineties: the villanelles of Ernest Dowson and such "mother" poems as Swinburne's "Mater Triumphalis" (especially lines 33-44 and 93-105), and Francis Thompson's "The After Woman." And its ancestors are such romantic treatments of this theme as Blake's "The Mental Traveller" and Keats's "La Belle Dame Sans Merci." Thus, Stephen's villanelle must be read partly as an effort in this recognizable sub-genre, where its compressed coolness compares quite favorably with the feverish looseness of Swinburne and Co. But the Leanhaun Shee, nevertheless, haunts Stephen's poem because it is a muse-poem. Joyce has unerringly selected for Stephen's single poetic effort in *A Portrait* a great poetical archetype— what Robert Graves has called the "single poetic theme."

Joyce, steeped in Catholic theology more strongly than in Celtic mythology, nevertheless knew his Yeats as well as anyone and knew most of the nineteenth-century Irish poets as well—as his essays on Mangan indicate. He might even have known a muse-poem such as Thomas Boyd's "To the Leanán Sidhe." In the "Villanelle of the Temptress" Stephen is writing a poem to his muse, who is a traditionally feminine and mythic figure, though the imagery through which she is presented is drawn almost exclusively from Catholic ritual and ceremony. He sees himself a priest of the imagination celebrating a eucharistic ritual of transubstantiation—the daily bread of experience becoming the radiant body of everlasting life—and a ritual of incarnation as well—in the virgin womb of the imagination the word is made flesh. And to render these qualities in his vision artistically he presents them in a rigidly prescribed esthetic form, the villanelle, in which the temptress-muse is worshiped in a eucharistic ritual. From the heart set ablaze by the languorous look of the temptress rises incense of praise. For the virgin who lured the seraphim from heaven a flowing chalice is raised in celebration.

The strange woman who tempted Davin has been recognized by Stephen, while writing the poem, as a "figure of the womanhood of her country." And so is Stephen's temptress such a figure. Like the Leanan Shee herself, Ireland is a female figure who destroys those who serve her. They call her Kathleen ni Houlihan or Dark Rosaleen or the Shan Van Vocht or the old sow that eats her farrow. Stephen's particular problem is to help the bat-like soul of this female to awake, to serve her without being destroyed by her; to forge in the smithy of his own soul the uncreated conscience of *her* race. He wants, among other things, to turn her from the enchanted Celtic Twilight to the daylight of his own time. The villanelle is half his self-dedication to a hopeless task and half a prayer for release from the pitiless muse and country whose service is his accepted destiny. The appearance of the milk woman in the opening scene of *Ulysses* starts Stephen's mind working along these same lines (pp. 15-16).

That Joyce intended the poem to be the product of genuine inspiration can be readily demonstrated by an examination of the manuscripts. In Trieste, during the years 1907 to 1914, Joyce kept a notebook in which he jotted down many thoughts and descriptions later used in *A Portrait* and *Ulysses*. Whole sentences and large parts of paragraphs on Cranly, Lynch, Buck Mulligan, and Stephen's parents come from his notebook, which Joyce began after he had abandoned the *Stephen Hero* version of *A Portrait*. The section of this notebook labelled "Esthetic" is directly relevant to Stephen's composition of the villanelle. Here are several entries from this section of the notebook:

An enchantment of the heart.

The instant of inspiration is a spark so brief as to be invisible. The reflection of it on many sides at once from a multitude of cloudy circumstances with no one of which it is united save by the bond of merest possibility veils its afterglow in an instant in a first confusion of form. This is the instant in which the word is made flesh.

There is a morning inspiration as there is a morning knowledge about the windless hour when the moth escapes from the chrysalis, and certain plants bloom and the feverfit of madness comes on the insane.

All three of these entries are intended as statements of Joyce's esthetic theory. The first phrase, "an enchantment of the heart," finds its way into Stephen's discourse to describe the moment when the esthetic image is first conceived in the imagination [*P*, 213]. The other two esthetic entries quoted here were employed by Joyce in the episode of the villanelle, and the first phrase was repeated there, making a bridge between esthetic theory and practice. Stephen woke early:

It was that windless hour of dawn when madness wakes and strange plants open to the light and the moth flies forth silently.

An enchantment of the heart! The night had been enchanted.

In a dream or vision he had known the ecstasy of seraphic life. Was it an instant of enchantment only or long hours and days and years and ages?

The instant of inspiration seemed now to be reflected from all sides at once from a multitude of cloudy circumstance of what happened or what might have happened. The instant flashed forth like a point of light and now from cloud on cloud of vague circumstance confused form was veiling softly its afterglow. O! In the virgin womb of the imagination the word was made flesh. [P, 217.]

The words and images are drawn directly from the esthetic jottings in the notebook, but they have been transformed from exposition to narration. Joyce has deliberately set out in his description of Stephen's inspiration to fulfill the theoretical requirements he had himself set up for such inspiration. The inspiration and the poem are both intended to be genuine. And the poem, after all, is a poem about inspiration. The emotions and sensations felt by Stephen in his spiritual copulation with the temptress-muse provide him with some of the vocabulary he employs in the poem. In his esthetic discourse with Lynch, Stephen remarked, "When we come to the phenomena of artistic conception, artistic gestation and artistic reproduction, I require a new terminology and a new personal experience." The episode of the villanelle provides him with both experience and terminology, locked in such a tight embrace that they produce not a theory but a poem. It is at this point that Stephen ceases to be an esthete and becomes a poet.

IV

❀◆

Explanatory Notes

KEY TO ABBREVIATIONS

The following abbreviations appear throughout the Explanatory Notes. Sources are cited fully except for the Joyce texts, which are listed in the Bibliography. Biblical quotations in these notes are sometimes from the Rheims-Douay translation of the Vulgate Bible and sometimes from the King James version. (Cf. note to 113.12.)

WORKS BY JOYCE

Critical Writings—*The Critical Writings of James Joyce*
D—*Dubliners*
FW—*Finnegans Wake*
Letters—*Letters of James Joyce*
P—*A Portrait of the Artist as a Young Man*
SH—*Stephen Hero*
U—*Ulysses*

WORKS BY OTHERS

Anderson—C. G. Anderson, "The Sacrificial Butter." *Accent*, XII (Winter 1952), 3-13.
Atherton—James Joyce, *A Portrait of the Artist as a Young Man*, edited with an introduction and notes by J. S. Atherton. London: Heineman, 1964; or letter to me, April 24, 1968.

Byrne—J. F. Byrne, *Silent Years: An Autobiography with Memoirs of James Joyce and Our Ireland*. New York: Farrar, Straus and Young, 1953.

Cath. Encyc.—*The Catholic Encyclopedia*, edited by Charles G. Habermann and others. New York: The Encyclopedia Press, 1913. 16 vols.

Clongowes Record—T. Corcoran, S.J., *The Clongowes Record: 1814-1932*. Dublin: Browne and Nolan, n.d.

Colum—Mary and Padraic Colum, *Our Friend James Joyce*. Garden City: Doubleday and Company, 1958.

Davitt—Michael Davitt, *The Fall of Feudalism in Ireland*. New York: Harper and Brothers, 1904.

Diary—Stanislaus Joyce, *The Dublin Diary of Stanislaus Joyce*, edited by George Harris Healey. Ithaca, N.Y.: Cornell University Press, 1962.

DNB—*Dictionary of National Biography*, edited by Leslie Stephen and Sidney Lee. New York: The Macmillan Company; London: Smith, Elder and Company, 1885-1901. 63 vols.

Ellmann—Richard Ellmann, *James Joyce*. New York: Oxford University Press, 1959.

Encyc. Brit.—*The Encyclopædia Britannica*, 14th edition. London and New York: Encyclopædia Britannica, 1929. 24 vols.

Fitzpatrick—Edward A. Fitzpatrick, ed., *St. Ignatius and the Ratio Studiorum*. New York: McGraw-Hill Book Company, 1933. (Includes English translations of the *Ratio Studiorum* and the *Constitutions of the Society of Jesus*.)

Gorman—Herbert Gorman, *James Joyce*, rev. ed. New York: Rinehart and Company, 1948.

Hall and Albion—W. P. Hall and R. G. Albion, *A History of England and the British Empire*, 3rd ed. Boston: Ginn and Company, 1953.

Harmon—A manuscript of annotations to the *Portrait*, prepared by Professor Maurice Harmon of the University of Notre Dame.

Hayden and Hartog—Mary Hayden and Marcus Hartog, "The Irish Dialect of English: Its Origins and Vocabulary," *Fortnightly Review*, LXXXV, New Series (April 1909), 775-785; (May 1909), 933-947.

Kenner—Hugh Kenner, *Dublin's Joyce*. Bloomington: Indiana University Press, 1956.

Mac Lochlainn—Mr. Alf Mac Lochlainn, Keeper of Manuscripts in the National Library of Ireland, helped me in the summer of 1964 to understand some things about Dublin speech and geography.

Monte Cristo—Alexandre Dumas, *The Count of Monte Cristo*. New York: A. L. Burt and Company, n.d. 2 vols.

Noon—William T. Noon, S.J., *Joyce and Aquinas* (Yale University Studies in English," Vol. CXXXIII). New Haven: Yale University Press, 1957.

O'Brien—R. B. O'Brien, *Life of Charles Stewart Parnell*. New York: Harper and Brothers, 1898. 2 vols.

OED—*The Oxford English Dictionary*, edited by James A. H. Murray and others. Corrected re-issue. Oxford: The Clarendon Press, 1933. 12 vols. and suppl.

Partridge—Eric Partridge, *A Dictionary of Slang and Unconventional English*, 5th. ed. New York: The Macmillan Company, 1961.

Prep. for Death—St. Alphonsus M. Liguori, *Preparation for Death*. Dublin: James Duffy and Company, n.d.

P. W. Joyce—Patrick Weston Joyce, *English as We Speak It in Ireland*. London: Longmans, Green and Company, 1910.

Ratio—See entry for Fitzpatrick.

Ryan—In the summer of 1964, in the Bailey in Duke Street, Mr. John Ryan—Dubliner, former Clongowian, present Joycean—helped me to understand several expressions in the *Portrait*.

Scholes and Kain—Robert Scholes and Richard M. Kain, eds., *The Workshop of Daedalus: James Joyce and the Raw Materials for A Portrait of the Artist as a Young Man*. Evanston, Ill.: Northwestern University Press, 1965.

Stanislaus—Stanislaus Joyce, *My Brother's Keeper*, edited with an introduction and notes by Richard Ellmann. New York: The Viking Press, 1958.

Sullivan—Kevin Sullivan, *Joyce among the Jesuits*. New York: Columbia University Press, 1958.

Thom's—*Thom's Business Directory of Dublin and Suburbs for the Year 1906* ("First Annual Publication"). Dublin: Alexander Thom and Company, 1906.

Vice Versâ—F. Anstey, *Vice Versâ: Or a Lesson to Fathers*. London: John Murray, 1920.

EDITORIAL NOTE

Lines in the text of *A Portrait of the Artist as Young Man* are counted from the beginning of the text on the page, and line spaces are not counted.

Epigraph: Et ignotas animum dimittit in artes. This picture of Daedalus "applying his mind to obscure arts" comes from Ovid's *Metamorphoses*, VIII, 188.

CHAPTER I

7.01 *Once upon a time.* The first two pages of *P* have been analyzed most ingeniously by Hugh Kenner, who points out that they "enact the entire action in microcosm." (See pp. 418-420 of this edition.)

7.04 *tuckoo.* Harmon suggests "cuckoo" as an appropriate name for Stephen. The baby cuckoo is an alien because the female lays her eggs in another bird's nest. Joyce's father wrote to him on January 31, 1931: "I wonder do you recollect the old days in Brighton Square, when you were Babie Tuckoo, and I used to take you out in the Square and tell you all about the moo-cow that used to come down from the mountain and take little boys across?" (*Letters*, III, 212.) The Joyce family moved from Brighton Square in 1884, when Joyce was two.

7.06 *a glass.* A monocle.

7.08 *lemon platt.* A twisted stick of lemon-flavored candy.

7.09-10 *O, the wild rose blossoms.* "The song is an old sentimental favorite, *Lily Dale.* The second line ought to be 'On the little green grave,' but this is a song taught to a very small child and so for *grave* is substituted the neutral *place.*" (Kelleher, "The Perceptions of James Joyce," *Atlantic Monthly*, CCI [March 1958], 84.)

7.21 *uncle Charles.* Joyce's great-uncle William O'Connell came from Cork to stay with the Joyce family while they were at Bray (1887-1892). (Ellmann, p. 23.) See 26.12, 60.01.

7.21 *Dante.* Mrs. "Dante" ("Aunt") Hearn Conway from Cork joined the Joyce family shortly after their move to Bray in 1887. (Ellmann, p. 24.)

7.24 *Michael Davitt.* Davitt (1846-1906) was an Irish revolutionist who founded the Land League, which aimed to make Ireland socialist.

7.25 *Parnell.* Charles Stewart Parnell (1846-1891) was the "Chief" of the Irish nationalist movement until he was named an adulterer in 1889. See 27.13, 31.23, 32.03, 36.20.

7.25 *cachou.* A silvered aromatic pill or pastille made of licorice, cashew nut, or gum, and used to sweeten the breath.

8.01ff *The Vances.* A chemist named James Vance and his family, Protestants, lived in the same building with the Joyces in Bray. "The Vances' eldest child, four months younger than James [Joyce], was a pretty girl named Eileen, and the two fathers often spoke half-seriously of uniting their first-born. Dante Conway warned James that if he played with Eileen he would certainly go to hell. . . ." (Ellmann, p. 25.)

8.07 *the eagles will come and pull out his eyes.* According to the epiphanies these are the words of Mr. Vance, and Joyce invented the rhyme which follows. See p. 267 of this edition.

8.17 *the prefects.* Teachers who have authority over a class or organization. Not to be confused with the "prefect of studies." (See 44.02.)

8.20 *the fringe of his line.* The "line" referred to is the "third line" (see *P*, 8.25), to which Stephen belongs because he is under thirteen years. See 11.10.

8.24 *Rody Kickham.* Twenty-two boys besides Stephen are mentioned in Chapter I, if "the Spaniard" and "the little Portuguese" are included. Many of them can be identified with Joyce's classmates from *The Clongowes Record*, pp. 165-297. In the order of the appearance of their names they are listed below, with their possible real-life counterparts and their years of attendance:

> Rody Kickham—Rodolph Kickham, Dublin, 1888-1893.
> Nasty Roche—George Reddington Roche, Athenry, 1883-1889. (Eight other Roches were contemporaries of Joyce at Clongowes.) (See *P*, 8.26.)
> Cantwell—John Cantwell, Dublin, 1888-1889; Thomas Cantwell, Clonmel, 1885-1891. (See *P*, 9.14.)
> Cecil Thunder—Cecil Thunder, Dublin, 1889-1894. (See *P*, 9.17.)
> Jack Lawton—John Lawton, Midleton, 1890-1896 and 1898. (See *P*, 10.02.)
> Wells—Charles Wells, Dublin, 1888-1890;

H. Wells, Dublin, 1888-1890. (See *P*, 10.29.)

Simon Moonan—No Moonans listed. (See *P*, 11.15.)

Saurin—Michael Saurin, Hill of Down, Westmeath, 1887-1893. (See *P*, 13.03.)

Fleming—Aloysius Fleming, Youghal, 1891-1894. (See *P*, 13.12.)

Paddy Rath—Patrick Rath, Enniscorthy and Argentina, 1886-1891. (See *P*, 13.31.)

Jimmy Magee—James Magee, Dublin, 1889-1892. (See *P*, 13.31.)

the Spaniard—José Arana y Lupardo, Bilbao, Spain, 1890-1892. (See *P*, 13.32.)

the little Portuguese—None listed. (See *P*, 13.33.)

[Peter Stanislaus] Little—Stanislaus Little, Monkstown, Dublin, 1886-1890. (His two brothers, Ignatius and Dominick, were also there in Joyce's day, but Stanislaus was the one who died.) (See *P*, 234.03.)

Athy—None listed. (See *P*, 25.01.)

Kickham's brother—Alexander Kickham, Dublin, 1886-1890. (See *P*, 40.13.)

Barnes—None listed. (See *P*, 41.21.)

Flowers—None listed. (See *P*, 41.22.)

Tusker ("Lady") Boyle—None listed. (See *P*, 42.9.)

Corrigan—None listed. (See *P*, 44.15.)

Dominic Kelly—Dominick Kelly, Waterford, 1886-1890. (See *P*, 46.22.)

Tom Furlong—Thomas Furlong, Dublin, 1889-1894. (See *P*, 49.25.)

8.26 *Nasty Roche*. See 8.25.

8.27 *greaves in his number*. Shinguards in his locker. (*OED*)

8.33 *Stephen Dedalus*. The name "Stephen" suggests St. Stephen, a Jew of Greek education who became the first Christian martyr when he was stoned to death after his conviction for blasphemy. (Acts 7:57-58.) He re-enacts the crucifixion, as Parnell later was to do, in Joyce's view. Joyce as well as Stephen identified himself with these and other martyrs. St. Stephen's Green in South Dublin, on the south side of which University College was situated, is also named for St. Stephen. (See *P*, 249.10, "crossing Stephen's, that is, my green.") "Dedalus" is usually spelled "Daedalus," a spelling which Joyce used when he first employed the name "Stephen

Daedalus" as a pseudonym when his first *Dubliners* stories were published in George Russell's (AE's) *Irish Homestead* in 1904. Daedalus was the mythical Greek inventor who built the labyrinth for King Minos of Crete to contain the minotaur. He and his son, Icarus, escaped from Crete by flying on wings which Daedalus fashioned of feathers and beeswax. Icarus disregarded his father's advice and in his pride flew too near the sun so that his wings melted and he plunged to his death in the sea. Icarus is also identified with Lucifer, another prideful soarer, so that Stephen's name suggests that he is martyr, maker, exile, Hebrew, Christian, Greek, and prideful sinner.

9.14 Cantwell. See 8.25.

9.17 Cecil Thunder. See 8.25.

9.21 the castle. The main building at Clongowes had been a castle.

9.28 peach on. "Inform on." (Partridge, OED.)

9.29 the rector. For detailed appraisals of the Reverend John S. Conmee, S.J., see "Clongowes and Father Conmee," *The Irish Monthly,* XXXVIII (August 1910), 424; Sullivan, pp. 15ff.; and Ellmann, pp. 27f and *passim.* Joyce liked him: see *U*, pp. 116ff. The rector is a kind of pope in the college: "It is the office of the Rector to take as it were the whole college on his shoulders. . . ." (*Constitutions,* Fitzpatrick, p. 92) His name is given at *P*, 59.05.

9.30 his soutane. A long, buttoned black gown with sleeves which is still the ordinary garment worn by Jesuits.

10.02 Jack Lawton's. See 8.25.

10.07 change the number. Stephen makes this change at *P*, 15.08. Joyce entered Clongowes on September 1, 1888. The Christmas holiday began that year on Thursday, December 20. Assuming that Stephen is running according to Joyce's clock and that he does not count the day of departure and that he changes the number the night before the day ahead, the day is Tuesday, October 4, 1888. Ellmann suggests, however, that Joyce "really was pushed into the square ditch or cesspool by a fellow-pupil and laid up with fever as a result, probably in the spring of 1891. . . ." (p. 27.) But since both Wells boys left Clongowes in 1890, it would seem more likely that the push took place in 1890. See 8.25 and 19.05.

10.11 from which window Hamilton Rowan had thrown his hat on the haha. ". . . Hamilton Rowan, a patriot and friend of Wolfe Tone [see 20.08], fled to the castle after his conviction in 1794 for sedition. He shut its door just as the soldiers were shooting, so that their bullets entered the door; then he threw his hat on the haha as a decoy, and let himself through a secret door into a tower room. His pursuers were fooled, thinking he had left, and he was able afterwards to make good his escape to France." (Ellmann, p. 29.) A haha is a fence or hedge or wall set in a ditch around a garden or park so as not to hide the view from within.

Joyce gave the name Richard Rowan to the hero of *Exiles*.

10.19 *Doctor Cornwell's Spelling Book*. "Doctor James Cornwell was the editor, alone and in collaboration, of an 'educational series' for young people." (Sullivan, p. 44n.)

10.22 Wolsey. English cardinal and statesman (1475-1530).

10.29 *Wells*. See 8.25 and 10.07.

10.29 *square ditch*. This ditch is not square; it is the ditch of the square. The square is an open water closet behind the dormitory with a slate trough running diagonally across it at the hypotenuse. The ditch is the cesspool for this w.c., just as the "square prefect" is its overseer. See *P*, 42.20 for "smugging in the square" and *P*, 43.11ff. for a partial description. For "slates in the yard" see *P*, 81.09.

10.30 *swop his little snuffbox for Wells's seasoned hacking chestnut, the conqueror of forty*. The contest was to swing one chestnut on a string against another swung by the opponent until one or the other smashed. "Conqueror of forty" probably does not mean that Wells's chestnut had smashed forty other chestnuts: it might, for example, have smashed four which were "conquerors of ten."

When Joyce was at Clongowes he had a tiny snuffbox in the form of a little black coffin. In later life Joyce dreamed that Molly Bloom threw a black coffin at Bloom and the little snuffbox at him, saying to each, "I have done with you." (Gorman, p. 283n.)

10.34 *Brigid*. The Joyce family had servants during John Joyce's palmy days at Bray.

11.01 *Mozambique Channel*. Mozambique, in what was Portuguese East Africa, was St. Francis Xavier's first stop on his way from Portugal to the East Indies. Stanislaus says of Dante that "besides teaching my brother to read and to write, with some elementary arithmetic and geography, she inculcated a good deal of very bigoted Catholicism and bitterly anti-English patriotism. . . ." (p. 7.)

11.02 *the longest river in America*. The Mississippi was explored by French Catholics.

11.02 *the highest mountain in the moon*. Dante's instruction is properly Catholic: many of the pre-space-age physical features of the moon were named for Jesuits by the Jesuit Riccioli of Bologna in 1651, based on the observations of his colleague Grimaldi, so that the moon became the "cemetery of astronomers" and the "pantheon of savants." (The Abbé Th. Moreux, *A Day in the Moon*. London: Hutchinson & Co., 1913, pp. 57ff.)

11.03 Father Arnall. In real life he was Father William Power, S.J., master of the elements grade during Joyce's time at Clongowes. (Sullivan, p. 36.)

11.10 lower and third lines. "The Third Line included boys under thirteen, the Lower Line boys from thirteen to fifteen, the Higher Line boys from fifteen to eighteen." (Ellmann, p. 31n.) See 8.20.

11.15 Simon Moonan. A fictitious name. See Kenner, p. 422, this edition.

Simon Moonan's name appeared as "Simon Mangan" in the first part of the manuscript of *P* and even the serial edition. Moonan's is the only name of all the Clongowes boys which recurs after the first chapter. However, one of the two Moonans mentioned in Chapter V is clearly not Simon Moonan. Named by the obtuse dean of studies as worthy of emulation for his high aspirations and perseverance, he might be Simon's father or older brother, since at *P*, 190.14-16, there is an ironic and obscure suggestion by Stephen that he, too, may be a "suck" (see 11.18). He would seem, then, to have been an alumnus for some years, since the dean is also advising Stephen to concentrate on taking his degree. Stanislaus, p. 189, says of him, ". . . it was generally rumoured in Dublin that the young law student had given early proof of his cleverness by writing leading articles contemporaneously for two newspapers of opposite politics. . . ." He also appears in the Aeolus episode of *Ulysses*.

The third Moonan could certainly not be identified with the second, though he just might be Simon. Donovan reports of him that he "got fifth place in the Indian." (*P*, 210.24.)

11.18 McGlade's suck. In real life McGlade was Andrew Macardle, S.J. The word "suck" is probably to be understood as synonymous with "sycophant."

11.20 prefect's false sleeves. The soutanes of the Jesuits in Joyce's day had a piece of material hanging from each shoulder down the back. One can be seen in the photograph of a group of University College students and teachers (including Joyce) printed in Gorman between pp. 184 and 185.

11.23 Wicklow Hotel. The Wicklow Hotel still stands in Wicklow Street, a few doors west of Grafton Street.

12.03 Go ahead, York! Go ahead, Lancaster! See Sullivan, pp. 79-80, for the Jesuits' encouragement of scholastic rivalry as a principle based on the *Ratio Studiorum*.

Father Arnall, oblivious of the part played by Ireland in the War of the Roses, treats York and Lancaster impartially. But Stephen wears the white rose of York, the traditional Irish side, while the leader of the Lancastrians, Jack Lawton, has a name which suggests the "new English" rather than Gael, Norman, Norse, or Fleming.

13.03 *Saurin.* See 8.25. His father is a magistrate (*P*, 26.06).

13.12 *Fleming.* See 8.25.

13.25 *That night at Dalkey the train had roared.* A pre-Clongowes memory. Dalkey is about nine miles southeast of Dublin on the C.I.E. Railway (formerly the Dublin and Southeastern Railway), from Dublin to Bray.

13.31 *Paddy Rath.* See 8.25.

13.31 *Jimmy Magee.* "Young Joyce must often have watched [Mr. Gleeson] and Jimmie Magee, . . . captain of the [cricket] team in 1891-92, perform brilliantly at the wicket. . . ." (Sullivan, p. 35.) See 8.25.

13.32-33 *the Spaniard . . . and the little Portuguese.* See 8.25.

14.04 *Tullabeg.* The Jesuit novitiate is at Tullabeg. It was formerly the site of St. Stanislaus College, begun in 1818 and merged with Clongowes in 1885.

14.07 *do you kiss your mother.* An "inside" joke. St. Aloysius Gonzaga, patron saint of James Aloysius Augustine Joyce, was too "pure" to kiss his mother. St. Alphonsus Liguori says that "St. Aloysius Gonzaga did not dare to raise his eyes to look even at his own mother. . . ." (*Prep. for Death*, p. 440.) See the argument about religion and mother-love between Stephen and Cranly, *P*, 242. Stephen's concern about mother-love is continued, of course, as one of the principal themes of *Ulysses* and *Finnegans Wake*. (See the *Ulysses* passages in this edition, pp. 300-309.)

15.29 *Class of Elements.* The *Ratio Studiorum* of Ignatius recommends that lower classes of a college be divided into five grades: three of grammar, one of rhetoric, and one of humanities. Covering the matter of the lowest grammar grade should take, he says, two years; apparently, one of rudiments, one of elements.

15.30-32 *Clongowes Wood College/Sallins/County Kildare.* "Clongowes Wood College was founded in 1813, in the pleasantest part of Kildare, and stands in the midst of beautiful and well-wooded grounds of 500 acres in extent. It is placed between the Great Southern and Midland Lines of Railway, Sallins, on the Great Southern, being 3½ miles, and Maynooth and Kilcock each 5 miles distant by road." (*Prospectus*, quoted in Sullivan, p. 231.)

16.34 *Mr Casey.* In real life John Kelly of Tralee, an Irish patriot who frequently visited the Joyces. See 28.09.

17.03 *poetry and rhetoric.* See 15.29.

17.26 *marbles.* The interior of the old chapel at Clongowes—floor, pillars, gallery, etc.—is made of wood, though the wood of the pillars is painted to simulate marble. Clongowians sometimes remember the pillars as being marble. (Ryan.)

17.30 on the hob to make punch. On the shelf at the back or side of the fireplace to make a hot drink, probably a mixture of whisky, hot water, sugar, and lemon juice.

18.06 Clane. An Irish parish and village in northeast County Kildare, between Clongowes and Sallins. The Clongowes chapel, now as in Joyce's day, is the parish church for Clane.

19.05 the boys in the dormitory. Sullivan (p. 31) explains that Joyce did not live among the older boys in the dormitories until his third year (1890-1891) at Clongowes, but had a room in the infirmary, a separate building, where he was under the immediate care of a nurse, Nanny Galvin, who also acted as governess. See 10.07 and 11.10.

A casual reading of pp. 8-27 would suggest that all the action at Clongowes before the Christmas dinner scene at Bray takes place in about twenty-four hours, from late in the afternoon of the seventy-seventh day before the Christmas holiday until late in the afternoon on the seventy-sixth, in Stephen's first year at school (1888 on Joyce's clock). There is no doubt that Joyce intends to give the impression that it is Stephen's first year: he is just getting acquainted with his fellow students, Nasty Roche asks him what his father does, he recalls "the first day in the hall of the castle" when his mother said good-by and when his father had told him "never to peach on a fellow." (*P*, 9.28.) But Wells probably did not push Joyce into the square ditch (*P*, 10.29) until the spring of 1890. Parnell's death, which is a part of Stephen's vision or dream in the infirmary (*P*, 27.13), did not occur until October 6, 1891. Little's death, about which he has a different kind of fantasy (*P*, 24.03), occurred on December 10, 1890. (See 24.03.) And the Roche who was probably Nasty's real-life counterpart left Clongowes in 1889, at the end of Joyce's first year. (See 8.25.) On the other hand, at least three boys—Thunder, Magee, and Furlong—did not arrive until 1889, two—Lawton and the Spaniard—not until 1890, and at least one—Fleming—not until 1891, on the assumption that the *Clongowes Record* is accurate.

It is clear, then, that Stephen's time is not Joyce's. It is interesting to know the time scheme of Joyce's life between the ages of "half-past six" and nine years because the knowledge helps us understand the artistic work of compression and distortion in the first part of Chapter I and elsewhere. But it would be wrong to let knowledge of Joyce's life interfere with knowledge of Stephen's.

19.17 A figure came up the staircase. The Browne family, from whom Father Peter Kenny had purchased Clongowes in 1813, included an ancestor who was marshal in the Austrian army and who died at the Battle of Prague in 1757. It was said that his ghost appeared frequently to the family servants. (*Clongowes Record,* pp. 39ff.)

20.02 the cars. These are no doubt four-wheeled hackney carriages, used at Clongowes to drive the three and one-half miles to the Sallins railroad station. See 15.30. The word "car" is derived from old Irish (*OED*). See 87.35 for "jingle."

20.08 Bodenstown. The parish on the Liffey River which contains Sallins. See 15.30. Theobald Wolfe Tone (1763-1798), the Irish patriot and a founder of the United Irishmen, is buried there, on the Sallins Road, only four miles south of Clongowes Wood Castle. (See 184.09.)

20.15 chocolate train. This image apparently dates from Joyce's earliest work on *SH*, now lost, for Padraic Colum (pp. 38ff.) reports that "one of the coterie that included Joyce and Gogarty" told him in 1904(?) that "Joyce's Meredithean novel" contained phrases like "the chocolate-colored train."

20.20 Hill of Allen. This is an unusually flat-topped hill with a pillar honoring Finn Macool, a third-century hero, not far from Sallins station toward Dublin and about four miles north of the Great Southern Railway.

22.18 Father Minister. "Among the necessary officials to be appointed by the Rector there is first of all a suitable Minister who is Vice-rector or master of the house, and who looks after all things which pertain to the universal good." (*Constitutions*, IV, x, 7, quoted in Fitzpatrick, p. 94.) Stephen (*P*, 48.09) thinks that the members of the Jesuit community confess to the minister, but this would be unusual and certainly not obligatory. Ellmann, p. 28, quotes a letter dated March 9, 1889, from "Father T. P. Brown, S.J., Minister and Prefect of Health," to Joyce's mother.

22.37 Brother Michael. In real life, Brother John Hanly, S.J.

24.03 when Little had died. Peter Stanislaus Little, whose grave lies just to the left of the gate inside the Jesuit cemetery. The grave is marked by a white cross with the inscription, "Sacred to the memory of Peter Stanislaus Little who died 10th December 1890 aged 16 years. RIP." See 8.25.

24.06 cope of black and gold. The cope is a long, semicircular vestment. The color of the cope is usually the color of the day in the Church calendar, but black and gold are the colors for the burial of the dead no matter what day it is. (*Cath. Encyc.*)

24.10 the main avenue of limes. A long arch of linden trees (limes) lines the road leading to Clongowes Castle.

24.15 Dingdong! The castle bell! Iona and Peter Opie, *The Lore and Language of Schoolchildren* (Oxford: Clarendon Press, 1959), pp. 33-34, list this as an example of "ghoulism" which comes about "when children are about ten years old" and "the outward material facts about death seem extraordinarily funny."

25.01 *Athy*. See 8.25.

25.14 *My name is the name of a town*. The small town of Athy, in County Kildare, is about twenty-six miles southwest of Clongowes.

26.12 *his granduncle had presented an address to the liberator there fifty years before*. The grand-uncle (actually Joyce's great-grand-uncle) was John O'Connell, father of William ("Uncle Charles"). See 7.21 and 60.01. The liberator, to whom Joyce may have been distantly related, was Daniel O'Connell, who successfully advocated the "Repeal of the Union" between Ireland and Great Britain in 1834. (*DNB*.)

26.16 *blue coats with brass buttons and yellow waistcoats and caps of rabbitskin*. According to the *Clongowes Record*, the uniform for festivals during the period from about 1816 to 1840 was "a cap made of rabbit-skin, a blue cloth coat with brass buttons, yellow cashmere waistcoat and corduroy trousers." The uniform was gradually modified and then abolished in 1850.

26.24 *a legend*. That is, a saint's legend.

27.13 *Parnell! He is dead!* Parnell died on October 6, 1891. See 19.05 for a discussion of the time scheme of the first chapter of *P*. "On Sunday morning, October 11, the 'Ireland' steamed in to Kingstown bringing home the dead Chief. In the forenoon there was a Lying-in-state in the City Hall. In the afternoon, followed to his last resting-place by a vast concourse of people . . . Charles Stewart Parnell was laid in the grave. . . ." (O'Brien, II, 352.)

27.29 *toasted boss*. Joyce explains: "This is a kind of foot-stool with two ears, stuffed without a wooden frame. The term is childish and popular. Compare the word 'hassock.' " (*Letters*, III, 129.)

27.30 *pierglass*. A tall mirror, such as one used to fill the space ("pier") between two windows. The one in the Joyce home in Bray extends from the mantlepiece almost to the ceiling.

28.09 *a birthday present for Queen Victoria*. See 16.34. "Kelly was in prison several times for Land League agitation, and John Joyce regularly invited him to recuperate from imprisonment . . . at the house in Bray. In jail three fingers of his left hand had become permanently cramped from picking oakum, and he would tell the children that they had become so while he was making a birthday present for Queen Victoria." (Ellmann, pp. 23f.)

28.16 *the Head*. Bray Head was visible from the Joyce house in Martello Terrace.

29.24 *Bless us, O Lord*. The grace ordinarily said in Catholic families.

29.32 *Dunn's of D'Olier Street.* Still doing business as a poulterer and game dealer at 26 D'Olier Street.

29.36 *the real Ally Daly.* Still rare slang in Dublin for describing the excellence of something. (Mac Lochlainn.)

30.01 *Mr Barrett.* See *P,* 43.35, where he is called "old Barrett," and *P,* 48.15, where he is called "Paddy Barrett." Sullivan (p. 92) identifies him with Patrick Barrett, S.J., who taught not at Clongowes but at Belvedere, where he taught not Joyce but Stanislaus in the class of Elements, 1893-1894. The designation "Mr" rather than "Father" suggests that, Mr Barrett is a scholastic not yet admitted to the priesthood.

30.32 *Mary.* Like Stephen's, Joyce's mother's maiden name was Mary Jane ("May") Murray.

31.23 *political discussion.* "John Joyce, James's father, was a fervent follower of Parnell for whom he worked as an election agent, an occupation for which his sociable temperament and ready tongue made him very suitable. In 1880 he had succeeded in getting two Parnellites elected as M.P.'s for the city of Dublin and, partly as a reward for this feat, had been appointed Collector of Taxes for the city. . . ." (Atherton, p. x.) See 70.21.

32.03 *The bishops and priests.* ". . . the day before Christmas of . . . 1889, Captain William Henry O'Shea filed a petition for divorce from his wife Kitty on the ground of her adultery with Parnell. He had tolerated the affair for ten years, and in 1866 accepted a seat in Parliament from Galway as a reward for keeping still. The decree was granted without contest on November 17, 1890. At first Parnell showed surprising strength in holding his party together; his lieutenant Tim Healy staunchly declared that the leader should not be abandoned 'within sight of the Promised Land.' But soon the pressure of Davitt, of Gladstone, of the Catholic bishops, and then of Tim Healy and other close political associates accomplished its purpose and, as Yeats put it, 'dragged this quarry down.' " (Ellmann, p. 32.)

32.16 *Woe be to the man.* Luke 17:1-2.

32.33 *the pope's nose.* A turkey's rump.

33.18 *Billy with the lip.* Archbishop William J. Walsh of the archdiocese of Dublin. Cf. "Gas from a Burner": "For everyone knows the Pope can't belch/ Without the consent of Billy Walsh." (*Critical Writings,* p. 243.)

33.18 *tub of guts up in Armagh.* Michael Logue (later a cardinal) was consecrated archbishop of Armagh in 1887. (*Cath. Encyc.*)

33.21 *Lord Leitrim's coachman.* Lord Leitrim, a landlord of evil repute, was murdered in 1877 with two attendants who tried to defend him in County Donegal by a farmer's son revenging a wrong suffered by his sister. The incident caused a fierce debate in the House of Commons. (Davitt, pp. 142-145.)

34.27 *county Wicklow*. Bray is in the northeastern corner of County Wicklow, on the southern border of County Dublin.

35.23-25 *a spoiled nun . . . convent in the Alleghanies . . . money from the savages for the trinkets and the chainies.* Dante "had been on the verge of becoming a nun in America when her brother, who had made a fortune out of trading with African natives, died and left her 30,000 pounds." (Ellmann, p. 24.) See 7.21. The convent may be the first foundation of the Institute of the Sisters of Mercy, from Dublin, which was in Pittsburgh, Pa. "Chainies" are worthless ornaments. (Harmon.)

35.30 *litany of the Blessed Virgin*. The Litany of the Blessed Virgin Mary is ordinarily said as an evening prayer. Among the many epithets it gives to Mary are "Mystical rose," "Tower of David," "Tower of ivory," "House of gold," "Ark of the covenant," "Gate of heaven," and "Morning star."

35.30 *Tower of Ivory*. See the preceding note. The source of the image is Canticles 7:14. Cf. *P*, 42.35.

35.30 *House of Gold*. See 35.30.

36.01 *tig*. Tag.

36.06 *Arklow*. About twenty-five miles south along the coast from Bray.

36.20. *The Paris Funds! Mr Fox! Kitty O'Shea!* These were "the funds of the Irish National League under the trusteeship of Parnell and others. In 1890 he was accused of misappropriating them." (Harmon.) Mr. Fox was one of the names which Parnell used in the "elaborately secret" intrigue with which he conducted his affair with Mrs. O'Shea. (St. John Ervine, *Parnell* [London: Benn, 1925] p. 125.) See 32.03.

37.24 *the Cabinteely road*. A road south from Dublin running directly to Cabinteely, a village at the foot of Killiney Hill.

37.26 *one night at the bend on the esplanade she had hit a gentleman on the head with her umbrella*. A real event. See Stanislaus, pp. 3f., 8.

38.05 *condemned to death as a whiteboy*. Ellmann (p. 10) confirms this as a fact from life.

The whiteboys were organized against landlords as early as 1769 in Tipperary, where landlords turned tenants out of waste lands which they had reclaimed. "They wore white shirts over their other garments as a 'badge of union,' and were called White-boys. They went about searching for arms, arresting and punishing those who refused to obey their laws in a most cruel manner." (David Bennett King, *The Irish Question* [New York: Charles Scribner's Sons, 1882], pp. 76f.)

38.06 *he would never let one of them put his two feet under his mahogany.* "His 'mahogany' means his dining table." (Atherton.) Ellmann (p. 10) gives this as a saying of Joyce's great-grandfather.

38.10 Touch them not. Zachariah 2:8.

38.21 *the time of the union.* On January 1, 1801, the Kingdom of Great Britain, formed in 1707 by the union of England and Scotland, became the United Kingdom of Great Britain and Ireland.

38.22 *bishop Lanigan presented an address of loyalty to the Marquess Cornwallis.* John Lanigan (1758-1828). Charles Cornwallis was viceroy to Ireland at the end of the eighteenth and the beginning of the nineteenth centuries. He helped put down the Wolfe Tone rebellion of 1798, and he proposed the legislative union of Ireland and England in the last session of the Irish Parliament (1800-1801). (*DNB.*)

38.24 *in 1829 in return for Catholic emancipation.* In 1829, principally as a result of the agitation organized by Daniel O'Connell, the Duke of Wellington as Prime Minister persuaded George IV to accept the Catholic Relief Bill, which freed Catholics from the restrictions of the Elizabethan penal code. However, "As Catholics won the right to elect men of their own religion to Parliament many of them lost the right to vote at all. The forty-shilling freeholders—small landholders, of whom there were some one hundred and ninety thousand—were disenfranchised in Ireland. Wellington had insisted on this minimum safeguard." (Hall and Albion, pp. 601-602.)

38.25 *fenian movement.* The Fenians, founded in 1859, were the "physical force" party in Ireland, officially called the Irish Revolutionary Brotherhood. See 202.02.

38.27. *dishonour the ashes of Terence Bellew MacManus.* Mac-Manus (1823?-1860) was an Irish patriot transported for treason. He died in America, and in 1861 his body was brought to Ireland and buried by the Fenians amid nationalist demonstrations, which were opposed by Cardinal Cullen. See 38.31.

38.31 *Paul Cullen.* See 38.27. Cf. the essay "Portrait," p. 260 of this edition.

Cullen (1803-1878) was made Bishop of Armagh, 1849; Archbishop of Dublin, 1852; Cardinal, 1866, the first Irishman named to the college of Cardinals; and ". . . a determined opponent of the Fenian brotherhood and all other revolutionary combinations. . . ." (*DNB.*)

40.03 *Hill of Lyons.* Three miles south of Celbridge. (Harmon.)

40.05 *Mr Gleeson.* See 44.16.

40.11 *fecked.* "Stole." (P. W. Joyce)

40.13 *Kickham's brother.* See 8.25.

40.16 *scut.* As a noun a scut is the short upright tail of a deer, hare, or rabbit, so that perhaps "turned tail and ran" is a close equivalent. Cf. *P*, 105.30.

40.35 *surplices.* A surplice is "a loose vestment of white linen having wide sleeves . . . reaching to the feet, worn (usually over a cassock) by clerics, choristers and others taking part in church services." (OED.) Stephen probably wore one as boatbearer. (See 41.01.)

41.01 *boatbearer, the evening of the procession to the little altar in the wood.* According to Sullivan, p. 33, George Roche was thurifer (*i.e.*, bearer and burner of the incense) and Joyce boat-bearer during Joyce's first year at Clongowes. The incense boat is a receptacle in which the incense is kept before it is placed in the censer to be burned. Cf. 158.25 and *P*, 158.25, where Stephen imagines himself as thurifer.

41.03 *censer.* "A vessel in which incense is burnt; a thurible." (OED.)

41.21. *Barnes.* Not in *Clongowes Record.*

41.22 *Flowers.* Not in *Clongowes Record.*

42.15 *Smugging.* Clongowes slang for a mild form of homosexual petting. (Ryan.) For the "square" (*P*, 42.21) see 10.29.

42.31 *Tusker Boyle.* Not in *Clongowes Record.*

43.18 *Balbus was building a wall.* This graffito, which Atherton says is from *Kennedy's Latin Primer*, remains obscure. The literal meaning of Balbus, "stammerer," and his occupation as mason or builder connect this Roman with Joyce's final multiple hero—H. C. Earwicker and Tim Finnegan in *FW*—who as Earwicker stammers and as Finnegan carries a hod. Joyce makes the connection early in *FW* (p. 4), introducing "Bygmester Finnegan, of the Stuttering Hand, freemen's maurer [*i.e.*, mason] . . . ," who as HCE is a "man of hod, cement and edifices. . . ." Later (p. 552) Joyce explains that "Blabus was razing his wall and eltering the suzannes of his neighbors: and thirdly, for ewigs, I did reform and restore for my smuggy piggiesknees, . . ." connecting Balbus with "smugging" as he does here in *P*, 43.11-18. See Cicero's *Letters to Atticus*, XII, 2, where Cicero complains that during the many Roman troubles of 47 B.C., while others are feasting or playing games, "Balbus is building [new mansions for himself]: for what cares he?" (The two best known "Balbuses" of Julius Caesar's Rome were from Spain and hence were, like the Danish Earwicker in Ireland, "outlanders." The elder Balbus was, like Earwicker, tried on obscurely motivated charges and was a considerable sinner. He kept a diary of his life and Caesar's which became the basis of Book VIII of *Commentarii de Bello Gallico* [cf. "The Calico Belly," *P*, 43.23], probably written by his friend Hirtius.)

43.33 six and eight. Three blows on each hand and then four blows on each hand. (Ryan.) See 44.26.

43.35 old Barrett. See 30.01.

43.65 twisting the note. In sentencing a student to be punished the master writes a note in Latin of the number of pandies to be given. The student then is "sent to the loft," where the prefect pandies him in accordance with the note. (Ryan.)

44.02 prefect of studies. "The duty of the Prefect is to be a general assistant of the Rector in the proper organization of studies . . . so that those who attend may make as much advancement as possible in uprightness of life, the arts, and doctrine, all for the greater glory of God." (*Ratio,* in Fitzpatrick, p. 143.) He is not responsible for corporal punishment.

44.15 Corrigan. Also known as "Big Corrigan." See 8.25.

44.16 Mr Gleeson. "There was nothing ambiguous about the real-life Mr. Gleeson. He was an athlete who excelled in all games but especially in cricket." (Sullivan, p. 35.)

44.18 able for. Capable of [handling]. Hayden and Hartog, p. 778, claim this as the "English of Caxton," still current in Ireland.

44.26 twice nine. The maximum number of pandies—nine strokes on each hand. It is the only pandying that also requires the student to "bend over" and receive blows on his backside. (Ryan.)

45.04 pandybat. The word "pandy" is from the Latin *pande,* "Stretch out!," the imperative of *pandere.* (See Father Dolan's order, "Hold out!," as he pandies Fleming, *P*, 49.06.) A pandy is a stroke upon the extended palm with a leather strap or tawse, ferrule, or rod. It is also called a "palmy." (*OED.*)

46.02-11 Mr Harford . . . never got into a wax. In real life Mr. James Jeffcoat, S.J., master of the Rudiments grade in Clongowes during Joyce's time there. When Joyce entered Clongowes Jeffcoat was only twenty-two, a young scholastic who, as Sullivan suggests (p. 36), was probably full of "patience and idealism" and therefore "never got into a wax."

46.16 monstrance. An open or transparent vessel of gold or silver, in which the host is exposed. The monstrance is often highly polished and decorated with cut diamonds and rubies.

46.20 benediction. The official Roman Catholic ceremony called Benediction of the Most Blessed Sacrament ("Benediction" for short) is usually performed in the evening. The Blessed Sacrament is incensed, removed from the tabernacle, placed in a monstrance, elevated, and adored by those participating in the devotion.

46.22 *Dominic Kelly.* This may be the same D. Kelly who sang the duet with Ignatius Little in the Clongowes Shrovetide program in 1890. The program is printed in Sullivan, p. 234. Critics have not thought of Kelly as a student, but it would be perfectly usual to have a student sing the responses. See 8.25.

47.09 *Gentlemen, the happiest day of my life was the day on which I made my first holy communion.* It is usual for Roman Catholics to receive their first communion during their seventh year, "the age of reason." The remark attributed to Napoleon suggests that this reason was fed on false information: Napoleon was an apostate and a notorious sinner.

47.19 *decline the noun* mare. *Mare* ("sea") is a neuter noun in the third declension, in which most nouns are feminine. Otherwise, it is regular, in the ablative as in the other cases.

48.10-11 *minister . . . rector . . . provincial . . . general of the Jesuits.* Stephen's notion of the order of command within the Company of Jesus is accurate. His notion of the confession of Jesuits is faulty: they choose confessors or are assigned to confessors from among their own.

49.20 *Father Dolan.* In real life Father James Daly. Joyce confirmed the pandying incident to Herbert Gorman. (Gorman, p. 29.) It is to be noted, however, that even if Stephen's punishment is unjust because he is not an idler, unwarranted because he has not been given precepts and warnings, and inequitable because he gets the same punishment as Fleming, who really is an idler, nevertheless the cruelty of Clongowes as Joyce represents it does not approach the cruelty of English public schools as they are represented in C. S. Lewis, *Surprised by Joy,* George Orwell, *Such, Such Were the Joys,* and Cyril Connolly, "A Georgian Boyhood," to name only three accounts which are roughly contemporaneous with Joyce's. Though wrongly punished by the prefect, Stephen does get justice from the rector; and other masters are represented as being kindly men, as indeed they are instructed to be in the Jesuit *Ratio Studiorum.* For example, even in the most severe punishment, where "it is not a sufficient remedy for the scandal given to expel from classes, let him bring the matter before the Rector that he may decide what further is fitting to be done. Still as much as is possible the affair must be conducted in a spirit of gentleness, with peace and charity toward all." (*Ratio,* in Fitzpatrick, p. 188.)

49.25 *Tom Furlong's.* "About this time [1890-1891] . . . he and Thomas Furlong, the second smallest boy in the school, were caught out of bounds raiding the school orchard, and word went round that 'Furlong and Joyce will not for long rejoice,' a pun that he became fond of in later life." (Ellmann, p. 30.) See 8.25.

49.26 tomorrow and tomorrow and tomorrow. Macbeth, V, v, 19.

53.30 Peter Parley's Tales about Greece and Rome. Joyce has combined the titles of two of the works of Samuel Griswold Goodrich (1793-1860), an American author who under the nom de plume of Peter Parley wrote (or had others write for him) hundreds of books used in schools. (Sullivan, pp. 43ff.)

55.35 saint Ignatius Loyola holding an open book and pointing to the words Ad Majorem Dei Gloriam. Ignatius Loyola (1491-1556), was wounded fighting for Ferdinand and Isabella and left lame. (See 186.17.) He founded the Society of Jesus in 1540. In an often reprinted painting he is shown pointing to the words *Ad Majorem Dei Gloriam* ("For the Greater Glory of God"), which became the Jesuit motto.

56.01 saint Francis Xavier pointing to his chest. Francis Xavier (1506-1552), was the first to join Ignatius. (See 107.27.)

56.02 Lorenzo Ricci with his berretta on his head. Lorenzo Ricci (1703-1775), was the General of the Jesuits beginning in 1758.

56.03 the three patrons of holy youth, saint Stanislaus Kostka, saint Aloysius Gonzaga and blessed John Berchmans. Kostka, 1550-1568; Gonzaga, 1568-1591; Berchmans, 1599-1621. Kostka and Gonzaga were members of the Blessed Virgin Mary sodality and its patrons. See 14.07, and *P*, 242.10-15.

56.06 Father Peter Kenny sitting in a chair wrapped in a big cloak. He purchased the Clongowes Woods grounds for the Jesuit order in 1813. (Ellmann, p. 29.)

58.18 the third line playground. See 11.10.

59.05 Conmee. See 9.29.

59.16 the pavilion. This building still stands across the playing field from the castle.

59.17 gallnuts. Excrescences produced on trees, especially oaks, by the action of insects. (OED.)

CHAPTER II

60.01 Uncle Charles. See 7.21. It was through William O'Connell's father, John O'Connell, that John Joyce traced a tenuous blood relationship to Daniel O'Connell, the liberator. See 26.12.

60.02 black twist. Tobacco made into a thick cord; a piece of this cord. (OED.)

60.23 summer in Blackrock. At the beginning of 1892 the Joyce family moved from Bray to 23 Carysfort Avenue, Blackrock, where they lived until late in that year or early in 1893, when they moved to Dublin. Blackrock is a small dormitory suburb on the coast south-east of Dublin (Ellmann, p. 34), about halfway between Sandy-mount, where Joyce and Gogarty lived in the Martello tower written about in *Ulysses*, and Dalkey, where Stephen (and Joyce) taught school.

60.27 *the house in Carysfort Avenue.* See 60.23. This house, with a recumbent lion over the door, is a long block from the main shopping street in Blackrock.

62.06 *prayed for the souls in purgatory.* According to Catholic teaching the souls of those who die with mortal sins unforgiven go to hell; those with no unforgiven mortal sins but with unforgiven venial sins go to purgatory until they have paid the penalty (penance) of their sins. Their "time" in purgatory can be shortened by the prayers of the living, and after the time is served, they go to heaven. See 147.18.

62.06 *grace of a happy death.* A "happy death" would mean that one would die with all his sins forgiven; he would then be in a "state of grace" and go directly to heaven.

62.18 *Munster.* The southwesternmost of Ireland's four provinces. The others are Connaught in the west, Ulster in the north, and Leinster in the east. The "Joyce country" is in Connaught, but several generations of Joyces had lived in Cork City, Munster, before John Joyce was born.

62.26 *a ragged translation of* The Count of Monte Cristo. By Alexandre Dumas. Apparently the translation was the same as the one published in two volumes by A. L. Burt Co. (New York, n.d.).

62.28 *dark avenger.* Edmond Dantes in Dumas's book, betrayed by Danglars, Fernand, Caderousse, and Villefort, spends fourteen years in prison, then escapes by being thrown into the sea in the shroud of the Abbé Faria. He finds the treasure of the Abbé in the cave on the Isle of Monte Cristo, purchases the island, and makes the cave a fortress retreat of Oriental splendor.

62.35 *Marseilles.* Mercedes's home in Marseilles is a "poor fisher-man's hut," "on the outside of which the sun had stamped that beautiful color of the dead leaf . . . and within, a coat of lime-wash, of that white tint which forms the only ornament of Spanish posadas." (*Monte Cristo*, II, 18. See 62.26.) The "sunny trel-lises" are those of Dantes's home, which Monte Cristo gives to the aging Mercedes.

63.11 *Madam, I never eat muscatel grapes.* In the *Count of Monte Cristo* Edmond Dantes returns to France. In Paris he begins to take his revenge on Danglars, Caderousse, Villefort, and Fernand, who has married Mercedes and become the Count de Moncerf. Edmond visits the Moncerf home, where Mercedes notices that he does not eat or drink anything. She determines that he shall and takes him for a walk in the garden. She picks a bunch of Muscatel grapes and asks him to try them. He refuses twice, the second time with the words, "Madame, I never eat Muscatel grapes." (*Monte Cristo*, II, 188. See 62.26.)

63.12 *Aubrey Mills.* The only friend Ellmann mentions Joyce as having in Blackrock is "a Protestant boy named Raynold who lived at No. 25" (p. 34), with whom he began to collaborate on a novel when he was ten years old.

63.13 *the avenue.* Carysfort Avenue. See 60.27.

63.20 *the castle.* This may be the castle Frascati, where the romantic Lord Edward Fitzgerald lived with his wife Pamela, a daughter of the Duke of Orleans. It is opposite Blackrock Park.

64.28 *tramtrack on the Rock Road.* The Rock Road is the extension of the Strand Road and Merrion Road which runs to the southern coastal suburbs, including Blackrock and Bray. Both road and tramtrack parallel the C.I.E. Railway from Dublin to Bray, on which Stephen had ridden in the days of his father's affluence. See 13.25.

65.15 *Two great yellow caravans.* A caravan is a covered carriage or cart. (OED.) Cf. "moving-van."

65.23 *Merrion Road.* See 64.28. Probably the Joyce family got off the train at the Amiens Street Station, just two blocks from Mountjoy Square. Joyce's fifth home, beginning in 1893, was at 14 Fitzgibbon Street, off Mountjoy Square, "the last of their good addresses." (Ellmann, p. 34.) The address has now sadly declined.

66.18 *the neighbouring square.* Mountjoy Square. See 65.23.

66.20 *skeleton map of the city in his mind.* Joyce's father said of his child, "If that fellow was dropped in the middle of the Sahara, he'd sit, be God, and make a map of it." (Ellmann, p. 28.)

66.21 *one of its central lines until he reached the customhouse.* Gardiner Street, at the south end of which stands the Custom House, on the north bank of the Liffey, a Romanesque, domed building designed by James Gandon.

66.33 *sunwarmed trellisses of the wineshops.* The plot against Edmond Dantes is conceived by Danglars and Fernand as they sit with Caderousse in the arbor before the Café La Reserve, where, also, at his betrothal feast, Dantes is arrested. (*Monte Cristo*, I, 34. See 62.26.)

67.03 *Christmas.* Perhaps the Christmas of 1893, the year the Joyces moved into Dublin. See 65.23.

67.14 his aunt. In life, Aunt Josephine, wife of William Murray, Joyce's mother's brother. The Murrays lived in Drumcondra, less than a mile north of Mountjoy Square. Joyce liked his aunt better than his other relatives and corresponded with her throughout her life after he left Dublin. (Ellmann, pp. 18, 139, 221.)

67.14 the evening paper. Probably the *Freeman's Journal*, for which William Murray's brother John ("Red") Murray worked in the accounts department, both in life and in *Ulysses*.

67.18 A ringletted girl. This may be Joyce's cousin Kathleen ("Katsy"), daughter of William and Josephine Murray, in whom he had a brief love interest. She was younger than Stanislaus, who loved her longer and better than Joyce. See 96.14. Ellmann says, however, that the scene took place on the other side of town, "presumably in his great-aunts' house on Usher's Island after Mrs. Callanan's death." (p. 87.) Ellmann is relying on an epiphany which was the first recording of this scene. (See p. 268 of this edition.) Usher's Island is a quay, not an island, that runs along the south side of the Liffey. (Cf. *D*, "The Dead.")

67.21 the pantomime. These were regularly performed in Dublin at the Gaiety Theatre.

68.23 Josephine. See 67.14.

68.27 Harold's Cross. South of the South Circular and the Grand Canal, near the Portobello Barracks. See 69.05.

68.29 spoils of their crackers. Party favors within a bonbon of crepe paper that also contains a fulminant which explodes when the cracker is pulled at both ends. (Harmon.) The children invited to the climactic party in Anstey's *Vice Versâ* (see 73.01) look like "little 'Kate Greenaway' maidens crowned with fantastic headdresses out of the crackers." (p. 341.)

69.05 She had thrown a shawl about her. See the *SH* passage, p. 276, and the epiphany, p. 268, of this edition. See 222.09.

69.25 He saw her urge her vanities. Emma is not unlike Mercedes, who "tapped the earth with her pliant and well-formed foot, so as to display the pure and full shape of her well-turned leg." (*Monte Cristo*, I, 18. See 62.26 and 222.11.)

70.10 new emerald exercise. This would probably be one of the several patriotic green exercise books popularized as the one hundredth anniversary of the revolution of 1798 approached, according to Mr. Mac Lochlainn.

70.12 A.M.D.G. Ad Majorem Dei Gloriam. See 55.35 and 71.04, for Joyce's own use of it.

70.13 E—— C——. The initials of Emma Clery, who is fully described only in *SH*. See pp. 274-76 of this edition. For a discussion of her real-life identity see 202.21.

70.15 *similar titles in the collected poems of Lord Byron.* For example, "On the Eyes of Miss A—— H——." Byron wrote this poem to Anne Houson, of Southwell, and his relation to her as suggested in his poems was not unlike that of Stephen Dedalus to Emma Clery.

The Works of Lord Byron, Poetry, ed. E. H. Coleridge, 7 vols. (London: John Murray, 1898-1904) was published during the period covered by Chapter V of *P*.

70.21 *second moiety notices.* A notice for the payment of the second half, or "moiety," an Elizabethan word which is one among many such words still current in Ireland. Perhaps this would be one of the notices which Simon (John) would send out, rather than receive, in his office as Collector of Rates. But by the Christmas dinner of 1891 he was already beginning to be in financial straits.

70.25 *Roderick Kickham.* See 8.25.

70.27 *Anthony MacSwiney.* Not in *Clongowes Record*.

71.04 *L.D.S. Laus Deo Semper* ("Praise to God Always") and *A.M.D.G. (Ad Majorem Dei Gloriam)*, ejaculations often put on student papers in Jesuit schools. Both appear on an early essay of Joyce's, "Trust Not Appearances," printed in *Critical Writings*, pp. 15-16, and in Ellmann, pp. 36-37. See 70.12.

71.16 *the corner of the square.* Mountjoy Square, near Joyce's fifth home at 14 Fitzgibbon Street. Both Belvedere College and the Jesuit church in Gardiner Street are within a few blocks of the Square. See 65.23 and 115.21. ". . . James [Joyce] entered Belvedere on April 6, 1893, in III Grammar, to become its most famous old boy." (Ellmann, p. 35). See 73.28.

71.20 *provincial of the order.* Father John Conmee had left the rectorship of Clongowes to become prefect of studies at Belvedere. "He was not yet Provincial of the Jesuit Order in Ireland; he became so in 1906-9. . . ." (Ellmann, p. 35.)

71.21 *christian brothers.* Joyce actually attended, for a brief period in 1893, the Christian Brothers' school on North Richmond Street. But Stephen did not. (Stanislaus, p. 52.) See 165.32.

71.36 *Maurice.* The name given to Stanislaus Joyce, who also attended Belvedere College. Maurice is a prominent character in *SH*. See 96.14.

72.16 *that job in the corporation.* In the city government John Joyce lost his easy and lucrative job as Collector of Rates when the office was abolished in 1892. (Ellmann, p. 34.)

73.01 *the Whitsuntide play.* "The play was F. Anstey's *Vice Versa*, and was probably given in May 1898. It dealt farcically with the theme of father against son that Joyce was to use to such good purpose in his later books." (Ellmann, p. 57.) The play is adapted from Anstey's novel *Vice Versâ, or A Lesson to Fathers,* published in January 1882, reprinted nineteen times that year and frequently thereafter for about forty years. *P* contains a number of verbal echoes of it.

73.02 *the small grassplot.* In the yard behind Belvedere House. (See 71.16.) The yard is now enclosed and cemented over.

73.04 *down the steps from the house.* That is, the back steps of Belvedere House, which lead to a yard around which the college buildings form a closed quadrangle now, but which was open on the east end in Joyce's day.

73.10 *the tabernacle.* An ornamented receptacle for the pyx containing the sacred host.

73.23 *secretary to the gymnasium.* Joyce was elected secretary of the newly opened gymnasium at Belvedere during his senior year. (Ellmann, p. 55.)

73.25 *the chief part, that of a farcical pedagogue.* Joyce did take this part. See 73.01 and 75.32.

73.28 *his second year at Belvedere and in number two.* Joyce entered Belvedere on April 6, 1893, in Third of Grammar. Anstey's *Vice Versâ* (see 73.01) was performed a little more than a year later. Joyce may refer here to the number of his room rather than his line: ". . . four classrooms numbered 1 to 4; being respectively for the senior, middle, junior and preparatory grades." (Byrne, p. 15.)

74.05 *a little troop of Neapolitan peasants.* Not in Anstey's *Vice Versâ,* but in the "first section of the programme." (*P,* 73.24.)

75.18 *Heron.* "Albrecht Connolly was the fop of Belvedere College. He wore a Norfolk jacket with flapless sidepockets and, as Joyce says, he carried a cane. But in *A Portrait* Joyce combines Albrecht's attire and his brother Vincent Connolly's face to compose the fictional personage Heron." (Ellmann, p. 762, n. 77.)

75.31 *Wallis.* Perhaps Vincent Connolly, Albrecht's brother. See 75.18 and 75.32.

75.32 *the rector.* Father William Henry. Vincent and Albrecht Connolly urged Joyce to take off the rector and he did so, as he did again at the beginning of "An Encounter." (*D.*) (Ellmann, p. 56 and n.) For an account of the performance and of Father Henry see Sullivan, p. 91; Eugene Sheehy, *May It Please the Court* (Dublin: C. J. Fallon, 1951), p. 10; and Ellmann, p. 49n.

76.22 *number one.* See 73.28.

78.09 *the* Confiteor. The confessional prayer. It takes its name from its first word (*Confiteor Deo omnipotenti . . .*) and is said by the server in the Ordinary of each Mass and by suppliants in the confessional.

78.20 *in number six*. See 73.28.

79.05 *Mr Tate, the English master*. "The lay teacher of English composition was George Stanislaus Dempsey. . . . He dressed unusually well, wore a moustache, and carried a flower in his buttonhole. His diction and manner were old-fashioned. . . . In later years [Joyce] and Dempsey corresponded. . . ." (Ellmann, p. 36.)

79.07 *heresy*. Stephen's heresy, in Mr. Tate's view, seems to relate to the question of whether a soul is granted adequate grace to reach the blessedness of communion with its Creator. The Church teaches that sufficient grace is available to every soul; therefore, those souls who do not approach nearer or even reach their Creator have rejected that sufficient grace.

79.32 *Drumcondra Road*. Joyce's seventh home, beginning about March 1894, was in Millbourne Lane, Drumcondra. Drumcondra Road is an extension of Dorset Street running northerly from the North Circular, across the Royal Canal and the Tolka River into Drumcondra. Cf. 80.05 and 82.13.

80.05 *Clonliffe Road*. A main street running westerly from Fairview until it ends by intersecting Drumcondra Road a few blocks north of the Royal Canal. See 79.32.

80.11 *Captain Marryat*. Marryat's books are still common in quay bookstalls in Dublin. His *Japhet in Search of a Father* (1836) is used as a tag in *Ulysses*, p. 19.

80.19 *Cardinal Newman*. "The discussion about Byron and heresy and the tussle with three of his classmates in *A Portrait of the Artist* is neither invented nor exaggerated. He must have been thrown heavily against barbed wire, for my mother had to mend the rips in his clothes so that he could go to school the following morning." (Stanislaus, p. 55.)

81.09 *slates in the yard*. The slates which made up the urinal trough in the "square" or "yard." See 10.29.

81.09 *sent to the loft*. Originally, perhaps, to the "organ loft," "choir loft," or "rood loft" in the gallery of the college chapel. But Ryan says that at Clongowes it means simply "sent to the prefect for punishment."

82.13 *Jones's Road*. A short street running south from Clonliffe Road to the Royal Canal. See 79.32 and 80.05. Stephen is heading for Millbourne Lane, Drumcondra.

83.09 *Doyle is in a great bake*. "His original is Charles Doyle, S.J., a scholastic assigned in 1897 to teach Third of Grammar at Belvedere. He was not, then, one of Joyce's teachers (Joyce having completed this grade of Grammar in 1893 . . .)." (Sullivan, p. 87.) To be in a bake is to be angry, though the distinction between a "bake" and a "wax" is not clear. In Anstey's *Vice Versâ* (see 73.01) angry teachers are said to be "in a bait" (p. 48.) "In a bake" may be a corruption of this, or vice versa.

83.22 *bally*. A euphemism for bloody (from 1884). (OED.) Heron's language—"deucedly" (*P*, 77.04), "your Governor" (*P*, 77.06), "by Jove" (*P*, 77.09), etc.—is that of an English dandy of the period, and much of it echoes that of the students in Grimstone's school in *Vice Versâ*. See 73.01.

85.04 *the band playing* The Lily of Killarney. From the opera by Julius Benedict (1862) based on Dion Boucicault's melodrama of Irish treachery. *The Colleen Bawn* (1850), based on Gerald Griffin's novel, *The Collegians* (1829), based on Irish life and legend.

86.10 *George's Street*. Great George's Street leads southward (toward the Liffey) at a right angle from Great Denmark Street, on which Belvedere College fronts.

86.25 Lotts. Still a Dublin laneway a short block behind the northern quays of the Liffey.

86.32 *a railway carriage at Kingsbridge*. Joyce accompanied his father to Cork in February 1894, when he disposed of the last of his properties. (Ellmann, p. 37.)

87.18 *Maryborough*. Now called Port Laoise, fifty-two miles from Dublin.

87.19 *Mallow*. A railroad junction about twenty-one miles from Cork.

87.35 *a jingle*. "One of Bianconi's long cars." (P. W. Joyce, p. 278.) See 20.02.

88.08-23 'Tis youth and folly/ . . . mountain dew. Brendan Behan sang a somewhat different version of this song on the recording "Brendan Behan on Joyce" (Folkways Records, FL 9826).

88.29 come-all-yous. Ballads which begin with these words, like Simon Dedalus's "O, come all you Roman catholics/ That never went to mass." (*P*, 35.12.)

89.04 *drisheens*. A dish beloved in Cork—"a sort of pudding made of the narrow intestines of a sheep, filled with blood that has been cleared of the red colouring matter, and mixed with meal and some other ingredients." (P. W. Joyce.)

89.09 *Queen's College*. Now University College, Cork. Joyce's father entered in 1867 and passed the first year of the medical course, but then he devoted himself to sports and college theatricals. He rowed in the college fours, ran cross-country, put the shot, and held the record for the hop, step, and jump. (Stanislaus, p. 24.) He spent time on dramatic performances and singing. He failed during his second and third years. Cf. 241.11.

89.12 *the Mardyke.* A "fine promenade" in Cork, says Ellmann (p. 37), though it is little better than an alley today. A few blocks from the university.

90.23 *the Groceries.* An ordinary grocery store, not remembered at University College today. It may have been licensed to sell alcoholic beverages.

90.26-30 *Harry Peard . . . Johnny Keevers of the Tantiles.* See the Trieste notebook, p. 297, this edition.

92.12 Queenstown. The port city of Cork, now called Cobh.

93.06 *slim jim.* Joyce says, "This is a kind of sweet meat made of soft marshmellow jelly which is coated first with pink sugar and then powdered, so far as I remember with coconut chips. It is called 'Slim Jim' because it is sold in strips about a foot or a foot and a half in length and an inch in breadth. It is very elastic and can be eaten by two people at the same time." (*Letters*, III, 129.)

93.25 *a lob.* A dialectal word meaning a "lump" of money or a nugget of gold. (*OED.*) In Ireland perhaps only a penny.

93.29 *Dublin jackeen.* Dublin diminutive of Jack; a worthless fellow.

94.07 *Dilectus.* Probably Richard Valpy's *Delectus* (1816), where, as Atherton points out, the sentence "*India mittit ebur*" (see 179.16) is used as an example.

94.08 *Tempora mutantur. . . .* "Times change and we change with them." Both versions are correct. John Joyce quotes the first two words in a letter to James in 1914. (*Letters*, II, 332.) Atherton points out (p. 244) that the phrase "was used by Robert Greene as the title of a poem, advising the reader to shun envy and ambition, which has as its second line, 'Proud Icarus did fall he soared so high.'"

94.25 *Yerra.* Sometimes spelled "arrah"; from the Irish *aire*, "take care, look out, look you." (P. W. Joyce, p. 61.)

94.30 *Sunday's Well.* A fashionable Cork suburb.

96.07-10 Art thou pale for weariness/ . . . *Shelley's fragment.* "To the Moon" (1824):

I

Art thou pale for weariness
Of climbing heaven and gazing on the earth,
Wandering companionless
Among the stars that have a different birth,
And ever changing, like a joyless eye
That finds us object worth its constancy?

II

> Thou Chosen Sister of the Spirit,
> That gazes on thee till in thee it pities . . .

96.14 *his brother and one of his cousins.* By "brother" the reader is no doubt meant to understand Maurice. See 71.36. The cousin may be Kathleen (Katsy) Murray. See 67.18.

96.15 *quiet Foster Place.* A tree-lined, dead-end street immediately behind the Bank of Ireland.

96.19 *orders on the governor of the bank of Ireland for thirty and three pounds.* Joyce won exhibitions during several of his years at Belvedere, but only in 1897 did he receive precisely £33. (Sullivan, pp. 98ff.)

96.31 *the house of commons of the old Irish parliament.* The new Bank of Ireland moved into Parliament House, which became unnecessary as the seat of government following the Act of Union in 1800.

97.02 *Hely Hutchinson and Flood and Henry Grattan and Charles Kendal Bushe.* They were all members of the Irish Parliament toward the end of the eighteenth century and were noted for their great oratory.

97.09 *keen October wind.* October 1897. On questions of "time" see 10.07, 19.05, 96.19, and 102.01.

97.13 *windows of Barnardo's.* Barnardo & Son, 108 Grafton Street, are still in business as furriers.

97.20 *Underdone's.* Ellmann (p. 40n.) suggests that this unpleasant name might be for the expensive Jammet's, still a leading restaurant in Dublin, catty-corner from Barnardo's, on Nassau Street.

97.33 *Ingomar.* A German melodrama by Friedrich Hahn, trans. Mrs. G. W. Lovell, 1851.

97.33 *The Lady of Lyons.* Edward Bulwer-Lytton's romantic drama in which Claude Melnotte, a gardener's son and poor poet, loves and wins Pauline Deschappelles by skillfully playing the role of the Prince of Como. When Pauline discovers his true identity, she rejects him, and he joins Napoleon's army, winning glory and the rank of colonel. He returns to thwart the villain and wins Pauline at last. See 99.23 and **Magalaner** and Kain, pp. 115-119.

99.23 *Claude Melnotte.* See 97.33. Melnotte provides a self-image for Stephen and Joyce quite like that of the Count of Monte Cristo, and in the deepest sense (that is, beyond the consciousnesses of the characters and perhaps of their authors, but not beyond Joyce's) their "identity problems" may be said to be Stephen's.

100.19 *the quarter of the jews.* The area near Mabbott and Mecklenburg Streets (now partially "redeveloped"), which Joyce made famous in literature as "Nighttown" in the "Circe" episode of *Ulysses*. See 181.29.

CHAPTER III

102.01 December. See Sullivan, pp. 125ff., for a discussion of Joyce's life relating to the time sequence of the end of Chapter II and the beginning of Chapter III. In life this December could only be 1898, the one year near the end of the century when December 3, the feast of St. Francis Xavier, fell on a Saturday. Cf. 10.07, 19.05, and 97.09.

103.16 the balefire of its burning stars. A balefire is a great fire in the open air. Sometimes it is confused with another meaning of bale as "fatal or evil fire." (*OED*.)

103.27 He had sinned mortally. Mortal sin is sin entailing spiritual death, and is sometimes called "deadly sin." See 106.09 for a list of them.

103.32 the fountains of sanctifying grace. Sanctifying grace is the state of habitual holiness, as distinguished from "actual grace," the transient help to act morally.

103.35 actual grace. See 103.32.

104.22 an illuminated scroll, the certificate of his prefecture in the college of the sodality of the Blessed Virgin Mary. Joyce was admitted to the sodality on December 7, 1895, and on September 25, 1896, he was chosen prefect, and his friend and rival Albrecht Connolly (Heron), assistant prefect. The prefecture was the highest distinction for a student at Belvedere. Joyce was elected to an unusual second term, which he served from December 17, 1897, until he left Belvedere in June 1898. (Sullivan, pp. 176ff.)

104.25 recite the little office. The "Little Office of Our Lady" is a liturgical devotion to the Blessed Virgin, in imitation of, and in addition to, the Divine Office. It was heard of as early as the eighth century and became obligatory for clergy by the fourteenth century. (*Cath. Encyc.*)

104.31 the psalms of prophecy. In the Vulgate (Rheims) numbering, Psalms 8, 18, 23, 44, 45, 86, 95, 96, and 97.

104.32 the glories of Mary. As Atherton points out (p. 245), this is the title of a book by St. Alphonsus Liguori and of a sermon by Cardinal Newman (No. 17 in the *Discourses to Mixed Congregations*), both of which are quoted from at 116.20 and 138.30.

104.35 her emblems, the lateflowering plant and lateblossoming tree. The apocryphal writings about Mary explain that she remained in the Temple after her presentation until she was fourteen years old. The high priest then called all the young men of the family of David and promised Mary in marriage to him whose rod should sprout and become the resting place of the Holy Ghost in the form of a dove. Joseph was the privileged one. (*Cath. Encyc.*)

105.01-08 *the lesson towards the close of the office* . . . suavitatem odoris. "I was exalted like a cedar in Libanus, and as a cypress tree in Mount Sion. I was exalted like a palm tree in Cades and as a rose plant in Jericho. As a fair olive tree in the plains, and as a plane tree by the water in the streets was I exalted. I gave a sweet smell like cinnamon and aromatic balm: I gave a sweet odor like the best myrrh." From Ecclesiasticus 24:17-20.

105.10 *the refuge of sinners.* An epithet frequently used of the Blessed Virgin Mary, in the Little Office, the Litany of the Blessed Virgin, and elsewhere.

105.17 *her whose emblem is the morning star.* The epithet "morning star" is used in the Litany of the Blessed Virgin; see 35.30.

105.23 *sums and cuts.* Joyce explains: "Schoolboy's abbreviation for problems set by a master to his class on the model of some theorum or problem in whatever book of Euclid's Geometry they are reading." (*Letters*, III, 129.)

105.26 My excellent friend Bombados. In the manuscript the name given here was first spelled *Pompados,* and this line was followed by another, "*My dearest and best Patake.*" The changes were probably made on the advice of Michael Healy, Nora Barnacle's (see Chronology under 1904, and ff.) uncle and a port official in Galway, as indicated by the following letter to him from Joyce in 1915: "I forgot whether I thanked you for having verified the quotation about our excellent friend Bombados. If I did not I do so now. I shall correct it on the proof—if I ever see one." (*Letters,* I, 86.)

105.30 *scut.* See 40.16.

106.05 *The sentence of saint James.* St. James 2:10: "And whosoever shall keep the whole law, but offend in one point, is become guilty of all."

106.09 *deadly sins.* The deadly sins (cf. 103.27) are lust, pride, covetousness, envy (or calumnious murmuring), gluttony, anger, and sloth. See Stephen's confession, *P*, 143-144.

106.26 *first beatitude.* Matthew 5:3.

106.27 *the second beatitude.* Matthew 5:4.

107.12 *after beads.* After communal recitation of the rosary. It consists of fifteen decades of Hail, Marys (*Ave Marias*), each preceded by an Our Father (*Pater Noster*) and followed by a Glory

Be to the Father (*Gloria Patrii*). One of the Sorrowful, Joyful, or Glorious Mysteries is contemplated during the recital of each decade. The rosary is divided into three parts, each consisting of five decades (of beads or prayers) and called a chaplet.

107.13 *special confessors.* That is, priests to whom the penitent regularly goes and to whom he is known.

107.27 *an old and illustrious Spanish family.* Especially on his mother's side. Francis Xavier was the son of Juan de Jasso, privy councilor to Jean d'Albret, King of Navarre, and his wife, Maria de Azpilcueta y Xavier, sole heiress of two Navarrese families. He was born at his mother's castle of Xavier at the foot of the Pyrenees. (*Encyc. Brit.*)

107.29 *They met in Paris where Francis Xavier was professor of philosophy at the university.* In 1528 Xavier was appointed lecturer in Aristotelian philosophy at the College de Beauvais of the University of Paris, where he met Ignatius of Loyola, also from the Spanish Basque country, in 1529. The other details of Xavier's life given below follow those reported by his Jesuit biographers. (*Encyc. Brit.*)

108.22 *simoom.* A hot, dry, suffocating sand-wind which sweeps across the African and Asiatic deserts at intervals during the spring and summer. (*OED.*) See Byron's *Manfred*, III, i, 128.

108.23 Remember only thy last things and thou shalt not sin for ever. The four last things are death, judgment, heaven, and hell. See *P*, 109.35.

108.28 *Father Arnall.* The retreat was led, according to Ellmann (p. 49), by Father James A. Cullen, a member of the Belvedere faculty. Cullen follows old Jesuit texts exclusively in his sermons. See Sullivan, pp. 138ff.; James R. Thrane, "Joyce's Sermon on Hell: Its Sources and Its Backgrounds," *Modern Philology*, LVII (February 1960), 177-198; Elizabeth F. Boyd, "Joyce's Hell-Fire Sermons," *Modern Language Notes*, LXXV (November 1960), 561-571; and James Doherty, "Joyce and *Hell Opened to Christians*: The Edition He Used for His 'Hell Sermons,'" *Modern Philology*, LXI (November 1963), 110-119. Thrane established that Joyce used Giovanni Pietro Pinamonti, S.J., *Hell Opened to Christians, to Caution Them from Entering into It,* as the main source of the sermons. But the sermons and meditations on hell by Jesuits from the sixteenth through the nineteenth centuries show a remarkable similarity in their order, imagery, phrasing, and quotation of Biblical passages.

113.12 *The stars of heaven were falling upon the earth like the figs cast by the figtrees which the wind has shaken.* Revelation

6:13. Revelation is called the Apocalypse in the Vulgate Bible, from which Joyce usually quotes in either Latin or English, often taking the quotation from the *Sodality Manual*, the missal, or some other source. However, he also copied the entire book of Revelation from the King James Bible. (Scholes and Kain, p. 264.)

115.03 *Addison, the great English writer, who, when on his deathbed, sent for the wicked young earl of Warwick.* Doctor Johnson gives the following account of the scene: "Lord Warwick [Addison's stepson, for whom he had served as tutor before marrying the dowager Countess of Warwick] was a young man of very irregular life, and perhaps of loose opinions. Addison, for whom he did not want respect, had very diligently endeavored to reclaim him; but his arguments and expostulations had no effect. One experiment, however, remained to be tried: when he found his life near its end, he directed the young lord to be called; and when he desired, with great tenderness, to hear his last injunctions, told him, *I have sent for you that you may see how a Christian can die.* What effect this awful scene had on the earl I know not; he likewise died himself in a short time." Samuel Johnson, *Lives of the English Poets,* I (Oxford: Oxford University Press, 1906), 422-423.

Joyce's use of the allusion is ironic, of course: Addison was a Tory, a flatterer of William of Orange, and secretary to the Marquis of Wharton when the latter was appointed Lord Lieutenant of Ireland. See 115.07.

115.07 *O grave, where is thy victory?*
　　　O death, where is thy sting?
I Corinthians 15:55. Joyce, however, quotes the lines as verse from Alexander Pope's "The Dying Christian to His Soul." This allusion to Pope, along with the preceding reference to Addison (*P*, 115.03), could be taken as a good illustration of the way Joyce ironically disparages both the understanding and literary sensibility of the priest, at the same time that Stephen, in a more complex irony, is "converted" by means of them.

115.21 *crossed the square.* Mountjoy Square. See 65.23 and 71.16.
115.27 *Emma.* Emma Clery. See 70.13 and 202.21.
116.20 *is not like early beauty . . . musical.* From Newman's *Glories of Mary.* Cf. 138.30, from the conclusion of the same work.
117.28 non serviam. See 246.37.
124.16 *the temple of the Holy Ghost.* The body. "Or know you not, that your members are the temple of the Holy Ghost, who is in you. . . ." (I Corinthians 6:19.)
125.25 *out by Malahide.* Joyce used this experience in the essay "Portrait" of 1904 (see p. 258 of this edition) and in *SH,* 156.15ff.

127.12 *book of spiritual exercises.* Loyola completed his *Book of the Spiritual Exercises* in 1548. It was designed to arouse a conviction of sin, of justice, and of judgment.

127.13 *composition of place.* Loyola's method or "exercise" of placing himself in the presence of God by calling material things related to Jesus before his mind—the wood of the cross, the smell of the sweat and the blood, etc.

134.27 *the act of contrition.* A formal prayer, beginning, "O my God, I am heartily sorry for all my sins. . . ."

137.05 *He had sinned so deeply against heaven and before God that he was not worthy to be called God's child.* Cf. Luke 15:18-19, 21. The decision of the prodigal son.

137.32 *Goatish creatures with human faces.* Reworked from an epiphany. See p. 269 of this edition.

138.30 *He prayed.* Atherton (p. 247) identifies this as the conclusion of Newman's *The Glories of Mary*. See 104.32 and 116.20.

141.12 *Church Street chapel.* "He [Joyce] did not confess in the college chapel; to abase himself before Father Henry was still too much to bear. He went instead, according to his sister, to the Church Street chapel. A Capuchin there listened to the tale from a boy, of a man's sins with sympathy rather than indignation." (Ellmann, p. 50.) P. W. Joyce points out (pp. 143-149) that in Ireland a Protestant place of worship is called a church, a Catholic church a chapel. (Cf. "Findlater's Church," 160.14, a Presbyterian church, and "Clontarf chapel," 164.13, a Catholic chapel.) The reason for the usage, he says, is that in penal days only Protestants attended church, while Catholics heard mass in the open air, later in huts and chapels.

142.09 *the brown habit of a capuchin.* The Capuchins, a branch of the Franciscan Order of Friars, wear a brown robe with a cowl, or *capuche*, sandals, and skull caps. The robe is fastened with a white rope cincture.

143.07 *God's yoke was sweet and light.* Matthew 11:30.

145.21 *the grave words of absolution.* The priest says, in Latin, "Absolvo te in nominis Patris et Filii et Spiritus Sancti. Amen."

145.25 *knelt to say his penance.* Modern penances ordinarily are merely the requirement of saying a certain number of prayers.

146.21 *ciborium.* The metal vessel shaped like a large stemmed wine cup in which the hosts are kept for distribution at the Communion of the Mass.

146.22 Corpus Domini nostri. "[This is] the body of our Lord."
146.26 In vitam eternam. Amen. "Unto life eternal. Amen."

CHAPTER IV

147.12 interleaved prayerbook. Stephen has apparently inserted between the leaves of his prayerbook leaflets printed with special prayers and petitions such as often carry special indulgences for the souls in purgatory.

147.18 ejaculations. Brief exclamations to God, the Blessed Virgin, or another, such as, "Lord Jesus Christ, have mercy on me!"

147.18 stored up ungrudgingly for the souls in purgatory centuries of days and quarantines and years. ". . . The literal surface of the passage was available to Joyce in the [*Sodality*] *Manual* where indulgences are carefully explained (p. 20) and a list of ejaculations provided (pp. 100-1) with a precise number of days' indulgence attached to each. The devotional arithmetic involved in totaling up these figures might pose a problem for one less naïve and more patient than Stephen Dedalus." (Sullivan, p. 137.) There are, of course, many manuals which do the same thing. Quarantines are periods of forty days in purgatory.

148.08 the amount of his purchase. The slogan was first used on cash registers built during the 1890s.

148.17 three daily chaplets. The rosary is divided into three parts, each consisting of five decades of *Aves* (preceded by a *Pater* and followed by a *Gloria*) and known as a corona or chaplet. See 107.12.

148.25 the seven gifts of the Holy Ghost. Wisdom, understanding, counsel, piety, fortitude, knowledge, and fear of the Lord.

148.26 seven deadly sins. See 106.09.

149.01 Paraclete. The Greek and Latin name for the (Anglo-Saxon) Holy Ghost.

149.02 To sin against Whom was a sin beyond forgiveness. The unforgivable sin is "blasphemy" against the Holy Ghost. (See Matthew 12:32, Mark 3:29, and Luke 12:10.) No one is certain what this sin is, though Catholic teaching most frequently suggests total despair, a final and invincible loss of hope in attaining a state of grace. (See 159.17.)

152.09 an old neglected book written by saint Alphonsus Liguori. Sullivan says (p. 135n.) that this may be either *Way of Salvation* or *Preparation for Death*, both of which are readings suggested by *Sodality Manual*, p. 397. But the quotations from the Canticle of Canticles (or Song of Solomon) which follow are used in Liguori's *Visitations to the Blessed Sacrament*.

152.13 imagery of the canticles. See the imagery which follows in this paragraph, all drawn from the Old Testament Canticle of Canticles.

152.16 *bidding her arise as for espousal and come away.* Canticles 2:13. See the epiphany quoted in this text, p. 269.

152.17 *a spouse, from Amana and from the mountains of the leopards.* Canticles 4:8.

152.19 Inter ubera mea commorabitur. Canticles 1:13, "He shall lie between my breasts."

153.17 *bidden by his confessor to name some sin of his past life.* Since some mortal sin is needed as "matter" for absolution, and since Stephen confesses none, the confessor makes this demand.

153.32 *the director.* Stanislaus confirms that this interview took place. ("Open Letter to Dr. Oliver Gogarty," *Interim*, IV [1954], Nos. 1 and 2, p. 51.)

154.26 *capuchin dress.* See 142.09.

155.07 Les jupes. "The skirts."

156.12 *muff.* An unformed bungler; one of the uninitiated.

156.17 *quiet obedience.* Obedience is the virtue of all others in which Ignatius wished the Company of Jesus to excel.

156.25 *I believe that Lord Macaulay was a man who probably never committed a mortal sin in his life.* The priest is "giving himself away" as stupid or uninformed in several respects in this epiphany. Every mortal sin is by definition "deliberate," and Macaulay's life was not spotless. He was very antipathetic to high Anglicanism, much more so to Roman Catholicism. (*DNB.*) Cf. the well-known remark about Joyce's patron saint, "In the opinion of his director, Saint Robert Bellarmine, and three of his other confessors, he never in his life committed a mortal sin." (Article on St. Aloysius Gonzaga, in Alban Butler, *Lives of the Saints*, rev. ed. [New York: Kenedy, 1956].)

156.35 *Louis Veuillot.* (1813-1883) Pale, aristocratic, and journalistic when compared with the flamboyant Hugo, Veuillot wrote delicate religious romances and supported the secular powers of the Church in France against attempts to limit them.

158.06 *the power of the keys.* Matthew 16:19.

158.25 *thurible.* A censer; a vessel in which incense is burned. Cf. 41.01-03.

158.25 *chasuble.* A sleeveless outer vestment worn by the celebrant at Mass over his other clothing. It would swing open only at the sides, not in front or at the back.

158.33 *the tunicle of subdeacon at high mass.* A wide-sleeved vestment worn over the alb (the long, close-sleeved robe of white linen) by subdeacons at the celebration of High Mass, and by bishops. The subdeacon prepares the sacred vessels and reads the epistle.

158.35 his shoulders covered with a humeral veil. Since a humeral veil is a shoulder veil, the expression is a tautology. The veil covers the hands when they are holding sacred vessels.

158.35 paten. The plate on which the bread is placed in the celebration of the Mass or eucharist.

159.01 stand as deacon in dalmatic of cloth of gold. The deacon is next in order below the celebrant at Mass. The dalmatic is the vestment which he wears over his alb.

159.03 Ite, missa est. "Go, the Mass is ended." Often considered humorously by the faithful, for the response is "Deo gratias" ("Thanks be to God"), but not by Stephen in his serious fantasy of power here.

159.16 the sin of Simon Magus. Simony; making a profit out of sacred things. See Acts 8:9-24. Simon Magus, a magician who wanted to buy from the apostles the power of giving the Holy Ghost to the faithful by the imposition of hands, is sometimes known as "the first heretic" or "the father of heresies." (See Kenner, p. 422, this edition.)

159.17 the sin against the Holy Ghost. See 149.02.

159.24 the imposition of hands. The laying-on of hands by the bishop in confirmation and ordination confers a fullness of grace from the Holy Ghost beyond that received in baptism. See Acts 6:6 and 8:16-18.

159.29 drink damnation to himself, not discerning the body of the Lord. I Corinthians 11:29.

159.31 a priest for ever according to the order of Melchisedec. Hebrews 7:21. Jesus, and hence all priests, are understood to belong to this order.

159.33 offer up my mass. That is, say the Mass with the special intention that God will reveal His will to Stephen.

159.35 a novena. A nine-day devotion.

159.35 your holy patron saint, the first martyr. St. Stephen Protomartyr.

160.03 Once a priest always a priest. Although a priest may for various reasons be relieved of priestly duties, he remains a priest.

160.05 the sacrament of Holy Orders is one of those which can be received only once. The others are baptism, confirmation, and, usually, matrimony. Those that can be received repeatedly are penance, communion, and extreme unction.

160.14 Findlater's church. A Presbyterian church at the head of Rutland Square (now Parnell Square), at right angles to Great Denmark Street, a long block from Belvedere College.

160.31 novitiate. Refers to both the state of being a novice in a religious order (a period of probation before taking vows) and to the quarters occupied by novices.

161.19 S.J. Society of Jesus.

161.28-29 Lantern Jaws . . . Foxy Campbell. Father Richard Campbell, S.J., a teacher at Belvedere.

161.30 the jesuit house in Gardiner Street. Next to the Church of St. Francis Xavier.

162.18 the bridge over the stream of the Tolka. Joyce lived near the Tolka in Millbourne Lane, Drumcondra. It is the river of the Dublin north side as the Dodder is the river of the south side. Millbourne Lane is the first turn to the left off Drumcondra Road beyond the bridge.

162.19 the faded blue shrine of the Blessed Virgin which stood fowl-wise. Although the old shrine is gone, a new one has been erected beside the bridge over the Tolka a few blocks from Joyce's former home in Millbourne Lane.

162.36 A group of his brothers and sisters. For a discussion of Joyce's brothers and sisters, see 174.26.

163.18 Fallon. The only Belvedere student identified by name. See Sheehy, *May It Please the Court* (Dublin: P. J. Fallon, 1951), p. 22.

163.27 his youngest brother. Joyce's youngest brother was George, born in 1887. If Stephen's youngest brother was born the same year, he would be nine years old here. See 174.26.

163.28 Oft in the Stilly Night.

> Oft in the stilly night,
>   Ere Slumber's chain has bound me,
> Fond memory brings the light
>   Of other days around me;
>   The smiles, the tears,
>   Of boyhood's years,
> The words of love then spoken.

164.09 Newman had heard this note also in the broken lines of Virgil. See Newman's *Grammar of Assent* (New York: Doubleday "Image Books," 1955, p. 79.) According to Atherton, p. 249, Joyce could have garnered all of the Newman quotations from a one-volume anthology, *Characteristics from the Writings of John Henry Newman*, William S. Lilly (London, 1875). See 165.21 and 176.13.

164.13 the gate of Clontarf Chapel. On Clontarf Road, not far from the bridge to the Bull. See 164.23.

164.20 the university. Joyce left Belvedere in June 1898, and entered University College, Dublin, that September.

164.23 He set off abruptly for the Bull. The Bull's full name is North Bull Island, a sandy island stretching from the north side of the mouth of the Liffey northeastward toward Howth. Clontarf means "Field of the Bull."

165.21 *a proud cadence from Newman.* From *The Idea of a University.* Cf. 164.09 and 176.13.

165.30 *He turned seaward from the road at Dollymount.* Dollymount is the area of Dublin northeast of Clontarf.

165.31 *the thin wooden bridge.* This bridge still leads from Clontarf Road to the Bull.

165.32 A *squad of christian brothers.* See 71.21.

166.27 A *day of dappled seaborne clouds.* Atherton (p. 249) identifies this as being from Hugh Miller's *The Testimony of the Rocks* (1869).

167.18 *the seventh city of Christendom.* A name given to Dublin during the Middle Ages.

167.20 *the days of the thingmote.* That is, when Viking kings sat in Dublin, thus beginning its millennium as the center of foreign domination of Ireland by Danes, Normans, and English. The basic meaning of *thing* is "public assembly."

168.04 *Bous Stephanoumenos! Bous Stephaneforos!* "Ox wreathed! Ox garlanded!" The name Stephen means "a garland."

169.01 *the fabulous artificer.* Daedalus.

169.03 *a winged form flying above the waves.* Icarus.

169.05 *a hawklike man.* Icarus.

170.05 *the great artificer whose name he bore.* Daedalus.

170.08 *the stoneblock.* This is on the south side of the "spine of rocks" (*P*, 167.12) which stretches eastward into Dublin Bay from the Bull Bridge. It is the only safe place for diving on the Bull, and it is still used for that purpose.

170.16 *He looked northward towards Howth.* Howth is the headland forming the northern end of Dublin Bay. "The incident actually occurred to Joyce about this time." (Ellmann, p. 56.) Joyce's first attempt to treat this scene was made in the essay "Portrait" of 1904. (See p. 262 of this edition.)

171.04 *faded cerements.* Graveclothes. Figuratively speaking, Stephen is dying and being reborn.

171.17 *ivory.* Perhaps the reader is expected to recall the association of "ivory" with Eileen and the Blessed Virgin. See 35.30.

172.09 *to recreate life out of life.* See *P*, 221.14, for Stephen's view of himself as a "priest of eternal imagination."

172.11 *fair courts of life.* See the essay "Portrait" (p. 263 of this edition).

CHAPTER V

174.01 *watery tea*. See Anderson, pp. 3-13. Stephen has become a priest of art. The watery tea suggests the wine of the Mass sacrifice. It is the Mass of Maundy Thursday.

174.02 *crusts of fried bread*. These might be said to represent the bread of the Mass sacrifice. (See 174.01.)

174.06 *box of pawntickets . . . the blue and white dockets*. The dockets might be said to represent the communion wafers for distribution to the communicants. (See 174.01.)

174.16 *lousemarks*. "His [Joyce's] clothes were generally unpressed and he still rarely washed [when at the age of 16½ he entered the matriculation class at University College, Dublin]. In a game at the Sheehys, asked his pet antipathy, Joyce replied, 'Soap and water,' and at a meeting of the Library Committee at University College it was probably he who voiced the opinion that there was no advantage in being clean. His sister Eva recalled that he prided himself that lice would not live on his flesh. . . ." (Ellmann, pp. 66-67.)

174.23 *The dear knows*. A translation of the Irish *Thauss ag Dhee* ("God knows"), for which the euphemism *Thauss ag fee* "The deer knows") is substituted. (P. W. Joyce, p. 69).

174.26-28 *Katey . . . Boody . . . Maggie*. John and Mary Joyce had many children; there is some doubt about how many. In *P* Stephen says, "Nine or ten. Some died," (241.03) and Joyce spoke of being surrounded by his "twenty-three sisters," while his brother Stanislaus says that "Mother had seventeen children of whom nine are now living." (*Diary*, p. 19.) Gorman (with Joyce's assent) says that there were "sixteen or seventeen children (five of whom died in infancy and youth) in eighteen years." (Gorman, p. 11.) Those who survived childhood were James, 1882, Margaret ("Poppie"), 1884, Stanislaus, 1884, Charles, 1886, George, 1887, Eileen, 1889, Mary ("May"), 1890, Eva, 1891, Florence, 1892, and Mabel ("Baby"), 1893. See Ellmann, pp. 20, 41.

174.28 *blue*. Bluing for clothes.

175.26 *kissing the tips of his fingers in adieu*. See 174.01. Stephen as priest of art celebrating a new Mass is kissing the altar representing Jesus. Since he has *become* Jesus, he kisses himself. (See Anderson, p. 6 and n.)

175.27-30 *The lane behind the terrace . . . the nuns' madhouse beyond the wall*. From May 1900 until 1901 the Joyces lived at 8 Royal Terrace, Fairview, Joyce's twelfth home. "This was the house, separated by a wall from the convent grounds, where they could hear the mad nuns' screams. . . ." (Ellmann, p. 70.)

175.31 Jesus! O Jesus! Jesus! See 174.01. The nun's ejaculation suggests both a thanksgiving for the "Mass" just ended and a naming of Stephen as Jesus.

Stanislaus Joyce underlines Joyce's interest in the Mass of the Presanctified: "It was as a primitive religious drama that my brother valued it so highly. He understood it as a drama of a man who has a perilous mission to fulfil, which he must fulfil even though he knows beforehand that those nearest to his heart will betray him. The chant and words of Judas or Peter on Palm Sunday, '*Etsi omnes scandalizati fuerint in te, ego numquam scandalizabor,*' moved him profoundly. He was habitually a very late riser, but wherever he was, alone in Paris or married in Trieste, he never failed to get up at about five in all weathers to go to the early morning Mass on Holy Thursday and Good Friday." (Stanislaus, p. 105.)

176.8 girls and women in the plays of Gerhart Hauptmann. During the summer of 1901, which Joyce spent with his father in Mullingar, he translated Hauptmann's *Vor Sonnenaufgang* (*Before Sunrise*) and *Michael Kramer.* (Ellmann, p. 89.)

176.12 the sloblands of Fairview. The sloblands were marshlands north of the Liffey mouth, drained to form Fairview Park.

176.13 cloistral silverveined prose of Newman. See 164.09 and 165.21.

176.14 North Strand Road. This road runs southwest from Fairview toward the Custom House on the north side of the Liffey.

176.15 the dark humour of Guido Cavalcanti. Italian poet (*ca.* 1255-1300), a contemporary of Dante.

176.17 the spirit of Ibsen. See *Critical Writings*, p. 65 and *passim.*

176.19 a grimy marinedealer's shop beyond the Liffey. Verdon, McCann & Co., 2 Burgh Quay and 3 and 13 City Quay—the only 1906 Thom's listing for yacht outfitters. Still doing business at the same address. Philip McCann, who was one of Joyce's baptismal sponsors and to whom he was related through his great-grandmother, John O'Connell's wife, was the owner or part-owner in Joyce's day.

176.20 the song by Ben Jonson. From the epilogue of *The Vision of Delight* (1617), where Aurora speaks the lyric about her lover Tithonus. Joyce read all of Ben Jonson's work in Paris in 1902-1903.

176.29 waistcoateers. Prostitutes of the lower classes. (Harmon.)

176.30 chambering. Sexual wantonness. Elizabethan English still current in Ireland. (See 180.32 and 182.11.)

176.35 Synopsis Philosophiæ Scholasticæ ad mentum divi Thomæ. Atherton says, "There are many similar titles; the nearest is G. M. Mancini's *Elementa Philosophiae ad mentem D. Thomae Aquinatis*, Rome, 1898 . . . which contains all that Joyce quotes." (p. 250.)

177.13 *near the hoardings on the canal*. The Royal Canal. The bridge on which the North Strand Road crosses it is the same one on which "Stephen" meets Mahoney in "An Encounter." (*D*.) Here, too, Joyce lost his virginity to a prostitute at the age of fourteen. (Ellmann, p. 48.)

177.13 *the consumptive man with the doll's face and the brimless hat*. For a discussion of this man as the type of the "disfigured Jesus" of the *Tenebrae* services, see Anderson, pp. 3-13.

177.22-23 *MacCann . . . squat figure in a shooting jacket and breeches*. In real life Francis ("Joe") Skeffington, who "invariably took first place in English" (Byrne, p. 54) and who changed his name to Sheehy-Skeffington, to show the equality of the sexes, when he married Hannah Sheehy (one of the "Daniel" sisters in *SH*). (Ellmann, p. 64.) Joyce called him the cleverest man at University College, after himself. (Ellmann, p. 63.) During the Easter uprising in 1916 he was "murdered by the British in Portobello Barracks, Dublin." (Byrne, p. 54.) "To protest against uniformity in dress he wore plus fours and was known as 'Knickerbockers.'" (Ellmann, p. 63.) In *SH* (p. 44) MacCann is called "Bonny Dundee," from Sir Walter Scott's line in "The Bonnets of Bonnie Dundee," "Come fill up my cup, come fill up my can."

177.24 *Hopkins' corner*. The corner of O'Connell Street (Sackville Street that was) and Eden Quay, where Hopkins and Hopkins still conduct business as a law firm.

178.06 *the desolate gardens of the green*. Saint Stephen's Green; on its south side the old University College buildings are situated.

178.15 *a severed head or deathmask*. Because Cranly represents John the Baptist in the secularized Christ-imagery of this chapter. See Anderson, pp. 10-11. For Cranly, see 191.09.

179.14 Ivory, ivoire, avorio, ebur. "Ivory" in English, French, Italian, and Latin.

179.16 India mittit ebur. "India sends ivory." The sentence is used as an example in Valpy's *Delectus*. See 94.07. (Atherton.)

179.17 *the shrewd northern face of the rector who had taught him to construe the Metamorphoses of Ovid in a courtly English*. Father William Henry, rector of Belvedere, called "Father Butler" in "An Encounter." (*D*.) See 75.32.

179.20 *He had learnt what little he knew of the laws of Latin verse from a ragged book written by a Portuguese priest*. Contrahit orator, variant in carmine vates. "The orator condenses, the poet-seers amplify in their verse." Atherton identifies the "ragged book" as the *Prosodia* of Emanuel Alvarez, S.J. (1526-1582).

179.24 *in tanto discrimine.* "In such a great crisis."

180.08 *The grey block of Trinity on his left.* The massive quad-rangle of Trinity College stands at the corner of Westmoreland and Nassau Streets, at the foot of Grafton Street, across from the Bank of Ireland.

180.12 *the national poet of Ireland.* Thomas Moore (1779-1852).

180.16 *It was a Firbolg in the borrowed cloak of a Milesian.* Both Firbolgs and Milesians are legendary Irish aborigines, the former dwarfish and primitive, the latter tall and handsome. The Milesians are said to have come from Spain and are referred to as the "dark Iberians." See 180.30.

180.18 *Davin.* In real life George Clancy. "The little tale in the *Portrait* about Davin's midnight adventure when returning home from the hurling match, is almost exactly as George told it himself." (Byrne, pp. 54-55.) While mayor of Limerick he was "foully murdered, by the Black and Tans at night in his home before the eyes of his family." (Byrne, p. 55.)

"Clancy was an enthusiast also for Gaelic sports like hurling, and therefore a great friend of Michael Cusack, the founder of the Gaelic Athletic Association." (Ellmann, p. 62.) Clancy appears in Joyce's early work as Madden; he is the only friend who calls Stephen by his first name.

180.30 *the rude Firbolg mind.* See 180.16.

180.32 *old English speech.* Stephen does not, of course, mean Old English (or Anglo-Saxon), but rather the language brought to Ireland by the Tudor and earlier invaders, and still used by country people. See, for example, 176.30 and Davin's expressions at *P*, 181.33, 182.07, 182.10, 182.11, 182.18, 182.27, 183.04, and 183.12.

180.34 *Michael Cusack, the Gael.* See 180.18. Cusack was the model for the "narrow-minded and rhetorical Cyclops in *Ulysses.*" (Ellmann, p. 63.) See 181.04.

181.04 *his uncle Mat Davin, the athlete.* Pat and Michael Davin were famous athletic Irish nationalists, the latter a founder with Michael Cusack of the Gaelic Athletic Association.

181.07 *young fenian.* See 38.25 and 202.02.

181.12 *the cycles.* The Irish heroic sagas of Finn, Ossian, Cu-chulain, Conchubar, Deirdre, *et al.*

181.20 *one of the tame geese.* In the last 150 years millions of Irishmen have left Ireland, reducing the population from more than eight million in 1840 to less than four million in 1964, the first year in modern times that the population has held its own. See 201.28.

181.29 dark narrow streets of the poorer jews. See 100.19.

181.33 disremember. To "disremember" means to "forget." P. W. Joyce says that it is "good old English; now out of fashion in England, but common in Ireland." (P. W. Joyce, p. 248.)

182.03 Buttevant. In northern County Cork.

182.04 a hurling match. Hurling or hurley is a fast, rough game which can best be pictured, perhaps, as a combination of football, baseball, soccer, hockey, and lacrosse. A small, hard ball is batted, rolled, or carried by means of a curved hardwood stick to the opponents' goal. See 182.07, 182.10, 182.11. Hurley, even more than other sports, is still associated with Irish nationalism and the Irish language.

182.07 stripped to his buff. This would ordinarily mean "to strip naked," but in Munster it means to strip "from the waist up." (P. W. Joyce, p. 227.)

182.07 minding cool. "Hurlers and football players always put one of their best players to mind cool or stand cool, i.e., to stand at their own goal or gap, to intercept the ball if the opponents should attempt to drive it through. Universal in Munster. Irish *cul* [cool], the back. The full word is cool-baur-ya, where 'baur-ya' is the goal or gap. The man standing cool is often called 'the man in the gap.'" (P. W. Joyce, p. 239.) See 182.04.

182.10 woeful wipe. "In Ulster, a goaly-wipe is a great blow on the ball with the *camann* or hurley. . . ." (P. W. Joyce, p. 351.)

182.11 his camann. The curved stick, also called a "hurley," used in hurling. See 182.04 and 182.10.

182.11 an aim's ace. "A small amount, quantity, or distance. Applied in the following way very generally, in Munster:—'He was within an aim's-ace of being drowned (very near). A survival in Ireland of the old Shakespearian word *ambs-ace*, meaning two aces or two single points in throwing dice, the smallest possible throw." (P. W. Joyce, p. 209.)

182.18 any kind of a yoke. "Any article or contrivance or apparatus, for use in some work. 'That's a queer yoke, Bill,' says a countryman when he first saw a motor car." (P. W. Joyce, p. 352.)

182.19 mass meeting that same day in Castletownroche. Perhaps for Land League agitation.

182.20 the cars. See 20.02, 87.35.

182.23-24 Ballyhoura Hills, that's better than ten miles from Kilmallock. The Ballyhoura Hills are in northern County Cork, Kilmallock in southern Limerick.

182.27 stopped by the way under a bush to redden my pipe. The uses of *way, under,* and *redden* are all Munsterisms. "An Irishman hardly ever lights his pipe: he reddens it." (P. W. Joyce, p. 311.)

183.04 She asked me was I tired. "The indirect question preceded by 'whether' or 'if' does not exist in Gaelic; it is rare in the mouth of an Irishman, who will say, 'I wondered was the horse well bred.' " (Hayden and Hartog, II, 938.) Joyce's father used this locution: "I wonder do you recollect the old days in Brighton Square. . . ." (*Letters,* III, 212.)

183.06 Queenstown. Queenstown (now Cobh) is the port of Cork City, several miles down the Lee River.

183.12 There's no one in it but ourselves. "In it" is a literal translation of "the Gaelic Ann (in it, *i.e.,* 'in existence') . . . *as ata sneachta ann,* lit., . . . 'there is snow in it!' " (P. W. Joyce, p. 25.)

183.25 handsel. The first sale of the day—an omen of success.

184.07 Grafton Street. Dublin's main shopping street, running from a few blocks south of the Liffey (from Trinity College and the Bank of Ireland) to Saint Stephen's Green.

184.09 a slab was set to the memory of Wolfe Tone. No doubt this is a recollection of a ceremony which took place in 1898, the centennial of the revolution of 1798, led by Tone. Even this tawdry tribute has disappeared since Grafton Street was widened to accommodate increased motorcar traffic, and Dubliners continue to decry the lack of an appropriate monument to Tone. (See 20.08.)

184.12 French delegates in a brake. The French had given Wolfe Tone and the Irish rebels ineffectual support in 1798.

184.21 the sombre college. The old buildings of University College are numbers 85 and 86 on the south side of Saint Stephen's Green, the latter the home of Richard Chapell ("Burnchapel") Whaley, father of "Buck" Whaley, the first a priesthunter, the second, known also as "Jerusalem" Whaley, a rake who walked to Jerusalem and played handball against its walls. With Buck Egan they performed, according to rumor, black masses in the future UCD buildings. (*DNB.*)

184.22 Buck Egan. See 184.21.

184.22 Burnchapel Whaley. See 184.21.

184.34 the dean of studies. Father Joseph Darlington. He is called Father Butt in *SH,* a name which has a special Irish meaning to designate a horse cart for potatoes, sand, etc. (P. W. Joyce, p. 228.) For J. F. Byrne's favorable impression of him see Byrne, pp. 28-29. For Byrne's description of the fire-lighting scene, which he says happened to him rather than to Joyce, see Byrne, pp. 33-34.

184.36 fireplace. A fine specimen of eighteenth-century ceramic elegance.

185.15 a levite of the Lord. An assistant in the Temple.

185.15 a levite's robe of plain linen. The Jesuit's soutane is probably of black cotton.

185.17 canonicals. The clothing prescribed by canon law for the clergy when officiating.

185.17 ephod. Priestly garb of the Hebrews, especially of the high priest.

186.01 Pulchra sunt quæ visa placent. Almost the words of Aquinas, who says "*Pulchra enim dicunter ea quæ visa placent*," "The beautiful is therefore said to be that which being seen [or apprehended] pleases." *Summa Theologica*, I, q. 5, a. 4, *ad Im.*) See Noon, pp. 22ff. and *passim*. Noon has surely underestimated, as Gorman overestimated, Joyce's knowledge of Aquinian thought. Sullivan provides a useful compromise. Joyce's "applied Aquinas" was a very early and accurate adaptation of St. Thomas's remarks on the beautiful to modern aesthetic questions. The work of the important Thomistic aestheticians—Maritain, Gilby, Gill, Little, and Duffy—would not be done until the 1930s and after. The novelistic point here is the irony that Stephen knows more about scholasticism than does the dean (in real life Father Darlington, the professor of metaphysics at University College).

186.07 Bonum est in quod tendit appetitus. "The good is that toward which the appetite is moved." The distinction between the beautiful and the good as understood by St. Thomas may be clearer if one considers a painting as apprehended "under the aspect of the beautiful and the good": in the first case one desires only to be pleased by beholding it; in the second, one wants to own it.

186.17 Like Ignatius he was lame. Byrne says that Father Darlington gave "the impression of having been an athlete." (Byrne, p. 28.)

186.19 the legendary craft of the company. The Company or "Little Company" of Jesus is another name for the Jesuits. "For the very many fables and false accusations that have grown up relative to the Jesuits, the reader should consult [Bernard] Duhr's [S.J.] *Jesuitenfabelas*." (Fitzpatrick, p. vii.)

186.21 It seemed as if he used the shifts and lore and cunning of the world, as bidden to do, for the greater glory of God. "No lectures should be given on those parts of books of humane letters which are contrary to virtue. The Society may use the rest as the 'spoils of the Egyptians.'" (*The Constitutions of the Society of Jesus*, Pt. IV, Ch. V, in Fitzpatrick, p. 70.)

186.25 with a firm gesture of obedience. Obedience is traditionally considered the special virtue of the Jesuits, as holy poverty is of the Franciscans.

186.27 Similiter atque senis baculus, he was, as the founder would have had him, like a staff in an old man's hand. The phrase is from the *Summarium Constitutionem* of the Jesuit order.

187.04 like looking down from the cliffs of Moher into the depths. These spectacular cliffs are on the west coast of Ireland about twelve miles south of Galway Bay. They face northwest toward the Aran Islands.

187.19-20 Epictetus also had a lamp . . . which was sold for a fancy price after his death. The name Epictetus ("acquired") refers to his slavery and may be appropriate for the servile dean who has acquired Catholicism by conversion. Like Ignatius and the dean, Epictetus was lame, according to Origen. He lived from *ca.* A.D. 60 to *ca.* 138. Lucian ridicules an admirer who bought Epictetus's earthenware lamp in hopes of becoming a philosopher by using it.

187.22-23 An old gentleman . . . who said that the soul is very like a bucketful of water. In his *Discourses* Epictetus refers to himself as "the old man." For the image of the soul as like a bucketful of water and outside impressions like light shining on the water ("When the water is disturbed it looks as if the light is disturbed —but it is not") see *Discourses of Epictetus*, Bk. III, Ch. 3.

187.25-26 he put an iron lamp before a statue of one of the gods and . . . a thief stole the lamp. Discourses of Epictetus, Bk. I, Ch. 18.

188.09 a sentence of Newman's in which he says of the Blessed Virgin that she was detained in the full company of the saints. "From Newman's 'Glories of Mary' . . . Newman is translating very literally *et in plenitudine sanctorum detentio mea* (*Ecclesiasticus*, 24:16): 'My abode is in the full assembly of the saints,' and this immediately precedes the Latin passage on p. 95 in the 'Little Office.'" (Atherton, p. 252.)

188.26-27 funnel . . . tundish. See 251.23.

188.32-33 Lower Drumcondra . . . where they speak the best English. Joyce's sixth home was in Millbourne Lane in Drumcondra not far from the Tolka River. The Joyces' neighbors were "farmhands and navvies." (Ellmann, p. 39.) See 162.18.

189.03 the wake of clamorous conversions. Father Darlington was an alumnus of Brasenose College, Oxford, M.A. 1876, and he had been an Anglican minister. During this period the Oxford or Tractarian movement was at high tide, and Newman, of whom Stephen has just thought, had floated into the Church on it.

189.08 serious dissenters. See 189.10.

189.10 vain pomps of the establishment. Father Darlington was an Anglican minister before his conversion. See 189.03. "Serious dissenters" eschewed the rituals, ceremonies, costumes, episcopal hierarchy, and other "popish" pomps of the Established Church of England.

189.12 six principle men, peculiar people, seed and snake baptists, supralapsarian dogmatists. These are very specialized dissenting sects representing the extreme "individualism" of interpreting the Scriptures, toward which Tractarianism was part of a widespread "corporate" reaction. Peculiar People, for example, is a religious sect founded in 1838 at Plumstead, England, which refuses medical aid, relying on prayer alone, because members feel bound by a literal interpretation of James 5:14. The sect takes it name from Deuteronomy 14:2. (*Encyc. Brit.*)

Supralapsarian Dogmatists are certain Calvinists who believe that God's decree of election of the individual to salvation determined that man should fall, so that there would be an opportunity of redeeming part of the human race. Sublapsarians, on the other hand, deny that the fall was part of God's original purpose in creation, and see the election of grace as a remedy for an existing evil. Jesuits tend, perhaps, toward the sublapsarian (semi-Pelagian) view, Dominicans toward the supralapsarian (Augustinian) view. (*Encyc. Brit.*)

189.15 insufflation. Breathing on a person (as in baptism) to symbolize or bring about the expulsion of evil spirits and the inspiration of the new spiritual life. "Spirit," as in Holy Spirit, means both "blowing" and "breathing."

189.16 the imposition of hands. The hands of the bishop, for example, are imposed on the postulant in baptism, confirmation, or ordination in order to give the Holy Ghost in full measure, a practice based mainly on Acts 8:17, 13:3, 19:6 and *passim*.

189.16 the procession of the Holy Ghost. One of the key theological questions which has tended to divide Christians from early times has been that of the "procession" of the Holy Ghost—whether the Holy Ghost proceeds from both the Father and the Son, or only from the Father. (*Encyc. Brit.*)

189.18 like that disciple who had sat at the receipt of custom. Matthew.

190.14 Mr Moonan. See 11.15.

190.19 Per aspera ad astra. "Through rough ways to the stars." This cliché was no doubt modeled (probably in the Middle Ages or Renaissance) on Vergil's "Macte nova virtute, puer, sic itur ad astra" ("Good speed to thy youthful valour, child! So shall thou scale the stars!"). (*Aeneid*, IX, 641.) Both Stephen and Joyce may be aware of this linguistic heritage, while the dean clearly is not.

190.29-30 *the name of worldlings . . . for having pleaded . . . for . . . the lax and the lukewarm and the prudent.* Cf. the story "Grace" (in *D*) for Joyce's fullest picture of Jesuits as apostles to the lukewarm ones.

190.35 *Kentish fire.* "A prolonged and ordered salvo or volley of applause, or demonstration of impatience or dissent (said to have originated in reference to meetings held in Kent in 1828-9, in opposition to the Catholic Relief Bill)." (*OED*.)

191.09 *Cranly.* In real life Cranly was J. F. Byrne, who has written his autobiography and memoir of Joyce in *Silent Years*. Joyce entered University College in the fall of 1898. Byrne had entered in 1895, but he stayed out during 1898-1899 to tutor two boys named Mooney. (Byrne, p. 39.) Joyce called Byrne "Cranly" beginning in 1898 after a "white Bishop," *i.e.*, a Carmelite bishop or archbishop of Dublin (from 1397 to 1417). He may also have been influenced by the name of one of the Joyces' nursemaids, "Cranly, a young woman whose people were decent fisher folk from Bray. . . ." (Sullivan, p. 37.)

191.14 *Leopardstown.* The main Dublin track for horseracing, northwest of the city.

191.15 *Moynihan's.* Moynihan's remark, "Chase me, ladies, I'm in the cavalry!" (*P*, 192.10) was in fact made by a young man named Kinahan in one of Professor Felix Hackett's lectures. The lecture presented in *P* telescopes two lectures given by Professor Hackett, one on electricity and one on mechanics, some months apart. (Ellmann, p. 308n.)

191.24 *In case of necessity any layman or woman can do it.* An irreverent allusion to the explanation of baptism in the catechism.

192.01 *W. S. Gilbert.* William Schwenk Gilbert of Gilbert and Sullivan operetta fame.

192.03 *On a cloth untrue.* From *The Mikado*. See 218.16.

192.17 *the portly florid bursar.* For a detailed portrait of the bursar see *SH*, pp. 23ff.

192.17 *the president.* For Stephen's discussion of Aquinas, Ibsen, and censorship with the president see *SH*, pp. 90-98.

192.21 *a case of conscience.* The *Ratio Studiorum*'s "Rules of the Professor of Scholastic Theology" suggest that such a teacher "content himself with a few general principles of ethics" and "omit any rather involved or detailed explanations." (Fitzpatrick, p. 163.) The "Professor of cases of conscience," on the other hand, "must refrain entirely from theological matters which have practically no necessary connection with his cases," though he may "define briefly some theological matter on which the teaching of cases depends." (Fitzpatrick, p. 165.)

192.23 *the plump roundheaded professor of Italian with his rogue's eyes.* See 249.01.

192.36 *F. W. Martino.* Probably F. Martin, who wrote articles on the chemistry of platinum. (Harmon.)

193.18 *A sharp Ulster voice.* A voice from the northern, in large part Presbyterian, counties of Ireland.

193.29 *the student's father would have done better had he sent his son to Belfast to study.* Belfast is the capital of Ulster. See 193.18.

194.13 *two photographs in frames.* One of Czar Nicholas II, the other of his wife Alexandra Feodorovna, granddaughter of Queen Victoria. See 194.33.

194.26 Ego habeo. "I have." Dog Latin.

194.28 Quod? "What?"

194.32 Per pax universalis. "For universal peace."

194.33-34 *the Czar's photograph . . . a besotted Christ.* Czar Nicholas II (1868-1918), in most respects a reactionary, nevertheless instigated the two international peace conferences held at The Hague in 1899 and 1906. Joyce attended University College from 1898 to 1902. The events here are probably from the spring of 1899; the first Hague conference was held from May 18 to July 29.

195.05-06 Credo ut vos sanguinarius mendax estis . . . quia facies vostra monstrat ut vos in damno malo humore estis. "I think you are a bloody liar, because your face shows that you are in a damned bad humor."

195.17 *A sugar!* Joyce explains: "A euphemism used by Cranley [sic] in as much as it begins with the same letter for a product of the body the monosyllabic term for which in English is sometimes used as an exclamation and sometimes as descriptive of a person whom one does not like." (*Letters*, III, 129.)

195.18 Quis est in malo humore . . . ego aut vos? "Who is in a bad humor—I or you?"

195.27 *Cranly's speech.* J. F. Byrne ("Cranly") was born and grew up in Dublin. He claims to have had a "pure Dublin accent." (Byrne, p. 149.)

196.01 *the progressive tendency.* Although Joyce "attended occasional meetings of a socialist group in Henry Street . . ." (Ellmann, p. 147) in 1904 and called himself a socialist in Pola and Trieste, he thought that the "progressive" concerns of biological, social, and political evolution exemplified in MacCann and Temple were not those of the artist, who is concerned with the spirit.

196.08 a lean student with olive skin and lank black hair. Temple, the gypsy-like student, who in life was John Elwood, a medical student with whom Joyce associated in 1903 after he had returned from his first flight to Paris to be present at his mother's deathbed. Irish gypsies in general are much less dark than their Continental counterparts.

196.18 the testimonial. Czar Nicholas II circulated petitions in European countries for world peace.

196.28 the Csar's rescript. A rescript is an order issued by a Roman emperor or by the pope in answer to some difficulty or point of law. The term was modernized for Nicholas's plea for world peace.

196.29 Stead. William Thomas Stead (1849-1912) English journalist, editor of the *Pall Mall Gazette* (1883-1889) and founder of the *Review of Reviews* mentioned in *SH*. He was an enthusiastic supporter of the peace movement.

196.29 arbitration in case of international disputes. "The second method put forward by The Hague Convention for the pacific settlement of disputes is Arbitration [the first was Mediation]. . . . A "Permanent Court of Arbitration" was set on foot at The Hague in 1900 in accordance with the organization provided in The Hague Convention." (*Encyc. Brit.*)

197.04 Marx. Karl Marx (1818-1883) wrote *The Communist Manifesto* (1848) with Friedrich Engels and *Das Kapital* (1867-1895).

197.12-14 Collins . . . John Anthony Collins. Anthony Collins (1676-1729) was an English deist, determinist, and freethinker born at Heston, Middlesex. He was a friend of John Locke. His *Discourse of Freethinking, occasioned by the Rise and Growth of a Sect called Freethinkers* (1713), which contains an indiscriminate attack on priests, brought an answer from Jonathan Swift. (*Encyc. Brit.*)

197.19 Lottie Collins lost her drawers;
            Won't you kindly lend her yours?
In 1891 Lottie Collins sang "Ta-Ra-Ra-Boom-De-Ay" in *Dick Whittington* at the Grand Theatre, Islington, and put the song on the lips of "every bus-conductor, errand-boy, and groom-de-ay in the town." (Iona and Peter Opie, *The Lore and Language of Schoolchildren* [Oxford: Clarendon Press, 1959], pp. 107-108.)

197.23 five bob each way. Moynihan is affecting to consider the name of the Middlesex philosopher as the name of a racehorse and offering to bet five shillings each on win, place, or show. (See *Letters*, III, 129.)

198.03 Pax super totum sanguinarium globum. "Peace over the whole bloody world."

198.31 Nos ad manum ballum jacabimus. "We shall play handball."

199.15 As they crossed the inner hall the dean of studies was in the act of escaping from the student with whom he had been conversing. Apparently this is one of the few instances in the *Portrait* of Joyce nodding. The dean of studies is described at *P*, 194.18 as "talking to a young professor, stroking his chin gravely and nodding his head." But here the "young professor" has become a "student," who is given the name Hackett at *P*, 199.21.

199.21 Mr Hackett. A Felix Hackett was "a classmate of Joyce" who later wrote an appreciation of Joyce's address on Mangan in the *Centenary History* of the Literary and Historical Society. See Colum, p. 26 and note.

200.11 reading his office. Each Jesuit is required to read certain prescribed prayers, devotions, and scriptural passages daily.

200.21 Jean Jacques Rousseau. The French author, a precursor of romanticism (1712-1778).

200.28 super spottum. "On the spot."

201.17 Lynch is awake. In real life his name was Vincent Cosgrave. "Vincent Cosgrave had a ruddy Neronic face and careless habits. He had a good mind but did not train it; he appraised Joyce shrewdly and early, and said to Byrne, 'Joyce is the most remarkable man any of us have met.' He was committed to idleness and rancorous unsuccess. As he grew older his character was to deteriorate further and his death in the Thames, presumably from suicide, was a blunt admission of futility." (Ellmann, p. 65.) According to Ellmann, Joyce became angry with Cosgrave because he stood by, "hands in pockets," when Joyce accidentally became embroiled in a fight in 1904 while they were walking through Stephen's Green together. Joyce, therefore, named him Lynch after a mayor of Galway named Lynch who had hanged his own son. Lynch leaves Stephen in the lurch in *Ulysses*, p. 585.

201.28 my little tame goose. See 181.20.

202.02 Long pace, fianna! Right incline, fianna! Fianna, by the numbers, salute, one, two! "Fianna" is the Gaelic name for the Fenians. See 38.25. According to Atherton, Stephen is quoting from their secret drill-book.

202.14 the office of arms. In Dublin castle. In Ireland there are two heralds or officers in charge of genealogies, coats of arms, etc. —Cork and Dublin—both under the Ulster King-of-Arms.

202.15 the tree of my family. "Joyce's father, John Stanislaus Joyce, owned a framed engraving of the coat of arms of the Galway Joyces, and he used to carry it along, grandly and quixotically, on his frequent *déménagements*. . . . Joyce represents him in

Ulysses [p. 557] as crying out, 'Head up! Keep our flag flying! An eagle gules volant in a field argent displayed. . . .'" (Ellmann, p. 9.)

202.17 *the league class.* The hero of *SH* attended the Gaelic League classes in Irish on Friday nights in O'Connell Street for some weeks. It was because of these meetings that he again began to see Emma and that enmity over her developed between Stephen and Father Moran. (*SH*, 60-68.)

202.21 *that certain young lady and Father Moran.* See 202.17, 220.04, and 220.06. This young lady appears in *SH* as Emma Clery (see the selections in this edition, pp. 274-76, 284-86), and in *P* as E—— C—— (p. 70) and Emma (p. 116). In real life, at least in part, she was Mary Sheehy, one of the four daughters and two sons of David Sheehy, M.P., whose home at 2 Belvedere Place Joyce began to frequent in 1896, his next-to-last year at Belvedere. "James and Stanislaus were there regularly, and at Mrs. Sheehy's invitation James several times stayed overnight. For Mary, Joyce conceived a small, rich passion which, unsuspected by her, lasted for several years. She queened his imagination in a way that, modest and a little abashed before him as she was, she could not have believed." (Ellmann, p. 52.) The Sheehy family corresponds to the Daniel family (in *SH*), which is placed in Donnybrook and includes "several marriageable daughters." (p. 42.) See 219.05.

203.15 *the days of Tone to those of Parnell.* That is, for a century, from the 1790s to the 1890s.

204.08 *Your soul!* Joyce explains: "A form of procope [apocope?] for "Damn your soul." (*Letters*, III, 130.) That is, part of the phrase is "cut off," or apocopated.

204.12 *Let us eke go.* See 204.20.

204.13 *passed back through the garden and out through the hall.* That is, they are re-entering the UCD building and going through the hallway toward the street on the south side of Saint Stephen's Green.

204.20 *This second proof of Lynch's culture.* Joyce writes: "Cranly misuses words. Thus he says 'let us eke go' where he means to say 'let us e'en go' that is 'let us even go,' eke meaning also and having no sense in the phrase, whereas even or e'en is a slight adverbial embellishment. By quoting Cranly's misquotation Lynch gives the first proof of his culture. The word yellow . . . is his personal substitution for the more sanguine hued adjective, bloody." (*Letters*, III, 130.)

204.26 *Aristotle has not defined pity and terror.* The terms "pity" and "terror" come from Aristotle's famous definition of tragedy in the *Poetics*, where their catharsis is said to be the end of tragedy, and where they are left undefined. Joyce first wrote his "dagger definitions" in aesthetics on his second visit to Paris during February and March 1903. The one for pity and terror reads: "Now terror is the feeling which arrests us before whatever is grave in human fortunes and unites us with its secret cause and pity is the feeling which arrests us before whatever is grave in human fortunes and unites us with the human sufferer." (*Critical Writings*, p. 143.) Cf. Stephen's slight revision of these at *P*, 204.32.

204.30 Horan and Goggins. Goggins was the name given to Gogarty in *SH*. According to Ellmann (p. 283) Joyce may have decided to cut him out of *P* in 1909. (Cf. 230.19.)

205.24 the Venus of Praxiteles in the Museum. The plaster copy of Praxiteles's Venus (admired also by Leopold Bloom in *U*) is no longer on display in the National Museum, across the quadrangle from the National Library.

205.27 that charming Carmelite school. J. F. Byrne ("Cranly") attended several Carmelite schools before entering Belvedere and then University College, Dublin.

207.06 They had reached the canal bridge. The bridge over the Grand Canal on Lower Baggot Street.

207.07 went on by the trees. A towpath runs along the canal beneath the trees which flank it, parallel to Herbert Place.

207.32 Pulcra sunt quæ visa placent. See 186.01.

208.07 Plato, I believe, said that beauty is the splendour of truth. This phrase is also quoted in Joyce's essay on the Irish poet James Clarence Mangan (*Critical Writings*, p. 83) and in *SH*, 80. According to Ellmann's note in Stanislaus, p. 148 (*Critical Writings*, p. 141n) Joyce came upon the phrase "in a letter of Flaubert to Mlle. Leroyer de Chantepie, March 18, 1857," where he also found the comparison between the artist and the God of Creation. See 213.03 and 215.15.

209.11 the corner of sir Patrick Dun's hospital. They have walked three blocks northeastward beside the canal and then turned left on Grand Canal Street. See 207.07.

210.06 He wrote a hymn for Maundy Thursday. It begins with the words Pange lingua gloriosi. Anderson points out (p. 6) that these hymns help to place this procession of Stephen and Lynch on Maundy Thursday, when the *Pange lingua* ("Now my tongue the mystery telling") is sung after the Mass when the second host, consecrated for the Mass of the Presanctified on Good Friday, is carried in procession. When the procession returns, Vespers are sung in the choir. See 174.01 and 210.09.

210.09 that mournful and majestic processional song, the Vexilla Regis of Venantius Fortunatus. See 210.06. Fortunatus's hymn for

Vespers in Passiontide, including Maundy Thursday. Fortunatus (530-609) was Bishop of Poitiers.

210.14-18 Impleta sunt. . . . Lynch sings the second stanza of the *Vexilla Regis*, "The mystery we now unfold," rather than the first. "Behold the royal ensigns fly" in celebration of Stephen's revelations of the mysteries of art. See 210.06 and Anderson, p. 6.

210.19 *They turned into Lower Mount Street.* They have taken the first left off Grand Canal Street, walked one block, and turned right on Lower Mount Street toward Merrion Square. See 207.06.

210.22 *Griffin was plucked.* This is English slang for "failed." The Irish equivalent would be "Griffin was stuck." (Mac Lochlainn.) Joyce is satirizing this affectation, as he does that of Heron at *P*, 83.22.

210.24 *Moonan got fifth place in the Indian.* Probably not the Simon Moonan of Clongowes. See 11.15 and 190.14.

210.25 *The Irish fellows in Clarke's.* Mr. Mac Lochlainn suggests that "the Irish fellows" might refer to Irish nationalists who gathered for years in the newspaper and tobacco shop of Thomas J. Clarke in Great Britain Street. Clarke became the first signer of the proclamation of the provisional government in 1916 and was executed by the British after the Easter Monday Rising.

211.09 *Donovan.* "Constantine P. Curran was goodhearted and controlled; Joyce granted his cleverness as well. *A Portrait* represents him as interested in food (he was inclined to be fat); he was also well versed in literature and architecture. Afterwards he became Registrar of the Supreme Court." (Ellmann, p. 65.)

211.15 *Goethe and Lessing.* Wolfgang von Goethe (1749-1832) and Gottfried E. Lessing (1729-1781). For Stephen's detestation of Lessing's work see *SH*, 33.

211.17 The Laocoon. Lessing's study (1766) of the limits of poetry and painting, based on an analysis of the famous statue of Laocoön and his sons fighting the serpents.

211.18 *idealistic.* The German philosophical school which includes Schopenhauer, Fichte, Kant, and others and of which Lessing could hardly be a member. In general the idealists followed Plato in holding that the real world is a world of divine "ideas," while the phenomenal world is a world of appearances, or "shadows" of it. Stephen, to a certain extent, is of the idealistic persuasion, but see 213.03.

212.01 *Aquinas says:* ad pulcritudinem tria requiruntur, integritas, consonantia, claritas. This is a paraphrase of *Summa Theolgica*, I, q. 39, a. 8, corp. See Noon, pp. 105ff.

212.08 *a basket which a butcher's boy.* Perhaps selected in preference to a grocer's boy because when Stephen arrives at the National Library, he will be symbolically crucified. (Anderson, p. 7n.)

213.02 *symbolism or idealism.* See 211.18. This is a nineteenth-century English Romantic or Platonic, rather than a twentieth-century, use of the word "symbolism," though Mallarmé, depending on Shelley, also used it this way sometimes.

213.03 *the idea of which the matter is but the shadow, the reality of which it is but the symbol.* Plato's metaphor for appearance as the shadow of reality on the wall of a cave can be found in the *Republic,* VII 514A-521B. It was accepted by the nineteenth-century Platonists and idealists, including Shelley. Joyce says in his letter to Dr. Alonso: "A reference to Plato's theory of ideas, or more strictly speaking to Neo-Platonism, two philosophical tendencies with which the speaker at that moment is not in sympathy." (*Letters,* III, 130.)

213.15 quidditas. "Whatness." See Irene Hendry Chayes, pp. 358-370, this edition.

213.17 *The mind in that mysterious instant Shelley likened beautifully to a fading coal.* In "A Defense of Poetry" Shelley says, "A man cannot say, 'I will compose poetry.' The greatest poet even cannot say it; for the mind in creation is as a fading coal, which some invisible influence, like an inconstant wind, awakens to transitory brightness; this power arises from within. . . ." Much of the spirit of Joyce's aesthetic comes from Shelley and D'Annunzio rather than from Aquinas.

213.22-25 *a spiritual state very like to that cardiac condition which the Italian physiologist Luigi Galvani . . . called the enchantment of the heart.* "Galvani [1737-1798] used the word *incantesimo,* enchantment, to describe the momentary cessation of heart-beat produced by inserting a needle into a frog's spinal cord. Joyce was perhaps struck by the contrast between the romantic word and the clinical fact." (Atherton, p. 253.) The phrase is repeated at 217.13.

214.10-11 *I have a book at home . . . in which I have written down questions.* This is, apparently, the "Paris Notebooks" (1902-1903), in which he had worked out the distinctions between tragedy and comedy, and between lyric, epic, and dramatic poetry. (Gorman, pp. 95-99.)

214.15 the bust of Sir Philip Crampton. The bust (now removed) of the famous surgeon (1777-1858) was laughed at by generations of Dubliners. William York Tindall named it the "degenerate artichoke."

215.04 *that old English ballad* Turpin Hero *which begins in the first person and ends in the third person.* Ellmann (p. 53) lists

"Turpin Hero" among the songs which Joyce sang at the Sheehys' Sunday evenings. No doubt his version was one derived from the street ballad of 1739, the year Turpin was hanged. It contains the phrase "Turpin Hero" and in a sense can be said to begin in the first and to end in the third person. (Arty Ash and Julius E. Day, *Immortal Turpin* [New York: Staples Press, 1948], pp. 128-129.)

215.15 *The artist, like the God of the creation.* Joyce found this metaphor in Flaubert's Letter to Mlle. Leroyer de Chantepie, March 18, 1857 ". . . *Madame Bovary* n'a rien de vrai. C'est une histoire *totalement inventée.* . . . L'illusion . . . vient au contraire de *l'impersonnalité* de l'œuvre. C'est un de mes principes: qu'il ne faut pas s'écrire. L'artiste doit être dans son œuvre comme Dieu dans la Création, invisible et tout-puissant, qu'on le sente partout, mais qu'on ne le voie pas." (Quoted in *Critical Writings,* p. 141n.)

215.21 *turned into the duke's lawn, to reach the national library before the shower came.* The lawn, by the Duke of Leinster's house, which stands on Merrion Square West in the same block with the National Library and the National Museum in Kildare Street.

215.28 *royal Irish academy.* What Joyce means by this is not clear to Dubliners, and the emendation of the British texts to "Kildare house" should probably be accepted, since it is hard to see who, other than Joyce, might have made it. According to Mac Lochlainn the Lord of Kildare lived in Leinster House at one time. On the other hand, he says that the art collection of the Royal Irish Academy became the National Museum collection.

215.29 *the arcade of the library.* That is, the columned porch of the library, called the colonnade in *P,* 234.13.

215.31 *Some girls.* See 216.23.

215.33 *Your beloved.* Emma Clery. See 202.21.

216.11 *midwifery cases.* Figuratively speaking, Emma, as Stephen's Blessed Virgin, can be considered both his mother and his girlfriend. The symbols, therefore, of the incarnation and the crucifixion are here combined. See Anderson, pp. 9-13, and 217.22.

216.20 *Ego credo ut vita pauperum est simpliciter atrox, simpliciter sanguinarius atrox, in Liverpoolio.* "I believe that the life of the poor is simply awful, simply bloody awful, in Liverpool."

216.23 *She was preparing to go away with her companions.* See the epiphany included in this edition, p. 270, and cf. *SH,* 183, reprinted in this edition, p. 283. On the symbolic level the comparisons are to the women with Mary at the foot of the cross.

216.25 *clusters of diamonds among the shrubs of the quadrangle.*

The quadrangle between the National Library and the National Museum. See the epiphany printed above, p. 270, and *SH*, reprinted in this edition, p. 283.

217.08 *as if the seraphim themselves were breathing on him!* Suggests that Stephen, crucified, dead, and buried, has ascended into heaven.

217.13 *enchantment of the heart!* See 213.22.

217.22 *In the virgin womb of the imagination the word was made flesh*. Every time the priest of the imagination transmutes the daily bread of experience into ever-living art the incarnation is reenacted. But Stephen is also becoming his own mother. See 230.17, for a discussion of the romantic and obsessive image.

217.35 *villanelle*. A poem made up of five three-line stanzas and a quatrain—all using only two rhymes—and with the lines repeated according to a regular pattern, as in *P*, 223.

218.16 *censer, a ball of incense, an ellipsoidal ball*. See 192.03.

218.29 *the soupplate he had eaten the rice from for supper and the candlestick*. For the suggestion that the soup plate may represent the grail (a flat dish) and the rice the presanctified host for the Good Friday Mass, see Anderson, p. 7n.

219.05 *reminded him of the lumps of knotted horsehair in the sofa of her parlour on which he used to sit, smiling or serious, asking himself why he had come*. "In spite of the entire absence of sympathy between the [Daniels'] circle and himself Stephen was very much at ease in it and he was, as they bade him be, very much 'at home' as he sat on the sofa counting the lumps of horsehair. . . ." (*SH*, p. 43.) Cf. *SH*, p. 155. Note that "her parlour" connects Emma with Mary Sheehy. See 202.21 and 219.08.

219.08 *the print of the Sacred Heart above the untenanted sideboard*. "During these recitations by Mr. David of 'national pieces' Stephen's eye never moved from the picture of the Sacred Heart which hung right above the head of the reciter's head. The Miss Daniels were not so imposing as their father and their dress was somewhat colleen. [Jesus, moreover, exposed] his heart somewhat too obviously in the cheap print." (*SH*, p. 44.) Cf. *SH*, p. 155. Once again the distinction between Emma and the "Daniels" girl (Mary Sheehy) seems to be collapsed. See 219.05.

219.15 *the victory chant of Agincourt*. Michael Drayton's poem, written in 1605, commemorating Henry V's victory over the French in 1415.

219.19 *the house where men are called by their christian names a little too soon*. "In this house it was the custom to call a young visitor [by his Christian name] a little too soon. . . ." (*SH*, p. 44.)

Next to this passage in the *SH* Ms, according to Spencer's note, p. 44, the words "fancy dress ball: Emma" are written in red crayon.

219.23 *that night at the carnival ball.* This does not occur in *SH*, but see 219.19, which supports the notion that Joyce kept an eye on *SH* while writing *P*.

219.25 *She danced lightly in the round.* A round dance. See the epiphany in this edition, p. 270, where the girl seems to be Hannah Sheehy, who along with her sister Mary helped make up the character of Emma.

219.27 *the chain of hands.* A "right and left" exchange of hands in a round or square dance.

219.29 *You are a great stranger now.* See the epiphany in this edition, p. 270.

220.01-.02 *a heretic franciscan . . . Gherardino da Borgo San Donnino.* Stephen may have thought that this thirteenth-century Franciscan "sounded like" a profaner of the cloister. Actually, although he was imprisoned as a heretic, he was a reforming type who wanted stricter rules for his order.

220.04 *the young priest.* Father Moran. Cf. 202.21.

220.06 *her Irish phrasebook.* Cf. 202.17.

220.30 *Jacob's biscuit factory.* Then, as now, at 28 and 30 Bishop Street. Biscuits are called "cookies" in American English. In *U* the citizen as Polyphemus hurls a Jacob's biscuit tin at Bloom as Odysseus-Jesus, who then ascends into heaven from the Hill of Howth.

221.08 *the latticed ear of a priest.* The small window in the confessional between the confessor and penitent usually is latticed to make vision difficult and physical contact impossible.

221.11 *a potboy in Moycullen.* Joyce originally wrote "Athenry." Both Athenry and Moycullen are towns in Galway. But while Athenry is a considerable market town with a fine medieval arch and wall, Moycullen is but a widening of the road.

221.34 *scarlet flowers of the tattered wallpaper.* A mock-heroic image alluding, perhaps, to the multifoliate rose in Dante's *Paradiso.* (See Canto XXX; the rose imagery throughout *P* is discussed extensively in Barbara Seward, *The Symbolic Rose* [New York: Columbia University Press, 1960], pp. 187-221.)

222.09 *Ten years before she had worn her shawl cowlwise.* If it is 1902 at this point in *P* (Joyce left Dublin in January 1903), this previous episode on the tram steps would have occurred when he was in his tenth year. See 69.05 and 222.33.

222.11 *tapping her foot on the glassy road.* See 69.25.

222.12 *It was the last tram.* See 69.05.

222.15 *They stood on the steps of the tram, he on the upper, she on the lower.* See 69.05.

222.22 *The brothers.* See 219.05 and 219.08. According to Ellmann (p. 52) and, apparently, Mary Sheehy's recollection, Joyce was more friendly with her brothers than with her. "His closest friend in the family was Richard Sheehy, a plump, humorous boy who called him James Disgustin' Joyce, and reminded him that the name Sheehy was an Irish variant of the name Joyce, but he was on good terms also with Eugene, a year behind him at Belvedere. . . ."

222.33-223.02 *the strange humiliation of her nature . . . dark shame of womanhood.* This seems to refer to menstruation and to suggest a continuous relationship with Emma during the "ten years." See 222.09.

224.05 *Molesworth Street.* Molesworth Street runs westward from the National Library on Kildare Street.

224.31 *A phrase of Cornelius Agrippa.* Author of *De Occulta Philosophia* (1531), which includes a discussion of bird auguries, chapters 54-56.

224.32 *shapeless thoughts from Swedenborg.* Emmanuel Swedenborg (1688-1772), a Swedish scientific genius who late in life turned to mysticism and psychic research, is here paraphrased from section 110 of his *Heaven and Hell*. In this book and in *The Divine Love and Wisdom*, he explains the divine signatures on nature as correspondences or analogies between the natural world and The Divine Mind. His New Church was a kind of "Protestant heresy."

225.09 *the hawklike man whose name he bore soaring out of his captivity on osierwoven wings.* The hawklike man, is, of course, Daedalus. "So complicated in his thought and in his prose, Joyce longed to sing; a dream of his youth was to be a bird, both in its song and in its flight. . . ." (Ellmann, p. 171.)

225.11 *Thoth, god of writers, writing with a reed upon a tablet and bearing on his narrow ibis head the cusped moon.* Thoth in Egyptian religion is "the scribe of the gods, measurer of time, and inventor of numbers; hence, the god of wisdom and magic. . . . He was identified with the Greek Hermes (Mercury)." (*Webster's New International Dictionary of the English Language*, 2d ed.; Springfield, Mass.; G. and C. Merriam, 1937.) The dictionary quotes S. Wiedemann: "The god who, above all, created by means of words, was *Thoth* . . . ," who is also identified with Hermes Trismegistus, who, according to the dictionary, is the "fabled author of a large number of works (called *Hermetic books*) most of which embody Neo-Platonic, Judaic, and cabalistic ideas, as well as magical, astrological, and alchemical doctrines."

225.28 Bend down your faces, Oona and Aleel. Spoken by the dying Countess in W. B. Yeats's *The Countess Cathleen*. She has sold her soul to the devil to save those of her peasants, who have sold theirs to pay for their poverty. In Yeats's *Collected Plays* the pronoun given to the soul in line 4 is "She" rather than "He." See 226.12.

226.12 *the night of the opening of the national theatre.* "On May 8 [1899] Yeats's *The Countess Cathleen* had its première. . . . A group of young students booed passages in the play which they considered anti-Irish; and when the curtain fell, as Seumas O'Sullivan has written, 'a storm of booing and hissing broke out. . . .' Joyce clapped vigorously. . . . As soon as the performance was over, Skeffington with others composed a letter of protest to the *Freeman's Journal*, and it was left on a table in the college the next morning so that all who wished might sign it. Joyce was asked and refused." (Ellmann, pp. 68-69.)

227.02 The Tablet. A conservative Roman Catholic weekly published in England.

227.12 Diseases of the Ox. According to Byrne this is not the title of a book but of a section or chapter. When Byrne (pp. 58-59) showed the chapter title to Joyce the effect was a "detonating expulsion of a howl that reverberated through the reading room" and caused Mr. Lyster, the librarian, to expel Joyce from the library.

228.05 *The captain has only one love: sir Walter Scott.* Stanislaus Joyce says that James "could not stand" Scott and Dickens. (Stanislaus, p. 79.) But cf. the "queer josser" in "An Encounter" (D), for whose taste in literature, including Scott, the nameless narrator feels an affinity.

228.19 *The park trees.* An imaginary park, somewhat like Lady Gregory's Coole, where Stephen imagines seeing an incestuous love.

228.33 *His father's gibes at the Bantry gang.* " 'Jibe' and 'jeer' have now in Standard English a distinct literary flavour; they are quite every day words in the vocabulary of Ireland. . . ." (Hayden and Hartog, p. 778.) The name "Bantry gang" was given to some anti-Parnellite politicians whose leaders, including Tim Healy, came from the village of Bantry.

229.21 *your intellectual soul.* Not a redundancy but an Aristotelian and Scholastic distinction between the "parts" of the soul—rational, animal, vegetable.

229.35 *Baldwin the First, king of Flanders. He was called the Forester.* On the contrary, Baldwin (ninth century) was surnamed *Bras-de-fer* (Iron-arm).

229.37 A *descendant of Baldwin the First, captain Francis Forster, settled in Ireland and married the daughter of the last chieftain of Clanbrassil. Encyc. Brit.,* IX, 356-368, gives no descendant of Baldwin named Forster or Forester or Francis—most of them were named Baldwin.

230.03 *the Blake Forsters.* Many Blakes, but no Forsters, attended Clongowes in Joyce's day.

230.08-14 *Do you what Giraldis Cambrensis says about your family?* . . . *Pernobilis et pervetusta familia.* "From a noble and distinguished family." Gerald of Wales visited Ireland in 1184 and wrote one of the earliest accounts of Ireland by a foreigner.

230.17 *Did an angel speak?* This question constitutes a blasphemy similar to that of Buck Mulligan's "Ballad of the Joking Jesus" ("My mother's a jew; my father's a bird") in the first episode of *Ulysses.* That is, Mary is impregnated by the word of the Holy Ghost as a "pigeon." Joyce first made use of this obsessive image in "An Encounter" (*D*), where the boys play truant to visit God (the Pigeon House) but instead encounter the "queer josser," which is pidgin English for God.

One of Joyce's sources for the "virgin womb of the imagination" idea or "artistic conception and artistic gestation" was surely D'Annunzio, whom he rather eccentrically considered to be the greatest novelist after Flaubert. As the "disdainful poet," Stelis, speaks to the "multitude," which "seemed to feel the divinity of the hour" in the first chapter of *Il Fuoco,* called "The Epiphany of the Flame," explaining Giorgione in apocalyptic terms, he undergoes "a singular bewilderment, almost a religious stupor, as if he had assisted at an annunciation." (Gabriele D'Annunzio, *The Flame of Life,* trans. by Kassandra Vivaria [Boston: L. C. Page and Co., 1900], p. 78.)

230.19 *Goggins.* See 204.30. Ellmann says that Joyce may have decided in February or March 1909 to eliminate Goggins (the name given to Oliver St. John Gogarty in *SH,* where in the portion now lost he played an important role) in revising *SH* into *P* and thus "put on Stephen's frail shoulders the whole burden of heresy in the book. . . ." (Ellmann, p. 283.) Goggins in *P* is characterized with such a limited number of strokes that it is difficult to tell from internal evidence whether Joyce did intend him to be Gogarty—he is stout (cf. "Stately plump Buck Mulligan," the opening sentence of *U*); he has a low wit ("I had it on my mind to say that," he says when Cranly calls him a "dirty devil"); and he shows "good humour" in not resenting Cranly's pushing him down the steps. But these are hardly enough. In broader terms Cranly is more like Mulligan, and in *Ulysses* Stephen points out to himself the similarity. In particular terms Dixon's question "Did an angel speak?" recalls Gogarty's and Mulligan's most memorable blasphemy "The Ballad of the Joking Jesus" ("My mother's a jew; my father's a bird") and "C'est le pigeon, Josef." See 230.17.

230.24 *a* paulo post futurum. A "state resulting from future act," a grammatical term.

231.26 *a ballocks.* A testicle.

232.08 *She passed out from the porch of the library.* See *SH*, p. 152.

232.17 *an evening when he had dismounted from a borrowed creaking bicycle to pray to God in a wood near Malahide.* See the essay "Portrait," p. 258, and *SH*, p. 156.

232.34 Darkness falls from the air. This line is misquoted, as Stephen realizes later (*P*, 234.07), from the "Song" by Nash from his play, *Summer's Last Will and Testament* (1600). The "Song" begins:

> Adieu, farwell earths blisse,
> This world uncertain is,

and is on the transitory nature of earthly life. Its refrain is:

> I am sick, I must dye:
> Lord have mercy on us.

W. B. Yeats quotes Nash's line in "The Symbolism of Poetry" (1900) as an example of "the continuous indefinable symbolism which is the substance of all style." (*Essays and Introductions* [New York: The Macmillan Co., 1953], p. 156.)

233.06 *the age of Dowland and Byrd and Nash.* John Dowland (1563?-1626) was an English lutist. William Byrd (1543?-1623) was regarded in the seventeenth century as the father of music. He wrote much church music, chamber and instrumental music, and songs and madrigals on texts by Ovid, Ariosto, Sidney, and others. Thomas Nash (1567-1601), English poet, prose writer, and dramatist. See 232.34.

233.11 *the cesspool of the court of a slobbering Stuart.* James I, who came to the throne on Elizabeth's death in 1603 would probably best fit this description: "That this uncouth James, with his driveling mouth and overlarge tongue, should have been the true son of the fascinating Mary Stuart and the handsome Lord Darnley seems almost incredible, despite the surprising tricks of inheritance." (Hall and Albion, p. 309.)

233.13 *dying fallings of sweet airs.* ". . . murmuring male-contents, whose well tun'd cares, channel'd in a sweete falling quaterzanie." (Nash, "Summer's Farewell.")

233.14 *kind gentlewomen in Covent Garden wooing from their balconies with sucking mouths.* This must refer to the district of central London noted for its vegetable and flower market rather than to the Covent Garden Theatre, which was not built until 1731.

233.32 *A louse crawled over the nape of his neck.* See 174.16.

233.37-234.02 *a curious phrase from Cornelius a Lapide . . . on the sixth day.* A "Jesuit author (1567-1637) of *The Great Commentary* on the Bible which explains, in a note on Genesis 1:25, that some 'creeping things' were not directly created by God but are generated from the nature of things created, so flies come from meat, maggots from cheese, and lice from human sweat." (Atherton, p. 255.)

234.09 Brightness falls from the air. Nash's line. See 232.34.

236.01 *why does the church send them all to hell if they die unbaptised?* According to Stanislaus some of Temple's bitterness was Joyce's. (pp. 10-11.)

236.21 *limbo.* See 236.01.

236.23 *a sugan.* "Straw rope." During the Tyrone War (1594-1603) a "league of Irish and Old English, under James Fitzgerald, the so-called *sugan* (straw-rope) earl of Desmond, took the field." (*Encyc. Brit.*)

237.10 *Neither my arse nor my elbow!* According to Mac Lachlainn, the expression is still used in Dublin to mean "neither this nor that."

237.26 *Come away.* An early poem by Joyce, dating from March 1902, owned in Ms by J. F. Byrne, has as its opening stanza:

> O, it is cold and still—alas!—
> The soft white bosom of my love,
> Wherein no mood of guile or fear
> But only gentleness did move.
> She heard as standing on the shore,
> A bell above the water's toll,
> She heard the call of, 'come away'
> Which is the calling of the soul.
>
> (Byrne, p. 65.)

Joyce first left for Paris on December 1, 1902. He returned to Dublin for the Christmas holidays and again on April 11, 1903, for his mother's funeral. He left again with Nora on October 9, 1904. These two departures are fused in *P*, in which Stephen is represented as leaving as soon as his university course is completed in April 1902, but after he had refused his mother's urgent appeal that he make his Easter duty—a request which she made on her deathbed in 1903. It would seem, in fact, that the "center" of the action near the end of Chapter V is the spring of 1903 rather than either 1903 or 1904, a year after George's death.

237.29 The birdcall from Siegfried. *Siegfried* is the opera by Wagner in which the hero, the son of Siegmund and Sieglinde, is brought up by Mime, the Nibelung smith. Siegfried forges the Nothung sword from the fragments of the sword of his father. With the sword he slays Fafner, the giant snake who guards the stolen Rhine-gold, and obtains the magic ring and the "Tarn-helm" which enables him to take any shape at will. He passes through the flames that surround Brünnhilde and wakes her to make her his bride. Joyce seems to be saying that Stephen is engaged in a similar heroic action. In *U* he will symbolically achieve his manhood (his freedom from his psychological attachment to his dead mother and his making of his father's potent sword when he smashes the chandelier in Bella Cohen's Circean brothel—see the headnote to the *U* selections above, p. 299, and the selection, pp. 305-309.) Here he is about to announce to Cranly that he will refuse his mother's request that he make his Easter duty.

238.08 jarvies. Drivers of hackney carriages or Irish cars.

239.06 I will not serve. See 246.37.

241.11-15 A medical student . . . and at present a praiser of his own past. Joyce's father was all the things which Stephen says *his* father was. The literary formulation of Simon may owe something to Stephen's "timeworn Horace," where he could read the discussion of character "types" in the "Epistle to the Pisos": "Many misfortunes beset the old man, whether because he is avaricious and miserly with what he has, and fearful in the use of it, or because he manages all his affairs faintheartedly and indifferently . . . is a praiser of times past, when he was a boy, and a reprover and critic of his juniors." (James Smith and E. W. Parks, *The Great Critics* [New York: W. W. Norton & Co., 1939], p. 119.) See 89.09.

242.10-11 Pascal . . . would not suffer his mother to kiss him. See 14.07.

242.20 Jesus, too, seems to have treated his mother with scant courtesy in public but Suarez . . . has apologised for him. Francisco Suarez (1548-1617) claims that Jesus's words to His mother at the Cana wedding, "Woman, what have I to do with thee?" (John 2:4) are courteous in Aramaic.

243.17 I fear many things: dogs, horses, firearms, the sea, thunderstorms, machinery, the country roads at night. "The only real weakness my brother showed as a boy was a terror of thunderstorms— a terror excessive even for his years. It was not merely a boy's fear of thunder, it was the realization and terror of death. . . . Until he was twelve or thirteen, my brother was always beside himself with fear during thunderstorms. He would run upstairs to our room, while my mother tried to calm him. She would close the shutters hastily, pull down the blinds, and draw the curtains together. But even that was not enough. He would take refuge in the cupboard until the storm was over." (Stanislaus, p. 18.)

243.31 *the penal days.* Following the defeat of James II and the Irish at the Boyne (1690) and Aughrim (1691) by William of Orange, the Protestant Dublin Parliament in 1697 and the English Parliament in 1699 "confirmed the settlement by which some three-quarters of a million acres passed to new owners. Thus the third conquest of the Irish nation [the others were by James I and Cromwell] within a century was achieved. The most illustrious names of the Irish nation disappeared from their country by attainder, death or voluntary exile. Those who remained owned only about one-seventh of the soil. The middle classes suffered exclusion from the corporations, trades and professions and the penal laws began with acts of the Dublin parliament in 1695 and 1698 which debarred conscientious papists from wearing arms, teaching publicly, and practising the law." (*Encyc. Brit.*, XII, 609.)

244.13 Mulier cantat. "The woman sings."

244.21 *the first words of a woman . . .* "Thou also wast with Jesus the Galilean." (Matthew 26:69.)

245.32 *wrangling with Doherty.* In the second draft of *Stephen Hero* Doherty is the name of a character apparently based on Oliver St. John Gogarty (like Goggins; see 230.19).

246.14-18 *the jesuit theologian Juan Mariana de Talavera . . . will also explain to you . . . or smear it for him on his robe or saddlebow.* The sixteenth-century Spanish Jesuit explains this in *De Rege et Regis Institutione.* (Atherton, p. 256.)

246.20 *the chastisement of the secular arm.* According to the theory of the Inquisition, offenders were not punished by the Church but by the state, its secular arm.

246.37 *I will not serve.* Stephen has consciously used the words of Lucifer that the retreat master used at *P*, 117.22-28. Since Lucifer means "light-bringer," the name of the morning star, the reader is probably meant to call to mind not only the fall of Lucifer and of Icarus, but also Shelley's moon "wandering companionless" (*P*, 96.09) and Nash's brightness falling from the air (*P*, 234.09). See Isaiah 14:2.

248.13 *Elisabeth and Zachary.* Byrne's mother had been dead since 1893. His father had died before his mother, when "Cranly" was three years old. Before moving to Dublin he had been a farmer in Wicklow. "Cranly" visited Wicklow on holidays and in summers. (Byrne, pp. 192ff.)

248.14 *Item.* Form used in wills. See Nash's *Summer's Last Will* *and Testament:* "Item, I give my withered flowers and herbes, Unto dead corses." (Lines 1972-73.)

248.14 *Read locusts and wild honey.* Mark 1:6. "And John was clothed in camel's hair, and a leathern girdle about his loins: and he ate locusts and wild honey." Cf. Leviticus 11:22.

248.16 *stern severed head or deathmask as if outlined on a grey curtain or veronica.* John the Baptist was beheaded. A "veronica" is a piece of cloth which received the imprint of Jesus's face when, according to an ancient legend, an old woman named Veronica wiped it with her handkerchief during the walk to Calvary.

248.17-18 *Puzzled . . . by saint John at the Latin gate.* The Roman Church of St. John Lateran, the station for Maundy Thursday. See Anderson, p. 11.

248.19 A *decollated precursor trying to pick the lock.* St. John the Baptist is the "decollated [beheaded] precursor." See Anderson, p. 11.

248.20 *Let the dead bury the dead. Ay. And let the dead marry the dead.* Matthew 9:19-22.

249.01 *little roundhead rogue'seye Ghezzi.* "The Italian lecturer [at University College] was a Jesuit, Father Charles Ghezzi, who had come to Ireland from a long residence in India." (Ellmann, p. 60.) (See 192.23.)

249.02 *Bruno the Nolan.* The famous Renaissance heretic Giordano Bruno (*ca.* 1548-1600). One of the fourteen books which Joyce reviewed for the *Daily Express* in the autumn of 1903 was J. Lewis McIntyre's *Giordano Bruno.* (*Critical Writings*, p. 132ff.) He refers to him throughout his work.

249.06 *risotto alla bergamasca.* Rice cooked in the style of Bergamo.

249.10 *Stephen's, that is, my green.* See 8.33.

249.12-14 A *quartet of them, soldiers, . . . tossed up dice for the overcoat of the crucified.* Matthew 27:35; Mark 15:24; Luke 23:34; John 19:23; Psalms 21:19. Only John mentions that there were four soldiers.

249.18 *Blake wrote:* I wonder if William Bond will die
For assuredly he is very ill.

From the first stanza of "William Bond":

> I wonder whether the Girls are mad,
> And I wonder whether they mean to kill,
> And I wonder if William Bond will die,
> For assuredly he is very ill.

The "moral" and final stanza:

> Seek Love in the Pity of other's Woe,
> In the gentle relief of another's care,

> In the darkness of night and the winter's snow,
> In the naked and outcast,
>   Seek Love there!

Cf. Gabriel Conroy at the end of "The Dead" (*D*). The quotation from Blake marks the terminus of a series in Stephen's development: "Among the older poets he had progressed from his boyish hero-worship of Byron through Shelley to Blake. . . ." (Stanislaus, p. 99.)

249.22 *a diorama in Rotunda*. The Rotunda at the head of O'Connell Street now houses a motion-picture theatre.

249.23 *William Ewart Gladstone, just then dead.* Gladstone died in May 1898. In an article on Parnell published in *Il Piccolo della Sera* on May 16, 1912, Joyce said, "To put it in a few words, Gladstone was a self-seeking politician." He then listed some of Gladstone's contradictory actions during a period of sixty years. His main objection to Gladstone, as he says in an earlier article in *Il Piccolo* (May 19, 1907), is that he "completed the moral assassination of Parnell with the help of the Irish bishops" while giving his watered-down Home Rule Bill a third reading in Parliament. Besides being a political opportunist and a moral assassin Gladstone was, in Joyce's opinion, a cultural pretender of light weight, "like an imposing major domo who has gone to night school." "Today how flimsy seem . . . the high sounding periods, the Homeric studies, the speeches on Artemis and on marmalade of Gladstone." (*Critical Writings*, pp. 193-96; 223-28.) See the essay "Portrait," p. 259.

249.25 *A race of clodhoppers!* Between this phrase and the crocodile meditation which follows, we have what may be the only example in *P* of an unconscious "echo," as distinguished from an allusion. "Do you not see," returned the count, "that this human creature who is about to die is furious that his fellow-sufferers do not perish with him? And, were he able, he would rather tear him to pieces with his teeth and nails than let him enjoy the life he himself is about to be deprived of. Oh, man, man! race of crocodiles!" cried the count, extending his clinched hands toward the crowd, "how well do I recognize you there, and that at all times you are worthy of yourselves!" (*Monte Cristo*, I, 396.)

249.28 *A long curving gallery*. See the epiphany in this edition, p. 271.

250.09 *Lepidus would say*. *Antony and Cleopatra*, II, vii. 29-31.

250.13 *drinking tea and eating cakes in Johnston, Mooney and O'Brien's*. Now, as in Joyce's day, a chain of cafés which does its own baking. This may have been the one listed in Thom's at Leinster Street (still the closest one to the National Library) or the one at 38 Saint Stephen's Green (no longer there).

250.17 *Shining quietly under a bushel of Wicklow bran.* Joyce explains: "An allusion to the New Testament phrase 'The light under a bushel.' " (*Letters,* III, 130.) See Matthew 5:15, Mark 4:21, and Luke 8:16.

250.19 *the cigar shop opposite Findlater's church.* A Protestant church at the head of Rutland (now renamed Parnell) Square. The cigar shop would be at the end of Great Denmark Street, about a block west of Belvedere College.

250.21 *the shortest way to Tara was* via *Holyhead.* That is, one has to leave Ireland to find Ireland. Tara is a hill in County Meath where kings and counselors once met in a large hall. Holyhead, England, is only 57 miles east of Dublin, about half as far as Liverpool.

250.28 *broke Pennyfeather's heart.* Joyce says, "In rowing. Compare Rower's heart. The phrase of course suggests at once a disappointment in love, but men use it without explanation somewhat coquettishly, I think." (*Letters,* III, 130.)

251.06 *Michael Robartes.* One of the "masks" of W. B. Yeats. The poem Stephen recalls is Yeats's "O'Sullivan Rua to Mary Lavell," the opening lines of which are, "When my arms wrap you round, I press,/ My heart upon the loveliness/ That has long faded in the world. . . ."

251.13 *a weary lover whom no caresses move.* See the epiphany quoted in this edition, p. 271.

251.13 *the sound of hoofs upon the road.* See the epiphany quoted in this edition, p. 271.

251.14 *the bridge.* See the epiphany quoted in this edition, p. 271.

251.15 *as they pass the darkened windows the silence is cloven by alarm as by an arrow.* See the epiphany quoted in this edition, p. 271.

251.23-24 *That tundish . . . good old blunt English.* See 188.26.

251.28 *John Alphonsus Mulrennan has just returned from the west of Ireland.* (*European and Asiatic papers please copy.*) The phrase "American papers please copy" is still used in Dublin newspapers after certain paid obituaries.

252.11 *the spiritual-heroic refrigerating apparatus, invented and patented in all countries by Dante Alighieri.* "I am sure however that the whole structure of heroism is, and always was, a damned lie and that there cannot be any substitute for the individual passion as the motive power of everything—art and philosophy included." (*Letters,* II, 81.)

252.25 *Away! Away!* These words appear in the third stanza of Joyce's translation of Verlaine's *"Les Sanglots longs"*:

> Away! Away!
> I must obey
>   This drear wind
> In aimless grief
>   Drifting blind.

(Ellmann, p. 79n.) Cf. Yeats's "Stolen Child."

252.26 *The spell of arms . . . the white arms of roads*. "The effect of the prose piece [in *SH*] The spell of arms is to mark the precise point between boyhood (pueritia) and adolescence (adulescentia)—17 years." (*Letters*, II, 79.) Cf. *SH*, p. 237, and the epiphany quoted in this edition, p. 271. In *P*, of course, it marks the point between adolescence and manhood.

253.01 *the reality of experience and to forge in the smithy of my soul*. As these explanatory notes should demonstrate, Joyce wrote about nothing but his own experience or the actual experiences of others. But the soul (which Joyce also calls the ego) is what enables him to "recreate life out of life" (*P*, 172.09). "He would create proudly out of the freedom and power of his soul, as the great artificer whose name he bore, a living thing, new and soaring and beautiful, impalpable, imperishable." (*P*, 170.04.) He saw himself as "a priest of eternal imagination, transmuting the daily bread of experience into the radiant body of everliving life." (*P*, 221.14). In the essay "Portrait" Joyce spoke of "that ineradicable egoism which he was afterwards to call redeemer." (See p. 251.) In 1902, according to Yeats, Joyce told him in an interview that "his own mind . . . was much nearer to God than folklore." (Ellmann, p. 107.) Even as early as the summer of 1900 he informed the citizens of Mullingar: "My mind is more interesting to me than the entire country," and that summer he dedicated his play *A Brilliant Career* "To My own Soul." (Ellmann, p. 81.) And as late as *Finnegans Wake* he represented Shem the Penman as "selfexiled in upon his own ego writing the mystery of himself in furniture." (*FW*, 184) While much of this kind of talk might be dismissed as mere pride and arrogance, much of it was seriously considered aesthetic theory derived from Shelley, D'Annunzio, and others, and Joyce formed both his life and his books from it. About to leave Ireland for the first time in 1902, he wrote to Lady Gregory, "I shall try myself against the powers of the world. All things are inconstant except the faith of the soul, which changes all things and fills their inconstancy with light. And though I seem to have been driven out of my country here as a misbeliever I have found no man yet with a faith like mine." (*Letters*, I, 53.)

253.03 *Old father, old artificer*. I.e., Daedalus, the pagan inventor. This prayer recalls *P*, 170.05.

Chronology

1882 James Joyce was born on February 2, at 41 Brighton Square West, Rathgar, a near suburb south of Dublin, to John Stanislaus Joyce and Mary Jane Murray Joyce. (See Notes, 7.7.)

1887 The Joyce family moved to Bray, a coastal suburb south of Dublin. (P, 7-59.)

1888 In September Joyce was enrolled in Clongowes Wood College, run by the Society of Jesus, about twenty miles west of Dublin. (P, 9.)

1891 In June he was withdrawn from Clongowes because his father had lost his job as Collector of Rates for Dublin. He wrote *Et Tu, Healy!* (not extant) on the betrayal and death of Parnell. (P, 70.)

1892 The Joyce family moved to Blackrock, about half way between Bray and Dublin. (P, 60ff.)

1893 Their fortunes declining rapidly, the Joyces moved to Dublin. (P, 65.) Joyce attended briefly the Christian Brothers' school in North Richmond Street and then, in April, enrolled in Belvedere College—Jesuit. (P, 71.)

1894 In February he visited Cork with his father to sell the last of the family properties. (P, 86-96.) In the spring he won the first of his exhibitions (cash prizes for scholarship, awarded in national competitions).

1895 He joined the Sodality of the Blessed Virgin Mary. He again won an exhibition.

1896 In September he was elected prefect of the Sodality, the highest honor at Belvedere. (P, 104.)

1897 He won an exhibition of £30 and a prize of £3 for the English essay. (P, 96.) He was re-elected prefect of the Sodality.

1898 In May, he played Grimstone in F. Anstey's *Vice Versâ*, taking off the rector of Belvedere. (P, 73-86.) The retreat at

Belvedere in honor of St. Francis Xavier took place November 30–December 3. (P, 107-146.) He graduated from Belvedere and entered University College, Dublin. (P, 165, 174ff.)

1899   In May he refused to sign the protest of University College students against Yeats's *The Countess Cathleen.* (P, 226.)

1900   He read "Drama and Life" before the Literary and Historical Society, published "Ibsen's New Drama" in the *Fortnightly Review,* and wrote *A Brilliant Career* (a play, not extant, dedicated to his "own soul") in Mullingar.

1901   He published "The Day of the Rabblement" (attacking the Irish Literary Theatre) in a pamphlet containing also an essay by F. J. C. Skeffington ("MacCann").

1902   He published "James Clarence Mangan" in *St. Stephen's,* the University College magazine. He graduated from the university with a degree in modern languages. (By this time he had begun to learn Italian, French, German, and literary Norwegian in addition to Latin.) He left Dublin for Paris to study medicine. Aided by W. B. Yeats and Lady Augusta Gregory, he met some London editors and published two book reviews in the Dublin *Daily Express.*

1903   He published twenty-one book reviews in the *Daily Express.* In April he was called home because his mother was dying. She died in August.

1904   He wrote "A Portrait of the Artist," an essay-story, on January 7. When it was rejected by the editors of *Dana,* he began to rewrite it as *Stephen Hero.* He published poems in the *Speaker, Saturday Review, Dana,* and *The Venture;* and stories ("The Sisters," "Eveline," and "After the Race") in the *Irish Homestead,* edited by George Russell (A.E.). He taught at the Clifton School, Dalkey; sang in the Feis Ceoil and won the bronze medal; lived in the Martello Tower, Sandymount, with Oliver St. John Gogarty. On June 10 he met Nora Barnacle. In October they traveled to Paris, Zurich, Trieste, and Pola, where he began to teach at the Berlitz School.

1905   Joyce and Nora moved to Trieste, where he taught in the Berlitz School there. Their son Giorgio was born on July 27. Joyce submitted the work of the preceding two or three years, *Chamber Music,* and *Dubliners* (save for "Two Gallants," "A Little Cloud," and "The Dead," yet to be written) to Grant Richards.

1906   Joyce and his family moved to Rome, where he worked as a foreign correspondent in a bank. He wrote "Two Gallants" and "A Little Cloud."

1907 They returned to Trieste. Joyce gave private lessons in English. Elkin Mathews published *Chamber Music*. Joyce wrote articles in Italian for *Il Piccolo della Sera*, a Trieste newspaper. Nora bore his daughter, Lucia, on July 26. He wrote "The Dead," and in September he began to rewrite the twenty-six completed chapters of the unfinished *Stephen Hero* in five long chapters as *A Portrait of the Artist as a Young Man*.

1908 By April Joyce had completed the first three chapters of the *Portrait*.

1909 Joyce visited Ireland. He signed a contract with Maunsel and Co. for the publication of *Dubliners* and returned to Trieste with his sister Eva. He went back to Dublin to organize the Cinematograph Volta. He published two articles, two poems.

1910 He returned to Trieste. The Volta failed. Maunsel and Co. postponed the publication of *Dubliners*.

1911 Joyce threw the manuscript of the *Portrait* into the fire in discouragement. Rescued by his sister Eileen, it was wrapped in an old sheet and laid by.

1912 With his family Joyce made his last trip to Ireland, visiting Galway and Dublin. He published four newspaper articles. The printer destroyed the edition of *Dubliners*. Joyce wrote "Gas from a Burner."

1913 He published one poem. Ezra Pound, encouraged by Yeats, wrote Joyce to ask for manuscripts.

1914 Dora Marsden (and later Harriet Shaw Weaver) published *A Portrait of the Artist as a Young Man* as a serial in *The Egoist* (London) from February 2 to September 1915, with two *lacunae* caused by Joyce's inability to complete Chapter V on the serialization schedule. Grant Richards published *Dubliners*. Joyce began to write *Ulysses* and *Exiles*.

1915 With his family Joyce moved to neutral Zurich, giving his pledge of neutrality to the Swiss authorities. He finished *Exiles*. He was given money from the British Royal Literary Fund at the behest of Pound, Yeats, and Edmund Gosse.

1916 He received a grant from the British Treasury Fund. B. W. Huebsch published the *Portrait* in New York.

1917 Joyce received his first gift from Miss Weaver, who eventually was to give him thousands of pounds. He published eight poems in *Poetry* (Chicago). He had his first eye surgery and spent three months in Locarno.

1918   He received a monthly allowance from Mrs. Harold Mc-Cormick. With Claud W. Sykes he organized the English Players. The *Little Review* (New York) serialized *Ulysses* from March 1918 to December 1920. *Exiles* was published by Grant Richards in London and by B. W. Huebsch in New York.

1919   *The Egoist* serialized five installments of *Ulysses*. Mrs. Mc-Cormick cut off Joyce's monthly stipend. Joyce and his family returned to Trieste, where he taught in a business school. He published one poem.

1920   He met Pound in Sirmione. Joyce moved with his family to Paris. The *Little Review* was enjoined from publishing *Ulysses* on the complaint by the Society for the Prevention of Vice that it was pornographic.

1921   Joyce agreed to have Sylvia Beach publish *Ulysses* in Paris. Pound, Miss Beach, Adrienne Monnier, Valery Larbaud, and others sponsored Joyce's career.

1922   *Ulysses* was published by Miss Beach's Shakespeare and Company on February 2.

1923   Joyce began to write *Finnegans Wake*.

1924   He published the first fragment of "Work in Progress" (*Finnegans Wake*) in the *Transatlantic Review* (Paris). He had severe eye troubles, which were to continue for the rest of his life. He visited Brittany and London. Herbert Gorman's biography of Joyce was published by Rinehart.

1925   Joyce published several fragments of "Work in Progress."

1926   Most of *Ulysses* was pirated serially in *Two Worlds Monthly* (New York). Joyce published more fragments of "Work in Progress."

1927   Between 1927 and 1938 seventeen installments of "Work in Progress" were published in *transition* (Paris) by Eugene Jolas. Many authors and others protested the piracy of *Ulysses* in New York. Shakespeare and Company published *Pomes Penyeach*.

1928   Joyce published parts of "Work in Progress" in book form in New York to protect the copyright.

1929   *Ulysse*, the French translation of *Ulysses*, was published. Shakespeare and Company published *Our Exagmination round his Factification for Incamination of Work in Progress*.

1930   Stuart Gilbert's *James Joyce's "Ulysses"* was published. Joyce began his four-year promotion of John Sullivan, the Irish tenor. He underwent more eye surgery.

1931   The Joyce family moved to London. Joyce and Nora were married on July 4. The family returned to Paris in September. Joyce's father died on December 29. More fragments of "Work in Progress" were published.

1932   Stephen James Joyce was born on February 15 to Giorgio and Helen Joyce. The poem "Ecce Puer," written that day, was published in the *New Republic* and reprinted in three other magazines. Lucia had the first breakdown caused by her schizophrenia.

1933   Lucia was hospitalized in Switzerland. The rest of the family summered on Lake Geneva to be near her. In New York Judge John M. Woolsey decided that *Ulysses* was not pornographic.

1934   *Ulysses* was published by Random House in New York.

1936   Joyce's *Collected Poems* was published in New York.

1937   The last "Work in Progress" fragment to be issued separately, *Storiella as She Is Syung,* was published in London.

1938   Joyce completed "Work in Progress."

1939   *Finnegans Wake* was published in May by Faber and Faber in London and The Viking Press in New York. When war was declared, the Joyces returned to France and stayed at La Baule and then St. Gérand-le-Puy (near Vichy) to be close to Lucia's sanitarium.

1940   The Joyces had to leave France for Zurich without Lucia.

1941   Joyce died on January 13 in Zurich.

Topics for Discussion and Papers

✿◇

FOR GENERAL DISCUSSION

1. As a way into some of the larger questions raised by *A Portrait of the Artist as a Young Man*, the student should first consider each word of the title. There may be little ambiguity in the word "portrait," for instance, but P. W. Joyce in *English As We Speak it in Ireland* points out that in Dublin the word "artist" means "character" or "eccentric." Does it have such a meaning in Joyce's title? Maurice Beebe contends that it is important to understand that the novel is a portrait not of *an* artist, but of *the* artist, yet when Joyce was writing *Ulysses* he told his friend Frank Budgen that the stress should fall on the last four words. Where does the stress fall and what are the implications?

2. Stephen says that "the artist, like the God of creation, remains within or behind or beyond or above his handiwork, invisible, refined out of existence, indifferent, paring his fingernails" (P, 215). Yet he does not seem indifferent when he thinks of "the patricians of Ireland": "How could he hit their conscience or how cast his shadow over the imaginations of their daughters before their squires begat upon them, that they might breed a race less ignoble than their own?" (P, 238). And Joyce ends the novel with the peroration, "Welcome, O life! I go to encounter for the millionth time the reality of experience and to forge in the smithy of my soul the uncreated conscience of my race" (P, 253). Are not these distinct views contradictory? Beebe sees the artist as a man divided "between the 'holy' or esthetic demands of his mission as artist and his natural desire as a human being to participate in the life around him." How well does this describe Stephen in Chapter V? If a rationale can be worked out for Stephen's artistic aims which include a didactic purpose, what is it? What does he want for Ireland?

3. Several generalizations can be made about Stephen's relations with females in the *Portrait*—with his mother, Dante, Eileen Vance, Emma Clery, the Blessed Virgin Mary, Mercedes, the prostitute, the flower woman, or the girl coming out of Jacob's biscuit factory. For instance, on page 14 Wells asks, "Tell us, Dedalus, do you kiss your mother before you go to bed?" and Stephen returns to the question in his conversation with Cranly in the last chapter, page 242, and to the basic issue again in the *Ulysses* selections in this volume. What difficulties does Stephen have in his love for his "nice mother"? To what extent might the entire *Portrait* be said to be an answer to Wells's question? Refer to Harry Levin and Richard Ellmann.

4. At the end of the *Portrait* Stephen's "natural father, Simon Dedalus, is left standing in the mystical kinship of fosterage. The Jesuit fathers, who supervised his education, no longer call him son. He has appealed from Father Dolan to Father Conmee; now he appeals from the Church to another paternity. His wings take him from the fatherland. . . ." (Levin.) And Hugh Kenner concludes, "And without a backward glance, he exchanges this father for a myth." What are the ramifications of Stephen's attitude toward his father? Formulate a rationale, for instance, for Stephen's psychological relationship to his father as it is suggested by his imagining himself as Parnell, Napoleon, Monte Cristo, and Claude Melnotte. Why does Stephen see himself standing toward his family "in the mystical kinship of fosterage, fosterchild and foster-brother"? (*P*, 98).

5. Kenner says that the "themes of the last forty pages . . . don't really focus" and that there remains a "moral ambiguity (how seriously are we to take Stephen?)" which makes these pages "painful reading." Is Stephen "indigestibly Byronic," as Kenner says, so that "to take him seriously is very hard indeed"? Or is he a hero with whom we can identify? What is *Joyce's* attitude toward Stephen? Refer to Wayne Booth and Robert Scholes.

6. "I am not afraid to make a mistake, even a great mistake, a lifelong mistake and perhaps as long as eternity too," says Stephen to Cranly of his decision to leave home, nation, and Church. (*P*, 247.) Levin recognizes the sermon on hell in Chapter III as "an ethical core for the book" and that "Stephen's ultimate text is the defiance of the fallen archangel: '*Non serviam!*'" ("I will not serve!") And Caroline Gordon (see Bibliography) goes much further in arguing that the novel is not about an artist "rebelling

against constituted authority," but is rather "a picture of a soul that is being damned for time and eternity caught in the act of foreseeing and foreknowing its own damnation." Is the *Portrait* a "Catholic novel" in this sense? Explain.

7. "As Joyce rewrote his book he seems to have transferred the scene of action from the social to the psychological sphere. . . . The final effect is that which Shakespearean actors achieve by cutting out all the scenes in *Hamlet* where the hero does not appear." (Levin.) Does anything remain of the social sphere in the *Portrait*? What is its function? Consider the economic decline of the Dedalus family. Or, more generally, discuss the relation of Stephen to the statements in Chapter V about Darwin, Marx, John Anthony Collins, Newman, Gilbert, F. W. Martino, W. B. Yeats, Giordano Bruno, and others—that is, to the cultural figures of his time and to those whose influence was most felt in his time.

8. Beebe places the *Portrait* firmly in what he calls the "Ivory Tower" tradition of the *Künstlerroman* (artist-novel) instead of in the "Sacred Fount" tradition, which is "rooted in the concept of art as experience" or the artist's involvement in life. Formulate an argument that shows elements of the Sacred Fount in the *Portrait*. Is the novel a *Künstlerroman* in fact or is it a *Bildungsroman* (a novel about the early development and spiritual education of the protagonist, who is not necessarily an "artist").

SPECIAL TOPICS FOR DISCUSSION AND SHORT PAPERS

1. Climaxes in the *Portrait* may be said to occur when Stephen rejects the invitation to join the order (162), or when he sees the "angel of mortal youth and beauty" wading by Bull Island (171-172), or offstage when he rejects his mother's request that he make his Easter duty. Is there a single climax? Where? If not (and assuming that books with climaxes may be said to be shaped like pyramids or hourglasses), what shape would be analogous to the *Portrait*? A circle? A spiral? Are the five chapters similar to the five acts of a Senecan or Shakespearean play?

2. Joyce wrote the first three chapters of the *Portrait* by 1909 and then, discouraged, tried to burn them. When his sister Eileen rescued the manuscript and tied it up in an old sheet, it apparently lay untouched for almost five years, until Ezra Pound asked to

see some of Joyce's work and praised the opening chapter highly. Would the book have had a certain completeness if it had ended with Chapter III? With Chapter IV? In either case, how would it have differed from the novel that we have? Is Chapter V an anticlimax that trails off into the whimper of the diary? What does it add to the *Portrait*?

3. The fifty-four-word sentence at the end of page 172 and the forty-eight-word sentence at the end of page 173 are "fine writing" —purple passages, Ruskinesque, Pateresque—in their participial construction, their imagery, and their vocabulary. In these respects they differ sharply from the "plain style" of the opening paragraph of Chapter V. Point out the particular differences. Levin mentions that such purple passages are placed "at strategic points in Stephen's development." Find other alternations in Joyce's style which coincide with changes in Stephen. What does Joyce accomplish by means of this technique?

4. Irene Hendry Chayes describes "the most conventional of Joyce's epiphany techniques" as involving "moments of revelation" which take up "residence in Stephen's consciousness with neither elucidation nor relation to anything beyond themselves." In the light of her essay, discuss Joyce's use in the final *Portrait* of the epiphanies reprinted in this edition.

5. Joyce frequently uses character "tags"—such as Eileen's hands and hair, Lynch's laugh, Cranly's figseeds, Davin's brogue, Dixon's signet ring, or the animal imagery associated with several characters —to sketch minor figures who help compose the portrait of Stephen. What else is Joyce accomplishing with this technique? For example, could its use be considered a kind of epiphany technique, as Mrs. Chayes suggests?

6. Work out the use of a single incident, such as Stephen's ecstatic prayer at Malahide, or the development of a character, such as Emma, where it appears in either the essay "Portrait" of 1904 or the *Stephen Hero* excerpts in this volume, and the final *Portrait*. Discuss the ways in which the tone changes in the three stages of the manuscript.

7. W. Y. Tindall defines a "symbol" as a concrete image which is "indefinitely suggestive" in its meanings. How do symbols such as "road," "cow," "rose," "water," "girl," and "bird" bear out the definition? How does Joyce use the imagery of air, water,

fire, and earth to help convey the meaning of the *Portrait*? Further, how is such imagery used structurally to shape the book?

8. Frank O'Connor comments that "the whole structure of the book is probably lost unless Joyce's notebooks give some indication of what it was, but I have an impression that Joyce wrote with a list of a couple of hundred words before him, each representing some association, and that at intervals the words were dropped in, like currants in a cake and a handful at a time. . . ." Discuss. In an essay that might be entitled "Joyce and Associated Metaphor" try to refute these charges.

9. The point of view from which the *Portrait* is told is crucial. How would the novel differ if the story were told by Cranly? By Mrs. Dedalus? By Mr. Dedalus? By Father Dolan? Or in the first person?

10. Trace the motif of death through the *Portrait*, paying due attention to the actual deaths mentioned (Parnell's, Peter Little's, Pottlebelly's) as well as to Stephen's thoughts about death and to implicit deaths, such as that of Stephen as St. Stephen Proto-martyr.

11. "Except for the thin incognito of its characters, the *Portrait of the Artist* is based on a literal transcript of the first twenty years of Joyce's life." (Levin.) If this is accurate, might it be said that Joyce is paying off old scores by placing his family, teachers, and old girl friends in a hell of his own devising, while putting himself on the roseway to paradise?

12. The "Early Comment" section of this volume provides a cross-section of first reactions to the *Portrait*. H. G. Wells is struck by its political climate at the end of his review; Edward Garnett calls it "too discursive, formless . . . unconventional"; and *Everyman* calls it "Garbage . . . Mr. Joyce would be at his best in a treatise on drains." Explain these points of view as a possible product of their times. What was the revolutionary nature of the *Portrait* when it first appeared?

FOR LONGER PAPERS

1. Although critics like Levin, Kenner, Tindall, O'Connor, and Ellmann make remarks in passing about the style or styles of the

Portrait, none of them attempts a detailed description of it. An accurate description would probably be the first one. One way to begin would be to catalogue the rhetorical figures (anaphora, epaniphora, chiasmus, and many others) with which the book abounds and then explain what purpose they serve. A complete list of them with examples can be found in Sister Miriam Joseph's *Shakespeare's Use of the Arts of Language,* and a briefer list in Stuart Gilbert's *James Joyce's "Ulysses."* Other possibilities for the description of style—the kind of diction, length of sentences, kinds of sentences, variety of sentence patterns, and so on—can be found in Edward P. J. Corbett's *Classical Rhetoric for the Modern Student.*

2. Compare Joyce's *Portrait* with another novel of adolescence, such as Meredith's *The Ordeal of Richard Feverel,* Butler's *The Way of All Flesh,* Maugham's *Of Human Bondage,* Lawrence's *Sons and Lovers,* Wolfe's *You Can't Go Home Again,* or Salinger's *Catcher in the Rye.*

3. Analyze the structure of the *Portrait* in detail, paying attention to the chapter divisions and to the separate sections in each chapter marked in the text with an extra space and asterisks. Include in the analysis some consideration of the expansions and contractions of narrative time, the use of flashbacks and set pieces such as the Christmas dinner scene or the trip to Cork, and the images of "passage" and "threshold crossing."

4. Not everyone agrees with Mrs. Chayes' essay on Joyce's epiphanies. Look up others listed in the Bibliography and write a fresh discussion of the epiphany, taking account of the different opinions held by Chayes, Scholes, Waltzl, Tindall, and others.

5. Five books which surely influenced Joyce in writing the *Portrait* are Meredith's *The Ordeal of Richard Feverel,* D'Annunzio's *The Flame,* Anstey's *Vice Versâ,* Dumas' *The Count of Monte Cristo,* and Lermontov's *A Hero of Our Time.* Compare Joyce's work with theirs to determine what it was that he was able to borrow and, in most cases, to transform.

6. Discuss Stephen's esthetic theory in *Stephen Hero* and the *Portrait.* A complete book and several articles on the topic are listed in the Bibliography. It is recommended that they not be considered the final word, even though some of them are very learned and detailed. For background information go also to other

neo-Thomist books on esthetics, such as those by Jacques Maritain, the Reverend Thomas Gilby, O.P., the Reverend James Duffy, and Eric Gill, the artist. Consider too the Platonic texts which most influenced Joyce in formulating his esthetic: Shelley's "Defense of Poetry," D'Annunzio's *The Flame*, and Yeats's "The Symbolism of Poetry."

7. Present as much evidence as possible from the text of the *Portrait* to support Ellmann's contention that the artist in Joyce's picture of himself becomes his own mother and father. Reread the passage in which Stephen's composition of the villanelle is presented (*P*, 217-224). Does this support Ellmann's argument? Compare the scene on Bull Island, where Stephen is "reborn" (*P*, 170-174).

8. The first five questions of "General Topics for Discussion" bring up some important issues in *A Portrait of the Artist as a Young Man*. Write a paper on any one of these topics, based on personal interpretation of the *Portrait*, and support the thesis with the text and the essays in this book.

Selected Bibliography

❀◇

BY KEVIN SULLIVAN

This bibliography is intended primarily for the undergraduate studying *A Portrait of the Artist as a Young Man*, though it includes also a complete listing of the texts by James Joyce and a generous selection of books and articles about his life and works.

If Joyce specialists are at times nonplussed, undergraduates may be totally perplexed by the sheer bulk of material (more than 100 items annually in recent years) that continues to accumulate around the man and his work. This bibliography aims to guide the student through most of that output to some of the best of it. First, however, a word must be said about Joyce bibliographies to which this bibliography is indebted.

The definitive bibliography of Joyce's own writings is by John J. Slocum and Herbert Cahoon, *A Bibliography of James Joyce, 1882-1942* (New Haven, Conn.: Yale University Press, 1953). This contains lists of books and pamphlets by Joyce; his contributions to pamphlets, periodicals, and newspapers; translations, manuscripts, musical settings for his work, and miscellaneous listings.

Among secondary source materials, Alan Parker's 1948 bibliography has been largely superseded by Robert H. Deming's painstaking work, *A Bibliography of James Joyce Studies* (Lawrence, Kan.: University of Kansas Libraries, 1964). Deming lists more than 1400 items in a comprehensive survey of the books and the periodical literature that appeared from the beginning of Joyce studies through December 1961. Checklists and supplements to Deming continue to appear regularly in the *James Joyce Quarterly*.

THE JOYCE TEXTS

Publications before 1941

Collected Poems. New York: Black Sun Press, 1936 (New York: The
  Viking Press, 1937).
> Includes:
> *Chamber Music.* London: Elkin Mathews, 1907; New York: Huebsch,
> 1918; New York: Columbia University Press, 1954 (ed. William York
> Tindall).
> *Pomes Penyeach.* Paris: Shakespeare and Company, 1927; New York:
> Sylvia Beach, 1931; London: Harmsworth, 1932; London: Faber and
> Faber, 1933.
> *Ecce Puer.* First published in *Collected Poems.*
> All three above are included in *The Portable James Joyce,* listed on p.
> 565.

Dubliners. London: Grant Richards, 1914; London: Cape, 1954; New
  York: Huebsch, 1916; New York: Modern Library, 1926. Included in
  The Portable James Joyce.

A Portrait of the Artist as a Young Man. The definitive text, corrected from
  the Dublin holograph by Chester G. Anderson and edited by Richard
  Ellmann. New York: The Viking Press, 1964. 253 pp. Included with
  different pagination in *The Portable James Joyce.*
> First appeared serially in *The Egoist* (London), 1914-15; New York:
> Huebsch, 1916. A first version—some 2000 words written in 1904 and
> entitled "A Portrait of the Artist"—is reproduced by Scholes and Kain
> in *The Workshop of Daedalus* and in the present edition.

Exiles. A play in three acts, including hitherto unpublished notes by the
  author, discovered after his death, and an introduction by Padraic Colum.
  New York: The Viking Press, 1951. 127 pp. Included in *The Portable
  James Joyce.*
> First edition: London: Grant Richards, 1918; New York: Huebsch,
> 1918.

Ulysses. New York: Random House, 1934 (Modern Library, 1940; rev. ed.,
  1961).
> Parts were first published serially in *The Little Review* (New York),
> 1918-20 and *The Egoist* (London), 1919. First edition: Paris: Shake-
> speare and Company, 1922; London: Egoist, 1922; London: Bodley
> Head, 1937, 1960.

Finnegans Wake. New York: The Viking Press, 1939, 1947.
> Early versions of several episodes appeared serially in *transition* (Paris),
> 1927-38, and in book form as *Work in Progress* (5 vols., 1928-37):
> *Anna Livia Plurabelle* (1928), *Tales Told of Shem and Shaun* (1929),
> *Two Tales of Shem and Shaun* (1932), *Haveth Childers Everywhere*
> (1930), *The Mime of Mick and the Maggies* (1934), and *Storiella as
> She Is Syung* (1937).

Posthumous Publications

Epiphanies. Introduction and notes by O. A. Silverman. Lockwood Memorial Library. Buffalo: University of Buffalo, 1956.
> Twenty-two items edited from Mss in the Lockwood Memorial Library.
> Scholes and Kain (*The Workshop of Daedalus*) reproduce these and
> add 18 other epiphanies from the Mennen Collection at Cornell Uni-

versity. These 40 epiphanies are all that remain of an estimated 71 originally composed by Joyce.

Stephen Hero. The surviving pages of the early draft of *A Portrait of the Artist as a Young Man.* Edited from the Ms in the Harvard College Library by Theodore Spencer. A new edition, incorporating the additional Ms pages in the Yale University Library, edited by John J. Slocum and Herbert Cahoon. Norfolk, Conn.: New Directions, 1963. (New Directions, 1944; 2d ed., 1955).

Letters of James Joyce. Edited by Stuart Gilbert. New York: The Viking Press, 1957; re-issued with corrections, 1966.

About 400 letters (19 written to or about Joyce) ranging from March 1901 to December 1940.

Letters of James Joyce. Edited by Richard Ellmann. New York: The Viking Press, 1966. 2 vols. Two additional volumes of *Letters* (1136 altogether).

The Critical Writings of James Joyce. Edited by Ellsworth Mason and Richard Ellmann. New York: The Viking Press, 1959. Fifty-seven items, some hitherto unpublished, dating from 1896 (a schoolboy essay) through 1937 (a manifesto in French on the moral right of authors), including Joyce's satirical verses, articles on Irish affairs, reflections on Mangan, Pound, Hardy, Svevo, etc.

Daniel Defoe. Edited from the Italian Ms and translated by Joseph Prescott. *Buffalo Studies.* Vol. 1, no. 1. Buffalo: State University of New York, December 1964. 27 pp. Text of 1912 Trieste lecture.

The Portable James Joyce. With an introduction and notes by Harry Levin. New York: The Viking Press, 1947. 760 pp. The revised edition of 1966 includes the definitive text of *Portrait, Dubliners, Exiles, Collected Poems,* selections from *Ulysses* and *Finnegans Wake,* and Bibliographical Note.

THE JOYCE JOURNALS

James Joyce Quarterly. Edited by Thomas F. Staley. Vol. 1, no. 1 (Fall 1963)—to the present. University of Tulsa, Tulsa, Okla.

James Joyce Review. Edited by Edmund J. Epstein. Vol. I, no. 1 (February 2, 1957)—suspended publication with Vol. 3, no. 1/2 (1959). Remaining files available from Gotham Book Mart, New York, N.Y.

A James Joyce Miscellany. Edited by Marvin Magalaner. First series (1957): James Joyce Society, New York. Second series (1959) and third series (1962): Southern Illinois University Press, Carbondale, Ill.

BIOGRAPHICAL MATERIALS

Books

Anderson, Chester. *James Joyce and His World.* London: Thames and Hudson, 1967.

Beach, Sylvia. *Shakespeare and Company.* New York: Harcourt Brace, 1959.

Byrne, John Francis. *Silent Years: An Autobiography with Memoirs of James Joyce and Our Ireland.* New York: Farrar, Straus and Young, 1953.

Colum, Mary and Padraic. *Our Friend James Joyce.* New York: Doubleday, 1958.

Edel, Leon. *James Joyce, the Last Journey*. New York: Gotham Book Mart, 1947.

Ellmann, Richard. *James Joyce*. New York: Oxford University Press, 1959. (Pp. 302-309 reprinted in this edition.)

Gorman, Herbert. *James Joyce*. New York: Rinehart, 1939; rev. ed., 1948.

Hutchins, Patricia. *James Joyce's Dublin*. London: The Grey Walls Press, 1950.

————. *James Joyce's World*. London: Methuen, 1957.

Joyce, Stanislaus. *My Brother's Keeper: James Joyce's Early Years*. Edited with an introduction and notes by Richard Ellmann. Preface by T. S. Eliot. New York: The Viking Press, 1958.

————. *Recollections of James Joyce by His Brother*. New York: James Joyce Society, 1950. Trans. by Ellsworth Mason from *Litteratura* V (July-September 1941), 25-35; (October-December 1941), 23-35. Also translated by Felix Giovanelli in *The Hudson Review*, 11 (Winter 1950), 487-514.

————. *The Dublin Diary of Stanislaus Joyce*. Edited by George Harris Healey. Ithaca, N.Y.: Cornell University Press, 1962.

Kain, Richard M. *Dublin in the Age of William Butler Yeats and James Joyce*. Norman, Okla.: University of Oklahoma Press, 1962.

Sullivan, Kevin. *Joyce Among the Jesuits*. New York: Columbia University Press, 1958.

Tindall, William York. *The Joyce Country*. College Station, Penn.: Pennsylvania State University Press, 1960.

Articles

Brophy, Liam. "The Stagey Irishman." *Apostle*, XLI (February 1963), 9-13.

Curran, C. P. "Joyce's d'Annunzian Mask." *Studies*, LI (1962), 308-316.

Curtayne, Alice. "Portrait of the Artist as Brother: An Interview with James Joyce's Sister." *Critic*, XXI (April-May 1963), 43-47. An interview with Eileen Joyce Schaurek.

Envoy. Special Joyce Number, V, 17 (April 1951).

GENERAL CRITICAL ESTIMATES

Books

Beebe, Maurice. *Ivory Towers and Sacred Founts*. New York: New York University Press, 1964. Pp. 260-295 and *passim*. (Pp. 3-18 reprinted in this edition.)

Brennan, Joseph Gerard. *Three Philosophical Novelists: James Joyce, André Gide, Thomas Mann*. New York: Macmillan, 1964. Pp. 2-55.

Burgess, Anthony. *Re Joyce*. New York: W. W. Norton, 1965.

Church, Margaret. *Time and Reality: Studies in Contemporary Fiction*. Chapel Hill, N.C.: University of North Carolina Press, 1963. Pp. 25-66 and *passim*.

Daiches, David. *English Literature*. Englewood Cliffs, N.J.: Prentice-Hall, 1964. Pp. 1-31.

————. *The Novel and the Modern World*. Rev. ed.: Chicago: University of Chicago Press, 1960.

Duff, Charles. *James Joyce and the Plain Reader*. With a prefatory letter by Herbert Read. London: Desmond Harmsworth, 1932.

Edel, Leon. *The Psychological Novel, 1900-1950.* Philadelphia: Lippincott, 1955.

Frank, Joseph. *The Widening Gyre.* New Brunswick, N.J.: Rutgers University Press, 1963. Pp. 16-19.

Givens, Seon, ed. *James Joyce: Two Decades of Criticism.* New York: Vanguard Press, 1948. New Introduction, 1963.

Goldberg, S. L. *James Joyce.* New York: Grove Press, 1962, 1963.

Golding, Louis. *James Joyce.* London: Thornton Butterworth, 1933.

Goldman, Arnold. *The Joyce Paradox: Form and Freedom in His Fiction.* Evanston, Ill.: Northwestern University Press, 1966.

Hoffman, Frederick. *The Mortal No: Death and the Modern Imagination.* Princeton, N.J.: Princeton University Press, 1964. Pp. 393-423.

Howarth, Herbert. *The Irish Writers: Literature and Nationalism, 1880-1949.* New York: Hill and Wang, 1958.

Humphrey, Robert. *Stream of Consciousness in the Modern Novel.* Berkeley and Los Angeles: University of California Press, 1955.

Jones, William Powell. *James Joyce and the Common Reader.* Norman, Okla.: University of Oklahoma Press, 1955.

Kenner, Hugh. *Dublin's Joyce.* Bloomington, Ind.: University of Indiana Press, 1966. (Pp. 112-133 reprinted in this edition.)

Kuma, Shiv K. *Bergson and the Stream of Consciousness Novel.* New York: New York University Press, 1963. Pp. 103-138.

Levin, Harry. *James Joyce: A Critical Introduction.* Norfolk, Conn.: New Directions, 1960. (Pp. 41-62 reprinted in this edition.)

Magalaner, Marvin, and Kain, Richard M. *Joyce: The Man, The Work, The Reputation.* New York: New York University Press, 1956.

Morse, J. Mitchell. *The Sympathetic Alien: James Joyce and Catholicism.* New York: New York University Press, 1959.

Noon, William T., S.J. *Joyce and Aquinas.* New Haven: Yale University Press, 1957.

O'Connor, Frank. *The Mirror in the Roadway.* New York: Knopf, 1956. (Pp. 295-308 reprinted in this edition.)

O'Faolain, Sean. *The Vanishing Hero: Studies in Novelists of the Twenties.* Boston: Little Brown, 1957. Pp. 170-204.

Russell, Francis. *Three Studies in Twentieth Century Obscurity.* Aldington, Kent: Hand and Flower Press, 1954; London: Defour Editions, 1961. Pp. 7-44.

Savage, D. S. *The Withered Branch: Six Studies in the Modern Novel.* London: Eyre and Spottiswoode, 1950. Pp. 156-199.

Seward, Barbara. *The Symbolic Rose.* New York: Columbia University Press, 1960. Pp. 187-221.

Smidt, Kristan. *James Joyce and the Cultic Use of Fiction.* Rev. ed.: New York: Humanities Press, 1959.

Stewart, J. I. M. *James Joyce.* London: Longmans, Green, 1957.

Strong, L. A. G. *The Sacred River: An Approach to James Joyce.* New York: Pellegrini and Cudahy, 1951.

Tindall, William York. *A Reader's Guide to James Joyce.* New York: Noonday Press, 1959.

———. *Forces in Modern British Literature, 1885-1946.* New York: Knopf, 1947.

———. *James Joyce: His Way of Interpreting the Modern World.* New York: Scribner's, 1950.

———. *The Literary Symbol.* New York: Columbia University Press, 1955. (Pp. 76-86 reprinted in this edition.)

Ussher, Arland. *Three Great Irishmen: Shaw, Yeats, Joyce.* New York: Devin-Adair Company, 1953.

West, Rebecca. *The Strange Necessity: Essays.* Garden City, N.Y.: Doubleday Doran. 1928. Pp. 13-54, 65-67, 187-209.

Articles

Beja, Morris. "The Wooden Sword: Threatener and Threatened in the Fiction of James Joyce." *James Joyce Quarterly,* II (Fall 1964), 33-41.

Benstock, Bernard. "A Covey of Clerics in Joyce and O'Casey." *James Joyce Quarterly,* II (Fall 1964), 18-32.

Beringanse, Arthur F. "James Joyce's Philosophy." *Cresset,* XXVI (October 1963), 10-15.

Block, Haskell M. "Theory of Language in Gustave Flaubert and James Joyce." *Langue et littérature* ([Société d'Edition "Les belles lettres," Paris], 1961), 305.

Chayes, Irene Hendry. "Joyce's Epiphanies." *Sewanee Review* (July, 1946), 1-19. (Reprinted in this edition.)

Duncan, Edward. "James Joyce and the Primitive Celtic Church." *Alphabet,* no. 7 (December 1963), 17-38.

Dundes, A. "Study of Folklore in Literature and Culture: Identification and Interpretation." *Journal of American Folklore,* LXXVIII (April 1965), 136-142.

Isaacs, Neil D. "The Autoerotic Metaphor in Joyce, Sterne, Lawrence, Stevens and Whitman." *Literature and Psychology* (New York), XV (1965), 92-106.

Kain, Richard M. "Joyce's World View." *Dubliner,* III (Autumn 1964), 3-10.

———. "Problems of Interpreting Joycean Symbolism." *Journal of General Education,* XVII (1965), 227-235.

Kronegger, M. E. "Joyce's Debt to Poe and the French Symbolists." *Review de Littérature Comparée,* XXXIX (April-June 1965), 243-254.

Liddy, James. "Coming of Age: James Joyce and Ireland." *Kilkenny Magazine,* no. 5 (Autumn-Winter 1961), 25-29.

MacDonagh, Donagh. "The Reputation of James Joyce: From Notoriety to Fame." *University Review* (Dublin), III, ii (1964), 12-21.

Modern Fiction Studies. Special Joyce Number, IV, 1 (Spring 1958).

Morse, J. Mitchell. "Joyce and the Early Thomas Mann." *Revue de Littérature Comparée,* XXXVI (July-September 1962), 377-385.

Noon, William T., S.J. "A Delayed Review, James Joyce, by R. Ellmann." *James Joyce Quarterly,* II (Fall 1964), 7-12 (review-article).

———. "*A Portrait of the Artist as a Young Man:* After Fifty Years," in Thomas F. Staley (ed.), *James Joyce Today.* Bloomington, Ind.: Indiana University Press, 1966.

Scholes, Robert. "Letter to the Editor." *James Joyce Quarterly,* II (Summer 1965), 310-313.

———, and Noon, William T., S.J. "James Joyce: An Unfact." *PMLA,* LXXIX (June 1964), 355.

Staley, Thomas F. "Joyce Scholarship in the 1960's." *Papers on English Language and Literature,* I (1965), 279-286.

Von Phul, Ruth. "A Sketch of the Artist as the Self-Parodist." *James Joyce Quarterly,* III (Summer 1965), 62.

A PORTRAIT OF THE ARTIST
AS A YOUNG MAN

Books

Andreach, Robert J. *Studies in Structure*. New York: Fordham University Press, 1964. Pp. 40-71.

Booth, Wayne C. *The Rhetoric of Fiction*. Chicago: University of Chicago Press, 1961. (Pp. 324-336 reprinted in this edition.)

Connolly, Thomas E., ed. *Joyce's Portrait: Criticisms and Critiques*. New York: Appleton-Century-Crofts, 1962.

Drew, Elizabeth. *The Novel: A Modern Guide to Fifteen English Masterpieces*. New York: Norton, 1963. Pp. 245-261.

Farrell, James T. "Joyce's *A Portrait of the Artist as a Young Man*," in *The League of Frightened Philistines*. New York: Vanguard, 1946. Pp. 45-59.

Feehan, Joseph, et al. *Dedalus on Crete*. Los Angeles: Immaculate Heart College, 1956.

Hancock, Leslie. *Word Index to James Joyce's* Portrait of the Artist. Carbondale and Edwardsville, Ill.: Southern Illinois University Press, 1967.

Hardy, John Edward. *Man in the Modern Novel*. Seattle: University of Washington Press, 1964. Pp. 67-81.

Karl, Frederick, and Magalaner, Marvin. *A Reader's Guide to Great Twentieth-Century English Novels*. New York: Noonday Press, 1959. Pp. 205-253.

Morris, William E., and Nault, Clifford A., Jr., eds. *Portraits of an Artist: A Casebook on James Joyce's A Portrait of the Artist as a Young Man*. New York: Odyssey Press, 1962.

Mueller, William R. *The Prophetic Voice in Modern Fiction*. New York: Association Press, 1959. Pp. 27-55.

O'Faolain, Sean. "Introduction," in *A Portrait of the Artist as a Young Man*. New York: New American Library, 1954.

Ryf, Robert S. *A New Approach to Joyce: The Portrait of the Artist as a Guidebook*. Berkeley and Los Angeles: University of California Press, 1962.

Scholes, Robert, and Kain, Richard M. *The Workshop of Daedalus: James Joyce and the Raw Material for A Portrait of the Artist as a Young Man*. Evanston, Ill.: Northwestern University Press, 1965.

Sprinchorn, Evert. "A Portrait of the Artist as Achilles," in *Approaches to the Twentieth-Century Novel*, edited by John Unterecker. New York: Thomas Y. Crowell, 1965. Pp. 9-50.

Van Ghent, Dorothy. *The English Novel: Form and Function*. Rev. ed.: New York: Holt, Rinehart and Winston, 1964. Pp. 463-473.

Articles

Anderson, Chester G. "The Text of James Joyce's *A Portrait of the Artist as a Young Man*." *Neuphilologische Mitteilungen*, LXV (Spring 1964), 160-200.

———. "The Sacrificial Butter." *Accent*, XII (Winter 1952), 3-13.

Bates, Ronald. "The Correspondence of Birds to Things of the Intellect." *James Joyce Quarterly*, II (Summer 1965), 281-300.

Beja, Morris. *Evanescent Moments: The Epiphany in the Modern Novel*. Ann Arbor, Mich. University Microfilms (*Dissertation Abstracts*, XXIV [January 1964]), 2903 (Cornell).

Brandabur, Edward. "Stephen's Aesthetic in *A Portrait of the Artist*," in *The Celtic Cross*, ed. by Ray B. Browne, et al. Lafayette, Ind.: Purdue

University, 1964, pp. 11-21. "Comment by Maurice Beebe," pp. 22-25.

Burke, Kenneth. "Three Definitions." *Kenyon Review*, XIII (Spring 1951), 181-192. (Reprinted in part in this edition.)

Cohn, Alan M. "The Spanish Translation of *A Portrait of the Artist as a Young Man*." *Revue de Littérature Comparée*, XXXVII (July-September 1963), 405-409.

Collins, Ben L. "The Created Conscience: A Study of Technique and Symbol in James Joyce's *A Portrait of the Artist as a Young Man*." *Dissertation Abstracts*, XXIII (1963), 2523 (New Mexico).

Doherty, James. "Joyce and Hell Opened to Christians: The Edition He Used for His 'Hell Sermons.'" *Modern Philology*, LXI (May 1963), 110-119.

––––––. "Daedalian Imagery in *A Portrait of the Artist as a Young Man*," in *Hereditas*, edited by Frederic Will. Austin, Tex.: University of Texas Press, 1964, pp. 31-54.

Donoghue, Denis. "Joyce and the Finite Order." *Sewanee Review*, LXVIII (Spring 1960), 256-273.

Gordon, Caroline. "Some Readings and Misreadings." *Sewanee Review*, LXI (Summer 1953), 384-407. [Also in her *How to Read a Novel*.]

Jack, Jane H. "Art and *The Portrait of the Artist*." *Essays in Criticism*, V (October 1955), 354-364.

Kaye, Julian B. "Who is Betty Byrne?" *Modern Language Notes*, LXXI (February 1956), 93-95.

Kenner, Hugh. "Joyce's *Portrait*—A Reconsideration." *University of Windsor Review* (Windsor, Ont.), I (1965), 1-15.

McCaughey, G. S. "Stephen Ego." *Humanities Association Bulletin* (Canada) XIII (1962-65), 5-9.

O'Neill, Bridget. "Joyce and Lemon Platt." *American Notes and Queries* (New Haven, Conn.), III (1965), 117-118.

Pearce, Donald R. "The Dinner Quarrel in Joyce's *Portrait of the Artist*." *Modern Language Notes*, LXVI (April 1951), 249-251.

Poss, Stanley H. "Stephen's Words, Joyce's Attitude." *Washington State University Research Studies*, XXVIII (December 1960), 156-161.

––––––. "A Portrait of the Artist as a Hard-boiled Messiah." *Modern Language Quarterly*, XXVII (March 1966), pp. 68-79.

Ranald, Margaret Loftus. "Stephen Dedalus' Vocation and the Irony of Religious Ritual." *James Joyce Quarterly*, II (Winter 1965), 97-102.

Redford, Grant H. "The Role of Structure in Joyce's *Portrait*." *Modern Fiction Studies*, IV (Spring 1958), 21-30.

Scholes, Robert E. "Stephen Dedalus: *Eiron* and *Alazon*." *Texas Studies in Language and Literature*, III (Spring 1961), 8-15.

––––––. "Stephen Dedalus, Poet or Aesthete?" *PMLA*, LXXIX (September 1964), 484-489. (Reprinted in this edition.)

Schorer, Mark. "Technique as Discovery." *Hudson Review*, I (Spring 1948), 67-87.

Schwartz, Edward. "Joyce's *A Portrait of the Artist as a Young Man*, V." *Explicator*, XI (February 1953).

Sprague, June Elizabeth. "Strategy and the Evolution of Structure in the Early Novels of James Joyce." *Dissertation Abstracts*, XXV (1934), 2501 (Bryn Mawr).

Thrane, James R. "Joyce's Sermon on Hell: Its Source and Its Backgrounds." *Modern Philology*, LVII (February 1960), 172-198.

Van Laan, Thomas F. "The Meditative Structure of Joyce's *Portrait*." *James Joyce Quarterly*, I (Spring 1964), 3-13.

Waith, Eugene M. "The Calling of Stephen Dedalus." *College English*, XVIII (February 1957), 256-261.